Joy Chambers utilised her love of history by beginning to write historical novels during her successful acting career in Australia. Over a dozen years on she continues to tell her stories and combines her writing with her business life as chairman of a group of companies owned along with her husband. Joy says, 'My life is in the entertainment business. A skilfully written book can be read on many levels but it should always entertain . . . I attempt to do that.'

Praise for Joy Chambers' novels:

'An epic saga and meticulously researched: this is an understatement. It is both these things and more . . . History skilfully combined with fictional characters' *Daily Telegraph*, Sydney

'Joy Chambers has written a real blockbuster' *Best*

'Brimming with drama and intrigue' *Publishing News*

'Written with an ease of style and sophistication' *Liverpool Echo*

D1354801

NONE BUT THE BRAVE

Joy Chambers

headline

First published in Great Britain in 2003
by HEADLINE BOOK PUBLISHING

First published in paperback in Great Britain in 2003
by HEADLINE BOOK PUBLISHING
A HEADLINE PAPERBACK
10 9 8 7 6 5 4 3 2 1

ISBN 0 7553 0521 3

Typeset in Times Roman
by Palimpsest Book Production Limited,
Polmont, Stirlingshire
Printed and bound in Great Britain by
Mackays of Chatham Ltd, Chatham, Kent

HEADLINE BOOK PUBLISHING
A division of Hodder Headline
338 Euston Road
London NW1 3BH

www.headline.co.uk
www.hodderheadline.com

Dedication

This book is dedicated to two groups of people: the boys of the RAF, in particular to Fighter Command and the inimitable Group Captain Douglas Bader DSO DFC whom I first met as a child and who corresponded with me until shortly before his death; AND the heroic band of male and female Operatives of SOE – Special Operations Executive – whose courage often defied imagination, and in particular to Violette Szabo (née Bushell) whose short brave life ended along with Denise Bloch and Lillian Rolfe in Ravensbrück death camp in Germany at the tender age of 23 years. She was awarded the George Cross posthumously and it was collected by her orphaned four-year-old daughter Tania.

Acknowledgements

To Reg Grundy OBE, my darling husband, whose discerning editorial thoughts enhance all my work and who has helped JB, Cash and Samantha blossom into life.
To my brother Dr John Chambers who reads all my work. To my friends: the very talented Douglas Kirkland who made the images for my cover and his wife, Françoise, who improved my French. To my cousins Patricia and Graham Muller.

And to those other very able people who assisted in my research or helped in various ways: Eva Thomas, Maggie Moore, Neil Freestone, Brian Foster, Grahame Bateman, my sister Coral Chambers, Duncan Whitehead, Chinni Mahadevan AND Special Thanks: to my friend who was one of those gallant men who flew Spitfires during World War II. He prefers to remain unnamed but he has been of invaluable help to me in my RAF chapters and deserves this approbation.

Chapter One

Close to Lille, Northern France: Monday, 12 October, 1914

The man halted to cough as rain, borne on the wind, settled onto the shoulders of his greatcoat and ran in trickles down the knapsack he wore on his back. He peered through the fading twilight along the path half hidden by the encroaching bracken on either side of him.

'Damn,' he said quietly to himself as he considered the sound of the guns. They were growing ever closer. He glanced back over his shoulder past the horse he led, to the indistinct lights of the little village where the noise of frantic activity reached him through the rain: people were hurling all they could carry onto drays and carts, children wailed and despair paraded on the closing darkness. He had no time to consider anything except the quest he was upon, and he strode swiftly on along the path towards the single thatched cottage lying separated from the other buildings by a short oak bridge spanning a water-filled depression.

Above him a branch quivered in the rising wind and discharged a shaft of water upon the sleeve of his coat. He shook it off, muttering something under his breath, and trudged forward.

As he hurried across the bridge the horse's hooves thudded behind him and he sighed, the sound now lost in the falsetto shriekings of wind, human cries and the advancing war. Now his eyes remained fixed on the glow through the window of the cottage ahead. This was his last hope.

Crossing the stones of the minute yard he rapped urgently on the door and above the wind he heard a child's cry from within followed by a female voice. '*Attendez un moment, s'il vous plaît. J'arrive.*'

Half a minute later the door opened and a woman, fragile and pale, stood clutching in her fine arms an infant dressed in a travelling coat and hat.

He instantly noted the weariness, the tautness of her mouth. He recognised her aloneness, substantiated profoundly in the glow of the interior lantern; the isolation from family and friends appearing almost tangibly in her face.

He watched her as she raised her eyes to his.

She froze and a cry of recognition escaped her mouth. '*O mon Dieu. John Baron! Tu es revenu!*'

She staggered as if she had been struck. He could see she was losing consciousness and he leapt forward and took the child from her as she sank to the floor.

The boom of a shell landing less than a mile away sent shudders through the decrepit cottage as he placed the little boy on the stone floor and took up the woman's wrist. Her pulse was normal though she looked ill-fed; she had fainted with the shock. The infant began to wail as the stranger stepped over his mother and swept his eyes around the room: open suitcase on a table, clothes and boxes strewn everywhere, broken toy on the drab sofa, worn carpet on the floor, faded framed pictures upon the walls.

Within minutes he had put as many clothes as he could force into the small case, picked up the black leather handbag that appeared to contain her valuables, taken some fruit from a bowl and bread from the table and pushed them into the pockets of his jacket.

He moved with haste, strapping the suitcase and the handbag to the back of the stallion's saddle to the accompaniment of the pathetic weeping of the infant beside his mother on the floor. Taking down the coat and scarf that hung on a peg near the front door he wrapped the woman in them by lifting her prone form into a sitting position against his own body.

The child continued his lament as the man drew the horse forward on its reins until its head was right inside the cottage

2

door. He lifted the little boy up into the saddle and took the woman in his arms, hefting her over his shoulder as he climbed upon the animal's back and eased her down into a sitting position in front of him with the child. He guided the horse as swiftly as was feasible back over the stones of the yard, and turned him to cross the footbridge onto the dirt road that led back through the village.

The mortar blasts were getting closer all the time. He was sure the city of Lille would fall to the Germans within hours. He must head south-west, away from the danger.

As a shell destroyed a clump of trees and began a fire somewhere in his vision to the left he attempted to take the horse into a trot, but the road was slippery with mud and he soon pulled the stallion back to a walk.

The war was very close and adrenalin forced his pulse to quicken, but there was great elation too, for he had found her: after all the searching, after almost giving up, he had found Antoinette Desaix and her little boy. Now he had to get them out of here.

Her head was tilted to view the turquoise sky through the boughs of the beeches where the summer clouds above, pursued by a loving breeze, collided with each other to bunch upon the horizon. The joyous call of robins and the trill of wrens drifted over the silken sound of oars from other canoes caressing the limpid waters of the river. She felt cushioned in the magic of the languid afternoon and everything around her compounded her happiness. Until these last months she could not have conceived of such perfection.

When she lowered her eyes they rested on the one who had brought the contentment into her soul. He sat at the other end of the boat, the oars resting at his side as they floated along under the overhanging branches. His straw boater had fallen forwards at a jaunty angle. He held an unlit cigar between his white teeth and now the face that had insinuated itself into the reaches of her soul broke into a grin as he asked, 'Is the Queen of Amiens enjoying her afternoon on the carefree waters of the Somme?'

3

She laughed. 'Was there ever one?'

'One what?'

'A queen of Amiens?'

'Well, possibly. You French had kingdoms all over the place, you know – Aquitaine and Lorraine and Brittany et cetera . . . all fighting one another, of course.'

She laughed again, a blissful sound that echoed its glee along the water. 'I think you'll find that they were duchies, my love, and what do you mean by *you French*. What about you English? You were all fighting one another too.'

'Yes, my darling, whatever you say.'

She trailed her fingers in the cool water over the side of the boat. 'I could sail along like this for ever.'

The boat slid by a fisherman on the bank removing his catch from the line; the fish wriggled as he dropped it into an open cane basket and lifted his sun-darkened hand to wave to them.

'I feel complete,' she said. 'You have completed me.'

'Ah, my sweet darling, and you have visited upon me such love as I did not know existed.'

She gave a tiny smile. Now was the time to tell him. The perfect time. 'John Baron?'

'Yes?'

'I am going to have our child.'

Antoinette was slipping in and out of consciousness, aware of the uneven movement of a horse beneath her, and somewhere the splintering sound of gun blasts; at times she thought she was sleeping but felt light rain upon her face. In the moments she was semi-conscious she recognised the soft vulnerability of her son clinging to her and then her mind acknowledged another larger, harder body which held her in firm arms. She felt unreal, suspended between living and dying. John Baron's arms were around her. A miracle had happened. Was she dreaming? She knew she had been ill, had been packing to leave ahead of the Germans. She tried to force herself into wakefulness but everything went black again.

* * *

The steam surged high in the air and rolled in a great swell along the platform as she held the infant John Baron up to his father at the carriage window. The man leant out and kissed the boy. 'I'll be back in a few weeks, a month or two at the most.'

'I'm happy the way we are. It's not important to me. You still can stay. Don't go.'

He laughed gently and lifted her hand to his lips as the train whistle blew. 'No, my precious Antoinette. You must be my wife, legal and proper as befits you. Our son's parents must be married to each other. I will manage a divorce somehow.'

'But we're happy. I don't care what people say . . .' Her fingers clung to his as she tried to keep up with the shunting train gathering speed. She kept pace for ten yards and then their hands broke apart.

His palm remained high out of the window. 'I love you,' he shouted across the fierce clickety-clacking of the accelerating train, and her answer was lost on the rising evening breeze.

Long after the train had disappeared and the platform emptied, she stood like a finely moulded porcelain figure, rigid in the descending dusk, hugging her son and looking along the track.

She opened her eyes to the black of night. She was no longer held firmly upon a horse, but was lying on something hard. A blanket covered her. As her eyes accustomed themselves to the darkness she made out a crude wooden madonna gazing harmlessly down upon her and realised she was in one of the tiny wayside chapels that the peasants built from gathered stones. Through the arch on the road's edge she could see a milky moon riding moodily upon the treetops. It had stopped raining.

Abruptly she remembered, and she sat up eyes replete with hope as she looked round for the man and her son. She crawled a few feet upon her knees and heard the snorting of the horse. She was about to call her son's name when a black figure appeared in front of her.

She rose up before him, her body taut with expectation. *'O mon Dieu! Ce n'était pas un rêve! John Baron, c'est bien toi!'* He had returned to her. She moved forward to cast herself into his arms but he raised his hands to stop her.

'I am not John Baron.'

She halted, her face twisted in confusion and fright as the figure lit a match and held it to the wick of a candle standing in a tin cup under the Virgin. Meagre though it was, the light from the single candle was enough to reveal his image.

She saw what he had said was true. Though he was the same height and shape as the man she had loved and there was a strong similarity in the bone structure of his face, he was not the same. She shuddered, knowing that the night had played a trick upon her; she felt vague and light-headed but she forced herself to control her feelings enough to ask in English, 'Who are you? Where is my son?'

He turned his head towards her. 'Your son is sleeping and we must move on soon. I'm John Baron's cousin. His father and my father were brothers.'

'His cousin? I am not understanding.'

'We were always alike; even from being small children. It made us very close, like brothers, though we were not.'

He could see the woman was bewildered. Her hand rose to her head as if she would faint again.

He gestured to the blanket. 'Perhaps you should sit down a little longer. I have water and bread, and some fruit I found in your cottage.'

A remote blast, menacing and portentous, rumbled across the hills and suddenly the infant woke and cried out. Antoinette hurried past the man into the darkness. The boy had been asleep on a coat taken from the man's knapsack and placed on a dry rock near the side of the chapel wall.

'Maman, Maman . . .'

'Oui, mon chéri, mon petit oiseau.'

Behind her the man picked up the blanket, blew out the candle and came to the stallion near the mother and child. As he took water and bread from his knapsack the first timid radiation of the dawn disturbed the dark horizon.

Antoinette accepted the sustenance and shared it in silence with the child upon her knee. Finally she asked the question that had been pounding inside her head. 'John Baron? He is all right?'

The man regarded her. 'No, he's not all right. I'm very sorry, he died in July. It was for him that I came here to find you. But the war . . .'

A sigh shivered from Antoinette. 'I knew. Even with this horrible war, he would have come back. He would have.' The bleakness had returned to her gaze. 'So you came to tell me?'

'Yes. I promised John Baron I would watch over the boy as my own.'

Her back stiffened and she put down the water-bag. 'What is this you say?' She stood and placed the child on the ground behind her.

'I'm a wealthy man. I can take care of your child, can give him everything. And I can take care o—'

'*Non!*' Antoinette broke over his words. 'I am his mother. You cannot have him. Go away. Please go now. We will make our own way from here.'

'You don't understand.'

A spark of defiance waxed alongside the entreaty in her eyes as she vehemently shook her head. 'It was kind of you to get us out of the village. But please, please do not do this. Go away now. *Allez-vous.*'

He stepped closer to her and in turn she stepped away from him, taking the child with her, fear making her bold. 'No, I say! *Jamais!*' Her fist rose in the air.

He smiled and held up his hands towards her. 'Antoinette, listen to me. I mean to take you both – you *and* your son – back to England. That's what John Baron wanted.'

Antoinette did not speak. Her mouth opened and closed. Her face looked as if it would crumple as her fist fell impotently to her side and the words finally broke from her lips. 'You mean to take us to England?'

'Yes, of course, that's why I'm here. Why else would I have brought the two of you away from the cottage?'

She stood there in disbelief with the toddler at her knee

and then the man smiled again. 'Antoinette, we must keep moving. The war follows us. I have passage out of Dunkirk in three days' time.'

Her face lost the weary look; a spark of life rekindled within her. She met Benjamin Chard's eyes and held his gaze for some seconds before she bowed her head in gratitude to him, her hands palms upward in supplication towards him. 'And yet . . . You, my saviour, I don't even know your name.'

The band of three continued on their way with as much haste as possible, mostly with the woman and child riding the stallion and Benjamin Chard leading them through the French countryside. The roads were choked with regiments of soldiers and refugees, their possessions piled high on horses, donkeys, motor bikes and bicycles, in dog carts and wheelbarrows – in vehicles of every kind. Benjamin soon realised that the Germans were advancing faster than he had been led to believe. He knew they had cut a sward south through eastern France and the rumour in the villages was that they were every day closing in on Paris. He began to be concerned that perhaps they had pushed across the Belgian border ahead of him just as they had done in 1870 and he became worried about getting through to Dunkirk.

By ten in the morning there was blessed sunshine and Benjamin was heading them towards the village of Armentières. The echo of the guns could still be clearly heard, but in a tiny settlement they entered, a semblance of normality reigned for they found a café still serving food. Though the line of waiting men and women was long Ben finally obtained some tea and cheese to go with the bread and fruit.

They sat on a tiny hillock at the side of the road while the endless stream of refugees passed. Antoinette shared her food with a peasant woman, large with child, who sat nearby on a flat rock.

'I'm afraid we cannot rest long,' Ben explained. 'The Germans are advancing all the time.'

She handed him a sandwich she had made from the bread and cheese. 'I understand. We'll get ready to go on.'

'Your English is excellent.'

'I went to school in England for six years; my father was in the Diplomatic Service, Monsieur Chard.'

'Benjamin, please. If we are to travel together, it would be better if we used Christian names.'

She nodded. 'Benjamin . . .' She said it in a musical way; he liked it.

Antoinette looked across at the tiny John Baron who had wandered a few yards away and was talking to himself. When she called him the child ran back to her and she hugged him close as he fell into her lap. She was really quite thin and small, but a little less frail today in the robust light than she had seemed in the dark of the night before.

The peasant woman and her companions lifted themselves from where they sat and moved on.

Benjamin stood and opened a saddlebag to place the water and uneaten food inside. He turned his head to Antoinette. 'I went to your parents' home to find you but no one would see me.'

She answered as she picked up the blanket upon which they had sat. 'My father rules everyone there.'

He thought she was about to cry and he went quickly on, 'I'd given up on finding you and had decided to leave France; then I heard someone mention your name and where you lived.'

She gave him an odd look. 'Who?'

'It doesn't matter.'

A knowing expression crossed her face. 'Ah, I see . . . a soldier told you.' She handed Ben the blanket and looked away above the rough farm buildings to the blue hills beyond before she picked up the child and mounted the stallion, her gaze focused as if she spoke to the hills and not to him. 'Since the war began I have taken care of my son any way I could.'

Benjamin was not judging her. He knew very little about her, but he sensed that she was intrinsically good. He stepped to the side of the horse and wrapped the blanket

9

around them and as he did so the little boy leant out from his mother's arms, the sun glinting in his baby's eyes – the washed blue colour of the sky on a cool autumn day – and he touched the back of Benjamin's hand.

Benjamin stared at the infant. This was John Baron's son, the son of the man he had loved as a brother. It was a fateful thing to have found him at last. Affectionately he ruffled the little boy's hair and the infant laughed, the innocent sound cheerful and pleasant in the adult's ears.

Ben smiled up at the woman, picked up the reins and took the horse forward at a quick walk. Marching towards them was a company of British soldiers and Benjamin called to a Lieutenant, 'Do you know if the road to Dunkirk is open?'

The Lieutenant blinked wearily. 'Shouldn't think so, friend. The enemy have moved to our flank and I think they're already only about five miles over there.' He lifted his hand to point and then swept it round across a line of verdant hills. 'Your best chance is to break from the road and cross that row of hills. You might be lucky enough to get round that way.'

'Do you know if Dunkirk itself is in danger?'

The officer threw his words back over his shoulder as he passed on. 'Last I heard, all the Channel ports were still open and free. It's around here that's dangerous. Regiments of reinforcements are coming up all the time but the Germans are in Lille now, we're told.'

Ben heard Antoinette's sigh even with his back to her.

They left the road and headed in the direction the Lieutenant had indicated. The small John Baron looked at the passing countryside with wide eyes. Up to now he had only vaguely been aware of his world and what occurred in it. He did not understand anything of his life or what happened around him, but every day his mother spoke of 'Papa' and pointed to a man in a silver frame. And while he was still only an infant and he could not comprehend or reason, he simply accepted what to him was the reality: that this man who now walked beside them and led their horse was Papa.

He had never been on a horse before and he delighted in the bumpy, jiggling movement, and enjoyed the breeze in his curls and the comfort and security of his mother's warm body against his back.

Benjamin led them along, his left hand on the reins. His shoulders were wide and strong like John Baron's had been, and as Antoinette observed the movements of Benjamin's body beneath his clothes she could almost believe it was her beloved who led the horse. As they passed by a copse of dark sycamores, he turned and looked back at her. She was recalling things John Baron had told her: there had been a cousin whom he loved and admired; they had grown up together and attended university together; they had travelled on the continent and to the ruins in Greece to witness the Acropolis and to stand at sunset on the golden shores of the wide Aegean Sea. Of course she realised now that Benjamin was this man.

Antoinette half-closed her eyes, lulled by the rocking vibration of the animal swaying her along. She knew they were travelling in haste and that the enemy were not far away, but the rustle of the fallen autumn leaves beneath the horse's hooves was soothing and she took solace in the sun warming her head and dancing across her shoulders. She had not felt a moment's contentment since her beloved had left her, and yet here, now, she was calm. It was all surreal: the passage of time did not seem like seconds and minutes, it was something else. She was only aware of the feel of her child's body against her stomach and the knowledge that John Baron's emissary led them to sanctuary. She was not sure how much time had passed when he spoke and sharply brought her from her reverie to open her eyes fully upon the world.

'There's a stream down there. I'll fill the water-bottle.'

She became aware again of the noise of guns in the nearby hills, and that men died and women and children fled. As they descended a long grassy slope to the running water, half a mile away to their right hundreds of soldiers moved in columns across the rise. Ben looked through his telescope. 'They're British and French.'

11

'Thank heaven.'

At the stream Antoinette sat on a stone and Benjamin filled the leather pouch water-bottle. The little boy watched in wonder as he made two paper cones from a page he took from a writing pad in his knapsack. He poured water into them and they drank. Afterwards he fed the horse then filled the crown of his hat and let the stallion drink while they ate some of the fruit.

The child was now tired of the hours upon the horse and he ran and rolled with delight in the grass. A little later Ben realised the boy was nursing something and he approached him. It was a tiny mewing kitten no more than a few weeks old for it had no teeth. He looked around for the mother or another cat but there were no other animals anywhere near.

'We must not delay, little man,' he said, removing the tiny form from the little boy's arms and putting it down in the grass. The child began to sob uncontrollably and Ben looked for support to Antoinette but she shrugged. 'Can we take it with us?'

'We've nothing to feed it on. It needs milk.'

'We could try it on mashed-up bread.'

With a groan he yielded and so they continued on with the delighted child holding the object of his desire tenderly in his arms. When the little boy slept his mother took the kitten, and when he woke he carried it himself. At times, young John Baron was fretful and complaining for he did not understand the need for the endless ride.

In the quickening twilight they halted at the top of a steep incline near a copse of mighty oaks, where, to the north-west, they could see flashes of flames in piles of smoke on the horizon, and hear the cacophony of the guns repeated across the hills.

The infant was once more asleep in his mother's arms and Antoinette looked down at him and spoke softly. 'I am frightened, you know – for him. Will we make the ship in time?'

Ben appeared more confident than he was. 'Yes, I'm sure we will.'

'But the guns sound closer to me.'

Benjamin agreed but, not wanting to alarm her, said nothing as he lifted his telescope to his eye. It was too dark to see much except the fires and he pointed down the hill across the railway track to a road where he could just make out a few refugees moving towards a convent. He knew exactly where he was now. 'That's where we'll rest awhile, at the convent, and if the nuns remain we'll get some food.'

He handed Antoinette the water-bottle and helped her balance the sleeping boy as she drank. The kitten was crying and he gave it a tiny piece of bread mixed with a little water.

As she returned the bottle to him she looked down at her son. 'He's still only two, will be three next month, on the eleventh.'

'He's a fine boy. Tall for his age.'

'Oh yes, and I named him after his father. He looks like John Baron, don't you think?'

Ben appraised the sleeping child. 'Indeed.'

And Antoinette gave him a gentle smile. 'Which means he looks a little like you as well.'

He was pleased to see her smile. 'Why, yes, I suppose so.'

In the brief twenty-four hours of their acquaintance, he thought he could see why his cousin had loved this woman. She was gentle and of a polite and agreeable nature, but strong; the strength that is found in those who don't give in to the whims of fate, but fight back.

He looked skywards. 'It'll soon be dark. Come on.'

In the encroaching night Ben could see there were loose stones all the way down the steep track and he asked Antoinette to dismount. 'For it's safer if you walk to the bottom.' He reached out and took John Baron and the kitten from her as she dismounted, but the child woke and began to prattle in his infant's way.

Soon the little boy began to wriggle in Benjamin's arms, insisting on being put down, and Ben placed the child and his tiny charge on the ground beside his mother as a boom of guns echoed in a long, ominous rumble across the row of hills to the north. Antoinette turned towards the noise.

13

'I'm positive they're closer than they were.'

He touched her reassuringly on the arm. 'I don't think so, but it's best if we keep moving along and don't delay too much. I'll lead the horse, you take John Baron and the cat.'

They both turned to gather up the boy and what happened next lurked forever in Benjamin's worst dreams. The child had moved away in play with the bouncing kitten and suddenly the animal bounded to the brink of the incline and sprang over the edge. The toddler ran after it, slipped forward, cried out and pitched face first over the steep incline.

Antoinette screamed as she threw herself after her son. He was some yards down the face, and in her desperation to clamber down to him she misjudged the damp ground and skidded, her weight pitching her forwards. Ben leapt after her as she tried to right herself but she hurtled headlong past the boy with hands outstretched flailing the air, rolling and tumbling over stones and through bracken all the way to the bottom of the hill.

Ben steadied himself and took up the shrieking infant and kitten to stand some seconds in disbelief. The light was receding quickly now and he could just make out Antoinette's inert body two hundred feet below. He began to descend when he heard the rattling approach of a munitions train, clattering inexorably along towards the woman lying motionless. Holding the weeping child and the wriggling cat in his strong right arm he used his left to help him slide and stumble down towards Antoinette.

As he righted himself at the bottom of the incline, he saw that Antoinette lay completely across the track. Quickly he placed the sobbing boy and the crying kitten down in the centre of a group of small rocks and ran to her as the noise of the train amplified and swelled around him. As the engine exploded by him and a gush of wind struck them he knew he had grabbed the woman and dragged her from the line. The train sped past on its way down the sloping valley floor.

He was lying on the ground, the woman on top of him,

and as he eased her away his stomach turned. Antoinette's right hand was missing and blood was spurting as if from a water-pipe in her arm.

He dragged off his jacket and his shirt, ignoring the enveloping cold of night, and tore his shirt into pieces. He pulled off his singlet and wrapped it round her wrist to stem the blood flow, then he strapped his shirt bandages over it and finally pushed her arm into the sleeve of his coat and tied the remainder of the jacket as tightly as possible around the ghastly wound.

He lifted her in his arms and only then did he hear the boy whimpering. The infant had climbed out of the stone enclosure and the kitten was at his feet. In the gloom beyond him Ben could see that the stallion had picked its way down the track and stood snorting about thirty yards away.

Gingerly he placed Antoinette's unconscious form on the ground and the child ran sobbing to her. '*Maman* . . . *Maman*.'

Calling to the stallion as quietly and calmly as his racing heart would allow, Benjamin gingerly moved to it and took up the reins. He thought to leave the cat there after all the horror it had caused, but he relented and soon he had it and the child up on the animal. Still in shock, but with infinite care, holding Antoinette draped over his shoulder once again, he mounted behind little John Baron and urged the horse along in the blackening night towards the road.

Chapter Two

Antoinette opened her eyes. Pain shot up through her arm; her head throbbed and her whole body ached. She felt she could not breathe – and there were moments when everything was obliterated and she was sliding . . . sliding: like nothing she had ever experienced before. Then the pain returned. At first her vision was blurred but finally she focused on the face hovering over her and she realised it was her benefactor's. His brow was wrinkled with concern.

Abruptly she remembered what had gone before and she attempted speech but the sound gurgled in her throat.

'Don't try to talk.' Ben gave a tender smile.

She looked down and saw her arm lying on the bedcover. Her right hand was wrapped in a huge bandage, like a massive boxer's glove. The bandage extended up her arm beyond her elbow. She realised something very bad had happened to her and the pain and the sliding feeling returned. She wondered where she was and tried to look around.

Ben spoke as if in answer to her. 'We're in the convent we saw from the hill. We've been here some hours. You tried to save your son and you fell down the hill. Antoinette, you've been badly injured, I'm afraid.'

'Where is . . .' Her voice croaked at last from her throat and tears broke from her lids to tremble across her temple to the pillow.

Ben answered quickly. 'John Baron's safe. He was not injured at all.'

'Thank God,' she whispered as she closed her eyes.

The Sisters gave her no hope: she had a number of broken bones including her left leg and some ribs; there was a deep laceration in her thigh above the break. One of the oldest

16

nuns, Sister Manille, had some medical training and she had attended to the wounds and bandaged them, all the time shaking her head and muttering to herself. She had found it almost impossible to stem the blood from the lost hand and even now a dark stain showed through the masses of bandages on Antoinette's arm.

John Baron had been comforted by two young novices and then been taken away to be fed. The child was disoriented and confused and Ben had asked that once he had eaten, he be returned to him.

The door squeaked and Ben turned to it as it opened to admit the Mother Superior and Sister Manille. The elderly nun crossed to the bedside and bent down towards Antoinette, who did not open her eyes. Taking up the injured woman's left wrist she felt the pulse, then placed the hand gently down.

The Mother Superior beckoned Ben to follow them from the room and outside in the corridor she spoke in her stilted English, the pristine white of her collar gleaming in the pale light from a single hurricane lamp. '*Monsieur*, my English *mal*. Sister Manille speak for me.' She shook her head and spoke in French to the older nun who in turn shook her head before addressing Ben.

Manille spoke competent English, had studied at the Sorbonne in her youth and worked for a time in an English hospital before returning to France to join the Order. 'Though it is a long time ago, I have some medical experience. The woman is dying. Her wounds are extensive and blood loss is great . . . much too great. We have nothing to help her here. We are told the Germans are only miles away and we must abandon the convent before long ourselves.' Her pale old eyes rotated towards the room where Antoinette lay. 'We cannot be sure exactly, but she won't live long – perhaps a few hours. We are sorry.'

'I understand.'

'What is your name?'

'Benjamin Chard.'

Sister Manille spoke again to the Mother Superior before turning back to Ben. 'The woman is your wife?'

17

Ben hesitated. So much had happened so quickly since they had arrived here at the convent that no questions had been asked; they had simply attended to the needs of Antoinette and the child. Nothing had been mentioned about why they were travelling together or what relationship they held. For a moment he calculated all the possibilities. Antoinette was dying, that was certain. If he did not claim the child he could find opposition from the nuns.

He had actually opened his mouth to reply when a door a few feet away snapped open and Ben and the two women with him swung towards it. One of the novices entered the hallway holding little John Baron's hand and when the child saw Ben he pulled out of the woman's hold and ran to Ben; and the words that issued from his mouth were, 'Papa! Papa!'

As the man lifted the boy in his arms he turned back to the nuns. The child had unwittingly established their relationship in the women's minds. Ben's voice sounded foreign to his own ears as he perpetuated the lie. 'Yes, she's my wife. We were on our way to Dunkirk where I have passage on a ship to England.'

Antoinette knew she was dying. She did not want to die but the pain kept coming in a consuming wave and it was too much to bear. When she tried to move it almost numbed her brain. She was sliding again, slipping from this life. She thought of her great love, John Baron Chard, and how she would soon be with him again. That consoled her. She kept having dreams – or were they hallucinations – that John Baron stood at the top of a long flight of steps and beckoned her with open arms. She wanted to climb them and be with him, and yet she did not want to leave their son behind. When she was more conscious she knew that Benjamin Chard sat by her bed and through the haze of pain she addressed him. 'Take John Baron,' she whispered. 'I give him to you. Bring him up as your son.'

From a long way off she heard Ben say, 'Antoinette, I don't want to leave you here.'

She succeeded in keeping her gaze upon his face; she

18

remembered the ship and that they had been making their way to it. 'Please, you must not miss the ship. Go now. I . . . know I am . . . dying. You must not stay.' She could no longer focus properly and Ben's image wavered in black surreal shapes before her, but she forced herself to continue. 'Promise me . . . Promise me . . .'

'What? What?'

'Bring . . . my son up as your own. Please.'

'I will.'

'Do what is best for him. And . . .' With all her remaining strength Antoinette raised her good left hand. On her third finger was a wide gold band. 'Take this for him.'

Ben began to remove the band gently from her finger and as he did so it separated into two. He realised it was really two smaller rings that fitted perfectly together. There were gold ridges running all the way round them, and a small V of metal extended out of one ring and slipped neatly into the opposing vacant shape on the other, making a whole.

Benjamin pulled the first ring away from its partner and sliding it from her finger saw the words *John Baron* etched in antique script in the interior.

Antoinette's voice was no more than a whisper now and Ben had to incline his head to hear her. 'The one remaining on my finger has inside it *Antoinette, my love always*. I must die with it. John Baron left both with me when he went away. Symbols of our love . . . fitting perfectly.' She gestured feebly at the band Benjamin held. 'Give it to my little boy . . . when he's a man.' Her hand dropped back to the bed and she closed her eyes.

Ben sighed deeply and leant forward and kissed her. 'I will do exactly as you ask.'

A single tear fell from her eyes as the door opened behind him and he looked round to see one of the novices. '*Je suis venue pour vous soulager, et pour veiller sur votre femme. Votre fils dort et nous avons nourri son chat. Soeur Manille vous attend.*' She pointed to the door.

Ben's French was limited but he realised the novice had come to watch Antoinette, and that the child was sleeping.

And he understood that Sister Manille waited outside, so he stood. '*Merci. Je reviendrai.*' He hesitated a few seconds, looking down at Antoinette's inert figure before he left the room.

Along the poorly lit corridor he made out the form of Sister Manille. When she saw him she halted by the single lamp and waited, lifting her arthritic fingers and clutching her rosary, the wide sleeve of her habit falling away to expose the back of her hand with its laced pattern of raised blue veins running from her wrist to her fingers. She spoke softly; there was an air of calm around her. 'What time does your ship leave Dunkirk?'

'Wednesday at noon.'

She made a sceptical sound. 'In less than two hours it will be dawn. You will have to travel at great speed to be there.'

'I do not want to leave my wife.'

The nun fingered the beads as she spoke. 'Monsieur Chard, forgive me for being blunt but if you remain even another *few minutes* I fear you will not make your ship. *Les Bosches* are virtually here. The brutal truth is that the war's upon us and you should save your son. We are hearing conflicting reports about Lille: it has fallen or is about to fall. We of the Sisterhood have no option but to remain in France, but you can go. It's pointless for you to stay here and lose your chance.

'Please understand. You can do nothing for your wife. That she has lived till now is a miracle.' She gave a forceful nod of her head. 'We will take care of her.'

'But I cannot leave knowing she's . . .'

The door of Antoinette's room creaked open and the novice who had been sitting with her stepped into the corridor, and upon seeing the older woman she called out nervously, '*Soeur Manille. La femme . . . Je pense qu'elle est morte.*'

The older woman held up her wrinkled hand. '*Restez calme. Je viens.*' She took a deep breath as she met Ben's eyes. 'It's time for plain talk, *monsieur*. Your wife is gone. She's with *Notre Seigneur*. We will do what needs to be done.' She motioned along the corridor. 'Now leave immediately or you'll not make your ship.' She lifted her eyes to the heavens and raising her rosary beads, pressed the metal image of Christ on the cross to her body. 'Save your son.'

Ben kept the horse at a steady trot, heading ever north-westwards along the winding road. Little John Baron had asked insistently for his mother but now was at last asleep in his arms. The blasted kitten was asleep too in a leather pouch on the saddle.

Where yesterday the roads had been full of refugees, they were empty of travellers now, a sign, along with the rumble of advancing guns, that the Germans were indeed close.

The boy's body felt warm and small leaning against him as Ben looked up at the sky. Lavish streaks of light leapt from the horizon and the moon's possession of the night was being challenged by the sun. And where, only an hour before, the Milky Way had proclaimed itself with an exuberant radiance across the galaxy, now the brilliance of dawn had already banished it from men's eyes.

The sensation in his chest would not go away. He had felt drawn to Antoinette, had acknowledged a tender regard for the woman his dear cousin had loved so greatly. The little boy in his arms was so vulnerable. In reality, alone in the world. Yet the child believed Ben was his father. What was Ben to do? He thought of his darling wife, Constance, taking her walk along Normandy Lane and by Eight Acre Pond; imagined her sitting at the parlour window tatting lace as was her way in the last hours of late summer evenings, looking out on the ever-changing waters of the Solent inlet. He saw himself opposite her, a glass of sherry in his hand, talking to her about the boatyard and the day's events.

They had hoped for a child of their own now for ten years without success. Antoinette had given him this boy to bring up as his own and he had promised the dying woman to do exactly that. He must do what was best for the boy. What good would it do for him to know the truth? Nothing would be achieved by that except sadness. To give little John Baron a lifelong sense of the loss of both his parents would be cruel and wrong. It stood to reason that he would not remember this. He was still only a baby; not yet three.

Suddenly Ben brought the horse to a halt. He was at a crossroads and he realised that the gunfire to his right was aimed at something up ahead. Explosions came from over a wooded ridge along the sealed road where he guessed a village must be. He looked up and flinched, for delineated against the dawn sky was a line of soldiers.

In a second he took stock of things. The child and the animal still slept. The road ahead to what he assumed was the village, ran through a wood but the dirt path to his left disappeared into a thicket of oaks about twenty-five yards away. He began steadily to edge the horse down to the left when he caught more movement in the trees back to his right. As a voice called, '*Halt! Wer geht dort?*' he instantly spurred his horse and made for the cover of the thicket.

The child woke and cried out as a burst of rifle shot rattled from the trees behind him but Ben kept his head down and charged for cover. He heard a bullet sing by his ear and as the stallion reached the safety of the shield of oaks he felt as if an axe thudded down on top of his left arm. He was slammed forward towards the horse's neck with such force that he dropped the reins and momentarily his grasp loosened on the boy, letting him swing out of his hold. Little John Baron screamed as he slipped sideways, and with searing pain shooting down to his elbow, Benjamin grabbed the falling child, pulling him back in close to his body and keeping his balance with his knees until he could again lift the reins.

Through the sturdy oaks Ben careered, clutching John Baron to his body. The dust rose in swirls under the galloping stallion's hooves as he charged along the path to cross a stone bridge and to round a hillock. He could see clearly now and the road led to high ground through clumps of trees snaking up a hill into the sun. He did not want to lose his way but he could not afford to remain in this part of the country with the enemy so close. He was in no fear of the soldiers following; they were making for the village he was sure of that, he had just been unlucky to run into them. Even so he did not slacken his pace until he knew he was about a mile from the crossroads.

The stallion panted noisily as Ben brought him to a standstill. The little boy's face was stained with tears and his body gave shudders every few seconds. And to Ben's amazement the blasted cat was still in the pouch mewing loudly.

Gingerly, keeping his left arm still, Ben dismounted and lifted John Baron to the ground. He checked to see the horse had not been grazed then took the kitten and knelt down to the boy. He spoke in his halting French, trying to console the child. '*Ne pas pleurer . . . petit camarade.*'

'*Maman,*' the boy began to sob and Ben took him in his arms and hugged him close. 'There, there, little man. We'll be all right. *Nous serons sur un grand bâteau bientôt.*'

'*Maman?*' The child whimpered again and when he saw Ben's blood-soaked sleeve he began to cry more loudly.

Ben put the cat down and assessed his wound. The bullet had opened his arm about four inches above his elbow and had gone clean through. He was bleeding profusely and he eased off his coat and removed his last spare shirt from his saddle-bag and ripped it as best he could, into bandages. He wrapped the wound and stemmed the bloodflow by tying a sort of a knot with his good hand and his teeth.

Putting his coat back on he took his water-bottle and held it for the child to drink before he took long gulps for himself. Finally he removed his felt hat which he had tied to the saddle the previous night, and again, filling the crown with water, gave it to the grateful stallion. Then he and the child and the cat ate some bread.

He looked at his fob watch: twenty-four hours left to reach Dunkirk. If he had to detour again it would be hard to keep up the pace and now he was wounded and his mount was tired. He felt very dizzy. He needed some sleep, just a few minutes – so did the stallion. Then they would be able to make the distance.

The child stood looking at him with huge tearful eyes. Just yesterday, little John Baron had a mother and today she was dead. It was all so bizarre and Ben felt exhausted. He forced himself to take out his compass and his map to calculate their whereabouts. He spoke aloud, as if the child understood him. 'Well, little fellow, as long as there are no Germans ahead of us, we might just make it.'

And as the guns back along the valley boomed their menacing orchestral accompaniment he took a rope from his saddle-bag and tied one end round the child's ankle and the other round his own wrist. He knew he was bone weary and had to sleep briefly but he could not risk anything happening to the boy. He would let the kitten take its own chances.

He secured the horse to a low branch and dropped to the ground. He could no longer keep his eyes open and a moment later he slipped into sleep.

He snapped into wakefulness. Instantly he sat up and looked around for the child. With relief he saw the boy's small form at the end of the rope asleep just a few feet away from where the stallion was cropping the grass. And there was the kitten, like a witch's familiar, lying not a yard from the child. Ben sighed and looked at his watch. It was after eleven; he had slept for over three hours!

He woke John Baron and fed him the last piece of bread and part of a biscuit he had found in his saddle-bag. What was left he gave to the mewing kitten. When he lifted them both into the saddle, the kitten wriggled as he placed it in its pouch but it soon settled, as if it knew this was all a serious matter of survival.

Once Ben was mounted he moved off at a walking pace. 'Now little man, we must get away from the war. À l'Angleterre et ma maison, nous allons.'

The child in his infant's custom repeated Benjamin's last words. '*Nous allons*.' Then he looked up at the man with him and said, '*Maman, Maman?*'

Ben could not explain anything to the baby. He bent and kissed John Baron's curls and murmured softly into them,

'Don't worry about *Maman*. *Tout va très bien*. Don't worry about anything at all, *mon petit*. We've got to keep our minds and hearts set on Dunkirk.'

Chapter Three

The early-afternoon sun twinkled spasms of gold through the trees onto Constance Chard's straw basket brimming with a galaxy of autumn colour: marigolds, Michaelmas daisies and chrysanthemums from the garden and wild roses from amongst the hedgerows along the lane. As she approached her front gate in the stone wall that surrounded their home, she halted to put down her basket and re-tie the blue ribbon that kept her wide-brimmed hat from coming off in the breeze. She smiled, pleased with the number of blooms she had found at this time of the year. Bending to retrieve her flowers she caught a movement along the lane and recognised Miss Brack's ungainly stride closing the gap between them.

Her husband's secretary wore her hair pulled back in a bun and she had obviously left the boatyard office in a hurry as she wore no head covering and the lead pencil she used so industriously all day long, still sat threaded in her hair above her ear.

'Miss Brack, what brings you here?'

'Telegram for you from Mr Chard.'

Constance shivered as she took the envelope. Benjamin had been away now for three months looking for Antoinette Desaix, John Baron's Frenchwoman. When the war in Europe had begun two months before, she had received a telegram from him saying for her not to worry herself, that he would stay away from any trouble; another had arrived ten days ago, stating that he had some new clues on the woman and that he would return home if they were not fruitful, or if the Germans advanced far into France. Well, the Germans were advancing daily and Constance was in terrible fear for him.

She was a reasonable woman and she knew that her husband had adored his cousin, John Baron. They had been 'soulmates' in the true sense of the word and the fact was that Constance, with her fair-mindedness, had understood when Ben had told her he must keep his promise to his dying relative and go to France. She knew that Ben would never rest if he did not. Cousin John Baron had left the bulk of his estate to her husband with the understanding that he take care of the Frenchwoman and in time pass the inheritance on to the child he had conceived with her. So Constance had seen Ben off to France with a heavy, yet understanding heart. However, when the war had begun and he had remained there, continuing the search for the woman, her feelings had at times been tinged with a little jealousy that his promise to his dead cousin could mean so much.

She tore open the envelope and read the message: *AM IN LONDON STOP MUST SEE YOU HERE STOP PLEASE COME RITZ HOTEL PICCADILLY SOONEST STOP ALL MY LOVE BENJAMIN.*

She lifted her eyes from the message. 'Thank God he's back.'

Ernestine Brack's severe face melted into kinder lines. She had worked for seventeen years for Benjamin Chard and if she adored anyone on the planet it was her employer. 'Oh, thank the Lord.'

The two women who were firm friends, even though socially removed, embraced in the lane.

'Where is he?'

Constance smiled. 'He's in London . . . wants me to go there immediately.'

Ernestine nodded. She did not know why her employer had gone to France. All he had told her was that he would explain it to her when he returned and that was good enough for her. She knew Benjamin Chard well, he was a man of honour and goodness, who treated his workers at the boatyard with equity and dealt honourably with all his acquaintances. She had joined him as an eighteen year old straight from the North London Collegiate School for Girls, and after all her years with him she could read him well. She had suspected that his trip to France might have had something to do with his cousin, for he had departed for France immediately after they had buried John Baron.

'You might catch the three-fifteen to London if you hurry.'

Constance answered, hastening up the path. 'I'll not miss it.'

Twenty-five minutes later a small brocade case had been packed and Constance was dressed to travel and tying her exuberant curls back in a ribbon when she called out, 'Come in,' to Ledgie's firm recognisable knock on the bedroom door.

Millicent Ledger entered, a small wiry Lancashire woman of fifty-eight with mild hazel eyes, a firm chinline and a flat nose – which had begun life slender and straight but had been broken when she was thirteen.

Ledgie had been with Constance all the years of her life. She had joined Constance's parents as nanny for their two-month-old baby and remained to perform a multiplicity of roles for the growing child and then the woman. Constance had been only twenty years old when her mother had died, and Ledgie, who had always been her major confidante, became her surrogate mother as well. And when in the following year the twenty-one year old had married Benjamin she had brought Ledgie along to live with them. In the nine years since, the strong-minded Lancashire woman had taken on the function of general housekeeper and also along the way, the entire household had come to rely upon her.

'Miss Constance?' the older woman began. For all the years before her marriage, Ledgie had called the young woman 'Miss Constance' and she had simply continued to use it.

'What is it, Ledgie?'

'Trouble.'

'What's wrong?'

'*She's* here.'

'Oh, I see. How inconvenient when I'm leaving for London in a few minutes.'

But Ledgie's quick North Country mind saw the bonus.

'Actually that's luck, m'darlin'. We should be able to get rid of her right smart.'

'Where is she?'

'In the front parlour.'

'Tell her I'll be down directly.'

When Constance opened the parlour door, Harriet Chard, the estranged wife of John Baron, stood with her ramrod stiff back to the room looking out through the elegant long windows to the miniature croquet lawn beyond. As Constance approached she turned and lifted the black veil from her face and swept it back over the brim of her hat.

'Well, Harriet, and what brings you here?' Constance attempted to sound polite but recalled the enmity from Harriet in their last meeting and did not hold out her hand.

'I've just heard that Benjamin's in France.'

'And who informed you of that?'

'Immaterial. Why is he there? Is there something I should know?'

'Harriet, I'm leaving for London soon. I don't have long.'

The visitor's eyes flashed with annoyance. 'Don't tell me a lie to get rid of me, Constance. I have a right to know why Ben's in France.'

'I don't really think you do, and in any case Benjamin's not in France and I'm not lying to you.'

Now Harriet's flawless skin began to colour with anger and a frown settled between her carefully arched eybrows. She had always been a beauty and when John Baron had married her a decade before, people from all over Hampshire had travelled into Bournemouth just to see her arrive at the church. She held a high opinion of herself and did not like to be corrected. 'Constance, do not play me for a fool. I know he's there. My sources are impeccable, if a trifle slow, for I also know he's been there months! We don't need to mince words.'

She tapped her gloved forefinger on the back of the nearest chair as she alluded to their last meeting. 'We know what a farce the reading of the will was and now I find out that Ben's been in France virtually from that day. I demand to know why, and what's going on?'

Constance had not suggested that her guest sit down and now as she replied she edged away back towards the door. 'I keep telling you, Benjamin's *not* in France.'

'Ah, then he's returned.'

There was a rap on the door and both women looked towards it. Ledgie opened it. 'Excuse me, Miss Constance, you must leave for Lymington Pier or you'll be late.'

'Thank you, Ledgie. I'll be there in just a minute. I'm sorry Harriet, I really don't have time for this.'

Harriet gave a scornfully dismissive glance at Ledgie's back as she closed the door. Swiftly she decided to try a different approach and her mouth drew into a counterfeit smile. 'Constance, we're relatives. Once we were something approaching friends. Can't you be honest with me and tell me? It's my right to know things concerning my husband. How can you condone such goings-on?'

Constance always found it amusing that Harriet used the words *my husband* and never John Baron's name. It had a strangely possessive impact upon the listener as if Harriet needed to convince herself of ownership. 'I've no idea what you mean and I must leave.' Constance took three firm steps to the door and took the handle.

This semi-dismissal had the effect of infuriating her visitor. 'Damn London! And don't you dare walk out on me! I know why Ben's in France and it's not right or fair. In fact, it's an outrage. I'm cruelly used – by all of you.'

Constance had had enough. 'Harriet, if anyone treated anybody cruelly, it was *you*. John Baron died in this house *with us* and yet you attended his funeral as the grieving widow. I'm afraid that did not sit well with me. I see it as no business of yours where Benjamin goes or what he does or whom he sees.' Constance firmly opened the door. 'Now I'm off to London soon. You know the way out. Good day.'

As Constance began to ascend the staircase to her bedroom she heard the sharp sound of Harriet's heels tap into the hall. The strident voice issuing through her lips was in acute contrast to her beautiful, well-proportioned mouth. 'If she gets anything that's rightfully mine, or Ben brings that whore anywhere near here, I won't be answerable for my actions.'

Constance made herself turn on the landing and look down at the woman in the hall. 'The last time I saw you, Harriet, you swore to make us sorry; today you tell me you won't be answerable for your actions. Surely even you can understand that this doesn't make you a welcome caller here.'

Harriet shot a look of malice up the stairs. 'I mean every word I say.'

Constance turned and hurried on to her bedroom. She hated confrontation, yet with Harriet it seemed it was ever that way. She remembered the day their cousin John Baron had come home from seeing her. He had already been sick with the lung disease that had killed him and he had sat by the fire, his shoulders drooping with defeat, his pale eyes weary. 'She's livid,' he had said, shaking his head. 'There's no hope that she'll ever divorce me; none at all. She'll never agree.'

It made Constance sick to think about what Harriet might be capable of doing if Ben had indeed brought the Frenchwoman *and the child* back home.

When the train arrived at Waterloo Station Constance caught a hansom cab to the Ritz. The doorman greeted her in friendly manner and ushered her in. The hotel had been built only eight years before and was very grand, though there was already evidence of the two months of war in the recruiting posters hanging in the wide foyer and the men in uniform passing through to the bar.

She was informed by a clerk behind a gleaming oak desk that she was expected and she followed the porter, a cheerful young man in a gold and blue coat who took her bag and whistled as he led her past the Louis XVI-style furnishings and along a wide corridor to ascend a marble staircase.

Throughout the journey she had wondered at the mystery. Why hadn't Benjamin just come home as they had planned? He had maintained all along that he would bring the woman and the infant home. Being childless, Constance looked forward to perhaps playing a part in the life of the infant John Baron had fathered.

She was not a person to moralise. The little boy existed and that was that. John Baron's marriage had been an appalling mistake and after five years of unhappiness with Harriet he had left her and England and gone to France where obviously he had met the French girl. Harriet had never forgiven him for leaving her.

Constance knew very little of John Baron's time in France. Occasionally when Ben received a letter he had shared its contents with her, but not always.

As Constance and the youth halted outside a room which had a silver 45 on the door, her heartbeat quickened.

The boy knocked and the door was opened by Benjamin who took the bag, thanked the youth, and brought his wife into the room, closing the door behind them. He kissed her warmly. 'My darling . . . at last.'

Constance closed her eyes and held him close and when he broke from her embrace in pain she regarded him with amazement.

Carefully touching his left arm, he explained: 'I have a slight injury, truly nothing to worry about – just a little painful.'

At that moment she caught a movement in the corner of her eye and turned to see a kitten jump from the lap of a small boy sitting on the sofa; his legs dangled in the air and at his side was a toy battleship.

She left her husband's embrace and moved across to the child, noting that his little mouth and chin and the shape of his clear, pale-blue eyes were all exactly like those of his dead father. She bent on one knee beside him and smiled and looked around the room for his mother. Before she could speak, Ben did. 'Constance, darling, just kiss the child in greeting. Say nothing for now.'

Dutifully she did so, though the child pulled away from her. Turning back to her husband she began, 'Where is his m—'

'No!' Ben cut across her, and Constance started in

32

surprise as the infant jumped to the floor and ran to Ben crying, 'Papa, Papa.'

Ben picked him up in his arms and kissed him and then handed his amazed wife a piece of paper. 'Read this darling, please, before you say another word.'

Constance read:

Darling Constance,

This is John Baron's son as you will realise. He has had great trauma in his short life and is very timid and afraid, and therefore I do not want to leave him even for a few minutes to explain things to you, hence this letter.

His mother is dead. She was mortally injured during our escape from France. The kitten was instrumental in causing the accident but the child has no understanding of this and adores it so I have managed to bring it with us for his sake. As you know, I promised his father to treat the infant as my own, but before his mother died she actually 'gave' the boy to me, and elicited another promise from me to bring him up as my son; and that means, my love, as 'our' son – yours and mine.

As you will see, little John Baron thinks I am his papa and needless to say I will never disillusion him. I want you to be his mother. He is still not three and will soon forget all that has happened if we are patient and loving. He is the child we have always dreamt about. I need you to want this, as I want it. We must be united. I have thought long and deeply and have analysed the matter to the nth degree and will explain everything in great detail to you once the child is sleeping. I do all this for the child's sake and the sake of the commitments I made both to his father and his mother.

My plan means that little John Baron will never know his real parents but he will still have 'real' parents . . . Us. He will know great joy and great love as 'our' son. We must believe as a patent truth that he will be even happier with us than he would have

*been with them. From this moment on I ask you to
act like his mother and as the days turn into weeks
and months the infant will forget his French begin-
nings and be ours completely. This way he will be a
normal little boy, legitimate in the eyes of the world
with no stigma attached to his name.*

And you will be the best mother in the world.

*Look at me, my darling wife, and smile your agree-
ment.*

Ever, Benjamin

Constance was dumbfounded. She had completed the letter
but still stood staring at it. She had come to London
expecting to meet Antoinette Desaix and her son; to
become the woman's friend and help her with support and
advice to raise her child. Instead she was presented with
a son of her own. She was to be *a mother*. Now, from this
minute.

Finally she dragged her eyes from the page and regarded
her husband. He was smiling.

'Benjamin, I'm stupefied.'

'Sweetheart, I've so much to tell you. When the boy's
asleep I'll reveal it all. What I need now is your smile. To
tell me we're in accord.'

John Baron began to babble in French and Ben laughed
and kissed the child, putting him down on the floor, but
the boy did not move from his side, and looked up at the
newcomer with wide eyes.

Constance stepped towards her husband and the child
clung to his trousers.

'Benjamin, this is hard for me . . . please understand.
Obviously you've had time to accept this.'

'That's not so, my love. Just days ago his mother was
alive. I've had to make immediate decisions and have had
no alternative.'

Constance dropped her gaze to focus on the boy. He was
regarding her with anxious eyes that seemed to be filling
with tears. What was the little thing thinking? She did not
want him to be afraid, especially not of her. In the letter

Benjamin had said he had suffered trauma and he looked so defenceless, pale and small.

She sank to her knees beside the child, though she did not touch him. 'Oh darling, you're only a baby. I'm so sorry, I hope I have not frightened you.'

Benjamin lowered himself until he too was on their level. He held the boy into his side as Constance warily put out her hand and ever so slowly lifted it to stroke John Baron's cheek.

John Baron did not cry, instead he smelt the pleasant aroma of flowers coming from the pretty lady on her knees. He liked the feeling of her warm fingers caressing his cheek. He did not understand what she said but now she took his hand and kissed his fingers and called him 'baby'.

His little mind was full of awful noises and riding a horse in the black of night, and falling and screaming, and big ships and men shouting and the wide water and big buildings and strange smells and lots of people. He had felt terribly frightened and he had wanted his mother; but he did not feel frightened here with his papa and the lady. In fact, he was conscious of a sense of comfort and security, and he watched as his papa kissed the lady's mouth, and then the lady was crying but smiling and laughing at the same time; and his papa was laughing and tenderly kissing the lady again.

And now his papa leant down and kissed John Baron's forehead and gently called him, 'my boy'.

Abruptly out of nowhere John Baron laughed too and as he was pulled lovingly into their arms and hugged between them on the floor the little kitten bounded over and climbed on Benjamin's shoe.

Chapter Four

While little John Baron slept that night as peaceful a sleep as he had ever experienced in his brief sojourn on this earth, and the tiny cat lay in a box on the floor beside him, his new mother and father talked of meaningful matters which were to alter all their lives.

Constance had insisted on seeing Ben's wound and hearing how it happened and bathing it while telling him how brave he was. Finally she agreed to drink a glass of red wine with him and sit near the window where the rain splashed on the glass overlooking the wide thoroughfare of Piccadilly.

She had removed the coat of her blue travelling suit and now her white blouse gleamed in the gaslight as she lifted her crystal glass and spoke of her fears about taking John Baron back to Lymington. '. . . for it will not be simple, my love. Harriet was there today. She knows you were in France and she knows why. She's vindictive beyond understanding and I was deeply concerned about bringing the mother and child home. But now, without Antoinette it will be impossible. How can we return with John Baron? How can we pretend we're his parents? Everyone will know. Even if we said we had adopted him in London, once Harriet found out I don't think we'd keep the secret a day.

'Darling, he looks like a Chard. Harriet would realise the truth immediately, and goodness only knows how she would react or what she would do. She's furious about the will, she's furious thinking that Antoinette exists, let alone if she knew about a child from the union.'

Ben nodded slowly. 'I've been mulling over all that, my darling, and that's why today I went to the Ministry for

War. While they kept me waiting over four hours I was lucky enough to have fifteen minutes with an acquaintance of mine, one Colonel Fleet, who's the right-hand man to Lord Kitchener himself.'

Constance's eyes narrowed. 'Oh yes?' She knew that Ben would want to do his part in the war effort. He had been a Captain training youths in the Territorials in Hampshire until he had retired from duty three years ago. She just hoped he had not done anything silly; he was well over the age to volunteer, thank God.

'Since the war started I've been wondering what I could do to help and after the talk with the Colonel this afternoon I believe I'll be in the war effort in a very real and significant way. And too, it's just what we need to keep John Baron apart from prying eyes like Harriet's.'

Constance leant forward. 'What have you done?'

'You know old Scammon has been trying to buy the shipyard for years.'

Jacob Scammon was one of Lymington's leading businessmen who owned hotels and inns, and large sections of countryside, one of his properties being hard by their boat-building yard. It was true, he had made Ben offers almost on a yearly basis.

'Well, my lovely Constance, I'm going to sell it to him at last. There's a yard that the government own up in Yorkshire near Bridlington Quay on the coast; builds small craft. Comes with a large house about a mile away, from what I'm told. The Ministry of War's going to expand the whole place; put in hundreds of workers so that they churn out small naval craft as fast as possible – lifeboats, cutters, launches, all manner of ships' boats. Kitchener himself has approved it and they were searching for a man to run it until this afternoon. You, my sweet, are looking at the new Manager.'

Constance lifted her hand to her head. This was going much too fast. Bridlington? A government shipyard? Ben the new Manager? 'What are you saying? What about our home, and Ledgie, Miss Brack – our life?'

Ben put down his glass and took up his wife's hand.

'Oh, sweetheart, I know this has been dropped on you like a bundle of bricks. But does it matter where we are, as long as we're together? We've no loyalty to Hampshire, both our families are from elsewhere. Can't you see it's the ideal way to bring up John Baron? We'll tell no one where we're going. In fact, we'll cover our movements.'

The shock on Constance's face hastened him to add, 'Of course, we wouldn't go anywhere without Ledgie, and Ernestine Brack too, she's the best secretary in England. But darling, it'll be just the place for us, well away from Harriet. We know that Ledgie and Brack will keep our secret. They're as trustworthy as the—'

Ben stopped short for his wife had burst into tears.

In an instant he brought her into his arms. 'Oh darling, please, what on earth are you crying about? Ssh, sweetheart, don't wake the boy. Tell me, for heaven's sake – what's the matter?'

Constance attempted to control herself, but her voice came in short bursts between her sobs. 'It's too much, Ben. This afternoon I lived in Lymington and we ran a good business, I managed a lovely house and was your wife. And that was my life. Now, a few hours later, I'm off to live in Yorkshire, you've a government shipyard to run, and I've got a son! My life is turned upside down, and I don't even like Yorkshire!' The tears were flowing in streams down her cheeks; she looked girlish and vulnerable in her distress and Ben kissed her eyes and wet cheeks and even her ear as she turned her face away.

He realised he had been thoughtless; in his joy at having worked out what he saw as a wonderful plan, he had forgotten about Constance's sensitivities and the possibility that she would not see things quite in the same light as he did.

'Oh, my darling girl, I'm so sorry, forgive me, please.' He kissed her again and again. 'I love you so. I did not mean to upset you. We've always been honest and straight-forward with each other and I, in my foolishness, thought I had worked out such a perfect answer to the problems that I wanted to tell you right away. I should have waited. Please don't cry any more.' And he held her close and kissed her hair. 'We'll do whatever you want. We can stay in Lymington. I won't take the government position. I should not have foisted it all upon you this way. I was wrong.'

Slowly his wife composed herself, and at last she spoke against his chest. 'Ben, I'm not sure. I just need time to think about it, that's all. This has been so fast. I feel as if I'm drowning.'

'My angel, I understand, forgive me. I know I acted hastily. Forget about it now and we'll talk of it another time.'

She looked up to him and he kissed the tears from her eyes as she agreed, 'Yes, that's right, let me sleep on it. I need to sleep on it.'

'Ah, my darling, you're the most wonderful wife in the world.'

Constance took a deep breath as she moved out of his arms. A few moments later she was calmer and she crossed to the door of the adjoining room, opened it gently, and disappeared within. Ben followed.

They had left a lamp burning low in case John Baron woke, and Ben noticed in the spread of wan light across the room that the heels of her shoes left tiny marks in the long pile carpet as she walked over it to stand at the side of the cot where the infant slept. She gripped the rail and looked down. The baby lay on his back breathing regularly: they watched the gentle rise and fall of his chest. One hand rested above the coverlet and there was a warm blush of deep sleep in his cheeks.

Ben stood on the opposite side of the cot as Constance spoke softly to the slumbering John Baron. 'We've lots to think about, little one.' She lifted her eyes to meet her husband's and she held out her hand to him. As he took it there was a loud knocking on the door of the main room.

Surprised, they looked down at John Baron, but the child slumbered on. Swiftly leaving the bedroom Constance closed the door behind them as Ben strode to the outside door and opened it.

'What the devil's all the—. Harriet!'

His cousin's widow stood there cool and beautiful. She wore a Parisian suit, the fashionable tan skirt to her ankle and the long jacket extending to calf-length. The coat was adorned at collar and cuff with sable and so too was her elegant travelling bonnet that dangled on a ribbon from her left hand. But all this elaborate sophistication was lost on Benjamin, and had he not been so agitated, he probably would have noticed the tell-tale hint of her dangerous mood in the action of her gloved hand closing and opening over the handle of the matching umbrella at her side.

Her cold gaze searched past Ben, greedily roamed the room, and came to rest upon Constance who stood a few yards behind him. 'So you thought you came to London on your own . . . Incorrect! I was on the same train.'

At this juncture Ben gestured for Constance to stay where she was and he stepped into the corridor and closed the door behind him. 'Harriet, what are you doing here?'

'I've come to see you, Ben – isn't that evident?' She parted her lips in what could have been construed as an intimate smile.

'Don't be coy with me, that won't work.'

'Aren't you going to invite me in?'

'It's obvious that I'm not.'

'You intend to keep me standing in this corridor?'

He sighed. 'If you wish to speak to me I'm happy to take you downstairs to the lounge.'

His visitor gave a laugh which turned into a sound of indignation on her luxurious mouth. 'Hell, Ben, I've come all the way from the New Forest to see my husband's French floozy and yet I feel you're going to deny me even that.'

Ben did not speak; his mind was racing.

'Benjamin, let's be frank. I know you've brought her to England. But I'll play your little game for now. We'll go downstairs and discuss it like civilised people.'

Ben led the way down the hall to the staircase and Harriet followed.

As they descended the stair together Ben glanced sideways at the petulant beauty who accompanied him and his mind darted back to the last time he had seen her. It had been the day after John Baron's burial at the reading of his will in the Bournemouth chambers of their solicitor, Robert Brine: a glorious July morning and the blackbirds had been feeding on the windowsill outside as the solicitor's good-natured face settled into sober lines and he drew on the string of the will he held in his hands.

Arranged in front of the legal gentleman were the beneficiaries: Benjamin himself, Constance, Harriet and Mrs Lamont, the housekeeper from John Baron and Harriet's marital home.

In his dispassionate tones Mr Brine read the names of the executors and the following formalities until he came to the specific bequests, when he hesitated and eyed his three visitors. 'The bequests are reasonably simple,' he informed them before he returned his gaze to the will. '"To my housekeeper, Mrs Gertrude Lamont, I leave two hundred pounds".' At this generosity Mrs Lamont exclaimed, 'God bless ye, sir, wherever ye are!'

Mr Brine coughed and continued. '"To my cousin-in-law, Constance Davina Chard, who has been more like a sister to me, I leave my mother's ruby and diamond necklace, the centrepiece of the necklace being a four-carat emerald-cut diamond".'

At this announcement Harriet moved slightly and folded her arms. Mr Brine went on, '"To my legal widow, Harriet Clara Chard, I leave Lissom Keep, the dwelling which we shared in Brokenhurst in the New Forest. It has given her more pleasure than it ever gave me. I also bequeath Harriet the stables and the horses I own on the outskirts of Beaulieu, for the only creatures I ever saw her show affection to were those horses. As she comes from wealth of her own, she does not need my money".'

Harriet's affronted intake of breath was loud in the ears of the gathered but she sat stiffly upon her chair while the solicitor finished the bequests.

'"To my cousin, Benjamin Chard, who has been as close as any brother to me, my life long, I leave my share in our boatyard and the remainder of my estate including the hotel in Lyme Regis, the bank balances, financial shares and the

41

property in south-east Queensland in Australia, which was left to me by my maternal grandmother. He knows what to do with everything and whom to take care of with it. I trust him absolutely and thank him for his constancy, his unwavering loyalty and his indubitable love for me".'

At this juncture Harriet stood. 'What a farce!' She stepped towards the amenable Robert Brine as if she would strike him, and at the same moment, as if they sensed her fury, the blackbirds eating on the windowsill flapped their wings in protest against the glass, rose and flew away. 'How could you have allowed him to perpetrate such a disgraceful act? You, a man with knowledge of the law who should have guided him. Instead, you allowed him to scorn me and treat me this way, and I'm his lawful married wife. You shouldn't be allowed to practise, you pettifogger!'

'Mrs Chard, please! We've not yet completed the reading.'

Harriet's expression altered completely. Gone was the cool flawless beauty and in its place was vitriol; her eyes became pinpoints of hatred and a florid veil swept up from her neck to her forehead. She spun round to Ben who had risen at her side. 'I will *never* forgive you. Never. You were always against me. It's all *your* fault.'

Ben held up his palm. 'This is no time for acrimony. We're all upset. Please, Harriet, let's just—'

'Go to hell!' The words were like gunshots. 'You'll be sorry for all this. I'll make you sorry, I swear.' And she lifted her gloved hand and pushed Ben aside as she swept by Mr Brine and out of the room.

In the silence she left, the solicitor's eyes blinked behind his glasses. 'I knew she'd take it badly. I told Mr Chard when he was making the will she'd take it badly.' He winced as if in pain. 'Calling me a *pettifogger* of all things!'

It was Mrs Lamont who replied from where she sat cross-legged in a brown leather wing-backed chair. 'She's got more'n she deserves. Why, that house and the stables are worth a fortune.' She sniffed and folded her arms. 'Mr Chard were far an' away too kind to her, if ye ask me, the way she carried on, screamin' at him an' demandin' all the time, drove him distracted she did until finally she drove him away altogether. And now that he's gone and treated me so kind I'll be leavin' her and be off on me own, I will. She's a right hard 'un to be around.'

Robert Brine exhaled loudly. 'Right, that's it then. We'll continue, shall we? It is customary to complete the reading, you know . . .'

And now as Benjamin eased himself into one of the plush chairs in the Ladies' Lounge in the Ritz Hotel and regarded his visitor, the events of that morning in Bournemouth were uppermost in his mind.

Neither of them spoke as a collector for the Red Cross passed between the tables. Ben put a shilling in the box and received a gracious smile for his generosity before ordering two glasses of gin and tonic, after which he sat back silently while Harriet toyed with the pins under the ostrich feather in her bonnet. She met his gaze as she placed the hat on the vacant chair at her side. 'So, what are you going to say?'

'Harriet, it is you who've come here! After our last meeting I would have thought you'd be trying to avoid me.'

'Ah. Well, I've had time to think since we last saw each other.' She paused for effect. 'I know about the child you have in the room upstairs.'

Ben's voice was strained. 'I see.'

Harriet was containing the rage she felt, but a tiny muscle beneath her right eye quivered involuntarily. 'It didn't take me long. I asked a few pertinent questions of some affable gentlemen here in the hotel, and I soon found out.' Her voice dripped with disgust. 'I'm offended by that, Ben, deeply offended. I am also offended by your act of bringing the mother of the illegitimate issue here. You see, Benjamin, you should have left them in France where they belong.'

'Yes, Harriet, that's pretty clear. But I intend to do as John Baron would have wanted.'

Her voice rose slightly. 'And what does that mean?'

'It means that I will do my duty, keep my promises and have compassion, an emotion which seems to be entirely foreign to you.'

Their drinks arrived and Harriet took a mouthful before she continued. 'How can you talk like that when you have what's rightfully mine?'

'I'm not going to let you annoy me. John Baron and I worked hard to get the shipyard where it is today; you did not contribute one iota towards it, so how is it rightfully yours?'

'I was his wife. The money, the property . . . he should have left everything to me.'

Ben groaned with frustration. 'This is old ground, Harriet.'

'Those two are going to share in what belongs to me, and that makes me very, very unhappy. I don't think you have any conception exactly *how* unhappy.'

'Look, the fact is I intend to do what's right.'

'Then look after me.'

Ben closed his eyes and sighed.

Seconds dawdled by and Ben opened his eyes and remained studying her. Over half a minute passed before Harriet asked, 'What part of the country do you intend to settle them in?'

Ben actually smiled. 'As if I'd tell you. As far away from you as possible.'

Harriet managed to part her lips in a matching display of satisfaction. 'Good, that suits me.' She took another mouthful of her drink and abruptly she confessed something that was so out of character that it made her listener think she was almost human, after all. 'I thought at first I wanted to see her; that's why I followed Constance up to London. All the way up in the train I believed I wanted to look on her face. Even when I knocked on your door I hoped she'd be in the room. But do you know? Now, just a few minutes later, I feel the opposite. I don't want to see her at all, not ever. Neither of them – her, nor the boy.'

He could not help himself and he shot back, 'So this way you keep the comfortable illusion that they don't exist?'

Harriet took another sip of her drink. 'Ah, but they do, don't they? And you in your foolishness have chosen them over me, your lawful relative.'

'God, Harriet, you twist everything. Do you ever see reality? I haven't chosen anyone. The truth is, you were left quite reasonably off. He did right by you whereas you did only wrong by him. In my opinion you deserve none of it.'

Her voice was rising. '*Deserve*, you say! What the hell do you know about deserve? Do *they* deserve? What was mine should have stayed mine. But no, you talk rubbish about promises and duty. Can't you see the child's illegitimate, damn you, and the Frenchwoman's nothing but a disgusting harlot. She's wantonly taken what I—'

'Keep your mouth shut about her!' Ben's voice had risen too and the people at the nearest table looked round. 'Damn it, Harriet, leave her alone, for God's sake. She's dead! She can't hurt you at all.'

Harriet thudded back into her chair. She said nothing for a few moments and when she did speak her voice was sedate and self-possessed again. 'So she's dead. Well, well, well. Now that makes me think about a deal of consequences. Oh yes, indeed. Well, dead or not, I'll never forgive her for spoiling my life and I'll never forgive you or that honey-tongued wife of yours.'

She nodded her head to herself. 'I'm beginning to see it. You'll keep *my money* for the offspring, eh?' She made a sound of mock mirth deep in her throat. 'Let me tell you something, Benjamin Chard. Listen carefully and take it in, and know I mean it. I want the necklace he gave Constance and I want the hotel and the nine thousand pounds I know John Baron had in Lloyds Bank and the three thousand he had in shares. All are rightfully mine. The rest you can keep. I want them turned over to me by the end of the month or I'll not be responsible for my actions.'

Ben shook his head in disgust. 'Were you ever?'

She did not speak while she finished her drink.

'There's a war on, Harriet. Men are dying and from what I hear, there'll be a lot more dead. Just for once realise how lucky you are and how John Baron, in fact, treated you more than fairly, far better than he should have. Forget your blasted myopia and self-indulgence and think about all that.'

She regarded him for a few seconds before she awarded him another of her faux smiles as she picked up her umbrella and her hat. 'You've got plenty of money of your own, you can share yours with the little bastard.' The venom that hung on each word seemed to droop tangibly in the air between them. 'Return what's rightfully mine by the end of this month. I've warned you and I mean it.'

Ben leant back in his chair and blew air from his mouth in a long resonating sigh. 'Harriet, haven't you got a train to catch?'

She did not reply. She ran her eyes across him in a dismissive glance before she rose and left the lounge, her proud head tilted skywards. Her departure was so swift that in thirty seconds the only sign of her in the entire Ritz Hotel was the aroma of her hyacinth perfume floating in the air.

When Ben opened the door to Suite 45 he found an anxious Constance waiting in virtually the same spot he had left her. She came forward and took hold of his hands. 'What did she want?'

'She wants the necklace, the hotel, the shares and the money John Baron had in his bank. She wants them by the end of this month.'

'What'll we do?'

'You'll keep the jewellery and I'll keep the rest, mostly for the boy as John Baron wished me to. She threatened me. She's filled with hate. She knows about the child and she made me so furious that I blurted out about Antoinette's death.'

'Oh Benjamin, darling, so now she knows everything. I've been worrying the whole time. Going back and forwards over everything in my mind, wondering what we should be doing for the best. The way she turned up like that, I couldn't believe it. But the one thing I know for certain now is, we must take John Baron away from her. We must! We'll start afresh, far from such people as Harriet, and we'll do as you suggested; the government boatyard and Yorkshire. I've come to terms with it all while you've been away.' She gave a long trembling sigh. 'And as well, we'll be helping Lord Kitchener with the war effort. Yes, you were right all along.'

Ben enfolded her in his arms and even though it hurt his left arm to squeeze her tightly, squeeze her he did. 'Thank you, angel,' he whispered into her curls.

For the next seventeen days there was little rest for Ben and Constance. For the first week Ben returned to Lymington, saw Jacob Scammon and arranged the sale of the property the old man had coveted so long.

Ben spoke in confidence to Ledgie and Miss Brack, and those two loyal souls took what they had been told to their hearts, to hold forever still. That very afternoon Ledgie began packing their belongings, and five days later she went up to London to help Constance with the child while Ernestine Brack began the task of organising their complete removal from Lymington.

Near the end of the second week Constance felt comfortable enough to leave John Baron with Ledgie – to whom he had taken quite quickly – and return to Lymington to help with the final vacating of the house. Ben had left nothing to chance; he had sold the house and shipyard intact, and the only pieces of furniture they took were Constance's Regency gilt and walnut desk which she had been given by her father for her twenty-first birthday and the Sheraton dining table and chairs which had belonged to Ben's parents. The employees at the shipyard and their friends in the town and county were informed that they were moving to London, which in the first instance they did.

By the end of the month, Harriet's deadline, they were entirely transferred to London. After five weeks in that city they told their landlord they were relocating to Scotland and in fact moved briefly to Coventry during the Christmas period, and then on to Yorkshire.

By 5 January, 1915 they were ensconced outside Bridlington Quay a mile from the government boatyard on the cliff above the North Beach of the watering place, and Ben was certain they had covered their tracks completely. They named the house Haverhill; it stood alone in meadows on a quiet road that led towards the great chalk cliffs of Flamborough Head and beyond. There was some work to be done on it, for it had lain vacant for a few years, but it had cedar panelling in the rooms and a spacious garden, and was surrounded by a high brick wall; all in all it was a fine dwelling and the most substantial by far for miles around.

It was three days later on Friday, 8 January that Ben rode a grey mare from Bridlington Quay across the emerald fields into the ancient market town of Bridlington a mile inland. At 126 Quay Road in a small stone building he found the Bridlington Register Office.

Open 10 a.m. to 3 p.m. It was 2.45 p.m.

Inside, a stooped gentleman of great age stood from a desk and as he came forward to greet Benjamin, an odour of whisky accompanied him.

'Are you the Superintendent?'

He shook his hoary head. 'Nay, sir. Mr George Harkinson – he be t'fellow you're after.'

'And where is he?'

'In Wales.'

'Oh. For how long?'

'Well, he's on his annual holiday, isn't he? Away a month or more and only just gone.'

'Who are you then?'

'I be the Acting Registrar. The Registrar himself's joined up.'

'But you can register the birth of my son?'

The man looked a mite offended. 'O' course I can. It's what I be here for, ain't it? Nowt's happened all day,' his eyes wandered to the wall clock, 'and then you come in at t'last minute and all. So we'd best be movin'.' He returned to his desk, bent down under it and took out a form, sat and picked up his pen, dipped it in the ink and looked up. 'Name of the child?'

'John . . . Baron . . . Chard.'

'Mother?'

'Constance Davina Chard.'

'Father?'

'Benjamin Blake Chard.'

'Date of marriage?'

'Twenty-sixth of June nineteen hundred and four.'

'Midwife in attendance at the birth?'

'Yes. Miss Millicent Ledger.'

Ben held his breath and the elderly gent frowned. 'Ledger . . . Never heard of her.'

'Oh, she's not in the district now.'

The man hesitated and eyed Ben for a moment: he appeared well-dressed, spoke properly, was obviously a gentleman. He looked down again. 'Date of infant's birth?'

'Eleventh of November nineteen eleven.'

The man raised his pale eyes again. 'My my, this is irregular. You be registering t'lad a bit late in t'day, aren't you? He's three turned from my calculation.'

Ben nodded. 'Yes, that's true. Meant to register him, of course, many a time. Just never got round to it until today.'

'My my, never got around to it, eh? And you look such an organised gent, but there you are, can't judge by looks. I've learnt that over a long life, I have.' He chewed the end of his thumb in thought. 'Don't know what to do about this an' all.'

'How do you mean?'

'Well, it be seven and six for being over forty-two days late. Can't imagine what it is for being three years late, but there you are.' He chewed his thumb again. 'I've never had such as this before.' His eyes wandered to the clock again. 'Can you come back Monday?'

'I'm afraid I can't.'

'Ee, my my. I suppose three years late be still over forty-two days, ain't it? So I suppose it still be seven and six.'

Ben took out his wallet. 'I'm happy to pay more.'

The old man waved his hand in the air. 'No, no. Let me think.' He continued chewing his thumb as his visitor took out a ten-shilling note and placed it on the desk. 'Ee, I can't be giving you change for that. We don't be holding that sort o' money here. That's two and six back to you and I don't have it.' He shook his head. 'My my, this is very

49

irregular, and what with Mr Harkinson away and all, and young Mr Taff, the Registrar, off in France . . .'

Ben smiled. 'Look, I realise how late this is. And I'm sorry to have put you to the trouble. Please take the ten-shilling note and pay the seven and six in. The extra two and six is for you.' He smiled benignly. 'I appreciate all this, really I do. And I must get it done today.'

'Oh, you must, eh? I see.' And now the man poked at the note with his forefinger. 'Three years late and it must be done today. My my, happen it's all reet, but I'll have to make a note about the irregularity here in the margin.' He spoke aloud as he wrote. '"NB. Irregular: late notification of birth of male child, John Baron Chard. Seven and six paid in for offence committed".' He sighed and looked at the clock. 'I suppose that should do it.'

'Oh yes, I'm sure it will,' Ben agreed.

The man continued to nudge the money with his finger. 'I reckon I've done right.'

His visitor swiftly concurred again. 'Oh, I'm certain you have.'

Ben felt a tingle of alarm as the old gent paused a moment seemingly in indecision, then he glanced once more at the clock and said, 'Aye well,' and pushed the sheet across the desk, pointing to the form. 'Write down your address here and sign at the bottom. Oh, and perhaps you should be writing "father" after the signature, please. We usually have the mothers in here, you know.'

Benjamin picked up the pen and did as requested while the man went on, 'Being there's a war on, I suppose irregular things do happen. My my, I daresay they do.'

'I'm sure you're right. Thank you so much, Mr . . . ?'

'Lacy. Egbert Lacy.'

'Thank you, Mr Lacy.' Ben took the carbon copy and returned the form back across the desk.

'Goodbye, Mr Lacy.' And without any more communication Benjamin disappeared promptly out of the door.

In the street he halted and heaved a sigh. Mr Lacy had not asked him where the child had been born. He had simply assumed he had been born in Bridlington at the address given! Ben looked up at the sky with a thankful expression. He had gone in believing he would have all sorts of trouble and he had met Mr Egbert Lacy! God bless him and all Assistant Registrars in the universe.

He was feeling so thankful that he strode along the High Street to the Church of St Mary and St Nicholas. He entered and halted by an easel, and read the description of the church pinned upon it.

St Mary and St Nicholas was a priory church of an Augustinian foundation during the reign of Henry I, son of William the Conqueror, Henry Beauclerc, 'Henry good scholar' as he was known. Some portions of it remain Old English original, probably built around 1120.

Ben glanced around. It was amazing to think that sections of this building had stood for 800 years. He felt a little odd, for he had not been inside a church since his wedding day, though Ledgie and Constance attended services regularly.

He walked slowly along the nave and sat down in the quiet emptiness. Weak rays of the dying January sun cast grey shadows across the pews as he picked up the *Common Prayer Book* and it fell open. He looked down and the words he read were:

. . . and grant that this child, now to be baptised therein, may receive the fullness of Thy grace, and ever remain in the number of Thy faithful and elect children.

He took it as a sign for little John Baron: a propitious sign. And giving a gentle smile to the altar, stood and walked out.

He rode home spiritedly. When he arrived at the harbour in Bridlington Quay he paused for a few minutes to breathe the damp cold air and to look down to the south, across the grey waters of the North Sea towards Belgium and France and the raging war, the bitter January wind lashing at the tail of his overcoat. He imagined the boys in the trenches over there, only about three hundred miles away, yet they might as well be on another planet: it would be hellishly cold in a hole in the ground tonight. He shook his head with the grievousness of it all.

He watched some fishermen coming into the harbour in

a long boat, their oars fighting the surges of the sea until they were safe within the wall before he turned his horse's head towards his new home.

After a few minutes his mind returned to what he had just accomplished. He felt a sense of justice about that, as if he had set right that which had been wrong. He had now given little John Baron his legitimacy and the fact was, that in Ben's mind, the fabrication of John Baron's English birth was not only justifiable, but entirely sanctioned by Antoinette Desaix and John Baron Chard. The two people who had given the boy life had in turn given the boy to Ben. What he had just done was not only warranted but valid.

As he brought the grey to a trot along Victoria Parade and on by his boatyard, he suddenly lifted his head high in the wind and he whistled 'The Farmer's Boy', a tune he had not thought of since he too was a boy and yet it rolled quite competently off his lips.

Chapter Five

John Baron stood at his bedroom window, his right hand automatically stroking Grenville, his cocker spaniel, which he had been given nine months previously when his cat, Moonbeam, vanished. She had been a wanderer always and was often gone for twenty-four hours, but when three days passed and she had not come home, his father searched for her in the byways, across the fields and into the town but Moonbeam did not reappear. Ben was genuinely sorry, for the cat had been such a survivor right from the moment in France when little John Baron found it.

Constance had told the child that Moonbeam had gone to live in a beautiful place with lots of other cats, and to console him for his loss they purchased Grenville, who quickly insinuated himself into the boy's affections.

John Baron lifted his left hand to shade his eyes from the surprisingly bright December sun as he stared across the wind-raked garden below to the wall and the thoroughfare beyond where a phalanx of soldiers marched in step along the road that led by North Beach and the boat-building yard to disappear in the distance.

Even though the wind was sharp and so strong that his fair curls lifted and uncoiled as he bent forward to rest his arms on the windowsill he did not mind, for he loved to hear the tramping feet of the soldiers, and to watch them passing by. There was what his mother spoke of as 'a camp' some miles to the north. He had heard the place they marched towards called 'Flamborough Head' and he certainly knew he had a head and that people had heads but he was not sure what a flamborough head was.

As well, he was aware of 'the war'. It was a lot of soldiers fighting and it was happening across the sea and the soldiers went there to beat the Germans. Everybody talked about the Germans, from Molly the maid to Paxton, the old man who did all the odd jobs and doubled as the gardener, and they never ever said anything nice so John Baron knew that Germans were terrible. Only this morning he had heard Ledgie say they were *not human,* and even though he was only just five years old he knew that particular phrase was Ledgie's common refrain when she thoroughly and completely disliked someone.

John Baron turned his head in the opposite direction to which the soldiers marched. His strong young eyes could make out the terrace houses on the foreshores behind North Beach where the boat-building yard lay. And he could imagine the rows of completed small craft lined up like large grey bananas on the beach waiting to be taken away in the big lorries that came every now and then.

A month ago on his birthday his father had taken him to the boatyard. It was always a special treat when that happened. He was excited by the noise and the activity, and he liked to watch the men smoke their pipes and talk as they sat along the sea wall at lunchtime.

Most of the men called him 'little master' and a few of them, who laughed a lot and wore checked cloth caps over their hair, addressed him as 'John Baron Boy'. Ledgie said they were 'common' and they should have more respect, but they made John Baron laugh and he liked them.

He had followed his father through the cobbled yard and into the office he shared with Miss Brack and another lady called Edwina, and to his delight Miss Brack had given him tea and cream cakes in honour of his birthday. She had made the cakes and each one was small and dainty. While they were there his father talked to Miss Brack about the sacrifice the soldiers in the trenches were making. He did not know what 'sacrifice' was but he knew it was something special from the way the grown-ups said the word.

After the tea-party his father took his hand and they entered the long shed where the boats were constructed. At one end the men painted the completed craft a grey colour.

They were all painted the same, a sort of green undercoat and then over-painted with grey. The painters had put down their pots and clapped their hands and called 'Happy Birthday!' to him. He realised he was the centre of attention and had laughed with joy. His father had taken him up a ladder and climbed into one of the bigger boats where he had then addressed the men briefly, saying it was his son's fifth birthday and that John Baron was indeed a lucky young fellow to be able to be involved so closely in the war effort. He had then lifted John Baron up to stand high on the bulwark while the men below were shouting out greetings to him. John Baron had begun to laugh and looked down at the sea of faces when suddenly for no reason at all he became terrified; he felt he was falling, falling, and the men's greetings in his ears turned into screaming and he dropped forward down into them.

Preston, the foreman, and another man had leapt into action and caught him, and his father had stood over him white-faced and felt his pulse before Miss Brack and Edwina carried him back to their office and fussed over him. After he had drunk some water and the dizziness had gone, he felt awkward and silly. His father used the word 'vertigo' when explaining to the men what had happened.

The occurrence certainly spoiled John Baron's afternoon, but by dinnertime that night he had forgotten all about it, and his mother and father had given him a train engine that Preston had made out of a piece of the wood they used to make the sea-craft. Preston had said that one small piece for the little master 'won't harm our boys at sea or in the trenches'. He had even discovered some red and yellow paint to decorate it with, and when John Baron opened the box he had exclaimed with delight.

The engine now sat near him on the window seat as he knelt watching the soldiers marching by, and when he jumped down to the carpeted floor, followed agilely by Grenville, he took it with him.

As he arrived at the top of the stairs the conglomeration of sounds from below reached his ears: the deep voices of the men and the occasional lighter female one riding over the top of them. He often liked just to sit on the stairs and listen to the adult voices.

As he descended the stairs to the ground floor he ran his fingers down the banisters and could hear a soldier's voice rising from below.

'You can say Ypres if you like, old man, but I can tell you now there was nothing like the viscid bloody mud in the Somme Valley when I was hit. God, my horse actually drowned in that! I can hear his whinnied screaming now as I look at you, and not a bloody thing I could do about it.' He hesitated. 'Best stallion on the blasted Front, too.'

John Baron daily heard of the Battle of the Somme. It had been going on since 1 July this year, and had only just ended three weeks earlier, the Allies gaining mere miles at the cost of over 600,000 men. John Baron was not aware of these statistics but he knew that most of the convalescing soldiers in his home had been wounded in that awesome battle. He sat down on the bottom step as one of the men turned and spied the child. 'Ah, there you are, Johnny B. What we're saying's not for the likes of your ears, young fellow. What have you been up to today?'

John Baron came forward smiling as Grenville ran up and licked Wakefield's hand. Wakefield was an airman who had crashed his aeroplane after a dogfight with the Germans and had lost his leg from the knee down as a result. All the men here were convalescing; all wearing hospital blue. John Baron's parents had handed over the entire ground floor of the house to the local military hospital, and it had been turned into a ward where recovering men stayed. They had thirty-one men here at present and Ledgie and Molly, the maid, cooked for them and for the household too. Ledgie called their lodgers 'men on the mend'.

Of all the wounded here, Flight Lieutenant Nigel Wakefield was John Baron's favourite and Wakefield in turn had become very fond of the boy. As well, the airman had struck up a fine friendship with Benjamin, for even though there were well over ten years between their ages, the two men had a lot in common; both being Cambridge men and both having travelled much upon the continent.

Wakefield's mother had been French born in Reims, his father English and he had volunteered for Kitchener's Army within two weeks of the outbreak of war. He had fought in the trenches in Flanders and after six months had transferred to the Royal Flying Corps.

Nigel Wakefield came swinging towards John Baron on his crutches. He was hoping to get a wooden leg soon. He ran his hand through John Baron's curls and the child lifted his face to his friend and replied to his question.

'I've been watching the soldiers march down the road and I've been playing with Grenville and with my train engine.'

'Good boy. That's the spirit, stay busy. Now, how about counting to twenty for me?'

Wakefield had taught John Baron to count and to say the alphabet in English and French. He had also taught him a little French song, 'Frère Jacques'. He had told Benjamin that Johnny B had a 'natural bent' for the French language and that his accent was perfect. Ben had smiled and nodded somewhat sagely at this news. John Baron was to begin after Christmas at the church school at Holy Trinity in the town, and Wakefield had told the little boy he would be so far ahead of the others that he would be the smartest in the class.

John Baron did as he had been requested and counted in French, and when he finished with 'dix-huit, dix-neuf, vingt,' a few men playing cards on the table nearby applauded.

The child preened and his cheeks coloured with pride as he pointed to the door with his engine. 'Do you want to walk in the garden with us, Lieutenant Wakefield?'

Wakefield grinned. 'Certainly, young fellow. I need the exercise.'

'You do indeed,' agreed one of the three nurses who came each day to the house from the military hospital.

Wakefield gave her a cheeky grin and followed John Baron and Grenville through the door. Grenville charged ahead to the suntrap between the outer wall and the gardener's shed and there, all with their faces up to the limited warmth of the rare December sunlight, sat a dozen of the wounded soldiers; some read, others just lolled in their chairs. Four had great bandages on their heads and bodies, six had arms or legs missing; one boy from Liverpool, Lieutenant Nelson, had both legs and an arm missing. And another, Captain Meere, always had a hand-kerchief over his face. He had 'been gassed' – that's all John Baron knew.

John Baron did not realise it, but at first Constance had tried to keep him away from the worst of the wounded, but Ben had known it would be impossible with so many invalids everywhere and he had simply said, 'The boy will see them anyway. Best he knows them as men, not as freaks in the distance. This way he will have some understanding of their bravery and the wonderful spirit most of them display.'

And it was true, there was something innately remark-able about each of the very badly wounded, their cheer-fulness transcending their physical disabilities to such an extent that it seemed as if they were not troubled by their crippling deformities. Of course in most cases it was an unspoken, heartrending bravado, but John Baron did not comprehend this and so he simply saw the broken men as jolly souls overcoming their disfigurement with humour and good spirit. If John Baron had been a little older he might have realised why his mother had tears in her eyes after she delivered a meal to Lieutenant Nelson or Captain Meere, but as he did not, it did not concern him and he treated the men as they treated him, with geniality and affection.

He ran by the men now in pursuit of Grenville who had hurtled by them giving chase to sparrows near the garden wall. A few of the soldiers called out greetings and Wakefield slowed down, coming to a halt near his friend Captain Blake.

As John Baron scuttled up to the dog he heard Ledgie's voice calling him from the scullery door. Obediently he ran across to join her. She had removed her apron and wore a green silk garment that the little boy recognised as one of the gowns she wore for special occasions.

'What is it, Ledgie?'

'Come with me, your father wants you.'

So back into the house John Baron trailed behind Ledgie: through the scullery where Molly stood at the sink washing piles of pots and pans; on past the kitchen and the multitude of wonderful cooking aromas that beset him, into the parlour where all the furniture had been removed and many soldiers' beds stood side-by-side, to finally issue out into the hall and pass by the convalescents playing cards and games at various tables and to again ascend the stairs he had so recently come down.

At the top on the landing Ledgie knelt down and stroked his face, the severe angles of her face softening with tenderness. 'Now me darlin', you go on along the passage to your daddy and mummy's room. They're in there and they have the special surprise I told you about. I'll be keepin' Grenville for a few minutes.' And she put out her hand and held the dog by his collar.

John Baron skipped along the landing and turned the handle of his parents' bedroom door. The first person he saw was his father holding out his hand. 'Ah, there you are, my darling laddie. Come and see Mummy.'

John Baron took his father's outstretched hand and looked beyond to the bed where his mother lay propped up on pillows and a strange woman in a grey dress and a white apron stood looking down at her. John Baron had not seen his mother since yesterday, and when he had asked for her this morning, Ledgie had told him she was away bringing home a surprise for him.

'Mummy, where have you been?'

Constance pushed against the pillows behind her back. 'Come here, sweetheart.' She opened her arms to him and he dropped his father's hand and ran to her side.

'Careful,' cautioned the lady in the white apron as John Baron went to climb on the bed.

'It's all right,' his mother replied as she bent forward to kiss him. His father lifted him up and sat him beside his mother. That was the moment when John Baron saw the crib: a tiny cot draped in white lace on the far side of the big bed. Because of the war there had been no lace to be found anywhere so Constance and Ledgie had cut up Constance's wedding gown and made the lace drapes themselves. It looked pristine and beautiful to John Baron's eyes, and as his father lifted him up into his arms and walked round his mother's bed towards it, John Baron realised this was the surprise Ledgie had told him about and he peered forward as his father halted.

Down inside the white lace bed, side by side slept two tiny little babies. John Baron had never seen anything like them before, they were so small and frail-looking and pink in the face. But the overwhelming feeling that swept through his youthful mind was the beauty of them with their tiny button noses and flower-petal mouths and the sweet little lace caps they wore. Except for his mother, he had never seen anything quite so beautiful.

'Who are they?' he asked.

Ben kissed him. 'They're your twin baby sisters.'

His eyes were wide with wonder. 'Really?'

'Yes, darling,' his mother spoke from the bed. 'They're your little sisters, Samantha and Vivian.'

'But where did you get them?'

'That doesn't matter now.' His father placed him firmly down on the floor. 'They're here and we'll all love them very much.'

'Can I see them again, please?' he asked, pulling his father's coat. And when Ben lifted him up to where he could see them once more the child gazed from one to the other. 'Which is which?'

Ben looked a little lost at this question and the lady in the white apron bustled to the side of the cot. She pointed. 'That one's Vivian and this one's Samantha.'

John Baron was fascinated. 'Will they live here?'

Now the lady with the white apron laughed and his father made an affirmative sound. 'They will, m'boy, and when they get a little bigger you'll play with them and teach them things.'

John Baron thought how nice that would be, though a part of him would have preferred two little brothers. Yet looking down from his father's arms upon the sleeping babies he had to admit he was happy they belonged here. 'They are very small,' he stated and his father returned him to the floor with the remark, 'They'll grow, laddie, just as you did.'

John Baron looked up at his parent. 'Was I that small, Daddy?'

'Of course you were. Now kiss your mother and we'll go down for luncheon, and if you are very good you can come back and see your sisters later on this afternoon.'

'Why are you in bed, Mummy?' the innocent child asked as Ben guided him to the door.

'I'm tired, darling,' his mother spoke from the bed. 'There's been a lot of work for me to bring your sisters to you.'

'Oh,' he replied acceptingly as his father took him into the corridor where Ledgie waited for him. 'Ledgie, have you seen them? There are two of them. My sisters.'

The woman bestowed one of her rare smiles upon him. 'Yes, me darlin' I've seen them, and right pretty they are and all.'

That night, after he had been in and seen his mother and kissed her good night and also kissed his little sisters for the first time, Ledgie had put another blanket on his bed and tucked him in and read him a little of his story, *The Ice Maiden*, before his father had come in to say good night. His father had left him with the words, 'Winken Blinken and Nod will soon be coming so I'll go along now. Good night, darling laddie.'

After his parent had gone John Baron lay snug in his bed listening to the winter wind making rushes against his window and the rain hitting the pane in gushes. There was a fire in his grate which kept the room cosy but he knew that often his mother and father went without the precious coal in their bedroom so that he could be warm; but tonight they too had a fire because of the babies. He had overheard Ledgie talking to Molly about the coal miners while they were cooking together in the kitchen. Ledgie had said the miners were on strike and coal was scarce. 'They aren't

61

human,' she had confided to Molly. 'Not when our boys are dying in droves across the seas for them, and freezing into the bargain, and they go on strike here at home in what's predicted to be the worst winter in living memory. They're worse than bad, worse than selfish, a plague upon the lot of them.'

John Baron did not understand a lot of what the grown-ups said, but he did feel sorry for the soldiers across the sea in France and he did hope that they would not freeze and that they would get some coal from somewhere to keep them warm.

But in his cosy room here with the fire crackling, the amazing event of the day was uppermost in his limited considerations. He still could not quite believe it. He had twin sisters, and they were here for ever. It had been a most startling event to go to his parents' room and have them turn up. He tried to remember what they were called but could only think of one name – it was Sam something; the other he had quite forgotten but he knew he liked their names and he felt quite contented about it all, happy about it all.

He drifted off to sleep snug and warm with their tiny sweet faces circulating in his mind, secure in the knowledge that he was greatly loved and, he correctly supposed, that they too would be.

Chapter Six

His seventh birthday was a day he always remembered. It stayed with him all his life, for it was imprinted on his psyche.

He watched as his small world erupted with elation.

'*It's over!*' was the cry that echoed across the streets; across the fields, the beaches and the cliffs; across the mountains and the rivers, the cities and the countryside. Everyone everywhere rejoiced.

The convalescent soldiers all began to sing and chant and slap each other with glee, and his mother, Ledgie and Molly and the three visiting nurses danced around the kitchen and the hall with those soldiers who had legs, and the ones who did not clapped their hands in time and shouted and called joyously through the house and out into the garden. Four bottles of champagne which Benjamin had been saving for a special day were brought out from the cold cellar and soon demolished by those lucky enough to be on hand.

In the yard men downed tools and thumped each other on the back and shouted and sang. The streets of Bridlington were congested with people and laughter, and the celebration extended up and down the land. Volleys of gunfire erupted across the nation and across the world down to the lands in the outreaches of the vast Empire, like Bermuda, the West Indies, India, Fiji, Australia and New Zealand. It seemed as if the whole world sang and Grenville was allowed to bark without restraint while John Baron and Samantha and Vivian were lifted high in the air throughout the day and kissed and hugged by all who knew them, and by many who did not.

Ledgie drank two sherries, the first alcohol that had passed her lips in a generation and as her cheeks flushed with exultation, she handed out indiscriminately the cakes and biscuits she had been jealously guarding and parsimoniously doling out in ones and twos in the past.

At luncheon Molly produced a birthday cake that she and Ledgie had made for John Baron by saving the flour, egg and sugar rations. It was only small but decorated with a little yellow boat with white sails and in the icing were written the words, *Happy Birthday Dear John Baron 11-11-1918*. One of the soldiers, a man called Reagan, gave him a red pencil and sketching pad, and a few of the others each gave him a penny. Constance produced a yellow scarf she had knitted for him by unravelling a cardigan that she did not wear and she put it round his neck and kissed him.

Even at his tender age John Baron was well aware he was lucky to get anything at all because he knew everyone was so conscious of saving for the war effort. And when he had eaten his cake and went wandering in the garden wearing his scarf and carrying his red pencil behind his ear, his sketching book under his arm and rattling his pennies in his pocket he was as happy as if he had received a room full of toys; for there was such overwhelming joy in the atmosphere around him that it pervaded all life.

At one point in the gleeful day Miss Brack took John Baron's little sisters and put them to bed for their afternoon nap, and Molly was seconded to watch over them; but as evening became night and the great excitement was still in the air John Baron left Grenville sleeping under the hall staircase and went out of the front door and through the tall iron gate into the road. After a few minutes Mr Brinkman's milkcart trundled slowly by, full of men and women drinking cider, and he climbed up onto the tailboard and was taken along down into the streets of the town where excitement reigned and frivolity was king. He was given half a sausage sandwich by the publican's wife at the George, where it seemed hundreds of grown-ups and children milled back and forth from the bar to the lounges and up the staircase until the pub seemed at bursting point with humanity.

When Wakefield found him two hours later, John Baron was sitting on the upright piano with his little friend Jimmy Fishburn, while Peg, the daughter of the house, thundered out 'It's a Long Long Way to Tipperary' as wildly as her fat fingers could push the keys.

Wakefield now had a wooden leg and he walked in rolling seaman fashion leaning upon his cane. After his convalescence he had been honourably discharged from the Air Force and had found a desk job in Scarborough, eighteen miles to the north. His friendship with Ben had become so close that he was now 'Uncle' Wakefield, a part of the family, and came every weekend to Haverhill.

Today was Wednesday and John Baron supposed, correctly, there were two reasons why he had come down to see them: that the war was over and that it was his birthday.

'All right, Johnny B? Let's go. *Allons-y*.' And although none of his words could be heard above the boisterous celebration, he lifted the boy down and tucked him under his strong right arm and carried him through the mêlée to the outside. There he placed John Baron on the footpath and in the yellow glow of light through the mullioned windows which turned his fair hair golden he shook his finger. 'Your mother was worried about you.'

John Baron defended himself. 'But Uncle Wakefield, they were all so busy having fun. I didn't think they'd miss me.'

'Ah well, that's where you got it upside-down, my laddie, for they did and they do.' He ruffled the boy's hair and gave him a smile. 'Anyway, Happy Birthday, *bon anniversaire*,' and with those words he took from his inside pocket a small wooden aeroplane. It was a perfect model with every detail intact from its double wings to the flat wide propeller and the red, white and blue ringed insignia on its side.

'Oh, it's just the best thing I've ever seen.'

'I made it for you – it's a De Havilland. I used to fly one and I've given you the same number as my old aircraft, 4573. Carved it out of a piece of wood.' Wakefield bent down on his good leg in the beam of light from the pub and tugged a small pulley in the tail, at which the plane's propeller began to turn. John Baron watched fascinated as the blades spun round.

'I love it!' he cried, picking it up and making a roaring sound as he swirled it through the air and, bursting into laughter, ran along the gutter.

'Now laddie, *nous allons rentrer à la maison.* We'd better waste no more time as there are quite a few people out on your trail and we might be in a spot of trouble, I'm thinking.'

Wakefield carefully mounted his stallion and lifted the boy up with his powerful arms. Fifteen minutes later by the light of a jovial moon, John Baron was back at Haverhill where his mother was too pleased to see him to chide him, but his father took him aside. 'You had us very worried, son. You've been missing for hours, and the sun long gone down as well. We went in all directions searching for you. You've caused a lot of upset on what is otherwise a day of absolute joy.'

John Baron thought it was unfair to expect that he should not have enjoyed himself too when all the grown-ups were. He attempted to put his point of view. 'But Jimmy Fishburn's still out. He wasn't sent for, and I was having such fun.'

Ben knelt down on one knee and looked in the child's eyes. 'It's not what Jimmy Fishburn does that concerns me. Why didn't you tell one of us where you were going?'

And the bright child answered, 'You would not have let me go.'

'Ah.' He gave the glimmer of a smile. 'Yes, that's probably true. Nevertheless I want you to promise you'll never worry us like this again. And on your birthday too.'

John Baron gave in. 'I promise.' Then he remembered his gift. 'I want to show you what Uncle Wake gave me. It's a model De Havilland. It's perfect!'

'All right, but first come along, Molly has your dinner ready.'

There were soldiers still all over the house chatting and

66

playing cards and drinking ale, and the mood of celebration was still very much alive though the atmosphere was more composed than it had been in the afternoon.

After his meal Molly took him upstairs and bathed him. This was always Ledgie's job and as she took off his shirt, pulling it firmly over his head, he asked where the other woman was.

'She's gone and knocked herself out, she has. First alcohol past her lips in nigh on twenty-five years, she told me. Well, it just put her to sleep, is what it did.'

'Oh.'

When he was between the sheets and Grenville was in his customary spot under his bed, Molly lit two candles and kissed him and removed the model plane from his hands. He had insisted on carrying it even during his bath. His face shone from the scrubbing it had received as he gazed up at Molly from the white pillow. 'Aren't you going to read me a story like Ledgie does?'

The straightforward girl shot him a self-conscious look. She hesitated then confessed, 'I don't read, John Baron. Can't read.'

John Baron, whose reading was coming along at a great pace, was shocked. 'Oh Molly! I shall teach you. It's easy.'

She bent down and patted his cheek. 'It's not for children to teach grown-ups anythin'. Now your mother will be in to kiss you shortly. Good night.' And she strode firmly to the door and departed.

He could hear soldiers' voices still rising up the stairs to his bedroom and he watched the door for his mother's entrance. But when Constance did come in just six minutes later, her little boy, exhausted by the day's unprecedented exuberance and the demands of his adventure, was dreaming, in a role reversal where he played the piano at the George and Peg the publican's daughter sat upon the piano with Jimmy Fishburn.

And so fifty days after his birthday, the meritorious 1919, the year of optimism and sanguine confidence, the year that put the ghastly 'war to end all wars' in the past, began with the hopes of all Europe and much of the world that a lasting peace had descended propitiously upon the planet.

But with the peace still came death. A virulent influenza raged in almost every country; had, in fact, begun even before the war ended and now it spread round the world without conscience.

As the afternoon closed in and the first edges of dusk crept across the cliffs near Bridlington Quay, Ben closed the door to the boatyard office and sliding the bolt, fastened the padlock. The March wind at his back came straight from the sea and urged him to wrap his woollen scarf more tightly round his neck and to pull his felt hat down over his ears. This was the second week he had kept the yard closed. Almost every household in Bridlington had been affected by the influenza and he had taken the course which seemed the safest; to keep the men at home in the hopes of not infecting each other. Besides, the yard had slowed greatly since war's end and he was in talks with the War Office about its future.

He drummed with his fingers on the box he held under his arm and paused, his eyes on the restless silvery grey waters of the North Sea. Yesterday they had buried Ernestine Brack. She had died from the influenza and Molly was still ill with it. Ben had been deeply affected by the death of his secretary. He remembered the day he first met the tall, lanky Ernestine in his office in Lymington and how she had proudly presented her diploma from the North London Collegiate School for Girls. She had been no Gibson girl – so much the ideal of the times – but she had been a bright-faced young woman eager to take her place in the male world of the workforce when the great majority of women simply married, bore babies and remained at home. He had always admired her for that. She had been a worker for women's suffrage and an admirer of John Stuart Mill, and he remembered how delighted she had been just a year earlier when women over thirty were given a vote in Great Britain. At the time he had heard her say, 'You know I do believe New Zealand of all places was the first country to give us the vote over twenty years ago.'

'Well Ernestine,' he said softly to the wind, 'you died having gained suffrage and you lived to see the great triumph over Germany even though you departed before your time.' He had just been into her orderly office and removed her personal items. He carried them now in a box under his arm and was about to deliver them to her nearest relatives, an aunt and uncle who were staying in lodgings down on the Promenade.

He turned from the sea and his contemplations to see Constance wrapped in a long shawl, a great scarf around her curls hurrying down from the road towards him. Paxton sat in a trap waiting for her.

'Connie?' It was his pet name for her. 'Why are you out in this wind?'

The anxiety in her face corresponded to the concern in her voice. 'I've come to find you.' She hesitated and he read her thoughts.

'Is something wrong with one of the children?'

'The girls. They seemed perfectly all right this morning, then at lunchtime they were both a little cranky. But now, in the last hour, they are obviously unwell.' Her voice rose in fear. 'Ledgie says she thinks it's the influenza and after burying dear Ernestine only yesterday . . .'

He wrapped her in his arms and kissed her. 'I'll go for Dr Campbell. You return home.'

'If you can find him. The poor man's so overworked it'll be a miracle if he doesn't come down with it himself.'

Benjamin propelled his wife in the direction of home. 'I'll be back soon.'

He found the doctor over at South Beach and brought him to Haverhill where the medico confirmed that the twins had influenza.

The household was dismayed by this news but Ledgie remained calm, following Dr Campbell's orders to keep the little ones warm but to use small cool compresses on their foreheads for the fever which accompanied the sickness, and to make sure they took plenty of fluid.

When John Baron asked to see his sisters he was told he must not, for they had caught the dreaded influenza.

After the initial shock Constance controlled her feelings and she and Ledgie nursed the babies in between taking care of Molly. Ben employed a local woman, Mrs Briely, to help relieve them, and as the rest of the week passed, the girls' condition remained unchanged, but Molly began to improve to the point where she left her bed and began to take part in light duties again.

It was a cool but dry Friday morning the following week when John Baron was playing catch with Constance on the lawn while Grenville kept scampering after any ball that was dropped. A few early spring wallflowers had exploded into colour and Paxton was on his knees in the rising blooms along the garden wall. John Baron ran by the gardener and caught the ball and paused before he looked up at his mother. His small face wrinkled as the diffident sunshine attempted to break through a cloud. 'Mummy, I haven't seen my sisters for such a long time. Please could I see them today?'

Constance bent and stroked his cheek and kissed his forehead. Benjamin had been adamant that the boy must be kept away from the twins, but looking at his pleading face upturned to her in such entreaty she almost gave in. 'Oh darling.' She bent down on her knees and drew the child into her arms. 'Daddy says you mustn't. You see, sweetheart, we don't want you to catch this dreadful sickness.'

'Will they die like Miss Brack did, Mummy?' the quick-witted child asked and his mother's face blanched before the boy's eyes.

He realised he had said something dreadful and he began to cry but Constance hugged him. 'Oh no, of course they won't. They aren't going to die. They'll soon be well and out here playing with you.'

'But Ledgie says Miss Brack died and so did Old Man Doon and so have thousands of others; she says it all the time.' The tears ran down his cheeks.

'Now now, sweetheart, forget about it.'

'But Ledgie says it's terrible.' He sobbed the words. 'She

said she didn't know why the Lord has let people live through the war just to be dying in the peace.'

Constance let out a trembling sigh. 'Darling, please, Ledgie says a lot of things which aren't for children's ears. Now, I'm sorry you can't see Samantha and Vivian but they'll soon be better and we'll all have a lovely time. We'll go over to Bempton Cliffs in the summer and have a picnic and see all the birds wheeling in the air in their thousands. You'd like that, wouldn't you?'

And the little boy nodded his head. 'But I want to see Sammy and Viv. I do so want to.'

'I'm sorry, darling, you mustn't.' The colour had come back into his mother's cheeks but there was a pensive look on her face and she swiftly wiped the corner of her eye before she stood to continue the game.

That night, after Ledgie had tucked him in and read to him and his mother had come in and heard his prayers and kissed him good night and gently closed the door, John Baron lay thinking, his child's reasoning at work and he fell asleep with a single thought in his mind.

He woke as the stealthy dawn began to delineate the roofs of Bridlington and the boats in the harbour. He slipped out of bed and Grenville woke immediately – as man's best friend does – then he crossed to the door and commanded his obedient companion to stay. Silently he passed along the hall to the point at the top of the stairs where he used to listen to the soldiers talking below. All was still. The only thing he could hear was the wind outside.

He hurried on down the hall to his sisters' room, his bare feet taking him silently over the Axminster carpet. He gently pushed open the door and looked inside. Mrs Briely's head nodded forward in her chair; she seemed to be asleep. He waited to be certain, watching through the crack in the door. His feet were cold so he kept lifting one up and putting it on his warm knee and then changing over. He could hear one of the twins moaning quietly and when he was quite sure the woman slept he opened the door wider and crept inside, crossing noiselessly to the two cots.

The lantern on the table and the burgeoning dawn

illuminated his sisters like duplicate wax figures; their golden hair gleamed and their perfect button noses shone. They looked somehow unreal. They both seemed to be asleep but it was Vivian who was moaning, her small fingers clutching the sheet. He wanted to kiss them both, he wanted to do that in case they left and went to heaven but he was not tall enough and could only reach through the wooden slats of the cots to touch them. He slid his hand in and touched Viv on the face and she trembled a little. Her cheeks were very hot under his hand. He looked back at the sleeping Mrs Briely as he moved across to Samantha and stood a moment looking at her before he ventured his hand in between the uprights and touched her too. She was breathing in a laboured fashion and she too felt hot where his fingers met her skin. He whispered, 'Please get better . . . please.'

Samantha's eyes opened and she recognised her brother. She lifted her hands up to him. 'Ja ba,' she cried in her baby's voice. 'Ja ba.'

Mrs Briely instantly awoke. 'Oh, my Lord God in heaven!' She was at least fourteen stone but she shot from her chair, her fat stomach wobbling with the ferocity of her action. 'What are you doing here?' She looked around for an accompanying adult and realised the situation. 'Oh no, John Baron. Out out, the master has forbidden it.' She began to steer him to the door while his little sister continued to call, 'Ja ba . . . Ja ba!' and began to cry.

Mrs Briely rushed him out of the door. 'John Baron, please go back to bed and tell no one about this.' She crossed herself. 'Promise me you'll tell no one?'

John Baron nodded and she gave him a shove in the direction of his room. 'Quick now, off you go before someone hears.' And he wandered back along the hall towards his room with the faint weeping of little Sammy fading behind him until it ceased completely with Mrs Briely's closing of the door.

John Baron said naught of his visit to his twin sisters and Mrs Briely kept the secret, which was not surprising. So another week passed while the spring made its entrance in an excess of field daisies that spread over the moors and the roadsides and meadows.

When Wakefield arrived for the weekend he played cricket with John Baron on the stretch of lawn near the gardener's shed where the soldiers used to convalesce in the sun. The adult was teaching the child how to drive the ball and John Baron had just hit a good shot when he saw his mother and father exit the scullery door and come towards them. Wakefield noticed too and a frown creased his forehead as he turned towards them.

Ben and Constance walked hand in hand but they seemed to bend forward as if a weight sat on their shoulders. When John Baron saw his mother's tears his chest constricted with fear.

Wakefield took the woman in his arms and hugged her as Ben dropped to one knee beside the boy. 'Your little sister Vivvy has gone to heaven.' And he wrapped the boy in his arms before he stood again.

'And Sammy too?' John Baron asked in his artlessness.

His father's mouth was set in a firm line to hold back his emotion. 'No, thank the Lord, darling little Sammy seems to be getting better.' And then tears welled in his father's eyes and seeing them the child began to cry.

Wakefield spoke and his voice was forced. 'There's been so much death. I'm so very, very sorry.' And the adults and the child straggled in sorrowful single file back into the house.

Six days later on a clear April morning, as the brilliance of the sky mirrored itself in the ultramarine North Sea and the Yorkshire meadows in full spring optimisim played host to golden rivers of daffodils, they buried Vivian in a miniature mahogany coffin that Benjamin carried on his shoulder. Constance leant heavily on his arm as her little girl went into the ground only a few feet away from Ernestine Brack; and as the bleak procession trailed from the graveyard she raised her eyes to the impervious eternity above and exclaimed, 'Benjamin, how can the sun shine this way on the day our little darling has left us?'

And her husband kissed her cheek through the black veil

over her face and wrapped his strong arm around her as he steered her past a weeping Ledgie to the carriage that awaited them.

Chapter Seven

Haverhill had been quiet that funeral morning. Not the still-ness that comes with peace and composure but the silence that arrives when a fearful happening is taking place. Molly seemed to creep about, her eyes focusing on her feet while Ledgie moved from room to room in her long black skirt shaking her head and mumbling to herself. Jake Preston the foreman and Paxton the gardener stood in sunshine at the front of the house dressed in black suits, their faces dour. John Baron had never seen Paxton dressed up before and the man looked ill-at-ease as he stood silently holding the horses' heads at the front of the carriage. Mrs Briely had arrived early to look after Samantha and John Baron, and she kept biting the side of her lip in distress as Ledgie took her into the kitchen proclaiming, 'I know as countless boys died in that horrible war, and tragic and all it was, I'll never get over it, I suppose, but it always seems a cruelty when a tiny life what hasn't got going is snuffed.' Ledgie continued to sniff and shake her head while Molly produced John Baron's breakfast and a cup of tea for Mrs Briely.

After breakfast Ledgie took John Baron and Grenville through to the front hall where they waited silently, John Baron's hand resting on Grenville's smooth back as he sat obediently at the boy's feet. A minute later Constance and Benjamin came down the wide staircase to the front foyer. They were dressed in black and Constance wore a hat with a wide brim from which a black veil hung down in front of her face. She lifted the veil as she took the little boy in her arms and kissed him. 'Be good for Mrs Briely, darling. She will look after you and Samantha until we come home.'

John Baron knew they were burying Vivvy for he had

75

heard Ledgie say so the day before and, as his parents left the house, he followed them down the stone steps and across the lawn to the drive where Paxton still held the horses' heads. As his father affectionately ruffled his hair in passing he looked up and squinted in the brilliant light of the clear April day. 'I'm sorry, Daddy,' he said, and Ben halted and turned back and lifted the child in his arms. 'We are blessed to have you, my son, you and Sammy.' He sighed and added, 'Little Viv will live forever in our hearts.'

As Paxton jumped up onto the carriage and drove the horses out through the open iron gates into the street, Mrs Briely lumbered out of the house holding little Sam in her arms and they all waved as the vehicle disappeared along the road. The corpulent woman beckoned to John Baron. 'Now come along, deary, we'll spend an hour in the garden as it's such a truly beautiful day.'

John Baron trailed behind Mrs Briely with Grenville at his heels as the rotund woman plodded round the corner of the house and down across the lawn to the garden shed where she had placed a canvas chair out in the sun. A blanket covered the grass beside it and on top lay Sammy's little doll and John Baron's cricket bat and ball beside three model aeroplanes, all made by Wakefield.

Mrs Briely put down Samantha, eased her weight into the chair and produced three gleaming apples out of the voluminous pocket in the front of her grey apron. They ate greedily, John Baron attempting to share his with Grenville, but the smell of apple did not appeal to the well-fed dog. For a time the little boy played with his baby sister, hugging her and rolling over on the blanket and onto the grass. Grenville joined in and the three of them frolicked together while Mrs Briely munched on a fourth apple she had found in another corner of her pocket.

John Baron thought of his other little sister as he laughed with Samantha in the warmth of the pure April sun, and while he did not exactly formulate the idea, he somehow sensed that he cared for Sammy almost more now that she was the one who was left.

Eventually Samantha toddled over to Mrs Briely's

massive knee and the woman picked her up and nursed her, calling, 'Don't go far,' to John Baron as he ran off making aeroplane noises with Grenville barking wildly.

It was the warmest day since the previous summer and fifteen minutes later John Baron returned to the blanket where Grenville lay down, his tongue hanging out. Samantha was asleep in Mrs Briely's arms and the woman's head was nodding. All were drowsy in the unaccustomed heat.

John Baron left his toys and wandered away towards the front of the house and the big iron gates which had remained wide open after the carriage had departed. He looked back as he turned the corner of the house, and the woman, baby and dog were still in the same position on the blanket. He counted the number of bricks in the base of the bird bath which stood near the circular drive and when he reached thirty-three he drifted down to the gates. He felt a little hungry and wondered what treat Mrs Briely would have for his morning tea. He had learnt that she always had a splendid choice of cakes and buns at tea-time. Ledgie often commented, ''Tis amazing how that woman makes such grand cakes with sugar and flour still so scarce!'

John Baron wandered out through the tall stone columns upon which the gates hung, and there on the far side of the road stood a lady. She held an umbrella in her hand and seemed to be watching him. A little way from her, underneath the arms of a chestnut tree, waited a horse and trap with a man sitting smoking in it. John Baron had never seen the man before. He had a beard and in contrast to the woman whose clothes were clean and neat, he appeared unkempt.

The boy watched as the lady crossed towards him. John Baron at seven was no connoisseur of style but he thought her dark blue gown looked better on her than any gown he had ever seen on a lady. When she was within a few feet she spoke. She had smooth pale skin and dark eyes. As she took off her hat the sunlight caught the colour on her mouth and John Baron thought she was very lovely to look at. Her luxurious pink lips parted in a smile as she asked, 'Are you John Baron?'

'Yes.'

'I'm your auntie. Is your mother home?'

'No, Mummy and Daddy are at little Vivvy's funeral.'

'Little Vivvy?'

'My sister.'

'Oh yes, of course, your sister. Hmm, very sad. Now tell me, dear, would you like to come with me, your auntie, for a little drive in that vehicle?' She pointed to the trap. 'We'll have a picnic. I've brought some lovely cakes with me.'

John Baron had only been for a picnic twice in his life. He recalled the events as wonderful merry outings. His mother had said they would go on one soon. He was enthusiastic. 'I like picnics.'

'Good. That's settled then.' And she put out a gloved hand to take his. He hesitated, looking back. 'Should I tell Mrs Briely?'

The lady laughed. 'Good heavens, no. It's your mother who has sent me to take you on the picnic. No need to bring Mrs Briely into a close family matter.' And she waved her hands to usher him towards the gig.

He did not know he had an auntie. In fact, he was not sure what it was, so he asked, 'What does Auntie mean?'

'Good heavens.' The lady smiled again and now her white teeth gleamed in the sunshine; everything about her seemed to shine and sparkle. 'Haven't Mummy and Daddy told you about me?'

He shook his head.

'Dear dear, and my being family and all. An auntie is a close relative, just a step beyond mother and father and sister. So you see I'm your auntie. I was very close to your father. Ah yes, I was truly particularly close to your father.' She hesitated as if deciding what to say next, then added, 'In fact, I'm your father's, how shall I say it? nearest relative really. That's it. I'm *his sister*. Now, you know what that means, don't you?'

'I had two sisters,' the child responded.

'Yes, yes, so I've learnt recently. Well, there you are, people all over the place have sisters, you know. It's a common thing. Anyway, I'm your aunt.' And she bent and lifted him up into the gig, sniffing as if something unpleasant assailed her nostrils as she spoke to the man holding the reins. 'We'll drive over to Flamborough Head.'

John Baron enjoyed the ride. It was exciting sitting next to the beautiful lady with the heat of the sun upon him and the rush of air passing him by. Daffodils and daisies dotted the green grass leading across to a single copse of trees near the Ancient British earthwork inaccurately named Danes' Dyke. The road ahead and behind was deserted; they passed no one, not a vehicle or a pedestrian all the way along the Point, even when they sped by the turn to the little village of Flamborough.

The wide blue sky presided over a pristine world and the verdant fields to left and right echoed with the shrill sound of seagulls cruising triumphantly in the air.

He could not help but smile, he felt so good, and yet momentarily he experienced a surge of guilt for he knew everyone else was so sad since little Viv had died. He really was sad about that too, but his seven-year-old heart could not help but be cheered by the effervescence of the clear spring day and this wonderful adventure with Auntie.

Two grey hares leapt out into the road as the trap rolled along past the old octagonal chalk tower lighthouse which had been built in 1674. The 'new' one, operational for over a hundred years, lay a few hundred yards in front of them on the Point of Flamborough Head.

His aunt gave an instruction to the driver: 'Pull up here.'

The trap rolled to a halt at the side of the road where the ground gently undulated in an ever-descending grass-covered slope towards the cliffs of Selwick's Bay in the distance. Auntie dismounted and took her handbag, umbrella and a small brown box with her. 'Wait here,' she barked at the driver who grunted his reply. 'Ye've got me for the day so what do I care.'

Auntie ignored this and called John Baron to follow her and the child jumped down from the vehicle and ran across the grass.

'I've got nice cakes in here,' she said, holding the brown box high in the air. 'Come on,' and she strode off in the direction of the cliffs, her sharp-heeled shoes sinking slightly into the lush grass with each step. Their only companions were the sea birds which continued wheeling in great circles, squealing their delight at the rare brilliance of the day as it gleamed its perfection upon the child who ran at the woman's side.

On the clifftop they halted and Aunt opened the box. John Baron took a deep loud breath of pleasure as he eyed the six round cakes with coloured icing and cherries on top.

'Take whichever one you want.'

He chose a chocolate one.

As he ate Harriet put down her umbrella and eyed him. It had taken years, all the years of the war, to find him, and now here she had him entirely in her care. She smiled at that and the innocent child looking up as he finished his cake caught the smile and replied in kind.

'Have another,' she said, holding the box out again to him. This time he took a pink one.

He looked so much like his father, her lawful husband, that it exacerbated her fury, and he had been brought into the world by that blasted French floozy. She found it easy to hate him even though he was a little child; quite easy. She clenched her teeth with such force that the muscles in the sides of her cheeks swelled momentarily.

'Aren't you going to have one?'

'One what?'

'A cake,' the child answered, pointing to the box. 'You haven't had one yet.'

'Ah yes, well I'm not interested in cakes. Bad for the complexion.'

John Baron shaded his eyes as he looked up. 'What's the complexion?'

Auntie sniffed, lifting her gloved index finger to her cheek. 'This, the texture of the skin.'

'You have nice skin,' the child commented.

'I know. Now come along and we'll have a walk. You can have another cake as we go.' And she picked up her umbrella and started off along the deserted cliff path towards Cradle Head.

The child ran in front of her. She did hate him so, hated him with an abiding rage. He was going to inherit all her money! He was going to own what was rightfully hers, the hotel and the shares that she should be able to pass on to whomever she wanted! It was all wrong. He should never have come into the world. His mother was a disgusting harlot and Benjamin and Constance were evil. Ah yes, Ben and Constance had a lot to answer for, and answer they would. Smug the two of them, thinking they were so clever, covering their movements. Coming to live up here in Yorkshire, away from any who knew them. And it had taken years all right, but she had found them. And found this little wretch who now bounded along. How all-consumingly she hated him.

Her eyes were pinpoints of enmity as they rested upon the back of the child who ran ahead waving his arms in the air. A moment later she looked behind. The entire coast was empty; not a soul in sight. The only objects in the world appeared to be the chalk tower and the lighthouse, and from up here she could only see half the lighthouse. There was nothing else at all up here . . . nothing except her and the child and the screeching sea birds.

Her gaze was fixed upon him as the boy halted close to the cliff edge and looked out across the North Sea. He turned to her and laughed. 'It's nice up here, Auntie. I like it. I wish Grenville could see it.'

'Who's Grenville?'

'My dog. He's five years old.'

The woman was thinking about what she was going to do. 'What can you see down there over the edge of the cliff?'

He glanced down the steep chalk face of the cliff to where a dozen gannets glided in formation above the aquamarine water hundreds of feet below. 'Birds and the sea,' he replied as she moved up behind him.

Abruptly the same odd feeling that he had experienced in the boat-building yard on his birthday years ago came

81

over the child. He felt dizzy and sick. He put his hand up to his head and lost his focus on the birds below.

In that moment Harriet stepped up to him, her gloved hands extended in front of her. 'Go to hell,' she said as she reached out to push him into eternity.

But in that flickering instant of a second he had lost his balance and fallen: the woman had not even touched him. He disappeared from view with a scream.

Harriet abruptly swung away from the precipice edge, knowing full well what she had intended to do. She did not look back but ran as fast as she could across the emerald grass and up the incline towards the trap waiting near the white tower in the distance. Her face was the chalk colour of the cliffs and twice she stumbled and nearly fell but she regained her balance and ran on, her handbag thumping on the side of her skirt as she went.

It was a long way back to the man sitting in the gig, and when at last she reached him, her companion spat and flicked away the stub of a cigarette. His bloodshot eyes closed with hers. 'Done the deed?'

'God damn you,' she retorted, leaning on the side of the cart panting, her pallor replaced by a high colour from her furious flight. 'He fell.'

The driver gave a guttural laugh. 'Oh yeah, he fell all right.'

'Hell, I mean it.' She climbed up beside him. 'It's true. Let's get back. Move quickly, blast your eyes.'

'Oh nice.' And he urged the horse forward.

'Hurry up, for God's sake. We need to return this and catch the one p.m. train.'

'And ye'll be giving me the rest of my money.'

'When we part in Hull, that was the arrangement.' And as the vehicle picked up speed she finally looked back. 'Oh God, I've left my umbrella behind.'

'So what?'

'Oh, I don't know. I'm just worried, that's all.'

'A bloody umbrella? Don't worry, no one can trace that.'

She lifted her gloved hand and it shook. 'I suppose you're right. Did you see anyone at all?'

'What? Out here? Don't be daft. This whole place is deserted for miles. There's been nobody at all since we picked up the boy. We seen nobody.'

'The lighthouse keeper? He might have seen me go over to the cliff face with the boy.' There was an edge of panic in her voice.

'Yeah, he *might* have, but crikey on a clear smiling day like this he'd not be aspectin' shipwrecks so he'd hardly be lookin' out, would he? And he couldn't have seen ye properly at that range. Ye were a long way off and over the hilltop. What are ye worried about? And even if he did see ye, so what? He don't know ye from nobody. And he ain't come runnin' out, has he, to say, "Eh lady, why'd ye push that kid orf the cliff".'

'I didn't push him, damn you, I told you he fell. He lost his balance and fell.'

Her associate grunted. ''Spect me to believe that? I'm not daft.'

'Oh, shut up.'

'Suits me,' her aide replied, bringing the horse to a trot and spitting vigorously down upon the side of the road.

They rode in silence, the vehicle rolling along at speed with Harriet's dark glossy hair blowing back across her shoulders, one of her gloved hands holding her hat in her lap and the other clutched tightly round the side rail of the seat. They saw no one until they came within sight of the turning on the right down to the tiny village of Flamborough.

'There's a man ahead walking this way.' Harriet's voice was shrill in the breeze.

'Yeah, I can see that. I'm not flamin' blind,' her cohort replied, striking the horse with his whip.

Two hundred yards later as they shot by the man, Harriet looked down at him. 'He was only a tramp.'

'Yeah, he don't matter.'

'He wasn't about before.'

'What do ye mean?'

'On our way out here. I mean we didn't see him before, did we?'

'For Gawd's sake, woman, of course we didna see 'im. Stop bloody worryin'. I'm tellin' ye not a blasted soul saw us. Now shut up, for the love o' Christ.'

Harriet turned her head and cast a malignant glance upon her companion. 'Oh, go to hell.'

'Yeah,' he replied, spitting once more on the side of the road and whipping the poor horse again. 'I probably will.'

Chapter Eight

When Constance and Ben, Ledgie and Wakefield returned to Haverhill with the rest of the household and their friends they found a distraught Mrs Briely.

'I only closed me eyes for a second, oh Lord and he was gone. Just up and disappeared into thin air!' She sobbed violently, her plentiful bosom shaking in tempo with her stomach.

It was too much for Constance: after burying her two-year-old daughter to come home to find her son missing. She collapsed and was taken upstairs immediately and tended to by Dr Campbell, who had been in the funeral entourage.

The house and garden were immediately searched, to no avail. It was soon decided that with the iron gates wide open the child had gone further afield and Ben and Wakefield organised search-parties from the twenty-nine mourners who had returned home to Haverhill with them.

The police were informed, the Constabulary in Bridlington consisting of a Sergeant and one Constable, who joined forces with the searchers. Sergeant Ruxton brought a disturbing note into the minds of all as he pulled on his beard and cleared his throat before he looked Ben in the eye. 'Mr Chard, I must say these things. The boy has now been missing many hours. So, one: he might have simply wandered away, in which case we shall find him. Two: he might have drowned, and three: he might have been abducted. If either of the latter are true, we have a longer and perhaps less fruitful search on our hands. I don't want to distress you more than is necessary but we have to take everything into account.'

Each search-party had a shotgun and it was understood

that if John Baron were found, then three rounds would be fired into the air.

The afternoon passed. And now that the searchers realised it was not going to be a simple matter they rode back to Haverhill and partook of a short refreshment before they resumed their task, this time carrying lanterns and water, axes and ropes; one individual even took a shovel on the back of his saddle.

Sunset that day was a glorious pot-pourri of lavenders, brilliant pinks and rose hues as the sun hurled its final shafts up into the streaming clouds that had appeared in the late afternoon and clung to the western horizon. It was talked about by those in Yorkshire for many years as the most beautiful they had ever seen. But the occupants of Haverhill and their friends did not notice, for little John Baron had not been found, and as the unrestrained sunset finally evanesced into what became a mild night, Ben and Wakefield and three teams of men continued up and down the lanes, criss-crossing the fields, holding their lanterns high and shouting the child's name.

Ledgie had watched over Constance since the medico had departed to join forces with those hunting for the child. Constance had been sleeping the better part of an hour before she opened her eyes to see the woman sitting beside her, holding her hand.

'Ledgie, tell me it isn't true.'

Ledgie sadly shook her head. 'I wish I could, me darlin'.'

'How could he have disappeared? What could have happened to him?'

Ledgie squeezed her hand and leant forward and gently stroked her cheek. She had tended Constance all the days of her life and Constance was the one person in the world who could truly touch Ledgie's obdurate heart. 'Now, sweetheart, don't be aworryin' like this. Remember how he wandered away on his birthday, Armistice Day, and Wakefield found him good as new. They're bound to find him. Now close your eyes and try to rest.'

'No, no I must not. I cannot rest while my little boy is out there somewhere all alone.'

And though Ledgie did her best to reason with her and then restrain her, Constance got out of bed and went into the fields with the older woman to seek for her son.

But as the hours passed, all returned empty-handed after combing the countryside, the town, the harbour and the beaches. Ben and Wakefield, recalling where the child had gone on Armistice Day, had ridden down into Bridlington Quay and spoken to the publican at the George, but no one had seen the child.

By midnight many of the seekers had given up for the night and gone home for a few hours' sleep, promising to return at dawn.

It was after two in the morning when Wakefield turned in the saddle to Ben who rode beside him. They were in the cow pastures outside the old town and ahead of them rode Larry Laughton and Dave Francis (two painters at the yard), both carrying lanterns.

'*Mon ami*, I think it would be best if we returned to Haverhill, so you can have some refreshment and an hour or two of rest. The pressure upon you is immense. You're exhausted. I know Larry and Dave will go on as long as you wish, they're good men, but they too need a short respite. We all do. We'll pick up again at first light.'

'All right, I know what you say makes sense, even though my heart's against it.'

And as they turned their horses' heads towards the north, Wakefield articulated what had been on his mind for many hours. 'Ben, have you considered what the Sergeant said?'

'That he could have drowned, or been abducted?'

'Yes. I've been thinking there were no signs of a child having been on the beach – no footprints, nothing. And I can't imagine Johnny B just wandering off to the beach. He liked company and if he had gone down into the town he would have headed again to the Promenade and the noise, to my way of thinking.'

Ben murmured in agreement. 'So what are you saying, Wakefield old man? That you think someone took him away intentionally?'

'I hate to say it but I do.'

Ben answered as he brought his horse up to a trot. 'Yes, I fear what you say is possibly so. Sergeant Ruxton will know more than we do about such things but I'm thinking that if John Baron were kidnapped then someone must have seen something or must know something.'

'Exactly. Come the dawn, we'll begin asking all over Bridlington if anyone saw anything unusual.'

Ben nodded in the darkness. 'The trouble is that being a seaside town, it's a place where strangers come and go all the time.'

'I know, *mon ami*, but we must begin somewhere.'

When Ben and Wakefield arrived home it was nearly three in the morning. Wakefield dismounted gingerly onto his peg-leg and Ben led the two horses across to the stables.

A few minutes later when they entered the front door they found Constance and Ledgie waiting up for them. Constance half ran across the floral carpet and cast herself into her husband's arms. He held her close and kissed her hair while she sobbed into his chest. 'Don't worry, my darling, everything will be all right. Now come along, we must all get a few hours' rest.' He met Ledgie's eyes. 'Wake me at first light.'

'Me too,' called Wakefield, heading towards his ground-floor room.

Four hours later Ben and Wakefield were back in the saddle. They rode out of the iron gates with their two companions of the night before and made their way along the lonely road that led from Haverhill to the crossroads. As the party neared the turning they saw a man riding down the high road from the town. When he came closer they recognised Vinney Hawke, an odd-job man who spent his days lazing on the harbour front smoking with a few mates. Ledgie scathingly described the group as 'loblollies and no-hopers'.

The man hailed Ben. 'Mr Chard, I've heard your wee boy's gone amissin'.'

'Yes. Been gone since late yesterday morning.'

'Well, I think I know summat as ye might be interested in.'

'Oh, what's that?' Ben and Wakefield both tensed slightly.

'I'd like a new saddle.' The man cast his gaze down. 'What with them automobiles takin' over, saddles aren't near as expensive as they used to be, but I still 'ave trouble affordin' one.'

Ben made an exasperated sound. 'Do you know something about my son or not?'

Vinney sniffed loudly. 'Reckon I do.'

Wakefield took out three guineas from his pocket. 'Here, take this for your damn saddle and tell us what you know, man, for God's sake.'

Vinney's rough palm closed around the money and a satisfied smile curled the corners of his lips as he lifted his bloodshot eyes. 'Last evenin' I be down at Mayberry's an' it was gettin' late, ye see.'

Wakefield shook his head. Mayberry's was a harbour-side tavern with a poor reputation where the riff-raff of Bridlington and environs gathered.

'Bein' a Friday night, there were a few fellas from places afar.' He wiped the sleeve of his garment across his nose, sniffing again. 'I'm supposin' the likes o' ye might call 'em tramps. Anyway, I knows one of 'em from years ago when I was on the tramp a bit meself. He told me he were sleepin' yesterday noontime in the single copse o' trees borderin' the Flamborough Head Road near Danes' Dyke.' Vinney gestured in the direction for emphasis. 'It be real quiet up there, not a soul in sight, and he wakes up all of a sudden and looks through the brush and trees to see rollin' by on the road, a trap wiv a man, woman and child sittin' up in it. He takes no notice o' that an' goes back to sleep . . .'

'For heaven's sake, man,' Ben gave voice to his frustration, 'get on with it, can't you?'

But Vinney did not speed up his narration; he sniffed and proceeded in the same monotone while Ben stretched the reins impatiently in his hands. 'Well, an hour later he wakes again and takin' to the road, continues his journey

89

in the direction o' the turn for the village o' Flamborough as he knows a gel there what might gi'e him an ale.

'There be not a soul on the road but himself and he enjoys the warmth o' the sun upon his old head. After he be walkin' for a bit an' comes up to the turnin' he be seekin'. . . well, along ahead o' him comes the very same trap. Beltin' towards him it be, and it passes him by like a bat out o' hell. The man be whippin' that horse mercilessly. And lo and behold! There be only the man and woman sittin' up in it. Now, me friend gets to awonderin' where the bairn has gone as there be nothin' along that road at all, nothin' except the lighthouse and them great high cliffs. It be real—'

But Vinney completed his tale to the morning air for Ben and Wakefield had spurred their stallions and headed off at a gallop towards Flamborough Head.

They rode furiously, followed by Larry Laughton and Dave Francis at their heels. When they came to the turn for Flamborough Head Ben called, 'I think it best to ride first to the lighthouse and see if the keeper knows anything.'

'Agreed,' shouted Wakefield as they sped round the corner and raced along the clifftop road.

They galloped along by Danes' Dyke, by the turning to Flamborough village, past the wide fields and the old octagonal chalk tower until they came down to the lighthouse sitting innocuously on the green and grassy Point. Within a few minutes they had ascertained from Mr Gunn the lighthouse-keeper that he had seen nothing the day before. 'You see, I like to draw birds and it were such a beautiful day, and the light so perfect I worked mainly on my drawings, never looked out the windows at all.'

Ben's face was drawn and his mouth set in a despairing line as they remounted and rode across the generous green slope leading to the cliff path where birds weaved and darted, screaming and screeching in the invigorating morning air.

'Who in hell could the man and woman have been?'

Wakefield shook his head. 'No idea, but Ben, we don't know that the child in question was ours.'

Benjamin looked round. 'I think we do, Wakefield. I think we do.'

'Mr Chard, shouldn't we be going for Sergeant Ruxton?' Larry Laughton exclaimed as he scanned the clifftops with his telescope.

Wakefield answered for his friend. 'If Johnny B's out here somewhere we'd be best to separate and cover as much ground as possible, not waste a man by sending him back for the police.'

'Right then, sir. Dave and I, we'll ride ahead and look. If the boy *is* out here somewhere, thank our Lord it was a mild night and this morning's not raining.'

'Indeed.'

As the two men set off north towards Cradle Head, Ben rode quickly to the cliff path where he dismounted and shouted John Baron's name, but with the constant crying of the sea birds his voice was lost.

Within half a minute Wakefield was beside him and they moved closer to the precipice together and looked down into the choppy water of Selwick's Bay.

There, on a substantial outcrop of chalk rocks some seventy feet down, they could see a child lying motionless.

Ben had to steady himself; he grasped his friend's arm. 'Oh God, Wakefield, I can hear him sobbing, I'm certain.'

Wakefield could hear nothing above the sounds of the sea birds, but in his heart he dearly hoped that it was not merely wishful thinking, but that Ben in fact did hear it, for it meant the child was alive.

'We'll soon have him.' He slipped his shotgun from its holder and fired into the air. Larry and David, who were already some few hundred yards north, turned round immediately and Wakefield reloaded and fired two more rounds to complete the agreed signal.

Knotting all their ropes together they had a length of about 120 feet.

Ben had remained at the escarpment face watching his son who still had not moved. And even though both Larry and Dave said they would go over the side, he insisted on being the one to be let down to the boy. 'If the locals can go over the side here to steal the birds' eggs, I can do it for my boy.'

Wakefield slapped Benjamin supportively on his back. 'I might only have one leg, but I've got the might of two in my arms.' And with the added strength of Larry and Dave and the pulling power of the four horses, they cautiously let Ben down the cliffside on the ropes.

John Baron was conscious and aware that his father had found him and as Ben reached him the little boy whimpered, 'I cannot move my arm or my leg, Daddy, and my head hurts.' Ben was uncertain of any further injuries but he realised the child had broken his right leg and dislocated his left shoulder.

With renewed spirit they painstakingly pulled the man and child back up, Ben protecting his boy to the extent that he scraped his legs and arms upon the cliff face many times and blood ran freely from his wounds by the time they finally had the two back on firm ground.

As the child continued weeping and the men consoled him, Ben confided to Wakefield: 'That the child has a broken shoulder and leg has probably saved him. If he were unscathed he might have moved in the long night and fallen to his death.'

It was a sobering thought and they kissed him and praised him, telling him what a truly courageous boy he was, and rode home holding him in their arms as carefully as they could while he drifted in and out of a restless sleep. They did not question him, preferring to get him home to safety rather than distress him further. At the turning to Haverhill Larry was despatched to bring Dr Campbell back.

The welcome at home was like the Second Coming. Everyone was jubilant.

The little boy cried and kept talking about the pain in his leg and shoulder, and while Constance would have liked to hug him and cover him with kisses she restrained herself and was content to sit beside him on the bed holding the hand of his unbroken arm and bringing it regularly to her lips and telling him how much she loved him. And when Molly caught the stoical Ledgie lifting a lace handkerchief to her eyes, Ledgie turned a withering gaze upon her and declared, 'I have my emotions like everybody else,' and Molly, to whom this was a revelation, whispered, 'Really?' and looked skywards and walked by.

Downstairs Ben and Wakefield conversed with Sergeant Ruxton until the doctor arrived. After he had set the child's leg and strapped his shoulder and given him a mild opiate, the little boy, exhausted from the pain and the night in the open, slept more peacefully. Dr Campbell informed a happy Ben and Constance that all other injuries were superficial and that with rest and care John Baron would fully recover.

Mrs Briely had not eaten since John Baron had gone missing, which had amazed the entire household, for the stout woman went no longer than an hour without food in her mouth. She had been crying in the pantry on and off since the day before and had refused to go home, preferring to remain at Haverhill to see what would eventuate.

Even though at first Constance had been angry with her, she could not bear the woman's anguish and her kind heart was such that when Ledgie stated, 'Serve her right. I hope she cries till her fat face thins down. Falling asleep indeed when she was supposed to be watching our babies!' Constance sought the woman out and patting her massive arm commiserated. 'I don't want you to continue upsetting yourself. You were very brave to stay here at Haverhill when so many people are blaming you for what happened. I admire you for that, so please, please stop crying now.'

But poor Mrs Briely continued to weep until the wonderful news came that John Baron had been found. As the child was carried into the house and taken upstairs she stood watching from the kitchen door and an hour later she came lumbering through the team of well-wishers who filled the front hall, to Ben who was in their midst. When he saw she wished to speak to him he took her aside. 'Mr Chard, it's terrible and all I've been feeling.' She stood screwing up her apron tightly in her big hands, her eyes red and swollen. 'And it's praying to the good Lord I've been, on the hour every hour. And praise be to Him for He led us to the child. Please, Mr Chard, will you be forgiving me for me negligence?'

Ben smiled at her. 'Of course we do, there's no need to ask.' And with his usual perspicacity added, 'Perhaps it wasn't your fault but ours, to leave you all alone like that with two charges so young and active. I now think that wasn't fair.'

The big woman sighed with relief. 'What a truly charitable thing to say.' Ben thought for one shocking moment that she was going to hug him as she went on, 'The missus said kind words to me too, even when some of the others were right scathing and upset me badly. You're good people and I'll never be letting you down again.' Then she gestured to the staircase. 'Would you allow me to go up and see the young man sometime?'

Ben nodded. 'Of course. When he wakes.'

So six hours later Mrs Briely trudged up the stairs and along the hallway to John Baron's bedroom to be met by Ledgie sitting guard and tatting lace, her bony fingers working the needle speedily. Her eyes narrowed. 'What do *you* want?'

'The master of this house has given permission for me to see the young one, and in his wisdom has forgiven me. So let me by.'

Ledgie made a sound of affront, her partisan dissension obvious as she muttered under her breath, 'Well, he might have, but I won't.' Nevertheless she stood and quietly opened the door to call to Constance inside. 'Your husband has seen fit to allow Mrs Briely up here. Do you want her in?'

'Yes, Ledgie.'

Constance beckoned her as Mrs Briely entered.

'Thank you, Mrs Chard.' The woman thumped across the rug to the bedside. 'I'm so pleased to see you young man. You gave me the worst start I've ever had in me whole life. I've been praying all the time I have since you disappeared and now you're back. It does me old eyes good to see you home, John Baron.'

John Baron turned his head towards the woman, and the morning sun dancing through the window played upon his hair and in his youthful eyes. He was in pain and pale from his ordeal but he still noticed the red and swollen eyes of the big lady and he thought she had been crying. Even at only seven years of age he was already the embryo of the just and fair adult yet to come, and what he replied to her now indicated his future qualities. 'Mrs Briely, I'm sorry to have worried you.'

The woman's face melted with affection. 'Tut tut, darling, I should have been watching you better. Anyway, you're home and safe now, thank the heavens.'

When Mrs Briely had gone, Ben came back in. Earlier, when John Baron had first awoken, the Sergeant of Police had briefly questioned the boy. What he had learnt then he now wished to enlarge upon.

He had told them all about his 'Auntie' and the man in the trap, and how they had gone to the place called Flamborough Head and eaten cakes and listened to the sea birds calling. Ben had heard it all with growing fear and had discussed it with the Sergeant, and now they queried the child again.

John Baron sat bolstered up with pillows and his broken leg and shoulder were resting on cushions. Constance had been about to scrape an apple for him, but she put the fruit and spoon down on the bedside table as Ben spoke to the child. 'Darling, Daddy and the Sergeant need to ask you some more questions about the people who took you to the cliffs.'

'About Auntie?' the guileless child asked.

'Yes,' answered the Sergeant. 'What did she look like?'

'She was pretty.'

'What colour was her hair?'

'I think it was very black,' and the little boy nodded to himself. 'Yes, it was and she had nice cakes. I ate a chocolate one and a pink one and then a . . .'

'No, darling,' his father broke in. 'Don't worry about the cakes. Tell us more about the lady.'

A tiny frown appeared on his forehead as the child

95

thought, then his eyes opened wider as he remembered. 'She said she was Auntie, that Mummy had sent her specially for me.'

Ben's eyes met Constance's across the child's bed.

'And she's close to you, Daddy. She said she was something . . . ah, something . . .'

'Yes, son?' the policeman prompted. 'She said she was what?'

'Daddy's nearest . . . I can't remember.' He turned his head to his mother. 'Can Sammy come in and see me?'

Constance patted his head. 'Of course, angel, as soon as you've answered the Sergeant's questions.'

Sergeant Ruxton was writing it all down. He lifted his gaze to Ben. 'Does any of this mean anything to you Mr Chard, sir?'

'No,' Ben lied.

'What was the man like?' the policeman asked.

'Smelly,' John Baron answered. 'I don't think Auntie liked him very much.'

The Sergeant subdued a smile. 'And so, son, you fell off the cliff – is that correct? Tell us about that.'

'Auntie was behind me. She smelt nice, not like the man. She had a pretty dress too.'

'Yes, yes, we understand that. But go on about when you fell.'

'I felt dizzy.' He looked up at Ben. 'I fell at the boat-yard too, Daddy.'

'Yes, darling, we remember.' Ben now knew that he did not want the Sergeant to delve any more. 'Don't you think the little fellow's had enough?'

The policeman pulled on his beard. 'Won't tire him, sir, just a couple of questions more. So the woman who called herself *Auntie* was waiting outside the front gate for you when you left Mrs Briely and your little sister asleep in the sun: is that correct?'

'Yes.' John Baron looked up at Constance. 'Mummy, you sent her for me, didn't you?' Constance stroked his hair but did not answer.

'Now, son, can you remember anything else that

happened on the clifftop?' the Sergeant continued relentlessly as Ben felt more and more inclined to halt the inquisition.

'She was near my back. She said . . . she said . . .' The little crease came back between his eyes.

'Yes, son, what did she say?'

'She was very close to me. She said . . .' But he did not finish. He began to cry and Constance stood to protest as the child finished his sentence through his sobs. 'I don't know.'

Constance kissed the agitated child to comfort him as Ben spun round on his heel. 'This is too much, Sergeant. I'll have to ask you to leave.'

'Righto sir, on my way.' And Sergeant Ruxton stood up. 'Never mind, sonny, you've answered well. You're a good brave boy and no mistake.' He glanced at Ben. 'Can I see you downstairs, sir?'

In Ben's study the policeman and Ben faced each other. Wakefield waited in the hall. 'Mr Chard, sir, do you know who this woman, or the man, might be?'

Ben shook his head.

'Funny, isn't it, that the woman would call herself *Auntie* like that – and say that Mrs Chard had sent her here? It would almost seem to me she might be acquainted with you, or your wife. And that for some reason the child was a definite target.'

Ben eyed the man in front of him: this country policeman was acting more like someone from Scotland Yard. He tried to sound dispassionate. 'Look, Sergeant Ruxton, we've all had a terrible shock. That our son's been found is all my wife and I are interested in.'

'But don't you want to catch the abductors?'

'Frankly, I don't think it's possible. Whoever they were they came and went, like will o' the wisps. My wife and I are satisfied that no harm has been done.'

The Sergeant raised his heavy eyebrows. 'Hmm? Really? You are, eh? Well, methinks a great deal of harm was done. Your son was kidnapped, sir. I just don't understand you.'

Ben remained impassive. 'Sergeant Ruxton, you don't

have to understand me. Just believe me. My wife and I are happy to leave things as they are. Please remember, we've just lost our baby daughter. My son's welfare is paramount and he's upstairs safe and sound.'

Ben and Wakefield accompanied Sergeant Ruxton to the iron gates and watched him ride off on his bicycle shaking his head. As he turned the bend in the road Larry Laughton came riding up from the other direction carrying an umbrella: a very fashionable blue umbrella with a detail of pleats around the brim. 'Mr Chard, I found this on the clifftop. Dave and I went back for one more look. It's a lady's.'

'Mmm, indeed it is.' Ben nodded, taking it in his hand. 'Thank you very much, Larry. You've been a great help to us all these past twenty-four hours. I don't know how to thank you.'

'No thanks needed.' He climbed down off his horse and Wakefield, who knew how Larry felt towards Molly, suggested, 'Why not go in and have Molly make you a cuppa.'

With alacrity Larry disappeared through the iron gates.

Ben held the blue umbrella and took his friend's arm, but before he had a chance to speak Constance came running out of the house onto the circular drive. 'Ben! Ben, I must speak with you.'

He excused himself, handed Wakefield the umbrella, and took his wife inside to his study. There was a distraught expression in her eyes as she related what she had just learnt from her little boy. 'Ben, the woman stood right behind him just before he fell. She said, "Go to hell".' Constance lifted her tear-filled eyes to meet her husband's gaze. 'It was Harriet, wasn't it?'

'Yes, I'm afraid so.'

'What will we do? I'm terrified. How did she find us? Oh Ben, what if she comes back? She tried to kill him.' Tears were now running down her cheeks and Ben folded her in his arms.

'Darling girl, don't worry. I promise you I'll think of something. Please please, it breaks my heart to see you cry.' He kissed her forehead. 'Now come on, I'm going to talk to Wakefield. Over the years he's proved we can trust him.'

Constance's eyes widened with misgiving. 'Oh darling, no. You don't mean to tell him *everything*, do you?'

He kissed her again. 'Connie, my love, I know Ledgie will take our secret to the grave, as did dear Ernestine, and I believe Wakefield too is that same calibre. I feel as close to him as I have to any man except my dead cousin. Now I already have a plan formulating in my brain but I want to be straight with him. I want to trust him; I know I can.'

As they stood looking at each other, the mellifluous call of a skylark floated in through the open window and Constance seized upon it as an omen. 'All right, sweetheart, whatever you think is best.'

Some hours later, as the lowing of cattle drifted across to them over the emerald lanes and byways of Yorkshire, Ben took his friend for a stroll in the fading light of evening. They walked in silence for a time, communing with the quiescence of eventide until they met a herdsman and his son driving their stock before them and the two friends raised their hands in greeting.

As the cattle and their keepers passed by, the two men turned a bend in the lane and walked under an overhanging beech. Finally Benjamin spoke. 'Wakefield, I want to talk to you seriously – more seriously than I have ever done before.'

'Go ahead.'

'I know who the woman was, who kidnapped John Baron.'

Wakefield halted beside him and met his friend's gaze. His steady brown eyes connected with Ben's honest blue ones in the quickening twilight. '*Oui*, I know that, old man. That was actually obvious to me.'

Ben sighed. 'Mmm, I thought it might have been. I think old Ruxton might have seen through me as well. But I want to tell you all about her; about why she hates us and why she would have acted in the extreme and dangerous way she did. I want to tell you many things – including how and why we came to Yorkshire.' He paused before he added, 'I want to tell you all this because I trust you and because I value your opinion on what I should do.'

Chapter Nine

That same night Ben came to his wife as she sat at her toilette. Ledgie had just left the bedroom after brushing out Constance's long hair, an act she had carried onward from Constance's childhood.

Ben bent down and kissed his wife's mouth. It was not a passionate kiss, for the sadness and trials of the last days had drained the two of ardour, but it was a tender kiss embodying all the love he felt for her. 'My dearest girl, I must discuss something with you now,' and he took her hands and drew her across the room to the window. It had begun to rain an hour before and the water on the outside of the window reflected minute rivulets in the lamplight.

Ben pointed through the window. 'Yorkshire. We spent four years of war here and contributed a valuable service for the Royal Navy which makes me very proud.' His wife snuggled into his side and murmured affirmatively as she laid her head upon his shoulder.

'We came here, my love, to remove ourselves from Harriet. And now she has risen up like the Phoenix before us again.'

'Ben, I'm terrified. I'll always be terrified. She's capable of anything.'

'As you know, I spoke with Wakefield this evening. Laid it all on the line. He now knows everything and just telling him made me somehow gather strength. You see, sweetheart, I have a plan in my head which I suppose I've been formulating from the minute I realised it was Harriet who had taken our little boy. I wish to discuss it with you before I explain it to Wakefield.' He turned to her and kissed her forehead and steered her to the bed and sat beside her.

A tear fell down Constance's cheek and her husband caressed it away with his fingers as she spoke. 'Benjamin, we don't know how Harriet found us.'

'No, darling, we don't. But now that she has, I want to make sure that she never does again.'

'What on earth do you mean?'

'I mean to remove ourselves from her once again. But this time permanently.'

'Permanently?'

'Where she will never be able to find us or our little boy; where our whole family will be entirely safe from all her venom and hatred.'

Constance's eyes were so wide the whites radiated in the lamplight as she listened.

Ben smiled. 'Australia.'

She gasped in surprise. 'Australia?'

'Yes. You must remember that my cousin left me the property in Queensland, a state of Australia, which had been bequeathed to him by his grandmother. I shall in turn pass it on to John Baron.'

Constance still did not speak.

'So you see, my darling, we have somewhere to go: far away where we can start afresh, on our own land. I looked up the deeds tonight and it's four hundred and fifty-eight acres, some of it along a stream called Teviot Brook, not far from a small town; I forget the name but we're set there for life. The government has been paying me these last four years and we've lived here at Haverhill rent free, so we've been able to save solidly. With my investments and the money I made from selling the Lymington yard we don't have a care in the world, I'm happy to say. We can sell the hotel in Lyme Regis and give a bonus to all our helpers and workers, and take our little boy and his sister and set sail for a new life.' He stroked her cheek as he bent his head towards her to look into her eyes. 'I have a strong feeling that Wakefield might come to Australia with us and I know Ledgie will, and . . .'

Constance abruptly moved out of his arms, rose from the bed and took a few steps across the room before she halted, her back to him. 'Ben, please . . . Yes, I'm worried about Harriet, in fact terrified about what she might be capable of doing. The last twenty-four hours have proved she has no conscience and I want to get as far away from her as possible. But Australia?' She spun round to face him. 'My life is England. My sympathies, my understanding, my soul . . . they've been given to me by this country, not some land I don't know thousands of miles away. I'm so frightened for our little boy.' Her hands came up from her sides in agitation. 'Why can't we go to Scotland or Wales or somewhere over here?'

'Connie darling?' He moved towards her.

'No!' Constance was adamant. 'You've already done this to me once before, packed me up and removed me from a place I loved, and now, just when I've come to terms with Yorkshire, just when I feel I like the people and belong here, you want to do it to me again. And you don't want to take me just anywhere. It's, oh my God, it's Australia! Only convicts went there!' Tears welled in her eyes and she marched away to the window where she leant against the cool glass and spoke again, her voice hoarse with emotion. 'My little girl's in the ground here. I don't want to leave her.' Her shoulders shook as she cried.

Ben said nothing for a time. When he did speak his voice too held the edge of tears. 'My precious darling, for that's what you are, I understand your feelings, really I do. I love you so and I love our lost little girl. I'm just mortally afraid that if Harriet could find us here she will find us anywhere in Britain. Yes, it would take her perhaps a long time as it did in this instance, but in the end we would be living in fear every day. Frightened to let John Baron out of our sight: fearful each day he left for school.'

Constance continued looking out onto the wet black night and did not turn around.

Benjamin sighed deeply and began preparing for bed while his wife remained at the window, her posture stiff, unyielding and constrained until Ben moved about the room putting out the lamps. When there was a moody light left from one single lamp he spoke again.

'Darling, I know this is hard for you, but Australia is filled with people just like us; not some strange alien beings. Convicts began the colonies, yes, but there were free settlers too, almost from the beginning. The majority are pioneers from here, our people, who've gone out there to carve a new land. Constance, hear me. I love you deeply and I want you to know that wherever you are is home to me and I promise you I'll not do anything if you truly do not want it. I'm just attempting to remove the menace of bloody Harriet once and for all from our lives, and from the life of our son.'

He could see she was still crying and he tenderly touched her shoulders. She did not recoil from his touch. 'Please don't cry, my lovely Connie, it breaks my heart to see you cry. Come to bed with me now and I promise you faithfully I'll not do anything you don't want.'

She turned into his arms and he kissed her damp cheeks and lowered his lips to her mouth. 'I love you. We'll talk no more of it.' And he led her gently across to the bed.

After that night, nothing about Australia was mentioned by either Benjamin or Constance, and a week passed during which time Sergeant Ruxton came again to Haverhill upon his bicycle to ask whether the Chards seriously wanted to drop the investigation regarding the kidnapping of their son.

Ben sent him away with the same response.

And so another week passed and it was a Saturday in May when the daylight had long declined behind the multitudinous clouds and a high wind was broaching the woodland behind Haverhill that Ben and Wakefield sat together as they often did on weekends after their evening meal. They could see their reflections in the glass of the French windows which were tightly closed upon the rain-soaked garden. It was well after eleven and Constance and the children, Ledgie and Molly had long gone to bed.

'This damned knee,' Wakefield began, rubbing the joint of his missing leg with his left hand and holding a whisky in his right. He laughed. 'Always worse when it rains.

Alcohol seems to be the only medicine that helps.' And he swallowed a large mouthful of his drink.

'Is there some pain all the time?'

Wakefield waved his hand dismissively. 'I'm all right. There're countless fellows worse off than me. But I must say that leaving one's leg behind in a crashed De Havilland in Belgium at age twenty-nine makes a man see what's important and what's not.'

'No doubt.'

'I decided then that being hit by that Hun was an act of fate to make me a better person. If the aircraft had burst into flames on impact with the ground I wouldn't be here telling you anything. I regard myself as lucky. We used to always say the wounded men had it made; they were the ones with the exit tickets out of hell. I began in the trenches and transferred to the Flying Corps and I'd been flying over Belgium and the bloody Somme Valley for a year when my ticket came; plenty of other poor buggers bought it and never came out. I can't complain.' He bent forward and massaged his knee again.

Ben nodded. 'That's exactly right – you don't complain. You're a good friend and a brave man, is what you are.'

Wakefield laughed again, a throaty sound. 'Why *merci, mon ami*.' His expression altered and he became serious. 'And thanks for allowing me to become part of your family. With both my parents gone and no siblings I'd feel like an orphan without the Chards – oh, and without Ledgie to boss me around.'

Ben smiled. 'She bosses us all, I suppose.' He quaffed his whisky and placed his glass on the table nearby. The wind made a charge at the French windows and they rattled. 'You've taken the place of my cousin John Baron in my eyes, you know that, don't you?'

Wakefield nodded. 'I do. And if I didn't appreciate it before, I do now after what you told me the evening we walked along the lane. I must tell you I'm mighty honoured by your trust in me. And,' he paused, 'I'll tell you again what I told you then. You must leave Yorkshire.'

Ben did not answer and Wakefield watched his friend.

He knew him well and he was very aware that Ben was deeply troubled.

'It's really the only course open to you.'

Ben sat seemingly concentrating on the rain hitting the glass and Wakefield went on, 'What do you think will happen with the yard?'

Now Ben spoke. 'How do you mean?'

'Will they close it? The government, that is.'

Ben stood and moved to the oak sidetable and there poured them both another whisky. 'I'm uncertain. The Navy still needs boats. Fact is, I've been asked to go down to London to a meeting with the War Office next week.' He studied the back of his hand for a moment. 'They'll certainly shut down a number of them, no doubt of that.'

'What will you do if yours is one?'

Ben shook his head. 'Don't know.' He moved back and handed Wakefield his drink.

Wakefield stretched back in his chair contemplating his companion. 'What's really troubling you? Is it the thought that Harriet will try again?'

Ben lifted his glass and took a drink. 'Ah, Wakefield. Yes it's definitely that, but it's something else as well.'

'What?'

'I can't tell you. I feel it'd be letting Constance down.'

'I see.' Wakefield nodded thoughtfully. 'She's a wonderful girl, your wife.'

'Yes, I know – that's why I won't do anything she doesn't want.'

'All right, don't say anything, then you won't have broken her confidence, but I can guess. She doesn't want to leave here, is that it?'

Ben shrugged.

'*Mais mon ami* you *must* leave. Unless you're going to put the police on Harriet's trail, and I now understand the overriding reason why you won't ever do that, for it's opening a Pandora's box, then Constance has no alternative. She's an intelligent woman – I can't understand why she doesn't see the obviousness of it.'

Ben sighed and ran the tip of his finger round the rim

of his glass. 'Look, old man, it's not that she won't leave.' He hesitated, drawing his lips together in a hard line before he added, 'The truth is, she just doesn't want to go where I want to go.'

And now Wakefield understood. 'Ah, I see.'

'I promised I'd talk no more of it and that was two weeks ago. I'll have to bring it up to her again, but I'll wait until after my meeting with the War Office and see what comes of that.' He gave a frustrated sigh.

'Can I say one more thing?'

Ben nodded.

'Is where you want to go a long way off?'

Ben nodded again. 'But we'll leave it there for tonight, my friend, if you don't mind.'

And they did. But a surprise ally revealed herself the very night before Ben was to take the train down to London.

Constance and Molly had just left to go to evening prayers at Holy Trinity Church. Constance had felt the need to go to midweek services since the death of Vivian, and it was Paxton who drove her down in the old Ford automobile which Benjamin had purchased just before the war.

It was a placid evening without the North Sea wind and Ben had been playing draughts with John Baron on the side patio overlooking the garden. The boy was amazingly adept at the game for his age and had just taken two of Ben's draughts when Ledgie came out through the French windows.

'Now young man,' she began, coming over to John Baron. 'Your sister Sammy's fast asleep and it's almost bath and bedtime for you so I hope you're winning.'

The boy smiled. 'I'm doing well.'

'Good,' she answered, ruffling his hair and then turning to his parent. 'Once I have my young man in bed could I have a word with you?'

'Of course, Ledgie.'

So an hour later when John Baron was tucked up and drifting off to sleep, the woman appeared through the door of Ben's study where he looked up from the notes which he was taking to the meeting with the War Office.

'Ledgie, please sit down.'

She slid into a chair and put her gaunt hands up onto the desk, her demeanour tense and her gaze penetrating.

Ben smiled. 'What is it?'

'Well, I know as I've never come to discuss anything with you in the past.' She cleared her throat. 'Because I've never needed to. I'm happy just caring for Miss Constance and yerself and the children, but I'm really worried for the first time in my life. I see Miss Constance is fretting, and I know that many a time in the past fortnight she's been about to tell me something, and then, no, she's held her counsel which is unlike her with me, as I suppose you be aware of and all. Into the bargain you seem thoughtful and concerned, and even Wakefield on his visits of late has not been his cheerful self. Now I know as we lost Ernestine and little Viv, and most terrible that is and all, but the abidin' upset that's just been the last straw for Miss Constance is Harriet.'

She lifted her hands palm upwards and studied them for a few seconds. For the first time Ben noticed the shape of her nails; they were perfect ellipses, really quite beautiful. It surprised him.

She took a deep breath and dropped her hands. 'I hope you don't think I'm out of place here, but I've waited till Miss Constance went to church to say this. *We have to get away from here.* We must! It's most dangerous to stay. Look what that Harriet did; no doubt meanin' to kill John Baron. My blood runs cold athinkin' on it. I fear the day will come when she finds out our darlin' is still alive, and it beggars belief to think what she could do then. I know it's bold of me to say such as this to you who is a wise man and thinks things out so clear and proper, and you'll just have to forgive me for being uppity, but we must leave Bridlington and get as far away as we can as soon as we can.'

Ben stood up and came round the desk to sit on it and face her. He patted her on the shoulder. 'Well said, Ledgie. I agree with every single word.'

And now her spark came back. 'Then why the devil haven't you done anything about it?'

Ben hesitated, but the anxiety and concern on Ledgie's face convinced him he should enlighten her. 'I will tell you.'

Ledgie listened, pursing her lips, her head pushed forward attentively, and when he mentioned Australia her mouth formed an oval of surprise but before long she was muttering, 'Yes, yes, it's the answer.'

'So Ledgie, you see I cannot force Connie to go. But now I've told you and a week ago Wakefield sort of guessed the situation though I didn't mention Australia to him. The hard part is I promised I'd not speak of it again and Constance hasn't brought it up to me.'

'Well, *I* haven't promised her,' the canny woman replied. 'I'll start on her this very night, I will.' She brought her finger up almost as if she were going to shake it at him. 'Mr Ben, why didn't you tell me this before?'

For a moment or two Ben did not know how to answer that, but he came up with a reply. 'I suppose I thought I was breaking her confidence if I told anyone.'

'Well, you wouldn't have been. She's just acting up. She's afraid of the unknown is all and she doesn't want to leave her wee girl here in the ground and be up and travellin' to the other side of the world. That's the truth of it. But I'll change her mind, for what you say is the answer right enough, no risk about it. And she loves you a mighty lot. To my mind she would have come round to your way of thinking, but it might have been too late and a dreadful something might have taken place in the meanwhile.' She paused and exhaled loudly. 'And we don't want that.'

'No, we don't,' Ben answered.

Ledgie stood and moved to the door.

'Ledgie?'

Her spare frame turned.

'Good luck.'

Suddenly she looked quite smug standing there in the glow of the fading day. 'Me, who's nursed her from bein' a wee spit of a thing no longer than me two hands joined, I can make her see reason don't you worry about that.' Her gaunt face broke into a grin. 'Now as I know what I'm meant to do, I can get on with it.' She shook her head. 'Australia, for the Lord's sake! Never in my wildest dreams did I think I'd be goin' *there*.'

Ben watched the straight little back disappear from sight and sat down looking nonplussed. 'Well Ledgie,' he said aloud, 'if you can do this, I'm eternally grateful, for I was at my wits' end.'

Five weeks later the Chard family set sail for the great south land on the 30,000 ton steamship *Safe Haven*, built at Harland & Wolff, Belfast, five years before.

They had given Grenville to Molly who was engaged to Larry Laughton. Both knew and loved the dog, and while John Baron had been saddened to leave his canine mate, he understood that they could not take him and he was consoled by the fact that Grenville would be replaced as soon as they arrived in the new land.

The travellers grouped together at the bulwark, Ben and Constance, side by side holding John Baron and Samantha in their arms. Next to Ben stood Ledgie and beside Constance stood Wakefield: he had decided he could not let his adopted family go to the other side of the world without him and they were deeply touched by his decision. 'The heat will do my knee a power of good,' he had stated. 'Besides, who would teach my Johnny B and little Samantha French out there? I must come if simply for that.'

As the *Safe Haven* edged out into Southampton Water, Constance turned to her husband. She wore a gold pendant on a chain around her neck which Ben had given her the week before. Inside he had placed a picture of Vivian cut from a large photographic likeness of the family, taken only months before the baby's death. Constance held the pendant between her fingers as she spoke. 'I'll always carry my little girl here. And now somehow, darling, I think I'm actually looking forward to it, after all.'

Ben kissed her forehead. 'As long as we're together, my love.' And she nodded in reply.

As Ben straightened up, he put out his free hand and touched Ledgie. The woman lifted her gaze to his and a message passed between them; no words were needed. They simply smiled at each other, and at the same moment John Baron reached out to his sister and took her small chubby fingers. 'We're going to Australia, Sammy, and it's a long long way.'

Chapter Ten

Southern Queensland, Australia: Tuesday, 10 December, 1930

Samantha mounted Aristotle, her grey stallion, and bent down to the girl who stood barefoot in the ubiquitous grey dust beside her.

'Thanks.' Samantha took the newspapers handed up to her. 'I'll see you on Friday, Veena.' Veena grinned and Samantha added brightly, 'It's my fourteenth birthday tomorrow.'

The girl's dark eyes became reflective. 'I've never had one.'

'What?' Samantha exclaimed in surprise. 'Never had a birthday?'

Veena shook her head. 'No.'

Samantha's smooth forehead creased in sympathy. 'Oh Veena, I'm sorry. I'll bring a big piece of my cake on Friday specially for you.' Sam guessed that Veena was probably a year or two older than she was and she determined that a time would come when they would decide on a day and make it Veena's birthday.

Veena smiled and loped away on her long dark slender legs, turning once to wave her hand high in the air.

Samantha lifted her arm in reply. Each Tuesday and Friday Veena picked up the *Queensland Times* newspaper from Kelly's general store over on the dusty main road and delivered it to Samantha as she came out of the tiny schoolhouse three miles from her home. It was a weekly routine that Benjamin had worked out years ago to be able to give the Aboriginal girl a little money. Veena's father, Jimmy Birnum, was employed as a horse-breaker and farmhand on Randall Slade's nearby property. He and Veena's brothers disappeared now and then for a couple of months and went *walkabout*, the practice which appeared to be in the psyche of the nomadic Aborigines, but Veena and her mother always remained behind on the Slade property.

Samantha liked Veena and sometimes on a Sunday the Aboriginal girl came to the Chard homestead, and spent the day there.

As Veena melded with the bushland around her to disappear in the distance Samantha brought Aristotle up to a trot, the pure country breeze circling around her and the hint of eucalyptus floating piquantly into her nostrils. She loved the bush and loved to breathe its roborant air; it lifted her spirits after the hours in the schoolroom and she began to hum 'I've danced with a man, Who's danced with a girl, Who's danced with the Prince of Wales' – a song she had decided to sing at the CWA – Country Women's Association – concert on Christmas Eve.

As the girl ascended what Veena's family called Erola Hill she displayed the skill and ease of one who has been riding since virtual babyhood; on her fourth birthday her big brother had lifted her up in front of him on his roan mare and set off at a pace down along the Teviot Brook trail. Samantha had laughed with pure joy at the stimulation of her first ride and now as she came to the end of her song, she remembered that initial day on horseback charging along, held safely inside John Baron's arms, and her mouth creased in a smile.

At that moment, as she reached the crest of the hill, and the smile still hung on her mouth, the object of her imaginings appeared round the clump of silky oaks down in the distance and came riding towards her.

She began to laugh with glee. 'John Baron, I don't believe it,' she shouted as she urged Aristotle forward to charge down the slope. 'I thought you weren't coming home for another week!'

John Baron had turned nineteen the previous month and had just completed his first year of studies in engineering at the University of Queensland. When his exams had ended he had gone away with his friend, Cashman Slade, who lived on the next property, to a gymkhana over the border in New South Wales.

Samantha continued to shout as she galloped down the hill towards her brother. 'You're home! Just in time for my birthday!' She brought Aristotle almost abreast of his horse before she pulled back on the reins and the stallion swept up his forelegs to beat the air.

John Baron laughed and raised his hands in mock protest. 'My heaven, Sammy, you still ride like a mad thing, don't you?'

His sister shrugged. 'I suppose so, but you shouldn't talk, you're worse than me. Anyway, how is it you're home a week early?'

'I wrote that letter deliberately so I could surprise you. You should know I wouldn't miss your birthday.' He leant forward and slapped her arm affectionately. 'Especially as you're turning fourteen, you poor old thing.'

The wide smile which had not left her mouth since she saw him, extended. 'Well, thanks. It seems such a long time since you were here.' Then in childish fashion she added, eyes alight, 'Mummy and Daddy have invited all my friends to the party tomorrow evening and Ledgie's cooked fairy cakes and cream buns and hundreds of yummy things to eat.'

'Good, I'm hungry already.' And John Baron turned his horse and they rode along the homeward path together.

Samantha felt happy and comfortable. It had always been like this between them. She knew that her friends mostly disliked their brothers, but for Samantha it was different. She had forever looked up to, and admired John Baron. He had never pulled her hair or hidden her toys or done the hundred upsetting things that boys usually did to girls. Samantha knew she was a bit of a tomboy and liked to do things with her brother, like playing cricket and climbing trees, but when she analysed it, she decided she was so attached to him because they were the only two children in the family. After little Vivian had died they had become

114

closer as each year passed and while she was a lot younger than JB as she called him, he had never treated her that way, never made her feel childish or foolish.

She remembered when she had turned nine and he had gone away to board at Grammar School in Ipswich she had cried on and off all night. She glanced sideways at him riding beside her and she concluded it was decidedly *nice* to have a *nice* brother.

John Baron turned in the saddle towards her. 'Cash and I came home on a Harley Davidson.'

'What's a Harley Davidson?'

'Just the most modern, smashing, and up-to-date motor bike.'

'You're a dare-devil you know, everyone says so and now you're riding a motor bike. Isn't it dangerous?'

'No, not if you know what you're doing.'

'But whose is it?'

'Well, we're sort of renting it. It's a long story, belongs to our flatmate Belcher.'

Dudley Belcher was from a wealthy Brisbane family and he owned everything from a Ford motor car to a racehorse. Samantha had heard her father tell her brother: '*Don't gather Dudley's tastes for your own.*'

John Baron smiled. 'Actually, Cash and I are thinking of buying one ourselves next year when he's at university too, that is, as soon as we can afford it.' He turned his head and looked skywards. 'You know Sam, I'm studying engineering, but one day I want to fly, like Charles Kingsford Smith. Gosh, when he completed that solo flight from England to Darwin a few weeks ago in just nine days twenty-two hours and fifteen minutes . . . I mean, the whole world took notice. And he was born right here in Queensland, you know – in Brisbane.'

Sam did not know and she eyed her big brother with wonder.

'Uncle Wakefield admires him too, and he was a fighter pilot in the war. Oh boy, what I wouldn't give to be up in the air right now.'

'Well, why don't you join the Air Force?'

His blue eyes clouded. 'Dad and Mum, I suppose. They're set on engineering for me. But one day I reckon I will.'

They had reached the creek path where the horses' hooves raised particles of dust to linger in the air behind them and the fiery December sunshine crystallised on the gum leaves above their heads, when Aristotle suddenly whinnied and reared up wildly in the air. Samantha, caught unawares, lost her grip on the reins, screamed and slid sideways. John Baron, in immediate reaction, mastered his own horse and caught her body, instantly urging his horse forward with his knees to a position where he could right his sister in the saddle. Even though Aristotle persisted in thrashing about, Sam managed to retrieve the reins and with her brother's help, regained control of him. As the stallion reared again John Baron now saw the death adder that slid away into the bushes.

For a moment John Baron thought Aristotle would still bolt but even though he continued to whinny and stamp his feet Samantha managed to quieten him. She looked in fear at her brother. 'What was it?'

'A death adder.'

'Oh no! Has Aristotle been bitten?'

'No, I'm pretty sure he hasn't or I think he'd have bolted for certain.' He climbed down and talked soothingly to Aristotle as he studied his legs. He could see no marks of any kind and the horse was calming down. 'Gosh, that was lucky.'

His sister looked down on him. Her eyes shone with unshed tears. 'Not luck at all. You saved me.'

He affectionately slapped her thigh. 'If you weren't such a good rider you'd have fallen off.'

'No, you saved me,' Sam repeated, swallowing hard.

A loud shout interrupted them and they both looked round to see a rider cantering towards them, his black hair gleaming like burnished ebony in the broad sunshine of the afternoon and his voice resounding along the trickling watercourse which was Teviot Brook. 'Hello, you two.' It was Cashman Slade, John Baron's friend. He approached at speed, riding with stylish ease.

Cash waved as they turned in his direction; he was fond of the Chard brother and sister. Sammy was a real nice kid and JB? Well, JB was as close to Cash as he supposed he would ever allow anyone to get. As he rode up and sharply reined in beside them, he glanced from brother to sister. Sam was pale and her pupils were dilated. 'You look terrible, Sammy. What's happened?'

John Baron explained. 'A death adder wrapped itself round Aristotle's leg, it's a miracle he wasn't bitten. He almost threw Sammy.'

'Shit, you don't say!' Now he gave his full concentration to Samantha. 'Excuse me, Sam old thing, didn't mean to swear. Poor Sammy. Those adders are dangerous, all right, though I don't think I've known one to latch onto a horse before – well not around here, that is.' He sprang out of the saddle to the ground beside Sam, raising his arms to her to help her down. 'Come on, let's take a look at you.'

Sam resisted. 'I'm all right Cash, truly.'

John Baron slapped his friend's arm. 'Leave her be.' It was typical of Cash to charge in and attempt to take over.

Cash grinned and shifted his attention from Sammy to Aristotle. 'All right then, let's have a look at Aristotle.'

'I've already done that, Cash,' JB countered, 'but if it makes you happy, go ahead.'

They rested until Sam felt comfortable to ride on and twenty minutes later they passed the clump of Moreton Bay ash trees that guarded the border into the Chard property. They had named it Haverhill after their home in Yorkshire. Constance had suggested it and they had all agreed. There was no fence on this side, though had they come in from the main road they would have passed through the wide gate and by the green and white painted sign reading:

Haverhill: Mr and Mrs Benjamin Chard.

Ledgie was on the verandah folding sheets when she saw the three riders passing by the grain sheds. She stood as they halted and dismounted to loop their reins over the hitching rail.

'I was nearly thrown by Aristotle! A death adder latched

around his leg,' Sam shouted as she climbed the steps two by two. 'But John Baron saved me.'

Ledgie took her by the shoulders. 'Heavens to Betsy. It's a brave girl you are. I'm thinking tea and scones might help you both over such an ordeal as that.'

Sam grinned. 'I reckon it would.'

'Me too?' shouted Cash hopefully as he took a great leap up the last four steps onto the verandah to land heavily beside Ledgie.

'Noisy beast,' she admonished. 'I'm well aware of your appetite, Cashman Slade. You can have five and no more!'

'You're a sweetheart, Ledgie, my old darling.' And he gave her a swift hug round her bony shoulders.

'Cheek!' Ledgie pretended to look in disapproval at him, when in fact she enjoyed Cashman's saucy behaviour. She turned to John Baron. 'Is he staying the night then?'

'We might allow him to, if he doesn't scoff all the scones.'

Cash gave an affronted grunt as they all traipsed after Ledgie into the kitchen where Crenna the housekeeper had scones and jam laid out.

By eight o'clock, an hour after the torrid southern sun had crossed the horizon, the family had eaten dinner and all sat in the wide comfortable lounge chairs busy at their various pastimes. Electricity had not yet reached them and they were uncertain when it would, even though the tall poles with the wires hanging upon them now stood on the corners of most of the towns throughout the land.

On the couch in the lamplight Samantha cuddled Tess the kelpie and at her right hand lay her Kodak Box Brownie camera. It was her prized possession; the one thing she valued more than anything in the world. She had become enamoured with photography two years before when she had seen the Box Brownie for the first time at the agricultural show in Ipswich, and Wakefield had bought her a book on photography. She was hoping for multiple rolls of film for her birthday tomorrow.

She touched her camera lovingly; all black and shiny, it reminded her of Cash's hair. She looked across at him as he lay upon the rug playing draughts with John Baron. At that moment John Baron spoke. 'I'll bet you a shilling I can lift that Harley Davidson off the ground with one hand.'

Cash leant in towards his friend and the errant lock of hair that regularly fell forward on his brow did so now. 'Oh you do, eh? Well, I'll take your bet.'

'Is that wise, dear?' asked Constance, looking up from her magazine.

'Which, Mum? Lifting the Harley or taking the bet?'

Both youths burst out laughing and Charity the silky terrier who nestled into Constance's side stood up and began to bark.

A few feet away from Constance Ledgie perched, pencil poised, doing the crossword puzzle from the *Queensland Times*. Crosswords had taken the world by storm a few years previously when the leading American and English newspapers had begun printing them every day. Ledgie looked over her spectacles and asked, 'A nine-letter word beginning with *d* having an *o* in the middle, meaning licentious.'

Samantha pointed to the draught players. 'Ask Cash, he knows everything.'

Cashman looked up in mock affront as Ledgie bit the end of her pencil and exclaimed. 'I've got it without him! *Dissolute.*'

'Who is?' said Wakefield, coming through from the kitchen and pausing to lean down and kiss the top of Samantha's head as he passed.

'No one unless it's you,' Ledgie answered, pointing to the bottle of whisky he carried.

'*Maintenant Ledgie, ma chère vieille*, what with the way of the world Ben and I need a little tipple occasionally.'

Ledgie shot a scathing glance at him. 'Lame excuse for your excesses. Have you been affected, I ask?'

'Not the point, Ledgie old thing. Stock markets have dropped, men have killed themselves because of it. All countries with a market economy are suffering. Look at those three blokes who came round asking for work this morning. They were all well-educated but had lost their jobs. Australia's not getting off scot free.'

'Prophet of doom!' Ledgie called to his back as he walked out.

The house was quiet, the dogs, Tess and Charity, were asleep in Wakefield's room as was their habit, and the clock in the hall was ticking industriously when Constance gently nudged her husband in his side.

'Ben?'

He turned to her in the bed. 'Yes, my love?'

'What did you tell those men who came by asking for work today?'

'That I was sorry but we had none to offer them.'

'Do you believe what the papers say? That there's going to be a world slump now and that everywhere will be affected? Wakefield seems to think so.'

He kissed her tenderly on the cheek. 'Yes, sweetheart, I'm afraid I do. People here are beginning to feel the pinch. I fear it'll affect everyone in some way sooner or later.'

'Will we be all right?'

He hesitated. He had lost money on stocks like so many had, but not everything. Years ago he had invested in land along the reaches of the Brisbane River and outside Ipswich. He still had money in solid banks here and in England. He kissed her again. 'We've got enough to fall back on. If we're sensible we'll weather it. But most of all I don't want you to worry.'

The years that followed took the world into the Great Depression, the worst in the history of the planet. All over the western world millions of people were deprived of their means of support when industry faltered and commerce suffered. Men lost their jobs in the cities and were subjected to walking the highways and byways, jumping freight trains and hitchhiking across country looking for work, begging for money and food. Reaching across continents, intelligent men, men of culture and men of standing suffered along-side their working-class brothers. Men who had never picked up a shovel in their lives toiled on the roads and professional men became stewards and deckhands on ships at sea.

Australia was no exception but those at Haverhill were relatively unscathed. Ben managed to keep the property going but with falling prices there were times when he did not cover his costs and he had to dip into his savings to continue, yet he and Constance made sure there was a meal for any who came calling, carrying their swags.

And so the occupants of Haverhill abided in their semi-sheltered haven of the countryside until John Baron's twenty-first birthday on Armistice Day 1932.

November that year brought sweltering heat day after day. The flies multiplied and Ledgie's limited patience collapsed. She marched through the house flicking her teatowel at them and using her old phrase of disparagement against the Germans during the war. 'They aren't human!' she cried, to the amusement of the household.

On Wednesday night 9 November, the heat was still unrelenting even as the sun went down. Ben and Wakefield had just come in from helping plough the northern fields and had washed and changed and joined the womenfolk and the dogs on the back verandah where Ledgie cooled herself and Constance with a large lace fan.

John Baron and Cash had arrived only half an hour before on their shared Harley Davidson and had unpacked and gone down to the still existing, though fast-diminishing water-hole in Teviot Brook. Sam, who boarded in Toowoomba at Glenee Girls' School, was returning the following day in good time for John Baron's celebration.

Ben handed Wakefield a whisky and sat down. 'Thank heaven there's a modicum of breeze just beginning.'

'You're an optimist,' stated Ledgie, using the fan ever more briskly as Constance wiped her brow with her white handkerchief. 'I'm doubting there'll be much relief tonight. The thermometer has sat between ninety-eight and a hundred and three all day long.'

As Wakefield took a mouthful of the alcohol he lifted his artificial leg and placed it on a wooden footstool. For years after the war he had worn a peg leg but in 1925 he had been fitted with an artificial ankle and foot by an Armenian doctor living in South Brisbane. At first it had been awkward to balance but Wakefield had persevered, and after many weeks it had worked well enough for him to walk, if not freely, then at least with a rolling gait reminiscent of a sailor, and this pleased him immensely. He looked around now at his companions and smiled. 'I know I've said it many times before and at the risk of constant repetition I'll say it again. The heat suits my leg, or what's left of it. Haven't had an ache in my knee since I crossed the equator.'

Constance nodded. 'Indeed, Wakefield, there's something to be said for warm climates.'

Ledgie sniffed. 'Not to my way of thinking, and if you do as much cooking as me, well then, you're just existing in an extensive oven is all. Oh, for a cold Yorkshire morning.'

Benjamin actually believed the years of heat had eased the pain in his upper arm where the bullet had entered in 1914, but he decided not to be drawn into this conversation. He looked around. 'Where are the boys?'

Wakefield poked his thumb in the direction of the creek. 'They're both down in the water.'

'Are you sure?'

'Is it important?'

'Very.'

Wakefield stood and stomped along the verandah to the far end where he could see past the sheds and trees to the two youths; one in the water, one on the bank. He came back and sat down. 'They're down there all right and it looks as if they're set for the night. They've got their towels and two hurricane lanterns already alight and standing on the rocks.'

'Good. Then first of all let's drink a toast to John Baron. There's a bottle of sherry behind you, darling.' He pointed past Constance and she turned to it. 'Pour yourself and Ledgie a glass.' He eyed the older woman. 'You will have a glass, won't you, Ledgie?'

She gave a birdlike squeak in affirmation. 'Yes, yes, all right. As it's a special toast to our own boy I'll break a golden rule.'

Constance poured the sherry, handed the glasses round, and they all raised them in the air.

'To John Baron.'

'To Johnny B.'

Ben put down his whisky and took a small velvet box out of his pocket and placed it on the low table before them. He said nothing for a few moments then he gestured to it. 'We none of us have spoken about a certain matter in all the years we've lived here. But it behoves me tonight to speak of it in these special circumstances.'

His listeners all glanced at each other, all knowing intuitively and instantly what the subject would be, and Ben's next words confirmed their convictions.

'We four have guided John Baron most of the days of his life and I'm absolutely positive that he has no memory whatever of the time when we were not his family.' He stretched out his hand to take his wife's fingers in his. 'Last night I conversed with my dearest Connie and we came to a decision. But we wish your agreement before we go ahead.'

Ledgie had stopped fanning herself and her body angled forward in attention. Wakefield still sat, leg on stool, leaning back sipping his drink, but there was the telltale sign of tension in the way his good foot tapped on the floor.

'You all know that his father, my cousin, left this property to me, and that I hold it in trust for John Baron to whom it is bequeathed, but in this box is the ring Antoinette Desaix gave me for our boy the night she died in the French convent. She was the true love of the one man I honoured above all others . . .' his eyes met Wakefield's '. . . at the time. Now, I don't dwell on that period of my life very often but in the last few days I've remembered it. I've seen her in my mind lying in the convent, ill unto death, the war all around, fear everywhere. I've heard her saying the words "*Bring my son up as your own. Please.*" And I replied, "*I will.*" Just before she died she asked me to pass on this ring to John Baron. She said to give it to him "*when he's a man*".'

Ben released Constance's hand, opened the box and took out the circle of gold, holding it in his palm. 'On Friday, our boy – our wonderful boy – turns twenty-one. He reaches man's estate.'

The sky was darkening swiftly as it does in southern climes and Ben looked round their faces in the settling gloom. 'We propose to give the boy the ring on the morning of his birthday. To tell him it's a family heirloom belonging once to my cousin whose name he bears, and now passed on to him. All of which is absolutely true.'

Silence hung in the thick hot air as Ledgie and Wakefield caught each other's gaze in the fading light and Ledgie exclaimed, 'Is that all?'

Constance was the one to reply. 'Well, yes, Ledgie, that's all. Why?'

The woman made a tutting sound, took a mouthful of her sherry, placed the glass on the table, picked up the fan and rapped it on the arm of the chair for emphasis. 'For heaven's sake I thought you were going to say you would be tellin' him the truth. I was in shock, I was! After all these years of his being entirely ours I thought you'd both lost your senses . . . I thought you were agoin' to tell him he's not your son and Sam's not his sister. Oh dear.' She raised her fan and began to shake it vigorously in front of her face. 'And givin' him the ring is all this is about. Yes, of course, no doubt about it, give him the ring. Certainly.' She lifted her head back and opened her mouth like a fish on a line. 'I feel quite faint if the truth's known, I do.'

Wakefield had begun to laugh softly. His body was shaking and rumbling sounds of mirth were escaping from his throat. Ledgie rounded on him. 'And what the devil's so funny?'

'I thought the very same thing, Ledgie old girl.'

Ledgie struck him with her fan as he went on laughing and talking at the same time. 'I couldn't believe my ears either. And it's only about giving the lad the ring.' He took his artificial foot from the stool and leant on his elbows and laughed heartily.

Ben and Constance could not quite see the funny side, but when Wakefield composed himself Ben acknowledged their thoughts. 'I'm sorry we alarmed you, for that was not our intention. We all agreed many years ago that nothing whatever would be gained by our boy learning the truth. I'm as convinced of that today as I ever was, perhaps even more so. He has a family and a life as our son. We've done what's best for him and will continue to do so.' He lifted the velvet box. 'Fact is, years go by and I never think of John Baron as anything but ours, our child, our flesh and blood. It's just that as his birthday neared I recalled my promise to a dying woman who was deeply adored by my own cousin, a fine and wonderful man, and I wanted you all to sanction that I carry out the pledge.'

'Hear, hear!' said Wakefield, gulping down the remainder of his whisky.

And as Constance turned and kissed her husband Ledgie stood up. 'All right, now that's over and we can all relax again, what about some dinner?'

'Good idea, Ledgie, *ma belle*.'

'Don't call me that,' retorted Ledgie as they all stood and ambled across the verandah to follow her indoors. Even the dogs moved lethargically.

Had one of them hastened instead of strolling, he or she just might have caught the edge of the shadowy figure that had stood and listened to much of their conversation and now slipped ahead of them through the dining room and across the hall to ease itself out of the side door and skim over the verandah, and down the steps into the quickening obscurity under the laburnum trees. But as no one did, Cash ran back the same way he had come: along the path by the sheds and around the gum trees to the brook where John Baron lay on a towel in the comfortable warm darkness. He lifted his fair head in the glow from the lantern. 'Did you get them?'

'I did.' Cash eased himself down and handed him a banana, looking intently at his friend. 'And may I offer an apple in addition?'

'Thanks. What are the family doing?'

'No idea, old man. I didn't make contact with a soul.'

The birthday was well chronicled by Samantha. She had begun immediately after breakfast by taking a photograph of them all in the yard by the hoop pine. In some she even made the dogs sit at attention.

At lunchtime she photographed John Baron alone. She made him pose with his right hand in the air to show off the gold ring his parents had given to him that very morning at breakfast. He had been intrigued by his name written on the inside and to everyone's surprise it had fitted perfectly onto his little finger.

Sam had experimented with a special new camera and lens which she had saved up for and bought in a curio store in Toowoomba. She used a whole roll of twelve photographic prints on what she called 'JB's ring photos' and would have liked to take more but rolls of film were expensive and money was scarce.

The party that night was attended by most of the district. The Chards had become a significant family for they employed local labour, participated in local events, and were involved in many of the associations in the area.

The School of Arts Hall in Boonah, the nearest town, rang with the sound of music from local musicians: a clarinet, a trumpet, a recorder and a banjo, with Cashman's brother Henry on the mouth organ and Mrs Thomas on the piano. They had just given an enthusiastic rendition of the melody 'Walkin' My Baby Back Home' and merriment and laughter were at a peak when John Baron was called to cut the cake, decorated with his name and a huge 21. As he did so Benjamin and Constance took the stage hand in hand and Cash's father, Randall Slade, called for silence.

When everyone had quietened Benjamin spoke. 'This is not a time for long speeches . . .'

'That's a fact!' shouted one of the Bell family from Couchin Couchin, the most famous homestead in the area.

'. . . and so all that's really needed to be said is that we came here from the mother country thirteen years ago, not knowing what to expect, and found . . .' he waved his hand in a circle '. . . all of you!'

Laughter broke out round the hall.

'You took us in and made us a part of this valley. And we know we made the right decision in coming here. This is home. We brought with us our two closest friends in the world and our two children.' He hesitated momentarily, and glanced quickly down at Constance, and they both thought of the child they had left behind. He went on, 'And tonight we're here to celebrate our son's birthday. Today he reaches his majority, on Armistice Day which has a certain significance for us all.'

'Too right!' shouted Alex Thompson and Gilbert Moreland who had both fought at Gallipoli and in the Somme. 'Hear, hear!' joined in Wakefield.

'So I'd like you all to raise your glasses to John Baron or JB as some of you call him. To wish him good health and long life. Happy birthday, son!'

Those gathered lifted their glasses and called, 'Happy Birthday, JB!' 'Good health!' and 'Long life, John Baron!' all at once.

'Speech, JB!' shouted Cash and the cry was taken up vociferously.

John Baron spoke from where he stood on the dance floor with Sam on one side and Julie Slade on the other. He lifted his right hand in the air as he spoke and the gold ring with the V shape in its edge gleamed. 'Thanks, everybody. I'm taking my father's cue and I'll keep it short. I'm having a great night. I vaguely remember living in Yorkshire but I've been here most of my life. This is my home and I'm proud of it. I'm glad you're all here to celebrate with me and an extra thank you for the gifts. I know this isn't a good time, what with the Depression and everything, but a couple of great things have happened this year. My hero Charles Kingsford Smith was knighted . . .' Cheers greeted this statement. 'And I'm turning twenty-one . . .' laughter and whistles followed. 'So thanks for a marvellous twenty-one years to Dad and Mum, Ledgie and Uncle Wake and my sister: the best family in the whole wide world! So now let's all just have fun and if anyone wants to meet me and Cash later on the front verandah we're taking bets on our being the best arm-wrestling team here.'

'You're on!' could just be heard above the cheering and cat-calling.

When the music began again Sam took John Baron's hand for 'The Pride of Erin'. 'Before you go outside, dance with me, JB.'

'Sure.'

They danced well together and Sam felt so proud in the arms of her big brother. 'I reckon you're the best-looking bloke here,' she said as he swirled her along.

'Ah get out, Sammy, what do you know about looks? You're only fifteen.'

Sam's offence was markedly obvious. She looked down her nose at him and hissed with disdain, 'I'm sixteen in a month, you pig.'

'Oh lovely,' answered her brother. 'One second I'm the best-looking bloke here and the next I'm a pig.'

Sam burst into laughter at this and in complete sibling harmony they revolved on around the floor.

At midnight when the party was still bubbling along and John Baron and Cash had won their bets and proved their strength, Samantha left her friends Julie Slade and Les Frith and moved out onto the verandah to enjoy the slightly cooler outdoor temperature.

Sam noticed Cash in conversation with two or three of the local lads and she wandered on down to them. They were laughing loudly at something Jake Clayton had said, but when she joined them Cash took her shoulders, turned her round and steered her back along the verandah.

'Come back, Cash, we're not finished!' shouted Jake as Cash replied, flinging the words over his shoulder, 'Yeah? Well, I have for tonight.'

'What's going on?' asked Sam as Cash took her around the corner out of sight of the group.

'Forget it, Sam. Sometimes the fellows get carried away.' Cash halted in a shadow. He looked down at her. She was dressed in blue silk and wore a matching band in her long hair. Around her slender neck hung amber beads. Her face was animated, she looked fresh and vital. 'Ah Sammy, m'lady, how old are you?'

Sam sighed. 'Why is everybody reminding me of my age tonight?' She pursed her lips before answering. 'I'm almost sixteen.'

Cash took her arm. 'Exactly. And at the risk of sounding like a schoolteacher, I must tell you that sometimes the blokes say things that aren't for tender ears such as yours. And it's not for you to be a participant.'

'So they were telling dirty jokes, were they?'

Cash grinned and mirth rumbled in his throat.

'Girls tell them too, you know,' she said.

He bent swiftly down and kissed her mouth. In her amazement she did not resist and his lips pressed into hers parting them gently, just enough for each to experience the wetness of the other.

Now she drew her head back. A pink flush flooded across her face. 'Cashman Slade!'

He released her and pointed to the door a few feet distant. 'So, back inside you go. For as desirable as you are, you're far too young for me.'

She moved off across the wooden floorboards and turned back in the golden light from the door. It rested in her brown curls and as she spoke a bold expression crossed her face and she lifted her right arm akimbo. 'What if I tell John Baron what you just did?'

His ebony eyes were lost in shadow, all Sam could see was a glint where she knew them to be. His laughter was almost sinister. 'Hell, Sammy, your brother doesn't frighten me. Fact is, no one does, my dear. And in any case, you should know me by now. *Pro bono publico* . . . I'll deny it.'

'You're rotten, do you know that?'

'Yes. Now get moving before I forget any limited restraint I have.' He watched the shimmering silk dress as she disappeared through the door. Sammy was growing into a wonderful-looking girl and she did not seem to be aware of it, which made her even more enchanting in a way. Cash took out from his top pocket a packet of Craven A and sidled on down the verandah to a vantage spot in the darkness where he could observe the party through a side-window. He lit a cigarette, contented in the obscurity of the warm night, and as he blew a swirling ring of smoke high in the air he noticed Sammy's blue dress swirl by on the inside of the window in the brisk steps of a barn dance.

The party ended around two in the morning and the family travelled home in 'Joe' as they called the 'ute', a Ford utility truck with a small cabin to sit three and an open back with two forms upon which Sam sat between her big brother and Wakefield. It had been a great success and everyone was still buoyed up. Wakefield, who had imbibed a few too many whiskies, insisted on speaking French all the way home and Samantha and John Baron indulged him and giggled and laughed as Joe rattled along.

'Your French accent is perfect, *absolument parfait*,' Wakefield said to John Baron and then added smugly, 'It should be after all the years I've been tutoring you.'

The young man laughed. 'You could be wrong, Uncle Wake. You haven't even spoken to a Frenchman for thirteen years. You might have forgotten.'

'*Jamais!* Don't be ridiculous, lad. My mother was from Champagne, I received a faultless accent from her, and you from me. You could pass for a Frenchman from Champagne, there's no doubt.'

Sam sounded offended. 'What about me?'

Her brother burst into laughter.

'What's so funny?'

'Your passing for a Frenchman from Champagne.'

This made them all laugh and Wakefield humoured the girl by declaring that her accent was . . . 'coming along'.

Sam did not mention to anyone about Cash having kissed her and when at last she lay between the starched sheets of her single bed in her neat pink room down the hall from her brother, she thought about it. In her life she had been kissed by three different boys and Cash was definitely her choice. She knew her girlfriends would be jealous because he was modish, and moodily handsome, and there was a rakish quality about him which made him fascinating.

But as she lay in the darkness looking at the pale lustre of her pink curtains she was vaguely cogniscent of a strange feeling; it played around the edges of her mind without taking shape. It had to do with John Baron and how she was so proud of him. It had to do with laughing and giggling with him and conversing in French in the darkness on their ride home, and with standing by him tonight when he had made his speech . . . And most of all it had to do with the proximity of him, dancing with him and being in his arms. She did not search too far into herself, she let her mind slip into the hallucinatory realm of sleep before her subconscious was unguarded enough to admit she wished her brother had kissed her too.

The following morning she had forgotten all about such an unacceptable illusion.

Chapter Eleven

Two years later: Christmas Eve, 1934

At 5 p.m. motor bikes and sidecars, horses and drays and a few utility trucks pulled into the side of the Church of England Hall in Church Street, Boonah. The performers and their amateur crews of dressers and backstage helpers all descended from animals and vehicles and gathered on the front steps for Sam to take a group photograph of them.

After she had recorded the amateur players for posterity her brother shouted, 'That's not fair! Sam should be in a photograph too.' So once again everybody returned to the steps and Sam took her place proudly beside her big brother, before they all dispersed to prepare for the evening.

At a quarter to seven Sam came out from the ladies' dressing room – an area on one of the side verandahs sectioned off with hanging sheets. She carried two sandwiches and headed round the corner where her brother and Cash, already dressed like aviators for the second act, sat on the back steps of the hall catching an agreeable breeze in the fast-fading light. As she came towards them she heard Cash say, 'Sam's grown into a positive *dream girl,* you know.' He laughed. 'She's a real corker.'

Sam halted.

John Baron did not answer immediately and when he did he sounded almost irritated. 'She was always beautiful right from the first time I saw her.'

'Oh?'

'In her cot in England. Just born. I was five. She was a twin.'

'And you remember that?'

'Yes.'

'You don't say. What happened to the other one?'

'Died of the great influenza.'

'You never enlightened me of that before.'

'No? Well, I'm telling you now.'

'Where were you born?'

'Oh, in Lymington, I think.'

'You think?' He looked away into the haze of fading day before he asked, 'Don't you know?'

'Well, yes I do, then – in Lymington. That's where we lived before the war and before we went up to Yorkshire where the twins were born, so I suppose I was born there.'

'But you don't remember living there?'

'No, I don't. All I remember is living in Yorkshire.' He delayed a moment before he said, 'Anyway, Cash, don't think about messing around with Sam. You've got your girl, or should I say *girls*, in Brisbane.'

'Hell, old mate, come on. I wouldn't *mess* with Sam, I feel a mite more serious about her than that. I mean, we've always been so close. I didn't tell you but I kissed her once a couple of years ago. Haven't followed up on it, though. She's been too young – up to now, that is.'

JB let out a curse. 'Damn it, Cash. I should slug you, really I should.'

'Ah, but you're my friend.'

'Don't count on that to save you. Sam's only just turned eighteen and she's my sister. Leave her alone, Cash. I bloody mean it.'

'Oh yes, indeed, she's *your sister*. How true.'

'Give up, Cash.'

Sam backed away while a silence hung between the two men on the steps. As she reached the corner of the verandah she saw her brother stand up and leave and she hurried back and went in behind the hanging sheets.

Even though it was a hot night, when the curtain rose at seven-thirty the hall was packed to capacity. And while a percentage of the assembly had been into Ipswich and enjoyed a night at 'Old Martoos', the moving picture-house where even 'talkies' were now appearing, and some had made the long journey into Brisbane to improve their educations with such professional touring company offerings as *No, No Nanette* and *The Boyfriend*, they were still unsophisticated in the ways of stage performances. Thus all acts, regardless of quality, were greeted enthusiastically.

The concert opened with 'Bye Bye Blackbird' sung by the local church choir, followed by John Baron and Cash presenting a comic sketch based on Charles Kingsford Smith and his co-pilot Charles Ulm. It was a great success and wildly acclaimed. Nine more acts preceded Samantha and John Baron in 'Tea for Two'. They danced and sang quite capably and when Samantha hit the final note and took John Baron's hand, clasped the hem of her filmy yellow skirt and bowed to the audience, they broke again into zealous applause.

As her brother followed her off the stage he gave her a playful shove. 'They loved us, Sammy, they loved us.'

'Accomplished act,' Cash congratulated them, and after the semi-confrontation she had overheard, Samantha was pleased to see her brother slap his friend on the shoulder and answer, 'Thanks, old man.'

Wakefield closed the green baize curtains for the end of the first half of the concert and the audience all proceeded out onto the long verandah lit by three lonely electric light bulbs all currently under attack from hundreds of moths. Yet there was enough of a glow to see the beer and the sherry, the soft drinks and pies on sale to raise money for the Country Women's Association which had been founded in Queensland in 1922 and had spread quickly across the state.

In this backwater of style the women mostly wore floral print dresses gathered or pleated at the waist though Samantha and Julie and the younger set displayed a little more knowledge by presenting themselves in the semi-modish A-line dress with short skirt above silk stockings. Samantha felt sorry for the men who all wore suits and ties, for even at 9 p.m. it was still 80 degrees.

Sam and her friends Julie Slade, Madge Clarence and the two Thomas girls, Coral and Clara, sat on the steps drinking creaming sodas. Samantha, Julie and Coral had all just completed their schooling at Glenee Girls' School in Toowoomba and were home for good. Clara and Madge were two years their senior and both engaged to be married.

At this juncture in the history of the world, the imprimatur of womanhood was to be wearing a diamond ring or a plain golden band. It was not unusual for girls as young as seventeen to be married, and they were regarded as heading for spinsterhood if they reached twenty-one without the distinction of an engagement ring. The young women were talking and laughing together, but all with one eye trained upon the group of males who clustered together at the bottom of the steps under the green canopy of a large jacaranda tree.

'Are they looking up at us?' asked Madge, sipping her drink.

Julie peeked sideways. 'Yes, definitely. That is, I think so.' She gave a sigh. 'You know, I reckon JB's the best-looking of the lot of them.' She glanced round. 'Come on. Let's vote on the best-looking. Who do you think, Coral?'

Coral gazed openly down at the males. 'I think my vote has to be for Cash. Yes, JB's nice and all, but Cash is dreamy: sleek hair, straight nose, so dark and interesting. Those intense eyes.' She made a moaning sound.

This made the girls giggle.

'Shhh, they'll hear you!' scolded Clara as Julie pointed to Samantha.

'What do you think?'

Sam ran her eyes over the group below. 'Jake Clayton has lovely white teeth . . .'

'Teeth?' Coral began to shake with laughter. 'Teeth aren't criteria for good looks.'

'I think they are,' Samantha rejoined. 'You must have good teeth to be truly handsome, but Coral's right about Cash – there's something magnetic about him.'

'So who're you voting for?'

'Well . . . I agree with Julie. My brother *is* the best-looking.'

They all shook their heads. 'You aren't allowed to say that.'

'He's your brother, that disqualifies your vote.'

'Ssh, watch out!' hissed Clara. 'Here they come.'

The group of young men had left the shadows of the tree and were making their way to the steps. The girls pushed themselves into a huddle to let them by and as they passed Cash paused. 'You'd better get a move on, ladies. The second act's about to start.' He ran his fingers through Coral's hair as he moved on.

'Cheek!' exclaimed Coral, but she blushed with pleasure all the same.

Cash looked back over his shoulder and called, 'Come on, Sammy, you've got to change.'

The penultimate act saw John Baron producing an excerpt from Oscar Wilde's 'The Importance of Being Earnest', with Samantha playing Gwendoline, Cash Earnest and Julie, Lady Bracknell. They were certainly a success, with Ledgie applauding wildly for she had been hearing Samantha's lines for weeks.

The night closed with a short speech from the CWA chairwoman and an invitation for everyone to take tea, coffee and pound cake, in the spirit of Christmas, free of charge.

People were soon on the verandah, pushing and shoving, and down in the yard the younger ones congregated together. Cash stood beside Samantha and when everyone else was occupied in conversation he whispered to her, 'Meet me round the side of the hall by the banana trees.'

She looked into his eyes. 'What?'

'You heard me.' And he moved swiftly away through the group.

Samantha frowned. That was Cash all over. Ever enigmatic and often downright rude. Nevertheless thirty seconds later she turned away from her companions and pushed back through the throng. The only person to notice her departure was her brother and he watched her until she reached the bottom of the wooden steps and Ledgie's sharp tones halted her. 'Now where are you off to, young lady? I'm rounding up the family. Your mother's dog-tired and tomorrow we have to cook Christmas dinner in this unforgivin' climate, so it's a night's sleep we're all needin'.'

Sam moved on, answering as she went, 'I'll be back in just a minute, Ledgie, really I will.'

'You'd better be.'

And with that Samantha hurried along the side of the hall, turned the corner to pass by a patch of long grass near the water tank and moved on to the banana trees lit only by the light of the moon.

'Cash?'

'Here.'

'It's so dark I can hardly see you.'

'I love the dark,' he replied, stepping out from the black shape of a banana tree. 'I've got something for you for Christmas. I wanted to give it to you alone.'

Her eyes were two round reflectors of the moonlight. 'What is it?'

He stepped in and took her in his arms and drew her to him, and just as two years before, she did not resist. He kissed her full on the mouth, opening her lips and kneading her tongue with his own. His arms felt strong and resilient.

After a few seconds she pulled away. 'Cash, stop it!' And she knocked his hands off her arms and stepped backwards. 'You kissed me like that at JB's birthday and now after all this time you do it again. What am I to be? Someone who means nothing to you for years but who's to be kissed when you damn well feel like it?'

Cash laughed quietly. 'Ah Sammy, my spirited Sammy, I couldn't control myself that night and would have kissed you a thousand times since but you were too young ... until now.'

Samantha's emotions were tumbling over each other. She knew she had enjoyed the caress but she was also annoyed that Cash assumed she would go along with it at his convenience. Then she remembered something.

'What about your girlfriend in Brisbane?'

'What about her?'

'You've got her, so why are you kissing me?'

'Because I wanted to. You've grown into a damn fine-looking specimen.'

'What a way to talk!'

'Sam, my so-called girlfriend is about to be superseded. And the way I feel about you, well, I'm hoping . . .' He stepped closer to her and put out his hand to touch her face.

'What's going on here?'

They both started and swung round.

John Baron stood a few yards distant. He was in shadow, but suddenly the headlights from a vehicle flashed upon him and bestowed his figure with a brief burst of light. Momentarily it seemed to radiate around him.

Cash stepped forward, sliding his hand sensuously along Samantha's back before dropping it to his side. 'Gosh, old man, with that bright light upon you, you looked like the Messiah Himself for a second there, halo and all. Very ingenious considering it's Yuletide.'

John Baron found his friend's eyes in the pallid illumination of the night. 'You heard me. I said, what's going on?'

Cash smiled. 'I was merely wishing Sam the compliments of the season. Is something unpalatable to you about that?'

John Baron did not answer but reached out and grabbed his sister's arm. 'I told you what I thought before. Come on Sam, Ledgie's damned annoyed.' He glowered at Cash. 'And if your intention's still to spend Christmas with us then behave yourself.' He steered his sister away and Cash followed on behind, his gaze upon the brother and sister, a quizzical expression on his face.

They could hear car and truck engines being cranked as John Baron's grip tightened on his sister's arm. He guided her round the corner of the building where headlights dazzled them and he shoved her hard in the back towards the dispersing crowd.

'Ouch! That hurt!'

'Serves you right. Move!' And he shoved her again.

People were calling out, 'Merry Christmas.' 'Wonderful concert.' 'See you in church tomorrow.'

Vehicles moved off and horses were urged away.

Ledgie was literally stamping her foot in her black laced-up shoe when they arrived at the side of Joe, the family ute. 'And where did you get to then, me gel?' Ledgie always dropped into her Lancashire accent when she was cross. 'Dinna you tell me you'd be back in just a minute?'

Ben had the engine running and he put his head out of the window speaking up to support Ledgie. 'You shouldn't have gone off like that, your mother's tired.'

John Baron gave Sam a final shove as Cash came sauntering up, and Ledgie poked him in the chest with a bony finger. 'And where have *you* been?'

'Sorry, Ledge old darling.'

She pointed to the back of the ute. 'Get in and don't backchat.'

The ride to Haverhill took forty minutes, most of it on unsealed road. In the front of the ute the soporific whir of the engine and the warm night soon had Constance asleep on Ledgie's shoulder, and in the back, Wakefield and Cash and occasionally John Baron talked on and off about the concert. Wakefield insisted on speaking French as he often did when alone with his youthful companions, and John Baron and Cash indulged him. Cash's French, while not as exemplary as JB's or Samantha's, was more than adequate, having flourished over the years under the guidance and tutorage of Wakefield.

Samantha did not join in the conversation. Instead she sulked, sitting silently mulling over what had happened, with the breeze blowing her long hair back over her shouders.

Yet by the time the ute had rattled along Haverhill's drive over the scarlet fallen flowers from the poinciana trees and pulled up at the front steps of the house to be greeted wildly by Tess and Charity, Sam's good humour had returned.

She wished everyone a Happy Christmas and Cash called, 'Good night, m'lady.' It was only John Baron who walked away from her without a word.

As the two young men went down the hall to their separate rooms, Cash put his arm round his friend's shoulder. 'Hey, JB, come on. I can't help it if I'm attracted to Sammy. I promise I'll not take advantage of her.'

John Baron managed a smile. 'Yes? Well, just make sure you remember your promise, that's all.'

In her room Sam brushed out her hair and washed her face and put on her pyjamas. She halted in thought for more than a minute, standing barefoot at her door before she slipped along the hall, tiptoeing by Cashman's room. Her parents, Ledgie and Uncle Wakefield were all remote, their bedrooms being on the far side of the house. She was at her brother's door with her hand in the air poised to knock when she recoiled. Cash stood in the darkness of the corridor ahead.

'Where are you off to, Sammy?'

Samantha hesitated in embarrassment. She pulled the two sides of the neck of her pyjamas together. 'God, Cash, I could ask you the same.'

'I'm going to clean my teeth – want to come?'

'Of course not.' She turned around and went back to her room as Cash's voice echoed behind her, 'Happy Christmas, Sammy.'

When Cash returned to the corridor he did not go back to bed. He had been intrigued by the way Sam had been hovering in the hall outside her brother's room; he felt anticipation, but he did not know about what.

As it was possible to circumnavigate the large house by walking around the verandah, he did so just for the sheer pleasure of being out in the night unknown to anyone.

The dogs always slept in Wakefield's room so he had been extra careful as he slipped by the older man's window. But Cash was comfortable in the darkness, the depth of night allured and fascinated him and he had a strong sense that something was about to occur tonight of which he, Cashman Slade, needed to be aware. He returned to his side of the house and leant on the verandah rail.

Fifteen minutes passed and nothing happened while he watched the moon cast ribbons of light through the slits in the torpid clouds of high summer. The warm night air all around him made him feel sleepy, yet he remained in the gloomy shadows until the moon slid again behind a thick wide cloud and the landscape blackened.

He crept along the verandah to stand where he could peer though JB's sash window. It was open to its full extent to give the interior as much air as possible. There was still the touch of a breeze, languid and weak, but it made the night bearable. One lamp burnt low near the bedside and illuminated his friend naked from the waist up, lying on his bed. Cash thought JB must be asleep and he had almost decided his expectations were false when he heard the door to John Baron's room open.

JB was *not* asleep, for he spoke. 'Who is it?'

Cash edged forward, as near to the window as he dared to go as Sam entered and closed the door behind her.

Sam paused when she saw her brother in bed, his back towards her, his face to the wall. One lamp cast a dull glow over his forty model aeroplanes, mostly made by Wakefield, hanging from the ceiling or standing on shelves above his reclining figure.

Cash watched fascinated as Sam crossed the rug and stood a few feet from her brother in the bed.

Sam felt very odd, but then she supposed that was natural in the circumstances; she could hardly recall her brother ever being angry with her before. She moved across the polished wooden floorboards to the rug.

'Who is it?' John Baron asked again without moving.

'Oh, JB, stop pretending. You know who it is. Me.'

Slowly he turned and sat up pushing the pillow behind his back. She could see he was naked to the waist.

She stepped closer to the bed, one leg of her pyjamas hitched higher than the other. He noticed the rounded shape of her breasts beneath the striped cotton material. He felt an odd sensation in his stomach.

'Why did you kiss him?'

Samantha took a sharp breath. 'So, you saw it?'

'Yes.'

'Then you saw that *he* kissed me.'

'I'd say you entered into the spirit of it pretty damn well.'

She shook her head and her hair moved on her shoulders while the shadows on the planes of her face made her appear much older. 'Look, I'm eighteen and Cash is

141

twenty-two. It's not illegal to kiss. He's sort of nice, you know.'

'He's got a girl.'

'He said he's finishing with her.'

'He's a damned liar and a flirt, and you're a fool.'

Sam flinched. 'What was that?' She looked sharply round to the window.

'What was what?'

'It sounded like something scraping outside on the verandah.'

John Baron shook his head. 'I didn't hear anything.' He gestured dismissively towards the door. 'Go back to bed.'

'Why are you so short with me? And why did you push and shove me like that tonight?'

Outside the window Cash scarcely dared to breathe now, remaining rigid in the night, his gaze intently upon them.

John Baron put his right hand up to his forehead. He was feeling hot. 'Look, Sammy, I've got a headache.'

'Oh, JB, are you all right?' Now her voice was worried, tender. She came to him and touched him lovingly on his head.

He pulled from her touch. 'Don't! Go away. You shouldn't be in here like this. You're not dressed.'

'But you're my brother. I've been with you in my pyjamas my whole life.'

He made a frustrated sound. 'You're grown-up now. It's different. Go away. Go to bed, Sam. Out.' He pointed to the door again.

A tear fell down her cheek. 'I don't like this. I don't want you to be angry with me. You're my best friend in the whole world. I feel unhappy. Please forgive me. I didn't mean to make you mad.' And as her tears continued she bent down and kissed his cheek.

This time he did not pull away from her. He had never felt anything as beautiful as this touch of her lips upon his skin.

His hands came up and took her shoulders, drawing them down to him. Her hands came up to cup his face between them.

They looked into each other's eyes and all Sam's wild imaginings opened up before her and became real as John Baron murmured his next words.

'I was jealous,' he said.

Sam thought she would remember this moment for ever. She leant in and kissed him.

Beyond the window Cash viewed with astonishment the scene playing out before him but he did not move. He could see and hear everything and his dark eyes narrowed while the hairs on the back of his neck prickled as he watched Sammy unrestrainedly kiss the man she believed was her brother.

Sam could feel the heat of JB's hands as they slipped down her back to grip her bare waist underneath the cotton material. He pulled her into him and held her against him.

They ran their hands across each other's body in carnal exploration and Samantha's loose clothes were cast aside. He hovered over her as she lay looking up at him, smiling up at him and he moaned as he kissed her again, his mouth lingering upon hers while his hands cupped her breasts. He moved over her and his body came down upon hers, pushing in between her open legs . . . and in that instant he realised what he was about to do.

'Oh my God, no!' He ripped himself from her grasp and stood up, clumsily snatching his pyjama trousers from the bed and stepping into them. 'Get out, Sam! What in God's name are we doing?'

Sam closed her eyes, her temples felt tight. 'I . . . I don't know. All I know is . . . I love you.'

He spun round. His face was white and a weird light burnt in his eyes. 'Don't ever say that again! Not like that. It's not natural. You're *my sister*. For Christ's sake, don't you realise what we were about to do?'

She sat up and he picked up her pyjamas and threw them at her. They hit her in the face. 'Get dressed. Get out!'

She began to cry softly as the moon, sliding out from behind the dense cloud, joined with the glow from the lamp to expose her upon the bed. She felt her nakedness and her eyes turned towards the moonlight. Momentarily she thought she saw something move outside but she was so overcome with what her brother was saying that her mind did not fully comprehend her vision.

'It has a name, Sam.' JB's voice had lost its excitement; it was anguished and quiet. 'It's a bloody disgusting thing called incest.' Perspiration was running in a trickle down his temple. 'We almost took a step into hell. Please get dressed and go now. And for God's sake, *never* tell anyone about this.'

She sat there breathing heavily, her breasts rising and falling with the intensity of her emotion.

'Get up, I said! Move, damn it.' He punched out at the air.

She lifted her body from the bed and he watched her put on her clothes, saw the beauty of her slender hips, her long legs and her full taut breasts and nipples disappear beneath the striped cotton material. He despised himself for not looking away.

She moved over the rug and paused on the bare floor-boards, aware of their coolness on the souls of her feet as she turned back to him. 'JB I know exactly what we were about to do. I know it's wrong. I know it's very bad, and that all the things you said are true. But you see, I didn't feel as if it were evil at all. Perhaps it's all my fault. Forgive me. You were right to stop us . . .' a moment later she added '. . . for I couldn't have.'

She crossed to the door and as her hand held the knob she heard him crying. She thought to go back and hold him, but she knew it was not allowed. She felt the tears drifting from her own eyes as she hesitated and said, 'I feel odd and terrible and I know no one would ever understand. But now I realise that I have always loved you, JB, and I always will, even though it's wicked.'

He heard her open and close the door. He detested himself.

After a time he felt calmer and rose from his bed. He walked barefoot along the corridor to the kitchen and out onto the back verandah and down the steps into the night. He wandered down to the brook and climbing onto the great stump of the felled gum tree near the remaining deep water-hole, he dived in.

When he surfaced he looked up where the moon had hidden itself again in the gloomy limitless sky. He floated there a long time with the water lapping around him, his lifeless eyes clouded with tears.

Back on the verandah of the house Cash stood holding the railing and watching the stream. He believed he could just make out JB's body floating in the water. He wondered if his friend intended to drown himself. He could damn well understand it if he did.

No wonder JB always jumped to excessive protective-ness over Sam: no wonder he had acted like a schoolteacher earlier tonight when he had caught them kissing. JB was bloody well in love with her! And they both believed they were brother and sister, and that their feelings were illicit and unnatural.

The fact that JB was not Sam's brother had remained Cash's secret. He had kept it to himself ever since he had overheard the Chard family discussion on JB's twenty-first birthday. But what he had seen and heard tonight was just as astounding a revelation.

Cash squeezed his lips between his forefinger and his thumb in thought. Poor old JB down there in the creek. He would be dying inside. Poor old decent, moral JB. Cash had the key to halt his suffering. The universe in its infinite wisdom had seen fit to enlighten Cashman Slade of the truth, and he alone was aware of the myriad complications.

He could liberate JB now, here tonight by revealing the facts to him.

But he would not do that. Fact was, he could not do that. Sam had somehow captured him. Hell, he had to face it: he wanted her for himself.

As an owl hooted in the trees by the grain shed, he shook his head and steadily peered into the night. '*No, JB, old man, we can't let you know the truth. You go on hating yourself!*'

He stood upright from the railing, a cold expression in

his eyes. '*So, Sammy, you let me kiss you but the one you want to give yourself to is JB. We'll just have to alter all that, won't we?*'

Cash watched the dark figure in the distant glinting water another minute while his long fingers toyed with his forelock, pulling it down over his brow and releasing it, then he shook his head, left the verandah and went back to bed.

Chapter Twelve

It was tradition that on Boxing Day the Chards and the Slades picnicked together. They took their two family utilities and piled one up with a trestle table and two long wooden forms to sit upon, and the other they filled with the children and food and drink and they drove the eight miles out to Lonely Man's Flat in the direction of the Logan River. There Teviot Brook opened into a deep pool which held water most of the year even when much of the water-course dried up. There was another popular deep water-hole on the far side of Boonah called Black Pinch where a lot of people went to picnic, but the two families preferred the seclusion of Lonely Man's Flat and it was here they spent the day.

The Slades arrived at Haverhill under a burning sun at ten in the morning and the men began to load up the back of the vehicles while the women went about putting the food into containers for the journey.

Samantha sat on the steps of the verandah watching and Julie came over to her and leant on the railing post. 'You look glum.'

Sam lifted her eyes. 'Do I?'

'I just said so. What's wrong?'

'Nothing.'

'Didn't you get any Christmas presents?'

'Of course I did.'

'Then what's up?'

'Oh, I don't know.'

'That time of the month, is it?'

Sam sighed, her chest lifting under the weight of the emotion. 'No, it's not. Look, Jules, just forget it, I'll be all right in a minute. I'll be back.' She stood and mounted the stairs to return into the house and Julie watched her go.

Sam went through the house to the kitchen where her mother was putting jam tarts into a tin.

'Oh, there you are, darling. Just finish this for me, will you, while I take the rest out to Mrs Slade.' Constance picked up the hamper of food and hurried out onto the back verandah. Her daughter's eyes followed her as she passed by the meat safe which hung where the coolest air washed up from the stream, keeping it at a relatively lower temperature than the rest of the house. As her firm footsteps faded, Sam lowered her eyes and continued with her task.

Every now and then she sighed. Yesterday had been the worst Christmas Day of her life. Oh, John Baron had been light and bright enough with everyone and no one in the rest of the family suspected anything. She believed it was only herself who saw the lifelessness in his usually animated eyes.

They had all gone into Christ Church in Boonah for morning service as was habitual on Christmas morning, and when they returned, the hot lunch had been served at the long Sheraton dining table which had belonged to Ben's parents, one of the few possessions which Constance had insisted on bringing out from 'the old country'.

Cash, who had studied JB steadily all morning, ate everything on his plate but John Baron merely picked at his food and his mother and Ledgie had fussed over him trying to tempt him. 'Come on, a young fellow like you not hungry? And on the Lord's day too. Try the potatoes, darlin', they're delicious.'

'They sure are!' exclaimed Cash enthusiastically.

After the plum pudding they had retired to the parlour and given out their gifts beside the tree. Sam wondered if anyone noticed that John Baron did not kiss her when he handed her his gift.

The rest of the day had been spent in pure Queensland Christmas tradition, re-looking at their gifts and lolling around in the shade. In the late afternoon the males had played cricket, Wakefield using Sam as his runner because of his missing leg. Sam tried hard to be normal but she felt ill most of the day and John Baron had avoided meeting her eyes and this morning he had done the same.

She sighed again as she put the last of the tarts in the tin, and Ledgie's relentless tones sounded from the verandah. 'Come along, Samantha. We're all ready now.'

When they arrived at the water-hole the men put up the tables and the women spread blankets on the ground near the bank of the river.

'Watch out for the ants!' Julie warned as Ledgie and her mother began to unwrap the food.

'Not just the ants, the blasted flies,' shouted her brother Henry, taking a long running jump into the water and splashing it high in the air.

Cash and Wakefield were sitting on a large rock with their fishing rods and tackle at their sides. Cash waved. 'Are you going to fish, JB, old man?'

'Be there in a minute.'

'Bet you sixpence I get the first bite.'

'I'll take that bet.'

Sam remained alone in the shade of a small eucalypt with the book of stories JB had given her for Christmas.

When things were settled and the three older women were sitting on a blanket talking and Ledgie had her tatting out and her needle between finger and thumb, Randall Slade took out a cigar and beckoned Ben.

Ben smoked a cigar perhaps three times a year and Boxing Day was one. The two men set off side by side for a walk and when they had lit their cigars and passed the second bend in the watercourse Randall tarried and faced his neighbour. Twenty-five years before, he had been the catch of the district: a man of medium height with a spectacular physique and dark Byronesque good looks inherited from his Italian mother, the fable hereabouts being she was the daughter of a disinherited Count. He had passed on his moody good looks to Cash and even now in his sixtieth year he remained a striking figure; and as he paused on the riverbank and puffed on his cigar, his still abundant eyebrows drew together disconsolately.

'Ben, I've gone and done it this time.'

'What's that, Randall?'

'There's no other way to say it. I've made some bad investments, very bad investments. Fact is, Ben, I think I'm going to have to sell the property and the farm to get out of the mess. These last few years have seen a lot go under and I'm afraid I'm to become another bloody statistic.'

Ben knew, as most folk in the valley did, that Randall was a gambler, wagering on horses, buying and selling antiques, even chunks of land at times. 'Are you sure?'

'Yes, I'm afraid so. Fact is, I haven't told the missus yet, nor Cash. Cash has just finished university, thank God, because I couldn't afford to keep him there: still haven't paid his last three months' fees if the truth's known. He'll just have to do whatever he can. We'll have to move to a smaller place and I'll have to get a bloody job in the coal mines or something. That's if there's a job for me to get.' He turned away and moved across to a flat sandstone rock where he sat looking at the dust on his boots.

Cash's laughter drifted down to them, followed by high-spirited voices echoing along the creek. A hot breeze lifted a dead gum leaf from the tree above Randall's head and carried it for a dozen yards, swirling in the air, before it settled in the dust.

'I feel bad about the farmhands and the blacks who break my horses. Got some really good blokes. Don't know what the hell they'll do.'

Ben thought of Veena and her family.

'There's no bloody way out, that's the rotten part of it.' Randall lifted his head. 'So this'll be the last Boxing Day we come out here, I'm sorry to say . . . after all these years.'

Ben moved a few steps and rested his foot upon a fallen tree trunk. He took a puff on his cigar while he thought. 'Look Randall, I might be able to help you with a loan. I can't manage a lot but I could let you have something until you get out of Queer Street.'

Randall raised his eyes. Ben noticed they were blood-shot. 'Ben, I'm in deep. I owe thousands.'

Benjamin's surprised intake of breath was clearly audible. 'Really?'

''Fraid so. Look, I appreciate your offer but unless you can lend me money to the tune of thousands, you can't help me.'

Ben slowly shook his head. 'Then I'm sorry, Randall, but I can't help you. Hundreds maybe, thousands, no. I've managed to keep my head afloat because I've had money to fall back on. When we didn't get the prices for the grain and the vegetables three years in a row I used some savings and dipped into money that's really not mine; which I have to pay back. After that I sold some of my best horses. Fact is, I've got enough for my family's needs, even some to spare; but not that sort of money.'

'Yeah, that's what I thought. Thanks anyway. Decent of you to offer. People look up to you, Ben. You came out from the Old Dart and a lot of blokes around here said, "What does he bloody well know about farming and horses and animals?" But you showed them mate, and I for one reckon you're all right.'

'Thanks Randall, I appreciate that. And I'm truly sorry I can't help you.' Randall looked down at his boots again.

Ben thought for a time then he touched his friend on the shoulder. 'Look, if after you've sold here you find you've got enough left to put up a cottage or something, Connie and I could let you live rent free on our land that's just sitting there over near Ipswich; can't do anything with it in this financial climate.'

Randall cheered a little. 'That's great, mate. I hope I can take you up on that. But at the moment I'm mighty bloody worried about telling the missus. She won't take it well. She's got used to having the things she wants: pulling her horns in won't suit her. And Cash, well it's turned out to be the bloody right moniker for that boy. He's forever spending, trying to live up to that flatmate of his – young Belcher. It won't come easily to him.' He hung his head down.

Suddenly Sam's voice reached them through the bush, 'Daddy, Daddy! Lunch is ready.'

Randall raised his head and grimaced. 'Best get back.' As he stood Sam entered the clearing.

'There you are, I thought I could smell cigars.'

Randall threw down the butt and tramped on it.

Ben gestured for his daughter to return to the picnic. 'Tell them we're coming.' As Sam disappeared, Benjamin touched his friend on the shoulder. 'Look Randall, I'll see what I can do about taking one or two of your hands over.'

Randall gave a wan smile.

'And you know that small disused cottage over near Cockatoo Hill? Well, Jimmy Birnum and his family can have that. Fact is, I don't have much work for him and his sons except the milking, but I do have a mare in foal and a few good horses left; might be able to pay him something to look after them. At least they'll have a roof over their heads and Veena and her mother will have somewhere to stay.'

Randall put his hand on Ben's shoulder. 'Thanks mate, so very neighbourly of you. I greatly value anything like that you can do; they're all good people.'

It was a singular lunch. Some, like Cash and his younger siblings devoured the food as if they were going on a hunger strike by day's end, whereas others like John Baron, Samantha and Randall Slade ate sparingly.

John Baron had studiously avoided being anywhere near his sister; and while he fished and swam in the river and acted as normally as he could, a despairing expression dwelt in his eyes. Yet it was only Cash who observed this and he knew full well the cause. After lunch he took JB aside near the riverbank. 'What's up?'

'What do you mean?'

'Well, you were quiet all day yesterday and today the same. Not still mad at me for kissing Sammy on Christmas Eve, are you?'

John Baron felt the pit of his stomach drop but he met his friend's look just the same. 'No, not at all. Fact is, Cash, I've been feeling badly about how I acted. I've no objection whatever to the attention you pay to my sister. Forget that I ever said otherwise. She's old enough to kiss whomever she damn well likes, and if you fall into that category, then good luck to you.'

Cash's face reflected none of his feelings. He asked casually, 'Are you serious?'

'Deadly.'

'And what's brought on this change of heart, old man?'

John Baron's troubled look deepened. 'Nothing. I've just thought about it, that's all.'

'Have you now? Well, that's better.' Cash smiled and his teeth shone in the brilliant sunshine. 'I was a mite constrained by your reaction the other night but you've revitalised my interest, so to speak. Thanks, old man.'

John Baron turned away and walked into the water with Cash's enigmatic gaze resting on his back.

In the mid-afternoon Ledgie, Mrs Slade and Wakefield dropped off to sleep on the blankets by the water's edge while Ben, John Baron, Cash and the younger Slade siblings went for a nature walk. Randall Slade sat on a rock making a pretence of fishing and Samantha, who had made an excuse when Cash asked her to go along with them, wandered off on her own.

Sam had walked for about a quarter of a mile through the bush wiping the ready tears from her eyes when she saw a form moving in the scrub. She halted and waited. A dark figure in a worn flowered print dress came out into the clearing.

'Veena, what are you doing here?' She had not seen the Aboriginal girl for about a year and Sam ran forward to her and gave her a spontaneous hug.

The girl lifted her hand to shade her eyes. 'Pleased to see you, Samantha.'

'Veena, I thought you'd gone into Beaudesert to work in service. Are you home for Christmas?'

The Aboriginal girl nodded. 'I'm a Christian.'

Sam touched her on the shoulder. 'Of course you are, I wasn't questioning that. I'm so pleased to see you.'

Veena, who had always been firm and slender, looked fatter; her girth had spread and her face had become almost

153

moon-shaped. Innocently Sam commented, 'You're not as thin as you used to be.'

The girl's face fell; her black eyes blinked. 'Yes.' She looked down at her body.

'But . . . but you look nice.' Sam attempted to remedy the situation.

Veena shook her head. Her shoulders sagged.

'Oh Veena, is something wrong?'

Veena placed her long fine index finger up beside her mouth and shrugged. 'Baby coming.'

Samantha's surprise was evident in her jumbled response. 'Oh Veena. I see. Are you? I mean, is there . . . ? Oh dear . . . Veena.'

'I come home. Dunno what else to do.'

Samantha was out of her depth. She said no more but took Veena by the arm and they strolled on through the scrub together. Sam was deeply depressed and bewildered about what had occurred between herself and her brother, and as sorry as she was about Veena's plight, a part of her was almost relieved to have the new situation to dwell upon.

They walked for a time in the mid-afternoon heat and halted in the shadow cast by a cluster of large rocks. Veena sat down upon a log in the shade of the granite overhang and Sam pulled up a stem of paspalum grass and chewed its exposed cream-coloured end.

'Mum's real mad at me.' Veena's eyes glistened with hovering tears. 'Said I was a dirty girl. Hit me real hard, hit me good.' She pointed to a mark on her upper arm.

Samantha moved over and sat beside her old friend. 'Veena, I'm so sorry. I don't know where they are but I've heard about people who can . . . well . . . terminate babies.'

Veena turned on the log to face Samantha. 'What's that – *terminate*?'

'It means they can end it, they can stop the baby from being born.' She whispered her next words. 'Well, they remove it from you, I suppose.'

Veena's shocked expression was a mixture of indignation and pain. 'You mean kill it?'

Samantha was not an expert on this and she faltered. 'Oh

Veena, I was only trying to help. I mean, I don't know much about it.'

Veena was adamant. 'I'm a Christian. Killing's a sin. I would never do that.'

'Yes, yes of course you're right. I know you are. Oh dear, I'm sorry.'

'Me too,' Veena answered bleakly as a tear dislodged from her eye and ran down her cheek. Sam took her lace handkerchief out of her pocket and handed it to her friend.

Samantha and Veena had always been content in each other's company. A few years before, there had been a teacher at the school who used to give the Aboriginal children lessons and Veena had shown how bright she was by learning to read and write. On Sunday afternoons in those days Samantha and Veena had read books together.

They both sat for a time looking into the heat haze that had risen in the distance, then Veena said, 'I don't know my baby's father.'

'Oh dear, really?'

'Yeah, might be a white fella might be a black fella. I dunno.'

Sam put her arm around the girl's shoulders. 'Oh Veena, I'm sorry.'

'Yeah, I done it with two blokes.'

Samantha heaved a big sigh and so did the girl beside her as she stood. 'Mum's real mad. Better get back now.'

Samantha stood too and Veena proffered the lace handkerchief.

'No, you keep it. I'd like you to have it. Veena, my schooling's over and I want to keep up my photography – you know, the photographs I take with that camera I have. I want to learn more, go to places and take more pictures. Fact is though, I haven't decided how to do that yet, so I'll be home for a while. Possibly a long time. So please come over to Haverhill and see me, anytime you like.'

Veena pulled her mouth into the resemblance of a smile. 'I'd like to come and see you.'

'Good. Come on Sunday afternoon, like you used to.'

'I will.' She moved out of Sam's grasp, waved and dissolved into the scrub.

By the time Samantha returned to the picnic site the bush walkers were straggling in and Randall Slade was packing the furniture in his ute.

The two families drove in tandem to Haverhill where the dogs came running out to greet them and they unloaded the vehicles and said their goodbyes. Randall held Ben's hand as they stood together near the bottom of the front steps. 'Thanks for listening to me. I'll have to break the bad news tonight.'

Ben nodded. 'If there's anything else I can do, let me know.'

'You're doing a lot by taking some of the boys and giving shelter to Birnum and his family. Thanks, Ben.'

'Let me know how you fare.'

'I will.' Randall withdrew his hand and walked to his ute, climbed in and drove away.

'I'll be seeing you, Sammy!' Cash called out, pointing dramatically at her as the Slades' vehicle entered the avenue of poincianas.

It was half past eight that same night when John Baron walked in the darkness up from the brook towards the house. He was within twenty yards of the back door when he saw his sister. She waited for him by a clump of she oaks.

'Sam?'

'Oh, JB, I must talk to you. This is terrible.' Her brow was puckered in the darkness and she twined and untwined the fingers of her hands as she spoke. 'I cannot go on this way. You haven't spoken to me since Christmas Eve.'

John Baron sighed. 'Sam, what the hell do you expect?'

'What does that mean?' Her voice was rising and he lifted his palm in the darkness to silence her as she stepped closer to him and took him by the arm.

He tried to shake free and to keep his voice low. 'Don't. You're my sister, damn it!'

She did not release him, she stepped closer. He could smell the freshness of her washed hair and the faint scent of jasmine about her. He felt the sensation overwhelming him again and loathed himself for it.

'Can't you feel it?' she said, lifting her face up to his. 'Hold me. Just hold me, please.'

At that second the headlight of a motor bike lit the sheds in the distance and the vehicle came roaring up the drive through the poincianas and around the side of the house to illuminate them both in its stark brilliance.

'Damn, it's Cash.' John Baron raised his hands in front of his eyes, 'Turn it off, damn it!' he called out.

The visitor obliged and jumped off the Harley Davidson positioning it against the water tank and striding across to the brother and sister.

'What's going on out here?' Wakefield's voice sounded as he appeared at the back door and leaning on his walking cane crossed the verandah and looked out into the night.

'It's only Cash, Uncle Wake. Sam's here too.'

Satisfied, Wakefield returned inside.

As soon as Cash came closer they knew he was distraught. 'God, JB, I need to speak to you!' He grabbed John Baron's arm and virtually pulled him away. 'I have to speak to him alone, Sammy.'

Sam watched their two figures move across the grass by her mother's flowerbed and around the corner of the house. When they had disappeared she slowly returned inside.

On the lawn at the side of the house in the gleam from the clear night sky Cash faced his friend. 'My father's broke.'

'What?'

'My father's broke . . . said I have to take a job, any job. Mum's near hysterical. The bloody property has to be sold. Shit.'

John Baron was amazed. 'But what's happened?'

'Dad said he's made some rotten mistakes – bad investments – tried to get out, made some bets he shouldn't have and got deeper in. The plain fact is the banks won't lend him any more money.' His face was pale in the bleak glow from the house and the sky. 'I'm done for. Don't know what I'll do.'

John Baron had been drowning in his own insurmountable problem but now he felt keenly for his friend. 'How much money does your father need? I mean, can someone—'

'He owes bloody thousands,' Cash cut him off. 'He's deeply in debt.'

'Oh hell, this is terrible. Your poor father.'

Cash flinched as if he had been hit in the face, and a hard line of resolution settled on his mouth. 'Bugger my father. He got us into this mess. That property's been in our family for three generations and now we're going to lose it. All because of his stupidity.'

John Baron knew his friend was overwrought and so was not going to argue about it. 'Surely there's something he can do.'

Cash shook his head and his black lock of hair fell onto his forehead. He pushed it back with a sigh. 'No. Seems he told your father today on the picnic.' His voice broke as he spoke. 'The bastard's a fool, talking of having to work in the coal mines. I mean, it's ludicrous.'

John Baron led his friend over to the steps on the side verandah of the house where they sat down. He felt the warmth of the wood beneath his hands; somehow he gained a certain solace from its touch. An owl hooted and the smell of eucalyptus borne on the breeze drifted into their nostrils.

A sigh rumbled from the young man at his side. 'But do you know what, JB? I'm not going to let him ruin my life. "Get some work, any work," he said. "Take a navvy's job on the roads," he said. Well, I'm not going to do that, oh no sir, not me. I'll get money somehow, real money. Blast Dad.'

'That's the spirit, old man, that's the spirit.'

'Cowardice was never a characteristic of mine.'

John Baron could not help it, he smiled in the darkness. 'You've convinced me.'

'Yes, well that's not a bloody Herculean task.'

'Thanks.'

Cash leant forward and put his head in his hands as his friend touched his shoulder. 'What's the most important thing to you, Cash?'

'Being rich.'

'It isn't to me.'

Cash brought his head up and his body round to face his companion. 'Easy for you to say, you're a real engineer – at least earning a living. I've had to rely on my old man all my life and now he's gone and misappropriated my bloody birthright. What do you propose?'

'Me?'

'Yes. What the hell should I do?'

'Oh God, I don't know. Wish I could help but can't think of a thing. I'm not myself tonight.'

Cash made a sniggering sound. 'Who is, my dear? Who in Hades is?'

They sat silently for a time listening to the sounds of the night. Insects flew about them and a billy beetle buzzed in and landed on John Baron's shirt-sleeve. It walked up his arm and he watched it in the gloomy night light until it reached his shoulder, then he lifted it between his fingers and held it inside his fist feeling the scratching clinging movement of its legs and wings before he opened his palm for it to escape into the darkness.

Finally they both stood at the same moment.

'Thanks for listening to me, JB. My life's altered from this night on. It'll never be the same again, all because of my ridiculous old man. It's a misnomer to call him a father.'

John Baron made a mild defence of Randall Slade. 'Do you think you're being fair?'

'I'm not interested in fairness. But I'll be what I want to be and I'll attain what I want to attain without my father's help. I swear it.' He held out his hand and John Baron took it.

'What do you want to do about the bike?' Cash inclined his head towards the Harley Davidson they had bought together and still owed money on.

'I'll pay it off, Cash.'

'And I'll remunerate you. Rest assured.'

'Yeah, when you can. Look after yourself, Cash.'

Cash took a step away and glanced back. His gaze drifted up onto the verandah where he saw Samantha standing looking down. He hesitated momentarily and then leapt up the side steps and confronted her. Sam had come outside again and her eyes were only for her brother who remained on the lawn. Cash was quite aware of this but he still took her hands in his.

'I've had a shock today, Sammy, but I won't let it break me. Fact is, it's made me determined to get exactly what I want. And you might as well face it, you fall into that category.'

He pulled her sharply to him and kissed her on the lips before he spun round and bounded back down the steps. He ran to the bike, started it, revved it, and rode away round the water tank, accelerating down the drive.

John Baron walked up the steps to the verandah where his sister met him. He put up his hand, fending her off in a gesture of protest. 'Don't say anything, Sam.'

She stood in front of him. 'What did Cash mean?'

'Ask Dad – he knows all about it.'

'Didn't you see him kiss me?'

'Yes.'

'Well?'

He pushed past her. 'You'd better get used to it, Sammy. I don't care who kisses you.' He made it sound as if he meant it.

That night when the house was silent Sam tiptoed down the hall and turned the handle of John Baron's door. It was locked. Always before she could tell her troubles to any of her family, especially to John Baron. She felt lonely and bewildered.

Silently she returned to bed where she concentrated on thoughts of Veena and her predicament, so as not to be drowning in her own. It was a still night and she felt breathless as she tossed and turned. Sleep, when it came at last, freed her for a few hours.

Chapter Thirteen

The following morning Sam awoke to the sound of the Ford utility being cranked. She jumped out of bed and hurried to the window, pushing her pink curtains aside just in time to see John Baron hoist a suitcase into the back of Joe.

She threw on her dressing-gown and raced down to the kitchen and out onto the verandah where her mother and Ledgie were standing. Her face was ashen and her voice quivered as she asked, 'What's happening, Mummy? Ledgie? What's going on?'

'John Baron's returning to Brisbane. Your father and Wakefield are taking him to the station.'

'Why? But he hasn't even said goodbye to me!'

'He said he thought you should sleep, sweetheart. He was being considerate. Didn't want to wake you.'

'Stop! Stop!' she shouted as she ran down the stairs and across the yard. Her father halted the vehicle.

She was crying now and her mother and Ledgie followed from the verandah as John Baron jumped out and came to her. He stood in front of her as she sobbed.

His voice was low; only she could hear but the sharp strain in his tone was clearly evident. 'Sam, please, for Christ's sake. Don't do anything silly. Just say goodbye. Be normal, Sammy, I beg you. Please.'

'You were leaving. You were leaving,' she cried, the tears streaming down her cheeks as her mother arrived and folded her in her arms.

'Now now darling, if any of us had known you'd take on so we'd have woken you straight away. Of course we would. Now say goodbye. There there.' Constance comforted her daughter and kissed her.

'He didn't mean anything by it, love,' Ledgie said, patting Samantha's shoulder consolingly. 'He was being thoughtful.'

'I'm sorry, Sam,' her brother said, 'I didn't mean to upset you.'

'When are you coming home?' she asked through her tears.

'Soon.'

'When?'

'Within a week or two. I'm just going back to town briefly, that's all. I arranged it before Christmas with Belcher.'

And as she stood with her mother's arms around her he leant in and kissed her fleetingly on her hot flushed cheek. 'Bye, Sam.'

'Bye, JB.' She lifted her hand to touch him, but dropped it to her side.

Through her tears she watched him walk away to the vehicle and climb into the cabin. He waved his hand in farewell and she did the same.

'I can understand how you feel, darlin',' Ledgie said, waving as Joe sped through the poincianas to the road. 'Your mum and I both got a surprise when he sprang it on us this morning as well.' She took Sam's hand. 'Now come on, sweetheart, let's go in. You can have your breakfast, there's a dear. Men often do funny things that we women don't understand. Brothers are no different at all.'

Samantha allowed herself to be led back into the house.

When John Baron said goodbye to his father and Wakefield at the station, he shook them firmly by the hand. His overriding thought was that he had to get away from his sister. He knew that he could not spend another night under the same roof with her.

He had risen at dawn that morning and waited for his family to appear. As usual the household began to wake around six o'clock and Crenna was first in the kitchen to put the kettle on, grumbling that the day was 'going to be a scorcher'. Wakefield came in and brought with him his usual good humour. '*Bonjour, mon cher garçon.*' He slapped John Baron on the back, sat down, and addressed Crenna. '*Bonjour, Crenna, quelle merveilleuse surprise m'as tu préparé pour le petit déjeuner aujourd'hui?*' Crenna, who in all the years still knew no French, simply asked, 'What do you want for breakfast, Mr Wakefield?'

Within a few minutes Benjamin came through from the hall and halted in surprise to see his son fully dressed and waiting for him.

'Good morning, son. Early for you, isn't it?'

John Baron stood. 'I want to talk to you, Dad.' He glanced at his uncle. 'You too Uncle Wakefield, please.'

Ben could see the boy was not himself and he turned and led the way down the hall to his study. Inside, the early-morning light streamed in through the large windows, bringing the leather furnishings to a shine, and as John Baron sat down on the edge of a chair it enhanced his light hair in its golden glow. Ben thought how marvellous the boy looked.

'I'm not sure how to say this, Dad, and I asked Uncle Wake here because I want him to know too; it's . . . well, I've got to leave Haverhill this morning.'

Wakefield sat down heavily in an armchair and automatically began to rub his knee, but he did not speak.

'Where are you going?' Ben asked, moving round to sit in his green leather chair on the other side of the desk.

'I'm going back to Brisbane to the flat today.'

Ben nodded without speaking.

His son coughed and went on, 'Yes. I don't have to be in the office until next Wednesday. And then after that, I reckon I'm going down to Melbourne.'

Ben eased forward on his elbows, meeting his son's gaze. 'What's wrong, lad?'

'Dad, there's nothing wrong. I'm just restless, I suppose.'

There was a silence during which Ben and Wakefield's eyes met.

'Yes, that's possible. You're a young man with the world before you and young people have a tendency to be unsettled, but I've never seen that in your character up to now.'

163

John Baron swallowed. 'Well, it's there.'

Ben stood up and moved beside his boy, hand on his shoulder. 'John Baron, you're twenty-three years old and you don't have to explain yourself to me or anyone else unless you wish to. It's just that I would hate to think you're hurt over something your mother, or I, or Wakefield have done.'

John Baron jumped to his feet in denial. 'Oh no, Dad, you've never been anything but the best. I've got the most wonderful family in the world. It's just that . . . Well . . . The truth is . . .' He hesitated and looked away.

'What *is* the truth, lad?'

John Baron realised he must absolutely convince his parent of his next words; that whatever he said now had to completely satisfy his father and his uncle otherwise he would have opened a Pandora's box.

He took a deep breath and turned to face his parent. What came out was an extemporaneous compound of invention and strains of truth. 'This has been coming on for a long time, Dad. I haven't mentioned anything before because, well it's very private . . . ah personal.' He hesitated before he continued. 'You see, there's a girl. I er . . . haven't told any of you about her because I know that you and Mum would think I was too young to get involved. I know Uncle Wake's always maintained that your twenties are for enjoying life and that responsibility should come later. Up to now it's been a bit of fun with this girl, ah . . . we've done things together, gone to places together. But now she wants to get serious . . . really serious. And I, the fact is, sir, I've realised that I don't want that. No, not at all.'

'Where is this girl?'

'Ah . . .' He hesitated. 'She's in Brisbane, sir.'

'I see.' Ben's mind was racing. Again he met Wakefield's eyes before he spoke. 'Son, this girl's not in any trouble, is she?'

John Baron's reply came out with a rush of breath. 'Oh no sir, nothing like that. It's just that she wants to get married and I don't. Look, the fact is, I've just got to get away from her. Truly I have. She's got it bad and I don't

164

want to hurt her any more. It's not fair to her, or to me or anyone. I've been mulling it over and I must get away. I've decided to go to old man Potter on my first day back and ask if I can transfer to the Melbourne office.' He raised his hands towards them. 'There, now I've told you everything.'

Ben thought for a moment. 'Do you believe you're doing the honourable thing by this girl, son?'

John Baron winced inside. 'I do.'

'Then that's good enough for me. Will Potter agree?'

'I think he will.'

'What's her name?'

John Baron paused, realising he was going to have to completely lie. 'I'd rather not say, sir.'

'What's her name, son?'

Long moments passed before he said, 'Sandra. Sandra Charters.'

Ben repeated it. 'Sandra Charters.'

The young man shuffled his feet awkwardly. 'You and Mum are the best parents in the world.' He glanced at his uncle. 'And I couldn't have a better uncle. You're all wonderful, and Ledgie too – and Sam, of course. Look! All I want to do right now is go back to Brisbane, pay Belcher my part of the rent, pack up and get organised.'

Ben nodded. 'Son, don't misunderstand, I'm all for your seeing other places, does a man good, opens his mind. It just seems a damn pity that you have to leave us because of some girl. I've always thought one day you'd travel, but to have to leave this way, well . . .'

'Oh, Dad.' Tears sprang to the young man's eyes but he held them back. 'I know what you're saying, and I suppose it's just come a little earlier than it otherwise would have, that's all.'

Ben took a deep breath and walked forward to his boy and folded him into his arms. He thought of everything that had brought them to this day – the long winding road of his boy's life – and when finally he stepped back he still gripped John Baron's shoulders firmly in his hands. 'You're old enough to know your own mind and Melbourne's not on the moon, son, but it'll still come as a bit of a shock to your mother and Ledgie. They won't see it like we do, I'm afraid.'

'I know, so I'd really prefer to simply say I'm going back to Brisbane today and I'll break the rest of it to them in a week or so. It'll be better that way. I mean, Christmas has only just passed and the time's not right.'

Benjamin did not answer immediately. He released his son and looked to Wakefield. 'Do you have anything to say, my friend?'

Wakefield stood and leant on his cane and addressed John Baron. 'This problem with the girl will blow over in time, these things always do, but for now I understand its significance to you, so while I'm not sure about the delay in telling the women, I accept you believe it's best. I'd like to keep you in Queensland but I agree with your father. It'll do you good. *Bonne chance, mon cher neveu.*'

Ben moved to the door with his son at his side. 'We'll miss you, lad, but as I said before you're not going to the moon.' He gave a wry smile. 'Though your mother and Ledgie will undoubtedy think you are.'

'I know, Dad.' John Baron hugged his father.

And when Ben opened the study door, the young man took a letter from his inside pocket. 'Oh, and give this to Cash, please, will you?'

Ben nodded. 'Cash has his own troubles.'

'Yes I know, but Cash'll think of something; he's nothing if not resilient.'

The train whistled and rattled along and John Baron leant back in the corner of the leather-bound seat and stared at the tiny pieces of soot on the window ledge. The carriage was empty but for himself. People were not on journeys at this time of the year. Those who could afford it were on holiday and those who could not, did not travel by train.

He thought of Sam, her face hot and flushed from her tears, and he closed his eyes with pain. No matter what, he knew he had made the correct decision. He was quite sure Sam did not realise what the results of their actions could have entailed. He did not blame her, she was still very young and in some ways yet a child. He blamed himself for having let his own emotions overrule him. He loathed himself for the attraction he felt towards her and knew the only answer was to stay away from her even if it meant leaving Queensland and his family.

He opened his eyes to gaze out of the window into the fields and the heat haze of the day. Deep in the penetralia of his mind he recalled something Ledgie had said to him when he was little and had been found out in a lie. *Oh what a tangled web we weave when first we practise to deceive.* That might be so, but he had to deceive his family. They were all good and moral and it would break them to learn of the incestuous leanings he had towards his sister and she in turn to him.

The train slowed down and creaked into Ipswich Station, and on a whim he rose from his seat, took down his suitcase and left the carriage. In the station-house things were quiet but he found one man on duty in the ticket office and asked if he could leave his suitcase there.

The man shrugged. 'I suppose so, mate. I'm on duty till three when my colleague takes over. The last train through 'ere goes at nine forty-eight tonight to Brisbane. You'll need to pick it up by then.'

'Yes, thanks. I will.'

He wandered out into the sunshine. This was the town where he had spent four years of his short life as a boarder at the Boys' Grammar School. It did not hold any special place in his heart but he had enjoyed his years here and it was an agreeable town of some 25,000 inhabitants. As he strolled round the corner into Nicholas Street and across the railway bridge to the Central Hotel he thought about Sam again. Many of the shops were open but there were few people abroad; it felt as if he had the town to himself and he was glad about that. He crossed the street and entered Bottle Alley, the dirt byway that led along the embankment by the railway line into Ellenborough Street. For a few minutes he halted in the byway and looked out over the railway line where in the distance he could see the two spires of St Mary's Roman Catholic Church.

When he exited the lane into Ellenborough Street he was not conscious of any particular destination but he turned right and crossed the railway bridge passing by a bakery on the corner, the agreeable smell of bread emanating through the door. Continuing on by a hotel and a stone wall with rings and bolts for hitching horses he crossed the street again and found himself at the bottom of the stone steps leading up to St Mary's Church. He stood there full of hesitation and uncertainty. He was not Roman Catholic; he had been brought up a Protestant, in the Church of England, and so he found it odd that he now half considered entering the portals above him.

Half a minute later he edged through the entrance and paused; it was cooler inside this sandstone building than out in the hot December day and that alone encouraged him to move into the last pew and sit down. Along near the altar he noticed only one other person, a woman in dark clothing moving down with flowers in her arms. He remained for a long time staring at the woman as she painstakingly changed the flowers before finally disappearing through a side exit.

He knelt down on the wooden form at his feet, hardly noticing the stained glass or the Virgin Mary or the ornate altar. He was asking forgiveness and for help to enable him to forget about his sister.

At one point he thought that he had fallen asleep for he seemed to wake with a start. He looked around but he was still on his knees and still alone. He wondered about the time and took out his fob watch. It was a quarter to two. His knees were sore but he was glad, he felt the need to be in pain. He was hungry but he remained kneeling.

'You've been here a long time.'

He flinched in surprise and turned to see a priest beside him.

'I . . . er . . . yes.'

'Why is that? Young men of your age rarely hang about inside a church.'

John Baron sat back. 'I just needed to be in here, I suppose, sir.'

'I've been watching you. I'm not a mind-reader, but it's apparent you aren't happy, my boy.'

'I've got things to think about.'

'No doubt, haven't we all? Do you wish to take Confession?'

John Baron's amazement showed in his face.

A knowing expression came into the man's eyes. 'Oh I see, you aren't Catholic. Then what, may I ask, are you doing here?'

John Baron rose to his feet, a flush of embarrassment tinting his cheeks. 'I . . . excuse me, sir. I know I don't belong here. It's just that I . . .'

'Oh, but you do. All men belong here. You, as much as anyone. Perhaps some of my congregation wouldn't think so but that's not my philosophy, my son, nor is it the Lord's.' He gave a gentle smile and John Baron felt reassured.

'What's your name? Mine's Leonard, Father Leonard.'

'John Baron.'

'A good strong name. Will you take Confession, John Baron? Believe me, acknowledging your pain will help salve your soul. It's an instrument for your salvation. I can listen to what's in your soul and through me the Lord will hear, and through me, He will forgive.'

It was obvious that the priest was a kind man, wanting to help.

'Come with me.' Father Leonard took his arm and John Baron did not pull away; there was a certain comfort in the man's touch. Down to a wooden box with a green curtain the Father led him. 'Go in and sit down, my son.'

John Baron did not doubt he had entered the church in search of some kind of solace to release him from persecuting himself: he moved into the cubicle and sat. There was a grille beside him and soon he realised the Father was on the far side of it.

'Speak, my son. What is in your heart that troubles you so? Tell me and be not afraid.' The tone of his voice was encouraging and the young man found it soothing.

He looked down at his hands. 'I . . . I . . . This is hard for me, sir.'

'I realise and I share your heartache. I can see there's great distress in your soul. Don't be afraid. Tell me what's wrong. The confessional is a most private place between you and God.'

John Baron hesitated. Seconds passed. He could see the dark figure of the religious man through the metal screen. The priest waited and John Baron sat looking ahead but no words came.

He felt the leaden oppression of his guilt and turning his head to the grille realised this was too simple: it could not be erased this way. 'I'm sorry, sir,' he said, and abruptly left the confessional.

Father Leonard followed him. He watched the young man stride along the nave between the pillars and out of the door, down the steps and across the street to round the corner. He shook his head and returned inside the church.

John Baron walked quickly back into the town. He bought some fish and chips in newspaper from Londy's Café in Brisbane Street and ate ravenously, walking back to the station.

The train he caught stopped at every station and at ten minutes to nine he descended onto the platform at Toowong and carrying his case out into the road, walked the short distance to his destination. When he knocked on the door of the flat, Belcher opened it. 'I thought it'd be you.'

'You did?'

'Yes. When Slade arrived about twenty minutes ago I had a feeling you'd soon be along.' Belcher pointed through to the kitchen. 'He's in there. Says his life's changed.' He gave a high-pitched laugh. 'I see a lot has been happening this jolly old, merry old Christmas.'

John Baron charged through to the kitchen. 'Cash?'

His friend was eating a banana, feet on the table, his roving black curl hanging down on his brow. 'Oh, thanks for the letter. As soon as your old man delivered it I left home and came here. I'd decided to leave anyway. Dad's a bloody Philistine. The kids are all of a dither and Mum's been hysterical since last night, and there's just so much I can stand of the woman blowing that bloody retroussé nose of hers. Anyway I have to make plans and I can't make them in that frenzied environment.'

'Hey, listen you two. I'm off,' Belcher called from the lounge room. 'There's half a bottle of champers left in the ice chest if you want it.'

Cash waved the banana skin in the direction of the voice. 'Righto, old man.'

They heard the front door slam and Cash winked at John Baron as he sat down. 'Good, now Belcher's gone you can enlighten me about this move to Melbourne you mentioned in your missive.'

'Can you take your feet off the table?'

'If I must.' He withdrew his feet and sat forward on his elbows.

John Baron shook his head. 'You've made a remarkable recovery since last night.'

'I recuperate fast. Don't digress from the subject.'

'It's simply what I wrote in the letter to you. I'm going to pack up, hopefully talk old Potter into transferring me and off I go.'

'But why?'

'Look Cash, there are some things I don't have to tell you.'

'Shit eh? I never was cognisant of that.'

'Well, become cognisant.'

'Do you mean all this?'

'I do.'

Cash wore a quizzical expression. 'So you don't want to identify the reason for your departure.' He gave a strange smile. 'My crystal ball informs me it's got something to do with a girl . . . Yes that's it, you're abandoning us because of some girl. Now who might that be? Come on, old man. Confess.'

'Leave it. You're too smart for your own good.'

Cash laughed. 'I reckon I am at that. I'm half tempted to come along.'

'What? Well, come.'

Cash groaned. 'But if I accompany you, old man, I won't be able to accomplish what I've resolved to do. You see

I've acquired an intricate knowledge of the suburbs of this city; I don't know Melbourne.'

'What the hell does that mean?'

'My value system places wealth at the top of the agenda. But now having passed my exams and graduated, finding a suitable paying position could take months, even years in this blasted Depression. So I've determined how to mitigate matters, pay the rent, pay off my half of the Harley and live here with Belcher and all that entails. In other words how to turn the inauspicious future I was facing last night into the howling success of my years to come.'

'You've managed to intrigue me. How?'

'Burglary.'

'Burglary?'

'That's correct.'

'You don't mean it.'

'Never been more earnest in my life.'

'But you're not a criminal. You can't rob people.'

Cash bent his head and his wayward lock slipped forward. He flicked it back with his thumb. 'We'll see.'

John Baron stood, walked to the ice-chest, opened the door, took out the half full-bottle of champagne, poured himself a glass and drank it. 'If I'm hearing correctly you actually intend to burgle homes to get money to continue living the way you enjoy.'

'Brilliant, isn't it?'

'God, Cash, you're shameless.'

'Pour me a glass, will you, old man?'

John Baron did as he was requested and handed it to him. 'Has it occurred to you that you might get caught – that you might go to gaol? Has this ever crossed that arrogant mind of yours?'

Cash's voice lost the laissez-faire tone. 'I won't get caught, JB.'

John Baron's head had begun to ache. 'I've had about all I can take for one day, Cash. I'm not used to hearing my friends tell me they're turning into criminals. I'm going to bed. Good night.'

'Good night, old man. Don't worry about me, worry

about yourself. For whatever it is that's made you take the rapid step of leaving Brisbane, isn't just a fancy. I know you too well for that. You can't dissemble with me. You've got a reason that you aren't telling. And as I said, it's to do with a girl. Yes, siree. In fact, my conclusion is that you of all people couldn't even . . .'

As John Baron closed his door Cash was still talking. He shook his head. He would miss Cash.

He undressed and washed his face deciding that Cash was not serious about becoming a burglar. Not even Cashman Slade with all his complexities could turn around after more than two decades of a moral and reasonable upbringing and become a thief for the expediency of paying his bills. He was so exhausted by the time he climbed into bed that even his muddled emotions could not keep him awake for long.

And as his friend finished off the champagne in the kitchen and went on a search for more, John Baron slipped into that blissful state of unconsciousness where guilt did not torment him.

Chapter Fourteen

Even though Samantha had finished her schooling and received what, for a girl, was a quite surpassing education, it was natural in the 1930s that she stay at Haverhill until she decided what she wanted from life.

The first few days after John Baron's departure she spent in her darkroom developing the film that she had taken at the concert on Christmas Eve. That day seemed an eternity ago, when she had been carefree and relished life.

As she developed three photographs of her brother she cried so much that the tears dripped into the water trays in front of her. 'JB, JB, what have I done? It was my fault. Oh please God, I'm so sorry.'

Her eyes were red and puffy when she came out into the light and she took Tess and Charity who were lying in the yard and walked down by the creek to sit in the sun in the hope that she could compose herself before going up to the house. When Crenna called to her that Ledgie was going into Boonah to do the weekly shopping Sam declined to accompany her.

'No Crenna, I'll be working in the darkroom, thanks.'

While Ledgie and Constance had both noticed Sam was a little quiet they had no idea of her true condition. And even though they had been surprised by her outburst the morning John Baron had gone to Brisbane they took it all in their stride and put it down to the fact that mood swings were not uncommon in eighteen-year-old girls. Each day Sam had lunch with them – her father and Wakefield were out mending fences – and she convinced the women everything was normal.

A week passed during which the New Year came in

quietly at Haverhill. And on the second day of 1935 Sam was out on the side verandah cataloguing her hundreds of photographs, when she looked up to see Veena sauntering into the yard. The dogs barked and Tess the kelpie came running to greet the Aboriginal girl.

Veena halted and smiled. 'You remember Veena,' she said as she stroked the animal's head.

Samantha called out as she descended the side stairs. 'Yes, she remembers everyone. I'm so pleased to see you, Veena. How are you?'

Veena stood bare feet planted in the dust. 'I'm all right. I'm gunna live with you, Samantha.'

Sam knew nothing of this. 'Who told you that?'

'The boss, Mr Slade. He said your dad said so.'

'Oh, well that's good. That's lovely.'

Veena grinned and inclined her head to the west. 'Yeah, in the little place by that long hill. Mum's real pleased. Said she can do it up real nice, better than our place now for sure.'

At that moment Constance came up from the chicken pen carrying a small bucket of eggs. 'Here, Mum, I'll take that.' Sam relieved her mother of the burden. 'Veena says they're going to live with us?'

'Yes, that's right. Mr Birnam is going to look after our coming foals, the boys are going to milk and Veena and her mother can do things for Ledgie and me.'

Veena nodded happily and Samantha entered into the spirit of the news. 'Veena, you know what? I can teach you about taking photographs.'

The Aboriginal girl liked the sound of her forthcoming alteration in circumstances. She grinned. 'Good.' She followed Sam back up onto the verandah and that was the start of the Aboriginal girl becoming Sam's photographic assistant.

A week later Sam and Wakefield helped the Birnum family move into their new accommodation. The small dwelling had been given a scrub from top to bottom, the roof mended and some spare paint used to turn the lounge room blue. The Birnum family were delighted. The cottage had four rooms, a wide verandah both back and front and a water tank and outhouse at the rear. Jimmy Birnum beamed with pleasure as he led his family up the wooden steps and through the front door. 'Good place. Mighty good.'

The very day they moved in John Baron came home to Haverhill. He rode in the gate on the Harley Davidson, bumped along the drive and pulled up close to the front verandah by the bold colours of the gerbera garden. Ledgie had seen him coming from her perch on the side verandah where she was sorting the fresh washing, the latest copy of *Good Housekeeping* from England lying beside her. She sped through to the kitchen calling Constance. 'Darlin', darlin', look who's home! John Baron's here.'

Both dogs darted out of the front door and barked a welcome as the young man climbed the wide front steps and bent down on his knee to allow Tess and Charity to greet him wildly. When he stood upright he dusted himself down and leant on the railing. With a sense of regret he gazed out through the vista of gums over the brown soil and the green bushes along the creek beyond where the afternoon sun coruscated on the silver water. He could see men in the distant fields. Haverhill was familiar, Haverhill had been his boyhood haven. But even as he knew he would miss it all, he was conscious of a certain building excitement about the coming adventure.

'Darling, there you are.' His mother came hurrying out of the door to wrap him in her arms.

As he hugged her he looked around quickly for Sam but only Ledgie appeared. After he had kissed them both they drew him inside. 'You must have a cuppa and some refreshment straight away,' Ledgie decided.

'I'll have a bath first, Ledgie, I'm covered in dust.'

When he had bathed and the kettle had been set on the fireplace and Ledgie had brought out meat and bread and a cake and scones, he casually asked, 'I know Dad and Uncle Wake will be at work but where's Sam?'

'She's with your uncle over at the cottage near Cockatoo Hill,' his mother replied, explaining about the Birnums moving in today.

John Baron did not show the relief he felt. All the way home he had dreaded seeing them all together for he could not trust Sam to behave calmly. After he had eaten he gathered himself and informed the two women that he had been transferred from the Brisbane office of Potter & Stephens to the Melbourne branch.

His mother made a sharp sound and Ledgie sat staring at him without uttering a word.

Finally he felt compelled to say, 'Won't one of you please say something.'

Constance did not speak but began to shake her head back and forth. It was Ledgie who found her voice. 'Ah now lad, so it's off to Melbourne, is it? You could be knockin' me over with a feather, you could. And what's brought this on?'

'I've been thinking about it for some time.'

'You could have warned us. Droppin' it upon your poor darlin' mother like this, out of the blue. Smack! It's enough to give a body a heart attack.'

His mother took out her handkerchief and wiped her eyes as she spoke. 'But you've only just completed the first year of your professional life. I thought you were happy in Brisbane. Why all of a sudden are you going so far away?'

'Mum, dearest Mum, things are not simple and it's not just *all of a sudden*. As I said, I've been tempted to do this for a while, and now's the time to do it. You know what Uncle Wake always says about enjoying your twenties and getting responsibilities later? Well, I reckon that's true.'

Ledgie made a harsh disdainful sound. 'Wakefield! Oh yes, that'd be right. Puttin' ideas into your young head, making you talk that silly language all these years with its mon sewers and madams. Fillin' your mind with aeroplanes and flying. Why you listen to him I don't know. And look at the way your mother's taken on so.' She stood up and came round the table to envelop Constance in her meagre sunburnt arms. 'There, there, me darlin', it'll be all right.' She kissed the top of the woman's head and eyed John Baron reproachfully.

The young man had known it would not be a simple

177

matter to inform his mother. He stood up, came round and knelt at her side where he hugged her. 'Mum, look, try to understand. I'm not going off to war or anything terrible, am I? I'm simply going away on an adventure while I'm young and have the wherewithal. Don't deny me that. I'll write all the time.'

Constance held onto him. 'My little boy . . . Oh, my darling little boy. I remember the first time I ever saw you with your little white face looking at me. You were so fra—'

Ledgie's head came up like a gunshot and she pulled Constance abruptly towards her, hugging her close and cutting across her words. 'Hush now darlin', say no more.'

John Baron simply smiled tolerantly. 'Well, of course you do, Mum, we were both there at the time.'

Ledgie continued in a consoling tone. 'There, there, sweetheart. He's young and we must accept that he has visions of his own as don't necessarily fit in with ours. Now come on, me darlin', we canna keep him to ourselves for ever. We *must* accept it. He has a life of his own to lead. Melbourne's still in Australia, after all.'

John Baron stood up and patted Ledgie's shoulder. 'Thanks, Ledgie.'

'And just how long are you going for?' she asked sharply.

'I'm *transferring* to Melbourne. I'll be living there.'

'Oh.' She pointed to the door. 'Now you'd better go and tell your father. He's down by the old barley fields. I'll take care of your mother.'

John Baron did not enlighten them that he had already told the men two weeks before. He walked to the door. 'Yes, I'll go and see Dad. And Mum?'

His mother looked up.

'I love you so much. Always know that.' He turned and crossed the verandah as his mother's eyes followed him.

Ben saw John Baron coming and he left two farmhands and jumped across the fallow mounds of earth to meet his son as John Baron halted the filly he rode and dismounted.

'Hello, Dad. As I promised I've told Mum and Ledgie I'm off to Melbourne.'

His father nodded slowly. 'I see. And how did that go?'

'Badly. Mum seems to think Melbourne's on another planet just like you thought she would.' He shrugged and kicked a piece of dirt with his boot. 'I was hoping you might have broken the news for me actually.'

His father coughed. 'Did you now? Well, I didn't because it's your responsibility, young man. You have to face up to those sorts of things yourself. That's a lesson in life, son. Remember it.'

'Yes, Dad, all right. Well, I did it anyway.'

'Did you tell her about Sandra Charters?'

John Baron blinked. 'No.'

'I think you should. At least your mother will then understand the impulsiveness of it all.'

'I'd rather not have to explain all that, sir. Telling Mum's not the same as telling you. She'd be even more upset. So I'd appreciate it if you and Uncle Wake would keep my confidence.'

Ben looked hard at his boy. 'I've never kept anything from your mother for long, son, so you'd better face up to telling her in time.'

John Baron was relieved to be released from it for now. 'I will, sir, in time. Perhaps I'll do it in a letter.'

'When do you leave Brisbane?'

'The day after tomorrow. I'm looking forward to it.' And now that he had come to this point, he believed he was.

'So you'll be building bridges in Melbourne soon.' Ben patted the young man's shoulder. 'Have you said goodbye to your sister?'

'No. I'm going over to see her now. Mum told me about the Birnums moving in.'

'Yes. I've managed to put on a couple of the Slade farmhands too. It's a terrible time for Randall and his family.'

John Baron thought of Cash and he looked skywards. There was really nothing he could add to this. 'Yes,' he replied as he took up the reins and remounted the grey filly.

179

Ben looked up and grasped the young man's boot. 'Are you staying the night? It'd please your mother and Ledgie and Samantha, I'm sure.'

'Gee, I've got a few things to do before I leave, and you know what? I feel as if it'd just be dragging it all out with Mum.'

Benjamin could see the sense in that. He nodded. 'Would you like me to come over to your sister with you?'

That was the last thing John Baron wanted. The paradox was that he wished with all his might he could just ride away without meeting her at all and yet he wanted desperately to be near her again. 'No thanks, Dad, but I'd like to see you again before I go.'

'In that case I'll be at the homestead.' His father turned to go but John Baron did not urge the horse away. 'Dad?'

Ben faced back to his son.

'Thanks for the way you and Uncle Wake have understood everything. I wish I could have given you all more time to get used to the idea.'

Ben nodded. 'Look, son, your happiness is the most important thing to me. I hope you have a wonderful time and that Melbourne lives up to your expectations and some of your dreams come true. I'm only sorry you had to leave because of a girl.' He sighed. 'But don't worry about us. Enjoy your youth.' He stepped back and tapped his son affectionately on the knee.

John Baron covered his father's hand with his own. 'You're the best father in the whole world.'

'And you've always been the best son.'

Samantha and Wakefield were riding along the bush path from the cottage when they saw John Baron coming the other way.

Sam's shout of delight echoed through the eucalyptus trees. 'JB, oh my heaven, JB!'

Wakefield waved. So Johnny B was back to tell his mother he was leaving home. '*Bonjour, mon garçon.*'

John Baron replied that it was good to see them both.

Wakefield glanced back at Sam and, continuing in

French, told her he would keep going to allow her to have some time with her brother. He took his horse on by as its hooves kicked up the dust on the path and he lifted his hand to John Baron. 'I'll see you at the homestead.'

John Baron turned in his saddle to his sister. Her lower lip trembled. 'I didn't know if you were ever coming back. I've nearly gone mad wondering.'

'Oh, Sammy. This is no good.'

'What do you mean?'

'Sam, look, we know how we both feel.' He looked away and then back into her eyes. 'You might think this sounds hopeless, but since I saw you last I've tried to redeem my soul.'

Sam was shaking her head. 'I don't want to hear that. To hell with your soul. All I know is that when you're in my life I'm happy. When you're gone, I'm bewildered. I'm lost. I know we can't be close like . . . like we were. But all I want is to have you here, to know you're around.'

'It can't be like that, Sammy.'

'But why?'

'You know why. You have to be brave. *I* have to be brave. You must live your life without me.' She was shaking her head as he went on: 'If I'm near you something bad is going to happen. The guilt would kill us. We couldn't live with ourselves.'

'I could.' She sank forward on Aristotle's neck. 'I could!'

He wanted desperately to hold her. His voice cracked with the strain. 'Well, that's the difference. I couldn't, Sam. I couldn't.'

He watched while she began to cry, tiny glistening waterfalls running down her cheeks, and when she steadied herself, he spoke rapidly. 'I'm going away, Sammy, where I can't just jump on my Harley and come back here. Where I can't just come home and see you whenever I want to.'

'Where?'

'Melbourne.'

Her body sagged. 'Melbourne?' she whispered it. 'But that's a thousand miles away, isn't it?'

'Yes.'

Aristotle stamped his feet and lifted his head and whinnied as if he too were in pain.

'Oh God,' she said.

A hot breeze came up from nowhere and her hair lifted from her back where it was tied in a ribbon. It wafted forward into her vision. She did not move; she just let her hair cover her face as she sat there weeping.

He edged forward on his horse to where he could reach her and brushed her hair aside. She looked at him with a lost expression then turned her head and kissed the back of his hand.

He stroked her tears away and she cupped his hand in both of hers and kissed his palm. She met his eyes as he withdrew his hand. 'What if I follow you?'

'Don't do that, Sammy. That would be wrong – selfish, silly.' He regarded her, concentrating on the way she sat the horse with her straight back as her hair undulated on her shoulders in the breeze. He noted the little indentation where her slender neck met her body and the smooth brown backs of her hands on the reins. He had many photographs of her but this picture he would carry with him.

'Goodbye, Sam.'

It took a long time before she managed to say it and all the while the breeze continued to stir her hair. 'Goodbye, JB.'

He brought his filly around and cantered away along the path. She watched him disappear and wondered what on earth would become of her.

For a long time she rode aimlessly: along Teviot Brook, across it, through the unending gums, up hills and down hills, by the old property line fence which had decayed over the years and was now just a series of rotting posts – until she came to the silky oaks and the brook again. She fancied she heard him starting the motor bike back at the house; she fancied she heard him ride down the avenue to the front gate and beyond onto the dirt road that led him away from Haverhill, away from her.

By the time she passed the milking sheds and the cows in the holding yard, and rode by the fruit trees and the water tank to the back of the house the short southern twilight was descending, and Wakefield, who had been sitting out under the green umbrella of a jacaranda tree, rose to greet her. Tess and Charity had been lying at his feet and they did the same, barking loudly.

'*Ma chérie*, you're late. We were just beginning to worry about you.'

'No need, *mon oncle*, I'm all right.' She made a massive effort to sound light-hearted. 'Did JB get away?'

'Oh yes, an hour since.'

'I hope he likes Melbourne.'

'Yes, me too. It'll probably do him good. Nothing like a bit of travel to broaden the mind. Would you like a game of draughts tonight?'

'Not tonight, Unc, I've some developing to do. Perhaps tomorrow.' She turned quickly away and swallowing hard led her horse over to the stables.

Chapter Fifteen

Four months later Samantha and Veena were down by the main gate to Haverhill on the lonely dirt track that eventually led to an intersection with the road into Boonah.

Lately Sam had been experimenting with taking landscape photographs and she had her camera set up on a tripod. It was one of her prize possessions: Uncle Wakefield had made it for her. He was a whiz with anything that needed to be fitted, made or fixed.

Veena was now large with her coming baby but even so she still liked to help Sam. Up until nearly six months she had ridden a quiet horse alongside Sam and Aristotle but now in her eighth they had to resort to taking the ute, so that Veena would not bounce around too much. Sam was a capable driver and they enjoyed their photographic outings together.

As Veena handed Sam her hat, Samantha recalled something from years before. 'Veena?'

'Yeah?'

'Do you remember once telling me you didn't know your birthday? Didn't know the day you were born?'

'That's right.'

'Well, I've thought of something.' She steadied herself and bent into the camera and pressed the shutter.

'What's that?'

'The day your baby's born. We'll know exactly what day that is and you can take it for your own birthday. Then every year you and your baby can celebrate your birthdays on the very same day.'

The girl beamed at this suggestion. 'Very good idea, Samantha.'

Sam continued to take photographs, talking as she did so. 'And you can have a party each year for the two of you.'

Veena, who had never had a party for anything in her life took this prospect to heart. 'Oh, I'd like that.'

Sam finished taking her shots and stood back from the tripod pointing into the distant olive-green hills. 'You know, Veena, I tried to get that mountain over there to dominate the picture but I'm just not sure about this lens.'

The practical Veena made a point. 'If you no get it, you no get it.'

Sam laughed heartily, unscrewing her camera from the tripod and handing it to Veena. Every now and then they took the camera out of the sun and placed it where Veena kept the film in the shade of a tree.

'You should sit down for a while, Veena, and take a breather.' Sam steered her friend over to the shadow of a large wattle tree where she helped her ease herself down onto a blanket before Sam settled herself too and took out a pencil and paper and wrote down some figures. Sam studied them, chewing the end of her lead pencil.

'This photography business is so expensive. If only I could make some money.'

Veena shrugged. 'Everything expensive.'

She was rubbing the side of her extended belly and Sam asked, 'Are you all right?'

'Yep. Sometimes get a kick, sometimes a little pain. Kid's busy.'

They both laughed.

For a time they said nothing, sitting silently until Veena shifted herself to a more comfortable position and shook off her sandals, stretching her legs beyond the blanket into the sun so they lay in a harmony of colour upon the dark earth. The skin on her shins gleamed as she glanced round at her friend. 'Samantha?'

'Mmm?'

'Do you think I'm a bad girl?'

Sam put down her pencil and paper. 'Why do you say that?'

'Getting into trouble.' She patted her belly. 'Mum says I'm a bad girl and my baby'll be bad too.'

'Oh no, that's not true. Please don't think like that. Your mother's just angry and hurt, that's all.'

'Yeah. But Veena was silly.'

Sam thought of her feelings for her brother and made a soft sad sound. 'We're all silly at times, Veena – all of us.'

'Bin thinkin' a lot since. Mum says I've made it hard for my baby. No father and all.'

'Perhaps that might be true, but remember your baby will live here at Haverhill where no one will call it names and we'll all love it so it'll have a big, ready-made family really, yours and ours.' She squeezed the girl's arm. 'Anyway, there are so many men here, your baby won't miss a father at all.'

This obviously cheered Veena immensely and her expression brightened just as the sound of an advancing vehicle reached their ears. Turning their heads they saw a car approaching with billowing dust rising around it in all directions. 'Oh Lord, Veena, close your mouth when it gets near, put your head down and pull up the blanket.'

But when it approached it slowed down completely so the dust was limited, and as it rolled to a halt alongside them a man poked his head out of the window. He was about thirty-five, his top lip covered in a dark moustache, and as he spoke, his eyes, which were slightly bloodshot, kept blinking in the strong sunlight.

'Good afternoon.'

'Good afternoon,' Sam replied.

'Look, I'm lost. Am I going in the direction for Kalbar?'

Veena started to giggle and Sam shook her head. 'No, you aren't.'

'Oh dear, damn it, that's what I thought.'

'You thought correctly. You need to turn around.'

Veena continued to giggle and bent forward on her rotund tummy.

He made an exasperated sound. 'How far away am I?'

'Oh, possibly ten miles I'd say. If you go back about

two and a half miles from here and turn right, that stretch will take you down to the main road.'

'Is it signposted?'

'No, it's not, but there's a big coolibah gum right on the roadside where you turn.'

He let out a long breath of frustration. 'What's a coolibah gum look like, for heaven's sake?' He gestured to Veena. 'What's wrong with her?'

Sam stood up. 'Nothing. I suppose she just thinks it's funny to get lost around here. She knows it so well, you see. Look, we can take you down to the turn if you like. All you need to do is follow us in the ute.'

'Would you? Would you be so kind?'

Sam helped the still grinning Veena to her feet. 'Sure we would.'

He turned his car around in the road while Veena climbed aboard the Ford and Sam took the crank out of the back, walked to the front of the engine and placed it in the crank-shaft. After a few hard revolutions the engine coughed into life.

'You do that pretty damn well for a female,' he called out as Samantha moved round the engine to the driver's seat.

'I do a lot of things well.'

The ute ambled along at twenty miles an hour while Veena rubbed the side of her abdomen where she felt the baby moving. Some minutes later they had the stranger at the turn-off.

Sam left the engine running and climbed down out of the cabin to lift her arm at right angles from her body and point along the side road. In her white blouse and delicate flower-printed skirt that clung to her brown legs and wafted about her calves in the gentle breeze the stranger thought she looked like some stately rustic goddess risen from the soil.

His eyes narrowed with admiration as she gave directions. 'Just keep going on this road; you'll come to a spot where you ford a creek. Once across that you'll arrive at the main road. It's a T-junction. Turn right, travel about four miles and you'll see the Kalbar sign.'

'Hey, thanks very much. I should introduce myself before I leave. Dexter Wilde at your service.'

'How do you do. I'm Sam Chard.'

'Sam?'

'Samantha actually, and this is Veena.' Veena leant out of the car window and grinned.

'Well, ladies, I noticed you had a tripod and a camera back there. Who takes photographs?'

'I do.'

'Really?'

'Yes. I know we were sitting in the shade when you came along, but I'd been taking landscapes up until then.'

He shook his head. 'You don't say.'

'You talk strangely.'

He smiled and she noticed a small dimple appear in his right cheek. 'Do I? Well, I've been around a bit: England, America, other places – you know?'

Sam did not know but she replied, 'Yes,' as she stepped back and lifted her right hand to shade her eyes. 'Goodbye, Mr Wilde.'

He disregarded the farewell. 'Listen, do you know much about photography?'

'Why, yes. I do my own developing and everything.'

He was leaning out of the window. 'Now this is a coincidence but I run a photographic studio in Brisbane. I'm what's called a "society photographer" if you like. People come in to have their pictures taken for weddings, twenty-firsts, baby christenings, important events.'

Sam's eyes widened with interest. 'My goodness.'

'I don't know what your work's like but you've got to be keen to be out in this heat taking landscapes. Fact is, I'll be on the look-out for an assistant in a couple of months; one of mine's leaving. I hadn't been thinking along the lines of a female and in any case you mightn't be interested, but if you are . . . you might be as good as anyone. Why don't you send me some of your pictures, let me see your style. My address is Market Street.'

Sam's mouth had dropped open and when she realised, she closed it instantly. She almost stammered her reply.

'Thank you. It's the sort of thing I've been hoping to do, I just didn't know how to get started.'

'Ah yes, knowing how, or knowing who? All very important in life.' He smiled widely and the sun glinted on his forehead. He nodded to Veena. 'Goodbye, Miss Veena.'

Veena was charmed. She smiled and waved.

'Goodbye, Miss Chard.'

'Goodbye, Mr Wilde.'

As the car drew away Veena pointed her thumb after it. 'Funny bloke. Swear he's got no legs, talkin' out o' the window all the time.'

Sam was still conscious of the weight she carried in her chest but for the first time since John Baron had gone to Melbourne she felt optimism. A little thrill ran through her. 'Oh Veena, this is a chance, a real chance for me. Did you hear him ask me to send him some samples of my photographs? I could have a job in Brisbane.' She was so elated she jumped around wildly then slipped into the driver's seat shouting, 'Oh yes siree!' and beeped the horn.

Veena entered into the excitement and began to whoop and shout, and the two girls drove down the dirt road laughing and hooting the horn all the way back to the tripod and the camera and the equipment.

By the time they had used up their last two rolls of film the sun was declining in the heavens and there was a rumble in the sky. 'Gosh, I think there's going to be a storm.'

A flash of light etched itself across the horizon to the west.

'Yep,' Veena nodded her head. 'It's comin' all right.' Then she added, 'My baby movin' a lot today. Feels lower.'

Sam contemplated her. 'Looks lower too.'

They packed up Joe the ute and took the camera, film and the important equipment inside the cabin with them. Sam threw the blanket over the tripod in the back, grabbed the crank and attempted to start the engine. But this time there was only an apathetic whine. She put all her strength behind it and tried again but there was still nothing. 'Oh, come on Joe,' she said, patting the engine flap. 'Don't do this to me. Not with a storm coming, please.'

189

But Joe was implacable. He would not start.

Sam came inside the cabin and sat down groaning. 'One minute I'm so happy I could sing all night and the next Joe behaves like a moron and I'm deflated. I suppose I'll wait a bit and see if he starts in a few minutes.' She looked round at her companion. 'Oh Veen, what's wrong?'

The girl was obviously in discomfort. She reclined against the door with her hand massaging her stomach. 'Just a little pain, Samantha. Be all right in a minute. Had a couple before. Nothin' really.'

'Oh dear. I'll have another go.' Sam sprang out and tried cranking the engine again. This time for a second or two it sounded as if it might turn over but it did not, and she stood there wondering what to do next. The wind had risen and the storm was moving towards them. She hurried round to Joe's window to talk to her friend. 'How do you feel, Veena?'

'Samantha, I'm sorry. The same. I've got a pain down here.'

To comfort her Sam began to pat Veena's arm. She was helpless unless the engine started but she was attempting not to panic. Within a few seconds she felt the first drop of rain. 'Oh dear, here it comes.'

Abruptly Veena bent forward, her hands reaching over her swollen stomach. '*Ohh.*'

A thunderclap sounded and rain descended upon them, big heavy drops with virtually no space between them, a deluge. 'Oh God!' exclaimed Sam. She ran round and jumped in Joe's cabin, pushing the window up to keep out the rain.

Veena was grimacing now. She did not want to alarm Samantha but she was having contractions. 'Dunno what the hell this kid's doin' but I wish it'd stop.'

Sam realised she was in a bad situation. She moved across the seat to her friend and put her arm around her and kissed her. She tried to sound calm. 'Veena, don't worry it's only a storm and they pass quickly.'

The girl could not answer, she was suffering so much she merely grunted.

190

A few minutes lapsed while Samantha comforted Veena as best she could and spoke optimistically about the storm's passing and how they would start the engine for sure and get on their way. Suddenly Sam realised there was a person outside in the rain. A dark form came to her side of the vehicle and opened the cabin door.

'What's going on? Why are you sitting out here in a storm?'

It was Cash! Like a miracle he had appeared out of nowhere.

He stooped in out of the rain as Sam exclaimed, 'Oh Cash, I can't believe you're here! I can't start Joe and I think Veena's baby's coming.'

Cash ran round to the other side of the ute, opened the door and took Veena in his arms. He moved swiftly to his car and placed the pregnant girl into the back seat and returned to Sam. 'Come on. Leave Joe here, let's get going.'

Sam grabbed her camera and the exposed film, tucked them up under her dress, and ran in the saturating rain to Cash's car and bounded in beside Veena. She dried her hands as best she could and carefully placed the camera and film on the passenger seat in front.

The rain was still pelting down as Cash started his car and edged it forward while Sam did her best to cheer her friend.

Cash spoke as he manipulated the vehicle on the wet dirt road. 'How long's Veena been in this sort of pain?'

'Only about ten minutes, but she mentioned other short pains earlier today.'

'And it's been kickin' me all the time,' the girl herself added between moans. Suddenly she gave a sharp scream and Sam flinched in alarm but asked as steadily as she was able, 'Veena, love, where does it hurt? Show me.'

Veena waved her hands erratically. 'All over. Oh Sammy, I think the baby's comin'.' And with that she fell back onto the seat. Beads of perspiration formed on her forehead and her eyes became glassy.

Samantha looked around. All three of them were soaked to the skin. There was a small cushion on the floor of the car, the only dry thing around, which she grabbed and pushed under Veena's head before she took up the girl's hand and began to stroke it gently. 'Now darling, don't worry. We'll soon be at the homestead.'

Veena continued to groan as another thunderclap rolled.

A few seconds later there was water and blood all over the back seat. 'Oh dear, you poor darling.' A flash of lightning accompanied her words, appearing to bounce off the bonnet of the car.

Samantha was now perspiring as much as Veena, small trickles of water running down beside her ears. 'Oh Cash, what'll we do?'

Cash spoke over his shoulder. 'All we can do, my dear Sammy, is stay calm.' He inclined his head in Veena's direction. 'Hang on, kiddo – please hang on. We're only about five minutes from Haverhill.'

Veena squeezed Sam's hand and ground out her reply. 'Five minutes . . . gunna be four minutes . . . too long.'

Cash's voice now held the edge of alarm. 'Sam, I can't halt. Have you got anything back there? I mean, anything to use?'

'Use? Hell, use – what does that mean? Even if I had something to use I wouldn't know what to do with it. Oh my Lord!' Sam's voice rose in alarm as Veena's tummy seemed to rear up in front of her eyes and then begin to alter shape. Sam ripped off her blouse as she realised that Veena's baby had declared that storm or no storm, it was going to enter the world right now on the back seat of Cash's car.

The photograph that Samantha took of 'Storm' that afternoon was possibly the first picture ever taken of a minute-old baby with umbilical cord still uncut, lying on a car seat. It was under-exposed for the light was poor but little Storm could be made out with an exhausted, but elated Veena in the background.

By the time Cash had driven them in through the avenue of trees blaring the horn all the way up to the front steps of Haverhill, the thunder and lightning had all but dispersed and the rain had abated.

And when Constance and Ledgie became aware that they had a newborn baby to attend to, they did as so many of their kind had done in the past and handled the entire matter with the competence and calm of pioneer women all over the world. Soon baby Storm was bathed and nestled in clean clothing and her mother the same, and Samantha and Cash had changed their wet clothing for dry. As a matter of course they sent for the doctor and he arrived within half an hour. After examining the mother and child he smiled warmly at Ledgie and Constance. 'My job was done for me and very well too.'

Before Veena dropped off to sleep Sam and Cash came into her where she lay in John Baron's bed. Sam took a deep soulful breath as she eyed the room: most of her brother's model planes with their rainbow colours still hung from the ceiling and stood on the shelves, some hats and belts remained on the hooks, and books were still stacked on the wooden desk. He had taken most of his clothes but his other possessions gave the room the illusion of being occupied. Sam had avoided coming in since JB left home and it was with mixed feelings she now crossed it with Cash beside her.

In the four months since John Baron had gone, Cash had altered. He had weathered his father's bankruptcy and had taken steps to shape his own life. His body had filled out, the slender boy had disappeared and the man was emerging. There was still the veiled expression in his black eyes, that would always be there, for the complications which made up Cash's personality were manifold and those who thought they knew him well, did not.

Veena looked up at them and lifted her hands to them. 'I'm lucky. You two so good. I'll never forget. Thank you.'

Sam smiled. 'All that matters is that you and baby Storm are well.'

'If Cash don't come along we'da been in a right mess.'

Sam agreed. 'Yes we would have.' She looked across at him. 'Thank heaven you arrived at that moment.'

Cash sat on the side of the bed holding his knee. 'You know, girls, something was telling me to come out here to

Haverhill for the last few days. Sort of prescient of me, really. Anyway, I decided it was time I showed off my new car to you all.' He laughed and the sound rumbled up in his throat. 'And now it'll take me a week to clean it.'

Sam laughed too, pointing out of the window. 'I don't think you need to worry; I saw Crenna and Uncle Wake heading out there with two big buckets of soapy water.'

'Oh splendid.'

'Storm's the right name,' Veena smiled up from the bed. 'It's just the right name. And I reckon I musta added up wrong. There we were thinkin' I was eight months, Samantha, but I musta bin nine.'

They all laughed and as Cash stood to leave he exhibited a side of himself that Sam had never seen. It surprised her as he paused and bending down, began to stroke Veena tenderly on the hair.

'That's a fact,' he said gently. 'And you were very brave. You showed what a strong woman you are.'

Veena's face filled with pride and pleasure and she covered Cash's hand on her hair with her own as she lifted her eyes to Sam. 'And Samantha, guess what?'

'What?'

'We know when my birthday is now.'

Sam agreed. 'Yes, we absolutely do.'

Cash looked perplexed at this turn in the conversation and Sam pushed him towards the door. 'I'll explain later.'

They left Veena to sleep, a calm sweet smile playing about her mouth as she watched them close the door.

As the years passed, 'the night Storm Birnum was born' became a marker in the annals of time for the people of the district, but on the actual night, out in the kitchen at Haverhill, Sam and Cash were just relieved it was all over. Sam poured Cash a whisky and they talked. 'Here, you deserve this. And I think I'll have one myself.'

'What? Started imbibing, have you?'

'No, but something like this doesn't happen every day. And I am grown up, you know.'

'Yes,' he said, winking at her. 'Indeed you are.'

'Guess what else happened to me today?'

'I wouldn't dare.'

Then she told him about meeting Dexter Wilde. And when she had completed her tale he sat back in the chair and grinned, raising his long index finger and shaking it at her for emphasis. 'Sammy, my dear, I believe you've an excellent chance of being hired.'

'Why thanks, Cash.'

'Yes, it will all fall in faultlessly. Come and live in Brisbane where I can court you properly.'

Sam appeared to be studying Cash but she was thinking about JB. She heard what her companion had said but she did not reply.

'Sam, did you hear me?'

She took a sip of her Scotch and water, replying in a faraway voice, 'So you're courting me now, are you, Cashman Slade?'

And he continued waving his finger in the air as he replied, 'Might be, perchance, m'lady.'

She stood and walked to the window where in the dusk a battery of moths flew in and out. Ignoring them she put her drink down on the sill and swung round to face him. She was about to respond when her father entered, speaking as he came. 'What an afternoon you two had! Cash, how fortunate you came by. Wonderful luck.' He noticed his daughter's hand turn to the glass on the windowsill. 'When did you take up drinking?'

'Oh Daddy, I haven't. It's just that I felt I needed something after all that's happened.'

'Well, don't make a habit of it. Ledgie will be horrified, to say nothing about your mother.' He gestured out of the window. 'That's a brand new car out there?'

Cash flicked a fly from the top of his glass. 'That's right.'

'Is it yours?'

'Affirmative, sir.' Cash decided he knew what Benjamin's next query was going to be, so he said, 'I borrowed the money from Belcher, as a matter of fact.'

Ben looked amazed.

'Don't concern yourself, sir. I pick up good jobs here

and there, you know, and I've been more than lucky on the horses. And Belch has so much moolah he doesn't mind if I don't pay him back for ages.'

'Cripes, he must be a good friend.'

Cash gave a slow smile and Ben could not help but remark, 'Seems a shame your parents had to sell their property. Pity they didn't have a friend like Belcher.'

'Yes, it was a shame, but that's life.' The young man took a long mouthful, finished his drink, and stood. 'But then my old man had you for a friend sir. You who allowed him to abide on your land in Fernvale.'

'That was the least I could do.'

Cash nodded to Ben. 'With your permission, sir, I'd like to take your daughter for a drive into Boonah and back in the aforementioned vehicle. I've got a friend there who's giving a party tonight at the School of Arts. Promise I'll have Sammy home by eleven or so.'

Sam stood, arms akimbo. 'Shouldn't you ask me, not my father?'

Cash stepped towards her and bowed. 'M'lady, would you do me the honour of accompanying me on a pilgrimage into Boonah tonight?'

Samantha grimaced. 'I suppose so. But I'll have to change my dress.'

'I'll wait outside,' Cash replied, making for the door. 'I'll find Wakefield and chat with him until you're ready.'

'Forget the *or so* and just have my daughter home by eleven,' Ben called out to Cash as he crossed the verandah.

As they drove into Boonah Sam admired the car's upholstery, smoothing her hand over the seat. 'Crenna and Uncle Wake did a wonderful job. The car's completely dry and smells so clean.'

'Mmm, not too many automobiles have such a baptism.'

'Wasn't Belcher absolutely wonderful to lend you the money for it?'

Cash emitted a curious sound and Sam looked round at him.

'That was something I thought best to make up for your father.'

'What?'

'I bought it myself. The fact is, there was a down payment and I'll have to make six more payments every second month for the next year.'

Sam was perplexed. 'But how can you afford it? Where will you get the money? I thought you had to be careful, what with your father's financial troubles and all.'

'Ah m'lady, as I mentioned to your old ma . . . er . . . your father, I've been very lucky lately with my betting on the night trots and the races. Fact is, I've had one or two wins that were so significant they positively liberated me from indigence.'

'Speak English, Cash! What's *indigence*?'

'Destitution, m'lady. Something we wish to know nothing about.'

'I didn't know you ever went to the races.'

'Ah well, there you are. I do. It's become one of my principal sources of income. It's how I'm paying for almost everything: rent, food, clothes. And I'll go on making money, too. I've devised what I reckon's a foolproof system.'

'My goodness. So what you told Daddy was a lie?'

'Ah . . . now, m'lady, I wouldn't call it that.'

'But it was. It was a straight-out lie.'

'Ah, don't be so exact, Sammy. It's not a redeeming trait. I just didn't want your father to ask too many questions. None of his business, really. Seemed the most uncomplicated thing to do at the time.'

Sam was shaking her head. 'For heaven's sake, Cash. I'll never understand you. You're . . . incorrigible.'

Cash turned, leant in towards her, and swiftly kissed her cheek. 'And you're beautiful. Now let's go to a party.'

Chapter Sixteen

December, 1935

Cash paused. Raised his head to listen, and exclaimed under his breath, 'Bloody hell!'

A car turned into the drive, headlights washing the front windows of the house and momentarily illuminating the room in which he stood: the oak bureau in front of him, the Axminister carpet under his feet, the stippled maroon and blue wallpaper.

He stuffed the gold necklace he held into the bag which hung from his belt and gathered up the fob watch and the five-guinea pieces which lay in the drawer in front of him as the engine was switched off and voices raised in merriment could be clearly discerned on the still night air.

Swiftly pushing the drawer back in, he crossed the room to the door as footsteps fell heavily on the front verandah. As he moved into the hallway Cash halted, trying to remember his bearings in the darkness while a man's voice reached him through the glass in the front door. 'I thought I left this verandah light on when we went out.'

'You did,' a female answered.

Cash hurried down the corridor. He bumped into something solid in the blackness and hesitated in uncertainty. Flashing his torch on and off he took in the open window some thirty feet distant through which he had entered.

'I'm sure I just saw a torch go on inside!' another male voice sounded as Cash hurried towards the window and a key turned in the lock.

As the door opened behind him, throwing a cool beam of light his way, Cash realised he had no time left. He ran to the window, vaulted up, and was climbing through it when one of the newcomers switched on the hall lamp, illuminating him.

'Hey you, stop!'

Cash half fell, half jumped through the opening onto the pavement at the back of the house as yelling and screaming followed him.

'Stop! Thief!'

In the pallid radiance of the night Cash ran across the tidy lawn, jumping rose bushes, clearing garden plots and heading for the fence. His pursuers, knowing their own house, had soon found their way out into the garden and ran after him still calling and shouting. 'Stop him!' There was just enough radiance coming from other houses, distant streetlights and the moon to see Cash's figure vaulting a hedge.

Not lessening speed, he darted under a mulberry tree and raced down the side of a brick house while the commotion followed. Lights came on in the building to his right and more shouting began.

Suddenly the adrenalin shot through him as a dog jumped out of the shadows. Cash fended it off with his jemmy but it came back at him growling fiercely and attempting to lock its jaws around the crowbar.

Cash kept running, still fighting off the dog, when a door opened ahead in the side of the brick house and a man dashed out wielding a hockey stick in his hand and yelling, 'Hold him, boy!'

With the dog behind him Cash charged the figure blocking his way. The man raised the hockey stick but Cash swung out with his hand, the impetus of his acceleration taking him straight into the newcomer to collide with him and knock him down.

The dog's jaw had closed around the jemmy and Cash wrenched it from his mouth and made for the fence ahead, but now the animal bit into his trouser leg and he felt a scrape of teeth along his calf as he dragged the dog to the palings and saw the street ahead. He climbed up, hitting back at the dog with his crowbar and the dog released his trousers but continued to bound up at him, snarling, barking and biting. A front window of a house across the street opened and someone shouted, 'What's going on?'

'Bugger!' Cash exclaimed as he fumbled the jemmy and dropped it. But he was over the fence and onto the footpath and sprinting down the road as the dog continued barking. More illumination appeared in his peripheral vision as he raced on, trying to avoid the pool of light from a streetlamp above. The general outcry behind him had widened now but he took the time to halt and look back. No one was to be seen yet, though he believed it would not be long. He ran to the first corner and turned it, letting out a sound of relief. Fortune was with him; the street was tree-lined and even though a car came along and he passed a man in a sulky, he was soon running in the gloomy shadows of the trees, pushing himself to greater and greater speed while the noise of his hunters echoed behind.

He swung round the next corner and kept on running with no idea where he was. He did not feel panic; in fact, he felt exhilarated. He had even enjoyed the rushes of adrenalin when the dog had attacked him. He knew the way out of this suburb was to continue downhill, so he kept on and finally as time passed he became aware that the commotion behind him receded. Within a few more minutes he was heading down a steep sloping street and feeling safe. He had kept the moon on his right hand and felt confident that he had distanced himself from those giving chase.

Soon he was into another downhill thoroughfare and he took the next turn and slackened to a walk. Even though it was after midnight, a few vehicles and sulkies drove by. He was perspiring freely but he knew where he was: on Hamilton Drive and the Brisbane River was in front of him.

In dark shadows he bent forward, hands on knees, and caught his breath before he removed his gloves and put them in his pocket. He slipped the bag of jewellery off his leather belt and tucked it into his inside pocket. Remembering the jemmy he had dropped, a smug smile drew the side of his lips upwards. That was why he wore gloves, to leave no fingerprints. He wiped his forehead and temples with his handkerchief, straightened his tie and took two deep breaths.

In the glow of a streetlight he looked at his watch: twenty to one in the morning. Then he smiled again to himself. He felt wonderful. He felt stimulated, alive! Could almost feel the blood coursing through his body. There was no one on the street and he jumped in the air and cried, 'Yes! Yes! Yes!' before he started walking at a quick pace along the river towards the Breakfast Creek Bridge. He believed that the occupants of the house would have telephoned the police by now, but he was not concerned. By the time police arrived at the scene he would be long gone. Another car and a couple of carts drove by and as he turned left over the bridge and kept up his fast walk towards the Valley he heard a tram coming behind him.

For a few moments he weighed whether to catch the tram or not. It would speed up his escape, but he decided against it. He had no regard for the expertise of the Brisbane police but finally one of their number must think to ask about tram travellers in this part of town on this particular night, so he let it rumble on by.

Cash hastened on until he turned at the corner of Wickham and Brunswick Streets and made his way up to where a half a dozen stragglers milled about outside Grady's Bar: Brisbane's 1930s version of a nightclub. He entered by the side door under a Chinese hanging lantern. First timers came in the front where Moira, a tired thirty-seven year old who wore bright red lipstick and smoked Ardath cigarettes sat taking the sixpence entrance fee. Habitués used the side entrance where they ticked a board and paid for the number of ticks at the end of the month: they were allowed in for fourpence.

Cash picked up the grubby piece of chalk, wrote his name and ticked the board. He proceeded through a curtain and looked around in the smoke haze and low illumination. The first person he noticed was the man he was looking for: Creedy Fulbrook. In the weak light Creedy sat with his back to the wall drinking his usual brandy, his wide arm resting on his massive stomach and what could be seen of his eyes in the layers of fat surrounding them, ogling the two dyed blondes who sat with him.

Cash crossed the dance floor and slid into a chair beside the fat man as the crumpled trio on the tiny riser in the corner took a break from playing their music.

'Evenin', Professor.'

'Evening, Creedy.'

Creedy waved his plump fingers across his paunch in a signal for the two females to leave. 'Get us two brandies,' he demanded as they stood and with eyes on the newcomer sidled away to the bar.

'What's happening?' Creedy showed tobacco-stained teeth.

Cash replied in a low tone, 'I've chanced upon some gold you might be interested in and some watches; a silver pendant set with a diamond, and a signet ring.'

'Sounds like the pendant and the ring'll be traceable. Might 'ave to send them off to Sydney to a fence down there. Depends how valuable they are. Mightn't be worth it. What sort of gold is it?'

'Chains. Eighteen carat. I didn't obtain all I set out for tonight, and the small cache I'm offering you is due to my early exodus from a certain house in Hamilton.'

Creedy shook his head and grinned. 'I love the way ya talk.'

'When can I show it all to you?'

The fat man thought for a few seconds during which time he patted the bottom of the blonde who had arrived with their drinks. 'Tomorrow, Professor. My place. One p.m.'

Cash bent his head as he lifted his glass and his wandering curl fell across his forehead.

Creedy's tiny eyes scrutinised his companion out of the rolls of skin. He extended his hand and flicked Cash's forelock. 'Lovely hair, Professor. Bet women tell ya that all the time. Bet women tell ya a lotta things, fancy-lookin' bloke like you.'

Cash moved his head from Creedy's reach, ignoring the compliment. 'I'll be at your place at one.' He took a mouthful of his brandy. 'Now, have you got the item I paid you for last week?'

'Would I forget?' He took a red velvet box from under the table and handed it to Cash who opened it and made an agreeable sound before putting it in his inside pocket. 'Looks like a good one.'

'It is. Bloody beauty and a whole carat.' Creedy took a swig of his drink and pointed. 'What happened to ya trouser leg?'

'Met a dog and then vaulted over a fence – the wooden kind, not the human kind. The dog did it.'

Creedy laughed and his entire body undulated with his mirth.

'Yeah, dogs are a menace in your kinda work. But you're a bad bugger for sure. You'll last. That's why I like ya. The only educated fella I've ever known and liked. Most of 'em are ponces.'

'An apt description of my counterparts.' Cash drained his glass and stood.

'Stay and have another drink.'

'Not tonight, old man. I'll behold your inimitable presence tomorrow.'

'All right, ya mad bugger. Be careful. I suspect from what ya said about tonight that ya nearly got rumbled.'

Cash took a deep breath and winked. 'Life's not dull. See you tomorrow.' He left the table and moved quickly away between the dancers to the exit.

As Cash disappeared, the two blondes immediately returned to the fat man's table, their gazes following the visitor from the room.

Twenty-four hours later Sam awoke, startled, from a nightmare. She had been dreaming about her boss again, Dexter Wilde. Sam had been working with him now for six months. At first it had been hard for her to comprehend that she was being paid to learn about something she loved. Dexter Wilde was well-known in the small world of Australian photography and, in September, Sam had even accompanied him and his studio receptionist, Jan Balfour, to Sydney

203

on an assignment for the premier fashion magazine *Australian Vogue*. While there she had gone with her boss to meet the editor of *Australian Women's Weekly*.

Dexter Wilde was a married man with an eye for beauty and he had made advances to Sam on more than one occasion. Within a month she had learnt not to remain at work after Jan and the male studio assistant, Leon Ware, had departed for the night. Sam believed she knew how to deal with Dexter Wilde and she also suspected that her boss had been conducting an on-again, off-again affair with his receptionist. But Sam reasoned that she loved photography and was prepared to put up with the occasional unwelcome proposition from Wilde to continue her chosen course.

Once during their stay in Sydney, after an afternoon at a photographic studio in Bondi he took her to a ladies' lounge for a couple of drinks. In the taxi returning to their hotel he kissed her against her wishes and later in the night when he had attempted to enter her room at the hotel she had bluntly rejected him.

In the three weeks she spent in Sydney Sam made her own set of photographs of city life, including a series on workers in factories, and people-movers like trams and trains. To her great delight and surprise her series of photographs had been accepted and published in *PIX*, a weekly pictorial magazine. For this Sam received the princely sum of five pounds.

Back in Brisbane she had recently received a letter from the picture editor of the same publication, offering her an assignment.

She had hurried in to see Dexter Wilde, who had been in the studio setting up reflectors with Leon.

'Mr Wilde, I've been invited by *PIX* to do a picture story for them. Listen to this,' and she read from the letter: '"*Your set of dramatic photographs published recently in this magazine has given rise to an interest in your work. It has been suggested that you do a series to illustrate a story we have commissioned on the commercial ships and wharfs of Sydney. If you are interested in this assignment please write to me at the above address*".' Her eyes were gleaming and there was a blush of high colour in her cheeks.

Dexter Wilde slowly turned round to her, a stub of a cigarette stuck in the corner of his mouth. 'That's great kid, just great. And I'll say myself you have a certain style in your pictures, yes you do.' He shook his head sadly and removed the butt and flicked it out of the open window. 'But it'd mean you'd have to travel to Sydney. I just can't afford for you to be away three or four weeks doing it. You'd lose your job here, kid. I'm sorry, but that's what it means.'

The light had gone out of Sam's eyes and she retreated. Later, when she was in the dark room, he came in and sidled up to her and put his arm around her waist. 'Sorry about the *PIX* assignment kid, but look, you've got a good job here. You can always come with me to Sydney when I go and that's at least twice a year.' He leant in towards her and she pulled away from him telling him to remove his hand. He had slid it down across her bottom with a coarse laugh. 'All right, Samantha. Look, you learn fast. You're set here with me for life. Why don't you just learn to be a little more accommodating? If you're reasonable I'll reconsider the *PIX* thing.'

She asked him to leave, and from that day on she had not entered the dark room without Leon Ware.

Lately she had begun to have these bad dreams where she was in the studio in the dark of night all alone with Dexter Wilde. As she came out of the dream, lying there under a single sheet in the heat of the December night, her heart was racing a little. By the light of the moon she turned to look at her bedside clock. It was half past midnight.

She started momentarily as outside her window the front verandah creaked under the weight of a footstep and a knock on the front door followed but she quickly calmed, suspecting it would be Cash.

She moved slowly out of bed, dragged on her dressing-gown and sauntered to the front door. When she opened it her suspicion was vindicated. 'You never seem to be able to come here at a decent hour.'

'I know, m'lady, but you're so appealing after midnight.'

'Is that Cash?' a female's cross tones sounded from the second bedroom.

'Yes, Leah. I'll keep him quiet. Go back to sleep.'

'Tell him to go home! If Mrs Tarrant knew, there'd be hell to pay.'

Mrs Tarrant was the landlady; an eighty-two-year-old widow who took single girls into her home for a moderate rental. She lived upstairs and had converted her downstairs into a two-bedroom flat with chintz-covered sofas and lace curtains. She had the distinguishing feature of being almost totally deaf, which pleased her two occupants immensely.

Cash eased past Sam, planting a kiss on her nose and speaking in low tones as he headed into the kitchen. 'Why is that female you share this flat with so hostile?'

Sam smiled. 'You can't blame a person for not welcoming you with open arms at half-past twelve.'

'I protest! It's twenty-five past.'

'You're incorrigible.'

'I accept the description as I always do. It's one of your favourite words.'

'Only where you're concerned. Anyway I don't have anything to drink.'

Cash looked amazed. 'You don't? I distinctly remember leaving half a bottle of gin here.'

'You didn't. You finished it all off before you left last time.'

He laughed and pushed back his hair which had fallen forward. 'Ah, then I'll have a cup of tea as a feeble substitute.'

'You can't stay long, you know. I've got to work in the morning. And the last I knew, so do you.'

Sam turned to pick up the kettle and Cash noticed the evening *Telegraph* newspaper opened on the table. A headline jumped out at him: BURGLAR ESCAPES IN HAMILTON HEIGHTS. He picked up the paper and as Sam filled the kettle and lit the fire in the stove to boil the water, Cash devoured the article:

*A burglar suspected to be the man who has system-
atically robbed wealthy homes in the prestige areas
of Ascot, Indooroopilly, Clayfield and Cooparoo
narrowly escaped in Hamilton Heights last night, Det
Sergeant Wilson of the Metropolitan Police told the
Telegraph today. The occupants returned to their
home around midnight to find the burglar still inside.
They gave chase but lost him. The first of the seemingly related thefts occurred in January this year. Last
night's raid was the seventh with similar modus
operandi. The thief waits until a house is empty,
usually when the wealthy occupants are out at a party
or function and then raids the home. Only money and
jewellery are taken. Entry is almost always through
a broken window at the back of the home. The criminal wears gloves and no fingerprints have ever been
found, though a jemmy was dropped near the scene
of the crime last night. Det Sergeant Wilson is optimistic. 'Criminals always make mistakes. This fellow
is beginning to and we are ready.'*

Sam turned from the stove. 'What are you reading?'

Cash folded the paper and put it aside. 'Nothing of any
import.'

She reached for the paper and opened it. For a terrible
second he thought she would point out the article he had
just read but she flipped the page and placed the newspaper
back down in front of him pointing with her long pink
fingernail. 'Look at that, doesn't it make your flesh crawl?'

He gazed down and read:

GERMAN FÜHRER'S ADDITIONAL LAW

*At the German Reich Party Rally of Freedom in
Nuremberg on 15 September this year – a misnomer
for the rally as this paper believes – the law for protection of German Blood and German Honour was
passed and included prison terms for marriage and
extra-marital intercourse between Jews and Germans
even if concluded abroad; the prohibition of German*

maids under forty-five years in Jewish households; and the withdrawal of Jewish civil rights. To this set of laws Adolf Hitler added a retrospective law that executions taking place in defence of the state require no explanation.

In a startling example of this additional law in force in Germany, our correspondent in Berlin recently came into possession of the following letter which was sent to Frau Ema Haebich of the Botnang district of Stüttgart on 18 Jan this year in reply to her enquiry about the fate of her son who had been arrested:

'In response to your enquiry sent to the Führer on 19 November, 1934 I inform you on behalf of the Political Police Commander of the Member States, Reichsführer SS Himmler, that your son, Walter Haebich, was shot by firing squad on 1 July, 1934 in connection with the Roehm revolt.

'As his execution took place in defence of the state, no further explanation is required.'

HEIL HITLER

(Signed) Captain of Police

Sammy shivered as she looked over his shoulder. 'What's happening over there is unbelievable.'

'Yes, poor buggers.'

'I feel so sorry for those people. The Nazi Party runs everything and that Hitler's plain evil if you ask me.' She gently stroked his shoulder. 'Aren't we lucky to live where we follow British law?'

He stood and took her in his arms. 'Yes, we certainly are. You have to choose your parents in this life.'

'That's silly.'

'Mind you, if I'd had any say I wouldn't have chosen mine.'

'Stop talking like that.'

He kissed her nose. 'Anyway, I'd certainly select you. And to think you're nineteen next week.'

'Mmm.'

He brought his lips down to her mouth and kissed her

tenderly. She returned the kiss then moved out of his arms over to the dresser where she took down two cups from the hooks on which they hung.

'And you excite me.'

She smiled. 'Thank you.'

'I must say it's been unremitting excitement lately one way and another.'

She put the cups on the table and moved to the ice-chest for the milk. 'Why? What's been happening?'

He did not answer as he sat down and looked at her a long time, his gaze dropping down her body to her feet and back up to her hair. He was silent for such an extended period she turned round from where she was now looking for the sugar.

'Cash?'

Finally he replied, 'I was surprised by some people who didn't like me.'

'Who? Where?'

He inclined his head and began to laugh, slowly and quietly at first and then amplifying into a full-bodied guttural sound that resounded round the kitchen.

Sam was amazed. 'Shh, even Mrs Tarrant's not that deaf. Quiet! What's so funny?'

He wiped his eyes, still shaking from his laughter.

Sam made a sound of exasperation. 'Are you going to tell me or not?'

Cash edged forward on the table and as his errant lock slid onto his forehead Sam automatically pushed it back. He took her arm as she did so. 'I'll tell you one day. It's not significant.' He bent his head and kissed the inside of her wrist.

She shivered as she pulled away from his lips and turned to the boiling kettle. 'Ah, so it's not significant; it's just hysterically funny.'

'Correct,' he responded.

'I suppose you were at those silly night trots again.'

'You could say that.'

She made the tea and they drank it. The only sound in the still night was the rattle of a tree branch on the kitchen window.

He stretched back, cup in hand, a sensual expression on his face. 'Sammy, I'm crazy about you.'

Sam met his eyes.

'There's no one else but me in your life, m'lady is there?'

She shook her head.

'Are you sure?'

'Of course.'

'Have you heard from your brother?'

Sam looked at him in amazement. 'Why? What's he got to do with it?'

'To do with what?'

Sam shook her head. 'Look, I'm not following this conversation.'

Cash stood up and came round to her, an unreadable expression on his face. He took her in his arms. 'You don't need to follow the conversation.' He kissed her, his lips lingering on hers and he spoke against her mouth. 'I've been taking you out all year now, Sammy.'

'Yes.'

'And it's your birthday next week.'

'Yes.'

He kissed her again and slipped his hand inside his coat, took out the red velvet box and handed it to her.

She lifted the lid and looked inside. 'Cash, I can't believe it. Is it real?'

'Now, m'lady, would I buy you anything that wasn't?'

'But this must have cost fifty, a hundred pounds! How could you afford it?'

Cash groaned. 'Will you stop talking about what it's worth and tell me you actually don't hate it.'

'Hate it? It's absolutely magnificent. It's beautiful. It's . . .' She removed the diamond ring from the box and held it as one would the Holy Grail. She met his eyes. 'I'm in shock.'

He smiled, took it from her and slipped it onto her third finger. 'Sam, this diamond's nothing compared with you.'

She raised her hand and the jewel sparkled in the electric light.

'Sammy, I know I'm impulsive, impious and improvident,

sometimes impolite, and often imprudent, but what I'm going to say is not impromptu, I've been thinking about it for months. Will you marry me?'

Samantha stared at him.

'Sammy, darling, answer me. This is not simply a birthday present, m'lady, this is an engagement ring.' He bent down on one knee.

A distant expression covered Samantha's face. She appeared to be looking right through the man on his knees in front of her. She was reliving the moments of being held in her brother's arms; feeding on the memory of his touch and the sensations she had undergone with him. A great sadness surged up in her and she inhaled and exhaled audibly.

Cash was reading her mind and he did not like what he read. 'As I said before, there's not anyone else, is there?'

She gave a sudden jerk of her head. 'Of course not.'

And now he spoke brightly, sharply. 'Good. For this isn't a melancholy question, it's a joyous one. Don't leave me here genuflecting before you. Can't you *plee-ase* answer me?' With his expresson beseeching, his arms outstretched, he looked so amusing there on the floor with his hair dangling on his brow that she gave a small smile.

'That's it, come on. Remember me down here. It can't take this long to say yes.' He took up both her hands in his, remaining kneeling and making a comic face. 'I'll end up with house-maid's knee and you, m'lady, will be the cause. Now this torment's gone on long enough. I crave a reply.'

Sam looked at the ring again. 'Oh, Cash.' She thought of all her friends out in the country: Julie and Madge, Coral and Clara. Madge and Clara were married now and Coral had become engaged in August.

She touched his forelock in a tender gesture. She had known him most of her life. All the girls she knew thought he was good-looking, and he was, definitely, in a moody vagabondish way. Her mother said he reminded her of a good-looking hawk – well, Sam could not quite see that but he was an attractive man and there was no doubt she

211

was fond of him. He was fun and unpredictable; and she had been going out with him steadily for the whole year. Life with Cash would not be dull. He had acquired a job at last with the Brisbane City Council after months of waiting and searching. It did not pay wonderfully in these desperate times of Depression but he seemed to lead a charmed life where the horses and night trots and grey-hound races were concerned: the ring on her finger was testimony to that. There was no doubt he could provide for her.

And there was one thing she knew as indisputable: she could never marry the one man she felt she truly loved, so she might as well marry the one who had asked her.

He was watching her with his inky unfathomable eyes. 'All right, Cashman Slade, I'll marry you.'

He smiled. 'Incontestibly wise of you, m'lady.' He rose up, and brought her to her feet, kissing her deeply as his hands ran down her body and slipped inside her dressing-gown to grasp her buttocks. He caressed her neck and spoke, his voice low and thick with emotion. 'I want you badly, Sammy. Now, tonight. I can't wait any longer.'

She could feel his rock hard youthful body through her light dressing-gown and a warm sensation swelled within her.

'Come on, Sammy,' he whispered, taking her hand and drawing her from the kitchen. He switched off the electric light and they made their way down the hall to her room at the front of the house.

Silently he closed her door behind them and brought her to the bed. She sensed that he took off his clothes and she could hear his accelerated breathing as she felt his hands remove her gown and pyjamas. He kissed her gently many times and called her *m'lady love,* then he tenderly pulled her down on the bed beside him.

As his mouth found her nipples a spasm of excitement exploded inside her and she began to tremble slightly while he whispered words of love to her and ran his lips across her neck and down her arms.

And when at last he brought his body down on top of

hers, the name that resounded with a mad consistency in her head was not the name that broke from her lips. 'Oh Cash,' she managed to say, holding him tightly to her. 'Oh Cash!'

He had loved many girls, but Sammy had been worth waiting for; and as Cash consummated his union with her two things pounded in rhythm in his head. *I'll make you love me, m'lady. I'll make you forget about JB.*

Chapter Seventeen

Seven months later: July, 1936

John Baron shivered. The bitter wind felt as if it came straight from the Antarctic via Bass Straight into Port Phillip Bay to hit St Kilda Beach and whip into his body as he crossed the street to enter the football field. It was just after dawn on a Saturday in July and had been raining all night until about half an hour before.

'Been waiting for you,' his friend Euston Marsh called as John Baron ran down to meet him and four of the team wrapped in coats and scarves. 'How do you feel today?'

John Baron gave a shrug.

He had taken Euston's bet in the club rooms last night when three brandies had done his talking for him and now the reality of what he had agreed to was overwhelming him.

Derek, a burly six-footer, handed the two competitors the home-made flags. The bet had been to see who could climb to the top of the grandstand and attach his flag and climb down to the ground first.

That afternoon the local team were playing South Melbourne and the two flags read in bold letters, red on white: *ST KILDA TO WIN*.

John Baron and Euston stood side by side, a hammer in their belts and nails in their pockets. The flags were attached to wooden supports which were to be nailed in three places to the roof.

'On your marks, get set, go!'

The two young men hurtled towards the one-storey wooden grandstand.

They climbed well even though both slipped a couple of times on the wet wood, and they arrived up on the roof close together. Derek, taking the matter seriously, watched through binoculars as the two protagonists nailed in their flags. Euston had difficulty and dropped a nail; it seemed to unsettle him and he slowed down.

John Baron had completed his task when suddenly he looked down from the roof to the men below and he halted altogether. He put down his hammer in the gutter and raised his hand to his head. He felt as if he were looking down from a high cliff and for a second he thought he heard seagulls screeching.

Derek exclaimed, 'Heck, JB looks as if he's going to fall!' And at that point John Baron turned and lay back on the roof and by the time he had recovered Euston had nailed in his flag and was beginning his descent. John Baron forced himself to climb down and jumped the last seven feet to thud into the wet ground, but Euston had beaten him and was declared the winner.

The two rivals were perspiring freely even in the cold wind, and Euston looked at his friend in amazement. 'I thought you had me beaten. What happened?'

'I fell off a cliff years ago, when I was just a kid in Yorkshire. I mean, I hardly remember much about it, but the whole thing came back to me up there on the roof.'

One of Derek's mates who had taken a side bet on him was quite upset. 'Hang! Really? You should see a doctor or something.'

But Euston was all smiles. 'I'm sorry about how you felt, mate, but can't say I'm sorry about winning.'

Derek handed the two ten-shilling notes to the delighted Euston who waved them in the air with elation.

'That's the first bet I've ever seen you lose,' Derek commiserated with John Baron. 'It came as a real surprise to see you lie back on the roof like that. Maybe you *really should* see a doctor.'

John Baron shook his head. 'No, I'm all right now. It just came over me up there.'

'Seems odd, doesn't it? If you felt like that up there,

how come you don't feel like that when you go flying every Sunday?'

John Baron was learning to fly with a pilot friend he had met on the train from Queensland to Victoria nineteen months before. He had flown solo now a few times. He shook his head. 'Don't know. When I'm up in the air I feel great. Must be different having the aeroplane around me.'

Euston, who had expected to lose and now had won, made a gesture. 'Come on, I'll buy you all breakfast at Greasy's.' Greasy's was the name the local lads gave to Gareth Greasley's Café near the beach which opened early and closed late.

'You beauty!' And the six young men ran out of the ground one behind the other.

That afternoon when St Kilda played South Melbourne the talk was all about the two flags with their messages flapping from the grandstand and who might have placed them there. The ground was muddy from the night of rain and it threatened again all afternoon but did not fall. St Kilda won the day and the team rushed off to Flanagans, the nearest pub, to get a celebratory drink before it closed. In certain states of Australia, there was no drinking in hotels after 6 p.m. and the bars became stuffed with men in that last hour. This phenomenon was known as 'the six o'clock swill' and when the barman yelled, 'Drinking-up time!' they knew that they had ten minutes to finish and leave.

'That's good,' Euston grinned, 'because it was my shout.'

'In that case we'll come round to your place tonight.' Derek laughed.

'All right, but bring something to drink. I can't afford a party on my own.'

John Baron returned to his lodgings where Mrs Rains, his landlady, sat knitting in front of the fire. She smiled up at him from beneath her grey curls and pointed with her knitting needle to the mantelshelf above the crackling fire. 'Two letters came for you today.'

He turned his head and even from where he stood twelve feet away, he knew the handwriting on both. He walked over and took them. 'I'll read them in my bedroom.'

'All right love, just as you like.'

In his room he switched on the lamp at the bedside, sat on his bed and opened Sam's letter.

Dearest JB,

How are you? You never write and I feel as if my letters go into a void somewhere. I know you reply to Cash so I'm sure you receive my letters too. I suppose I understand why you don't answer but it still hurts.

Well, I've gone and done it now. Messed up things properly. I'm pregnant to Cash and I'm nearly three months gone. Neither of us are thrilled about it – having a baby really wasn't on our books so soon, but we're getting married pretty quickly as you can imagine.

Fact is, we're getting married on 1 August. Oh God, JB, what can I say to you? Come home for my wedding. I must see you just once before I'm a married woman. Please come home. I know why you don't come back but Mum and Dad just cannot understand. It would really make them so happy to see you even though their daughter has let them down. To think that Veena and I have found ourselves in the same boat – only difference is we don't know who little Storm's daddy is. Well, if this kid turns out as cute as Storm we'll be lucky.

Cash is doing well. His job pays meagrely but he does fantastically on the horses – seems to have a magic touch with anything that has four legs and runs. Mind you, he had a quiet spell early this year for a couple of months but he's back in the money now. I have a spectacular engagement ring which I told you about before and now I'll have a gold band to match.

Mum and Dad are good though they went into shock when we made the announcement. Can't blame them either but Mum's insisting on a proper wedding. She said it's the least we can do – she's going to tell everyone the baby is premature when it comes! I don't think she'll fool anybody but it'll make her feel better.

We went home last weekend. Ledgie is still the same as ever and Unc Wake is wonderful – hit me with French the whole time I was there saying I had to keep up! Heaven knows why. But it makes him happy. He bought me a book on a photographic exhibition held in a museum in New York. I mean, can you imagine it? Photos on display just like paintings. It's amazing. He never stops talking about the time he spent down with you last year.

Well, I guess that's it. Please come home for my wedding. I need to see you so very badly. I'm sad so often when I think of you. Just to see you again, just once more is all I ask.

Your ever-loving sister,
Sam

He held the letter and sat looking down at his hands, the gold ring he had been given on his twenty-first birthday gleaming on his little finger. He stood and walked to the window and opened it. The rain was splashing on the windowsill and the air was damp and icy cold yet he sucked it in as if it were his last chance to breathe. He felt sick to think of Sammy pregnant; sick to think of her in Cash's arms, making love to him and being his. And yet he had no right, no right at all. He put his head out in the rain and let the cold drops fall on his face and in his hair in some forlorn belief it would wash away his despair.

He had made excuses not to go north to Sam and Cash's engagement party last December, just as he had made an excuse not to return to Haverhill at Christmas. But no reason would be acceptable this time. How could he possibly not go to his own sister's wedding? There was no justification. Saturday 1 August was twelve days away.

He recalled Wakefield's month in Melbourne with him the previous October. They had spent such a happy time being together and when he had left to go back to Queensland he had asked John Baron if Melbourne were to be his permanent home. 'For we miss you badly, Johnny B, and it's difficult in these hard times for us to come and visit you. Your father and mother are needed constantly on the property. I'm the only one who can take a holiday, and I can't afford to come every year. Why don't you come back to see us, even if only for a little while.'

John Baron went to his bathroom and dried his hair then changed his drenched shirt and his trousers and opened the other letter. It was what he had assumed it would be. A message from his father telling him of Sam's imminent marriage and the request that he come home to be there for it.

He sat down and replied.

When he came past Mrs Rains on his way out that evening she was listening to the wireless. She looked at him. 'You look nice, dear, hair washed and all. Cleanliness is next to Godliness, as my dear old mother used to say. Now take an umbrella, it's still raining.'

He shook his head. 'I don't mind the rain.'

By the time he arrived at Euston's the cold wind had driven the heavy clouds away to release the shine of a milky moon. The whole team and many of the supporters were there. Beers were consumed like water and couples danced the charleston on the front verandah. Mrs Marsh was 'a good sport' who liked to see the young ones enjoying themselves. She wandered around handing out small meat pies she had baked that afternoon when she knew the team had won. JB was given drink after drink for he had scored the final goal and when he did sit down in the front room with Euston and his girlfriend, Eva, the noise was so loud that talking was almost impossible.

Nell Ward, a friend of Eva's, came over and sat down next to him. He knew she was attracted to him and Eva had arranged dates in foursomes with herself and Euston, Nell and John Baron, a few times in the past. As the girl attempted conversation above the tumult his mind was in Queensland at Haverhill, visualising Sam riding along with her hair blowing forward in the wind as it had the last time he had seen her. He imagined her straight back and the gentle hollow at the base of her sun-browned throat. He saw her swimming in the Logan while Tess and Charity barked at the birds flying low across the water. He envisaged her lying out in the grass in springtime under the gums by Teviot Brook with the wattle downstream bringing forth their golden flowers.

He pictured her taking photographs, giving him instructions on how to stand and where to look and laughing with delight when he obeyed.

When Euston and Eva rose to dance Nell looked at him with her big expressive eyes sending undeniable messages and he stood and escorted her out to the front verandah. He did his best to engender enthusiasm but by half past ten when all his mates were either drunk or heading in that direction, he made his excuses to leave.

Nell and Eva confronted him in the front hall where he was thanking Mrs Marsh, and Eva, a forceful girl who knew how pretty she was and was used to having her own way, spoke up. 'Aren't you going to see Nell home, John Baron?'

For a moment John Baron hesitated and Nell began to pick up her handbag and jacket.

Quickly he stayed her with his hand. 'No, Nell.' Then he leant across and kissed her cheek. 'Sorry, I'm not much company tonight.' And turning on his heel he walked into the front room, slapped Euston affectionately on the shoulder and shook hands with Derek and a few of his mates, before he left the smoke-filled house.

A week later he was on a train travelling by the green hills and valleys of Victoria. He changed trains at Albury because of the differing railway gauges between the states and when he arrived in Sydney he spent a night in the YMCA. He walked along Pitt Street to Circular Quay where ships had berthed for 160 years and he stood looking up at the great coat-hanger of Sydney Harbour Bridge. His engineering firm had been involved in part of the building of it and he remembered old man Stephens who had been at the opening ceremony three years earlier, amusing the entire office with his description of the fellow called De Groot riding on his horse through the cordon of startled police and officials. Before the amazed onlookers had time to stop him De Groot had severed the ribbon instead of allowing the Premier to perform the deed.

The last time John Baron had been in Sydney was with Cash on a brief holiday when they were at university. It was easy to like the city with its magnificent busy harbour and the green foreshores of the Royal Botanical Gardens and the pretty Point called Lady Macquarie's Chair. He knew that Sam had been here on an assignment with her boss a couple of times. His sister was having some success in the photographic world and making a name for herself.

He arrived in Brisbane at the Melbourne Street railway station early on the morning of Thursday, 30 July. Outside he caught a tram and alighted near Edward Street, walked up the hill to the hotel run by the Temperance League on the corner of Ann Street, took a room, bathed and changed clothes and ate breakfast. He caught the 10.20 a.m. express train from Central Station out to Ipswich and changed trains for Boonah. As the train picked up steam out of Ipswich Station he observed the twin spires of St Mary's Church and recalled the day he had meditated in the silence there and met Father Leonard. He closed his eyes as sadness and regret washed over him once more.

On his arrival in Boonah he visited Hardy Medcott who ran the stables in Park Street and who delivered the mail to some of the properties once a week. John Baron had decided to hire a horse and ride the miles out to his home but Hardy persuaded him to accompany him in his old jalopy for he had to pass Haverhill's front gate on a delivery of mail to the Thomas farm.

Hardy knew everything that went on in Boonah and its environs, and he informed his passenger that 'the whole darn district is waitin' for ya sister's weddin'. We'll all be at the church, that's for sure.'

As he turned in at the Haverhill sign, John Baron halted him. 'Stop, Hardy. I'd rather walk from here.'

Hardy pulled up. 'But it's close to half a mile in and you've got a suitcase.'

'I'd like the walk, really I would. There's a cool westerly blowing; it's the day for exercise.'

Hardy shrugged. 'If that's what you want, lad.'

John Baron waved him off and headed in along the dirt road. It was gratifying for him to be out here alone walking into Haverhill. His eyes were hungry for everything he had not seen for nineteen months: the tall silver-grey gums with the multi-colours in their peeling bark, the native cherry trees dotted here and there in the scrub and occasional kurrrajong towering over the olive-green gullies; the winter sun assailing the hills in the distance and the ever-bright sky above him so different to the moody changeable skies over Melbourne. Yes, he had missed his home.

Three or four crows swooped by and for a few moments as he walked along his mind seemed to play a trick on him and he saw in the great open spaces of south-east Queensland another view, from a window out over a garden of colourful flowers to a brick wall and emerald-green fields. He realised it was where he had lived as a small boy in England. He did not recall anything very much except the soldiers who had lived in the house: Uncle Wake had been one. He was reminded about his fall from the cliff. He thought of the lady who had called herself 'Auntie' and the exciting ride in the trap, the cakes and the abundant grassy slopes. He knew that event had happened after the war. His father had told him the woman was a distant relative and that they had no idea why she visited that day.

A minute later he spied part of the big wooden house with its encircling verandah nestling in the distance and he knew all the people he loved dearly in this world were congregating there.

In one fashion he was pleased that the walk had delayed his entry into Haverhill and yet in another he wanted to hurry for he was impatient to see his father and mother and Wakefield and Ledgie. He dreaded, and at the same time, yearned to see his sister.

He thought of Cash who had been his best friend all his life, but he had never understood him. In a certain sense John Baron would choose Cash for Sammy's husband above all comers but at the same time, he could not help but think Cash was unsuitable.

The house lay ahead of him through the vista of the poincianas and he could see the grain shed through the trees. He fancied he could hear the dogs barking in the distance. He put down his case and stood there looking at his home and wondering how much time would go by before he saw this view again.

He found himself humming 'Tea for Two' and recalled the Christmas concert when he and Sammy had sung and danced together. He saw her stepping out and turning towards him to take his hand, her skirt billowing in the air . . .

Suddenly there was a shout and a figure waved on the verandah. It was Cash. He jumped the seven front steps to the ground and came running towards him. John Baron picked up his suitcase and met his friend halfway down the drive. Cash enfolded him in his arms. 'Welcome home, JB. It's been too long.'

'Thanks, mate.'

The bridegroom took the suitcase and they walked side by side back to the house.

'We didn't know when you'd arrive so guessed sometime this afternoon, and because Sam and the women are so preoccupied with dresses and veils, the interior of the church, flowers, catering and all that, they're in Boonah and I'm relegated to guarding the homestead.' He gave a playful groan and placed his arm round John Baron's shoulder as they came to the front steps. 'We'll be engaging in the formality of a bucks' party tomorrow night at the Empire Hotel in town. Julie and I are staying down the road at the Thomases' place.'

'Right. Where's Dad?'

'With Wakefield in the grain shed, I think.'

'Good. I'll drop my bag in and go and see them.'

They mounted the stone steps and as John Baron followed Cash through the familiar rooms he was glad to be home.

'How was the journey from Melbourne?'

'Good. I stayed overnight in Sydney.'

'Sydney eh? I'm taking Sammy there for our honeymoon. The great metropolis!'

Walking down the hall John Baron gave his friend a playful shove. 'I've missed you, that's for certain.'

'The feeling's mutual, old man,' Cash responded and marched on to the bedroom, opened the door, and placed the suitcase on the bed as John Baron entered and looked around. Cash took hold of John Baron's shoulders. 'Gosh, some things are immutable – us for instance, our friendship. And now we're to be brothers-in-law. Of course you understand I want you as my best man?'

John Baron nodded. 'Yes, I do.'

'Thanks, JB. It's important to me that I have you at my side.' He paused then added, 'And I think it's important to Sammy too.' He fell silent, just staring at his friend. Then he gave a sudden laugh and slapped John Baron on the shoulder. 'Now shall we go over to the grain shed?'

The two older men were delighted to have their boy home and they halted work and returned to the house with him where Crenna wrapped John Baron in her massive arms and insisted that afternoon tea would soon be ready.

After they had drunk their tea at the big wooden table in the brightly painted kitchen, and eaten most of the pumpkin pie specially made by Crenna for the homecoming, John Baron changed from his travelling clothes and accompanied the men back to work. 'I want to do something manual, Dad. I've missed it.'

'Wonderful, my boy. Let's go down to the stables where I said we'd give Jimmy Birnum a hand this afternoon.'

Inside the stables they toiled along with Ben, Wakefield, Jimmy Birnum and his son Jake, grooming a number of the horses that had been out working on the farm during the day. Cash helped for about half an hour then set down his brush. 'It's time for me to drive into town for the women. Coming, JB?'

'No, old man. I'll stay here.'

Cash walked out into the sunshine and John Baron followed him, halting him with the words: 'You do love my sister, don't you?'

Cash paused. He turned back and leant on a hitching rail between them. 'An understandable question.'

'Answer it then. Don't try to be clever. Do you love my sister?'

Cash tossed his head and his black forelock dangled in cavalier fashion on his brow. He straightened. 'I have *always* loved your sister.'

'Is she going to be the only woman in your life?'

'Now JB, what's this – the Inquisition? Why would I need any others?'

John Baron's eyes narrowed. 'Make sure you keep it that way.'

Cash's eyes narrowed in response. 'You've always been protective of Sammy, JB. *Overly* protective, one might say, and yet you left her and rushed off to Melbourne. Strange, that.'

'What the hell does that mean?'

'It means I wonder why you went away.'

'I know you do.'

Cash smiled; one of his singular half-smile half-smirks, then lifting his wrist, looked at his watch. 'I'm going.'

'One more thing.'

'Hell, JB, what now?'

'Before I left here, you told me that you intended to become a burglar.'

Cash inclined his head to the side steadily regarding his friend; his expression was now completely unreadable, a conundrum.

'I'm informed of your huge success at the races. I mean Mum and Dad and even Wakefield and Ledgie write to me about it. You win on the horses, the dogs, the trots with seeming ease.'

Cash shook his head. 'Ah no, old man, there's nothing easy about it. Believe me.'

'Wakefield told me when he was in Melbourne that you'd made good money on the re-sale of some blocks of land you picked up for a song out of your winnings.'

'Mmm?'

'You do come by the money that way, don't you?'

'Be explicit, old man.'

John Baron stepped up to his friend. 'I want to hear it

from you that you have amazingly good luck at the races and that you didn't become a bloody burglar like you said you were going to the Christmas before last.'

Cash brought his head up straight and spoke out of the side of his mouth in a flippant manner. 'I take it you wouldn't readily consent to your sister's union with a thief?'

'Bloody right. So let's get that straight.'

'As we're both putting things plainly, old man, your sister *has no option but to get married.*'

John Baron's voice rose. 'I know that, for Christ's sake! And you're both damn fools to have allowed it to happen. I just don't want her to be making two blasted mistakes.'

For a moment Cash looked skywards, flicked his curl off his forehead with his thumb in a comical dramatic action and ran his fingers through his thick black hair. He laughed and his expression was easy, accommodating, friendly. 'In that case, old man, relax. I'm not a burglar. I assert it.'

'I prefer you to swear it, Cash.'

Cash paused. 'As you prefer me to, I do.'

'So you do have amazing luck then? That's all true?'

'Well, occasionally I have a dry spell, but principally fortune smiles on me.' He laughed again. 'But I work at it, old man. I've got systems coming out of my ears.'

John Baron gave a murmur of relief and Cash slapped him light-heartedly on the shoulder. 'So now we've approved of my credentials I'm off to town.'

As Cash walked away John Baron remained motionless, watching his friend's long stride until he disappeared from sight; then with a thoughtful shake of his head he returned inside to continue working beside his father and his uncle.

And that was where Constance, Ledgie and Sam found him two hours later when they returned from Boonah. Cash drove his Ford right up to the stable door and the women all alighted and entered across the hay-covered floors.

Constance wrapped her arms around her son and cried while Ledgie repeated, 'Home at last, home at last,' dabbing her tears with a lace handkerchief. But even as he hugged his mother and Ledgie it was Sam's eyes he gazed into over their shoulders.

She waited there a few feet away with Cash's sister Julie, who was to be one of the bridesmaids; though John Baron's eyes saw only his sister standing in the late-afternoon sun as it extravagantly animated her auburn hair and the glow of her skin. She wore a pale flower-patterned dress and her silk stockings shone on her legs. Her body was slender just as it always had been and there was no swelling of her girth as yet. Her feet were planted in the golden hay of the stable floor and she did not move until his mother and Ledgie had hugged and kissed him and calmed down, then she came forward, her hands outstretched to take his. 'Welcome home, brother mine.'

He took her hands and they both felt the tingle in their fingers.

'Hello, Sammy. You're gleaming.'

She quickly stepped into his arms. 'You're gleaming too,' she replied softly in his ear, holding him to her heart. He kissed her swiftly on the forehead and released her, turning immediately to Julie in one movement and hugging the surprised girl quite fiercely to him.

Julie kissed him. 'Why JB, how nice. It's good to have you home.'

He did not look back at Sam though he felt the heat of her gaze upon him and at that moment he lifted his eyes and saw Cash leaning on the door jamb watching him. Abruptly Cash grinned. 'So, JB, your salutations are over? Ready, girls – Mrs C? Hop in the chariot and I'll take you back to the homestead.' He moved over to Sam and slipped his arm around her. 'This way, m'lady.'

The women left, and John Baron and the two older men followed on foot.

Cash and Julie departed for the Thomas property just before dinnertime and along with the rest of the family, John Baron strolled to the car to see them off. He was patently aware that the prudent move would be to return swiftly inside with his parents, but now that he was close to his sister his resolution was weakening.

While the family said their goodbyes and Cash kissed Sam and bounded into his Ford, John Baron stood in the yard watching with Ledgie at his side.

Cash leant from his car and smiled oddly at him. 'Be good you two,' he quipped, pointing to JB and then to Sam, before he accelerated across the yard.

As the car disappeared Constance and Ben, Wakefield and Ledgie, headed back to the house, but the brother and sister remained in the yard.

'Are you coming?' Constance called to her children as she climbed the steps to the verandah.

'In just a minute, Mummy,' Sam replied. The westerly wind was rising and the fleeting Queensland dusk was fading into a cold night as her hand crept into John Baron's. All of his will told him to release her and return to the house.

'It's so good just to be beside you again,' his sister said, her voice low and melodious to his ears.

They did not look at each other, they simply stood facing in the direction Cash's car had taken. He began to speak and then halted. Finally he asked, 'Sammy, are you going to be happy with Cash?'

She squeezed his hand. 'Yes, I'll be happy. He sort of suits me, you know. I've decided that if I can't have the one I want then I must have the one who wants me. Most of my girlfriends think he's dreamy, and I've always liked him. Gosh, I mean it's always been the three of us . . .'

Now he turned to face her and he gazed into her eyes in the dying light of the evening. He realised this was all incautious, all foolish, and for some seconds neither of them spoke, until suddenly she whispered, 'Come,' and took up his other hand in her free one and drew him across into the darkness at the side of the verandah by a tall hoop pine.

She nestled her head on his chest. 'Oh God, how I've missed you.'

He kissed the top of her head breathing in the exquisite smell of her. 'And I you.'

They remained holding each other in silence as the moments passed; neither wanting to move, their bodies pressed together in the wonderful comfort of the shadows. When at last she lifted her mouth to his, he began reasoning again. He forced himself to step away. 'Sam, stop. You're carrying Cash's baby. This wasn't right before and it's not right now. In fact, if it's possible, it's worse now.'

Her face was flushed and she gave a little nervous laugh. 'Yes, yes of course, you're right. And believe me I do feel a lot for Cash. He attracts me, that's for sure.' Her voice grew louder and her tone was over-bright. 'We're going on a great honeymoon . . . Three weeks in Sydney, you know.'

'That's good. It's important for you both.' He stepped further away from her, out from the shadows into the mild illumination coming from the house.

Suddenly the pitch of her voice dropped again, tender, coaxing. 'Walk down to the brook with me, just once more. There's still a little water left from the rainstorm we had last week. It smells fresh and clean down there. Come on, JB, please. Just for a few minutes. Please . . . I know you want to.'

The temptation was beginning to overwhelm him. He could make out her hands lifted towards him.

He spun round on his heel to face away from her. He spoke, not looking round. 'You must realise I don't trust myself. And I don't trust you, at all.'

'I knew you'd say that.'

He trudged slowly up the steps to the verandah. When he halted at the top she spoke to his back. 'I'm so sorry. Forgive me. I'm hurting you and it's the last thing I want to do.'

He turned to gaze down at her from the verandah; the light from inside the house seemed to play about his fair hair and she was reminded of the night at the Christmas Eve concert when he had caught Cash kissing her; when Cash had said he looked like the Lord Himself with a halo.

'We're hurting each other,' he answered in a low voice. 'You're going to be a wife and a mother. Concentrate on that, Sammy.'

'You look wonderful, JB. Just seeing you is . . . enough.' Her sigh was loud on the night air. 'You're resolute, good, just and ethical, and I must be glad of that.' She folded her arms across her body and held herself.

He continued looking down at her for a long time before he said, 'It's cold out here, Sammy. Very cold. Too cold. Come inside.'

Crenna had done herself proud and cooked John Baron's favourite food: tomato soup, chicken and dumplings and coconut pie. Constance had insisted on the best linen being used and Wakefield made a speech of welcome to the home-comer while Ledgie even played 'Land of Hope and Glory' on the piano, a recital which was usually heard only at Easter and Christmas.

There was a chill throughout the wooden house and the only really warm rooms were the kitchen where the wood stove emitted a pleasant cosiness, and the lounge, where a fire crackled in the brick fireplace. So for a time while the women cleared away, everybody remained in the kitchen, after which they all retreated to the lounge where they sat and talked. Wakefield lit his pipe and Constance poured whiskies for all the men. 'I'll even have a small one myself,' she said and while Ledgie did not comment she made tut-tutting noises in the background as she sipped her cup of tea.

'I'll have one too,' pronounced Sam from where she sat beside Wakefield.

Ledgie almost choked on her tea, looking askance across to Constance. 'Are you going to allow that?' she asked, adding in an undertone, 'In her condition.'

Benjamin thought it was time he took charge of his family and as he accepted his glass of whisky from his wife he lifted his index finger towards his daughter. 'Samantha, you're about to be married and that brings certain respon-sibilities, thinking for yourself and your family being one of them. Now I don't know much about whether you should or shouldn't drink from a medical standpoint; your mother would know best about that, but as a married woman you'll be running your own home and I wouldn't like to think that you'll be sitting up drinking whisky every night.'

John Baron leant back and closed his eyes.

Sam met her father's gaze. 'Daddy, I won't be "sitting up drinking whisky every night". I just felt that with the stress of the wedding and everything . . . well, that I'd have a drink. But forget about it, I don't want to upset anybody.'

'That's right, love,' her mother replied in conciliatory fashion. 'I'll make you a nice cup of tea.'

Ledgie put down her cup and picked up the newspaper. 'Good that's settled so let's do the crossword.'

After a few minutes Ben took the opportunity to lead his son away. He was brimful of happiness to have John Baron home and he wanted simply to talk with him alone.

In Ben's study the father and son sipped their whisky and Ben looked over his glass. 'So will you be returning home, my boy? I assume that the affections of Sandra Charters are no longer a worrying issue for you.'

John Baron almost said 'Who?' when he recalled the name of the imaginary girl he had made up for his father nineteen months previously. He groaned inwardly; deceit was not natural to him. He forced himself to reply, 'That's true, sir.'

'And now might be the time to tell your mother of the real reason you went to Melbourne?'

The young man exhaled loudly. 'I'd prefer to let that lie actually sir, especially as I've decided Melbourne's not for me any longer.' He had been mulling over an idea for the last few months and now that he had come home and seen Sammy again he knew he had to do it.

His father looked expectant.

'But I'm not coming home. I've got a bit of the wander-lust and I've a hankering to see England. I've decided to try and work my passage on a ship. I know a bloke in Melbourne who got a job as a deckhand just a couple of months ago.'

Benjamin sat studying his son. He was remembering all the reasons they had left England and come out to this country: Harriet being at the forefront. But he was sure that by now even Harriet's hatreds should have eased and in any case he was unconcerned about her ever having contact with his boy. There were around 40 million people in England, after all. So if his son wanted to see the old country he would have to let it happen. He had no desire for his boy to go even further away, but the plain fact was he had not seen John Baron since January the previous year so he might as well have been overseas. 'I see, son.'

'Dad, I've become used to living away from home. I feel as if I want to see things and experience more of the world than I have up to now. I know I'm lucky to have a job here in these uncertain times but I've got to do what I feel is right.'

'And you're sure it's England you wish to visit?'

'I'm sure. It's where I was born.'

'Son, I know I said I was all for your seeing other places when you went to Melbourne, but England's another matter. We've all been hoping you'd return home, you know.'

'Yes, I suppose I do.'

'There's a lot of unrest in Europe with constant strife in almost every country and political extremists all over. The world Depression's giving rise to all sorts of problems. This Adolf Hitler bloke in Germany, *the Führer* as he calls himself, has now sent his troops into the Rhineland without interference from anyone. He's rabidly anti-semitic and a very dangerous man. Since he murdered all his opposition two years ago he's absolutely in control. This Nazi Party he leads is hardly a political party; it's like an army, uniformed and organised on military lines at all levels, and no opposition parties allowed. You've only to read the papers to know all that. He has his eyes on European domination, if you ask me.'

'Dad, what you say is true, but England's not Germany, and I feel as if I must go now, while I'm young. I don't want to wait.'

Ben sat silently looking at his boy, then he shook his head in a defeated manner. 'Your mother won't like it. She's still not reconciled to your being in Melbourne.'

John Baron knew this. 'True. But she'll take it better now than she would have before.'

Ben gave a wry smile and stretched forward on his desk

tapping the wood with his sunbrowned finger. 'It seems whenever we're in this little sanctuary of mine that you're telling me you're off somewhere.'

'I'm sorry, sir. Please don't think I'm not grateful to you and Mum . . . and Uncle Wake and Ledgie too. I've had the best upbringing a man could wish for and you're all the most wonderful family in the world. But Dad, I'm twenty-five in a few months and it's time I saw the world.'

Ben swallowed, made a sound of acceptance in his throat, and sat upright. 'So, in that case, how long are you staying here now and when do you intend to leave for England?'

John Baron thought immediately about the three-week honeymoon, so he answered promptly, 'I'm staying at least three weeks. I think I'll write a letter of resignation while I'm home and work out my notice when I return, so I suppose I'll be leaving after that.'

'All right, my boy, let's talk about other things. At least you'll be here with us for a few weeks, I'm glad of that.'

'Sure, Dad.' And before his father could say any more John Baron added, 'Oh by the way, sir, I don't want to say anything to the others while the wedding's so close, there's enough emotion floating around already. So if you don't mind keeping it under your hat I'll tell everybody next week.'

'What about your sister and Cash? They won't be here.'

'Don't worry about them, Dad, they won't be concerned. They've got each other. I'll write to them; that'll be the best way. It's Mum and Ledgie I'm really thinking about.'

Chapter Eighteen

At 4 p.m. on Saturday 1 August, Samantha stepped out of Cash's Ford in the late-afternoon sun, crossed the dirt foot-path with Julie Slade and Coral Thomas holding her veil and dress up off the ground, and entered, on her father's arm, Christ Church in Boonah. Townsfolk lined the way wrapped in jackets against the westerly wind; a big wedding was always a magnet to country folk even in the chill of winter, and Sam's had caused a stir.

The previous night when Ledgie had been brushing out Constance's hair she had confided to her, 'I wouldn't say this to anybody, dearest, but I'm thinkin' I'm not sure about our Sam wearing white, you know? It's meant to symbolise purity, after all.'

Constance had given a small moan. 'I know, Ledgie. But she was desperate to be a real bride and after all, it's only we who know she's in the family way. She doesn't look it at all and people won't be aware for some time. And anyway, I told you before, I'll be maintaining that the babe is premature.'

Ledgie made a scoffing sound. 'You'll be afoolin' no one, my precious.'

Yet the bride was one of the most bewitching figures ever to be married in the county of Ward. The country folk stared at her as she glided up the steps in her lace and silk with clusters of orange blossom over each ear.

Sam had indicated to her family that she had fallen in the bath a week earlier and sustained marks on her legs and an extensively bad bruise on the back of her neck. It had been of concern to Ledgie and Constance how to hide the discoloured skin on her neck, but finally they were satisfied after covering it in vanishing cream and face powder, and when the veil was put on it was completely disguised. In these days of Depression Constance and Ledgie, having metamorphosed into redoubtable country women, had utilised a spare lace curtain for the elegant veil, and no one was the wiser.

Sam's dress was white silk, and while Ledgie might be disapproving of its colour she had sat up every night for a fortnight tatting the tiny lace flowers which had been sewn all over the bodice. Sam's waist was still slender and the dress was flared to the floor trailing just a few inches behind her in a short train and adding more than a vestige of glamour as she strolled up the aisle.

John Baron stood beside Cash at the altar. They both wore dark suits with white shirts and identical maroon ties. A few feet away, Mrs Thomas played the *Wedding March* on the organ, her fingers lifting in extravagant movements six inches from the keys.

A number of Cash's old university friends were in the pews behind his family including Dudley Belcher who had driven up in his brand new Austin. The world Depression had not seemed to affect the Belchers who had their money mainly in picture-houses throughout Queensland. Belcher had also kindly agreed not to return to the flat he shared with Cash in Brisbane until Monday, which meant that the newlyweds would be alone there on Sunday night after spending the wedding night in an hotel in Peak Crossing, a tiny spot before Ipswich.

Cash looked around and when he saw his bride he made an appreciative noise but John Baron continued to face ahead concentrating on the sun spots on the back of the Reverend Michael's hands holding the Common Prayer book. He felt overwhelmed by the event; his feelings were tumbling over each other and he was sorry that he had come home.

Cash, at his side, had watched him closely while they waited for Sam's entrance. There was a wrinkle somewhere in Cash's heart that held real sympathy for JB, but he could not allow it to become a valley; that would never do. He desired to have Sam for his wife, and along the way that meant maintaining the secret.

He had to hand it to JB though, he was holding together pretty well; the man had guts. When JB and Sam had greeted each other in the stables on Thursday he had seen that their feelings had not much altered in the twenty months apart. That had disturbed him right enough, but he was willing to take the chances he realised all this entailed. Sam was having his baby, she had to care for him to be in that condition, didn't she? Well, maybe it wasn't love yet, but he was prepared to take the risk that in time attraction would transform into love.

As he turned back to the minister and his eyes briefly met his best man's he felt confident; he winked and John Baron replied with a pseudo smile.

The service began and the minister's voice intoned throughout the church. He was a gentle man and caring of his parishioners and was happy to see the two young people joining together. John Baron handed over the ring without dropping it and watched with a bleak almost disassociated feeling as Cash kissed his bride.

There were fifty guests but the remainder of the church was full with locals and Hardy Medcott, good as his word to John Baron, stood in the back pew with his wife and two daughters all agog.

The whole Birnum family were there. It had been one of Sam and Cash's express wishes. As Cash put it. 'Veena is Sammy's friend and also her country photographic assistant. We want her there and we want her family there; and in any case little Storm is our good luck charm.' So Storm was dressed in pink and white lace and sat almost quietly on her mother's lap throughout the wedding ceremony, falling asleep when the bride and groom disappeared to sign the register. Veena's three brothers giggled and dug each other in the ribs when the married couple stopped to talk to them as they walked down the aisle arm-in-arm after the ceremony.

From the time she entered the church Samantha had tried to catch her brother's eye but his gaze was elsewhere. And as the bridal procession made their way from the church to the stirring music of the organ, one old woman who had come in especially from Mount Alford spoke aloud the thoughts of so many. 'I've never seen a prettier pair in me life. Him with his black hair and eyes and her all dolled-up and flower-like.'

The two bridesmaids looked elegant in pale green and for once the bride was hampered as a photographer. Unable to take her own wedding pictures she had seconded her brother, and the stiff formal photographs in the fashion of the day, on the stairs in the hall of the Australian Hotel in High Street were all taken by John Baron while the bride dictated the proceedings from the centre of each picture.

The wedding breakfast at the Church of England hall was sumptuous for Depression times and the guests all in their finery enjoyed four delicious courses. Constance had been adamant. 'I know it's hard times but our only living daughter is getting married and I want a nice wedding with all the trappings.' So the local baker had been brought in to help and liquor flowed and everyone forgot that they were in a world Depression for a little while.

A high standard in toast-making was set when Benjamin spoke first as the father of the bride in an eloquent and often amusing speech. After talking for some time about the attributes of his daughter and reminding them that she had been born a twin, he praised Cash and then ended with the words, 'Cash is getting a gem, a real diamond in my opinion. Yes, they are both very young but they'll grow and mature together. They're both serious-minded young people with an eye to their futures. I wish them love and immense happiness.' At that stage Cash turned into John Baron's ear and whispered, 'Was he speaking about me?'

John Baron had been proposed as the one to give the toast to the bride and groom, but he had declined, reasoning that he was an engineer not a speech-maker and so Wakefield had been deputised. He rose to the occasion giving a sensitive insight into Sam's life and making the guests smile and call out 'Too right!' when he said he had known the groom since he was eight years old but that he was still a mystery. He closed by saying that until today's sumptuous repast he had agreed with Jean-Baptiste Molière. *'Il faut manger pour vivre et non pas vivre pour manger.'* But now I have altered my mind.'

Cash's brother Henry was the first to shout, 'In English for us illiterates, please!'

This made everyone laugh and consequently Wakefield translated, 'One should eat to live, not live to eat!'

Cash's father and mother had come over from Fernvale where they now lived in a modest little home on land owned by Ben and Constance, and where they eked out a living by running a few dairy cows and some pigs. Randall Slade looked like a broken man and was decidedly uncomfortable when he rose to speak, his discourse being almost curt. 'Samantha's a beautiful bride and Cash is a lucky man. I and my wife wish them a happy marriage and hope that they enjoy good health and long life.' It had not gone unnoticed by many of the assembled that Cash had swiftly kissed his mother and not spoken at all to his father.

When the bride and groom stood for the bridal waltz, everybody cheered and indeed they proved worthy of it; the handsome pair danced in pleasing harmony to a Strauss waltz.

Mrs Thomas, having divorced the organ for the piano, played with gusto and many of the guests soon joined in the dancing until the hall echoed with laughter and high spirits.

When Cash kissed Sam and moved away to find another drink, Sam crossed to where John Baron fox-trotted with Julie. She tapped her bridesmaid's shoulder. 'Excuse me, Jules, but this might be my last chance to dance with my brother – so if you don't mind?'

Julie looked as if she did mind but she acquiesced.

John Baron took his sister in his arms and to any highly perceptive person watching, she seemed to melt forward into his embrace. He spoke quietly, his eyes never leaving hers. 'Do you think this is wise?'

Sam lifted her face up towards his and answered softly,

'Not even I have the guts to do anything you wouldn't like in the middle of a dance floor on my wedding day.'

His temperature was rising and he pulled gently at the knot in his tie. 'I wish you great happiness, Sammy.'

'And I wish you the same.' Briefly she rested her head on his chest.

'Don't do that Sammy, please.'

She raised her head. 'I'm sorry. I don't want to upset you.'

'You don't upset me.'

She inclined her head and looked up into his eyes. They danced for a minute or so without speaking each conscious only of the other, before Sam said, 'I wonder if there's a planet in the universe where it's acceptable?'

He knew exactly what she meant. 'Perhaps.'

'I wish we were there.'

He did not answer.

'Goodbye, JB.'

'What do you mean?'

'I've got this feeling that I won't see you for a long, long time. I know it somehow in my soul. Look after yourself, my dearest. And please just promise me one thing?'

He swallowed hard as she caressed the side of his neck above his celluloid collar.

'What's that?'

He could see tears brimming in her eyes; he did not want her to be sad.

'You haven't written me one letter in all the time you've been in Melbourne; please promise you'll write to me, even if it's just once a year. Make it for my birthday. Please.'

His voice broke a little as he replied, 'I promise. I remember your very first birthday, Sammy. That's one of the things I do recall about England. You and little Viv.'

And now a tear swelled over Samantha's lid and ran down her cheek. And he halted and they stopped dancing, though he did not release her but continued to hold her in his arms.

'Don't cry, sweetheart,' he said tenderly. 'It mightn't seem like it but Cash has a side that's strong and caring and I've a sense it's all centred on you. That makes me happy.' He lifted his hand and brushed away her tear. 'He's all sorts of strange things, but he does love you, I'm truly positive of that.'

'And I suppose I love him too, well I reckon I do, but . . . It's just different with you.'

He gave a nod in understanding. 'Goodbye, Sammy.'

Her response was a whisper. 'Goodbye, JB.'

'Hey, what's this?' It was Cash at their side, a flush of four rums igniting a glint in his unfathomable eyes. 'Brother and sister, and little sister in tears? This is a discordant note at a blithesome event. M'lady, what the devil's going on between you two?'

Sam dragged her gaze from her brother's. 'Oh Cash, I haven't seen him for so long. I've just been married. I'm having a baby. I'm emotional, I suppose.'

Cash slipped his arm around her and pulled her possessively to him. 'Mm, I suppose so too.' He shot a dismissive look at his new brother-in-law. 'She's my wife now, JB old man, you don't need to worry about her any more.'

For some reason John Baron had the sense that Cash meant a lot more than he said.

Cash's odd expression remained as he turned to his bride and kissed her forehead. 'Now dance with me or I'll begin to suspect you'd prefer to dance with your brother.'

'Don't be silly,' she replied, taking his hand.

Cash held her tightly as they moved off in step and he pressed his face into her hair. Silently he repeated, 'You're mine now Sammy, all mine,' in time to the rhythm of the music as he watched JB's back disappear through the dancing guests.

At eight o'clock the newlyweds retired to the Australian Hotel and changed into their going away outfits. Sam wore a pale blue skirt with a matching knitted jacket and a flowered skull cap and Cash changed his shirt and tie for shades of blue to match his wife's clothes.

They hugged their family and friends and Wakefield's final words to them were, 'Keep up your French, *mes enfants*, whatever you do. Write to me, that's one way.'

'I will,' Samantha promised.

'Too right,' agreed her husband.

Ledgie in an unaccustomed display of affection for anyone other than her darling Constance, kissed Sam and hugged Cash to her lean frame quite fiercely.

Sam nursed little Storm who had been fast asleep in her grandfather's arms for hours and as she hugged Veena close the young woman whispered, 'Thank you for everything and specially for givin' me a birthday.' Veena had done as Sam had suggested, and on Storm's first birthday on 3 April Veena too had celebrated the day, taking a guess that she was twenty.

Sam kissed her. 'You gave it to yourself when Storm was born.'

She waved to the gathering of people in the dark night illuminated only by the light thrown from the hall and three torches held high by Wakefield, Ledgie and Henry Slade, the groomsman. Cash's Ford was decorated with coloured paper and a *Just Married* sign embellished with a string of cans hung from the back bumper bar.

When Cash shook John Baron's hand and said, 'Nothing stopping you from finding a girl of your own now,' John Baron could not help but answer, 'What does that mean?'

Cash laughed in the wavering light thrown from the torches. 'Isn't it time you had a nice girl of your own, old man? You've always been *such* a good brother and protective of Sammy. No need to be any longer; you can find someone of your own now, eh?' He laughed again and then his expression altered. 'I do love your sister, JB. That's like a universal truth. Between you and me, I wanted her, and I do strive to get what I want.' And he slapped John Baron's shoulder and spun away.

The couple entered the car and it clattered down the dark street to be revealed for a moment in the soft pool of light from the streetlamp as it rounded the corner and disappeared out of sight.

Constance hid her face in Ben's shoulder as they walked back through the mêlèe into the hall. 'Our little girl's a married woman and she's not even twenty until December.'

'I know, darling, I know. Life's funny Connie, and we all have to accept what we get. But I'm sure Cash will take care of her.' Ben lifted her arm through his and kissed the top of her head. 'Now, we still have each other and we're surrounded by wonderful people; let's take comfort in that.'

With her free hand Constance touched the gold pendant she wore. It was the one Benjamin had given her when they had left England seventeen years before: inside was the sepia image of Vivian, her other little girl. 'Now I've lost them both,' she murmured as Ben kissed her again and led her back inside.

John Baron remained on the footpath until all the others had straggled away. The music had begun again, and 'I Only Have Eyes for You' drifted out of the door to him. He guessed that some of the younger guests would be enjoying themselves for hours yet.

He was unsure how he felt. His little sister had united with Cash. He had meant it with all his heart when he had told her he wanted her to be happy; he really did, more than anything else in the world.

Even living in Melbourne there was the potential of simply jumping on a train to come up here and see her. He had to forget about Samantha Chard Slade: fill his life with substance and excitement. He knew he had done the right thing in deciding to remove himself entirely from this country, right away from her. He leant back on a telegraph pole and watched the dimly lit corner where the Ford had turned right into High Street out of sight. He thought about Cash's parting statement. He had felt at the time that there was some veiled message in it, but the more he considered it, the more he decided he must have been wrong. That was simply Cash. Surely Cash could have no idea how he really felt about his sister? It was impossible. Cash had said he loved Sammy and that consoled JB. If ever Cashman Slade had loved anyone, it appeared to be his sister.

As he stood there, back against the pole in the dark of the Boonah winter night with the levity in the hall behind him, he turned his mind to what he wanted to do when he arrived in England. He knew it now: he wanted to fly. Uncle Wake would be delighted.

He remained outside until a few drops of rain, borne to him on the wind, licked the skin of his face and he returned to the hall to find his uncle on the back verandah drinking a glass of wine, and there they conversed in French for a time. 'For Johnny B, you and your sister and Cashman are the only people in the whole of south-east Queensland who speak my mother's native tongue to me. And I don't see much of Sammy and Cashman these days.'

A little later as the family left for home John Baron strolled to the car alongside his uncle who flicked his walking stick up in the air and pointed back in the darkness. 'I'm delighted you're coming home with us, but I thought you'd be remaining a while longer the way Julie Slade was eyeing you earlier.'

John Baron gave a weak laugh. 'Uncle Wake, has Dad told you what I want to do?'

Wakefield turned to him in the darkness. 'Do you mean about going to England?'

'Yes. I just knew he wouldn't be able to keep it to himself. I'm going to tell Mum and Ledgie next week. I reckon they'll both act up; I'm prepared for that. I hate hurting them, but at least they've become used to the fact that I don't come home every weekend.'

Wakefield cleared his throat. 'Oh, you believe that, do you?'

They were at the ute's side and Ledgie fussed as she searched for blankets to cover the two men who would ride home in the open back.

Randall Slade and his wife and the Birnums all piled into Randall's old truck and they followed the Chards with John Baron and his uncle huddling together against the cold in the back of the vehicle. As Joe the ute ambled along John Baron confided, 'You of all people know that my whole life I've loved aeroplanes and flying. I suppose you and Sir Charles Kingsford Smith were my heroes.'

'Ah laddie, now Kingsford Smith, he was a real hero, flying like that across the world in his Southern Cross. He and Charles Ulm, and Hinkler – all brave men. Did so much for aviation. But me? I was just a fighter in the war.'

'I don't know how you can say that! You were brave and courageous. Fought in Flanders and then went into the Royal Flying Corps. You were shot down and lost your leg. You could be bitter and angry, but you're not. You're wonderful.'

Wakefield said nothing.

'I mean it, Uncle Wake. I've admired you all my life.'

Wakefield reached out and squeezed John Baron's arm. He held it a long time. 'Thank you, Johnny B. *Merci*, my dearest boy.'

'And because of you, probably even more than because of Kingsford Smith, I know what I'm going to do when I get to England. I'm going to join the Royal Air Force.'

'*Ah, mon cher garçon*, I've wondered how long it would take for you to make such a decision. I've seen the way you've loved aircraft and flying since you were a wee spit of a thing and I made your first toy De Havilland for you. I never encouraged you outright for I respect your parents too much. They wanted other things for you. So you became an engineer for their sake, but I continued to speculate on how long you would stay with Potter and Stephens.'

Wakefield did not want his dear boy to go to England. He feared what a lot of people were beginning to fear: that Adolf Hitler had ambitions far beyond German borders, and he thought of twenty odd years before when he had joined the Royal Flying Corps. He sensed that another war could be looming and he worried for the young man beside him, but he was a rational man and rightly supposed that JB must follow his own leanings.

He turned to his companion in the darkness beside him. 'You'll be a fine pilot, Johnny B, I know you will, but you could be one here in Australia. You don't need to go away.'

'I know that, but please understand I must.' In the darkness Wakefield could not see the smile beginning on the young man's mouth but he could sense the kindling excitement and intensity in him as his nephew added, 'Yes, I'm going to be a *real* pilot, just like you were.'

* * *

244

As Cash and Sam rolled along the road towards Peak Crossing where they were to spend their wedding night in the single hotel there – the Exchange Hotel, a rambling country establishment run by an old friend of the Slade family – Cash's arm went around his bride, and believing that it was now or never to make the best of things, Sam snuggled a little closer into him.

The following day, Sunday, they would be travelling to Brisbane to the flat Cash still shared with Dudley Belcher; though they would find their own home on their return from their honeymoon.

Cash gently pressed his wife's shoulder. 'You know, in all the haste and excitement we haven't talked about whether you should keep on with your photography or not.'

Sam sat bolt upright. 'What on earth do you mean?'

'Hey darling, don't flare up. Hush now.' He pulled her back into him. 'What I mean is, you might find it difficult with a baby in the house. They do tend to be fractious, you know.'

'Oh Cash, what the hell does that mean?'

'Fretful, cranky, not easy to manage. A bit like you at the moment.'

She dug him in the ribs.

'Ouch! Look, m'lady, think about it. For instance you can't go into Wilde's Photography Centre every day and nurse a baby, can you?'

Sam sighed. 'Oh Cash, I know that, but I couldn't give up taking my pictures, I'd die. I was just hoping we could work something out. Perhaps even start my own studio or something. I reckon I know enough.'

'Hell, that'd be hard work.'

'I don't mind. And I could get someone to look after the baby. Or I could do assignments. I think *PIX* would give me half a dozen a year.' She made a sharp disgusted sound and wriggled in closer to her new husband. 'Anyway, Wilde's despicable. I'm never going back there – ever.' She paused before she added, 'I've been going to tell you about something and I . . . well, I haven't.'

'What's that, m'lady?'

245

She hesitated. 'Well . . .'

'Well what?'

'Do you remember I told you he's been having an affair with Jan the receptionist?'

'Yeah.'

'I'm not sure how to tell you this.'

Cash halted the car with such force on the brakes that they both shot forward, dust billowed all around from the dirt road and Sam nearly hit the windscreen. 'That bastard hasn't been trying anything on you, has he?'

Sam attempted to gather herself.

He turned to face her in the weak glow thrown backwards from the headlights. 'Sammy, what are you attempting to say?'

'I'm trying to tell you he's forced me to kiss him a couple of times and . . . Look, he's just a dirty old man. I haven't been into the dark room without Leon his other assistant, now for ages.'

'Why?'

'A while back I even had a few bad dreams about him but that's nothing. Actually I sort of took him as a joke, that is – until I told him I was marrying you.'

As time passed, Sam would learn to recognise the placidity which now descended over Cash as seriously ominous, but these were the early days and she had no experience of it, so when he said, 'Tell me all about it, everything, so I understand,' in a dispassionate and unruffled tone, she did so.

'Last Wednesday week I asked him for four weeks off, including this week and the three for the honeymoon. He was really annoyed, complaining strongly that a few days' notice for a month off wasn't acceptable. Then I told him I was getting married to you today and so I had to take the time, and that was all there was to it. He looked at me really strangely and asked if I *had to get married*?'

'I told him it was none of his business and he gave a dirty laugh and said that any girl who comes to work and says she's getting married in nine days' time has to be pregnant. Anyway, he reluctantly agreed I could have the time off so that was that.' She took a deep breath and paused.

Cash encouraged her gently. 'Go on, m'lady, tell me the rest.'

'Well, that evening, Leon and I had to finish printing two sets of wedding photos and so we stayed back together. That didn't worry me, we often do that; Leon's nice. About half-past five Wilde and Jan headed off together as they often do and Leon and I bought some sandwiches from Mal's café in Charlotte Street then went back to work. It was well and truly dark and cold and we were hurrying to finish the photographs when Leon came over really ill. He vomited and almost fainted and looked terrible . . .'

Abruptly Sam broke off and began to cry.

Cash took her in his arms and kissed her wet face. 'Now, now, m'lady. Everything's all right. Just complete your tale and you won't ever have to tell it again.'

She looked up into his eyes. 'Cash, I've been all right until right now, I really have. I wasn't even going to tell you about it. I thought I was over it. It's just that starting to recount it to you has made me . . .' She began crying again.

'Yes, sweetheart, I understand, but you must tell me. Come on.'

'Well, Leon was in such a bad way that I made him go home. It would have been about nine or so by then and knowing that Wilde would be impossible if we hadn't finished the job I said I'd complete it and close up myself.

'Leon made me lock the door from the inside and he went. I suppose it was only about ten minutes later when I heard the door being unlocked. It was Wilde. He closed the door and stood leaning on the wall smoking a cigarette, then asked where Leon was. I lied and said he'd just gone out for a minute and he was coming back. He gave a sort of sinister smile as if he knew better. That's when I realised he must have been watching the place. He came over to me and said now he knew what sort of girl I was, having to get married and all. That if I were *doing it* with you then I could *do it* with him.' She hesitated and turned her head into her husband's chest and he kissed her forehead.

'He threw the cigarette down and I went to pass him to go for the door but he grabbed me.' She cried a little and Cash stroked her tenderly on the hair.

'He ripped my blouse and I'm not sure . . . I think he pushed me onto the floor. I was screaming and he was on top of me. That's when I got the bruises – he was practically choking me to shut me up. I thought I was done for when all of a sudden Leon was back. He was wielding something –I think it was a studio lamp. Anyway, Leon hit him with it and Wilde jumped to his feet, yelling that I was a whore and that we were both sacked. Then he was gone. I was so upset but Leon calmed me down, helped me and saw me home.

'Leon told me he had felt an eerie sensation when he got up to Eagle Street and something had made him come back even though he still felt sick.' She wiped her face with her hand and Cash lifted it and kissed it lovingly.

'Don't worry, sweetheart. The bastard will pay.' He held her close and whispered tender words to her, calling her m'lady and saying how she was the most beautiful girl in the world.

Now that she had emptied herself of the account, Sam composed herself. 'Thank you,' she said softly.

'You forget all about it. It's over now for you, m'lady. All over.'

'What are you going to do?' Her voice wobbled again.

'Not sure, but the bastard will get what's coming to him. I'll make certain he thinks twice about attempted rape in future.' Then he gave a gentle laugh. 'Hey come on, this is an historic moment, our nuptial night.'

He steered the Ford back onto the dirt road and accelerated, laughing again. 'Belcher, the little beauty, donated us a bottle of champagne. Do you know how stupendous a feat it is, m'lady, even to discover the whereabouts of champagne in these trying times? If the redoubtable Exchange Hotel sports an ice-chest in the establishment, we'll cool it and perhaps even you can have *one* glass, Mrs Slade.'

And now Sam sighed and thought suddenly about her

new name and sank back into the seat murmuring, 'Yes, that's a good idea, without my parents to watchdog over me.'

That night Cash kissed his wife tenderly and drew her into the waiting bed where they drank their champagne and lay in each other's arms. Cash made love to his wife and Sam responded. She had always been attracted to Cash and now she had decided she would love him. He was the father of the seed that grew within her, the man with whom she was aligned. JB was unattainable, always had been, always would be, but this man was right here in her arms. There was an old saying, 'If you can't be with the one you love then love the one you're with': that would be her motto, and as she truly believed her new husband loved her, she was willing to live in the belief that in attempting to return it, she in fact would do so. Their slender athletic bodies came together and ignited. Later Cash stroked her naked-ness and whispered, 'Sammy, I want you again,' and the hotel's best room was host to their youthful endurance.

The following day they drove down to Brisbane, stopping in Ipswich to eat their sandwiches in Queen's Park up on a bush-covered hillock, for in respect of the Sabbath, there were no shops, businesses or cafés open. In the noonday sun they climbed to the top of the rise where Cash turned and kissed his new wife and Samantha laughed and quixotically named the spot *Mount Farest*. 'Because it's far away from worldly care and it's where we rested.' He took her hand and they meandered comfort-ably back to their vehicle and drove up the charming white concrete road dotted with black stones which had been built by men doing relief work during the earlier years of the Depression.

Cash pulled Sam closer as he drove down Chermside Road to the Five Ways intersection and turned right into Brisbane Road for the last twenty-three miles of their journey to the Brisbane suburb of Toowong.

It was just over an hour later when they drove into the yard of the flat to be greeted by the next-door neighbour,

Art Brown, who was mowing his front lawn. He ceased his work and leant over the fence. 'So you're back, Cashman.'

Cash introduced Sam. 'Salutations, Art. This is my bride.'

Art lifted his hat. 'How do you do,' and as Cash ushered Sam up the front steps he called back to his neighbour, 'I'm looking forward to my second night of wedlock spent peacefully in front of the wireless with my wife.'

'Good idea,' Art replied.

Hence it was with some amazement that Sam heard her husband say, as nine o'clock approached and they sat in front of the wireless singing along to 'Goody Goody', one of the year's most popular songs, that he was going out.

'What – on a Sunday night? Where to? And it's freezing out there.'

Her husband bent down to where she sat, feet up on a stool, and kissed the nape of her neck. 'M'lady, it's important. I can't explain right now. Trust me.' He crossed to the door and turned back, grinning. 'Have a hot bath and a cup of tea, go to bed, and read a little. I'll be in your arms before you know it.'

'But I don't want to stay here alone, and it's only my second night of married life.'

'M'lady, I assure you I wouldn't relinquish a few hours with you unless it were absolutely necessary.'

'Are you taking the car?'

He shook his head. 'Due to my own laxity I'm almost out of petrol and there are no garages open on Sunday.'

'How long will you be?'

'I'll return by the witching hour.'

'Midnight? Where on earth can you be going?'

'Don't interrogate me.'

'I'm not.'

'You are.'

'God, Cash, you're incredible.'

'Thanks, m'lady. Makes a change from incorrigible.' He closed the door and was gone.

Cash caught the last train into the city and alighted in Brunswick Street where he waited fifteen minutes before he caught a tram out along Bowen Bridge Road. When he disembarked he traversed two dark streets: Sunday nights were quiet times, a lot like being becalmed at sea.

He had brought Sammy to his objective to deliver some prints about six months ago. It was a brick house with a hedge at the front, and nestling in a large block with trees. As he paused by the front fence he guessed it must be close to ten.

Taking three deep breaths he reconnoitred the outside of the house. He knew that no dog was kept; one thing for which he was grateful. There were lights in some rooms and he took hold of the sill and pulled himself up to look in a front window. It was a bedroom and it was empty. Silently he passed round to the side and did the same again. Reflected light from a corridor within showed a lounge room but it too was vacant. He raised himself a third and fourth time to look into what appeared to be empty bedrooms. Passing round to the back he eased himself by the outside toilet and the bushes that surrounded it to mount the steps and gaze through the window to the lighted kitchen. Wilde, in a blue sweater, sat at the table, a periodical open in front of him. He seemed to be alone in the house just as Cash had believed he would be, for he knew the man was living apart from his wife.

He was drinking beer out of a Flag Ale bottle and he gave a wide smirk at something he was reading and ran his hand across his moustache as he turned over the page.

Cash tapped gently on the back door.

The occupant of the house lifted his head inquiringly.

Cash tapped again.

Putting down his drink the man crossed to the door.

Cash tapped a touch louder.

The door opened. 'Who's out here?' He peered into the darkness.

The man's face registered shock as, in one rapid movement, Cash stepped forward and pulled him out onto the porch, hitting him hard in the stomach and sending Dexter Wilde stumbling back against the wall.

'What the Christ?' Wilde regained his balance holding

his hand to his middle. Then he recognised Cash. 'Slade, what the bloody hell are you doing here?'

'I'm here to teach you to leave my wife alone.'

'I don't know what you're talking about.'

Cash lashed out and grabbed him again, hitting him so hard that Wilde half-fell, half-stumbled down the four steps onto his back lawn.

'You bastard!' Wilde spat.

Cash followed him and swung another punch as Wilde scrambled to his feet and hit back in defence. Cash grabbed his arm and they grappled together, stumbling sideways across a garden bed and spewing dirt everywhere.

Suddenly Wilde broke free and pulled a pocket-knife from his trousers. 'You shit!' he yelled as the blade flicked out. 'Coming here to teach me something, eh? We'll see.' He lunged forward, swinging the blade. Cash spun to the side avoiding the point, but Wilde rounded on him and swung the weapon in an arc across his body almost catching the front of Cash's jacket. In that second Cash attempted to grab his opponent's wrist with his right hand, but the older man knew how to handle a knife for he reared back and twisted his wrist out of Cash's grasp to bring the blade back up menacingly between them. Cash hit out with his left hand as Wilde swept the knife across between their bodies and Cash felt the graze of its point catching him fleetingly on the side of his neck.

Both men were desperate now and Cash threw up his right hand again. This time it latched firmly around his adversary's wrist and Wilde suddenly dropped the blade. They dived for the knife but Wilde reached it first and now they grappled together on the ground, Cash grabbing at Wilde's wrist to gain the blade and to hurl it out of reach.

Grunting and groaning, the two men tumbled across a second garden bed. Wilde was on top of his assailant now and was forcing the razor edge closer and closer to the younger man's neck. They were both tiring fast, and in a violent gathering of all his might, Cash drove the man's hand away from himself.

Wilde gave a grunt and then what started as a scream

ended in a gurgling half-groan as he collapsed onto his opponent.

Cash extricated himself from beneath Wilde's body and rolled him over. He knelt there panting, perspiration beads covering his face, looking down at the man, a tiny trickle of blood seeping into his shirt collar. It was two or three seconds before he realised he could see only the handle of the knife; the blade was lodged completely in Wilde's chest and blood had begun to ooze from the wound.

There was no movement from Wilde. He lay in the cold pallid light cast across the garden from his kitchen window. It was obvious he was dead.

'Hell.' This was not what he had come for: he had come to give the bastard a hiding, not to kill him!

'Dexter?' A woman's voice resounded through the back door. 'What the devil's going on out there?'

Electric twinges of adrenalin blasted through Cash as he bounded to his feet. He watched the female push the door open. She stood there, backlit by the illuminated kitchen, her body clearly exposed in a filmy nightdress. 'Dexter? I said what the devil's going on?' She took three steps across the porch, raising her hand to her eyes to look out into the night. 'Where are you?'

Cash turned and ran.

He raced down the side of the house and out into the street. As he charged off down the sealed road he believed he heard the woman's scream and he imagined her bending over the dead man. This brought him to more speed and he fled along the two dark streets he had traversed to come here.

So there was a bloody woman in the house all the time. Where the hell had she been? In the bathroom?

He knew he had to think clearly about what to do now. He soon reached the point on the main road where he had arrived earlier by tram. Being after ten on a Sunday night the trams had ceased to run and he halted under a tree. Fortunately even the main road was dimly lit and devoid of traffic.

He was aware that his fingerprints would be on the knife

253

that had killed Wilde: the first time ever he had allowed such a thing to happen. He berated himself for not extricating the knife but consoled himself with the knowledge that he was not a wanted man so the police did not have his prints on file.

He was not frightened; it was not in Cash's nature, even though tonight's operation had gone dreadfully wrong.

He always experienced elation after a burglary and indeed the night he was caught in the house in Hamilton Heights he was positively exhilarated when he had outrun his pursuers. He loved darkness, clandestine actions and secrecy; they fanned the fire of his soul, and tonight's exploits fell wholly into those categories. He was angered by the fact that Wilde had pulled a knife but at the same time the entire turn of events excited him.

He felt little sorrow for what he had done. In his reasoning it had followed naturally from the fight. If Wilde had not pulled the knife, he would not be dead. 'I was trying to throw the bloody knife out of reach,' Cash explained to the night as he began to run along the gutter.

He believed that even if the woman had a telephone in the house and had called the police it would be some time before they arrived. He continued running in the direction of the city and within ten minutes he could see the lights of the Brisbane Hospital and an idea came to him.

A smile settled on his mouth as he darted across the relatively wide road and ran up into O'Connell Terrace at the rear of the hospital. When he arrived at the area behind the children's hospital where those of the staff fortunate enough to own a vehicle parked, he chose a small utility truck close to the entrance. He soon had it started. He took his gloves from his pocket and put them on: he was not going to leave his fingerprints anywhere for a second time in the same night!

Stealing vehicles was a relatively new crime and Cash was well aware that having this mode of transport gave him great versatility and allowed him to complete his still forming plans. He drove along Gregory Terrace through Spring Hollow and halted in the murky shadows of a warehouse at the end of a seedy thoroughfare called Love Street. Highly aware of the hour, Cash dashed along to an old wooden two-storeyed dwelling and up the side steps three at a time. On a completely dark landing he knocked seven times and repeated it.

The door opened and a dim beam of electric light hit him.

'Oh, it's you, Professor. Bit late, isn't it?'

'Are you alone?'

'Yep. Always alone Sunday nights.' Creedy took off the horn-rimmed glasses he had been using to read and held the door for Cash to squeeze by his rotund belly into a kitchen with a tailor's bench for a table in the middle. One electric bulb hung over it, illuminating the newspaper he had been reading and reflecting on grubby curtains that once had been white.

'Gawd, ya're sweatin' like a pig. Look like ya've run a bloody marathon.' He pointed with his thick forefinger to Cash's collar. 'There's blood on ya collar. What happened?'

Cash touched the side of his neck and there were no smears on his fingertips: the blood had dried on the small cut he had sustained. 'Nothing significant,' he replied, 'I need a gift. Something special. A bracelet or a brooch.'

'Shit, ya've stolen enough of those yourself. Didn't ya keep any?'

'Creedy, that's rhetorical. Do you have something?'

Creedy took up the glass of sherry he had been drinking and gulped a large portion. 'Want a drink? Ya look like ya need one.'

'I'll have some water.'

'Water? Jees, ya're desperate all right.' He pointed with his thumb to a soiled sink in the corner and his visitor went over and turned on the tap, splashing water up onto his face and drinking out of his cupped palms. He took off his shirt and rinsed out the small bloodstain on his collar as he continued speaking. 'Look, I haven't time to be sociable, mate. I have to keep moving. Now a piece of jewellery, I beseech you. Untraceable, obviously.'

The fat man raised his eyebrow quizzically. 'Come on. What've ya been up to, Professor?'

'Look, Creedy, I just need the jewellery. I'm not going to give you a discourse on my private Sunday-night life.' He wiped his hands on his trousers as he spoke. It was at that moment he noticed his bare right wrist and realised his watch was gone.

'Hell!'

Creedy was laughing and lumbering over to a dilapidated wooden dresser. He turned smartly, which was a feat for a man of his size. 'What was that?'

'Nothing.' Cash looked away, his heart accelerating and then, suddenly remembering he had not worn his watch tonight, a sound of relief escaped his lips.

Creedy sniffed and gave him a long searching look. 'What's goin' on? You in trouble, Professor?'

'No, not at all. It's nothing. I thought something had happened but I was wrong. Come on, Creed, where's the jewellery?'

The big man continued studying him for a few seconds before he moved to the dresser and pulled out a drawer. He delved through some boxes, took hold of something and brought it back to the table, placing it down.

'Creedy, it's a masterpiece.'

'Yeah? I know. It'll cost ya twelve quid.'

'Christ, old man, that's an impediment to the transaction. How about five?'

'No.' He shook his head.

'Seven?'

'I'll take eight. It's worth a bloody sight more.' He poured himself another sherry and flopped into a chair that groaned under his weight. Lifting his beady eyes to his visitor he added, 'Ya can pay me after ya come back from ya little trip.'

Cash paused; his fingers drummed in mild agitation on the surface near the turquoise and sapphire brooch. 'Who enlightened you about that?'

Holding the full glass of sherry in his right hand, Creedy picked up the half-empty bottle in his left and took a long swig. 'A little bird. So ya went and tied the knot. Ya didn't tell ya friends ya were gettin' married, Professor. I'm real hurt I wasn't invited to the big do. Felt left out I did, like ya were ashamed of me.'

'Creedy, you're hardly in my coterie of close friends. You and I see each other on a business basis.'

'Ah well, in that case the price for the brooch goes back to twelve quid.'

'Shit, Creedy, that's just immoral expediency.'

'It's what?'

'Stop taking shameful advantage of me.'

Creedy burst into laughter and his eyes closed to disappear entirely between rolls of fat. He bent forward on his blubbery arms and rumbling with mirth took another swig from the bottle. 'I love the way ya talk, Professor. I surely do. *Immoral*, yet? Ya use the word as if ya were a high court judge himself. And because ya always give me such a bloody good laugh I'll settle on eight quid after all.'

Cash nodded and took up the brooch as Creedy hit out playfully at his unruly forelock. 'Love ya hair, Professor. Bet ya new wife loves ya hair.'

Cash pulled away from the fat man's reach and pocketed the jewel while Creedy gave another loud guffaw. 'It's not only ya hair, Professor. I reckon ya're very pretty – all of ya. Knew a bloke what looked like you in prison once. Ah, what a bloke.' And as he continued shaking with laughter Cash walked to the door.

'Sure ya don't want ta tell me where ya've been tonight, Professor?'

Cash did not answer, but placed four pound notes on the table. 'I'll have to compensate you for the rest on my return . . .' he opened the door and spoke as he closed it '. . . *from my little trip*.'

As Cash disappeared Creedy called, 'I trust ya, Professor,' and poured out another sherry, a knowing expression taking the place of his rumbling laughter.

At fifteen minutes past midnight Cash walked at speed down the darkened street in Toowong to the flat. He had abandoned the small utility truck near Roma Street Station and run all the way along Milton Road to his home. He was sweating profusely. He had done all he could now and felt confident that his suberterfuge with the gift would fool Sammy. Mounting the back steps he opened the kitchen door and entered the flat.

His new wife's voice resounded from the bedroom. 'Is that you, Cash?'

'Affirmative, m'lady.'

She came through the hall door as he switched on the light. She wore pyjamas and looked fresh and clean. 'My heaven, the perspiration's running off you like water. Where on earth have you been?'

He sat down on the nearest chair and took the box out of his inside pocket. He put it down on the table and opened it. 'To obtain this for you.'

Sam's eyes widened in surprise. 'But I don't understand.'

'I had to cross the city to an acquaintance of mine, an erstwhile jeweller who occasionally still makes these. I wanted to give it to you so you could wear it on your honeymoon. And as I'm wingless I couldn't fly, hence when the trains and trams stopped for the night I ran much of the way.'

The frown Sam already wore deepened. 'But, darling, you could have gone for it tomorrow.'

'He's leaving Brisbane tomorrow – going to Bundaberg. Oh, m'lady, you haven't even told me whether you approve of my great journey?' He pointed to the brooch.

'Oh Cash, I love it. It's absolutely beautiful. This sort of jewellery's so expensive. I don't know what to say. You're too extravagant.'

'Not where my wife's concerned.' He pinned it on her pyjamas making her smile.

'Oh Cash darling, I missed you and I still don't quite understand it . . . And running home this way. You're exhausted. But thank you.'

She kissed him gingerly on his damp cheek. 'I don't really care about receiving gifts and you didn't need to go to all the trouble of going out and getting this for me, you know.'

'Ah but I did, m'lady, truly I did.'

Chapter Nineteen

September, 1937

John Baron sped along on his motor bike through Gerrards Cross, Buckinghamshire, heading south. Even the lowering sky that threatened rain did not dampen his mood. He felt released and free, and though he was aware of the burden of loving his sister, much of the time he had been able to sublimate his thoughts of Sam since being in England and thus his life had altered.

He had left his ship from Australia in Marseilles early the previous November and travelled for three weeks through France, where it had surprised and delighted him when people verified that his accent was first-rate. He had visited Champagne and spent his birthday in Reims where Wakefield's mother had been born, and he had visited a number of war cemeteries and thought of all the men who had given their lives in the Great War. It had made him reflect on the current state of Europe and how his parents had wished him not to come here. The Spanish Civil War rolled on and now that he was here he realised that people in Europe gave lip service to peace but speculated on war.

He had a week in Paris and succumbed to its charm, wandering through Montmartre and along the Seine and writing long letters to Wakefield about it all.

He took a ferry from Calais to Dover and the first thing he did on English soil was to write to the Air Ministry. While he waited to hear from the Royal Air Force, the King had abdicated on 10 December and his brother George had become sovereign. It was all because of a twice-divorced American woman whom Edward loved. JB felt sympathy for the King: love was not something that could be dictated and kings were not impervious to such feelings. The British people were polarised about it.

Before Christmas he was given a preliminary interview by a panel of five officers of the RAF at the Air Ministry in Adastral House, Queensway, London. There were a lot of questions, and an old Cambridge man with a monocle looked down his aquiline nose and asked, 'And so, young man, oblige us with the reasons why you might, just might, be suited to be a pilot.'

'Well, sir, when I'm flying I feel as if I were born to be in the air, in the cockpit of an aircraft. I see very well and I've been told my reflexes are acute. I believe I'm very fit, I have no illnesses and I have no responsibilities, no wife, no girlfriend. These things make me believe I'm the right sort of material for a pilot.' Three of the panel nodded which JB took to be a good sign and the Cambridge man commented, 'I met your Kingsford Smith once and I have to admit he knew how to fly. Perhaps it's natural in Australians.'

John Baron did not know whether this was a joke or not, but he took a chance and answered, 'Well, if it is, sir, then perhaps you should take advantage of it.' This was met by a brief rumble of laughter from the chairman of the panel and some uninterpretable looks from the others, but when he issued once more out into the chill damp air of Queensway he felt he had done his best. Next he submitted to a stringent medical examination at the RAF Central Medical Board in Gower Street.

To his delight, within the month he had received a letter instructing him to report to the Elementary and Reserve Flying Training School at Hanworth, London Air Park. Here he spent two months as a pupil pilot before he went on to the RAF Depot in Uxbridge for two weeks of drilling and training in the customs of the Service, as well as the fitting for his uniform.

Uxbridge had been followed by six months at a Service Flying Training School at South Cerney near Cirencester where he spent two terms, the first a Junior term in converting to service types and all forms of advanced flying: low flying, night flying – greatly relying on instruments and formation flying. After that came a Senior term in applied flying including bombing, navigation, signals and gunnery.

There, after his very first few circuits with his instructor Sergeant 'Cracker' Day – a diminutive man with a lugubrious expression which misrepresented his happy nature – it was apparent that John Baron's Melbourne lessons had given him a good knowledge of handling an aircraft. Cracker immediately sent him up solo and instead of weeks in the Blackburn B2s, Cracker soon had his protégé flying Hawker Harts and Audaxes.

Now, as John Baron sped along on his motor bike he thought of how he had departed from Cracker the previous morning.

'You'll soon be a Flying Officer, sir,' Cracker had said, taking his hand and grinning. 'So give 'em all you've got down at Northolt.'

As they had walked out to John Baron's waiting motor bike with his belongings tied to the back, Cracker slapped him on the shoulder. 'You're a good pilot, sir. No, in fact you're one of the best I've ever seen. You didn't need me to teach you much but there are two things I'd like to think you did, in fact, learn from me.'

'I'm listening.'

'Don't be one of those flyers who talks about *kite*s or *plane*s. *Aeroplane* or *aircraft* are the words you should use in referring to the machine that will be a part of you as surely as your soul. So, sir, give it some respect.'

The young man recognised the good advice. 'Yes, I understand. What's the other?'

Cracker pursed his lips and eyed his ex-pupil silently for a few moments. 'The other is: don't do aerobatics below two thousand feet. All right?'

John Baron had believed his little airshows at what he thought were discreet distances from the aerodrome, had taken place for his own private benefit. Now he knew better. Cracker could have reported him and had not.

261

Grateful, he grinned. 'Yes, Cracker. Thanks.'

Cracker shook his index finger. 'Believe me, sir, you'll live longer if you follow my advice and you're too good a darn pilot to end your career before it begins. I knew a spiffing good pilot in thirty-one, name of Bader, who insisted on taking dares and flying low, and he ended up without legs and out of the Force.'

'I take your point, Cracker.' He had left the Sergeant standing in the floating autumn mist outside the mess and rode away on his motor bike giving a long wave of his hand.

There were four free days before he needed to report to Northolt and so he spent them riding around the country-side of Oxfordshire and Buckinghamshire visiting the little villages, eating lunches and dinners in wayside inns and staying in tiny pubs. He walked the country footpaths by woods and streams and at times just stood and admired the chocolate box scene beauty of the land. In these quiet moments he thought of his loved ones at Haverhill so far away; and always then Sam stole into his mind, and he would catch his breath and try to think of other things and dismiss the ghostly visits from his sister.

On the day he was due at the airfield he headed in towards London, the largest city in the world with 8.2 million souls.

He came out of Gerrards Cross travelling comfortably along the undulating slopes and a little while later on a long gradual rise he laughed out loud, and as a few drops of caressing rain cooled his face, he overtook a small grey lorry at close to 45 m.p.h., his laughter lost on the wind.

Suddenly his vision was completely filled by an oncoming car travelling at great speed. Horns blasted and men's voices yelled and even as he swerved to avoid what he now realised was an MG, he knew he had miscalculated badly. The oncoming sports car missed him by a finger width and careered noisily into the lorry behind. And as John Baron's bike shot off at a tangent from the road another motor bike, appearing as if from outer space, collided with his back wheel, resulting in both riders being thrown from their seats to go soaring through the air.

When John Baron came to he was lying on his back covered with sticks and bare branches and a discarded five-gallon oil tin perched precariously in a bush above his head. He now realised the lorry had hidden the crossroad ahead and he had failed to see the swiftly converging vehicle.

He sat up to calculate whether he was hurt or not. He was in a ditch and fortuitously the bracken had broken his fall. Gingerly he rotated his neck from side to side and as he could move his arms and legs he assumed there were no breakages. He had a pain in his left shoulder and his left knee was hurting but he stood up perfectly well, if a little shaky, and looked upon the scene of devastation in front of him.

His bike was lying against a tree trunk. The rider of the bike from outer space was wobbling towards him, trouser-torn and holding his head: his vehicle lay on its side in the road and had lost its front wheel. The driver of the lorry was standing hands on hips surveying his twisted bumper bar which had the damaged nose of the MG lodged against it.

A strong smell of oil and petrol wafted on the air as John Baron extricated himself from the bracken and climbed up the side of the ditch to the road.

'Are you the silly bugger who passed me?' the lorry driver, a big man in grey overalls, shouted angrily, waving his hands in the air and John Baron walking slowly towards him, nodded.

'Christ! I'm late already. Look at this. What the hell did you think you were playing at?'

John Baron could not readily reply to that and the rider of the bike from outer space came unsteadily over to him. 'Where the devil did *you* come from?' At first his accent sounded Irish.

'Up the hill, of course,' John Baron answered. 'I was passing the lorry.'

'Well, that wasn't real smart when you were heading into an intersection,' the bike rider responded, dabbing the graze on his forehead.

John Baron was about to defend himself when the lorry

driver bore down on the newcomer. 'And why the hell did you come into an intersection at that sorta speed? It's a wonder you weren't bloody killed.' He shoved the man in the chest and the man shoved him back. John Baron raised his hands to restrain them.

'Come on now, none of that, steady on. Let's act in a civilised manner.'

'Civilised?' exploded the big man. 'All I was doing was driving along minding my own business and I meet you three maniacs. I'm supposed to be at my depot by two o'clock!' He was now bright red in the face and he smacked JB's hands away and turned round to exclaim at the MG driver. 'And you, you're nothing but a lunatic the way you raced into the intersection!' And he marched over to the car where the driver remained seated inside.

'I'm still not used to driving on the left side of the road,' the rider from outer space confided to John Baron.

'Ah, you're American.'

They followed the grey overalls to the side of the MG where a pair of bold eyes under a high brow above a freckled round face looked out at them, but before the man could speak the lorry driver continued to extend his wrath. 'Look what your bloody car's done to my bumper bar.'

'Hang on, old man, I suspect my car's not getting off scot free,' the freckled face replied.

'But you're to blame,' the big man shouted.

'And you're a clot,' retorted the MG driver.

The lorry driver growled in offence and his hand went in the window as if he were going to drag the speaker through it.

'Hold on.' John Baron grabbed the sizeable arm.

'Listen,' exclaimed the MG driver, 'I don't like your bloody attitude.'

'Oh my Gawd!' The big man in overalls pointed down inside the MG, his fury subsiding. 'You poor bugger. Hang on, we'll soon have you out!' He pulled the door of the MG open. 'Quick, let's get this fella outta here. He's broken his ankle real bad. Better get an ambulance.'

John Baron looked down at the MG driver's trousers and

to his surprise he saw the man's right foot and shoe were twisted at a ninety-degree angle away from his leg.

The lorry driver had opened the door and was kneeling down to look at the broken ankle, but the man in the MG said, 'I'm all right.'

'All right? But you can't be.'

And now the driver of the MG began to laugh. The big man's face dropped. 'Are you daft? How can you laugh?' He glanced up to John Baron and his companion. 'Give me a hand with 'im.'

The MG driver glanced longsufferingly skywards. 'Please just move away so I can get out.' And as the man in overalls stood he lifted himself up from the seat to a standing position on his left leg. He balanced by holding onto the door beside the car.

The lorry driver's face blanched. 'Bloody hell, your right foot's still in the car.' And sure enough there it was, in sock and shoe, lying on the floor.

John Baron was still dazed but he noticed that the clutch was where the accelerator should be and vice versa and all of a sudden he understood. 'You've got an artificial leg.'

The man nodded. 'The fact is, old boy, I've got two.'

'Gor blimey,' the big man exclaimed, driving his fist into the hood of the car for emphasis as the MG driver eased himself round to sit on the bonnet.

At that moment two police constables arrived and interviewed them one at a time; the lorry and MG were moved off the middle of the road and excuses were made and statements taken.

The big man's vehicle was driveable and he sped off irritated and grumbling about being late. The MG's radiator was intact and its engine started even though it had a broken grille and a dented bumper bar. John Baron's motor bike had miraculously survived with only a few scratches though his belongings had shot in various directions. The other bike was badly damaged.

When the police departed the three men faced each other. The rain that had continued to threaten now began to fall and the American's hair glistened as he faced them. 'It's all right for you two but my bike's had it.'

'All right, you reckon?' shot back the MG driver. 'Not blasted likely. Fixing the front of my car and repairing my foot's going to set me back a bit.'

'Look, what if we all chip into a sort of pool?' John Baron suggested.

The American thought for a moment. 'I suppose so. It's one way of doing it.'

'I'm on my way to Northolt air base, you can contact me there.'

The American looked surprised. 'You don't say? I've just been assigned there myself, with the newly formed 85 Squadron. I've just completed my training at South Cerney.'

'Lucky blighters,' spoke up the MG driver. 'Used to be in the RAF myself but now it appears it's full of Yanks and Australians.'

'Thanks a lot.'

The American eyed them both. 'About time we were formally introduced. My name's Forest Russell but my friends call me "Twig".'

'Right. My name's John Baron Chard, but my friends call me "JB".'

'And my name's Douglas Robert Steuart Bader, and strangely enough my friends call me . . . "Douglas".' They all laughed and it eased the mood. Douglas Bader handed JB a card. 'You can get me at Shell Oil.' He slid himself back into the MG and looked up at them. 'Be careful because you're two of the worst bloody drivers I've ever met.'

'You fall into that category yourself, old man,' John Baron declared. 'Are you certain you can drive that thing without a foot?'

Bader grinned. 'I like a challenge.'

John Baron and Forest watched the MG bounce off in a sort of jump start and roll off along the road.

'Hope he makes it.'

'He will,' John Baron replied as he pumped his foot pedal and the engine coughed and started. 'Reckon I know just who he is. My instructor mentioned him. Crashed doing low aerobatics in 'thirty-one. It was a dare to beat-up the airfield, I think. Lost both his legs. '

Twig was impressed. 'You don't say?'

'Anyway, I'd better take you into Uxbridge – probably the nearest place we'll find a garage.'

They found one and the owner sent a truck out to pick up the bike; but not before they had to pay two pounds deposit. JB paid one, Twig the other.

It was dark when the two new acquaintances reached the main gate of the areodrome and reported in.

The following morning Pilot Officer John Baron Chard drew flying kit and was walking back to his room with log book, helmet, goggles, Sidcot flying suit and immaculate black flying boots when he saw Twig coming along the corridor.

They met and halted. 'Doing anything Friday night?' the American asked and John Baron replied in the negative.

'A bunch of us are going over to the Orchard at Ruislip. Want to join us?'

'Yes. Thanks, I'd like that.'

'You'll need to give me a lift. It's really your blasted fault my bike's in the garage, you know.'

'Well, we won't argue about that.'

So the next Friday evening the new friends found themselves in the company of several Flying Officers and a couple of other Pilot Officers in the congenial smoke-filled bar of the Orchard pub, and there they continued to cement their friendship by both laughing at each other's jokes. On the following Saturday JB took Twig down to Uxbridge to pick up his bike. They had been invited to spend the night at one of their comrades' homes in Camberley, Surrey. There was a house party going on and a group of their compatriots would be there.

They had lunch in a pub and both drank four beers. When they arrived at the garage, the mechanic was still working on Twig's bike but he was assured it would be ready within the hour.

'No point in waiting for me,' Twig said. 'The guy says an hour but it might be two or more – you go on.' He leant on the side of the garage door and began to whistle 'Way Down South in Dixie'.

'Right, I'll see you in Camberley,' JB shouted as he set off onto the road. He sailed along through Windsor Great Park and on southwards by Ascot. He was nearing the village of Bagshot when suddenly he felt thirsty and on seeing a roadside sign reading *The Pantiles: Morning Coffee, Lunches, Cream Teas, Open till 5 p.m.* he brought the bike to a standstill and parked near three cars on a stretch of gravel in front of what looked like a converted barn with leaded windows set in a garden dotted with ornamental trees. People – in the main women – sat at small tables.

He thought they would surely sell lemonade and he strode briskly in through the door and virtually slammed headlong into a man who was exiting, talking back over his shoulder as he did so.

They rounded on one another.

'You!' John Baron exclaimed. 'I don't believe it!'

It was Douglas Bader. 'Hell, JB, you're always running into me.'

'From where I see it, Douglas, you're always running into *me*!'

They shook hands.

'What are you doing here?'

'Ah . . . My fiancée helps the owners out as a waitress now and then.' Douglas turned and called to a slender girl carrying a cream tea on a silver platter. 'Come and meet an Australian, darling. He could do with an introduction to a cultured English girl.'

The girl breezed over. She had a fine-boned face and a small mouth that was quick to smile.

'Thelma, meet JB.'

'How do you do?'

'I'd appreciate a lemonade if it's all the same to you.'

Thelma pointed to an empty table near a terracotta pot brimming with lilac. 'Take a seat.'

'He's the Australian I told you about, darling.'

'Oh. The one in the accident?'

Douglas nodded.

Thelma gave a longsuffering look skywards. 'Douglas is always having them. He's quite a dab hand at accidents. You're just the most recent in a long list.' Douglas looked affronted and she hit him playfully on the arm. 'I forgive him though.' As she moved away she said, 'I'll be back shortly.'

John Baron sat and Douglas eased into a chair next to him. 'I'm afraid Thelma's right. I've had more than my share of car accidents. Last year near Virginia Water I even stopped to see if I could help in a two-car collision and before I could get out of the MG a bloody motor bike and side-car head butted it.'

John Baron began to laugh.

And Douglas, seeing the funny side, joined him.

'Well anyway, I'm glad to see your foot's back on your leg.'

'This is an extra set I keep for emergencies. The other's still being mended. How are you settling into the Air Force?'

And JB told him. They were still seated at 5 p.m. when the Pantiles closed and Thelma came over in her coat ready to leave. Since their collision, John Baron had learnt more about Douglas Bader and now Douglas enlarged on his story and revealed that he had refused a desk job in the Air Force after the loss of his legs and that he missed flying more than anything. His perpetual dream was that one day he would fly again.

John Baron spoke about himself, how he had been born in Lymington, had migrated to Australia with his parents after the war and had returned to England, 'to visit the land of my birth', as he put it.

They also discussed Franco and Mussolini, Hitler and Stalin and the fact that war seemed inevitable. 'I know it might sound odd,' Douglas confided, 'and I'm no warmonger, but the minute this war starts with Hitler, and I reckon it will, I'll be back in the air.'

By the time Thelma took Douglas's arm and they left the Pantiles the two men felt a certain comfort with one another. And as they all crossed the lawn to where the MG was parked on the gravel a little way from JB's motor bike, John Baron pointed to it. 'I really should have recognised the broken grille and dented bumper bar.'

'Yes,' rejoined Douglas. 'Being the cause of them, you should have.'

'Unfair!'

'I'm hoping to have it repaired this week,' Douglas called as he opened the door for Thelma, 'so you and Twig will be hearing from me.'

John Baron breezed along behind Douglas and Thelma for a time until suddenly Douglas put his hand outside the window and signalled a halt. Car and motor bike slowed down and pulled to a standstill on the verge.

JB dismounted as Douglas hitched himself up out of the sports car and with his distinctive rolling gait ambled back to the bike. He grinned widely. 'Look, JB, don't ask me why I'm doing this for I hardly know myself, but Thelma and I are getting married next Tuesday morning and I'd like you to be there if you can.'

JB extended his hand. 'Firstly congratulations. Secondly I'd love to be there.'

'Do you play golf?' Douglas asked suddenly and John Baron, who had begun playing since joining the Air Force answered, 'Yes, but my putting's awful.'

Douglas looked delighted. 'Great. Then I should be able to beat you.'

'Has that got anything to do with the wedding?' John Baron queried with a frown.

'No,' his companion beamed, 'but it should have something to do with the game of golf I'd like to play with you after our fortnight's honeymoon down at the Lizard.'

The following Tuesday morning, 5 October 1937, John Baron presented himself at St Mary Abbott's Church in Kensington London and amongst relatives and friends witnessed the marriage of Douglas and Thelma. The legless groom had been granted permission to stand throughout the ceremony as it was a physical impossibility for him to kneel, and as Douglas placed the ring on his bride's finger John

Baron thought of the last wedding he had attended the year before in Christ Church, Boonah, 13,000 miles away. He could not help but wonder how his sister was; he was very aware of her coming birthday and decided that he should write her the promised letter soon.

He watched Thelma taking her vows, her slender shape not unlike Sam's.

After the ceremony people took photographs outside the church and the best man, Geoffrey Darlington, drove John Baron the short distance back to where the wedding breakfast was held, 12 Avonmore Mansions, the home of Thelma's mother and her husband, Lieutenant-Colonel Addison.

Champagne was handed around and all began to consume it steadily. After an hour Douglas was very obviously enjoying himself and as he kissed Thelma on her dainty nose Mrs Addison confided to John Baron as she handed him a canapé, 'My son-in-law doesn't usually drink and he's had four already.'

'Well, I suppose a man doesn't get married every day,' John Baron rejoined and Douglas, who had overheard the remark, laughed loudly, his candid gaze upon his new friend.

Later as the married couple began their preparations to leave, Douglas lurched through the hall to pick up his coat and met John Baron. 'JB, old chap, delighted you came.'

'Yes, me too.'

Douglas looked around; there was no one else in the hall. 'I'm going to tell you something nobody else knows.' The freckled face glowed from the champagne. 'No one other than Thelma, that is, but I need you to swear to secrecy.'

John Baron had drunk his own fill of alcohol and this seemed to him a perfectly normal request. 'Sure, I swear.'

'I heard you say before that you supposed a man doesn't get married every day.'

'Yes.'

'Well, I've been married before.'

John Baron shrugged, assuming that Douglas had either lost his previous wife or been divorced.

Douglas's eyes shone in the hall light hanging above. 'To Thelma . . . four years ago today exactly. We've been husband and wife all that time. Didn't want to wait till the family thought we had enough money; just went off and did it in Hampstead Register Office. Desperately in love, wanted to be together. Funny I should tell you, I suppose, but today I needed to say it to somebody and I can't inform any of them, you see?' He gestured back down the hallway.

'Yes, I do.' John Baron nodded seriously.

'But this was special. Nice ceremony, nice people. Today was for us *and* for them. A celebration. But keep it under your hat, old man.'

'I will. And thanks for telling me.'

Ten minutes later the guests saw the happy couple off to Cornwall amongst loud good wishes, affection, laughter and waving; and the following day in the *Daily Mirror*, under the caption *This man has courage* appeared a photograph of the 'newlyweds' walking out of the church.

A fortnight later John Baron and Douglas played their first of many a game of golf together.

Chapter Twenty

Three months later

Samantha ran up Seven Shilling Beach, known in local Sydney parlance as Seven Bob Beach. It was a tiny cove between the eastern suburbs of Double Bay and Rose Bay, and not overly frequented.

In her black swimming costume – the legs of the fashionable suit covering her thighs – she looked slender and stylish as she fell down onto a towel beside Cash and lifted her face to the sun. It was early summer and the temperatures were already in the high eighties during the day so the couple had become habitués of this sunny hideaway within walking distance of their home.

Her husband turned his bronzed body round to hers. 'We'd better go soon or I'll be late.'

After half a year without work Cash had finally found a job as an engineer in a foundry and had been there some months; not that being jobless seemed to worry him, he still did amazingly well at the races for his luck appeared to have migrated with him from Brisbane. His working hours varied and today being Saturday he was covering the afternoon and evening shift.

Samantha and Cash had relocated to Sydney a few months after their honeymoon. There had been a number of reasons for the move: Cash had fallen in love with the city and Sam knew that she had gone as far as she could in photography in Brisbane. She no longer cared for pretty shots of babies and brides; she wanted to tell stories in photographs, to take pictures which showed how people acted, laboured and lived; *photographic illustration* and *exhibition photography* were her desired aims. And too, the murder of Dexter Wilde had played a part in their decision, for Cash had been adamant that it was in Sam's best interests to forget about her association with him.

They had been notified of the murder on their honeymoon in Sydney and Sam had even been interviewed by the metropolitan Criminal Investigation Bureau, though needless to say she could tell them nothing. On their return to Brisbane she had been interviewed again by the local branch of the CIB.

The Brisbane interview had taken place in the flat they still shared with Belcher in Toowong, on an afternoon a week or so after the return from their honeymoon.

It was one of those Brisbane spring days when the sky is pure blue and the earth sparkles.

There had been a loud knock at the door and Cash answered it to find two big men standing on the porch, their Panama hats over their eyes. One removed his hat and eyeing Cash at the same time asked, 'Does Samantha Slade née Chard live at this address?'

'Yes, who wants her?'

The man showed his identification. 'Detective Sergeant Tom Noble and Detective Ron Seymour. We're from the Criminal Investigation Bureau. Is the lady in question home?'

Cash nodded. 'Ah, plainclothes police. Look, she's already been interviewed in Sydney. Is this necessary?'

'And who are you?'

Cash rested against the door jamb, an indifferent expression in his cold eyes as he looked from one to the other. 'I'm her husband.'

Ron Seymour, a wiry man with a small moustache, put away his identification and Tom Noble moved a step closer. 'Can we come in?'

Cash did not move. 'My wife's pregnant and I'm worried about her condition. There's nothing she can add to what she told the Sydney Police.'

'I think we're the better judges of that, sir. So if you'll move aside . . .'

Cash slowly complied but pointed with his index finger to the mat and the two policemen wiped their feet and entered to see Sam coming forward into the hall.

'This is my wife. These blokes are from the police, Sammy.'

Sam surprised them by shaking their hands – few women did this sort of thing – and the Sergeant gestured into the lounge room behind her. 'We've a number of queries, Mrs Slade. Perhaps it would be better if we all sat down.'

As Sam led them in he continued, 'I know you gave a statement to the Sydney boys, Mrs Slade, but there are a few things we want to clarify.'

Sam eased herself into a chair and Cash moved across and sat on the arm next to her, his hand on her shoulder.

The Detective Sergeant fell to watching what transpired and Ron Seymour conducted most of the interview. He flicked the pages of a notebook, ran a lead pencil down a list and lifted his eyes to Sam's. 'Now Mrs Slade, for the record we need to go over some things one more time. We're doing the same with everyone we believe knew Dexter Wilde well.'

Sam nodded.

'How long had you worked for Mr Wilde?'

'About fifteen months.'

'And you parted from his employment for what reason?'

'She was getting married,' Cash replied.

Noble now entered the interview briefly. He raised his hand, palm towards Cash. 'We'd prefer your wife answered, sir. Your turn will come, as we believe you knew him too.'

'Well, of course I did. He was my wife's employer.'

'So Mrs Slade,' Seymour repeated, 'you left his employment for what reason?'

'As my husband said, I was getting married. I'm having a baby. I couldn't stay on.'

'So your departure from his employ was amicable?'

'Well . . .' Sam paused.

'It's been suggested by others who worked for him that perhaps you and he had not been on good terms.'

'Look, Detective,' Cash interrupted, 'what are you suggesting? That my wife murdered him?'

The policeman gave a small laugh and gazed pointedly back to Sam. 'Were you on good terms with your employer?'

Sam sighed. 'Nobody was really. He came on to any girl who worked for him. He was a real ladies' man. I suppose you could say I'd had enough of him and that's one of the reasons I left, but the main one was that I was getting married, just as I said.'

'Thank you,' Seymour replied, writing something in his notebook. 'And so where were you the night he was killed?'

'I was here. It was the night before we left for Sydney on our honeymoon.'

'And your husband was here with you?'

Cash's hand tightened almost imperceptibly on Sam's shoulder and she answered, 'Yes.'

'Neither of you left this flat all night?'

'That's right.'

Detective Sergeant Noble now looked up to Cash. 'You agree with that, Mr Slade?'

'Obviously.'

'Well, it checks out with what your neighbour Mr Brown told us. He said your car was in the yard all night.'

'Good of him to notice,' Cash responded.

The two policemen nodded simultaneously and Seymour continued, 'Neighbours do notice things.' He lifted his finger to Sam. 'Mrs Slade, do you know of anyone who might have held a grudge against your former employer?'

Sam hesitated. 'I suppose there could be people, but I don't exactly know any.'

'What about the women whom he'd *come on to*, as you put it?'

'Well yes, there might be one or two but I wouldn't know who.'

'You worked with Leon Ware?'

Sam nodded.

'He says that Wilde assaulted you one night and that he saved you.'

'Now look here, this isn't fair . . .' Cash began.

'Please, sir, let the lady answer.'

276

Sam sighed. 'It's true. When Dexter found out I was getting married because I was having a baby, I suppose it made me fair game to him and he waited until I was alone and came into the studio. Yes, he attacked me. If Leon hadn't come in, well . . . it would have been worse.'

'And you knew of this, sir?' The detective lifted his eyes to Cash.

Cash took his hand from Sammy's shoulder and crossed his arms before he answered. 'It was the reason that we decided my wife wouldn't go back to work for him.'

'Did you ever have words with Wilde over that incident?'

Cash edged forward on the arm of the chair. He spoke coolly, calmly, objectively. 'I didn't know the man very well. When I found out about the assault I decided that he was scum. I didn't want Sammy anywhere near him. I thought to come to you and press charges, but my wife didn't want that so we went on our honeymoon. Had the man not been killed, I might still have convinced her to do something about it.'

The detective nodded. 'But you were angry about it?'

'I don't get angry,' Cash replied.

'How sensible,' Detective Sergeant Noble interjected. 'Many a crime's been committed in anger.' He gestured to the detective to continue and Seymour looked down at his book first then back up to Sam.

'Right, Mrs Slade, so the last time you saw him alive was the day you left working for him: Wednesday the twenty-second of July, nineteen thirty-six.'

'Yes.'

'And Mr Slade, the last time you saw him? When was that?'

'I'm not sure. It would have been many weeks before his death. One of the nights I picked my wife up, I suppose. I did that occasionally.'

'So five, six weeks, before his death?'

'Mmm, that's probably factual.'

Noble bent forward, knees on elbows and looked at Sam. 'Did you ever hear anyone threaten him?'

'No, I never did.'

The two visitors looked at each other and then rose together as if on cue. Noble spoke again as they walked to the door. 'If either of you think of anything that might be significant, give us a phone call, please.'

As Cash opened the door and as the two men exited into the pleasant breeze blowing across the porch, he asked, 'What do you signify as *significant*, Sergeant?'

'Oh, anything at all. The smallest thing might help.'

'Do you have any leads on who might have done it?'

They put on their hats and started down the steps, Noble calling back over his shoulder, his voice rising, 'Not much at this stage, Mr Slade, but we will have. We usually get our man.'

Cash closed the door and turned to Sam. She came to him and put her hands on his arms, looking up into his eyes. 'I hate lying to them.'

Cash gave a dismissive glance at the door. 'They're arrogant, Sammy; it's a facet of any copper's personality. So don't feel any remorse where they're concerned.'

'I don't. It's simply the difference between right and wrong I'm thinking about.'

'Well, please don't regard it as lying.' He kissed her forehead. 'Yes, I know I went out that night, to obtain your gift, my love. Can't you see the bloody police would make a mountain out of that? I mean, Dexter Wilde was no paragon, probably deserved his fate if the truth were known, but hell we don't want to get involved in anything that we could regret, now do we?'

'No, of course not. I suppose you're right. But it's just a shame we can't tell the truth. I know I'd feel better if I did.' She paused. 'And we never discussed pressing charges against Wilde either.'

'Didn't we? Then we should have.' He kissed her again; this time on the mouth and he patted her expanding stomach. 'Come on, m'lady, forget about them. Baby Slade wants his mother to listen to his father.'

Sam had smiled and allowed herself to be led away to the kitchen for lunch but she did not eat much and complained of indigestion.

Within five hours of the police visit she had miscarried.

It was a shock to both of them and while Samantha had been saddened by the event, surprisingly it was Cash who was the more deeply distressed. He had been grave and withdrawn, and said that he thought the police questioning had so disturbed Sam, it had brought on the miscarriage, and even though Sam half-heartedly protested that it was not so, this had been another strong motive for their move to Sydney.

Sam had been loath to leave her family and Haverhill, but in the end Cash had prevailed. They had left Queensland in early November and within two weeks had found a flat on New South Head Road which led out of King's Cross along the eastern beach suburbs.

Sam, who was known to the editorial staff at *PIX* magazine for her previous assignments with them, had made her first approaches there and received a trickle of work, but she very quickly landed a job with a studio run by Bob Buckland, a talented photographer who was an associate of Harold Cazneaux, a man sometimes called the 'father of Australian photography' and who had photographed the metropolis and its social scene for decades.

Buckland had allowed Sam to use the studio facilities and equipment after hours, and soon recognising her talent, had become a sort of mentor, introducing her to Cazneaux and a number of his peers including Max Dupain, a modern young man not unlike Cash to look at, who was making swift headway in the photographic world of Sydney.

Buckland's wife was French, the first French girl Sam had ever met and it was with delight that Françoise Buckland realised she had someone in Australia with whom she could converse in her native tongue. Françoise helped Sam with current French idioms and they often had coffee together in the small café across from the studio, where they spoke entirely in French much to the consternation of the other patrons.

Bob Buckland agreed for Sam to take her own assignments as long as they did not interfere with her work for him, and after six months Sam realised that even with the disadvantage of being female, she was becoming known.

She longed for her own studio and a chance to really show what she could do in the unaccommodating man's world of photography. It was Cash who helped alter her prospects when he informed her he had won spectacularly on the horse races through a risk-taking bookmaker who had allowed him to bet for high stakes. He financed her and she rented a small space in King's Cross to use as a studio. So after almost a year under Buckland's tutelage she had left with his blessing and begun her solo endeavour with the thrilling news that she was to work with *Vogue Australia* on a series of fashion stories.

She had suggested to Cash that she bring Veena and Storm down from Queensland so that Veena could work in the studio with her, but Cash had denounced the idea as frivolous. 'Please be sensible, Sam. How the hell would Veena fit in here? Have you lost your senses? And little Storm . . . It would be most unfair to take her from a wonderful country home to this city.' So she put on a part-time assistant in the form of Greg Davies, a teenage boy who was a keen photographer and knew the Bucklands well.

In the élite company of the New South Wales' Photographic Society exhibition of 1937 two of her art photographs were shown. And on the strength of that she had been able to send some of her work to England to the London Salon of Photography. Sam felt confident about her chosen field of endeavour and her excitement and enthusiasm grew daily.

And now on Seven Shilling Beach as her husband reminded her that he must not be late for work, she smiled and gathered up her towel and belongings. 'All right, darling.' Rising to her feet she slipped into her cotton skirt and blouse and stood waiting for Cash to put on his trousers.

Within fifteen minutes they were back at their flat and Cash was opening the lock on the front door below the art nouveau coloured glass panel. Cash bathed and departed for work throwing Sam a kiss from the front door.

He strode down to the tram stop and stood waiting, leaning on a lamp-post feeling the hard wood on his spine and watching the comings and goings of people and vehicles along New South Head Road. Down the side street he could see a group of boys playing cricket. He had liked cricket at school and excelled in what they called Physical Training, winning all the gymnastic prizes.

Cash was enjoying living in Sydney. It had been kind to him. He had a healthy bank balance – four, in fact, all under different names. He had robbed homes and businesses in various parts of Sydney, always randomly choosing his victims, but once chosen diligently doing his groundwork. His movements had been as far away as Wahroonga on the North Shore to Watson's Bay in the eastern suburbs, though the eastern suburbs were his favourites: easier to return home or to his little mate Danny's place in Rushcutter's Bay where he kept his working clothes and left his tools. He smiled when he thought of Danny Defoe. The little man idolised him, showed what a smart bloke he really was. He called Danny's place his 'safe house', the phrase the old bushrangers in the previous century had used about pubs and homes that had given them shelter.

Though unlike the bushrangers of old he was rigorous in keeping his after-dark occupation to himself and his single trusted liaison, Danny. No doubt there were some of Danny's acquaintance who might be suspicious about him, but they couldn't be sure, and that's the way he would keep it. He had learnt a lot since his Brisbane days when Creedy and most of Creedy's mates knew the truth.

As his tram came along he ran and bounded aboard before it had come to a halt. After all his fence-vaulting, roof-walking and wall-climbing, swinging aboard a moving vehicle was child's play. As he took a seat near the back he thought of Sam. He had been able to set her up in a studio. She was thrilled about that and it made him happy to help her; he loved that girl.

Suddenly his mouth drew down. A while back he had made a bit of a scene over a photo of JB that Sam had framed and placed in their bedroom. Since that event she was aware that he knew, or suspected, her feelings for JB. And he had found a letter from him in her purse – that hadn't helped matters either.

Cash reckoned Sam did love him, it was just that the bloody ghost of JB walked around with them. He really believed that if the baby had come along things would have been different; it would have cemented their marriage and she wouldn't have had the time to daydream about a bloke on the other side of the world. In his moments of benevolence, which were rare, he felt a tinge of sorrow for JB, not for Sammy because he adored her and felt she was lucky to be loved so much, but his old friend was all alone and far away. When he thought like that he would alter the direction of his meditations.

The conductor arrived and he paid the fare, then leant in the corner of the wooden seat and closed his eyes for a time. When he opened them the vehicle was climbing the hill to King's Cross by the various shopfronts and businesses.

His mind reverted to Sam. He dreamt of a day when Sam would love him exclusively, just Cashman Slade. What a day that would be! Well, things were pretty good at the moment, perhaps the day was coming soon. He smiled and closed his eyes again.

In the flat a few miles back along New South Head Road Sam finished her coffee and went to the tiny spare room. She was working on a series of amusing shots she had taken of house painters and was hoping to place somewhere.

After hours of poring over her pictures loupe in hand, she rubbed her neck and spine and drifted into the kitchen to put the kettle on again. She sat looking out of the back window across the treetops and houses below to the harbour in the distance where ships and small craft moved across her vision. She badly missed Haverhill and her parents, Ledgie and Uncle Wake, but this view somehow comforted her; she liked to imagine the destinations of the distant passing craft and she pictured Europe and exotic ports in the Orient. Whenever she sat here alone coffee in hand, eyes upon the remote blue water, she caught herself thinking of JB, and today was no different.

As her lips touched her cup she pictured JB in his Royal

Air Force uniform, flying aeroplanes up in the sky. She took a deep breath to quash the tightness in her chest and wondered if she would ever see her brother again. On his birthday last month, the eleventh of the eleventh, she had made her own pilgrimage to the cenotaph and placed a rose there.

A week ago she had received a letter from him for her coming birthday. It was the second year he had kept his promise. He had told her all about his life in the Air Force and his two new friends, one a man who had lost his legs in an aeroplane accident and the other an American flyer. He had signed it the same way as the one last year: *Always, JB.* which had made her cry and she had taken it and hidden it at her studio, for the one JB had written to her the previous year had disappeared out of her wallet a month ago just after the first dispute that had taken place between her and Cash.

The altercation had occurred after her mother had sent her a photograph of JB in uniform taken beside his aircraft. Sam had framed it and placed it on her bedside table but that very evening when she had returned home it was gone. She had challenged Cash about its disappearance and her husband had replied in a strangely detached way, saying that he did not want a photo of his rival in their bedroom. When Sam had asked angrily what he meant by such a statement, he had crossed the room and come to within inches of her face and completely dumbfounded her.

His tone had been calm, chillingly calm as it always was when he was infuriated, and the expression in his black eyes had wounded her. 'I discern much that you are unaware of, m'lady. I always have. There are enough complications in daily living without the added complexities of your unnatural attraction for JB – *that's* what I mean. I am offended by a photograph of your brother in *our* conjugal home. Is that clear enough for you, Sammy, or do you want me to continue?'

Sam had been astonished and could not find words to answer. To that very moment she had received no inkling that Cash knew anything of her disturbing feelings for her brother. She had stood there in shock looking at him until he left the room.

The photograph had never returned and a few days later she had realised JB's birthday letter had been taken from her wallet, though she dared not mention it.

That was when she had begun to watch the post and when the current letter had been delivered she had taken it immediately to her studio and hidden it amongst her canisters of film.

Ever since the dispute Cash had acted perfectly normally to her, but she continued to brood on what he had said and the fact that he was aware of what she had believed was secret.

Cash was an enigma. She knew that now. They had been married over a year and in that time it had become apparent how solitary he was; not lonely, but alone. He spent so much time on his own; he did it by choice, isolated himself.

She guessed that tonight he would probably go to the trots at Harold Park when he finished work at 9 p.m. Rarely did he come straight home. She could hardly mind for he so often won, but she just wished that sometimes he would take her, and even though she had suggested it he never did.

Since they had been in Sydney Sam had made many friends, but as far as she knew Cash had none. She thought perhaps the loss of their child had affected him more than she had understood. Yet she never broached the subject with him, partly because Sam herself was guilty about it. She hardly dared admit it, but she was not really sorry about the miscarriage. In her honest moments she admitted the awful truth that she felt released, able to be carefree and motivated about her work.

Everything stemmed from the mess she had made in caring for her brother. She had married Cash because she had to and she thought she understood him simply because she had known him the greater part of her life, but that was not so. She now realised Cashman Slade was not easily fathomed.

Still thinking about her husband and her brother she left

the kitchen and dressed for the evening. She had agreed to meet a few friends including Max Dupain and his girlfriend, Olive Cotton, who was five years Sam's senior, at the Royal Oak Hotel in Double Bay at 4 p.m.

It was beginning to rain as she left the flat so she decided against taking a tram and was soon hurrying around the side of the block of flats to the lane behind where the garages stood.

She parked within forty yards of the hotel and once inside she found Olive and Max, Françoise Buckland, a girl called Maria, and an American, Lenny Lambert Cundy. They conversed animatedly and drank castildas, a delicious cocktail with a brandy base made by Henry who ran the bar and would not reveal the recipe. He clung to a story that his Spanish grandmother had whispered him the secret on her deathbed.

Sam enjoyed herself. She liked the busy pub, and Max and his companions were exciting and avant garde. She was in awe of Max Dupain's pictures and one she had studied in his studio recently Sam had thought wonderful. Max had taken it on holiday at Culburra, a small place near the Shoalhaven River. It showed the head and shoulders of a man sunbathing; a powerful study of outdoor life in the sun which Max really had dismissed as 'a snap'; but Sam believed it was so much more.

She had been flattered when Max had said, 'There's an innocence about you, Sam, you see things that way. And that innocence comes out in your pictures, you know. There's a magic in that.'

Olive, a girl with kind eyes and straight hair that she wore parted and curled on the ends, was herself an accomplished photographer and Sam felt awkward when Max paid her such a compliment. Olive was possessive of Max and Sam feared she did not approve of Max's praise of her. In truth Sam admired Olive's work though Max was very much the star of the pair.

They had all speculated for a time about the situation in Europe. It seemed to fill people's conversation so often these days. Lenny was of the mind that Europe was decadent. 'Full of dictators' as he put it, and he thought that Hitler and Stalin were intending to divide Europe between them and that Mussolini in Italy was really a puppet for Hitler. While the two men theorised Sam drifted into thinking about JB over in the Royal Air Force and how he would be at the forefront of any war that might occur, and for a time she fell silent and became introspective, but Lenny brought her abruptly out of her reverie with a hug.

'What was that for?' She looked sharply at him.

'Because you were obviously deep in thought and it was time you took more notice of me.'

They all laughed and had another drink.

At the early 6 p.m. closing time they left the hotel, all complaining about the heat which seemed worse in the still evening, and Max and Olive and the two other women waited outside in the street while Lenny saw Samantha to her car.

Lenny had worked at *Time Magazine* and the *New York Post* and was very suave and sophisticated; he had flirted with Sam from the first day he met her with Françoise in a coffee shop in Rowe Street in the city where the art crowd hung out. He opened the door of the Austin for Sam and inclined his head. 'Nice motor car.'

'Thanks.'

'Wouldn't like to drive me home, would you?'

'I thought you and the others were going back to the city for dinner?'

Lenny smiled. 'We were, but I'd rather be alone with you.'

'Lenny, I'm married.'

'I know. So's a lot of the world.'

At that moment a tram came along and Max shouted to Lenny.

'Go on,' Sam pointed. 'Off you go. Max is calling.'

'You won't drive me home then?'

'No.'

His mouth drew down in disappointment. 'I'll call round to the studio and see you tomorrow.' And he made to turn away, but just as he did he rounded back on her so fast that

286

she started as he swiftly kissed her lips and then ran off towards the tram.

Sam stood there in surprise and as he mounted the tram with his friends he lifted his hand to wave in the ambient light of the night.

Shaking her head, she answered with a wave of her own and sighed as she slid into the driver's seat of the car. 'Men!' she murmured to herself.

It was so hot that she opened the glove box to find the paper fan that she knew was kept there. In the glow of the street-lamp above she searched for it but instead she felt two wristwatches under her fingers. Lifting them out she held an all-gold watch and a silver one on a leather strap. A frown creased the smooth skin between her eyes. Why would Cash have two watches in the car? She turned the face of the gold one over and in the illumination from outside on the telegraph pole she read: *Ernest Young*. She reversed the other and there in classic script was engraved *To Ernest with love*.

How odd that Cash would have two items belonging to a stranger; well, at least Sam had never heard of Ernest Young. For a few moments she sat frowning reflectively.

Not long after, as she brought the Austin into the lane behind the block of flats her mind turned to Dexter Wilde's murder, and when she ran along the cement path to the front door there were other half-formed thoughts drifting at the edge of her consciousness; thoughts that had to do with Cash and his activities, things she could not actually name but that made her uncomfortable. They remained with her as she entered the flat and passed through to the kitchen to make a light meal. But after she had eaten a ham sandwich and drunk a cup of coffee and settled in the lounge to listen to the wireless, she was back to normal.

And that was where Cash startled her when he entered an hour later. He had come silently through the front door and into the lounge room without a sound. 'Sammy?'

Sam jumped. 'My Lord, Cash, don't do that. You nearly gave me a heart attack.'

'Hello, m'lady. Can't help it, I'm the strong, silent type.'

'Very funny.'

'How about a drink?' He bent down and kissed her.

'Sure, though you smell like you've had a few already. I made you a ham sandwich.' She stood and he followed her to the kitchen.

'Thanks, I could do with one. Haven't eaten. Went to Harold Park to the trots after work.'

'Thought you would. Did you do any good?'

'Sort of.'

'What does that mean.'

'Now, m'lady, that means maybe a few quid. Enough to take you out on the town next week.'

Cash ate his sandwich ravenously and she made him another, telling him of her evening

'You enjoy Max's company, don't you?'

She nodded. 'Of course. I've learnt a lot from him. He's so gifted.'

'Who's Lenny?'

'A Yank, friend of Max.'

Cash stood from the table, rinsed his plate and headed to the door. 'I'm tired, m'lady. Let's go to bed.'

Half an hour later as she lay in Cash's arms, her head on his chest listening to his heart steadily beating, she asked, 'Who's Ernest Young?'

'Beats me.'

'Then why do you have two of his watches in the glove box of the Austin?'

Cash had been running his fingers through her hair and now his hand hesitated. He broke the silence of the darkened room with his reply. 'Oh heck, those watches. Yes. Right. Did you use the car this evening then?'

'Yes. It was raining so I didn't want to catch the tram.'

Cash took a deep breath and gently removed her from his chest as he turned over. 'I didn't recognise the name for a moment because poor old Ernest was not an acquaintance of mine. A bloke I know lent them to me on approval. I think Ernest was his cousin, anyway he's gone west. Died a few weeks ago apparently. This bloke I know inherited the watches and wants to realise on them.'

'Yes, they look expensive. But why would you want to buy watches engraved with another man's name?'

Cash rolled round towards her. 'Now, darling, you can always erase a name. Fact is, I've decided I don't want them anyway. I'll return them to him tomorrow.'

'What's the name of the man?'

Cash gave a rumbling laugh. 'What's this – the Inquisition?'

'No, I'm just interested.'

'Danny Dixon. Funny bloke, always peddling something.'

'Does he work with you?'

Cash lifted his body over hers in the darkness and kissed her mouth. 'No, he doesn't work with me, Miss Inquisitive. He's a not very discriminating fellow I see periodically at the races.' He ran his hands up and down her spine, pulling her gently up underneath him to where his palms cupped her bottom. 'I love you, m'lady,' he whispered sensuously.

'Not tonight, Cash,' Sam answered, sliding out of his arms. 'I'm not feeling really well.'

'What's the matter?'

'Nothing. I'm tired, that's all.'

'It's not like you, to be like this.'

Sam sighed. 'Please Cash, I'm tired that's all.'

'You didn't seem tired when you were cross-examining me a minute ago.'

She did not answer.

'That's what you're mad about, isn't it?'

Sam took a deep breath and it rustled out of her mouth on the still heat of the night. 'Don't be silly. Good night.'

Cash reacted by sitting up with his back towards her, feet on the floor. 'I'm not being silly.' He hesitated and added with sinister calm, 'I'm being very serious. Perhaps you'd rather your brother was in the bed.'

Sam felt the rush of blood to her face. 'Go to hell!' she exclaimed, pulling the sheet over her body and turning to the wall.

Cash languidly lifted his body from the bed. So Samantha had finally caught him out; she had not believed his story about the watches. He wondered if there had been other times when she had doubted him? He could hear cars passing along New South Head Road but also he was aware of the clock ticking on the mantelshelf at the far end of the room: it was the first time he could recall hearing it and suddenly it irritated him. He moved across, picked it up and lifting it high in the air, smiled and smashed it to the floor.

Sam jerked straight up in shock. 'What the hell? What have you done?'

'Got your attention.'

Her heart raced as she snapped on the bedside lamp. 'You've broken the clock.'

He stood over the smashed pieces, his black forelock dangling on his brow, his expression making her feel deeply uncomfortable. 'Bugger the clock! Good night, Sammy.' He left the room.

Sam sat in the lamplight clutching the sheet. She felt ill and lay back upon the headboard.

She did not believe what Cash had told her tonight, and now all the half-formed suspicions that had floated vaguely in her mind for the entirety of her marriage, began to take substance. Where had he really gone the night of Dexter Wilde's murder? He had brought her home the brooch all right, yet it had always seemed mighty odd that he had to go and obtain it that very night, the night of the killing. He had lied to the police about his whereabouts and she too had lied to them to protect him. And the amount of money Cash always had; right back from his university days!

Everyone she knew had suffered through the world Depression, yet somehow Cash always had *cash*! Did it all actually come from the races as he maintained? She had seen his various systems for winning neatly printed out on his lined writing pads, but that could be just to convince. And if it were fact that his money came from betting, how on earth did he continue to have such amazing luck, year after year? Did he really go to the races at all? If he did not, then where did he go? Where did he spend those nights? Where did the money come from? Who was Ernest Young and how did Cash come by his watches? Was Cash some kind of thief?

She heard Cash open a bottle of something, she assumed beer. She really wanted one herself but refrained from going out to get it. After a few minutes she rose and went to the bathroom and drank some water. When she returned to bed she left the light on and fanned herself for a time but Cash did not return. Finally she put out the light and drifted into sleep.

The following morning when she woke she was alone. There was a note on the kitchen table:

Sammy,
   Gone out early. Sorry about the clock, I'll buy a new one today. I didn't mean to upset you – never have. I'll be home by six tonight and I'll take you to Princes. I love you, m'lady.
   Cash.

Princes was the most glamorous and expensive restaurant in the whole of Sydney, downstairs in Martin Place in the centre of the city.

Sam held the note and moved to the window where she stood for many minutes looking out to the harbour as if mesmerised. Finally she shook herself into wakefulness, left the window and put on the kettle.

Chapter Twenty-one

England: July, 1939

Feet on the rudder pedals, hand on the control column, John Baron watched the aircraft ahead and smiled. To his right were trailing white clouds and to his left across the four 303 Browning machine guns mounted in the eliptical wing, soaring along at his side, were Twig and Flying Officer Paul Richey, a Londoner whose mother was an Australian. They had become friendly after an evening in the mess when one of the boys had been ribbing John Baron as a 'colonial' and Paul had come to his defence saying, 'If you count JB a colonial then count me one too, for my mother was born out there.'

John Baron was in a Spitfire, Twig and Paul in Hurricanes which they all usually flew. Yesterday a single Spitfire had been flown into Tangmere, their home airfield, which lay in Sussex between the South Downs and Selsey Bill on the English Channel, and where John Baron's newly formed squadron shared the base with Number 1 Squadron and Number 43 Squadron and the General Reconnaisance Squadron – Number 217.

The boys in the mess had mounted a lottery to see who would fly the Spitfire on the current exercise: a dawn flight over the North Sea. John Baron had been amazed and thrilled when his name had been chosen. Subsequently eleven of his comrades had offered him all sorts of bribes to give up the flight to them; one had even offered a night out with his girlfriend! But the temptations had been resisted.

It was magical at fifteen thousand feet in his Perspex

bubble canopy, the mullet-headed cowling over the Merlin engine did not allow for exceptional visibility but John Baron thought it was perhaps an improvement on the Hurricane and it handled like a dream. He still felt the influence of the variegated green and russet shapes of the home fields of the earthly planet as he caught sight of them through the openings in the cloud below. He did not feel separate from this aircraft, he did not feel as if he piloted it, he felt rather as if he were an extension of the Supermarine Spitfire, an integral living part of the aeroplane he flew. In fact, as he looked across to Twig and lifted his finger in silent greeting he felt invulnerable.

The cockpit was compact; three feet wide and even less from instrument panel to the back of the armoured rear panel behind his seat. He was snug and feeling powerful in his flying suit, headgear and goggles as Squadron Leader Bull Halahan gathered speed and used full throttle to climb: up they went aiming at infinity, eighteen, twenty, twenty-one, twenty-two, twenty-three thousand feet. They flattened out at twenty-five thousand and looking down, JB saw the ground again.

Even before the Prime Minister, Neville Chamberlain, the advocate for appeasement, had met Adolf Hitler in Munich a year earlier, the British High Command had realised there was no trusting the German leader and that there would be 'no peace in our time' even though Chamberlain had stated it so definitely. So the RAF had been on alert, expecting war and practising war drills. Winston Churchill, who had been warning the world for years of the real intentions of Hitler, had condemned the Munich agreement between Chamberlain and Hitler as a 'total and unmitigated defeat' for democracy. Now, a year later, with the German army openly mobilising along the Polish border and Czechoslovakian and German Jews pouring into Great Britain, John Baron, along with most of the world, realised Churchill was right.

After a wonderful spring the summer of 1939 was overcast, wet and chilly and it was into a cloudy July sky at 0700 that John Baron had been scrambled in the exercise to intercept Bomber Command aircraft. And now, sailing by bunching cloud, they were heading across the coast over the North Sea.

John Baron tried not to think of a coming war. Intellectually he realised conflict must begin, and soon, and as he had been trained to be a pilot, he would be in the thick of it. Pilots would die.

He was pleased his family were so far away from Europe. He imagined Samantha as he had seen her so many times riding along Teviot Brook upon Aristotle, her hair undulating on her shoulders in the thick hot Queensland breeze and he consciously decided not to think of dying.

He almost flinched when the radio telephone crackled in his earphones and the voice of Bull Halahan sounded. 'We'll fire the one hundred and sixty rounds into the sea.' This was the first time their eight machine guns had been loaded, and as John Baron waited his turn to tilt and sweep down to empty the twenty rounds from each gun into the gleaming silver water he felt privileged to be flying the Spitfire. Not that the Hurricane was a country cousin by any means; it was a sturdy, reliable and manoeuvrable aircraft and was the first fighter plane to fly at over 300 m.p.h.

It was simply that now, experiencing the Spitfire for the first time, it felt lighter and faster with its thinner wings reducing the air resistance. John Baron knew its top speed was 362 m.p.h. and everybody said it was definitely a match for the German Messerschmitt Bf109 which was touted as the acme in combat aeroplanes, and as he fingered the firing button on his control column, he wondered what it would be like to actually fire at another aircraft.

He took a deep breath, recalling the previous night and the article he had read by Winston Churchill in the *New Statesman*. He had stated that the Magna Carta, Habeas Corpus and The Petition of Rights were the indispensable foundations of freedom. That debate and questioning – the basic features of democracy – far from hindering the conduct of a war frequently assisted it by exposing weak points. John Baron had thought deeply about that and agreed. It was easy to see that dictatorships brooked no investigation or challenges, that Hitler, Mussolini and Stalin would conduct matters without interference from anyone. Churchill's article had ended with a sentence pointing out that while war was horrible, slavery was worse and that he believed the British people would prefer to go down fighting than live in servitude.

John Baron knew that Australia would join Great Britain when war began, and had he still been living out there he would have volunteered anyway, so he took some perverse comfort in the fact that when it came he would have been involved one way or another.

And when in turn he banked and swept down to race above the choppy waters of the North Sea, pressing the firing button and emptying the bullets into the waves below he was aware of a surge of something akin to invincibility.

Half an hour later the squadrons dropped through cloud low over the South Downs and came into land.

Easing back on the throttle . . . slowing down . . . wheels down . . . flaps down . . . sinking towards the earth, slide back hood, holding speed at 90 to 95 m.p.h., feeling that comfortable position where the reassuring bump of aircraft meeting ground made John Baron grin as he rattled and rumbled along the 1500-yard runway that ran north-east to south-west. In his vision were the two new runways of 1600 yards that were nearing completion. The Rolls Royce Merlin liquid-cooled engine purred as he taxied in and switched off the ignition and came to a standstill, undid his safety and parachute harnesses and jumped out onto the wing.

Twig in his Hurricane halted beside him. 'Hey JB,' he shouted, a wide smile on his face. 'How was it?'

'Bloody beautiful.'

'It looks an absolute dream. Does it handle like they say?'

'Better.'

'Hey, I loved killing the North Sea! You bet!'

As they headed off the field Twig pointed his thumb to his Hurricane. 'It's a great aircraft but what you just flew somehow looks even better up there.'

'Too right. I'm a lucky blighter to have flown it. Only nine squadrons with them, Bull Halahan said in the mess last night, and this one goes back to Duxford this afternoon.'

Twig looked longingly at the Spitfire. 'Yeah, well I bet Halahan makes an excuse to take her up before she leaves. He was dying to win that blasted lottery.'

As they waited on the edge of the field for Paul Richey to taxi in, JB shielded his eyes from the sunlight and looked over the sea of aircraft now all neatly lined up like powerful metal insects. He pointed to the Spitfire. 'Reckon R.J. Mitchell would've liked to see that Spitfire up there over the North Sea this morning.'

'Who's R.J. Mitchell?'

'He's the bloke who designed the Spitfire. Reginald Mitchell.'

'Oh?'

'Died in thirty-seven so never saw them in production.'

Twig took out a cigarette. 'You don't say? What rotten luck. Who designed the Hurricane?'

'Sydney Camm, Hawker's chief designer, you illiterate Yank.'

Twig rolled his eyes and blew a stream of smoke at JB. 'Thanks.'

As Paul strode towards them John Baron confided in his friend. 'You know, I actually get vertigo – have been that way always. I even fell off a cliff as a kid, and almost toppled from a roof a few years ago, but when I'm in an aircraft I have no sense of it at all.'

Twig regarded John Baron thoughtfully. 'Probably because you're encased in your own little flying castle.'

'Yes, that's what I think.'

When Paul joined them they stood momentarily together in the warmth from a sudden burst of sunlight before making their way to the debriefing hut nestled beside the newly built station workshops.

The following week as JB was about to leave his room to meet Twig and Paul in the mess, Clive the batman knocked on his door. 'Phone call for you, sir.'

John Baron made his way down the dimly lit corridor

to the corner where the phone sat in an alcove under a photograph of Betty Grable in a red and white swimsuit.

Douglas Bader's animated voice came down the line. 'JB, I know you chaps are on twenty-four-hour alert at the moment but a few of us are going over to an inn near Sandwich on Friday night and staying for lunch nearby on Saturday. Friend of Thelma's lives there and we've all been invited for a bit of a shindig – tennis, swimming in the Stour. Thought if you and Twig weren't on operations you might like to come?'

Before John Baron could reply Douglas went on, 'Apparently there's a golf course pretty close.'

'If you're going, there would be. We're on thirty-minute alert at present and one twenty-four-hour pass a fortnight. But we might swing it.'

'Perfect.'

'Hang on,' John Baron smiled down the phone. 'Where's Sandwich?'

'Near Tegwell Bay.'

'Where's that?'

'Near Sandwich.'

'Silly bugger.'

'About a hundred miles from you as the crow flies. To the north-east, in Kent.'

'How are we supposed to get there?'

Douglas laughed. 'Take the station flight?'

This was an aircraft normally used for navigational exercises and which all the pilots used socially. In Tangmere's case it was a little two-seater low-wing monoplane trainer which was a useful runabout. The boys referrred to it as 'Maggie'.

'Yes, I could get Maggie, I suppose.'

Douglas sounded mildly disgusted. 'JB, of course you could.'

'Making an excuse for twenty-four-hours' use might be a bit of a feat.'

'Now look, you clot, I haven't played golf with you in a month. Geoffrey's going to make up the foursome so you and Twig must come.'

John Baron knew Geoffry Darlington: he had been Douglas's best man. He smiled resignedly as his friend went on, 'And afterwards we'll whip around to Thelma's friend's place for lunch. You can fly back to the airfield on Saturday afternoon.'

John Baron smiled into the telephone. 'If I can get Maggie we'll be there. What's the nearest airfield?'

'Manston.'

'All right. We'll fly into Manston and you and Geoffrey can pick us up.'

On Friday a single day of summer seemed to suddenly find the British Isles and the sun shone and the breeze sliding across Tangmere to the South Downs seemed to carry ozone in straight from the Channel.

The duo flew away a few minutes after five and crossed from West to East Sussex and on through Kent to land at Manston, south-west of Margate on the slab of land known as the Isle of Thanet.

They were picked up by Douglas and Geoffrey and after stopping in a wayside pub where John Baron, Twig and Geoffrey drank ales and Douglas lemonade, they made their way to the grey stone inn resting not far from the Roman ruins at Richborough.

Inside they wandered past a seventeeth-century bar and fought their way through the haze of smoke to discover Thelma and Jane Cardrew, the hostess for the following day's lunch, a well-dressed girl with large expressive eyes and wavy hair which shone in the electric light. Thelma introduced them and explained, 'Dinner's set for eight tonight and there'll be eight of us; a dozen at Jane's place tomorrow.'

They dispersed to their rooms. They had taken over the entire inn which comprised just seven rooms and they met again in the low oak-beamed dining room for the convivial meal. John Baron found himself between Jane and Geoffrey. Twig sat on the far side of Jane with a bespectacled man called Grantley across from him, while a woman called Marian made up the group.

'It's kind of you to invite two fellows to lunch tomorrow

when you've never met us,' John Baron said to Jane as a plate of savoury smelling duckling was placed in front of them.

'Oh, you come highly recommended,' she laughed. 'Not that I'd take too much notice of Douglas, he's an absolute rogue, but Thelma I do listen to.'

'Well, that was lucky for us.'

After a lot of laughter and good humour the gathering broke up around eleven and as Douglas rose from his seat he placed his arm round Thelma's slight shoulders. 'I think it's good night for me. Have to be on the course by seven in the morning.' Suddenly he caught his foot under the chair and stumbled sideways. He looked momentarily as if he would plunge to the floor and Grantley grabbed his arm to steady him but Douglas threw it off with a growl. 'I'm all right, damn it. Leave me alone!' Grantley, abashed, mumbled something about 'people not being grateful' and most of the others in the party turned quickly away.

During the exchange Thelma had remained still and now as she walked beside JB to the foot of the stairs that led up to the bedrooms, she whispered, 'He'd rather fall than be helped.'

John Baron had known his legless friend for two years and was patently aware of the determination and pride that drove the man; he patted her arm. 'Yes, I know.'

Douglas stomped up the stairs ahead and Grantley, with a sidelong glance at the legless man's back, moved into the bar with Jane, Twig and Geoffrey.

In a tiny room with oak-panelled walls, slanting roof and a dormer window covered by a red white and blue flowered curtain, John Baron spent the night and was woken with toast and tea at six and by quarter to seven the golfers were at the course and on the first tee right on schedule. The fine weather of the previous day had deserted them and the sky was overcast though no rain fell.

Whenever John Baron was with Douglas he was reminded of Wakefield. Both men had overcome the handicap of losing limbs and both had a spirit which was seemingly dauntless. Wakefield still rode horses and played cricket and helped run a large property, and Douglas with the even greater handicap of both legs lost, his left above and his right below the knee, had made himself walk without any aid, play golf, drive a car and live a normal life. It was strength of character and resolve that kept Douglas upright, and John Baron smiled as his friend hit a fair ball off the first tee, almost straight down the middle.

Two hours later Douglas stomped off the eleventh green, putter under his arm and asked John Baron, 'Now are you glad you came?' They were playing Stableford as a team against Geoffrey and Twig and were one point in front.

JB laughed as Douglas asked, 'What was the wager again?'

'Thirty shillings each,' Twig advised them.

'Trust a Yank to be clear about the finances.'

Twig swung his club at Douglas who swashbuckled aside nearly losing his balance. 'You'll be sorry.'

And at five to eleven as the caddies trailed them off the 18th green Twig and Geoffrey in fact handed over their three pounds to the winners who had held their single point ahead. They smiled as Twig began to defiantly whistle 'Way Down South in Dixie' as they walked to the club house.

They had a quick drink at the '19th hole' and left the club house with Douglas puffing enthusiastically on his pipe. As they piled their clubs into the boot of the Swift and Douglas lifted his bag of clubs, John Baron noticed the initials DB in small gold studs on the handle. He pointed. 'Do you know, it's just occurred to me what we should call you.'

'What's that?'

'DB for *Dogsbody*. We should call you Dogsbody.'

'How utterly bloody charming of you.'

They all laughed, but it stuck and from that day on the golf course, the three men who were there with Douglas called him 'Dogsbody'. Little did they realise that it would stay with Douglas and become a very meaningful nickname.

Jane Cardrew's parents' house stood to the west of Sandwich back off the road in five acres with a swathe of

300

beeches on two sides, and the narrow Stour River flowing at the back. As they passed the sign reading *Castlemere* and pulled up to the front steps of the Victorian façade Twig commented, 'Your friend Jane definitely does not live in a dump.'

They were met by a maid and taken out to a redbrick terrace overlooking a croquet lawn where Jane and Thelma were handing around drinks to the other guests. Lunch was served promptly at twelve-thirty upon a long polished table.

On John Baron's right side sat Meryl, a woman of perhaps thirty with extravagant make-up and fair hair plaited around her forehead and caught with a sparkling red clip above her right ear. She told him that she had known Thelma for years and that she was related to the Earl of Carlisle and she made her feelings known on many matters during the lunch. 'Hair needs to catch the eye, must be dramatic,' she opined, holding up her glass for her fifth refill of claret before revealing that she owned two hair-dressing salons in Ashford. When the topic of war came up as it always did, she passed her long red fingernails across her eyes wearily. 'Can't we talk of something else? It's all you get at dinner parties and luncheons these days.' She looked round the table. 'War, war, war. The last one only ended just twenty years ago. I thought that's why Mr Chamberlain went to Munich last year – to avoid it.'

Douglas shook his head. 'Meryl, don't you read the papers? Unfortunately it's the most likely event I see on the horizon. Children under twelve are now being sent out of London. What do you think that means?'

'I don't know. It's all too depressing. Sometimes I think Mosley's right,' Meryl replied with a slurring of her words. 'At least he's trying to keep our boys from getting killed.'

There was a negative rumble of voices and Geoffrey leant across the table. 'That's not right, Meryl, you're just being controversial. You don't mean that.'

'How do you know what I mean?' Meryl pointed at him with her scarlet fingernail.

Thelma's eyes turned to the ceiling as if she had heard all this before and Douglas replied, 'Meryl, for heaven's sake, Mosley and his Blackshirts are blasted traitors supporting Hitler, and if you ask me Hitler's going to try to enslave Europe; and the world if he can. He's anti-semitic: that's been obvious for years and it won't just stop there. After the Jews it'll be others. This Aryan purity he's on about. Churchill's right, sadly there'll be a war and pretty darn soon.'

Meryl's eyes blinked and her vermilion nail now shot forward at Douglas. 'Oh, you just want to fly again. You've said before that the first thing you'll do if a war comes is to get back in the air. You'd like a damn war. You and Churchill. Everybody knows that.'

Thelma's knife and fork clattered on her plate. 'That's a horrible thing to say, Meryl. Take it back. Why are you like this when you drink?'

Meryl tapped her nails loudly on her saucer. 'Like what?'

The atmosphere was thickening as Douglas put out his hand to calm Thelma with his eyes on Meryl. 'You've got one thing absolutely right, I do want to fly again and I'd give anything to do it. It's the greatest wish I have, but I halt at the desire to plunge the entire continent of Europe into a war simply to get my own way. As for Churchill, he was the only one in this damn country who saw what was happening and who tried to warn us long ago. And since Munich, only a blasted ostrich with its head in the ground could think there isn't going to be a war. If you drank less claret, old girl, your judgement wouldn't be so bloody distorted.'

'How dare you! I'm not drunk,' Meryl bristled, knocking her glass of wine in her haste to point her roving finger-nail once more at Douglas. Grantley, with lightning speed, caught her teetering glass of claret but some of it had spilt on the white tablecloth. Jane jumped up as Grantley patted Meryl's hand consolingly and took her side. 'Isn't every-body entitled to an opinion? All Meryl's done is to say what she thinks. There's no need to get personal.'

Suddenly Thelma exploded. 'Personal? Grant, have you lost your senses? Meryl was as personal as it gets. She always does this.' She looked directly at the woman.

'You're drunk and you're being stupidly inflammatory.' Thelma was not easily roused, but she looked as if she were going to rise and slap her.

A hush descended over the lunch. Geoffrey coughed and poured wine into as many glasses as he could reach while John Baron made a valiant attempt to clarify the situation.

'Look, the truth is that now Churchill's back in the government I think most people feel more comfortable. I do for one. As for flying, we all love it. It's in our blood and in our psyche. But the point surely is that we've been preparing for war for ages. The air-raid precautions system was put in years ago, Anderson bomb shelters have been distributed throughout the country, and zig zag trenches dug in parks. There've been "blimps" – you know, barrage balloons – over London for nearly twelve months and the latest is we're being issued with identity cards. Czechoslovakia's been overrun and German troops are stacking up on the border of Poland and looking to the Low Countries. Come on, everybody! No one here's stupid. Sadly, war's as plain as the noses on our faces.' He turned to Meryl and Grantley as he finished, 'And whether Douglas flies again or not is a totally separate issue from any of that.'

Meryl sniffed, and Grantley answered, 'You bloody well would take his part.'

John Baron shook his head. 'Forget it, Grant. Any rational person knows that what Meryl's said here today is drivel.'

Meryl's face was now the same colour as the fingernail she poked sharply into JB's shoulder. 'You can go to hell.' She looked blearily at them. 'You all stink.'

'Oh lovely.'

Now everybody began to talk while Jane dabbed at the red spot on the tablecloth with a damp serviette. Twig, whose voice carried at any time, took a turn making himself heard above the babble. 'Come on, fellas, we're not warmongers, but the fact is that in the RAF we're on thirty-minute alert now, day and night. What does that tell you? It's a mighty serious state of affairs, that's what. JB and I were lucky to get this twenty-four-hour pass we're on. Have to be back by five this afternoon.'

Jane made a sound of disappointment at his elbow and Twig looked quickly round at her and slid his arm along the back of her seat.

'So,' shouted Douglas rapping the table with his fist, 'QED.'

At that moment the maid came in with dessert and a unified sigh of relief was heaved.

Conversation began again in halting fashion and stumbled along. Dessert was a delicious chocolate parfait in a long glass which deserved compliments, and gave the table a safe topic for a few minutes.

Nobody sat after the sweets, coffee and tea were refused and all left the dining room. Jane was disappointed at the way the lunch had ended but as Twig offered her his arm she took it with a smile. Grantley and Meryl headed hand in hand down to the Stour talking about taking a swim and most of the others eyed the tennis court.

There was a suggestion of a breeze and the sun had come out from behind the clouds as Douglas drew out his pipe. 'No activity for us. I'm going to sit with my lady wife on the terrace and enjoy some sunshine. Thank God Grantley and Meryl have gone to drown in the Stour.'

They all laughed and a swift look darted between Twig and Jane; it seemed to impart that they too desired to find a sunny spot away from company so John Baron took his cue. 'I'll go for a stroll around the grounds for half an hour. We'd better leave then, Twig. The Wingco will have our hides if we're late.'

'Wingco' was the airmen's parlance for the Wing Commander, in this case a diligent Scot called Macarthur who lived by the rule book but had a reputation for fair play.

Reluctantly Twig agreed. 'All right, I'll be ready.'

John Baron strode across the croquet lawn with the sun warming his back. He stood for a time looking in the fish pond where he could see carp racing back and forth under the reeds and lily pads. A frog croaked somewhere and he meandered on by the dark shape of a sycamore tree and halted near an ornamental bird-bath by a low wall covered in ivy.

Suddenly, someone said, 'Well, hello.' He turned sharply to an empty view, then he thought to look up. Two shoes dangled a few yards from his face. He lifted his eyes to the sleek grey slacks and the slender body. For a heartbeat he saw Sam sitting on the branch above!

'Did I startle you?' she asked, taking a bite of an apple.

It was not his sister of course but a girl with the same olive skin and shock of Sam-like hair tumbling to her shoulders.

'No. Just for a moment I thought you were someone else.'

'Not an old girlfriend, I hope.'

'No.'

'Good. For it's not a recommended start to remind men of their former loves.'

'Oh, isn't it?'

'No. People want to be loved for themselves.'

'Yes, I suppose you're right. Who are you anyway?'

'I'm Alex.'

'That's a boy's name.' He thought of Sam, that was a boy's name too.

'It's short for Alexandra. What's yours?'

'John Baron.'

Her eyes twinkled in the sunlight as she gnawed on her apple, her legs swinging. 'That's a boy's name as well.'

They both laughed.

She still reminded him of Sam. She even had the same high cheekbones and forthright gaze, though the flippancy in her manner was quite different. John Baron gestured back to the house. 'Do you belong here?'

'Yes, I'm the youngest daughter. You're probably here at my sister Jane's invitation. She's the socialite, and she gathers smashing-looking men. Then there's Kate, she's the studious one, and away at university. I'm still treated like the kid sister which really is awful. I'm not a baby.'

'You're a tonic.'

'What does that mean?'

'It means you've entertained me.'

'Daddy says I'm shameless.'

'He's probably right.'

'It's the times,' she suggested. 'All this talk of war would make anybody shameless.' She pitched her apple core into the trees.

'Should you do that?'

'The squirrels will eat it.' She put out her hand. 'Will you help me down?'

She tilted forward and he caught her as she slid down into his arms to meet his body with a thump. 'Oops, shouldn't have physical contact on first meeting.'

'Who says so?'

'*Good Housekeeping* magazine. Mummy gets it. It tells you all sorts of things.' He noticed she had remained in his arms to give him this information and he continued to hold her until she stepped back. 'Thanks for helping me down.'

They began walking back towards the house and she glanced up at him. 'How long are you here for?'

'Another ten minutes.'

Alex's mouth turned down. 'Oh.' She was silent for a few seconds before she inquired, 'Where are you going?'

'Back to the airfield at Tangmere down near Chichester.'

'Are you in the Air Force then?'

'Yes.'

'Are you a pilot?'

'Yes.'

'Isn't it dangerous? I heard that pilots get killed in accidents all the time.'

What she said was true; his own squadron's average was one death per month. Just last week in a night operation Damien Clark, a boy from Edinburgh, had become confused and dived down a searchlight beam. He had hit the downs at 380 miles an hour. He shrugged as he replied, 'Yes, it can be dangerous sometimes.'

'Where are you from? You don't sound exactly English.'

'Australia.'

'My. How wonderful.'

They rambled on for a minute or so and reached the croquet lawn. Alex halted and John Baron paused at her side. He could see Douglas and Thelma sitting facing the afternoon sun but there was no sign of Twig and Jane.

Alex crouched down and picked a buttercup. She remained there as she informed him, 'It's my birthday in a month, Thursday the twenty-fourth of August actually.' She was peering at him with unashamed admiration.

'Oh, and how old are you?'

'That's another thing *Good Housekeeping* says you shouldn't ask.'

'What? A lady's age?'

'Yes.' She stood up holding the buttercup.

'Ah, but you're still a girl aren't you?'

She sighed. 'No. Not any more, for I'll be twenty-one.'

'But now you get to vote and make up your mind about all sorts of things.'

She laughed and struck him gently with the flower. 'I do half of that already. Daddy's giving me a party, not large just thirty or forty.'

'What do you call large?'

'Well, when Jane had her twenty-first, a hundred people came. We had a marquee over there,' she pointed with her buttercup past the croquet lawn, 'and a band and a singer. But Daddy says in the current world situation, what with the threat of war and all, that's not appropriate. So there won't be a fuss, just a few of my friends and a lot of my cousins and relatives.'

'What do you do?' John Baron asked for something to say.

'I'm a telephone exchange operator. I work in Canterbury during the week. Sometimes I stay at my aunt's. She's a God-awful woman but I'm used to her. Anyway she's away most of the time either up in London or somewhere else. Goes to France a lot. Bags of money. Third husband, you know the type.'

He did not, but he made an affirmative sound as he noticed Twig and Jane sauntering round the corner of the house.

John Baron felt something tug at his sleeve. It was Alex. The evening sunshine kindled a touch of fire in the abundant waves of her hair. She was so very like Sam.

'Will I see you again?'

He did not reply and she took a deep breath. 'Will you come to my birthday party?' And before he could answer she rushed on. 'I know I'm being awfully forward.' She waved the buttercup at the terrace. 'If it's fine weather we'll dance over there. Mrs Blake, she's our cook, will make nice canapés and cakes and . . . Do you like champagne?'

'Sometimes.'

And now she frowned and became serious. 'I'm sorry if I've put you on the spot. You don't have to come . . . truly.'

He did not know what to reply. He knew another twenty-four-hour pass would be impossible though he might be able to fly up here for a few hours on some spurious reconnaissance flight; but he thought it was all a bit hard and was about to say so, when she tossed her hair back over her shoulder, sighed and looked away. Even her profile was reminiscent of Sam's. He felt a rush of tenderness towards her and heard himself say, 'Yes, I'd love to come. I don't think it'll be easy but I might be able to get up here for a few hours.'

She rounded on him triumphantly. 'Oh, thanks awfully.'

'Give me your telephone number and I'll let you know.'

Chapter Twenty-two

On Thursday, 24 August, John Baron and Twig flew again across the green hills and dales of Sussex and Kent in Maggie to Manston airfield. Since 1 August, all leave at Tangmere had been cancelled and the base had stepped up preparations for war but Twig, who was a mastermind in harmless deception, had managed to elicit an order for a manoeuvre for himself and a second pilot which required a reconnaissance flight over the Kentish coast and a landing at an airfield. That the second pilot was JB and that they happened to choose Manston as the airfield was merely a coincidence.

Summer seemed finally to have found the British Isles for they flew in perfect conditions and when they landed, a Sergeant in overalls carrying a clipboard and pencil met them as they jumped down from the aircraft.

Twig hailed him like a friend. 'Afternoon, Sergeant, great weather we're having at last. Need to refuel. Heading back to Tangmere. We'll be off now and return in a few hours.'

The Sergeant looked dubious. 'You're not supposed to leave the airfield, sir.'

'What? Since when?' Twig asked, looking in the direction of the main gate where he knew Jane waited for them with her wide smile and an Austin Seven.

The Sergeant tapped his pencil on his clipboard. 'Last couple of weeks.'

Twig gave a disappointed grunt. 'Look, Sarge, fact is there's a girl outside waiting for us. I can give you a phone number where you can reach us if any problems arise. We're only going seven miles down the road, can be back here in no time.'

The Sergeant shook his head. 'New regulations. No one's to leave the airport during refuelling, sir.'

John Baron and Twig exchanged glances and Twig took the plunge. 'You married, Sarge?'

'Why . . . er yes.'

'Well, it's like this. That girl at the gate's my bride. Only got married last Saturday.' He gave a forlorn glance towards the main gate. 'Come on, you know how it is. This is my last chance to see her. Word is, our squadron's off to France any day.'

The airman hesitated and Twig jumped right back in. 'Come on, old man, we'll be back almost by the time you've had her refuelled. No one's going to be any the wiser. I don't know what I'll do if I don't see my wife again.'

The Sergeant pointed at JB. 'Why the devil's he got to go too?'

'He's engaged to her sister.'

John Baron looked quickly away to hide the expression that crossed his face.

'Blimey!' exclaimed the Sergeant.

'Come on, old man. Look, here's the telephone number where we'll be.' Twig took his pencil and wrote the Cardrews' home phone number on the side of the form attached to the clipboard. He looked up. 'Are you going to be on duty all evening?'

'Yep – till midnight.'

'Good. I'm Russell and he's Chard.'

As they walked away the airman called, 'Here, what if somebody in Requisitions asks where you are?' and John Baron shouted as they kept walking, 'Say to your knowledge we're here on the airfield.'

As they strode past the sandbags that guarded the perimeter of the field John Baron turned his head to his friend. 'So now you're married and I'm engaged. Jane *will* be interested.'

They both laughed spontaneously. 'Well, hell, he was never going to agree otherwise.'

At the main gate a Corporal came out of the guard hut

to meet them and Jane stood waving beside the Austin fifty yards away.

'We're refuelling.' John Baron pointed over his shoulder to the distant Hawker. 'We'll be back in about three hours.'

The Corporal extended a clipboard towards them. 'Names, please.'

The two looked again at each other and John Baron took it quickly and wrote two names down. 'You seem to have a lot of clipboards at Manston,' John Baron commented as he returned it to the Corporal.

The man saluted and as they hurried down towards Jane, Twig asked, 'What did you sign on that thing?'

'Speke and Burton,' JB replied and Twig burst into laughter.

Jane and Twig greeted each other with obvious affection. She had travelled down to Chichester on two previous weekends to see Twig who had been able, by his great skill with double talk, to leave the airfield and see her for a few hours each time. On the second visit Jane had brought a letter for John Baron from Alex in which she wrote that she was hoping he would be able to come to her birthday party.

'How long can you stay?' Jane asked as they drove off across the flat Kent countryside.

'A few hours.'

Jane half-turned her head to John Baron who sat in the back. 'I swear you've been the birthday girl's only topic of conversation this last month. I think Mummy's worried. Alex has never shown such an interest in any fellow before.'

John Baron did not reply. He was uncertain whether he was pleased to be here or not. After his promise to Alex a month ago he had experienced second thoughts but Twig had been mad keen to see Jane again and had persuaded him to come. If Alex had crossed his mind at all it was in the hope that when he next saw her she would not remind him so much of Sam.

But John Baron was to be frustrated in that wish for when they arrived at the Cardrews' into a warm cloudless evening and he saw Alexandra standing with four or five

311

people on the front steps she looked so much like Sam that he drew his hand across his eyes and focused again.

Seeing them Alex ran down the steps to meet the car, almost skipping the last few steps to John Baron's side as he opened the door and climbed out. She looked fresh and animated; her face breaking into a delighted smile. 'I've been waiting for you. I'm so glad you could come.'

'As I mentioned on the telephone – sheer luck. Twig's the bloke you have to thank.'

She laughed. '*Bloke*'s such a funny word.'

'It's what we say instead of *chap* where I come from.' He handed her a parcel tied with a pink ribbon. 'Happy birthday.'

'Yes, Happy Twenty-first, Alex,' agreed Twig. 'I've got something for you too, but Jane and I'll take it inside.' They departed arm in arm and John Baron was left with Alex, her eyes alight as she surveyed the parcel.

'Can I open it here, now?'

'Of course.'

Inside was a 6-inch high porcelain deer painted blue and white with tiny turquoises pasted into the centre of the large round eyes. The face was pretty and somehow comical at the same time. He had bought it in Chichester at an antiques shop.

'Oh, it's just beautiful.'

'I'm glad you like it.'

'I do.'

As they crossed to the steps Alex held the deer close to her body. She felt like crying. She had never experienced this sort of abrupt emotion before and wondered what on earth was happening to her. She looked sideways at JB's profile as she swallowed hard. She had been on tenterhooks ever since she had asked him to her party – half expecting him not to come. But here he was. She supposed he was quite old really, he must be at least twenty-seven or eight, but that was not a fault; to Alex it was exciting.

She halted by a terracotta urn and he paused at her side. 'Shouldn't we go in?'

Alex shook her head. 'Not just yet. Couldn't we stay out

here a little longer? Tell me something about Australia. Where's your home over there?'

He did not reply, for a five-seater Swift came whizzing along the drive and screeched up beside them. 'Happy Birthday, Alexandra!' two young women shouted, before climbing out, rushing over and kissing her.

Alex covered her disappointment at the interruption and accepted their greetings before dutifully introducing John Baron to them.

Patricia and Carolyn Blackburn were high-spirited twins and after the introduction they linked arms with Alex and John Baron and enthusiastically bore them up the steps and into the house where 'The Lambeth Walk' swelled out from a gramophone and couples stepped out to it on the terrace while other people milled about talking, champagne in hand.

Alex still held the china deer in her cupped hands as if she carried the Koh-i-nor Diamond. 'I must put this somewhere safe,' she decided aloud, extricating John Baron from Patricia's continuing grasp and turning him towards a woman in her middle years wearing a lavender georgette gown clasped with a diamond on her bodice, who bore down upon them.

'Good evening, Mrs Cardrew,' the twins chanted and ran off towards the drinks table.

Alexandra smiled at the woman. 'Mummy, this is JB.'

Mummy's small eyes were covered with ivory rimmed glasses and her dark hair, streaked with grey, was pulled back in a bun. 'How do you do?' She held out her hand and John Baron took it.

'John Baron Chard. How do you do, Mrs Cardrew.'

For a moment Lillian Cardrew frowned and paused, but her recovery was so swift that the reaction was lost in the quick smile and warm handshake that followed. 'I believe you've come all the way from Tangmere.'

'Yes.'

'I'm sorry I didn't meet you when you were here before. We – my husband and I – were away for the weekend.'

'Mummy and Daddy like to go up to London for the shows,' Alexandra explained.

313

'Do I get an introduction?' asked a young woman who looked a lot like Lillian Cardrew.

'Of course. JB, this is my sister Kate.'

'Oh, you're the one who's chosen the university career?'

'Mmm,' she smiled and held out her hand.

'Now what's this?' Alex's mother inquired, noticing the deer her daughter held.

'JB gave it to me. Will you please put it somewhere safe, Mummy? While we dance?' She passed the object delicately into her mother's care and took John Baron's hand.

Lillian cast a disapproving glance at her daughter and Alex defended herself. 'If I don't dance with him he might ask someone else.'

John Baron smiled at Mrs Cardrew and Kate, and Alex led him away to the terrace where they were intercepted at the French doors by a swarthy young man in a dark suit and red tie. 'Oh JB, this is Trevor Braithwaite. Meet JB Chard.'

The two men shook hands and before any conversation began Alex gently pulled John Baron onto the terrace. Trevor's eyes followed them closely as the two moved off in step.

A sweet smell of honeysuckle wafted up to John Baron as they moved in unison and Alex tilted her head back to look at him. He felt a catch in his throat. Her body even felt like Sammy's in his arms.

'Do you like my dress?'

He had not noticed it. He looked down. It was a pale blue silk caught up at the shoulders in little pleats. He liked blue. He remembered Sam all in blue at his own twenty-first birthday party. What a wonderful night that had been. He carried that picture of her encapsulated in his memory; how they had danced together that night – she had felt like an angel in his arms swirling along with him. He saw her in the Pride of Erin, laughing and smiling at him . . .

'I said do you like my dress?'

'Oh? Sorry.' He returned his attention to Alex. 'Yes, it's quite lovely.'

'Why is it that you don't convince me?'

'Of what?'

'That my dress is lovely.'

'But it is.'

'Am I?'

He smiled at her. 'Yes, you are.'

'But I should have waited for you to tell me, I suppose.'

'Yes, you should.'

'But then you mightn't have.'

He began to laugh and she laughed too as he propelled her on, the evening sunlight kissing their faces.

Alex had been about ten when she first heard her aunt say *Nothing ventured nothing gained* and it had stayed with her, becoming a sort of catch-phrase; that's why she had invited JB to her party the first day they met. The allure had begun for Alex the very moment she had spied him walking by the sycamore tree. A feeling began almost tangibly as if a switch had been flicked on somewhere inside her. It had been followed by the horrible thought that he might be married or in love or something awful like that but the gods were with her, for here he was in her arms at her party, and he had come all the way from Tangmere and brought her a most beautiful gift. Alex was enraptured; she was not on the stone terrace of her childhood home but in the radiance of a magical cloud, cloaked in bliss, veiled from reality by the feel of his arms around her and the music charming away her senses.

Suddenly JB stopped dancing and Alex lurched into the present. Trevor stood with his hand on JB's shoulder. 'My turn with the birthday girl,' and he whisked Alex out of JB's arms and off across the floor. John Baron caught a glimpse of Alex's miserable expression before she was hidden from view by the other couples around her.

'Hello.'

He turned to see Jane, Twig and Patricia drinking champagne. 'Come on, we'll get you a glass.' As they wandered across to the trestle tables serving for a bar Jane pointed back to Alex. 'That's her old boyfriend. His family and ours go back a long way, so Mummy and Daddy were rather pleased when they seemed to hit it off, but since you came into the picture my baby sister's affection has waned.'

Patricia agreed. 'Yes, JB, we've all noticed it. You manage to appear in her conversation on an hourly basis.'

John Baron really did not want to hear this. He mumbled something about 'being flattered' as Jane handed him a glass of champagne.

The champagne was a good vintage which Nicholas Cardrew had been keeping for this very occasion, and as Twig picked up one of the bottles to read the label he spoke his thoughts to his companions. 'This is a pretty good drop. We'll have to tell old Simmons in the mess to get some of this in.'

Jane laughed. 'I doubt the RAF will be buying Pol Roger 'twenty-eight for the likes of you, Twig Russell.'

John Baron lifted his forefinger towards his friend as Twig emptied his glass. 'I don't want to be the voice of reason, but we do have to fly an aeroplane this evening.'

Twig grinned. 'Then don't be. The voice of reason is always a fun-killer.'

'Oh, I love this song,' Jane said as 'That Old Feeling' rose from the gramophone and her sister sailed by, laughing on the arm of a young man.

'Then let's all dance.' Twig lifted his hands towards Jane.

'Excuse me.' They turned to find Lillian Cardrew standing behind them. 'There's a telephone call for either Flight Lieutenant Chard or Russell.' She pointed through to the front hall.

'I'll take it,' John Baron replied and Twig dropped Jane's hands to join him. 'I'd better come too.'

'Excuse us.'

As they disappeared to take the call, Patricia wandered away and Alexandra left Trevor on the terrace and came inside to her mother and sister. 'Where are they going?'

'It was Manston airfield on the telephone.'

Alex's mouth drew down. 'Oh, I do hope there's nothing wrong.'

Out in the hall John Baron replaced the receiver and Twig eyed him expectantly.

'It was the Sergeant; said Tangmere called to see if we'd

landed there and to tell us to return without delay. Something about a lecture tonight for all officers. Apparently no one has asked where we are but he reckons we should hot foot it back and take off smartly.'

Twig sighed. 'Hell, it will be hours before we're back at Tangmere.'

'Yes, but we'd better get moving in any case.'

'Well, that's the end of the champagne for tonight.'

They re-entered the drawing room and when Jane saw the expression on Twig's face she murmured, 'Uh oh,' into her glass as John Baron spoke.

'Alex, I'm sorry. Mrs Cardrew, Jane, we're to return to the airfield immediately. Have to fly back to Tangmere without delay.'

'Oh no. Is it war?' Lillian Cardrew asked, a small sound of fear escaping from her throat.

John Baron shook his head. 'No, Mrs Cardrew. Nothing like that's been said. I'm so sorry to have to depart like this.'

They shook Mrs Cardrew's hand, and Alex and Jane accompanied them out of the front door into the evening sunshine.

Twig and Jane headed across the drive into the shadow beneath the beeches and John Baron shouted, 'Hey you two, you've got one minute, that's all.'

Alex pulled on the sleeve of his jacket. 'This just isn't fair.'

'I'm sorry, Alex.'

'I haven't read anything in *Good Housekeeping* which covers this sort of thing.'

He could not help but smile, she sounded so very child-like in her disappointment.

'And now you're smiling as if you really want to leave.'

She certainly said exactly what she was thinking. He shook his head. 'That's not true.'

She hoped with all her heart he meant what he said, but she was very unsure. 'And you didn't tell me anything about Australia at all. Please just tell me something before you go. Now, while Jane and Twig are at it.'

317

He could not help but smile at her again.

'Where did you live?'

'In Queensland.'

'That's a nice name. Go on. What's your home like? Please.'

He glanced over to where Twig was kissing Jane under the broad overhang of one of the trees while at his side Alex continued, 'Another minute here with me won't do the RAF any harm. Just tell me something about where you live.'

'All right.' He thought for a moment. 'My home's in south-eastern Queensland by a stream called Teviot Brook. Well, it's a stream some of the year; in the dry spells it turns into a series of small water-holes or disappears altogether. Gum trees grow along the banks and you can smell the eucalyptus on the breeze – it seems to waft across the land from the dark hills that cling to the horizon. The house has a wide verandah all the way around and kookaburras – they're birds – used to wake me in the morning. Summer's a solid arid heat with occasional thunderstorms. In winter the westerlies blow. It's an olive-green and grey land, unlike this emerald country. We plant crops and grow grain, and we've a couple of hundred dairy cows, a few pigs, a lot of horses and some cattle. My father and my uncle had no experience of animals or farming before they went there but they run a profitable property now. It's called Haverhill and at dusk you sometimes see wallabies or kangaroos coming down to the water. In spring the yellow wattle trees flower and the bush comes to life with wild flowers . . .' He broke off and fell silent.

'It sounds wonderful and as if it means an awful lot to you.'

'It does.'

'Then what are you doing here?'

'That's for another day.' He cupped his hands over his mouth and called, 'Come on, you two!' and the lovers reluctantly left the trees and came over arm in arm and climbed into the car.

Alex wished with all her heart that she could go to

318

Manston with them and see them off but Jane gestured to the house. 'Shouldn't you get back to your other guests?'

For the second time in less than an hour Alex felt as if she could cry. JB was looking at her in a most peculiar way and she decided to be bold again. She positioned herself where John Baron's body hid her from Jane in the driver's seat. She felt all hot and bothered and she just took the plunge. 'Heck JB, I know I've only seen you once before but it's my birthday after all and I don't know when I'll see you again.' She inhaled deeply and whispered, 'Couldn't you kiss me just once?'

He had never met anyone like her. She was obviously smitten by him and of course that was gratifying but his feelings were still in disarray, even after three years completely away from Sam. There were times when he told himself he had to find a nice girl, in fact, must find a girl, yet he had not met anyone who could hold a candle to his sister. And here was this kid who looked so much like her, right here with him asking him to kiss her . . .

Alex felt his hands take hold of her shoulders and then the blue sky disappeared as he bent down and covered her lips with his.

She was transported again, living in the dream of the moment, sinking into fantasy . . . And then too quickly it was over and he stood back from her.

'Look after yourself, Alex.'

Suddenly a car weaved noisily into the garden and pulled up at the bottom of the front steps. Alex looked around at it as John Baron slipped into the back seat of the Austin and Jane eased it into gear.

Alex turned back to the Austin's window, her heart's yearnings displayed so obviously in her eyes. 'You *will* telephone me, won't you?' she asked.

He replied, 'I will,' and Jane accelerated down the drive.

Now Alex knew she was crying. She lifted her fingers to wipe away a tear as a sharp voice filled the space behind her.

'Alexandra, who on earth was that?'

Alex turned to see her Aunt Harriet and her father standing beside the newly arrived vehicle.

Harriet at fifty-nine was as fashionable as she had been twenty years previously. She wore a grey shot-silk dress with a black and white checked collar. Her shoes were covered in the silk of her dress and her handbag and gloves were black and white to match her collar. On her ears were two substantial rubies that her current husband, Edward Barrington, had brought back from South America for her fifty-fourth birthday.

Before Alex had time to gather herself her aunt exclaimed, 'Who was that man?'

Alex did not reply.

'Speak up, answer me, who was he? What's wrong with you? Cat got your tongue?'

Alex sighed and hesitated before she answered, 'Which man?'

'The one who was *kissing* you.'

'He's a friend of mine, in the RAF. He was just recalled to Manston.' A tear rolled down Alex's cheek and she brushed it away with the back of her hand.

'What's his name? Tell me this instant what's his name?'

'For heaven's sake, Harriet, why is all this so important?' Alex's father strode over and placed his arm around his daughter. 'Can't you see Alexandra's crying?'

Harriet frowned and her chin came down as she eyed Alex. 'Oh, is she? Crying? No, I didn't notice.' Her voice became a mite less severe. 'So Alex dear, come on then, who was he?'

'His name's JB.'

Her father gave her a quick hug. 'Oh, you mean the fellow you met when Mum and I were in London?'

Alex nodded.

Her father took her hand. 'The one you're keen on, eh my darling?'

Harriet sniffed. 'Will you two stop all this and tell me the man's name!'

Alex complied. 'His name's John Baron, John Baron Chard.'

The look that passed between Harriet and Alex's father

went unnoticed by Alex for she was so full of JB's departure, and when her father turned to her again and gave her a hug, she tried to smile.

'You're upset by his departure, my darling?'

'Oh, I don't know, Daddy, I suppose so.' She gave a deep sigh. 'But I'd better get back to the party.' And she hurried away up the steps and into the house.

Harriet was holding her chin in thought and she stepped closer to her brother to confide her feelings. 'I knew it as soon as I saw him. He looks exactly the same. Didn't you see him, Nicholas?'

'No, Harriet, I didn't.'

'How could you miss him? He was kissing Alexandra, for heaven's sake!'

'Yes, I saw that, but I didn't see *him*.'

Harriet gave an exasperated intake of breath and waved her gloved hand in the air. 'Well, he's identical to my *first* husband. And his name's the same!' Her neck was turning pink and a telltale nerve twitched in her still lineless cheek. 'He has to be the child of that dreadful French floozy!'

'Do you really think so?'

'Oh Nicholas, use your brain. He looks the same and has the same name. Why wouldn't any rational person think so?'

'Could be, I suppose. I remember once, years and years ago, you finally found out they'd gone to Australia and you were all for following them. I'm glad I talked you out of that.'

A dismissive sound escaped Harriet's lips. 'Nicholas, you're my young brother and so I'm fond of you, but you've never talked me *out of*, or for that matter, *into*, anything in your life.'

Nicholas was used to his sister: he did not react to this. He remembered her first husband John Baron, though he had not really had a great deal to do with him. Harriet had wedded him when Nick was only eighteen and he was not really clear on the ramifications of the marriage, but he always knew there had been great ructions when John Baron left her and went to France, only to reappear a few years later and die within months of his return. His sister had never forgiven him for leaving her, and there had been a violent dispute over John Baron's will. Not that it had stopped her from marrying twice since. Her second husband, a lead mine owner, died in a fall and she married again, a race-horse breeder whom she seemed to live with only intermittently, spending most of her time between their house in St John's Wood in London, a villa in the South of France and a country house near Canterbury, while her husband, Edward, appeared to spend most of his time in Salisbury.

Castlemere saw Harriet mostly at weekends when she motored up to harass them all. Nick and Lillian put up with her: Nick because she was his flesh and blood and Lillian because she loved Nick. The girls had long ago become immune to their Aunt Harriet.

Nicholas took his sister's arm. 'Come on, Harriet, we're here to celebrate Alex's birthday. Let's forget about this. There's nothing you can do about it.'

'That's what you think,' Harriet said under her breath as she allowed her brother to take her up the steps into the house, and as they entered the hall she commanded aloud, 'You'd better bring me a glass of champagne straight away. I need to consider many things.'

When John Baron and Twig arrived at Manston, Twig kissed Jane in hearty fashion once more before they left her at the gate and ran by the Corporal who was still on duty.

Passing through the Nissen huts to the airfield they found 'Maggie' refuelled and waiting, and within three minutes more they had started the engine and were gathering speed along the airfield for take-off.

Forty-five minutes later they landed in Tangmere, and Redleaf, JB's mechanic, came running over. He hailed John Baron from under his sandy moustache as they climbed out onto the wing and jumped to the ground.

'I'll put "Maggie" to bed. Message from the Wingco for you to report to his office.'

'Shit,' Twig commented. 'Hope we're not in for it.'

Wing Commander Macarthur was known as a man who expected a lot from his men but who at the same time was not a strict disciplinarian and allowed his boys a certain amount of freedom as long as they played fairly with him. When the two pilots reported to him he asked, 'When did you two land?'

John Baron replied, 'A few minutes ago, sir. Came straight here.'

The Wingco tapped a pile of maps on the desk in front of him and stood up. He was well over six foot and seemed to loom over them in the small room. 'Why did it take you so long? My information is that Manston was contacted at 1915 and it's now . . .' he looked at his watch '. . . 2132.'

Twig answered this time. 'Beats us, sir. We flew out immediately we were told.'

Wing Commander Macarthur knew his pilots well. He gave them a long searching look. 'You hadn't left the airfield, had you?'

'We were being refuelled for quite some time, sir. They don't seem to work as swiftly at Manston as they do here.' Twig answered again, looking intently at the small window behind the officer's head. 'You know how it is, sir. A message is taken and it isn't always delivered immediately. Some people go out of their way to act without delay – others, well, they seem to just take . . .'

'Yes, yes. All right, Russell, we don't need a discourse on the actions of airfield personnel. And I'm not so far past it I can't tell when you're wriggling out of answering a question.' He walked back round his desk and sat.

They stood in front of him in silence as he shot a piercing look to Twig and then to JB before he spoke again. 'Squadron Leader Crandle, who's been working closely with Squadron Leader Coop, the Assistant Air Attaché in Berlin, called in here this evening – he's just left. He gave us an in-depth lecture on the Luftwaffe. You two missed it and were obvious by your absence.' He lifted his forefinger at them. 'Who authorised this reconnaissance flight you took over Kent anyway?'

Twig exhaled and answered, 'This office, sir.'

Wing Commander Macarthur looked from one to the other of his pilots. 'Oh really? I'd like to see the authorisation form.'

Twig shuffled his feet and John Baron wished he were invisible. The officer continued to eye his charges from beneath his dark brows. 'If you weren't such damn good pilots, I'd delve into this one . . . *really delve into it*. Do you understand me, Russell?'

'Yes, sir.'

'Do you understand me, Chard?'

'Yes, sir.'

'Flight Lieutenant Richey took notes this evening, I believe. Get them from him and study them.' The Wingco pointed to the door. 'This airfield's on twenty-four-hour alert and I expect you to take that seriously. No more reconnaissance flights. No more missing vital lectures. Got that?'

'Yes, sir.'

He saluted and his two men replied in kind before they hurried out of the room.

'Phew!' Twig drew his finger across his throat. 'We were nearly for it.'

'Yeah, but we survived. Come on, let's get a drink.'

'Let's get two.'

Alex slept with her porcelain deer on her bedside table every night onwards from her twenty-first birthday. She named the animal 'Johba' and it was somehow comforting for her to whisper, 'Good night, Johba,' before she went to sleep each night.

On Thursday, 31 August, a week after her birthday, the telephone rang in the front hall and she answered it smartly: she had remained in the house each night in case JB should call.

She felt a tingle of delight as she heard his voice. 'It's John Baron Chard here, can I speak to Alexandra, please?'

'Oh, JB it's me.'

'Well, hello. How are you?'

'Oh I'm well, just wonderful, thanks. How are you?'

'Busy. War drills every day. On duty most of the time. Flew to Scotland and back this afternoon. The consensus is Hitler'll move into Poland any minute. Anyway, to happier things: how did the rest of your birthday party go?'

A sober expression crossed her face. 'Oh, it was nice.' She was remembering how she had run up to her bedroom after he had gone and cried with disappointment at his sudden departure, and then washed her face, renewed her lipstick and returned to the party. 'Everybody stayed till about eleven or so, then went home . . . being a week-night and all, you know.'

'Yes. What other gifts did you get?'

'Some perfume and a few scarves, a pair of silk stockings from Jane. Somebody gave me a fountain pen. Mummy and Daddy bought me a new handbag . . . lots of nice things.'

'They all sound great.' Then he coughed. 'I really called to thank you for inviting me and to say sorry I had to leave that way.' He paused. 'The squadron's ready and prepared to leave England, so I suppose this is goodbye.'

She thought her heart had stopped beating. She tried to say something but there was no sound.

'Alex? Are you there?'

She took a long breath. 'Yes.'

'So look after yourself.'

'JB?' A sort of squeak came out of her mouth along with his name.

'Yes?'

'Would you . . . could you . . . write to me from wherever you go?' She bit her lip as she waited for his reply.

There was another more noticeable pause before he replied, 'Yes, I will.'

She was doing it again – crying. A tear was rolling down her cheek. She was angry with herself. She was not an emotional person – well, not normally, and she thought how ridiculous it was that she kept crying whenever he was near her – even when it was only his voice on the telephone. She mastered herself. 'Look after yourself, JB.'

'I'm sure I'll do that. Give my regards to your mother. Oh, and to Jane.'

'I will.'

'Bye, Alex.'

She heard the click of the telephone receiver and the line went dead. 'Fly safely,' she said to herself as more tears crept over her lids. 'Oh God, I'm such a fool,' she spoke aloud as she hurried to the foot of the stairs.

'What did you say, dear?' her mother asked, coming in behind her.

'Nothing, Mummy.'

'Who was that you were talking to on the telephone?'

'JB,' she threw over her shoulder as she continued on up the stairs, her mother's gaze following her.

In her room Alex closed the door, moved to her bed, picked up the china deer and kissed it, then held it to her chest and lay down. She knew she was mad about JB and the trouble was she really had no idea how he felt. Hell, he had only seen her twice and spoken to her on the telephone twice. What kind of a romance was that? It was all on her side, no doubt, and she had been so brazen asking him to kiss her and all. He probably didn't even like her and she kept crying about him. It was maddening really.

She sat up and with a deliberate motion wiped her eyes. 'Alexandra Cardrew, it's time you were sensible,' she said aloud.

She thought of her Aunt Harriet and how she had wanted to know all about JB. Not that there was much she could tell her, except that he came from Australia and had lived on a property called Haverhill. Her aunt had asked about his parents but she knew nothing about them. She had revealed that JB was based at Tangmere in Sussex and that as far as she knew he was in England alone. 'Why do you want to know about him?' she had inquired of her aunt, and Harriet had wasted a thin smile upon her and replied, 'I'm always interested in your young men, dear.'

As her aunt had shown no interest whatever in any of her previous boyfriends, this came as a surprising statement to Alex. But she did not concentrate upon it and put it down to Harriet's eccentricity which was legend throughout the family.

As Alex sat clutching the deer and staring at the pale

lemon curtains of her room, her door opened and Jane entered. 'Mummy said she thought you were crying.'

'What if I am?'

'She asked me to come in and look after you.'

'I'm all right.'

Her sister sat on the bed beside her. 'So you think you're in love, do you?'

Alex turned a horrified expression upon her. 'No, I don't.'

'Phooey. Kate told me you came up here and bawled when he was called back to base on your birthday. You're my little sister. I can see through you. Look at you now.' She pointed to the deer in Alex's grasp. 'Holding onto the deer he gave you as if it were the Messiah's robe. You're transparent.'

Alex hated to be transparent. She sniffed, pushed her sister aside and stood up from the bed, placing the deer firmly down near the bedside lamp. 'You think you know everything.' She walked over and knelt on the padded seat to open the window. Skylarks called beyond the river and Alex leant out into the fading evening.

Jane came and knelt beside her and now her voice was sympathetic. 'You've only seen him a couple of times.'

'Yes.'

Her elder sister slipped her arm around Alex's shoulder. 'Do you know something else?'

'No – what?'

'I've only seen Twig a few times too, but I'm pretty keen on him as well. Fact is, very keen on him'

Alex turned her face to her sister. 'Yes, I would hope so, the way you kiss him.'

Jane made a noisy lovelorn sound. 'I got a letter from him in yesterday's post. He said he wants to see me, the first chance he gets. Said whenever he manages leave he'll head straight here. He signed it with two kisses.'

Alex drew in her bottom lip. 'Gosh. Aren't you lucky? I asked JB to write to me, but I'm not sure he will.' She stared at her sister and added, 'I've never felt this way before.'

'Really? What about Trevor?'

'Nothing like this.'

'And Ron Howard, you used to moon over him a year or so back.'

'He was all right. But JB's different altogether.'

Jane ran her finger along the windowsill. 'You know, my first real romance was with a fellow called Peter Barlow. I was about seventeen or eighteen, I suppose. He worked in the Canterbury library.'

Alex began to giggle.

'What?'

'Kate and I used to think he looked like a horse.'

Jane's mouth dropped. 'You mean things – you never!'

'We did.' Alex dug her in the ribs and now as her giggle turned into a full-blown laugh she bent further out of the window and Jane, uncertain whether to be affronted or not, continued to kneel beside her until finally she saw the funny side and she too began to laugh.

They could see the skylarks sailing high on the breeze as the dusk hastened up along the narrow Stour from Pegwell Bay. And the sisters' laughter rose until the sound of their merriment rang over the garden to the river; girlish and free, unconstrained and vital, it drowned out the skylarks' evening melody.

Twelve hours later the world knew: GERMANY INVADED POLAND AT DAWN THIS MORNING.

Crowds of people pushed into Downing Street and waited for Prime Minister Chamberlain to come out and speak. Of the thousands milling in the streets of London many were Czech and German Jews; refugees from the Nazi persecution in their home countries.

In the mess at Tangmere, JB, Twig and Paul stood together with a group of pilots and their Squadron Leaders as Wing Commander Macarthur informed them they would remain on constant alert and to expect the order to relocate to France at any time.

'There'll be no leave so telephone or write to your loved ones. We are given the understanding that war with

Germany is a probability within the next few days.'

In the brief silence that followed they looked at one another with that certain expression that men carry when they suspect they are about to enter a maelstrom.

Forty-eight hours later the maelstrom was entered: after all the pacifying of Hitler, after all the years of talk and speculation, after all the warnings and conjecture, Great Britain issued an ultimatum to Hitler to pull his troops out of Poland by 11 a.m. on Sunday, 3 September, 1939 or face war with Great Britain and France. Hitler did not reply in any fashion and at 11.15 all the officers at Tangmere collected in the officers' mess to hear the Prime Minister's mournful voice inform the nation: 'This country is at war with Germany . . .'

John Baron spent the afternoon packing, every now and then lifting his head to look out of the window to the woods beyond the blast-protection pens around the newly laid perimeter track. At one point he rested on the windowsill and felt the calming breeze that flowed across from the Downs and stirred the long grass outside. It was somehow surreal to think a war had begun when the sky was a turquoise blue and banners of white cloud drifted harmlessly over the woods beyond.

The orders to fly out to Northern France came through that same afternoon and they were to depart at 0800 the following morning.

Before he picked up Twig and Paul to go across to the mess at 1900 he telephoned Douglas.

'So it's finally begun.'

'Yes.' Douglas's voice held a brittle edge with excitement riding beneath. 'And JB, I know my boss at Shell's got my name on the list of indispensable workers debarred from call-up. Think he thought he was doing me a favour. Well, I've got to get off that. I have to fly again – I must. I've still got a few friends at the Air Ministry – I'll descend upon them from tomorrow morning.'

'What about Frederick Halahan – wasn't he your Commandant at Cranwell?'

The Royal Air Force College at Cranwell in Lincolnshire was where Douglas had done his initial training.

'He was,' Douglas replied.

'Isn't he an Air Vice Marshal now or something? You could write to him.'

'I intend to, old boy, and I'm going to write again to Charles Portal, the Air Marshal. He's the one who told me a few months ago that if ever a war came I'd have a chance at getting back into the RAF.'

'Good going. I'll be waiting to hear.'

'What about you? What's happening?'

They knew there was a telephone censor listening so John Baron replied, 'We'll be at readiness from dusk tonight. And we've orders to fly out in the morning.'

Douglas paused. 'Ah, I see. I won't ask you where to, but I reckon I know. Good luck, old chap, and say the same to Twig.'

They said their goodbyes and Douglas told him he was sending Thelma out of London down to the Pantiles where her family had a bungalow.

As John Baron hung up he saw Twig coming down the corridor towards him. They knocked on Paul's door and the three strolled across to the mess together.

John Baron and Twig were called to readiness as the sun went down and they waited in their own blacked-out crew room; most talking, some playing cards and others just drowsing. Nothing happened though they heard some Hurricanes from Number One Squadron take off at about 2200. Later they were informed that Paul had been in the scramble. German bombers had been sighted over the Dutch coast, but Paul and the others had found nothing and had returned at 2300.

During the wait in the crew room John Baron wrote two letters: one to his parents, Ledgie and Wakefield, and one to Samantha and Cash. Later he lodged them with the airfield post and returned to his room to find his batman, Kelly, finishing his packing.

He slept deeply and was awoken with tea by his batman who brought the information that seven Whitley bombers were supposed to have landed at dawn on their return from bombing the Ruhr Valley but only two had come in. There was heavy ground mist and they had been led in with Verey lights which had been fired off from the airfield.

'Gawd knows where the other five are,' Kelly said. 'Makes you realise the war's started.'

John Baron looked thoughtful. 'Yes, it does.'

As the batman turned to leave he halted. 'Oh sorry, sir, nearly forgot, this came in for you in a bag of mail this morning.' He held out a letter.

John Baron saw immediately it was from Sam.

The first few paragraphs were about him: how she hoped he was all right and that she was fascinated by his friend Douglas Bader whom he had told her about the year before in his birthday letter to her. While her wish was that all the talk and the theorising of a coming war would prove to be merely that, she thought Hitler was a total evil and at some point would have to be stopped if he were not going to ruin the world, and she prayed that JB would be safe if in fact a war did begin. She mentioned she was well and hoped he was.

It was the second half of her letter which was the disturbing part.

I must tell you that I have left Cash. It's been coming for a long time and in fact I haven't been home to the flat for a couple of months now. Lots of reasons. I think mostly his fault; but no doubt a bit of mine as well. He was always an enigma, as you know, and finally I couldn't live with him any more.

He somehow found out how I feel about you – yes, I still do – well, you would have known that, wouldn't you? Trust Cash to find out. That certainly helped to undermine the wedded bliss, I can tell you. There were other things but they don't matter now. It's over. Yes, I feel sad in one way because we had some really good times, but there – that's Cash; he ruins everything.

The other thing is I've got a new bloke, called

Lenny. He's American – worked for Time Magazine. *I'm really excited because he sent off a letter about six weeks ago with some of my photos to the Pictorial Editor at* Time, *and if we hear anything positive we'll be heading off. If I'm lucky I could be on my way before you receive this letter. Lenny makes me laugh and he's pretty good-looking, and I'm enclosing his New York address for you just in case I go there. If I do I'll write once I'm there and let you know.*

If I'm off to America I'll go home to Haverhill and tell them face to face. Now that will be something I can probably do without. I don't think Mum and Dad or Unc will approve of me and Lenny! And I just know exactly what Ledgie will think – oh dear!

I know what you're thinking too, but JB, I have to do this. I'm stagnating in Sydney, really I am, and with Cash so close – well, he could probably talk me round if he catches me in the right mood and honestly I don't want that. I want a real career and New York can supply me with that, I feel it right through me.

I know some of this will be a bit of a shock but please understand.

I miss you like hell.

Stay safe for me, my darling brother. And please please please write more than once a year,

Yours,
Samantha

John Baron placed the letter down on the desk at his bedside and moved to the window. The morning sun was trying to exert itself through the mist outside.

He felt sad for his little sister. She wrote as if she were entirely sure of what she did but he felt an ache of responsibility for her right down inside him. He knew she was floundering. Yes, perhaps she would go to New York and do well, but at least when she was with Cash, John Baron had known she was with somone who loved her; enigma or not.

Who the hell was this bloody Lenny?

He sank forward on the glass of the window pane and felt the coolness on his warm forehead. *Sammy, Sammy. I'm in a war and you're probably already in New York. Oh Sam, what's to become of us?*

Chapter Twenty-three

Sunday, 3 September, 1939: Sydney

Thunder rolled as Cash slipped down the drainpipe at the back of the shop. He had become adept at climbing, and entering and leaving places by first-floor windows when necessary, as it was tonight, for there were bars covering the glass on the ground floor. Looking left and right in the night, his keen eyes saw the yard was empty so he dropped the last five feet to the ground. Swiftly he pocketed his gloves, and replacing his slipper-like soft climbing shoes with his rubber soled sandshoes, he clipped them to his belt under his coat alongside his jemmy and the leather bag of loot. His eyes searched the black night again before he slipped across the yard to round a corner of the adjacent building and edge along the side of it through the narrow access which took him to a lane and from that to the street.

Once in the street he walked casually across the bitumen, jumped the gutter and began to run in the darkness downhill along the footpath. Even though he was dressed entirely in black, including a black cap, he avoided the pool of light from the street-lamp and turned the corner into a wider road of houses where he loped along, passing under a line of trees for a hundred yards. His hand rested on the valuables under his coat and a smile rode his mouth in harmony with the feeling of elation pulsing through him.

That was when his heart missed a beat. A torch beam abruptly hit him out of nowhere.

'Halt!' shouted a bodyless voice. The stream of light came from his right-hand side and instantly Cash guessed the holder of the torch to be at a distance of about forty yards across the road.

In one continuous movement Cash spun round and raced back behind the trees the way he had come as four or five voices shouted in unison after him and the shaft of light wavered along the street in an attempt to pick him up.

He kept the trees between himself and his hunters and hit his stride doing close to a twelve-second dash to the corner as the ray from the torch flickered across him and hit him solidly again as he turned back into the street he had run down so merrily mere seconds before.

The police, for obviously that was who they were, were all shouting and running wildly after him. He heard yelling up ahead now too, in seeming answer to those behind, and as his brain began working again he swiftly realised they did not know where he had been or they would have been waiting at the bottom of the drainpipe for him. His best chance was to return there and scale one of the fences into what he knew was a quiet group of houses. He hurtled uphill across the road as the police came round the corner and the torchlight continued its search for him.

'There he goes!'

'Into that laneway.'

Feeling the first drops of rain Cash charged down the lane and slid into the narrow access he had just exited as he heard men exclaiming: 'This way! Quickly!'

Cash now realised the police had staked men around the streets of Paddington and probably even in a wide net of some square miles in an attempt to catch the man who had become known as 'Sydney's Stealth Burglar'.

Unlike his hunters he knew exactly where he was and with his heart pumping and the stimulation of being chased lifting him to even greater speed in the darkness than his pursuers could possibly muster, he reached the back of the building he had just robbed and ran to the six-foot stone fence to scale it. Suddenly there were raised voices on the other side of the wall. He came to an abrupt halt.

He dared not risk going over the fence after all. His mind raced in assessment and he made a decision and slipped off his sandshoes. There was no time to change into his climbing slippers, the cops could be here any moment if they saw the narrow access; so he threw his shoes under a bush against the stone fence and began in his socks to ascend the drainpipe. He could hear the police running by on the far side of the building. Down they charged to meet a brick wall. 'He must have gone over this!' he heard a voice opine clearly in the night.

The sounds of men vaulting the wall now reached him. Then he heard a dog begin to bark in the distance, and the policemen's cries lifted in continuing theory of his whereabouts.

Cash was sweating profusely as he shinnied up the pipe; it was so much more difficult in his socks than his specially prepared slippers but he closed his mind to the nearness of the police and concentrated with all his prodigious determination on getting up to the window. Lightning flashed in a brittle silver flare, delineating the fence and trees and the roof of the house next door. Cash swore under his breath as he heard a new voice cry, 'Hey, what about down here?'

He knew they had found the passage at the side of the building!

Immediately loud grunts, from men sliding and scurrying down towards him, echoed in the night. Abruptly thunder filled his senses and he scrambled up further to come abreast of the window he had jemmied open earlier.

It began to rain as he reached out towards the sash window and gave it a push with his right hand. The lock being broken it opened easily and now he could hear the men below approaching the yard as he lifted his leg towards the opening.

Cash's body hung between the pipe and the windowsill when the first policeman came panting into the yard below him and threw a probing arc of torchlight across the grass and bushes and along the fence.

Suddenly the rain intensified as a second arrow of light shot into the yard. Cash strained every muscle in his being to slip his body astride the window as one of the policemen shouted, 'Hey, what's this?'

Cash's pulse raced.

'A bloody sandshoe! And here's another!'

He could see the two arcs of light penetrating high in the trees and could hear the shouts. 'These sandshoes'll be his. He came down here, all right.'

'Might have gone over the fence!'

'If he has, Drayton and Clark'll have him.'

Cash willed himself over the sill and as his shin scraped along it thunder rolled again and the illumination began systematically to climb the building towards him.

The thunder masked his grunts as he hurled himself through the opening, hit the floor, rebounded, and dragged the pane down just as the window was lit clearly from below and the gleam penetrated inside.

Cash held his breath as the beam passed on then returned to wash across the window again before disappearing. And now he smiled. *Missed me, you bastards!*

He edged to the glass and looked down. Light danced all around the yard again, and while he watched the police scramble through the bushes and over the fence Cash wrapped his handkerchief around his bleeding shin and let out a long relieved breath. Yet there was no fear in him; there had been none right from the moment he had been intercepted in the road. Yes, he had felt the electrifying excitement of being chased, yes, he had felt the unadulterated thrill of making his escape, but he had not felt fear; that had never been his companion; right from being a child there had been nothing he had truly feared.

But he was annoyed, and the events disturbed him. The single occasion he had been on the run before had been when he was surprised in the house in Hamilton Heights, Brisbane. Eluding his hunters that time had come relatively easily except for the dog that latched onto him. But tonight was different. The police had a net out for him and they were serious. He needed to re-think a lot of things. From all he read and saw at the flicks, the police in the USA carried guns. If that had been the case in Australia tonight he could have been shot.

His quick decision to come back here had saved him.

He had chosen this Paddington barber shop to rob when he had been the last customer in for a haircut on a Saturday morning five weeks previously. The shop closed at noon and at about eleven forty-five the barber's assistant had unlocked a drawer behind the counter and added up the notes and silver within. He then inquired whether he should leave it 'to bank on Monday as usual?'

The barber replied, 'No, I need it to pay for my new wireless set. It's being delivered today.' And the youth put the earnings in a brown paper bag and left it on the counter and went whistling down the staircase and out of the door. Cash had acted as if he had seen and heard nothing but gambled that this would remain the conduct of the barber; to bank the money each Monday, and that hunch had paid off. Tonight when he had forced open the drawer he had taken twenty-five pounds in cash and notes. He had also jemmied open the door from the barber's downstairs hallway into the side room of the antique store below. There he found no money but much he would have liked, yet he limited himself to jewellery and three small, solid gold fili-greed boxes.

He remained at the window watching the deluge, the rain spattering on the pane in the vague ambient night light of Sydney, his shin throbbing, his elbows on the sill and his long smooth hands cupping his chin. Now the cops had his shoes, and in Brisbane they had his fingerprints from the knife that had killed Dexter Wilde. Maybe it was time to move on. Go to Melbourne or get away altogether to New Zealand. He could even follow JB, Sam's phantom bloody lover, over to the Old Dart. But what about Sam? His eyes clouded with melancholy, and a strange half-wistful look crossed his face, to be swiftly replaced with a sneer. Sam would not go anywhere with him. Hell! He and his wife had become strangers. She was leaving him, wasn't she? With that Yankee bastard she had become tied up with. *Going to New York to further her career* was the excuse she gave him!

If only he had realised where Sam's photography would take her he never would have embraced it. He had lost her to it, to her dream and the strange set of people she mixed with; photographers and artists, most of whom were self-opinionated pseudo-intellectuals who bored Cash with their trivial prattle. He had come to detest phrases like: photographic optimism, conscious nationalism, subjective and arbitrary images, photographic illusion, constructed and desegmented pictures: what, if anything, did those blasted terms mean? Most of what Sam's friends spent hours arguing about, Cash thought was pretentious mumbo jumbo.

He crossed the room and sat in the barber's chair vaguely aware of his reflection in the darkness.

Theirs had become a fractious relationship. It had been their third wedding anniversary last month and what a day that had been. He gave a quick sad smile as he relived 1 August.

It had started badly. Sam had stayed with Françoise and Bob Buckland the night before, as she had tended to do of late, and Cash had visited her at her studio around eleven in the morning.

It had been a bitterly cold Tuesday and he had worn a sweater under his blazer and driven the Austin up to her studio and parked in the street outside. When he opened the front door he handed Greg, Sam's young assistant, five shillings, and told him to have an early lunch. Cash had gone through to the back and found Sam adjusting the lighting. She was standing on a wooden crate reaching on tiptoes up to a grid in the ceiling, her long body stretching enticingly in front of him. He felt something inside – he guessed it was love.

She looked round in surprise. 'God, Cash, what are you doing here?'

'Do you know what day this is?' He leant on the wall. Sam regarded him. 'Yes, I do.'

She had to admit he was a good-looking devil. He made her feel decidedly vulnerable, the way he lounged there with his black forelock dangling on his forehead and his mouth set in a grim sort of smile while his blasted unreadable gaze rested on her. She looked away; she would not allow herself to be drawn in again. Sam had had her fill of Cashman Slade. She stepped down to the cement floor.

'Well?'

'Well what?'

'Aren't you going to kiss me?'

'No.'

'What the hell happened to us, m'lady?'

She met his eyes. 'What happened to us, Cashman Slade, was that you became a bloody burglar and a liar. Oh, as long as I was all Miss Innocence everything was hunky dory, but when I started to question you, when I went six nights in turn to the trots and the dogs and combed the stands, the bars, the grounds and the betting ring, and you were never there; when I finally worked out where all the money you have came from and I challenged you about it . . . And you lied again. That's what happened to us! Oh yes, and then on top of all your lies there's your damn fixation on my brother and how you *assume* I feel about him. That's what happened to us, Cash. That's what damn well happened.' Tears filled her eyes and she turned away. 'And I want no more of it.'

Cash stopped leaning on the wall and stood upright. He spoke dispassionately, quietly, and Sam had long ago learnt to recognise that meant he was furious. 'Sammy, let's get one thing perfectly clear, shall we? I do not *assume* how you feel about JB.'

She swung round to face him.

'I know.' He gave a cool grunt of disgust.

She closed her eyes and turned away

'For God's sake, girl, I've always known.'

'What does that mean?'

He still spoke rationally: it was the import of his words that carried the jealous fury. 'It means I married you knowing all the while that you were in love with your own bloody brother, for Christ's sake.'

Sam shook her head. 'But . . . how could you know?'

He made a small exasperated sound and walked the few steps to the window and looked out onto the bleak day where a sparrow jumped along on top of a woodpile; everything in Cash's vision was grey like the feeling he carried inside. He faced back to her. 'Hell, Sam, I've known for years. I saw you, that night after the Christmas concert when you would have let him screw you for God's sake. I saw everything.'

Sam's face altered colour; her eyes were disbelieving. For a moment she dropped her head in shame and then she looked up at him and shuddered. 'You *saw* us? You *spied* on us?' Her voice rose. 'God in heaven, Cashman Slade, have you no honour at all?'

'Perhaps not, but hell, girl, let's not start to moralise. Your record's more than discredited.'

Sam's face crumpled and tears welled in her eyes. 'Oh yes, I'm the evil one. Not you, the liar and the thief. There's *nothing* wrong with you.'

'I didn't say that. There's a lot wrong with me.' He walked the few steps back to her.

'Bloody right,' she sniffed. 'I could go to the police right now. I *should* go to the police right now. You've no idea how I feel. None. And you don't care.'

He silently watched her weep while inside, he himself wept and continued to hide the key to unlock her pain. A great part of him wanted to comfort her and hold her, to take her in his arms and say he did understand; that he did care and it was all right. That she could love JB; that it wasn't incest at all.

But he did not move. For while he knew it was absurd, he longed to believe she would come back one day, be his again, that their life together would continue.

Finally she calmed and she raised her gaze to his while they stood there impotently facing each other as the seconds passed; both consumed with the appalling reality of all that had been said.

Unexpectedly a call split the void of silence between them. 'Sam, where are you, darling?'

They both spun towards the door as Lenny ambled through it. When he saw Cash he halted. He looked to Sam. 'Visitor, my dear?'

In a move so fast that neither Lenny nor Sam saw it coming, Cash lashed out and hit Lenny full on the jaw with what was an explosive right hook carrying all of Cash's

341

pent-up emotion. The American dropped like a felled tree to the ground.

'Now what've you done?' Sam sank on her knees beside the unconscious man.

'*Visitor, my dear.*' Cash mimicked the prone man's words. 'No, I'm the *husband* mate, you're the bloody *visitor.*' Cash nudged him with his foot. Lenny lay still, and blood began trickling from his mouth.

'Sadly, I think the bastard will live.'

Sam looked up, and again tears built up in her eyes. 'Go away, Cash. Just go away.'

'Sure, I'll go.' And now he wanted to hurt her, to frighten her: he wanted her so damned much it pained him inside. But he just had to hurt her. 'Stay cognisant of this, m'lady. You've lived off stolen goods your entire married life. You're an accessory. I *could* say you were a partner in it all. So don't do anything as idiotic as putting the law onto me.'

He turned but quickly looked back, a multitude of emotions drowning him. He had to take a breath before he went on, and his voice choked slightly as he spoke. 'And I do know how you feel. Fact is, I'm in torment too, though no doubt you hadn't noticed. And that bloody ratbag on the floor isn't worthy of you.' He bent forward and touched her hair but she withdrew from his hand. He stood there a second or two looking down at her and then hurried towards the street door throwing the words, 'Happy anniversary, m'lady,' grimly back over his shoulder.

The rain still fell on the window as Cash became aware of his shin throbbing. He shook his head. Sammy had left him permanently after that débâcle. He knew she went to Queensland to say goodbye to her parents and Ledgie and Wakefield, and he was aware she was meant to leave for New York any day now with the ratbag Lenny. There were still quite a lot of her possessions in the flat; he was not sure what he would do with them if she did not take them. Anyway his life with Sammy merely reflected the blasted mess the world was in: Germany had invaded Poland the day before yesterday and no doubt Britain would have to declare war on that maniac Hitler soon. Australia wouldn't let Britain down, so who knew what the hell would happen? He had to start thinking about himself now; especially after tonight. That had been serious. And he still needed to get out of here.

He took out his torch and flashed it on his wrist to look at his watch: 4.30 a.m. He had been here in this room about three hours. He thought by now the police would have removed their stake-out from the area and would regard him as having escaped. Cops hated getting wet: they had probably called it quits at the beginning of the downpour, weak buggers.

He did not shinny down the drainpipe this time but took the slight risk of being seen coming out of the front door into the street. Earlier in the night he would not have dared to be so bold.

The rain had abated to steady drops by the time he slipped across the street and gingerly passed downhill. Instead of turning the corner and running along where the beam of light had hit him earlier, he took a side street and went a different route, running all the way to Rushcutters' Bay. He was cold and wet when he arrived before dawn at a dilapidated small house in an alley directly behind Sydney Stadium. The stadium had been erected in 1910 to stage the world title fight between the American fighters Jack Johnson and the great white hope, Tommy Burns, and now was where the Sydney hoi polloi gathered each week for local fights and where Cash met a lot of his seedy associates.

The rain had long ceased when Cash eased himself by the broken-down Vauxhall that blocked the front of the house, and, panting from his exertion, opened the unpainted door with the key.

'Who's that?' came a grating voice from within.

'Only me, Danny,' replied Cash.

'Bloody late, aren't ya? I was worried.'

'Yes. Cops were crawling all over the place.'

'Shit, eh? They didn't get ya but.' A small wiry man of about fifty crept out of his iron cot, grabbed a coat and came forward to the first of the three rooms. He lit a lamp. 'Christ, it's bloody cold and you're soaked.'

'Yes, well it happens that it was raining the last few hours, Danny old dear.' As he spoke Cash was removing his belt, his leather booty pouch and his jemmy. He handed the crowbar to Danny and put the pouch in an open case on the floor then he took off his drenched black clothes and placed them over a rail to dry and rubbed himself down with a towel.

'Lucky ya've got me to come to, lad,' Danny said, lighting a cigarette. 'Now ya can get on home in dry clothes all respectable like.'

'Yes, Dan – thanks, old mate.'

'Gawd, what did ya do ta ya shin?'

'Scraped it along a windowsill.'

'Here, I've got some Dettol somewhere.' Danny began delving into a cupboard and came out with the antiseptic. He poured a little in a dish and filled it with water and Cash dabbed his shin.

He gave ten pounds of the stolen money to Danny who grinned widely, showing broken teeth.

'There are two gold boxes and jewellery in there.' Cash pointed to the pouch. 'Should get a couple of hundred for that and you'll get your share, mate. Look after it.'

'Comin' to the fight tonight?' Danny asked, clearing his throat.

'Probably.'

'Good. I'll sit wiv ya then.'

'Sure. See you around six.'

'Beaudy.' Danny began to cough and splutter, but he took another draw on his cigarette and blew a long trail of smoke into the air.

Cash picked up a Minton porcelain cup and poured himself some water from a crystal jug. They sat together on a silver tray: all items Danny had come by one way or another, and stood incongruously on a wicker table against the wall.

Cash placed two more logs in the grate and built up the fire. 'For heaven's sake keep warm,' Cash said as he left. 'And eat something instead of smoking.'

Danny's peel of laughter followed him through the front door.

As Cash walked, dawn broke over Sydney town. The sky was filled with golden stretching arms of light escaping through the breaking clouds and reaching upwards from the gilded horizon. The harbour's calm grey waters lapped the sodden beaches and the first ferry nosed its way across from Manly to the city in the arriving day.

Cash looked across the street to the glistening limbs of the bare trees on the harbour side of New South Head Road as he strode by the gutters awash from the night's rain. He headed up Bellevue Hill towards Double Bay and onward.

The dawn of day did not cheer Cash as it did so many of mankind. He preferred the close of day and his anticipation of what the approaching dark hours held. Days he existed through; nights he lived.

But on this September morning as the first tram rolled by him he felt the sting of exhilaration and he began to lope up the long hill. He had evaded the bloody wallopers again! Tonight his good mate Danny would find the right fence for him at the fights and by midnight the deal would be done, then he and Danny could celebrate with a beer. Danny had become his sort of semi-partner. Cash took the risks and Danny got rid of the stuff. For this he paid Danny well and he had come to completely trust the half-Aboriginal man who adored him. They had met at the fights shortly after arriving in Sydney and the association had just grown.

As Cash gained the crest of the slope his thoughts turned to Sam. He wondered if he would ever see her again. 'Damn it, m'lady,' he said aloud as a tram came along behind him and he ran across the road and skipped easily onboard.

'Hey, you.' It was the conductor.

'Speaking to me?' Cash asked.

'Damn right. What you just did is dangerous.'

Cash met his eyes as the man came down the aisle of the tramcar to him. 'For you probably.'

'Smart aleck eh? Why is it you people who get up early are all smart alecks?'

Cash grinned. 'Makes you one too then.'

The conductor, hoist upon his own petard, sighed. 'Look, mate, just pay the fare. Where are ya goin'?'

'Five stops.'

The conductor took the money, handed him the ticket and walked back along the vehicle shaking his head.

When Cash alighted he ran down the hill and into the front yard of the block of flats, bounded up the steps and into the foyer, leapt up the nine steps to the next landing, opened the door and wandered in, throwing his key into the dish on the hall table.

'Sammy!' He halted in surprise.

'Hello, Cash.'

Then he saw the boxes and the two suitcases.

'I came for the rest of my stuff.'

'So I see,' he replied.

'I can guess where you've been,' she said with disgust.

'Can you now? I didn't know you were acquainted with Danny: he's a bit too normal for the sort of company you keep.' He passed through to the kitchen and she followed him.

Sam gave a rumble of frustration in her throat. 'Have you heard the news?'

'And what news would that be, m'lady?' he asked, filling up the kettle.

She sighed. 'While you've been out, no doubt robbing some poor innocent victims, a war's started.'

He put down the kettle. 'Ah, I see. Well, the world's been expecting it. That bloody Hitler's a maniac for a start.'

'Britain declared war on Germany yesterday and we have too. I heard Mr Menzies on the wireless last night.'

'That'll certainly alter a lot of lives.' Cash lit the flame and placed the kettle on the stove. 'So we're at war, Sammy. Does that mean you won't go to Yankee land, that you'll stay here with me and be a good wife, and support the war effort?'

'Give up, Cash.'

'Still going then, are you?'

She nodded.

'I doubt the Yanks will be declaring war, not with all the stuff I read about isolationism. Even that blasted aviator, Charles Lindbergh, is convinced of the Luftwaffe's superiority and campaigning to keep America out of the war.' He shrugged 'So there you go, Sam, running off to a neutral country with your boyfriend, eh? Leaving us here to contend with things. That's the spirit!' He walked to the dresser and took down a cup and saucer.

'Damn you, Cash. I'm going to New York because I want to learn, to be more than I am here. To be somebody in the photographic world – the real big world.'

'Just coincidence that Lenny the lover's going too?'

'I don't have to explain myself to you.'

He gave her a long slow look. 'There was a time when you liked to.'

Before she said any more there was a rap on the front door.

Sam turned. 'That'll be my taxicab.' She left him. He listened to her footsteps on the hall carpet and heard her open the door.

'Oh yes, could you take those boxes and those suitcases? I'll be out in just a minute.'

'That's what I'm here for, lady.'

She came slowly back through the hall and stood regarding him. Neither spoke while the sun mounted the windowsill and in its exuberance lit Sammy's face.

Cash eyed her.

Finally she took a deep breath. 'I only came back to Sydney yesterday, but while I was at Haverhill saying goodbye, Mum told me that two plain-clothes cops had been there looking for you.'

Cash chewed the side of his lip in thought. 'Did she tell them where I live?'

'Of course. She doesn't know you've anything to hide.'

'When was that?'

'Sometime last week.'

She picked up her purse from the kitchen table and hesitated. She looked clean and vital and so very young in the brazen sunlight. 'Goodbye, Cash.' She held out her gloved hand.

He felt a small tremor somewhere: perhaps where his heart was. 'Farewell, m'lady.' He took her extended hand.

'You'll be all right, Cash, war and all.'

'Yes, I will.' He smiled. It was a perfectly controlled, self-possessed smile.

'But you'd better get away from here fast.'

'Yes, I will,' he repeated.

'Look after yourself.'

'Yes I will,' he said again, letting go her hand.

She hesitated. Her bottom lip trembled. She looked as if she wanted to say more and he dearly wished she would, but she turned smartly and walked down the hall. He heard the door open and close.

He stood without moving at all for some seconds then his mouth set in a tight line as he crossed to the window and opened it, leaning on the sill to feel the comforting heat of the sun on the skin of his face as he regarded the morning. 'Nothing good happens in daylight,' he whispered as a tear wobbled on his eyelid before it fell to make a minute splash on the back of his hand.

In the taxi Sam sat head down. She was crying. She could not help it. She felt bad. It had been over with Cash for months, but saying goodbye had been so much harder than she had thought. They had said horrible things to each other as usual but it had still been awful at the end. Lenny had been against her going to the flat at all. They had argued over it, but she had gone anyway. She had been quite adamant actually. 'We were husband and wife, for heaven's sake. I have to say goodbye to him.'

And telling them at Haverhill. What a business that had been. She had informed them of her arrival in a telegram:

Coming home stop Something important stop Arrive Thursday depart Saturday stop Sam

When she had driven into the front yard in Hardy Medcott's ute they were all sitting on the front verandah like a committee. Even Crenna was there in her apron.

Sam felt annoyed. God, what do they think I am? A naughty child coming home?

They had stood in unison and walked down the steps to her, the dogs barking and making an awful din. Her mother wrapped her in her arms. 'Darling, you're all right, aren't you? We've been so worried.'

'Gosh, Mum, yes. I'm tip top.'

They had all seemed to sigh at the same time, and then she felt sorry for being annoyed with them.

'Is Cash all right?' Benjamin asked.

'Yes, but that's part of what I've come to tell you.'

It was with trepidation that she finally faced her mother, father, Ledgie and Wakefield round the scrubbed kitchen table. Crenna had made tea and then conveniently departed.

Sam regarded them: the four wonderful people who had nurtured her, brought her up and given her the values she held. Her father and mother had not really altered and if anything Wakefield looked younger than the last time she had been home; it was Ledgie who looked more frail and much older. Sam had never known how old she was, for the woman kept that information like a military secret, but she had to be over eighty. Nevertheless there was nothing frail about Ledgie's character and it was the little woman who put down her cup firmly on the table-top, placed her hands flat beside it and said, 'Why are we avoidin' asking the child what's going on?'

Benjamin cleared his throat. 'We're not avoiding it, Ledgie, we were waiting for Sam to begin but you're right in that it's time she did.' He lifted his eyes to his daughter's. 'So, Samantha, what is it?'

She told them.

She did not mention about Cash's being a burglar but she did say he had lied about where he spent his time and that it had undermined her feelings for him. When she arrived at the point about leaving him altogether Constance had begun to weep and Ben's arm had slipped comfortingly around her while Ledgie patted her hand.

Sam had tried to be as honest as possible about her departure to New York and had justified it by expressing her need to further her career. Explaining Lenny had been the complicated part.

'He's . . . well, he's a friend of mine and he can get me an entrée into photographic circles there. He knows the editors at *Time Magazine* and the *New York Post*. He wrote to the Pictorial Editor at *Time* and sent some of my photos.' Here she could not hold back the excitement in her voice. 'The wonderful thing is they actually liked my work.' She looked around their faces with uncontrolled glee. 'I've been offered a position – only a line photographer at first but don't you see what a break this is for me? New York!' She was smiling widely at them, but no one was smiling back.

She faltered and fell silent.

It was her father who spoke their unified thoughts. 'So Samantha, you've come home to tell us you've tired of your husband and therefore are leaving him and going to New York with an American who can help further your desire for recognition in the photographic world?'

Sam's smile had disappeared. 'Heck, Dad, that's a bit curt.' She glanced at Wakefield. 'Unc, you've always supported my ambitions. Tell him.'

Wakefield shook his head. 'This is different. There's no doubt of your talent, but leaving for America . . . Sammy, there's going to be a war any day now. That's as sure as the nose on your face, and you'll be thousands of miles away like your brother already is. And then this business of leaving Cash . . .'

'Oh God,' Sam broke in. 'If you only really knew the man. You don't have any conception of what he's like. Nobody does.'

Benjamin rapped the table with his fist. 'That might be so. And even if we accept that after merely three years of marriage you're giving up on it, how on earth do you think we could be pleased that you're sailing off to New York with this Lenny Lambert Crumby bloke?'

'Cundy,' Sam corrected.

'Cundy then! Sam, Sam you're young; this is all a mistake. Oh yes, you've lived a few years in Sydney but that doesn't prepare you for the world!'

Constance shook her head in bewilderment. 'It was bad

enough that John Baron upped and went like that, but you, too . . .' She began to cry again.

'She's a little blighter,' was all Ledgie could manage to articulate.

And so the round table meeting had floundered and died and Sam had gone walking along the brook and conjured up pictures of yesterday and JB when her world had been a beautiful place.

The following day she rode over to see Veena and Storm and spent the afternoon lounging on the grass on a blanket, catching up with Veena's life and playing with Storm who was now four and the possessor of a determined personality and wavy hair above big bold eyes. The little girl had been timid with Sam at first but within half an hour all restraint had evaporated.

'You spoil her, Sam,' Veena had said as Sam unwrapped the two dolls and the pink hat and bucket and spade she had brought.

'I like to, and I'll send you a dress from Fifth Avenue, New York,' she laughed as the child ran and fell onto her lap.

For some minutes, there in the sun on the blanket with the smell of eucalyptus on the breeze and a kookaburra laughing on a branch of a silky oak and little Storm digging into the russet earth with her spade, Sam thought about the child she might have had: the little person who might have been. A surge of sadness overwhelmed her and she looked away from the tot at play and wiped the corners of her eyes. Perhaps if it had been born things might have been different; but she knew as soon as it came to mind that she would still have been ambitious and wanted her dreams, and Cash would still have been the great complexity; the liar and thief. She sighed. The world was full of sorrow and the human condition was no happy legacy, so perhaps not bringing a child here could be construed as the great kindness.

She left Veena and Storm as the afternoon waned and arrived back at Haverhill to hear the news that Germany had invaded Poland.

'Will you still go to America?' her mother had asked, obviously close to tears again, and Sam had sighed and said, 'I'm sorry, Mummy darling, but yes I will.'

So there had not really been any pleasant conclusion, nor any effective acceptance of Sam's decisions, on her visit to Haverhill.

And now she sat in the back of the black taxi on her way to Lenny's flat in Kirribilli across the Harbour Bridge and this afternoon she would leave on the SS *Paragon* for Fiji, Pago Pago, Tahiti, the Panama Canal, Miami, Bermuda and New York.

She wiped her eyes and looked up to see the taxi driver eyeing her through the rear-vision mirror as he opined, 'Yes, love, I feel like cryin' too, what with the war and all.'

Chapter Twenty-four

Harriet frowned, smoothed her gloves and eased back in the taxi as the vehicle puttered out of Chichester towards Tangmere airfield. The taxi driver had bargained with her for the fare and in the end they had agreed to three shillings which she believed was exorbitant for the six-mile round trip. She had seen no alternative as this was the single taxi on the rank outside the railway station on her arrival from London.

She was watching the bald spot on the back of the driver's head as he half-turned and lifted his left hand off the wheel to shake his finger in emphasis. 'Don't know what's going to happen to us now this war's started. They're goin' to bring in petrol rationin' and that'll be the end of taxis then, won't it? I mean, how can we take folks to a destination if we ain't got no petrol, well, unless we get special treatment. And of course we should, shouldn't we? I mean, we're a necessary form of—'

'Would you please keep quiet!'

The man started. 'There's no need to be rude.'

'Listen to me, Mr Whoever you are. I'm paying you an excessive amount to take me to Tangmere airfield. I believe the charge is highway robbery. I did *not* pay you to talk to me. Your fee is to take me where I wish to go, to wait for me and return me to the station. I have a great deal on my mind and do not wish to converse with you about taxis, the war or anything else. So please resist speaking and take me to Tangmere.'

'Well I'll be blowed!' the driver exclaimed. 'I've never had such a fare.' But he fell silent all the same.

From that point on Harriet ignored him. She had been

thwarted in her quest to contact Flight Lieutenant Chard and finally had to take the step of travelling to see him. She tapped her gloved fingers together as she thought of the events which had brought her here.

Last week when she had attempted to elicit the telephone number of the airfield she had met with opposition. The stupid girl on the exchange would not give her the number, had said she was not allowed to give out any telephone numbers of any air bases in the whole of Great Britain; that they were 'classified information'. Harriet had demanded to speak with the supervisor who in due course had come on the line and been just as resistant as her subordinate.

After that Harriet had tried to coax it out of young Alex who worked at the telephone exchange in Canterbury by saying she wished to call a few RAF stations to track down a person she used to know. She mentioned Tangmere as one of them but the child had been just as infuriating as the others by confirming it was classified information. When Harriet had suggested that surely for her own blood relative she could make an exception, the girl still had not cooperated. 'I couldn't actually find out myself, Aunt Harriet. Even the supervisors wouldn't know that sort of thing.'

Harriet had felt like shaking the little fool, but had resisted.

So she took another avenue and called her old friend Maisie Laverstock. Maisie's husband was high up in Fighter Command, a Marshal or something or other; but important, she knew that. Harriet had told Maisie that she needed to speak urgently to a pilot at Tangmere, a man called Flight Lieutenant Chard. When Maisie duly inquired why, Harriet told her she wished to discuss Alex with him: 'The child is infatuated and I need to see what the Lieutenant's intentions towards her really are. She's in my care during the working week you see, Maisie, and I do feel so responsible.' Maisie was a romantic and this was enough for her.

Finally after three days of waiting Maisie's letter had come informing her that the airfield's telephone number was unobtainable. Harriet could feel her blood pressure rising, but she calmed herself when she read that Maisie believed her connections were good enough to have a pass issued allowing Harriet to enter the aerodrome and meet the Flight Lieutenant.

For the first time in a week, Harriet had smiled.

The pass arrived on Friday attached to a note which advised her that Flight Lieutenant Chard had been notified of her pending arrival and that the interview must be no longer than half an hour as all pilots were on twenty-four-hour alert.

And then yesterday – the war had started. The whole thing was infuriating. Harriet had telephoned Maisie only to be told that she was away from home and not expected back for some days.

Harriet decided to take a chance and had caught the train to London and on to Chichester, the nearest town on the railway line to Tangmere.

The minute she had seen John Baron Chard at Castlemere on Alex's birthday she had been overwhelmed by the need to fulfil her incompleted work of twenty years before: not that she would attempt to remove the grown man from the planet, but she owed it to herself to inform him of the truth. If he did not know his origins, then it was her duty to divulge them. If he did know them, then she would alert him to the fact that what he had lived upon should by rights be hers and that Benjamin had cruelly used her.

The child who had turned into Flight Lieutenant John Baron Chard had blighted her life by being born. It was all a disgrace and the years had not altered her sense of injustice.

She closed her eyes in remembrance of that day so long ago when she had been at the boy's side as he fell from the cliff. Yes, he had simply fallen without her hand making contact with him. And she had run away believing him smashed to death on the rocks below.

Her nostrils quivered in recollection of the odour from Strapper Keating, the ruffian she was forced to associate with for the day. A crude piece of goods he had been, but he had served his purpose and been handsomely paid for it.

355

She remembered the silence that had followed; no mention of anything in the newspapers when she had expected some report of the boy's death. She had even ordered the *Bridlington Free Press Newspaper* for weeks afterwards but no article of any kind had ever appeared. Then in August she had dared to return to the town and found out that the child lived and that the Chard family and their hangers-on had sailed for Australia.

For months she had not slept a wink at night wondering whether or not to follow them, and her health suffered dreadfully. The doctors advised against a long sea voyage and valiantly she had fought back from the bitter betrayal. Then one Christmas she met Bertie Brownlow, a mine owner, and had busied herself in marrying him and all that entailed. Then the silly fellow had fallen and killed himself. It was at his funeral she met Edward and of course matters had progressed from there. But she had never forgotten her first husband, and she would never forget the treachery of the French harlot who tempted him away from her and created the demon child who had become Flight Lieutenant John Baron Chard.

Harriet winced as she opened her eyes and cast them once more upon the September day. Finally she could repay something of what that offspring had put her through.

A few minutes later the driver slowed down and pulled in beside a guardhouse surrounded by barbed wire. Without speaking he turned round towards her, resting his right arm on the steering wheel, an unfriendly expression on his face.

Harriet ignored this. 'Wait here. I have no idea how long I shall be but I won't be over half an hour.'

She climbed out and walked to the guardhouse. Three armed men stood inside and a Corporal came out to Harriet who made an ostentatious display of taking out her pass and handing it to him.

He looked at it and nodded. 'Just a minute, madam.' And as he made to leave he paused and turned back. 'Do you have your identity card?'

Harriet shook her head. 'No. They haven't yet been issued where I live.'

'And where's that, madam?'

'I live in St John's Wood, London and the South of France and Salisbury and Canterbury.'

One of the uniformed men inside the hut who had overheard the conversation stepped out. 'Four places and not one identity card, madam?'

'And who are you?'

'Sergeant Macelroy, madam.'

Harriet made a rumbling sound of annoyance in her throat. 'Sergeant Macelroy, my official residence is in Canterbury, Kent and my understanding is the cards are to be issued this week. But what on earth has that to do with all this? I've a pass with today's date on it signed by the proper authority.'

The Sergeant held out his hand and the Corporal gave it to him and took his opportunity to slip back into the guard hut.

'Ah, Mrs Barrington, is it?'

Harriet heaved a sigh. 'Obviously.'

'Yes, Mrs Barrington, this seems to be in order. It's just that since yesterday we've been advised to check all passes against the carrier's identity card.'

Harriet inhaled and exploded. 'For heaven's sake! I've travelled all the way from Kent to see this Flight Lieutenant Chard – a pilot here. I was informed I needed a pass only, no mention of anything else. It's been issued by a very important person, a Vice Air Marshal or whatever you call them . . .'

'Air Vice Marshal, actually Mrs Barrington.'

'Yes, well, an Air Vice Marshal then. He's a good friend of mine, an intimate acquaintance. Now stop fooling around and let me by.' Harriet's gloved finger waved at the gate.

Sergeant Macelroy replied as he handed the pass back to Harriet, 'I'm afraid it's become academic whether I let you by or not, Mrs Barrington.'

Harriet slammed her umbrella down so forcefully next to the Sergeant's boot that he moved away from her.

'Don't you dare toy with me, you Sergeant you! I'm here for Lieutenant Chard and I shan't be leaving without seeing him.'

Sergeant Macelroy forced himself to remain calm. 'Madam, you can't see him. He's gone. His squadron flew out this morning. If you wish to see a pilot in One, Forty-Three or Ninety-Two I can accommodate you today, and who knows for how long? But your Flight Lieutenant Chard's flown out.'

Harriet was momentarily nonplussed. 'Gone?'

'Yes, Mrs Barrington, the country's at war.'

'I know that! All right, where have they gone and when are they coming back?'

'I'm sorry, madam, I can't give you that information.'

Harriet shot a withering look at him. 'Typical narrow-minded military reply. You must think me as dense as yourself. Obviously they've been sent to France.' She tapped the umbrella against her leg. 'Damn it.' Then, giving him a dismissive glance she turned on her heel and marched back to the taxi. 'Return me to Chichester,' she commanded.

Sergeant Macelroy watched the vehicle until it turned the corner out of sight before he re-entered the guard hut. 'Hell, what a woman. With a few more like her the Germans wouldn't stand a chance.'

The following day Harriet made certain she was issued with her identity card, after which she strolled around to Lyon's Tea House where Lillian Cardrew waited for her at a table near a window. On the wall behind was a poster depicting a hand full of coins, some of which were falling from the fingers and turning into bullets. The words beneath were *Turn Your Silver into Bullets at the Post Office.*

After the greetings Harriet ordered tea and scones, and while they waited Lillian asked, 'So what was the urgent matter you wished to discuss with me?'

Harriet's gloved finger flourished in the air. 'The fellow that Alex's taking an interest in.'

Lillian nodded; she had half-expected this. She and Nick had already spoken about John Baron. Nicholas had enlightened his wife of Harriet's belief that he was the son of her first husband. Not that Lillian knew details about Harriet's first marriage. When she had met and married Nick, the

358

original John Baron had been away in France. All Lillian knew was that the man returned to England in 1914 and died shortly afterwards. She had never met him. But of course she knew of him and of Harriet's obsessions about him, that was why she had been taken aback when she had learnt 'JB's' full name at Alex's birthday party.

'Lillian, I want you to promise you'll never speak a word of this to Alex. You or Nicholas. I don't want the child to learn of my interest in this fellow she's keen on. What I want is for you to inform me the minute you know she's off to see him again.'

'Why would that be?'

Harriet looked down her nose at her sister-in-law. 'There are certain matters that must be addressed. I know his squadron's been sent off to France, of that I'm certain. I won't tell you how I know, Lillian, for that's none of your business, but it's imperative that I'm informed where he is the moment he returns to this country.' She paused as the tea and scones arrived, then began again. 'Now Alexandra is sure to tell you and I expect you to contact me without delay.'

Lillian put her hand to her temple as if she felt a headache coming on. 'Let me get this clear. You don't want me or Nick to tell Alex anything about your interest in this young man?'

'Correct.'

'And you want us to pass on to you where he is, if and when Alex finds out.'

'That's it absolutely.'

'So that you can go and see him?'

'Possibly.' Harriet poured tea for herself and took a scone as Lillian watched.

'Do you realise that my daughter thinks she's in love with this boy?'

Harriet's nose wrinkled. 'What's that got to do with it?'

Lillian eased forward on her chair to meet her companion's eyes. 'Everything.'

Harriet looked nonplussed. 'Lillian, I'll say it again. I *must* see that man whenever he's back here, even if he's up in Scotland. I must know and your daughter's the only person I'm aware of who might find out. So when you know, you tell me.' She stirred sugar in her tea, and mustering a smile, added, 'There's a dear.'

Lillian took a deep breath and turned her head to the pristine daylight coming through the window. She sat that way for thirty seconds while Harriet ate her scone.

'Harriet?'

'Yes dear?'

'I'm not going to get into an extended discussion with you about this and I'm not going to get into an argument, but one thing I must say. I've known you for a long time and the only reason you wish to see John Baron Chard is to make mischief. My daughter's feelings are important to me and I'll not have her hurt. I don't know if Alex will ever see him again or hear from him again but if she does, I'm not going to tell you anything. And if the worst comes to the worst, Harriet, I'll have to apprise Alex of why you're so interested in the man she cares about.' Lillian took another deep breath. 'Now I've said how I feel.'

Harriet's mouth formed a perfect oval. She replaced her cup on the saucer and dabbed the corner of her lips with the checked serviette. 'Lillian, I'm astounded! Have you no sense of proportion?'

'Harriet, I think we should talk of something else, otherwise I'm leaving you. I've a lot of grocery shopping to do anyway.'

Harriet fixed her sister-in-law with a glare. 'Then off you go, now, before you injure me any further.'

Lillian shook her head as she picked up her handbag and lifted her gaze. 'No one's injuring you except perhaps yourself. A war's just started, awful things will happen. Think about what you might be able to do to help your country and don't dwell on things you can't alter. Try to forget the past, that's my advice.'

'And when did you ever give any advice that was worth hearing? You and Nick are good at holding opinions on things you know nothing about.'

Lillian gave a long suffering look skywards and rose. 'That's as may be. Bye bye.'

And as she turned to walk away Harriet sniffed and said, 'I'll see you on Saturday dear. And do let me know if Alex tells you anything.'

On the other side of the world Cash and Danny Defoe made their way unsteadily along the side of the Sydney Stadium in pitch blackness. They leant on each other, Cash's arm round the diminutive man's shoulders.

'Mind your step here, matey, the place is full of bloody holes. Could easy break yer ankle,' Danny warned as he took a puff on his cigarette.

'Wouldn't want to do that, Dan, my dear,' Cash replied. 'A broken ankle in my line of work would be a serious threat to our financial well-being.'

This apparently was hilarious, for Danny burst into laughter and Cash joined him as they came wobbling and weaving to Danny's front door. For a moment Cash thought his companion had disappeared but then he realised Dan was down on his haunches and his fingers were seeking in a hiding-place for his door key.

'Got it.'

'Ex . . . tremely dex . . . dex . . . terous of you,' Cash giggled as Dan placed the key in the lock and opened the door, switching on the single light bulb which hung in his front room.

Danny squashed his cigarette butt on a saucer. 'Now, matey, a fire. I'm bloody cold – can't even feel me bum.'

They both began to laugh again as Danny threw some logs and newspaper in the grate. Cash wagged his forefinger at his friend as he put a match to the paper. 'Did you know, my dear Danny, that *bum* was used as the sh . . . shortened form of bumbailiff?'

His friend fell into the nearest chair wailing with laughter. 'Bumbailiff . . . bumbailiff – what's that?'

Cash tottered a step backwards, hit a wicker table then slid onto a stool. 'A bumbailiff, my dear Dan . . .' He started laughing again until finally he managed to inform his companion, '. . . a bumbailiff was an official . . . who was originally employed in arresting people . . . and such officials being the lowest form of life, my dear Danny . . .'

'Certainly,' shouted the little man.

'. . . Bum was the right word for them. Now, as bumbailiffs made approaches from behind, from the posteriors – also known as the bum – perhaps that's why they – the ubiquitous *they* – added bum to bailiff as a prefix, then shortened the word to . . . *bum*.' He brandished his right hand high in the air for emphasis while Danny exploded once more into peals of continued mirth.

'You know everything Cash, Jees, you really bloody do.'

Cash bent his head in his hands. 'Thanks for the confidence. Think I better get some sleep, mate. Must be pretty late.'

'I reckon.'

Within ten minutes the small abode was quiet, the only sound the crackling of the fire in the grate.

And when Danny brought his companion a cup of tea at eight in the morning Cash opened his eyes and groaned. 'Heck, Danny, where did we go last night?'

'We went lotsa places. You were drinkin' like a fish.' He handed over the tea and Cash sat up and accepted it.

'Yeah, Danny old man thanks for taking me in.'

'Taking you in? This is your place as much as mine. Ya paid for it. And the blasted cops won't find ya either.'

'Yes, I'll be all right here for a day or two but soon I'll have to move on.'

Cash had survived a narrow shave the previous day. He had taken to heart Sam's warning about the police and had shifted many of his belongings down here to Danny's on Monday morning after she had gone. Then he had visited his landlord, paid up his rent, and told him he would be leaving for Perth within a day or two. This was a plant in case the police came; Cash had no intention of leaving for the west.

Around noon that day he visited the Woolloomooloo wharves and discovered that the only ship bound for New York was the SS *Paragon*. It was to sail at four that afternoon and he made the assumption Sammy would be on it.

Around three-thirty he returned to the dock and hung around in the darkened doorway of one of the warehouses with a clear view of the ship. All passengers were aboard by then and the long gangplank was being stowed. People milled on the wharf and waved up to their friends or loved ones on the decks but there were no open displays of excitement, no shouting or calling out. Depression floated in the air and the fact that the country was at war clouded the expressions of all those in public places.

At one point Cash saw Sammy. As the ship's long ropes detached from the bollards and were dragged aboard, she was in a group on the main deck aft and she pushed to the bulwark and looked briefly down to somebody before waving once and turning away. There was no sight of Lenny the rat.

Cash watched the ship as it separated from the wharf before it slowly turned its great bulk round and sailed down the harbour.

He stood on the wharf, a stiff detached figure with his eyes on the waters of the harbour while the sea breeze stirred the errant lock of hair on his forehead.

He remained that way until the SS *Paragon* was out of sight then he walked sluggishly back along Woolloomooloo to MacLeay Street, and up through King's Cross where he called into the Snake Pit, a busy bar. He had two schooners of beer and felt sick in the stomach so he drank no more and walked the three miles home in the dark. He listened to the wireless for a while, slept fitfully and woke early. He showered and dressed and as dawn was breaking he heated a tin of baked beans and poured them on toast. He had just taken his second mouthful when he heard a knock on the front door.

Long ago he had drilled through the wall in the front hall and made a spy hole to see who was outside. He could not see clearly for there was only vague electric light thrown from the stairwell, but the two men at his door were heavyset and tall, then he recognised them – the detectives who had come to interview Sammy in Brisbane!

Moving with speed and silence he passed through to the bedroom and picked up his wallet, three bank books and two chequebooks. He slipped them into a pocket of a jacket from the wardrobe, put it on and glided along the corridor to the spare room. He crossed to the window passing three of Sammy's enlargements still on the walls.

Voices were raised outside his front door and he suspected that the police had woken the neighbours in flat three opposite.

Pushing up the window he heard loud banging and he waited no longer. He mounted the sill and climbed out. The window was eleven feet from the ground and he eased himself down the wall and hung by his hands before he dropped to the ground. He was along the side of his block of flats and over the fence and running along the back of the next block by the time the police jemmied open his front door.

Cash came out onto New South Head Road and crossed it. He was deciding whether to cut up a side street and steal a car when he saw a tram rattling along towards the city. It slowed down and halted at the crossroads and he ran over and climbed aboard.

Taking a seat at the back next to the window he watched as the tram sped by the end of his street. Looking along he saw the police vehicle pull out from the kerb in front of his building and drive away. He turned his head to study the car while it paused at the entrance to New South Head Road as if the occupants sat in indecision. A moment later it made a right turn and followed the tram.

For a few heartbeats Cash actually thought the detectives might realise he was on the tram but the police car slowly overtook it and cruised on by.

Cash had come straight to Danny's and remained indoors for the rest of the day. When darkness fell they went out for a few drinks which had evolved into a lot of drinks and on into their eventual insobriety.

But during it all Cash had been thinking, and in the way that we all can mull over matters in our sleep and come up with the answer the following morning, Cash too, had done that, even in the heavy slumber of the drunken man.

He sipped his tea and rolled his eyes and groaned again. 'Better have some water too, Dan.'

'Coming up. Had that ready as well,' his comrade replied setting down a Coalport porcelain jug and a crystal glass beside him. 'I've got bacon and eggs and toast ready for ya as well. That'll fix ya.'

Cash sniffed. 'Yes, it might. Smells great. You're a wonder.'

After two glasses of water he felt slightly improved and after four slices of bacon, three eggs and three pieces of toast he felt almost normal except for the fuzziness just behind his eyes.

'How come you don't suffer from hangovers, Danny old man?'

'Dunno, just never have. Me old mum didn't either, and she could drink me dad under the table.'

While Danny lit another cigarette Cash enlightened his friend, 'We know the cops are onto me, Dan, so I've decided to leave Sydney. Now, I told my landlord I was off to Perth so once they've spoken to him my hope is they'll believe him. And if they don't, then with their mentality I reckon they'll guess I've gone to Melbourne or Adelaide. But wherever I go there's one thing that'll be different.'

'What?'

'They'll be looking for Cashman Slade; and he's going to simply evaporate.'

'Huh?'

'Cashman Slade is going to metamorphose, my dear Danny.'

Now Dan's confusion was complete. 'Meta . . . what?'

'Change – alter. Cashman Slade's going to become *Ashley Wade*, and I'm going to join up.'

'What, the Army?'

'Yes. Look, my old dear, I've got no choice. Being in the Army's not my ideal but those bloody cops don't give up. They're onto me now . . . want me for something I did in Brisbane. Though what happened was actually an accident. Typical of them to be after me for something I didn't plan, and not after me for all the stuff I did plan and did do! But imagine it, Dan, me, behind bars? I don't bloody think so! So the war has to be my way out whether I like it or not. The Army's the only place I can get lost. I'll change my name and volunteer. I might even be sent overseas.'

He eyed his friend earnestly as the fingers of the morning sun strayed through the worn lace curtain and found his face. 'The way I evaluate it all, is this. I've got four bank balances, Danny. One's in my real name and I virtually emptied that a month ago. The other three are in separate names, one of which happens to be Ashley Wade. I leave the money in that one, for that legitimises me, makes me a real person. I've already got a chequebook in Wade. The other two accounts I'll close today. I'll keep some money and the rest I'll leave here with you, my friend. You can use it when you need to and keep the rest for the future.'

'Jees, Cash.'

'So that's it really. Last night was our goodbye party, old man.'

'Damn it, I'll come with ya. I'll join up too.'

Cash laughed and a gold filling on his eye-tooth glinted in the sunlight. 'You can't join up. You're fifty this year; they don't take blokes your age!'

Danny ground out his cigarette on a plate. His dark face twisted with emotion. 'Heck, Cash, ya the best mate I ever had. Ya just up and trusted me. Snap! Like that. No one ever did anythin' for me before you. I was just pilferin' here and there. Pinchin' car headlights and wheels and stuff, and along ya came and made me life . . . well . . . somethin'. Them robberies you do, boy, some of them are right top class. Ya're a real master of the art, ya are. Now I'm a bloke what's had no education, but ya've taught me a lot, sure as sure. Me old grandma what was an Abo and all, she used ta say, "Dan, when ya find a true friend they don't care about what ya've got, they just care about what ya are – I mean inside like, they can see inside ya".' He sighed.

'That's how I feel about ya, Cash. I can see inside ya, and what's there's real bloody good.'

Cash smiled. 'And what's inside you, Danny, is real bloody good too. Your gran was a very wise lady.'

Dan nodded, his eyes glistening. 'Yeah, I reckon she was and all. And I'll tell ya one more thing.'

'What's that, Dan?'

'I know ya well like, and I know the main reason ya got drunk last night was because ya wife's gone. I don't know how ta say this so I'll just spit it out. She was a damn fool and all for leavin' ya and that's a fact.'

Cash met his friend's eyes. 'Ah Danny, old man, it wasn't all her fault.' He turned his head into the morning sun again and stared at the smeared window pane. 'She was m'lady and I let her down. I'm a bugger to live with and that's a fact.' He smiled ruefully. 'I reckon life's a journey in darkness with just a few beacons of light along the way. And as most of us wander through wearing a blindfold, how the hell can we know when we arrive at a beacon?'

'Jees, matey, you say such great stuff.'

'You know what, Danny? Now I've managed to remove the blasted blindfold I sense that my Sammy was a beacon. But . . .' he snapped his fingers in the air and pointed behind him '. . . but now she's gleaming back there in the distance somewhere and I'm heading on into the blasted darkness.'

'Jees.'

Cash stood. 'So I'll be off to close the bank accounts, mate, and then I'll be back to say goodbye.'

Dan rose beside him and took hold of his friend's arm. 'Are ya sure they wouldn't let me join up with ya but?'

'Danny, *I* won't let you. You're safer and better off here. I'd be worried about you all the time if you were in the Army, and hell, as I told you anyway, you're too old.' He patted his companion's arm. 'Now I'll be back after the war and then we'll do something wonderful, something we've never done. Maybe take a long sea voyage and sit on deck, watching the sunset and be waited on. What do you reckon?'

Danny grinned. 'You beauty. I'll be ready and waitin' here for ya, Cash.'

'And Dan?'

'Yeah, mate?'

'I don't like the way you cough and I'm no medical man and so I'm not at all certain of this, but I reckon it could be the cigarettes affecting your lungs. Try and give them up.'

Danny looked askance. 'Give up me cigarettes?'

'Yes. Drink as much as you like but *try* to drop the fags.'

'Shit, mate.'

'Well, give it a go.'

Danny sighed. 'You really think I should?'

'I think you should. For me.'

Danny screwed up his face and sniffed loudly. 'Hell, Cash, I dunno where ya get these ideas, but . . . all right.'

Chapter Twenty-five

Sam lifted her head as the key turned in the lock. She put aside the *New York Times* and rolled over. Fom the bedroom she had a clear view to the front door and as Lenny opened it and came in she sat up.

'You there, Sam?' he called, flipping the key into the crystal bowl on the hat stand.

'Yes.'

He dropped the parcel he carried and took off his jacket, draping it over the back of a chair, and came through to the bedroom.

As Sam moved off the bed the strap of her petticoat slipped down her arm. Len took hold of her and bent down and kissed her shoulder then moved his mouth lower towards her breast.

She side-stepped out of his grip. 'Don't, Len.'

'What's wrong?'

She made a despondent gesture with her hands. 'I don't know. It's just that I've been reading about the war in Europe. It's escalated all of a sudden. Norway's been invaded and now it seems like Hitler's going to move into the Low Countries. My brother's over there and I don't feel like being mauled when good men are in danger.' She picked up her dressing-gown and put it on.

Len turned sharply towards her. 'Mauled? For Christ's sake, is that what I do to you? Maul you?'

Sam closed her eyes and lifted her right palm. 'No, look I'm sorry, wrong word.'

'Too damn right it was the wrong goddamned word!'

'I didn't mean that. It's just that the war upsets me so much and I feel like—'

'Hell Sam, that's all I ever hear from you these days. "The war in Europe – my brother – the war in Europe – my brother." You're like a stupid gramophone record. Do you know when the last time was that I walked in here and you smiled at me?'

She did not reply and he yelled, 'Do you?'

'No.'

'It was a bloody long time ago.' He took out a cigarette and lit it. 'I'm going down to the Algonquin. Babs and Marty and Jennifer are coming. What about you?'

The Algonquin Hotel was where New York's literati and the social elite gathered. Babs and Marty were wealthy friends of Lenny. Jennifer was a freelance writer and occasional night-club singer, and though he had never admitted it Sam suspected she and Lenny had been an item at one time, for whenever Jennifer saw Sam she acted in a cool formal fashion towards her.

'No, I'm tired and I've got that assignment in New Jersey tomorrow. I think I'll get a good night's sleep.'

Len loosened his tie and headed to the bathroom. As he opened the door he dropped the next sentence over his shoulder in an undertone. 'Margaret and Caldwell are coming as well.'

As he disappeared Sam followed him.

She stood at the door watching him disrobe.

'Margaret – Bourke-White? Caldwell – Erskine?'

'Mmm.' He stepped into the bath and sliding the shower curtain across between them, turned on the water.

For a time Sam watched the movement of his body through the semi-opaque curtain and then left the bathroom. Margaret Bourke-White was as near to an idol as Sam had. She was one of the finest women photographers in the world and a pillar of *Life Magazine*, had been one of the four original photographers employed when the magazine began three years before. She was married to Erskine Caldwell who was best known for his ribald rustic southern novels, *Tobacco Road* and *God's Little Acre*; and for constantly being in the news fighting censorship on his books. He had worked in Hollywood and knew everybody.

Sam had met Margaret, or Maggie as some of her intimates called her, on New Year's Eve at a party given by Babs and Marty.

Samantha crossed the bedroom to the window and looked out. She could see the top of the Empire State Building, the world's tallest, opened nine years previously and gleaming now in the setting sun; it commanded the city skyline with its 102 storeys. She took her eyes from it and cast them to the pavement where people streamed back and forth. The buildings were all skyscrapers and the street below was in shadow, but it was ever the same; New York was a constantly moving, vibrating stream of people coming and going. She had found it so exciting for the first few months. Lenny had taken her to places she had never imagined existed and the day they had been to the World's Fair was imprinted on her memory.

When she actually landed the job at *Time Magazine* she had been ecstatic. She had been so grateful to Lenny and had shown it, and last Christmas saw them in each other's arms and, as she had believed at the time, in love.

But now as April turned into May Sam was unsettled. Len was back working on the editorial staff at the *New York Post* and their schedules often differed, and while she still found him attractive and they had their laughs and good times, their cultural differences had begun to get in the way. Like tonight when she was so concerned about JB and Hitler and England and all that. Whenever she brought up the war, all she received from Len were platitudes, followed by his frustration and then his anger.

She watched the roving crowds in the street below and decided she must go with Len. She could not miss out on a chance to be with Margaret Bourke-White.

She crossed to the wardrobe and took out a white crêpe de Chine dress cut low at the back with a simple skirt that fell to the knee. As she removed it from the hanger she touched the blue silk dress she had worn to JB's twenty-first birthday party. She did not wear it any more, of course, it was sort of old-fashioned and not sophisticated but she had never been able to throw it out.

371

She sat for a moment on the side of the bed looking at it and thinking of JB. She wrote to him each month even though she only received one letter a year from him for her birthday, as he had promised at her wedding. Actually that was not true: she had received one other, it had taken over six months to arrive because it had been sent first to the flat in Sydney. That one had been written to both her and Cash on the very day war was declared. It had been forwarded to Haverhill and onto New York. It was not really informative except for saying the squadron was off to a war zone, that he was well and that he did not want them to worry about him. He had signed it *Your loving brother and brother-in-law, John Baron.*

Her birthday letter had arrived in New York in January. It had been much longer, five pages, and she had read it avidly. In fact she had read it so often she almost memorised it. Much of it had been about his friends, some leaves he had taken, and about the boredom of flying reconnaissance flights and dawn and dusk patrols. After the fall of Poland in just three weeks last September there had been very little real fighting. But from what she read in the *New York Times* tonight German forces were building up heavily on the borders of Holland and Belgium preparing for advances into those countries.

She gave a tiny mournful sound as she remembered JB's last paragraph in her birthday letter.

I think of you often and wonder how you are. I have to say I was saddened when I knew you had left Cash, for as difficult as he might be I do believe he loved you – and that's what I want for you, Sammy: love. I hope your dreams come true but don't lose yourself along the way. You are so precious and so wonderful, I would hate to think of anything changing you. He had signed it *Always, John Baron.*

She softly repeated the words as she sat staring at the blue silk dress. 'Always, John Baron.'

'What was that?' Lenny asked, coming through from the bathroom drying his hair.

'Nothing, just wondering what to wear.'

He gave a hoot of derision. 'I knew you'd come. Maggie Bourke-White can get you where you won't go for me.'

She did not reply and slipped into the crêpe de Chine.

At the Algonquin smoke and chatter filled the air, almost drowning out the singer who was trying to make headway with 'The Very Thought of You'.

Jennifer, Babs and Marty were there and so too was a sunbrowned polo player from Long Island they simply called Scottie.

Sam ordered a gin sling and Len a whisky. 'What time are the author and Maggie meant to arrive?' Len asked, leaning forward to light Jennifer's cigarette.

Jennifer glanced towards the door. 'Shouldn't be long. I said we'd all be here by nine. Though they're often late.' She smiled round the group and her eyes settled on Lenny. 'Did you like their most recent book? You know, the one they collaborated on?'

'*North of the Danube*?'

'Yes, that's it. What did you think, darling?'

Len drew on his cigarette. 'It was pretty well done. Though I think I preferred their previous one.'

'You mean *Have You Seen Their Faces,*' Sam spoke up, taking a sip of her gin. 'It was good.'

Jennifer puffed on her cigarette and blew out a perfect smoke ring as she conferred a forced smile upon Sam. 'Ah, so you're a fan, eh?'

'Of hers? Yes.'

'Oh, look at those,' Babs squealed, her voice high with excitement and they all turned to see a dancer near them wearing turquoise silk flowing pants with little silver bows bobbing up and down upon them. 'Aren't they just the thing. The last time I saw anything so wonderful was by the pool at Eden Roc.'

'Oh, I love that place,' Jennifer informed them, running her fingers through her golden hair. 'Cole and Clifton were there last year at Sara's. She and her husband rented a villa at Cap D'Antibes.'

Len bent forward and whispered in Sam's ear 'That's Cole Porter and Clifton Webb she's talking about, not sure who Sara is. Cap D'Antibes is in the South of France. It's quite the place these days.'

Jennifer looked straight at Sam with an unconvincing smile before she said, *'Est-ce que vous avez visité le Sud de la France?'* It was obvious she had thought to make a fool of Sam by asking her if she had been to France.

Jennifer's smile faded swiftly as Sam replied that she had not but she had been to other exotic places. *'Non, mais je suis allée dans les pays exotique comme Australie, Fidji, Hawaii, Panama et les Bermudes. Et vous?'*

Babs and Marty hooted with laughter, Scottie smiled behind his hand and Jennifer went pink in the face. She blinked, puffed on her cigarette and turned her attention to Lenny.

At ten o'clock there was still no arrival of the celebrity couple and so too at eleven when Sam stood from the table and said good night to Scottie. The other four were merrily stepping out on the dance floor to an upbeat version of, 'All I Do is Dream of You'.

'Aren't you goin' to wait to see Len before you leave?'

Sam shook her head. 'He's having too good a time, he won't want to leave. Please tell him I'll see him at home. I have to be up by six.'

'Wow, that's early,' Scottie decided as Sam picked up her pocket book and left.

Outside she waited for a cab and suddenly at her side was Scottie. 'Thought I should see you home. Jennifer's supposed to be with me but it's pretty obvious she'd prefer to be with Len.'

It was true: the two 'old friends' had danced most of the night together.

A cab pulled up and Sam got in. Scottie slipped in beside her and when it arrived outside her apartment block he paid.

They walked up the fifteen steps to the building. 'I love red doors,' Scottie announced as Sam opened it and he followed her inside. Sam turned to him. 'Well, good night. Thanks for seeing me home. I usually walk up. We're on the fifth floor.'

'Hey, you're energetic. And I must see you to your real door, Sam. Hope it's red too.'

'It's not.' Sam started up the stairs and he followed again. At her white door he took her in his arms and kissed her. Sam did not resist. He felt good and solid and smelt of something quite pleasing.

As they broke from one another he grinned. 'What about one for the road? A nightcap. Come on, Sam, we're both disappointed in our dates.'

Dates? For God's sake, I sleep with the man.

Sam met his eyes and spoke. 'Len's hardly my date. I live with him. Here behind this white door.'

Scottie had not realised this. 'Oh. Then what the hell's he doing tonight all over Jennifer?'

'Making me feel bad.'

Scottie's warm hazel eyes rested on her. He wore a fashionable moustache and his hair was blond and sleeked back. His clothes reeked of Park Avenue and he could have been an advertisement for the model young New Yorker. And in truth he did seem quite nice. Sam made a decision. 'Come on in, Scottie, let's both have a nightcap.'

Scottie had two small whiskies and left. He kissed her gently again at her front door and said, 'If ever you don't live with this guy, look me up, Sam.'

Twenty minutes later Sam climbed into bed and went immediately to sleep but woke some hours later and looked at the clock: 3.20 a.m. No Lenny. From that point she slept fitfully and when she rose at six he was still not home.

As she showered and dressed, the words that kept repeating in her head were her brother's: *I hope your dreams come true but don't lose yourself along the way.*

Harry Grenville, her assistant for the day, arrived at seven-thirty and drove her to New Jersey. Usually she worked alone with her Speed Graphic camera, her pride and joy, but when she was taking pictures for a story the magazine sometimes supplied her with an assistant. Sam concentrated on photographing the operations in a fish cannery for the next eight hours but when she took coffee breaks she kept thinking of JB and hoping he were safe. How badly she missed him, how badly she missed her mother and father and Ledgie and Uncle Wake. She remembered the day she had told them she was coming to New York with Lenny. She knew how sad they had really been. She knew they only wanted what was best for her but they did not understand. Here she was, the only Australian woman photographer in the whole of New York, and her family neither realised, nor appreciated what she had done. She completed her assignment and they were back in Manhattan as the sun was setting.

At eight o'clock there was no sign of Lenny, and Sam sat drinking coffee with all her misgivings in her mind. What she wouldn't give just to see JB, or even Cash for that matter! She thought about Cash and how everything had gone wrong; she wondered if he ever had really loved her. She had to admit they had enjoyed some fine times, even with all the aggravation. She pictured Cash on Seven Bob Beach smiling at her with his wayward lock of hair dangling on his forehead. JB and Cashman had always been in her life. She had loved JB and married Cash; and yet when she looked back on it she supposed at times she had loved Cash too – and now she had neither of them. She wondered what had become of her husband. Of course he had been impossible, but she did hope he was all right and that he had not been caught by the police.

She picked up a magazine carrying her photos and flicked through it. She was proud of her position at *Time*. She had only joined them four months ago, and she was the only woman in the department, but already she was being noticed and given assignments she knew usually went to the more experienced. But when she analysed it she probably wasn't proud of living here with Len.

The door rattled and she heard him enter and drop his keys in the crystal bowl. She turned as he arrived in the living room.

'Where the hell were you last night?'

He took off his coat and hung it on the usual chair before he sat on the arm of a brocade sofa and gazed steadily at her. He was wearing a shirt and a pair of trousers different to those of the previous night.

'I stayed with Jennifer. She's a friend of mine, and unlike you she smiles, and she doesn't continually harp on about the war in Europe. It was a pleasant change.'

Sam took a noisy deep breath. 'You know what, Lenny, it's time I said a few things to you.'

'Shoot.' He lit a cigarette and crossed his legs.

'I gave up a marriage to come here with you. Oh yes, it wasn't much good, I'm aware of that and I was fired with ambition and you were the one who really got me the position with *Time*.' Tears welled in her eyes but she fought them back. 'And I'm grateful to you for that. I wanted to come, I wanted everything New York offered . . . I was excited by the thought of being a photographer here, by being with you, meeting famous people, being somebody.' She drew her fingers across her eyes and hesitated briefly while he remained silent. 'The real truth is, I was brought up to believe a man and woman got married and stayed married.' She shrugged and waved her hand, bringing it back impotently to her lap. 'I know you might be laughing at me inside, Lenny, but living here like this . . .

'Oh God, I know your friends here don't give a damn whether we're married or not. Most of them aren't, anyway. But you see? I'm still legally married to Cash and I thought I was all grown-up and sophisticated, but . . .' She covered her mouth with her fingers and attempted to control her feelings. 'But I'm not. It might be normal for you to live with one girl, eat, sleep, see her naked and all that . . . and then go off and have sex with another like you did last night, but it's not that normal to me.'

A tear escaped and rolled down her cheek and as Len moved off the sofa and came over to her she held up her hand to keep him back. 'No, Lenny. Let me finish. It's all become clear to me today. I love my job and I'm proud of what I've achieved. But I'm so confused. You're a nice guy but you don't want to marry me. And even if you did, the truth is, I don't want to marry you. I'm mixed up all the time these days and worried about all the people I love.

'This is your world and you fit in it, but it's not mine. My heart's with the people at war far away in Australia and in England. I want to help them. And Len, I mean it, thanks for sleeping with Jennifer. I know what I have to do now.'

Len blew a torrent of smoke into the air. 'Great speech, kid. Do you mean it?'

'Yes, Lenny, I do.' She wiped her eyes and spoke quite calmly. 'I'll leave tomorrow.'

'Where will you go?'

'First to my boss. See if they'll give me an assignment and send me to London. If they do I'll go and work my heart out and if they don't, I'll go anyway.'

Len reached out and patted her hand. 'Listen Sam, we had some real good times. You don't have to leave. We can give it another go.'

She gave a brief smile. 'No, Lenny. Let's part while we're still friends. I'll sleep in the spare bedroom tonight, unless you want me to leave straight away?'

He shook his head vigorously. 'Don't say such a dumb thing. For Christ's sake, kid, you were my girl till last night.'

They both laughed at that, and as Sam stood and moved to the bedroom to pack, he walked along with her. 'Look, if you have trouble convincing *Time* to send you to London, I just might be able to do something for you somewhere else.'

She spun round. 'God, Lenny, you've done enough for me. But thanks anyway.' She smiled, it was a genuine smile and she meant it.

Len sighed. 'If you'd given me a few more of those you wouldn't be leaving, you dumb girl.'

She reached out and touched him. 'Ah, Lenny, yes I would be. It would have taken a little longer, that's all.'

The following morning Samantha saw her boss.

Lester Arnott took stock of her from behind his dark-rimmed glasses. 'What's wrong, Sam? Broken up with your boyfriend?'

Sam shook her head. 'It's not like that, Lester. I'm an Australian. My country's at war. They're fighting Hitler along with England. My brother's in the RAF. My mind's on it all the time. I love my job, I like New York, but I'm in trouble. I want to do something . . . *more*. I reckon if I could take photos of what's going on over there, my heart would be in it. I'd be really trying to get something special for *Time*. How people feel. Our readers would see it from my point of view, an Australian in London. It'd be good. I'd make sure it was.'

Lester was from Brooklyn; he had come into the newspaper business the hard way, from the bottom. He liked Sam Slade but she had only been with the unit just on four months.

'Listen, kid, you're turning into a swell photographer but we've already got guys over there. Good photographers with twenty years' experience. Our readers don't know where Australia is, kid, let alone want to see anything from an Australian's point of view. Take my advice and keep it to the American point of view!'

'Well, of course, yes, certainly I would. That was just a slip of the tongue.'

'Sam, I can't recommend sending you to London in any case. You haven't been here long enough. Besides, I've got a budget to work to. That's it. You can see my position.'

'Yes.'

'Sorry, kid. Now look, I've got a good little job for you. There's been a ruckus down at the Statton Island Ferry and . . .'

'Lester, I'm sorry, I quit. I'll work out whatever notice you want, but I'd actually prefer to quit right now.'

'Now look, kid, I don't think you really understand what you're doing.'

'Yes I do, Lester. I'm handing in my notice.' She gave him a proud grin and left his office.

That afternoon Sam decided to try other avenues.

The first was *Newsweek* magazine. She presented herself there, told them who she was and what she wanted, and sat and waited for an hour before a woman in black crew-neck sweater and black trousers came out.

'Samantha Slade? I'm Carter Brinkwood. This way.'

In an office papered with photos Sam explained that she was a photographer and had been working for *Time*. That made the woman look more closely at her. 'So what are you doing here?'

Sam pushed twelve of her photographs across towards her and the woman gave them a quick glance as Sam answered the question.

'Well, I'm taking a chance. The truth is, I want to go to London. I'd like to have my fare paid and I'd like to be working taking photographs over there. I've seen the articles and photographs that have appeared in all the magazines, but I've got an idea for a series of shots on the children. I'm calling it "Children in War".' Sam had only just thought of this idea seconds before and she noticed Carter Brinkwood's expression alter slightly. 'If I don't do it for you then I'll offer it to *Life* or *Fortune* or somewhere else.'

The woman picked up Sam's photographs and flicked through them. She took out a packet of cigarettes and lit one. She proffered the packet across the desk and Sam shook her head.

'So why aren't you offering this little gem to your editor at *Time*?'

Sam coughed. 'Fact is, I don't work there any more. They wouldn't send me to London, so I left.'

Carter Brinkwood took a deep draw on her cigarette and spoke as the smoke came out of her nose and mouth at the same time. 'Why are you so all fired up about going over there?'

'The war's on my mind most of the time. My brother's there. I'm an Australian . . .'

'I wondered what the hell that accent was.'

'. . . And I know that the way I feel would push me forward. I'd put my heart and soul into "Children in War" and I'd deliver great pictures.'

The woman looked through the twelve photographs again. Then she stood and picked them up tucking them under her arm. 'Look, I'm making no promises,' she tapped the photos under her arm, 'but these are good and I'll have a talk to the editor who'll make the decision. Come back on Friday, say around noon?'

'Oh yes, thanks, certainly I will.'

On Friday at noon Sam re-entered Carter Brinkwood's office. She felt ill with nervousness as the woman who was dressed entirely in black again, offered her another cigarette which she declined. 'Sam, I've spoken to *Time* since I saw you last.'

Sam's face dropped. 'Oh.'

'Lester Arnott said your work's swell. Fact is, he's sorry to lose you.'

'Oh?' Now Sam dared a small smile.

'*Newsweek*'s prepared to pay for your fare to London and we'll pay fifty per cent towards your accommodation. I think that'll have a proviso of not more than thirty shillings a week. We'll give you six weeks from the date you arrive to get the photographs back to us. You can write a piece to go with it if you want, which we may or may not use. If we like your pictures, we'll publish them and we'll think about offering you a job. But there's no pay until that point. Is this acceptable?'

Sam could not find her voice. She nodded and Carter Brinkwood held out her hand.

In another minute Sam was out in the street. Her heart was pumping. They were paying her fare! That was enough! She could manage in London for six weeks. She'd knock their eyes out with her photographs.

As she walked away she skipped a few paces in her elation. She would be in London, that's what mattered! She would be taking her beloved photographs for another prestigious magazine. She would be in the war zone, not removed from it and guilty, but over there. She would be proud again. And most of all, the overriding thrill, she would be closer, so very much closer, to JB.

Chapter Twenty-six

The world had watched when Poland collapsed within three weeks of the initial German Blitzkrieg upon it on 1 September, 1939. Long on valour, the Poles had fought with all they had which was very little: they mounted cavalry charges against the might of the tanks and even fought with bottles and stones.

Blitzkrieg was a strategy of 'lightning war' using surprise and relying on the independent operation of mobile armoured units hitting ahead of the main armies and supported by air attack. The Poles had fought back with outmoded biplanes and troops who were outnumbered and outgunned by modern puissant weapons. Since the Fall of Poland the Jews in particular, and the population in general, were being forced by the Nazis into death and labour camps. Some of the Polish Air Force had escaped to Britain where they were forming their own squadrons.

After the invasion of Poland the fighting had lulled for the months of winter. The only real action saw a British victory when the German battleship, *Graf Spee*, was destroyed by a force of weaker cruisers. Hitler and Stalin had formed a secret pact and had agreed to carve up Poland, and while the Germans occupied Poland they had made no moves on France or the Low Countries. Their next attack had come upon Denmark and Norway, the following spring of 1940. Those Scandinavian countries had fallen swiftly.

When John Baron's squadron had been ordered to France at the outbreak of the war they had been stationed west of Arras, not far from the headquarters of General Gort, the Commander-in-Chief of the BEF – British Expeditionary Force – who had made the Château of Habarcq, 'without water, light or loo', his home. It was well-known that Gort, a realist and courageous man, deliberately lived with the windows open during the cold weather to harden himself and get used to privation.

And the winter of 1939-40 proved cold. For many months the airfields had been covered with mud and ice.

John Baron had been delighted to receive a letter from Douglas at Christmas, and even more delighted when in his friend's legible but florid hand he received the news that Douglas had been readmitted to the RAF.

> *So JB, old man, I'm back in the air. My first solo was in a Tutor on 27 November almost eight years since my crash. It was 1530 and there was cloud at 1500 feet and a south-west wind was running. Do you know, I flew away on my own from the few aircraft in the air and I think you'll understand when I tell you that I simply 'had' to roll the aeroplane at 600 feet. I'm not really sure why, even in reflection. But it probably had to do with erasing the ghost of my crash!*

Much of the time John Baron had found himself digging trenches and latrines and sitting around bored while the long cold months had drawn out in waiting. On weekends the airmen would go into Arras and get drunk as young men are wont to do. John Baron would laugh, practise his French, pick up colloquial sayings and be delighted when the locals praised his accent. The pilots often landed their Hurricanes on other airfields and spent evenings meeting up with squadrons who flew Blenheims, Battles and Lysanders.

On one of these 'drop-ins' to Rouvres, John Baron and his comrades met the most famous RAF pilot of the time, Edgar James 'Cobber' Cain, a twenty-one-year-old New Zealander and the 'darling' of the war correspondents who had made his exploits popular. He had already been awarded the DFC and had more 'kills' than anyone else in the RAF: being five. He was the boyfriend of the English actress Joyce Phillips and this added to his popularity. Meeting 'Cobber' and having their photograph taken with him was one of the highlights of the dreary winter for the boys of John Baron's squadron.

Only occasionally had John Baron seen the enemy. Invariably they had been in Ju 88s, Dorniers and Heinkels and usually they were single aircraft at very high altitude appearing to be on reconnaissance. The Germans had paid particular attention to the Franco-Belgian border and the Ardennes forest region.

April saw the airfield blossoming into a lush green strip and the squadron suddenly found itself in long spells of 'readiness' awaiting the arrival of enemy aircraft. The pilots passed the time on the edge of the airfield, basking in the sun when it appeared, sitting in the tents and huts if it rained and spending hours in the air on dawn and dusk patrols. And with the advent of April the Messerschmitt fighters had appeared, although they also had flown very high and had only participated in aerial combat when pressed into it by the RAF and the French fighters.

In May everything altered. It could have appeared fateful that Winston Churchill became Prime Minister and formed his coalition government on 10 May, 1940, the day that the Germans launched 'Operation Sickle Stroke' and attacked Holland, entered the Ardennes into Luxembourg and Southern Belgium, and pushed into France. Thrusting through that section of France's border lands that the French Marshal Henri Philippe Pétain had dismissed with the words, 'This sector is not dangerous.'

'Tally Ho,' Twig's voice crackled over the radio. 'Southwest.' *Tally Ho* meant enemy aircraft sighted.

'Viking to Eagle. Where? I can't see the bastards,' David Flinders, the Squadron Leader replied from the Hurricane ahead. They had been in the air day and night since the German Blitzkrieg into the Ardennes three days before, their principal missions being to escort the British and French bombers in their attempt to destroy the pontoon bridges across the River Meuse where the German armies now massed upon its banks.

They had successfully escorted two British bombers

home and were now returning to their own airfield outside Arras. The losses in the low-level attacks on the bridges from the German anti-aircraft artillery had been high; the previous day, John Baron's squadron had lost two machines and three had been badly damaged, and they had been small in comparison to some.

'There underneath you. Starboard, four o'clock. Above that bastion of grey cloud. There's a bomber in the centre.'

John Baron, who was the Red Section Leader, spied them. 'Got them. More than a dozen of them escorting it and they haven't noticed us yet.'

'Yes, got them,' repeated David Flinders 'Have you, Blue Leader?'

Blue Section Leader, Henry, Garner, a New Zealander who at twenty-nine was the old man of the squadron, replied, 'Yes. Only nine of us but what the hell.'

'You're right, I don't think they've seen us. Let's go in.' David Flinders rocked his wings signalling for them to close in tighter as he turned to starboard and dived in an arc down on the enemy from astern.

The fourteen Messerschmitt 109s continued on without deviation, and John Baron searched the skies as they roared down towards them, checking that they were not going to be attacked by others, to date unseen.

As the Hurricanes closed in, suddenly the 109s wheeled in sections of three and four to right and left, going swiftly into aircraft-line-astern. John Baron marked one of the rear aircraft, and, peripherally aware that the others were marking their own bandits – as they called the enemy – he held behind his chosen 109 as it turned tightly to the left, breaking from the pattern of line-astern formation. The 109 steepened its angle in an attempt to throw off John Baron but with the manoeuvrability of the Hurricane, he easily wheeled inside the enemy, sticking to his tail as the 109 weaved and began to dive.

John Baron clung to him and suddenly had the Messerschmitt perfectly in his reflector sight – wing-tips touching the horizontal bars. He had practised this a hundred times, and he pressed the firing button in short bursts.

The bullets ripped straight into the 109! Yellow pieces flew off the engine cowling and a lump off its tail, and in another few seconds the 109 began to stream oil and black smoke. John Baron shot by its starboard wing and saw the pilot fighting wildly to contol his machine before it headed into a steep dive, down, down, racing towards the earth, plummeting into a death roll and dipping oddly before it reached a wide gap in the cloud where it lurched into a spin and its tail slewed sideways and fell off. John Baron watched with sick fascination as it disintegrated and went to earth, smoke and fire pouring behind.

He saw no parachute open and as it hit the ground in a balloon of red and orange flame he realised he was sweating copiously. He could taste the salt on his lips. He did not know how to feel. It was his first kill. He had told himself many times to simply think of the enemy aircraft as 'it' and that the pilot did not exist: not to give the pilot any thought. He was simply 'the Hun'. It had to be this way, he did not want to think of a human being inside that burning horror making its way to the ground. He wished with all his heart he had not seen the pilot panicking to control the machine.

Abruptly Twig's voice blasted in his ears, high-pitched over the radio. 'Break! Break! Now!' He had given no call sign so JB did not know whether it was for himself or another but reacting immediately he swung away plunging downwards. Then he saw them in his rear-vision mirror – two 109s on his tail, the leader not more than 100 yards astern as the Hun tightened his turn to hold onto John Baron.

All JB could do was lose height in a tight spiral.

'Koala! Get out! Get out! Use the cloud!' The Squadron Leader's voice blasted in his ears. John Baron's call sign was Koala and he knew he had no time. Tracer bullets flashed past his eyeline as he raced down for the cloud and plunged recklessly into it in a steep dive but he felt a thudding impact and the Hurricane lurched.

Oh God! I've been hit. Where? In the tail? In the wing? Not the fuselage please! How could this happen right after my first kill?

Thundering into the heavy cloud below him at around 350 m.p.h. he had not had time to trim the aircraft or set the throttle to give the correct rate of descent. All the instruments were going mad!

He wrenched back on the throttle as he precipitated through the vapour, falling, falling with the impression of being pulled down into a vortex and hurtling into oblivion. His mouth was dry and hot and he began to feel desperate.

Calm. Calm. *Think*. If he had been hit badly he would be on fire by now but he did not believe he was. He was still pulling back fiercely on the throttle to reduce speed and now the altimeter finally stopped unwinding and he decelerated to 100 m.p.h. The green interior of the cockpit seemed to alter to a deathly grey. He was confused, disoriented. Was he climbing? The controls showed he was at 7000 feet. He was dizzy and continuing to sweat profusely. Still in cloud. How much blasted cloud was there?

And then he burst out into daylight, feeling sick and aware of the nose of the Hurricane dropping and slewing sideways in a weird dance across the horizon. Am I going down?

He acted automatically: full opposite rudder, stick forward, centralise the controls. Blissfully he realised he was not in an uncontrollable spiral but in a normal spin, and a few seconds later the aircraft started to respond. Come on lady, good, good, beautiful, you little beauty! You little ripper!

The Hurricane's nose lifted, he was horizontal and steady and he was not on fire. God, what a beautiful aircraft! He could kiss it, really he could.

He looked around and saw nobody; below him was France. He was solo sailing along beneath the cloud at a comfortable 200 m.p.h.

Finally holding steady at 5000 feet, and employing his rear-vision mirror and remaining swivel-eyed to check the sky, he headed for home. He kept thinking of the 109 in flames plunging down to the earth.

It was not until he pushed back his hood in customary fashion – hoods were always back for take-off and landing in case of accident – and came in to land that he saw black dots at about 3000 feet to the north which crystallised into his brother aircraft returning.

And as he bumped and rolled to a halt he undid his harness and parachute and looked around. No ground crew. He was getting tired of this. How many times in the last few days had he come back to find the French ground crew missing? The fitters and riggers, or 'Erks' as they were known, had simply disappeared. And today he had flaming holes in his aircraft!

John Baron could understand that the French were utterly demoralised by Hitler's Blitzkrieg into their land, but he thought they should not give up so quickly.

After the long months of waiting, the invasion had come through the Low Countries. The French emphasis had been on the Maginot Line, a solid system of impregnable concrete and steel defences built between 1930 and 1935 which stretched from Luxembourg to Switzerland and which the Germans had completely avoided.

While German paratroopers had dropped from the skies, Panzer Divisions had plunged into Holland and at the same time entered the Ardennes, the semi-mountainous and heavily wooded frontier of Southern Belgium and Northern France. From there they had pushed on with a rapid advance. Entry through the Ardennes had been obvious to some but apparently not to French and Belgian High Command who considered it impassable and had left it weakly defended by only Reserve Divisions of the Belgian Second and Ninth Armies. Commanded by the French General Corap, the Reserve Divisions were being wholly overrun and presently withdrawing.

John Baron took off his helmet and goggles and jumped out of the cockpit onto the wing to examine the damage to his aeroplane. He found the holes in his tail as he had suspected. He could fly it, that was for sure, but he needed some running repairs. They had been scrambled many times in the last four days and he knew it would happen again, if not tonight then tomorrow morning.

He jumped down to the ground as Twig, Henry, and five

other pilots, 'Rattler' Matheson, a boy from the Falkland Islands, Tony Allen from Rhodesia, and three English pilots, Lefty Rowlands, Fred Sanders and Walter Franklin came rumbling up one after the other.

Twig bounded out onto his wing. 'You got one and so did I. We saw yours hit the deck.' He pointed his thumb over his shoulder at Henry. 'The Old Man winged one and Rattler damaged the bloody bomber as well.'

John Baron stroked the wing of his Hurricane lovingly. 'She took a hit in the tail, but brought me home. In fact, I was thinking up there how I could kiss this little beauty.' And suddenly he leant forward and kissed the wing while the others hooted and laughed.

'Has anyone seen the Squadron Leader?' Fred Sanders asked from under his bushy black moustache.

They shook their heads.

Henry glanced to Twig. 'I thought he was right behind you.'

'Shit, he can't have bought it. Not David, he's too good a flyer.'

The day before, David Flinders had shot down a 109, and the previous autumn a Luftwaffe Dornier 17. He was an experienced pilot who had been with Number 19 Squadron at Duxford before the war, the first squadron ever to be equipped with Hurricanes.

David's non-appearance dampened the mood and they stood on the edge of the field looking skywards and talking. Suddenly Walter saw three French ground crew over by one of the Nissen huts.

'I'll go and grab these blasted erks before they get away. My guns need washing.'

As he darted off, they heard an engine in the air, spasmodic and coughing, but definitely coming in their direction. A minute later over the tops of the trees, his engine cutting in and out, smoke trailing from him, sped David Flinders. They could see him waving to them as he shot over their heads entirely missing the airfield and thudding into the next field where his Hurricane jumped and floundered, slewing and skidding and finally ramming its nose

389

into an ancient oak. The pilots watching sprang in the air, screamed with joy and ran towards the aircraft yelling and shouting.

They clambered over the stile beween the airfield and the Hurricane, and as they charged towards him David stood up out of his cockpit, stepped onto the wing, ceremoniously undid his helmet . . . and bowed.

His men went hysterical with laughter.

They were not scrambled that night and John Baron and most of the squadron lingered in the mess, a brick shed beside a row of Nissen huts used by the mechanics. While talk, alcohol and congratulations flowed for John Baron, Twig and Rattler's successes and David's survival, the mood was sober, for the French Front was collapsing fast and the Germans were bludgeoning onwards and threatening Sedan, on the right bank of the River Meuse.

'How could Reynaud and his generals have been so blind as to have ignored the Ardennes?' asked one of the men.

David Flinders shook his head. 'Hard to say. Twenty years ago the French put up a good fight. Perhaps it's all too much for them this time, like déjà vu, and they're simply war weary.'

'But sir, I heard France has mobilised one man in eight. That's an awful lot of fighting men.'

'I believe that's right, but who knows? Perhaps at the expense of quality: size doesn't necessarily mean efficiency. All this inactivity for months on end, we've all experienced it . . . Boredom sets in. They say the French Reserve Divisions here in the north are only given one day a week of instruction, training and marksmanship. If so, that's serious inefficiency.'

'God, what are they doing the rest of the time?' asked Rattler Matheson.

Harry Fairbanks, a South African and the baby of the squadron at nineteen, supplied an answer. 'Drinking wine!'

This resulted in a rumble of laughter.

'That's all very well but the small countries are being smashed up one by one like matchsticks.' Henry Garner thumped his fist into his palm in emphasis. 'The BEF'll be surrounded if the French don't rally and hold the Nazis back.'

'One hundred per cent right,' agreed Tony Allen. 'The infantry'll be surrounded all right.' He had an atlas opened in front of him and he traced his finger along the section of the Dyle River where the British Expeditionary Forces were entrenched. 'This is where we are, right in the middle.'

John Baron was looking over his shoulder, brandy in hand. 'Well, thank God Churchill's finally in charge.'

And Twig, who had become a student of British politics, raised his glass in the air. 'Yes, siree. I'm a boy from Florida and I knew nothing about Great Britain till I arrived in London. But I can tell you he's swell, just the man for the job. Knows his history, makes great speeches, likes a drink, likes a cigar, likes a laugh, and bloody-minded into the bargain! A perfect choice to go up against Herr bloody Hitler.'

This brought a round of laughter, for Twig had never used the word 'bloody' until his arrival in England.

'Why the hell did you leave Florida anyway Twig, old man?' asked Walter Franklin. 'I thought your State Department back in the good ol' US of A didn't approve of foreign enlistment.'

Twig pursed his lips. 'You're right they don't.'

'Then how come you and "Pussy" Palmer are here?'

Cyril 'Pussy' Palmer was from Cleveland and was flying with Number 1 Hurricane Squadron, their brother squadron in France.

'We're unique,' Twig laughed.

'That's what I'd say about you, Twigsie,' Tony Doyle shouted. 'You're bloody unique all right, though I heard there's a Puerto Rican with two fifty-three. Aren't Puerto Ricans Yanks?'

Twig nodded. 'Well, yes, it's a Territory like you British guys have. They're US citizens – have been for about forty years, I think.'

'So then, there're a few of you *unique* Yanks in the RAF.'

Harry Fairbanks put his beer on the bar and lifted his forefinger for emphasis. 'Actually Grifter down in Operations told me that he knew of an American who came over to join up pretending to be a Canadian so as not to get into trouble with your Yankee authorities.'

'Probably right.'

'Good on him,' shouted Arnie Townsend, the comedian of the squadron. 'So that makes at least four of you, Twigsie old boy! And we're very much obliged.'

'Hey, let's not forget the initial question to Russell. You still haven't told us why you left the sunshine and came here.'

And now most of the boys round the bar took up the cry. 'Yes, Russell, come on, why *did* you leave Florida? What's a southern boy like you doin' fighting with us?'

John Baron knew the reason, and he also knew Twig was still a little sensitive about it.

'Come on, Twig, tell us the truth. Your mob aren't even in the flamin' war.'

John Baron began to fill the gap of silence. 'He's here because he's here. Got tired of all the sunshine and good weather and decided to come to the charm of the rain for a bit.'

Twig held up his hand. 'It's all right, JB.' He looked around the bar and shrugged. 'The fact is, I'm here because the great love of my life at the time, Mary Beth Moran, up and married another guy.' His friends unanimously moaned in mock pain. 'I was a commercial pilot and I still wanted to fly so after a couple of months in London, the lucky RAF got my services.' He smiled meekly. 'I was destined to be with all you dear sensitive souls!'

Sounds of derision and catcalls met this announcement as Twig lifted his hands up in the air for silence and added, 'And do you know what, fellas? Losing Mary Beth bothered me for years until I met this great little English girl who's changed my life! Now come on, let's have another drink.'

'Good idea!'

Later as the two friends walked back to the bunkhouse,

Twig took John Baron's arm. 'I was glad I got that off my chest tonight.'

'Do you mean Mary Beth?'

Twig paused by a blacked-out window in one of the Nissen huts and John Baron discerned his eyes in the night light. They were both swaying a little from the excesses of the evening. 'Yeah, I haven't wanted to talk about it but tonight I thought, What the hell, who's Mary Beth anyway?'

'That's the spirit. You had a ca . . . tharsis.'

Twig hiccuped. 'A cartha . . . what?'

'Catharsis, release of pent-up emotions.'

'Shit, did I?'

They rambled on for a few yards. 'You know what, JB?'

'What?'

'I like Jane Cardrew, I mean I like her an awful lot. Can't keep my hands off her.'

'So I noticed.'

'She writes to me every second day. And now that this fighting's hotted up, well, it makes a guy think.'

'About what?'

Twig hiccuped again and stood still. 'About whether I should be making her a respectable woman.'

'Too deep for me, old man.'

Twig gave a soft snort. 'What about you?'

'What about me?'

'You and Alex. Jane says she's got it bad for you.'

John Baron took hold of his friend's arm and moved him on. 'I think we should digscuss this when we're sober.'

Twig began to giggle. '*Digscuss* – you said *digscuss*! Yes siree, we'll digscuss it when we're sober.'

'Sure.' And both laughing they meandered on to the bunkhouse.

Half an hour later John Baron lay hands behind his head listening to the night. He had drunk three glasses of water before going to bed for he knew they would be in the air again at dawn. The last few days had matured him. He understood now what killing in the air was about. The infantry there on the ground lived in constancy with the battle, poor devils, whereas a pilot went into the foray, fought, and if not brought down, returned to home base where the proximity of death disappeared. He was back to normality: his belongings around him, a proper bed, the drinks in the mess, the conviviality. It was all a bit surreal.

A strong wind rushed at the walls of the hut and every now and then a window rattled. His mind ranged over many things and settled upon Alex. She wrote to him almost as much as Jane did to Twig and was now mentioning joining one of the women's auxiliary services though she was doing important work with the telephone exchange. She moved round Kent to airfields censoring their telephone calls. She had asked for his advice though he had not yet replied.

He had not seen her since he left England even though she had hinted about coming to Paris if he could get leave. Twig and Jane had met in Paris a few weeks previously and Jane had suggested in a letter to Twig that they make it a foursome. But John Baron had found an excuse not to go. His feelings for Alex were ambivalent. Oh, he was attracted to her, no doubt about that. She was so physically similar to Sam that it was impossible for him not to be. Yet there were strong differences between them, and he found himself wondering if the contrasts pleased or displeased him. One thing was a fact, he liked receiving her letters, and in a fashion looked forward to them.

He listened to the wind. The window rattled again and the hut creaked. He missed Sam. Now that she had left Cash and gone to New York he dearly hoped she would be happy and successful. He thought perhaps he should write her a letter, after all she continued to write once a month to him. He would tell her about his first kill today and how he felt; the shock of seeing the German trying to control his aircraft, the weird unreality of being in the spin in cloud and the bliss when he came out of the dive into the sunshine.

He actually moved on his bunk and half rose to get out of bed and write the letter, but he fell back on the pillow. What good would it do other than to keep cementing a bond that was futile? No! He would write only for her birthday.

He wondered how Cash had been affected by Sam's departure? He had written a letter of commiseration to Cash late last year but the letter had been returned to him. Cash was no longer at the flat in Rose Bay.

Then about a fortnight ago in a letter from his father he had learnt a little about Cash. His parent had included a one-page note they had received.

Dear Mum and Dad Chard, Uncle Wake and Ledgie,
Well, Sam has been in America now for many months. I'm sorry our marriage was a failure and I'll carry a torch for your daughter always.
I thought you might be wondering where I am. Well, no names no pack drill. I'm all right, don't worry about me. When haven't I been all right?
You might not hear from me for a long time but I'll be thinking about you. If ever you see my mother, please let her know I'm well and tell JB when next you write that I'll get around to dropping him a line one day.
Yours ever,
Cashman
PS Give Storm a hug

Apparently the envelope had been postmarked Hobart and thus the family believed the Tasmanian capital city to be Cash's whereabouts, but John Baron had other thoughts. He knew from his parents that two detectives had been out to Haverhill looking for Cash not long before the war started and Sam had insinuated in her letters that Cash had been on the wrong side of the law. This reminded John Baron of his friend's threat to become a burglar all those years ago.

Yet at Haverhill outside the stables two days before he had married Sam, Cash had sworn to him that he was not doing anything illegal.

But that was Cash. With him anything could be possible.

He could not help but wonder about his old friend. What a character! He had a way about him all right. Even managed to get a record amount of smiles out of Ledgie!

John Baron rolled over still listening to the wind and

thinking of days gone by. Just as he drifted into sleep he imagined Cash behind him on Belcher's Harley Davidson shouting in his ear, 'Faster, JB. Go faster!'

Cash looked around at Corporal 'Curly' Dunne in the breaking dawn chill as a feeble trickle of light wavered through the pale candlebark gums to sprinkle the first touches of day upon the rise where they had bivouacked on the seemingly endless New South Wales plains outside Bathurst.

He sat on a rock, studying a map by torchlight and arching his back in an attempt to remove a sore spot, the result of the night's hard mattress – the uneven ground beside a dried-up water-hole.

He heard a rustling noise and looked up.

'Sergeant Wade, here's your tea, just made.' The man's tired, bloodshot eyes blinked as he handed the tin mug to Cash.

Cash had joined up as Ashley Wade; a name that sounded a lot like Cash Slade and one to which he thought he would react. The first mouthful of hot sweet liquid slipped blissfully down Cash's throat as he placed the map flat on the dirt, flicking torchlight across the paper.

'Sit down, Dunne, I want to show you something.'

The Corporal crouched beside him.

They were on a manoeuvre. It had begun at 1800 the day before. The 'enemy', two platoons of B Company under the command of Lieutenant Barry Jarrold, a schoolmaster before he had volunteered, had route marched to a disused farmhouse two miles from the tiny town of Blainey where they were now in residence. The two opposing platoons that included Cash and Corporal Dunne were under the command of Lieutenant Colin Turnbull – a graduate of Duntroon, the Australian Military College – and they were to attempt to capture the house and its occupants.

Turnbull's two platoons had been dropped in lorries twelve miles from the farmhouse and the Lieutenant had divided his men. Cash led one third of the command and his orders were to approach the target from the north and to attack at 1500. At the same time Turnbull would divide the remainder of the men and half of those – deployed from the south – would join Cash's assault. While the enemy were resisting this two-pronged attack Turnbull would bring in the rest of his command and overwhelm the farmhouse.

Cash looked at his compass and traced their position with his forefinger. 'We're here.'

'That's right,' agreed Dunne.

'And when the Lieutenant left last night he went in this direction.'

'Yes.'

'There's something funny about his proposed entry into enemy territory. Didn't he say he would go up this ravine?'

'Yes.'

'Well, I studied this map most of last night and I reckon that'd be a perfect place for landmines.'

If one of the dummy landmines were trodden upon, it would be deemed that all troops within a radius of fifteen feet were classified as dead or injured, taking them out of the attack. And as there was one observer for every ten men, he would ensure fair play.

'Gawd, why didn't Lieutenant Turnbull think of that?'

'You tell me.'

Dunne's bloodshot eyes reached skywards. Lieutenant Colin Turnbull unfortunately did not inspire esteem in his men. He had got off to a bad start by getting them lost on a couple of exercises in the Blue Mountains yet he was constantly attempting to impress. Too often he was heard to boast of his Great Uncle Ben, whom he claimed was Ben Hall, the most famous of the bushrangers in the early 1860s, when those outlaws were known as 'The Wild Colonial Boys'. The truth was that to the average Australian soldier, especially most of those in Cash's company who were country bred: stockmen, farmhands and horsemen born to the rifle, this would have been a meritorious connection. Each of this steady-eyed, bronzed, long-striding breed gave grudging respect to the outlaws of old, but Lieutenant Turnbull overdid it all, using any opportunity to regale the boys with gilded stories of his 'mother's uncle'.

And when the men had seen him in civilian clothes sporting an old Anston .58 calibre pistol in his belt and alleging it had been taken from Ben Hall's body when he had died in a hail of police bullets down by Goobang Creek near Forbes, they had scoffed at him behind his back. The pistol had *B.H.* engraved in the wooden handle and most of the boys joked that he had engraved the initials there himself. Turnbull was heard to say, 'That handgun means the world to me.'

So as Corporal Dunne's eyes rolled, Cash said nothing, but he was concerned about the probability of the land-mines.

'Get the Lieutenant on the radio, Corporal.'

'Righto, Sarge.'

Cash moved along with his Corporal to where Private Hector Milbank, a muscular bricklayer from Narellan, reached the Lieutenant on the radio and Cash spoke.

'Lieutenant Turnbull?'

'Yes, Wade, what is it?'

'I've been studying the map overnight and I think that ravine K could be a dangerous entry point. Looks ideal for landmines to me.'

There was a long silence at the other end of the radio.

'You there, Lieutenant Turnbull?'

'Of course I'm here. Is that all?'

'Well, I reckon the dried-up creek beds H and M could be mined as well so I'd make an approach over W, Dogwood Hill, if I were you.'

Another silence before Turnbull's voice, sharp and impatient, crackled, 'Remember there's to be no radio contact after thirteen hundred. Oh, and Sergeant Wade, when you speak to me over the radio or in person, call me *sir*. Understood?'

Dunne and Milbank made faces at the radio and Cash answered, 'All understood. Over and out . . . sir.'

By 1300 all of Cash's platoon were in place. Cash and Dunne took out two forward enemy sentries and moved up into a strong position for the assault. Precisely on 1500 they attacked.

'Where are the others, for Christ's sake?' exploded Dunne as Cash and his twelve men ran doubled-up across the dusty broken ground leading up to the farmhouse.

Five minutes later it was all over. Lieutenant Jarrold's two companies had won. The attempt to seize the farm-house had failed and as Cash by then had realised, Turnbull had ignored his advice, taken his men in by the ravine and one of the dried-up creek beds, and lost half his forces to landmines.

Back at the main camp on parade the following day Turnbull informed them that there was no leave that weekend. There was a long groan from the soldiers.

'And none the following weekend.'

An even longer groan met this announcement.

'That's enough!' Turnbull shouted, a flush of red rising up his neck above his uniform. 'You went and got your-selves killed in the exercise, what do you expect? Drinks all round? You'll stay in camp and drill. We'll make soldiers of you yet.'

The final insult presented itself on the second weekend that the men remained in camp. At 1600 they saw their brother soldiers going off for the weekend on motor bikes and in lorries while they drilled on the parade ground. Then at 1730 as a cold wind entered the camp along with the dusk, Cash's platoon were marching across to the mess hut when Lieutenant Turnbull stepped out of his hut in fancy dress.

They all knew the officers were going to a Red Cross fancy dress ball that night in Bathurst to raise money for the war effort, but as Turnbull emerged from his door it took the marching soldiers all their resistance not to break ranks and charge him. He wore a flat-crown cabbage tree hat with red velvet band, a showy red shirt, white kerchief tied around his neck, leather bandolier across his chest and cord breeches tucked into knee-high black boots with his pride and joy, the ancient Anston .58 calibre pistol, at a rakish angle, in his belt. Cash, who was knowledgeable on the bushrangers knew he looked far more like the flam-boyant Johnny Gilbert, who had been Ben Hall's partner, than Ben himself, who had dressed much more quietly and similar to a gentleman farmer.

The soldiers began to boo as Turnbull strode down from his hut to a jeep in the distance.

Cash halted the marching men and turned round to them. 'Listen, boys. Leave it. We don't want any more of his spleen turned on us. Forget it.'

Corporal Dunne scratched his freckled cheek and gave a grunt of anger. 'Turnbull's a dickhead, Sarge. You warned him about those mines and he took no bloody notice and now we're the ones payin' for his mistake and he's off to a flamin' fancy-dress party. He looks like a fool and he's a bloody let-down to Duntroon and that's a fact. You're a thousand times more of an officer than he'll ever be.'

There were general rumbles of agreement at this statement as they stood and watched Turnbull ride away.

The following Tuesday morning Cash and the B Company Sergeant and Sergeant Major were called in to face Lieutenant Turnbull. He sat in his day tent behind his desk upon the duckboard flooring, his face blotched with red and purple spots of rage and his temper obviously close to precipitating out of control.

He stammered when he spoke. 'I . . . I've called you all h . . . here, because I've been bloody-well burgled here in camp. No doubt about it. Last night! And I want you, no, I *order* you, to find out who's responsible.'

Cash replied in a dispassionate and authoritative manner. 'Burgled, sir? That's a serious charge to make against your own men. Are you absolutely sure?'

Turnbull stood up and bumped his leg on the corner of his desk in his haste. He groaned in pain as he met Cash's eyes 'For Christ's sake, Wade, I know a burglary when I see one. My great-uncle's pistol's gone.'

The non-commissioned officers in front of him thought he was going to cry for his face seemed to crumple.

'That's an heirloom, an irreplaceable piece of history, of inestimable value to this country.' He shook his head and grimaced as if in pain. 'Perhaps I should have offered it to the National Gallery. I just could never bear to part with it.'

Sergeant Major Flynn spoke. 'Was anything else taken, sir?'

'Yes. Yes. My entire month's pay, my solid gold cufflinks, given to me when I graduated from Duntroon, and my solid gold watch . . . and my father's silver fob watch and my gold signet ring.' He hesitated. 'There could be other things – I'm not certain yet.' He sank back on his desk in defeat and his hands fell limply to his side.

The Sergeant Major rubbed his chin in bewilderment. 'But your room's on the upper floor of the only two-storeyed building in camp, sir. The officers' mess is opposite with traffic coming in and out all the time. There are sentries at the main gate twenty-four hours a day and that's right opposite you. If anybody were going to rob a place, robbing yours doesn't make sense. It's the most difficult target in the whole camp – even the Commanding Officer's quarters are on ground-floor level.'

Turnbull looked as though he would explode. 'Sergeant Major,' his voice trembled on the edge of hysteria, 'I want you all to comb the camp. I want those objects found and I want the culprit here before me!' He pointed through the tent flap in a desperate gesture. 'Enlist any help you need. Now get out and get moving, all of you!'

They did.

As the three non-commissioned officers left the Lieutenant's company the Sergeant Major reiterated his surprise that such a difficult objective as Turnbull's room would be chosen. 'The fact is,' he stated as they passed through a broad band of sunshine near the cook tent, 'the only way in would be to shinny up that drainpipe at the back of the building and you'd have to be a blasted professional burglar to even attempt it.'

Cash smiled to himself as he answered. 'You certainly would, Sergeant Major. Nobody but a professional burglar would dare to attempt it!'

The orders were followed and the camp turned upside down, and when Colonel Maxwell and Major Anderson arrived by jeep that afternoon and were confronted by the disarray they asked for a complete explanation which a still jittery, barely coherent Lieutenant Turnbull did his best to give them.

The stolen goods were never found.

Colonel Maxwell and Major Anderson were capable men. They kept a keen eye on the whole regiment and while they sympathised with their subordinate officer over the loss, they privately believed that the Lieutenant had handled the aftermath of the burglary injudiciously and that Turnbull had in fact probably brought the robbery upon himself by his attitude to his men.

A month later Lieutenant Turnbull was transferred to a desk job in Sydney and Major Anderson called Sergeant Ash Wade into his tented office. Anderson was English, born in Africa. He had married an Australian girl and had run a farm not far from Young in New South Wales. He had enlisted early in the first days of the war and was as fit as any man in the regiment and he recognised that Cash was a match for him.

'Wade?'

'Yes, sir?'

'I notice on your record that you went to school and university in New Zealand.'

Cash hesitated. 'My family lived there for a decade.'

'Right. What did you graduate in?'

'I'm an engineer sir.'

'Marvellous – we need engineers. The Colonel and I have had our eyes on you and we believe you're officer material. So you're off to become one. There'll be six months' to a year's training in it.' He smiled. 'We'll push you through as there's a war on. Now there's talk of the regiment being sent abroad, to the Middle East or perhaps Singapore or Malaya. The Japs have been the aggressors on this side of the world since their invasion of Manchuria nine years ago. Their current war with China and their open support for Hitler and Mussolini in Europe all lead us to reckon they've got their eye on a lot of the Pacific including

Australia. But my guess is that it'll be six or nine months before we go anywhere. So you might come back to us.'

'I'd like to come back, sir. And . . . ?'

'Yes?'

'Can I refuse to become an officer?'

'No.'

'Right then, sir.'

Chapter Twenty-seven

Monday, 20 May, 1940

Winston Churchill cleared his throat in that manner which always drew attention. The members of his War Cabinet, who had been in discussion, turned their eyes to him.

'Gentlemen, I do believe that as a precautionary measure the Admirality should assemble a fleet of small vessels in readiness to proceed to ports and inlets on the French coast. Admiral Ramsay at Dover should be alerted.'

Anthony Eden leant forward on his elbows. 'Prime Minister, do you really believe it will come to an evacuation of the British Expeditionary Force? It's almost unthinkable.'

Winston's gaze settled on his Secretary of State for War. 'I know what you say, but we have to face the fact that the German armoured divisions are pouring towards Amiens and Arras, and curling along the Somme towards the Channel. These hideous scythes are encountering little or no resistance and I'm shocked by the utter failure of our allies to grapple with the German advance.'

His blue eyes searched the faces before him as he continued in phlegmatic tone. 'Thus to me we seem to have two fearsome alternatives. One: for the British Army, at all costs and without French or Belgian cooperation, to cut its way south to the Somme – a mammoth task that begs for more troops than we have, and one which would involve a rearguard action and protection of both flanks. I've spoken to our Commander-in-Chief and he doubts he could perform this task without help – and there is none to be had. Two: to fall back on Dunkirk* and face an emergency sea evac-

---

*Dunkirk: Operation Dynamo: see *Endnotes*, page 811.

uation under hostile air attack, with the absolute certainty of losing all our precious artillery, vehicles and equipment.'

Winston's fingers toyed with the signet ring on his left hand as his cabinet waited for his next words. 'Perhaps you're right that it's unthinkable, Anthony, but I fear we must evaluate the unthinkable. And therefore steps must be taken now in case evacuation becomes the only way of saving the BEF and regrouping to continue the fight against the German monster.'

General John Standish Surtees Prendergast Vereker, the sixth Viscount Gort, and 'Jack' to those close to him, the Commander-in-Chief of the British Expeditionary Force in Europe, stood with his hands behind his back, a drawn expression tightening his moustached top lip while his fingers roamed across the map of Europe on the wall in front of him.

He had dashed off a quick note to his wife Marjorie at 0600 in which all his frustrations and concerns had been swiftly stated. He had signed off with the words: *I'm sorry for the luckless Low Countries who have no quarrel with anyone but who are condemned as usual to be the cockpit of Europe. The BEF is surrounded by armies withdrawing before the German onslaught and to think our son Sandy is here and our future son-in-law too. May God keep them safe for us.*

The General moved to the window where his cup of tea stood on the sill. Picking it up he sipped his tea as he looked through the grimy cracked glass into the fading light. He had arrived in his new command post in the small village of Premesques between Lille and Armentières after abandoning previous headquarters in Arras and Waghnies to move ahead of the German advance.

For a few moments he watched two sentries who stood in front of great lengths of barbed wire and piles of sandbags near the small pool in front of the château. At the edge of the sandbags wild daisies grew in profusion: it was an incongruous sight.

When the German Blitzkrieg had begun he was dismayed

to discover, contrary to what he had been led to believe, that there was no French strategic reserve to be had; that they existed only on paper and anything remotely resembling reinforcements had been concentrated behind the Maginot Line. The French were reeling in disbelief at the massive German thrust through their country.

With his eyes staring through the host of tiny daisies pushing for an existence beside the sandbags, General Gort's mind wandered back over recent days.

On 13 May, Queen Wilhelmina and the Dutch Government sought refuge in England.

On 14 May, Gort had travelled to Willbroek Fort in Belgium to visit King Leopold of the Belgians. He had found the King anxious-eyed and deeply depressed: his army was in tatters and streaming westward before the German advance. Gort had said what he could to cheer the monarch.

On 15 May, the Luftwaffe had reduced the defenceless city of Rotterdam in Holland to rubble and the Dutch Army completely capitulated. The French had replaced General Corap with General Giraud, but such moves had come too late and many of the French Generals fought openly with one another. This had surprised Gort.

By 17 May, the Germans had reached the Oise River and Brussels fell to enemy hands after repeated devastating air attacks using high explosives and incendiary bombs. A day later, in the south, the Germans were making bridgeheads across the Somme.

On Saturday, 18 May, Paul Reynaud, the French Prime Minister attempted to fortify his High Command by recalling Marshal Petain – of Great War defence of Verdun fame – from his ambassadorship in Madrid and inviting him to join the Government while the Prime Minister personally took charge of the Ministry for Defence.

By Sunday, 19 May, the British were attacking south of Arras and the Germans surrounded the French troops in the town of Cambrai. General Giraud was taken prisoner and General Weygand, aged 73, who had been recalled from the Levant, replaced General Gamelin as Commander of the Allied Forces.

On 20 May, the 2nd Panzers had reached the English Channel near Noyelles and the retreating French 7th Army, totally demoralised, had been routed. The Germans occupied Amiens.

On 21 May, General Weygand, trying his best to unify his troops, had come up with a highly improbable counter-attack plan and bravely announced his intention of a French defence of a 'Weygand Line' along the Somme-Aisne even though the Germans had bridgeheads at points across it.

General Gort was a realist, he had moved troops in an effort to support the plan but in his heart he believed it would need the French army to be somehow magically revitalised.

On 22 May, in a desperate bid the French Prime Minister met with Winston Churchill and British High Command. They had agreed to a counter-attack by the British and French towards Bapaume using 8 divisions, with the Royal Air Force giving day and night support to the battle.

Then today, 23 May, General Gort was given the depressing news that the Germans were in Bologne and heading north up the coast towards Calais.

Gort mechanically emptied his teacup, took his staring eyes from the redoubtable daisies and turned round to General Sir Henry Pownall, his Chief of Staff, who waited by his desk. 'The message I received from Mr Churchill this morning pointed out there will be a moment when the Panzers, tired by the constant push, must rest. That will be the time to attack if we can.' He walked back to his Chief of Staff. 'Are the men on half rations yet?'

'Orders were given this morning sir.'

'We too must do the same.'

'Right, sir.'

Gort crossed to the wall map. His fingers roved over Northern France. 'I'm moving as many troops as I can but the men are exhausted. We're holding our own right flank at the moment but if I'm to make a southward drive as is proposed, I'll need both flanks protected and a rearguard action.'

'Sir, we don't have the support to do it. Disaster's all around. The roads are blocked not only by the retreating armies but by refugees as well. We're delaying the Panzers with some units of our Twelfth and Twenty-third divisions but they can't continue indefinitely. We've men in the field fighting rearguard actions who've never been near the front line before: medical orderlies, PT instructors, chemical warfare units, cooks, any able man who can fire a rifle. I'm told a bunch of our padres actually defended the bridge at Bergues and none of them had ever touched firearms before.'

Gort gave a tired smile. 'The French cavalry corps under Prioux have given a great account of themselves. They're now fighting along with us. He's one Frenchman who never says die. And so are de Gaulle and Molinie in Lille.' He snapped his fingers. 'I wouldn't give a jot for the rest.'

There was a rap on the door and a messenger came in. 'Radio message, sir.'

Gort took the form and read it. He spoke as he left the room and walked along the corridor with Pownall at his side. 'The two divisions at Arras have fought like lions and held up the Panzers for nearly four days. Apparently the vigour of our defence has surprised the Germans for they've brought up reinforcements. But there's only a narrow corridor to the west still open to them. I must withdraw them tonight.'

Henry Pownall sighed. He knew his Commander was trying everything he could.

'Has Lieutenant Colonel Bridgeman drawn up a last resort plan for a withdrawal to the sea?'

Pownall nodded.

'Ask him to bring it to me.'

'Yes, sir.'

Three days later General Gort, tired and drawn, stood again in front of his map in typical attitude – legs apart and hands behind his back. He had slept little in the past two weeks and last night not at all. He had watched the French and Belgian armies fall back consistently. This very afternoon

408

he had received urgent calls for reinforcements from his own Generals. In Belgium General Alan Brooke, who was attempting to hold the arterial road from Comines to Ypres, was in desperate need of more troops and tanks, but there were none to send. The men in the garrison at Calais were fighting like demons against overpowering odds and in the south the Germans were in St Omer, Aire, La Bassée and Lens.

Gort was aware the Panzers to the west had halted, apparently for respite. He also knew that King George had asked for this very day to be a national day of prayer. Personally he believed the time for prayer had passed.

The door creaked open and he looked round as General Pownall entered.

'What time is it?' Gort asked.

Henry Pownall looked at his watch. 'Eighteen thirty hours.'

General Gort's eyes closed momentarily. He was not a man given to showing his feelings but the weight of the emotion he felt was so great that his voice quivered as he began to speak.

'It's a grave hour, Henry, and I must make a grave decison. I'm here, the War Cabinet isn't, the Prime Minister isn't. I've no instruction from higher authority, but I know what I must do. My responsibility for the safety of the men of the British Expeditionary Force who are almost completely surrounded by the enemy, outweighs my obligations to the French High Command. I must save my men from death or captivity.

'There'll be no more talk of a British offensive. We'll plug the gap to the north if we can and we'll march to the sea. Evacuation's our only chance.'

John Baron rolled over. His eyes opened and he was wide awake. He did not struggle back to consciousness as once he had. He leapt out of bed, automatically buttoning up his tunic and strapping on his revolver. He heard Squadron Leader David Flinders's voice above the general uproar. 'Moving out! The Huns are coming again! I want you all in the air before dawn. Any unflyable aircraft – turn them over in the bomb craters and burn them!'

Guns were booming in the distance as he hurried out of the hut into the darkness, where he saw Twig coming towards him. 'We're at it again?'

'Hell yes. Not sure where to this time.'

The Squadron Leader's voice lifted once more. 'I know you're tired, but move. I want the main road party out in fifteen minutes.' That consisted of the petrol tankers, a buckboard, a Commer van, and four lorries for the station troops, kit and equipment. 'The French sappers have told me they'll blow the bridge in half an hour!'

They knew they were the last squadron still in France. The fact was that all squadrons of the RAF, except for them, were now operating from Britain.

Before they took off again, David Flinders gathered them around him. In the shadows of the night his fair hair sneaked out from under his helmet as he buckled his chinstrap. He looked jaded but a warrior-like glint still sparkled in his eyes. 'This is our final operation in France. Apparently the brass hats have taken note of our fourteen days of continuous day and night action and they think we should be rested. Anyway we're the last squadron here and this is the last airport open. My orders are for us to make a final patrol of the beaches. After that we fly home. You're to take leave. Out of the fray for at least a month, I'm told.'

The pilots eyed each other. They were jumpy and morose a lot of the time these days but they had become a band of brothers; been blooded in this constant day and night operation. They hardly dared believe it, that they would fly back to England today, not to have to live on their nerves with the sleep deprivation and the perpetual strain of the day and night patrols and their inevitable losses.

As John Baron looked round the faces with him, many sporting five or six days' beard, he pictured those who were missing: Harry Fairbanks, the squadron's baby had been shot down two days previously, and was missing over the Channel: Lefty Rowlands had been hit, crash landed and was in a hospital in Paris, and Rattler Matheson had been shot down over De Panne, crash landed on the beach, broken his leg and was believed to be in a hospital ship on his way back to England. Fred Sanders had been hit on two separate missions and both times had crash landed, the second time he had been wounded and was currently being evacuated home. Walter Franklin had been killed a week ago; he had been hit over the beach at Calais and the Squadron Leader had seen him bail out and watched helplessly as a German Dornier shot him before he landed. Tony Allen had been shot down and killed over the Channel.

'What airfield do we head home to?' Henry Garner asked.

'Lympne in Kent. Now let's go.'

They climbed into the air, away from the gleam of gold that inched over the horizon behind them. John Baron wondered if the road transport would get through. So many of the arteries were blocked hopelessly now as vast masses of troops and transports poured back to what was becoming known as the 'Dunkirk Perimeter', a section of defended coast which continued to shrink back around Dunkirk as the BEF and the French army withdrew.

As John Baron's Hurricane swept along behind David Flinders leading the squadron, a dense cloud of smoke from burning oil tanks blotted out the actual port of Dunkirk and over to the north of the smoke, he saw a bunch of Heinkel 111 bombers being escorted by Messerschmitt 109s.

'Tally Ho!' he called into the radio as he turned his reflector sight on and the gun button to 'fire' while the squadron immediately gave chase. In the diving, weaving, sweeping battle that ensued John Baron took care of a Heinkel as did David Flinders and Twig; and Henry Garner and Sergeant Johnny Clowes bagged 109s. This time no one was lost. It was miraculous.

John Baron had added another to his score: four in twelve days! He could not help but feel elated; that made six in all with his two previous kills. It was an amazingly high score for the amount of days he had actually been in action.

He took a sweep down over the beach at Bray Dunes where he saw long lines of men, thousands of them, human chains neck deep in water, wading out to vessels, and flew low over a hospital ship marked with a red cross.

A haze of burning oil seemed to stretch like a strip of ribbon across the Channel in front of him and as he pulled back on the throttle and gained height he saw six Spitfires coming out of it; they passed him to his right and as he looked across at the leader he was certain it was Douglas Bader and he was sure he saw *Dogsbody* painted on the fuselage! John Baron smiled to himself. Bader was a Flight Lieutenant with 222 Squadron these days.

He looked around for his own squadron and could see the Hurricanes over to the west heading for home and he automatically swung his gaze round to the east before following them. In that moment he saw a lone Junkers 87 dive bomber, or a 'Stuka' as they called it, the abbreviation for the German, Sturzkampfflugzeug. With its big intimidating black crosses on the wings and swastika on its tail it was going in low over a beach to the south of Dunkirk heading towards the lines of helpless men in the water, and without consideration he brought his aircraft round and dived down towards it.

He came in fast as it was strafing the soldiers below and when it saw the Hurricane it arced away sharply but not before John Baron's thumb had jabbed at the firing button and his guns in the wings had squirted bullets.

He missed it and the enemy aircraft streaked away inland. 'Damn you!' he said aloud and shot after it. He followed it, weaving and rolling, pressing the firing pin when he was within range. They raced in tandem across the French countryside and the Junkers entered a cloud with John Baron on its tail. As they emerged from the grey vapour he had gained on it and he saw little brazen flashes issuing at him from the bomber's glasshouse. John Baron gave it another burst of fire and the little flashes stopped. *Good, I got the gunner!* Where just a few weeks ago, he had felt sick knowing he had killed a man, it was completely different now. He had seen so much horror and destruction wreaked by the Germans; had lost friends who were dear to him because of them – it had hardened him. His job was to shoot down Nazi aircraft and that was what he would do, as often as he could!

The enemy steep-turned and dived away as John Baron sped by. He guessed he would still have about 80 rounds left to each gun and began to make a turn for England and home.

He was breaking to the left and thinking how everything in the air happened so fast when all of a sudden something hit him!

There was a bang and it was as if the aircraft's tail were in some giant's hands being waved around. Abruptly the machine lurched and the nose dropped. He fought to gain control. He thought he could smell fuel and he was in a dive. He pulled back on the stick as he saw the Heinkel that had hit him sweeping away to the right.

He tried not to panic but the Hurricane was heading for the ground and remembering the last time he had been in a spin towards the earth he gathered himself and took a deep breath as he fought against the nose's desperate bid to point downwards.

The ground was speeding up at him; he could hear the hissing of the air over the roof of the cockpit. There was a hole in the windscreen to the left of the bullet-proof section and as he pulled back with all his strength on the throttle and to his eternal relief the nose inched up, he looked around and saw the gaping hole in his right wing.

'Shit!' His head spun from right to left. *No fire yet! Thank God.*

At least the aircraft had come out of the deathly earth-wards spiral.

He was sweating profusely as he looked at the instruments: air speed was not registering at all, the others seemed normal. Now the engine began coughing, cutting in and out and he was losing altitude fast. After another minute or so the engine gave a sort of whining scream and cut out all together. He was gliding across treetops, he saw a stream then two tanks and soldiers. 'Oh Christ!' He spoke aloud to the green interior of his cockpit. 'Germans!' He sped over a village or what was left of it, a road junction, across

413

an open field, a harrowed field . . . He pulled back on the hood handle but nothing happened. *Hell, it's jammed.*

As he held off over a burnt-out farmhouse and outbuildings he continued to pull back on the hood handle but nothing moved. *God, I'm going to be stuck in here.* He braced himself as he felt the massive jolt of hitting the ground followed by the Hurricane bouncing up twice in the air in showers of dust. The final impact of the tail thudding down to the earth slewed the aircraft into a tree and everything around John Baron went black.

Chapter Twenty-eight

John Baron opened his eyes. He must have blacked out for a minute or so with the impact. His left shoulder felt tender, perhaps it had hit the side of the cockpit. It was the one he had dislocated all those years ago when he had fallen from the cliff.

The first thing he saw was the engine smoking. God, he did not want to be burnt! He had to get out. With rising panic he remembered the sticking hood handle. He pushed it again. This time it slid back smoothly and he groaned with relief; the jolt of the crash must have loosened it. He whipped the pin out of his Sutton harness, unclipped his parachute and stood up.

He knew he had seen Germans back there and they had seen him. He grabbed his maps but did not turn off the petrol or main engine switches before leaping out on the wing and down to the ground.

He was not injured, just sore, and though he felt shaky he could not afford to hang around here. He ran towards the perimeter of the field to a lane where he gazed rapidly left and right. Two cows eyed him from fifty yards along the lane, but they were the only life he could see. He wondered where the hell he was. He knew northern France pretty well after eight months of flying in and out of the aerodromes here, and if only he could find a signpost or perhaps even see a landmark he recognised he would be able to get his bearings. He could hear distant guns that gave him an idea he was not too far away from the fighting.

He looked back at the Hurricane's smoking engine. If it began to burn and exploded, the Germans he had seen would know exactly where to come. He had to get away from around here and fast: to make for Dunkirk and the beaches. He tapped the inner pocket of his flying jacket: the compass that he invariably carried would be valuable now as the afternoon sky was beginning to cloud over. He crossed the lane and entered another field heading west as he glanced at his watch: it was 0802.

He ran across two fields and came to a hedgerow where wild roses weaved their way in profusion through new green shoots. He eyed them; so small and pink and lovely, in their dainty beauty they symbolised everything that was normal . . . and yet nothing was normal!

He felt slightly sick and his shoulder began to ache. The hedgerow ran on one side of a road with trees and bracken opposite. It appeared to be a lonely country byway in a sparsely populated area. Obviously those peasants and country folk who lived here had departed in advance of the German army.

He cautiously crossed the road. The sound of an approaching vehicle prompted him to dive into the bracken and a minute later a lorry rumbled by, swastika looming ominously on its side. God, how he hated that symbol!

When it had disappeared he rose and looked cautiously both ways. He was about to move off when he heard the sound of more vehicles in the distance and he fell back onto his stomach. After another minute or so, two armoured cars trundled by while he eyed them from the bracken. This was a busy road!

He studied his compass. To head north-east he would need to cross open land. It was risky with this major road nearby but he had to keep moving for in his flying suit he was a beacon to the enemy.

He waited another few minutes and started out. For an hour he walked over field after field, all adjoining with only tall poplars and bracken separating them. The countryside looked familiar to him but he could not see a landmark he recognised anywhere. He concentrated on listening for vehicles or other sounds of approaching enemy and his eyes swivelled right and left, and back and forth constantly. Fortunately this action was ingrained into him from flying, though it was more difficult when walking, especially with a tender shoulder.

Three times he halted to watch aircraft high in the sky. How he wished he were back up there.

When enemy vehicles passed on the perimeter of the fields he lay flat down in the dirt. He saw a number of farm buildings to the west but they were not in the direction he needed to go and detouring would mean crossing roads. He could still hear the boom of guns in the distance; there were battles going on all around.

He had to get out of his flying gear and into civilian clothes! He was in German-occupied France and must shed the appearance of a British pilot.

It was hard walking across the untilled fields and as he halted for rest he noticed a set of farm buildings directly ahead about a third of a mile away. Warily approaching he could see they were deserted and as he came closer he noticed a road beyond.

A few trails of smoke emanated from the collapsed roof of what looked like a grain shed. It had obviously been on fire though the house and barns looked intact. He walked stealthily on by a tractor and started in surprise. There, on the ground before him, was a body, obviously dead. The man lay on his back with a congealed wound in his chest. He looked like a farmer and death was only some hours earlier, but flies were already massing on the wound. He hurried by to a kitchen garden when suddenly his heart missed a beat. A duck flew out of a broken window right beside him, wings beating wildly. John Baron's hand went to his revolver and he wheeled around looking for what might have startled it but there was nothing.

The back door was open and he entered the house. He would wait here during the remaining hours till dusk. It was a very basic farmhouse with three rooms downstairs and he assumed bedrooms above. In the kitchen a chair lay on its side and signs of hasty departure were all about. Drawers and cupboards were open, broken plates were on the floor and utensils had been left on the table. He moved through to the other rooms where items of clothing were strewn about and boxes and half-filled sacks were lying in confusion on sofas and on the floor. In an upstairs bedroom he changed his clothes and found two pairs of shoes.

He tried them on. Damn! They were too small. He went through to a second bedroom but this appeared to have been inhabited by women. So he had to keep wearing his black flying boots! He looked at himself in a mirror as he tied a checked kerchief around his neck. Yes, he believed he could pass for a Frenchman.

It was well after noon when he heard motor bikes. He froze and his head jerked back at the sound. He crossed to the window. Germans! Four of them. They rode into the yard and dismounted.

John Baron's eyes searched the room for a way of escape, but the only exit was back down the stairs. Then one of the soldiers spoke, his voice loud in the silence of the house and yard.

Only one word was recognisable: *Wasser* – water. John Baron calmed his racing heart. They were looking for a drink, not him! He guessed they were probably despatch riders, key men in the co-ordination of the German front-line units.

He watched through the curtain as one walked over to the dead body near the tractor and then moved on to the rear of the smoking barn. Another entered the kitchen and the one behind the barn soon gave a shout. He must have found a well.

John Baron continued to watch and the soldier who had entered the kitchen came out with four mugs as a voice yelled angrily from the well. Amongst the words John Baron identified the phrase '*Französische Schweine!*' – 'French pigs!'

He assumed the water must have been bad, and his suspicion was verified when the soldiers tramped back to their motor bikes cursing. The one with the mugs threw them at the kitchen windows, smashing the glass as they rode out.

Alone again he looked into the distance towards a cluster of small stone cottages beside an open area that appeared to be a playing field. And then he saw a church spire beyond.

He recognised the place! The boys of the squadron had played on it many times. It had no official name but it was about two miles or so from the town of Cassel where the squadron had been based at the airfield for three months in the winter.

He took out his maps and studied the area. He was probably only about sixteen miles from Dunkirk! But with the BEF falling back to the town, he wondered how far beyond Cassel the enemy were now.

It would look best if he carried some goods in a bag of some sort; he would be more believable as a French peasant that way. So removing a pile of male clothing downstairs he filled one of the sacks and stuffed a pillow and a mug and plates in on top. Then searching down a stone corridor he discovered a bicycle leaning against the wall. Wonderful! At dusk this would help him cover a few miles in a hurry. To his dismay it had a flat tyre; probably the reason why it remained.

He searched nearby for a pump, opening cupboards and drawers and he smiled when he did in fact find a box containing bicycle pump and attachments, pliers, wire, screws, and a hammer but the smile faded when he filled the tyre and he could hear the air escaping. It was punctured!

Now he searched for anything with which to mend it but was not rewarded though he did come across a jug of cider in the cellar. He drank some before putting the remainder aside for later.

He ventured into the yard and hesitated beside the dead man. He thought to bury him but decided against it. Instead he covered him with a blanket, at least that would keep the flies away for a time.

One of the barns was virtually empty; in the other were piles of hay and a discarded saddle. Strips of leather hung on the wall and beside them horseshoes. He went back to the house.

He heard vehicles on the road outside and each time he stood still in alarm until they passed. He knew he should rest and he lay down and finally drifted into a troubled sleep.

* * *

On the other side of the Channel Alex toyed with a slice of tea cake. She just could not eat, not with the great evacuation of the soldiers of the BEF going on just fifty miles away.

She thought of the men piling onto the beaches around the town of Dunkirk while German Stukas, raining death, dive bombed them. She had heard on the wireless that the RAF were protecting the men by engaging the enemy in the air but that there were not enough anti-aircraft batteries or British fighter aeroplanes to cover the defenceless men on the beaches. That of course had brought her to thinking of John Baron, which was not unusual; he was on her mind many of her waking hours.

Alex had heard aircraft overhead regularly since 10 May. Being so close to Manston airfield and virtually on the Kentish coast they could not help but hear the droning of aeroplanes day and night. Especially as the airfields and the ports were the main targets for the Luftwaffe.

Alex had been on shift work and had arrived home at Castlemere to find her mother gone to Ramsgate. Lillian Cardrew was a member of the WVS, Women's Voluntary Service, who were taking care of returning evacuated soldiers. Alex's father was in Dover. He was in one of the Weekend Lifeboat crews and had been called in to help with the troop evacuation. He had closed down his Canterbury legal office and gone to Dover the previous day and they had not heard from him since.

'Your mother phoned.'

Alex looked up as her Aunt Harriet strolled into the room. She wore a grey and white silk shirt and grey garbardine slacks. She had announced on Sunday afternoon that she intended to stay the week and not return to her Canterbury house which had been a surprise to all of them as she usually left on Monday mornings.

'She said she might not be home until nine tonight. She's getting a lift back with somebody, can't recall who. Some military vehicle, I think.'

Jane was not home either – Alex was uncertain where she was. Her sister was a part-time receptionist for her father but with his office closed she was not working.

Harriet eased herself into a chair and managed a thin smile for her niece.

Alex left the cake and as she stood to remove the plate Harriet said, 'Now dear, no need to rush off. Tell me how you are.'

Alex halted. 'Are you all right, Aunt Harriet?'

'Now that you ask I do have a slightly sore neck. Must have been the angle it was on when I rested earlier.'

Alex had asked because it was such an amazing occurrence to have her aunt inquire about her well-being. She could not recall this happening before in her life.

Harriet rubbed her neck as she watched Alex rinsing the crockery. 'Have you heard from that young pilot friend of yours?'

'Yes. He's in France. I just hope he's safe.'

'I suppose they'll all come back home now, with this evacuation business.'

'Yes, I suppose so.' Alex moved to the door. 'I'd best be off. I want to write some letters.'

Harriet lifted her eyes. 'Do let me know if your pilot comes home. I'd like to think he got back to us all safe and sound.'

Alex frowned. There was definitely something wrong with her aunt; showing an interest in two separate people all in the same morning. She answered as she walked out to the hall. 'Yes, all right, but perhaps you should see the doctor, Aunt Harriet. There might be something really wrong with your neck.'

In the front hall she met Jane taking off her hat and coat.

'Afternoon,' Alex said and her sister replied, 'Where's Mummy?'

'In Ramsgate and if you didn't stay out most of the day you'd know.'

'I've no wish for an argument,' Jane responded as she passed by into the drawing room.

Alex was mounting the stairs when the knocker on the front door was rapped.

She opened the door to Terry Keys, a businessman who ran pleasure boats the other side of Sandwich.

'Good afternoon, Alex. Is your father in?'

'No, he's in Dover.'

'Ah. Right. Dick Lacey and I – well, we're going along the Stour to talk to owners of pleasure boats. Your father runs a twenty-footer, doesn't he?'

'Twenty-two, actually.'

'I'm surprised you can turn it round this far upstream.'

Alex smiled. 'We manage.'

'Well, as your father's not in. I'd better keep moving.' He dipped his felt hat and moved to the steps.

'Mr Keys, wait!'

The man turned back.

'What did you want Daddy for?'

Keys gave a grim smile. 'We've been contacted to round up what boats we can. To sail them down on the tide to Ramsgate where we're meeting up with a fleet of fishing boats and going across to help. The first fleet of small boats is set to go out this evening and more later if we can get enough.'

Alex shaded her eyes against the afternoon sun as it streamed through the beeches to the west of the house. 'To help? Do you mean to go to the French beaches to assist in the evacuation of our boys?'

He nodded. 'Uh huh.'

'And you say you're going out this evening and tonight?'

'We are, lass, on the tide, that's why I thought your dad might be able to come but it seems like he's already doing his bit.' He heaved a sigh. 'I met some of the boys who were evacuated today. They're desperate over there. Need small craft to ferry the troops from the beaches to the larger ships waiting off. Bloody Germans are strafing them all the time. Sea's red with blood, they say. Hard to believe on a beautiful calm day like this.' Keys waved his hand in farewell and ran down the steps to his lorry.

Alex stood on the top of the steps as the vehicle rattled down the drive to the road. She thought of the soldiers waiting on the beaches and being strafed by German aeroplanes. She knew Mr Churchill was rallying the nation. He spoke in such a way that you believed him. You wanted to do as he said and he made you feel that if everybody was determined then you really could beat the Germans. She had read a speech he made in the House of Commons on 13 May. It had really stirred her and made her wish with all her heart she could do more.

She had cut it out of the newspaper and she carried it with her:

'I have nothing to offer but blood, toil, tears and sweat . . . You ask what is our policy? I can say: it is to wage war, by sea, land and air with all the might and with all the strength that God can give us: to wage war against a monstrous tyranny, never surpassed in the dark, lamentable catalogue of human crime. That is our policy. You ask, what is our aim? I can answer in one word: victory, victory at all costs, victory in spite of terror; victory, however long and hard the road may be; for without victory there is no survival . . . And I say, "Come, then, let us go forward together with our united strength".'

Alex hurried back into the house and found Jane sitting on the terrace with Harriet. They both had sherries in front of them.

'Bit early for that, isn't it?'

Harriet looked appalled. 'Good heavens, child, it's never too early for a sherry.'

'Jane, get dressed. We're going to Dunkirk.'

Jane blinked in confusion and Harriet raised her eyes, an expression of mild interest crossing her face.

'Come on, get moving. The *Capability*'s sitting on the river at the end of the garden this very minute. I can handle her just as well as Daddy, and with you to help me with the ropes and to throw out the anchor we'll be as good as any craft out there.' She screwed up her mouth with emotion. 'God, Jane, let's do it!'

'Do what?'

'Sail *Capability* downriver to Pegwell Bay, meet up with Mr Keys and the fishing fleet and get over to Dunkirk to do what we can to help, for Mr Churchill, for all of our soldiers stranded over there. Oh Jane, they're going to be Hitler's prisoners if we don't! Think about JB and Twig, and let's do it for all of them! They need us!'

423

Jane was astounded. 'But we're girls, we're not men. They won't let us go.'

'Don't be such a defeatist. We're adults. We'll dress like men in Daddy's clothes and perhaps they won't even notice. Anyway, if we sail *Capability* down to Pegwell Bay I don't see how they can stop us.' She pulled her sister to her feet and drew her into the house.

With eyebrows raised Harriet watched them go as Mrs Blake, dressed in hat and gloves, came out. 'I'm off home now, I'll be back for dinnertime. How many of you will there be?'

Harriet looked in amazement at the woman. 'How on earth would I know?'

Mrs Blake, who had suffered Mrs Barrington for many years, took no offence. 'And did I hear right? Did young Miss Alex say she's off to Dunkirk?'

'She did.' Harriet sipped her sherry. 'Bring me some cheese before you leave would you?'

Mrs Blake ignored the request. 'But Mrs Barrington, that's dangerous. They could get killed. What will Mr and Mrs Cardrew say? This is right terrible.' She pointed after the girls. 'Mrs Barrington, please, you must go and stop them.'

Harriet yawned. 'I'll do nothing of the sort. They've both turned twenty-one. You stop them if you must, but for heaven's sake bring me the cheese first.'

John Baron woke to the sound of a heavy vehicle. He sat straight up, but it rumbled on by.

The sun was heading towards the horizon and he hurried downstairs and made ready to leave. He was taking a box of matches and a sharp knife from the kitchen cupboard when he realised there was a small lean-to outside and went out to investigate. Hanging on a nail was a bicycle wheel fitted with a tyre! The spokes of the wheel were rusty and the tyre was flat but daring to hope that the wheel was an old spare for the bike inside he ran in with it. The wheel was the correct size! And as he pumped the tyre he prayed it would stay inflated. This time there was no escaping air and with a groan of relief he wheeled the bicycle outside.

He picked two ripe tomatoes and pulled up five carrots from the kitchen garden and pocketed them. Then tying his sack across the handlebars he wished a silent goodbye to the dead man and remaining vigilant in the fading light set out on the road.

The clouds of the morning had cleared away and he watched flocks of birds in the sunset making their way to havens for the night. His shoulder was still sore but he had all his mobility so he knew it was sound. He kept turning down lanes and making for the soccer field with the echo of the guns becoming nearer.

He halted on a gentle slope when he was a couple of hundred yards from the field. He would avoid the Nazi-held Cassel over to the left where there was a glow in the sky; probably part of it was burning. Steenvdore was to the right but he would ride straight ahead in the Warmhoudt direction.

He eyed the deserted playing field as night enveloped him. He and Twig had bicycled out here to play soccer; well, he had played, Twig had watched. He was quite familiar with this area. There were main road junctions which he would need to avoid, but even in the darkness he thought that possible. Taking out his maps he dropped them on the ground, not needing them now, and no French peasant would be carrying maps written in English. He decided to take off his dog tags, but did not throw them away for they were his only means of identification if captured so they were slipped down inside his boots.

He started off in the direction of Warmhoudt but soon realised there was a battle going on ahead of him. In fact, at that very minute, Warmhoudt was being tenaciously defended by the 2nd Royal Warwickshires. He remembered a detour which avoided the town by a wide margin to the north-east. It ran through a half-mile of dense oak-wood that eventually headed in a direct line towards Dunkirk. He thought of Anna and Fleurette, two sisters he and Twig had met who lived with their parents in a mill on the stream that ran at one edge of the wood.

Believing that once through the wood he must come across the BEF during their fall back to the environs of Dunkirk he pedalled on at a slow but even pace; his night sight was good and the sky was clear. He headed north-north-west on winding lanes and small roads and across fields when need be, stopping to carefully light a match and check his bearings from time-to-time. The battle was now close on his left-hand side but he did not come in sight of any humans until he approached a main thoroughfare leading away from Warmhoudt. At first he was uncertain what was going on then he realised the road was choked with refugees: young and old, many with babies, all bewildered, all carrying their possessions in their arms or on carts, horses, even wheelbarrows; the fortunate on bicycles or in an occasional vehicle. Children wailed and some of the desperately weary had left the road and built campfires. Their faces were pictures of tragedy as they hunched together in grim rings in the firelight.

He asked more than once if any of them knew the extent of the German advance. They merely told him what he knew – that they had taken Cassel and were fighting the British in Warmhoudt.

He pushed his bike along the main road at the sluggish pace of the refugee column until he found the winding lane which led off to the oakwood. He knew that once through the trees and over the bridge on the millstream he would turn sharply right to a junction of two highways; after that came another lane which ran in the direction he desired.

At some point he must meet up with the British infantry.

He set off again, chewing a carrot from his small vegetable cache and pedalling at a steady speed in the weak but sufficient ambient night light, some of it supplied by a battle over to his left where flares were going up. The air was a comfortable temperature and it played about his face and neck. His shoulder was no longer aching and if there were no war and he were not in this dilemma he could almost have enjoyed the night ride.

As he gained the oaks he was forced to dismount and walk: it was pitch black under the trees. He felt a rush of sadness for Anna and Fleurette and their parents; they could even have been amongst the refugees streaming along the road.

After about ten minutes he thought he could discern the end of the oaks and the outline of the bridge ahead, so he remounted. He had not ridden forty yards when a blaze of torchlight illuminated him from the left side. '*Halt! Wer geht da?*'

John Baron's instinct was to flee but realising instantly he had no chance and would be shot in the back he halted and climbed off the bicycle. The streak of light hit him from behind, and as he eased the bike down to the ground, he slipped his revolver out of his belt and dropped it under the front wheel before turning round and walking back towards the holder of the torch.

'*Wer sind Sie und wo gehen Sie hin?*'

John Baron could see nothing. He shaded his eyes and made the assumption that he had been asked who he was and perhaps where he was going? He answered in French that he lived on the outskirts of Cassel and was taking his leave of the area.

The holder of the torch dropped his beam a little lower as a second German soldier, a Private, stepped forward into the swathe of light and spoke. John Baron answered exactly as he had previously. The Private had not shaved for some days and looked weary as he began somewhat unenthusiastically to search John Baron.

During the body search John Baron took the opportunity to look studiously through the trees. He could see firelight about seventy yards away beyond the ancient trunks of the oaks where men moved about near the black shape of an armoured car. Down the gentle slope to the stream and on the far side about 100 yards left from the bridge was another fire and two tanks. He remembered it was the 6th Panzers who had been coming this way. This was probably a forward unit.

The soldier with the torch said something else and John Baron recognised the words 'French peasant'. Good! At least they believed he was French.

The soldier who had searched him lifted the compass out of his pocket and held it up to the man with the torch whose arm came out to take it. John Baron saw the insignia: it was that of a Sergeant. He rolled the compass over and for a moment alarm seized John Baron until he remembered he had purchased the instrument here in France and not in England.

The Sergeant eyed his detainee as he pocketed the compass. A few seconds passed before he gestured for John Baron to get on his bike and go.

With growing relief John Baron walked away. He had actually bent down to retrieve the bicycle with the beam of light still upon him when he heard '*Halt!*'.

Shit! What now? John Baron stood up very slowly as the two soldiers walked up to their French peasant.

The Sergeant used his rifle barrel to lift the hem of John Baron's trouser leg and he tapped the black boots beneath. '*Was sind dass? Sehen aus wie Fliegel Stiefel.*' John Baron stiffened inside; he did not need to understand the language to know that the German was questioning his wearing of a pair of flying boots.

In the glare of the torchlight, doubt now filled the enemy faces where before there had been merely boredom. The Sergeant brought the compass from his pocket and revolved it in his hands again before he turned back to his sentry and, marching past him, said enough for John Baron to realise that he was going to fetch a Lieutenant who spoke French!

The remaining soldier stood a few yards from his captive holding the torch in one hand and his rifle in the other.

John Baron knew there was no time left; the French-speaking Lieutenant would question him and they would take him prisoner for certain now. The Sergeant was in the trees on his way to the campsite. It was now or never!

JB looked away from the glare. He knew the Private held the torch in one hand, his rifle in the other and he waited until he was sure the Sergeant was well away towards the campfire before he bounded forward and knocked the torch out of the soldier's hands, kicking out hard with his right foot, imagining he was back on the rugby field in Melbourne. The torch flew into the grass and as the man tried to bring up his rifle John Baron's boot connected with his thigh and the soldier fell to the ground. There was enough illumination from the discarded flashlight for John Baron to grab the man's rifle as he fell. And as he dashed towards his bicycle he threw the rifle into the grass and the German on the ground began to shout.

A group of soldiers at the campfire scrambled to their feet and the Sergeant turned back.

John Baron was at his bicycle. He began to lift it as the soldier on the ground regained his feet, still yelling for help. He knew his pistol had been under his front wheel. He brushed his hand in the grass, found it, and leapt upon his bicycle as the soldier came running towards him.

John Baron fired over his head and pedalled away while the soldier fell back to the ground to avoid being shot.

The Sergeant charged to the road, gun blazing as he came. Bullets hit the trees and ricocheted off stone and into water, beams of light bounced off the trunks to his left as John Baron pedalled across the bridge; the bedlam behind him urging him to furious speed.

Another spate of bullets struck a trunk near him and one whipped past his cheek. He came off the bridge pedalling at such a pace that he could not slow down to turn right and he slewed sideways, throwing dirt high in the air as the sack of goods slipped from the handlebars and thumped to the ground. He recovered in a moment, leaving the sack behind, and continued his furious flight as bullets thudded in the trees and bracken all around.

The engine of an armoured car started up and men were running behind him firing Bergmann submachine guns and shouting and calling for him to stop. The uproar echoed on the night air as if it were a whole division following him.

He wheeled right again, and was pedalling so fast down the lane he was bumping violently along, but he dared not slow down.

He kept repeating certain things like a litany in his mind in an effort to calm himself: he did not believe they had seen him enter the lane, so to follow him they would disperse in a number of directions; they could not follow him down here in a wide armoured car; they could not chase him in tanks; and finally to ease his panic: how long would a tired forward unit of Panzers search for what after all, could just have been a French peasant on a bicycle?

Still bumping crazily along, slipping and sliding and almost falling, he managed to keep upright and to his relief the clamour of his hunters was fading when he came to a pot-holed patch of ground and was forced to dismount and walk.

He had no compass now but he was sure of his position and, as the minutes passed and he began to breathe more normally, he became increasingly certain that the Panzers had abandoned the chase.

Hours later, after keeping the noise and lights of battle to his left and behind him, and as the first glimmers of lemon crystallised on the horizon, weaving the promise of the coming morning, John Baron met another column of French refugees, shuffling dispiritedly along.

But, interspersed with the fleeing citizens, he saw lorries, jeeps, motor bikes and men in uniform. He had found them, the British and French infantry, pressing diligently on towards the beaches around Dunkirk.

The evening before, Alex and Jane had sailed down the Stour to Pegwell Bay on the evening tide.

Harriet accompanied them over to the wooden landing on the river at the back of the garden. The prospect of her two nieces dressed as men, sailing the *Capability* down to Ramsgate to help in the evacuation of hundreds of thousands of soldiers on the other side of the Channel with the likelihood of their being strafed and even killed, motivated her to see them depart.

With a grey jacket and jaunty scarf round her neck, she leant languidly upon the bole of an elm and lit a cigarette as the two sisters climbed aboard the *Capability*. With an enigmatic expression Harriet watched the procedure, popping the cigarette into the long black holder encrusted with tiny diamonds which her second husband had bought her in Paris.

Alex had made sandwiches and tea in two Thermoses and had taken all the fruit from the kitchen bowl. She placed them in the half-cabin and after a few attempts started the engine. When it was running steadily Jane threw off the ropes and the boat drifted away from the landing.

'Do we look like men, Aunt Harriet?' Alex called from the back of the half-cabin where she stood at the wheel.

Blowing smoke out in a long thin stream Harriet replied, 'Men? No. Strange corruptions of boys? Perhaps.'

'If Daddy and Mummy are worried about us,' Jane shouted stowing the ropes in the aft locker, 'please tell them that if we can, we'll telephone home from Ramsgate as soon as we're back.'

Harriet stepped forward and sat down on a garden seat. 'If I remember.' She gave a weak smile as Alex manipulated the craft beautifully, turning it around in the water and setting off downriver.

Jane waved but Harriet did not respond. She sat smoking until the *Capability* disappeared round the first bend and when she had finished her cigarette she dropped it from her manicured hands into the river and strolled back to the house.

When the girls reached Pegwell Bay and began to head across to Ramsgate Pier in a mild sea, they underwent their first encounter with the war. Alex pointed to the east where, in the distance, they saw aircraft, some diving towards the water.

'Oh my Lord, they'll be the ruddy Luftwaffe strafing some of our ships!' Jane exclaimed.

Alex looked through her telescope and saw two destroyers entering the harbour. 'They're all filled to the brim with soldiers. Oh my goodness, the one in front's on fire. We'd better go and help.' And following her pointing finger Jane saw smoke floating skywards. As they drew closer they perceived that the fire was forward and the stern of the ship was in danger of going under water as the soldiers huddled in it. But fortunately the *Prudential*, the Ramsgate lifeboat, was already alongside and a second small craft was standing off, and soon men were scrambling down ropes to them. As the *Capability* came within range a sailor on the burning ship yelled into his loud hailer, '*Capability*, can you come alongside!'

Alex brought her boat nearer. 'Steady as you go,' the sailor called again. 'Prepare for men to come aboard.'

And holding her as steady as she could on the lee side of the burning ship and fighting the wheel to stay away from the other small craft already there, soldiers began dropping into the *Capability* from above.

'Lord,' said the first soldier onboard, 'you fellas are life-savers. Hit by the bloody Luftwaffe halfway across and we've been slowly burning ever since.'

'Thought we'd just got within sight of home to flamin' drown,' another said as he hit the deck.

'We'll soon have you ashore,' Jane replied in the deepest voice she could muster, and when the *Capability* was low in the water with her human cargo Alex set off across the now choppy harbour.

It was a relatively short trip into the pier and the exhausted soldiers lay about on the deck in silence most of the way, except for one who shouted, 'She's going under now!' and they all looked round to see the destroyer sinking, the smoke and flames now eclipsed by the churning water rushing over it.

When they came to Ramsgate Pier and disembarked the soldiers thanked their saviours.

'You're a great lad,' one of them said, thumping Alex on the back as he climbed ashore. 'What's your name?'

'Alex,' she answered quite truthfully.

'Well, thanks, Alex. We're in the Queen's Own Royal West Kent Regiment, and it's heaven to be home on English soil. It's hell back there.'

Alex waved and Jane watched them go, a gloomy look on her face.

No sooner had the infantrymen been welcomed and departed along the pier than the *Capability* was hailed again by a man wearing an air-raid warden's armband, a tin hat and a beard. He held an official-looking black folder and beside him stood a short fellow in a Ramsgate Life-boat cap. The bearded man spoke. 'Saw you out there giving a hand to the *Redoubtable*. Thanks. Are you chaps here to go across to Dunkirk?'

'Yes,' Alex replied from under her sou'wester. 'We were going to meet Terry Keys and the fishing boats.'

He turned from them and shouted along the pier to a group of men one of whom answered, 'They left about half an hour ago. They were in the first assembly out from here.'

The bearded man looked back to Alex. 'Never mind, we've got a good chap off to the beaches right now. You can go in tandem. We'll rope you to him to save petrol on the way over. He's just had a bite to eat and a kip in the *Merrie England* and now he's ready to go.'

The girls knew that the locals called the Funfair Ballroom the *Merrie England*, and that it had been taken over by the authorities.

The short man spoke. 'His name's Fisher – used to be in the Navy, Good Conduct Medal and all. He'll look after you lads as best he can. Do you want a pint of ale before you go?'

'No thanks,' Jane replied gruffly.

'Why aren't you fellas in the Army anyway?'

Jane immediately busied herself with the ropes in the stern and Alex coughed and replied, 'I'm only seventeen and my brother's got bad eyes. Should be wearing his glasses really but the sea spray fogs them up.'

The bearded man nodded. 'Right, well, you're doing your bit now.' He pointed downwards with his black folder. 'Wait here, there're five more craft going across with you. It's a bit of a round trip to avoid enemy aircraft but you'll be there before dawn.'

As the two men moved away Alex faced her sister with a grin. 'Gosh, I didn't know I could lie that easily.' But Jane was not grinning back. A deep furrow sat between her eyes. 'Alex, it's all right for you. You've always been a tomboy but I'm scared. I'll admit it. The Luftwaffe are firing real bullets and dropping real bombs.' Her hand trembled as she lifted it over her mouth. 'I don't think I want to go.'

Alex thought her sister was about to cry; she began to reply but Jane cut her off. 'It was all right back there at home, you bullied me into it and I let you, but now, here . . . After seeing the *Redoubtable* on fire and the soldiers and everything . . . Well I know it's real and—'

'Look, Jane, just try – please.'

'No! For heaven's sake we're female, we're not expected to do this. Fact is, if they knew they wouldn't let us.'

Alex took her sister's hand. It was cold. 'Listen darling. I'm scared too, and what you say about being female . . . well, yes, they might stop us if they knew, but for heaven's sake, what about JB and Twig?'

'What about them?'

'Do you love Twig or not?'

'I think so.'

Alex sighed. 'Well, I *know* how I feel about JB. And I've only got to think of his being one of the men waiting on the beaches and I'm certain of what I've got to do.'

Jane gave a frustrated moan. 'They're in the RAF – they won't be on the beaches.'

'But what if they were?'

Jane shook her head. 'Oh God, I don't know.' She gazed agitatedly about and began to climb out of the *Capability*.

Alex attempted to halt her. 'Where are you going?'

Jane shook her off and jumped ashore. 'I just can't do this. I'm not as brave as you.' She began to cry and hurried away.

Alex watched her disappear. 'Oh hell!' she said to herself looking bleakly along the pier to where Mr Black Beard waved his folder at the Captain of the second destroyer, now tied alongside. She wondered what on earth she was going to do when into her vision came Jane, hurrying back towards her.

Jane's face was full of despair. 'Oh God, Mummy's up there.'

'Where?'

'Just as you come off the pier there are about twenty of

them, the WVS with tea and coffee and hundreds of soldiers all sitting around. Mrs Davidson's there and so's Meryl's mother.'

'Did they see you?'

'No.'

'Look Jane I—'

'Oh, shut up,' Jane responded, jumping into the boat. 'I'll just have to come now.' She blinked to hold back the tears and her large hazel eyes glistened as she pointed her finger at her sister. 'I'll never speak to you again if I get killed,' she declared, striving to give a wan smile.

Alex slapped her affectionately on the arm. 'That's the spirit, darling.'

At that moment Mr Beard shouted to Alex, 'Up here, *Capability*! Bring her forward and we'll attach you to the *Night Errant*.'

Alex glanced back at her sister. Jane looked tense but she untied the ropes from the pier bollards. 'I'm ready.'

Soon the *Capability* was roped to the *Night Errant* with the five other small craft lined up behind. Within another half an hour the little flotilla sailed away from Ramsgate Pier into the silver water of the English Channel, heading for Dunkirk.

Chapter Twenty-nine

Dunkirk was ablaze when John Baron arrived to the north of the town. A haze hung over everything and spread out in all directions. The smell of oil was overpowering and he could hear explosions emanating from the harbour itself and assumed correctly that demolition of the port installations was in progress.

The column of BEF he had joined had been dived upon by Stukas just after dawn. He had found himself in a ditch for half an hour with some boys of the Fifth Division. Led by General Brooke they had held Comines in Belgium for three days against overwhelming numbers but as the Belgians withdrew northwards and then capitulated, the Fifth Division had taken over the protection of the flank of the BEF extending the vital corridor of life that led to Dunkirk. They were good-humoured even in the misery of retreat, and as the dive bombers came in they defiantly fired back with their Lee Enfield rifles in stubborn refusal to allow the Luftwaffe free rein.

At first they assumed John Baron was French but when he related his story they told him that there had been a failed British counter-attack the afternoon before, aimed at retaking Furnes seventeen miles to the north-east of Dunkirk. 'The Dunkirk perimeter's shrinking right back and the beach at La Panne's gone now . . . impossible for embarkation there,' Jake Hughes from Leeds informed him. 'We heard that the boys in Calais hung on until the twenty-seventh, God bless 'em all, or we'd have been cut off to the south and the Germans would have been in Dunkirk by now. Our only bridgeheads to safety left are the adjacent beaches to Dunkirk. The Huns have got all the other coastal batteries.'

It was hard for John Baron to accept the apocalyptic scene before him as he walked over the rise above the sea. Hundreds of discarded vehicles edged the beach like a grim grey lace pattern; and beyond, thousands of soldiers stood or lay in zigzagging columns all over the sand, and thousands more, like human threads, stretched out into the murky dark water. A pall drifted across everything and through the haze out at sea large cruisers and destroyers, ferries, hospital carriers, minesweepers, gunboats, sloops, torpedo boats and large motor boats of all descriptions, rode at anchor – some on fire from German bombs. While corvettes and trawlers, yachts, lifeboats, fishing vessels and even small pleasure boats dotted the spaces between the strings of men, picking them up and ferrying them to the larger vessels. The tide appeared to be going out and the lines were so long that near the beach they stood in ankle-deep water while half a mile out, men were up to their necks. As he eyed the spectacle he dispiritedly shook his head. It would take a whole day to move from the end of a line on the beach out to the ships!

He had flown over these beaches only twenty-four hours earlier, but the devastation and the number of soldiers had increased beyond all belief.

A Sergeant Major was barking orders and his men were driving abandoned vehicles in a row, end to end, across the beach and into the sea. John Baron realised they were forming a makeshift bridge for soldiers to walk across as the rising tide came in.

Then suddenly John Baron was the focus of attention of the Sergeant Major. 'Hey you, Frenchman! You can't hang around here.' He pointed towards the port. 'You'd better get on into Dunkirk proper. We're only taking infantry aboard here, not civilians. Off you scarper.'

'I'm an RAF pilot. My Hurricane was shot down in German-held territory east of Cassel. I changed my clothing in an abandoned farmhouse.'

The soldier pursed his lips. 'How do I know that? Where's your identification?'

John Baron was once more wearing his dog tag and was

about to reveal it but the sound of an approaching aircraft halted the conversation and he looked around for shelter, quickly throwing himself down in the sand under the nearest vehicle. He recognised the whizzing, whirring sound of the Stuka. It came in over their heads and bullets spattered in the sand around him while down on the beach the men without cover fell with hands over their heads.

As the first Ju87 was quickly followed by two companions the Sergeant Major took cover beside John Baron. They heard a scream to the left followed by a groan and explosions threw sand up all around them.

An exhausted unit of the Royal Artillery fought back from a beach battery, and when one of the Stukas was hit in the wing a rousing cheer lifted from the beach. As John Baron pulled himself out from under the jeep two soldiers were being carried away. He noticed now that there were red stains all over the sand.

The Sergeant Major crawled out beside him and as they stood up he smiled. 'I believe you, matey.' He pointed at his companion's feet. 'Those boots are pure RAF standard issue.'

John Baron gave an enigmatic grunt. Only a few hours previously the boots had given him away and now they were taken as proof of his true identity.

'You should take off that bloody kerchief for a start,' the Sergeant Major advised him, and pointing to the revolver stuck in his belt, added, 'and make your revolver more obvious. See if you can get a uniform off a dead man, you'll be less likely to be stopped again.'

John Baron did remove the kerchief and he tucked the revolver in the front of his belt near the buckle, but he could not bring himself to remove a uniform from a corpse. However he wore a tin hat that he found half-buried in the sand and picked up a Lee Enfield rifle to carry over his shoulder.

He joined a queue and moved in snail-like fashion, and as dusk fell there was a concentrated attack by the Luftwaffe. He was in the middle of the beach by then and without cover all he could do was throw himself down like those about him. Some of the bombs were blessedly muffled by the sand, but there were still plenty to maim and damage, and the totally defenceless men were killed or not killed, depending on their luck. The wounded were picked up and the dead were left to lie where they fell; or float where they fell; there was no time to spend on corpses.

John Baron went through various moods as he edged across the Dunkirk beach past the wounded and the dying and the already dead: hate for the enemy, fury and frustration, then fear and panic, and ultimately the philosophical state of acceptance where there were simply three alternatives to his existence: injury, death or complete survival. He became almost cavalier about it and began to make conversation with the man in front of him, Hector Tait, a Royal Engineer.

They talked that night on the sand side by side, and Hector told him about his home in the New Forest. 'Ringwood, it's a nice little place on the Avon. We used to swim in the river in July and August.'

John Baron smiled and said, 'I was born in Lymington.'

Hector laughed and his nose crinkled. 'You don't say. Ringwood's no more than ten miles away. We were neighbours, you and I, JB.'

Hector brought out a piece of chocolate which he divided with his new friend and as morning dawned John Baron broke his last carrot in half and they shared it. But the haze of coming day brought yet another wave of hell from the Luftwaffe. And as they brought their heads out of the sand and used their rifles in a vain attempt to fight back, the soldiers nearby began cursing the RAF for not being present. John Baron tried to explain that the RAF were engaging the enemy day and night, but the superior numbers of German machines made it impossible to defend the beaches all the time. 'And much of the conflict takes place up there,' he pointed to the sky, 'where you can't see it from here. Believe me, the RAF are fighting constantly.'

'Well, it doesn't look that bloody way to me,' one soldier growled, his hair dripping sand.

'Listen, I know that the RAF are up there battling for

you. Let me tell you something, mate, a fighter aircraft uses so much juice flying over here and back to Britain that it's only got about fifteen minutes of air time above the beaches.'

'How do you know?'

'Because I'm in the bloody RAF and my squadron was the last one to leave France yesterday. I was shot down.'

'Yeah?' spoke up one of the other soldiers. 'Well, the way we see it, you fellas haven't done your bloody share.'

John Baron thought then of his friends: Harry Fairbanks, missing, Lefty Rowlands badly burnt, Rattler Matheson in hospital, Fred Sanders badly wounded and Walter Franklin and Tony Allen dead. He shook his head and eyed the soldiers with their belligerent faces.

'You couldn't be more wrong! Two hundred and sixty-one Hurricanes were despatched to France to fight with you blokes and I can tell you at the last count that I know of, there were only seventy-two left. So mate, don't bloody well talk to me about doing our bloody share!' He turned away and Hector patted his shoulder and told the soldiers to, 'Shove off!'

It was all surreal, surrounded by terrified faces, with bombs falling from the sky and exploding, spitting death across the black water and a noise that engulfed everything. John Baron thought of his mother and father, of Haverhill and home. They did not seem real. Did Sammy and Uncle Wake and Ledgie really exist? Or was the only truth this unrelenting nightmare of water and death and screaming and the incessant noise of bombardment?

And so he edged along, one step after another, and eventually by 0800 he and Hector were in the sea. By 0900 he was knee deep in water and by 1000 thigh-deep with hand on Hector's shoulder, and up ahead about 50 yards away at last, were boats pulling men up to ferry them to a cruiser more than half a mile distant.

Around 1030 there was another violent assault from above. This time seven Stukas came in low over their heads and John Baron and those around him sank down in the water, attempting to make themselves the smallest targets

440

possible, and as the bombs exploded around them and bullets spat into the ocean, Hector groaned and sank forward.

John Baron grabbed him. 'Hec, Hec, are you all right?'

'Don't know,' came the reply. 'Can't feel my legs.'

The water about Hector was a dirty scarlet. JB took Hector in his arms and now his left shoulder began to ache again but he ignored it.

'I don't think I'll make it,' the man said as John Baron held him and staggered forward to the nearest of the small boats but it had been hit and was on fire and men were leaping off it into the water. There was shouting and groaning and yelling all around and the bloody Stukas were coming in again.

'Can't feel anything now, JB,' Hector said, a sudden glassy appearance in his eyes.

'Hang on, mate,' John Baron answered, fear catching in his throat as he staggered towards the next boat crying out for them to take Hector. He thought he could see a sailor in the stern waving at him to keep coming forward. Men were falling all around and the water was churning with bullets and pieces of shrapnel. Bits of wood flew off the boat that was on fire and John Baron fought with all his strength to push through the sea of bodies, flotsam and blood – carrying his newly found friend. *This must be what the end of the world is like; the end of the world in the Book of Revelations!*

John Baron's whole universe became centred on striving through the sea to the sailor in the stern of the small launch ahead. On through the choppy grey water, through the destruction. Closer and closer came the arms that reached out to take his friend.

He was aware that Hector was groaning and he said again, 'Hang on, Hec, hang on.' He stumbled, but the water, now up to his waist, balanced him and he looked down into his friend's face as the man opened his eyes, and amongst the tumult and confusion smiled up at JB who carried him. It was a beautiful smile, brotherly, intimate. And as it faded John Baron felt Hector's life fade in unison. The body in his arms went limp and the lifelight died in Hector's eyes just as he reached the wide brown hands that groped down from the small ship to take the man from him.

It was in that last second as he delivered Hector up, that he thought he heard his name cried from afar, 'JB! Over here, JB!' and he turned his head but suddenly he felt powerful hands upon himself and he was lifted and brought into the small craft.

He lay on the deck beside the dead body of his short-time friend, and when they came to the cruiser and were taken aboard he tried to insist that they take Hector too.

The Petty Officer spoke gently but firmly. 'I know he was your friend lad, but we must take live men back home, not dead ones. Now move along forward so we can get you home to Blighty.'

As he made his way to the bow John Baron did not look back; he preferred not to know what they did with Hector's body.

Alex and Jane had no conception of the maelstrom they were entering. They sailed across the Channel at night towed by the *Night Errant* without incident at a steady six knots, and when Fisher called through his loudhailer to ask if they were all right, they replied that they were. Each slept while the other steered, and about an hour before the sun rose they drank the tea and ate their sandwiches.

Realisation hit them both when the Luftwaffe attacked them as they approached the beaches at dawn.

An enemy aircraft dive-bombed them and when the bombs went wide but the bullets spat across the *Capability*'s aft, severing one of the ropes, Jane began to cry silently. The tears simply flowed down her face. She did not say anything. She did not remonstrate with her sister, she just wept.

Alex herself was feeling dismay but she spoke courageously enough. 'Jane, darling, we're here. We can't alter that so let's be as brave as we can. I'm ever so glad you came with me. Thank you.'

And when at last they discerned in the pall of smoke

and haze ahead, the moles at the port in the distance covered with men and the big ships riding at anchor, some already wrecked and sinking from the constant air raids – and the small ships and the lines of soldiers reaching towards them in the sea: when they comprehended much of what floated in the water was dead bodies and that many craft were in flames, when they saw the water red with blood and heard again the Luftwaffe swooping down upon them, Alex turned to her sister, eyes wide with disbelief. 'Jane darling, forgive me for bringing you here. I had no idea, no idea at all.'

Jane lifted her red and swollen eyes to meet her younger sister's, and amazed her by replying, 'It's like you said before, Alex, we're here, so let's get on with it.'

Fisher stayed as close to them with the *Night Errant* as he could; he had decided they were good lads. The sea was choppy but not from a rising wind, just from the activity upon it and young Alex handled the little boat well. All the other ships' crews were men in their middle years used to the sea and some even used to war, having fought twenty years before. Thus Fisher remained with the *Capability* and he shouted instructions to them. 'Go in as close to the beach as possible but don't run aground. Lift as many soldiers out as you can but don't overload. The *Capability*'ll take about fourteen safely, I reckon, so don't take more. Count them. We're here for eight hours or until all the large vessels depart, so ferry as many as you can to the big ships. I'll hail you when the time's right, then we'll both pick up a load of our own and we'll sail back together to Ramsgate. Understood?'

It was Jane who replied to him. 'Understood. We'll do our best.'

And so the initiation of Alex and Jane took place at Dunkirk. They turned into women that day. They looked death in the face; saw men drown in seas crimson with blood; lifted all ranks and creeds into their craft and confronted how men acted caught up in the brutality of survival.

As often as they filled the *Capability* and sailed out to a warship or other sizeable vessel and discharged their human cargo, there were still more men remaining, eyes large with fear or hope, waiting their turn patiently or impatiently, clambering, scrambling into the *Capability,* their first link with rescue and deliverance.

Alex began to feel automated, as if she were existing in an unreality, a nightmare from which she would wake to find herself back in her bedroom at Castlemere, with the golden curtains moving in the breeze on the window seat and her mother's voice floating comfortingly up from the front hall. And then a man would scream or a bomb would explode and she knew it was not a bad dream but a real and tangible hell that she had come to and in her naivety, brought her sister.

It had been many hours since her hair had fallen down under her sou'wester and she had abandoned wearing the hat and simply tied her hair back with some twine to keep it from her face. Jane's hair was short and she, too, no longer wore her hat but pushed her hair back behind her ears. Some of the soldiers had been amazed to find that girls were their deliverers while others, deep in shock, and internalising their fears, had not even noticed. On one of the runs out to the destroyer *Golden Oak* an officer had shouted at them, 'What the hell are you two doing here?'

And Jane had replied, 'Doing our bit.'

When Donald Fisher on the *Night Errant* realised who his two lads really were, he simply shook his head. It was too late to do anything about it, they were here and he could not help but think what bloody fine specimens of women they were.

It was sometime between ten and eleven, in the middle of a raid by seven Stukas when the sea was agitated with bullets, exploding bombs and blood, that Alex saw John Baron.

The *Capability* was about thirty yards from a fishing boat that had been strafed and was in flames. Men were screaming and Alex was pale with fear but still fighting to keep control of her vessel in the moving sea as Jane helped soldiers to scramble aboard. The warship behind was returning cannon fire to the Ju87s as they swooped destructively in over the small ships and Alex cast her eyes across the fishing boat as an exploding bomb flung water and debris high in the air and a hail of lead zapped across the sea in front of her. There, waist-high in the sea holding a soldier in his arms and making for a service launch, was the man she loved.

As she watched he staggered but righted himself and pressed on towards the launch where a sailor leant out of the aft, arms stretched towards JB and the man he carried.

As he reached the launch Alex screamed, 'JB! Over here, JB!' and he paused and looked around but at that moment he was lifted into the vessel and she saw him no more. She watched through the smoke and flames and churning water as the launch moved off and with heart pounding she turned back to face the task of controlling the *Capability*. In the turmoil she spoke aloud. 'Oh Lord, I'm glad I came. He was in the sea after all.'

At two in the afternoon most of the large ships had sailed away and Donald Fisher called again through his loudhailer, 'Alex, fill up once more and follow me. We head for home.'

They came under fire from the shore batteries as they passed to the south of Dunkirk on their homeward journey but the shots went wide, and now in a gathering sea Alex admitted she was completely fatigued from her long hours at the wheel. Suddenly she found two Sir Galahads in her little band of evacuees, Bill Mason and Arthur Gedge from A Company, 2nd Battalion, Royal Norfolk Regiment who both knew how to handle boats. They took over and sailed the *Capability* the rest of the way. Alex and Jane fell asleep in the stern and woke around midnight to see two destroyers come alongside and escort them back to Ramsgate.

As they came to the harbour and the dark shapes of the pier and other ships materialised Bill turned from the wheel to Alex. 'I think you should be the proud Captain of the *Capability* as we bring her in.'

Alex smiled and took over and brought her little ship into harbour behind the *Night Errant* and up alongside the pier.

Men with flashlights appeared and officials hailed them.

'Well done, Captain!' one of them shouted to Alex, and Bill Mason slapped her on the shoulder affectionately.

There was cheer and bustle all about. They were coming out of the bad dream at last.

'Welcome home, lads. There's plenty of refreshment after your ordeal, hot tea and coffee, ale and food inside the second building on the left as you go ashore.' A man bounced torchlight round the weary faces. 'Come along. We'll soon have you in clean clothes and after a kip we'll get you down to the station.'

Before the fourteen soldiers in the *Capability* disembarked they stood around the two women and applauded. Arthur Gedge spoke for all of them. 'You're the finest women in the world, God bless you both, and God bless the *Capability*.' Then they gave three tired cheers and climbed ashore.

Alex could feel the tears she had resisted so long begin to form in her eyes as Bill Mason turned to her. 'Alex, if ever you want to get married, come and find me. I'll marry you in a minute.' Then he jumped ashore and knelt down on the pier and kissed the wooden planks.

'Home in God's country!' he exclaimed and as he stood up and waved to them, he added, 'Thanks to you two.'

His tall figure moved away through the other soldiers in the darkness and Alex felt the tears edge out from her eyes and fall in streams across her face. She turned to Jane who stood beside her, face dirty, hair dishevelled. 'I'm sorry, Jane,' she sobbed and her sister took her in her arms.

'No, don't be. I'm all right now. I'm glad we went, truly. It was one in the eye for those Nazi pigs.'

The two sisters stood hugging each other and Jane whispered, 'I know you think you saw JB because I heard you call his name,' and Alex lifted her weary face to her sister.

'I did see him, darling, he was there, in the water holding a man in his arms.'

Jane thought her sister must have been hallucinating but she did not argue and suddenly beside them on the wharf they heard the composed voice of Donald Fisher; the voice

446

that had kept them steadfast and steadied their nerves for the last twenty-four hours. 'Now then you two, come on. You'll be the toast of Ramsgate when we get inside!'

Chapter Thirty

It was three in the morning and a milky moon rode the clouds above No. 10 Downing Street. Winston Churchill put aside the speech he had written for the Commons and before he rose from his desk flicked open a book of paintings to his right hand. He sometimes used it as a paperweight when the windows were opened and the breeze blew in. It was a miscellaneous collection of Victorian works, all portraits. He ran his hand over a painting on one of the glossy pages in front of him. It was of General Gordon of Khartoum and depicted the great man standing on the walls of that city. It appeared to be late in the day for the sun slanted on the buildings and it was entitled *The Last Watch*, presumably capturing him the evening before he was massacred by the Mahdi and the latter's fanatical troops. In habitual mode Gordon held his Bible in his right hand, his field glasses in his left. The artist, a man named Dickenson, was not fêted or acclaimed but he had caught an expression in Charles George Gordon's blue eyes that spoke of a destiny, of resolution in the face of fear. The look was a mixture of resignation and serene strength, as if he clearly saw his fate but was not afraid of the death which awaited him. It was one of Winston's favourite portraits and he lingered a moment over it. Years before, he had written in lead pencil at the side of the picture, *The whole fury and might of the enemy must soon be turned upon him.*

Winston stood to leave, and suddenly murmuring something to himself, sat back down and added another sentence to his speech.

He looked up to see Clementine before him in her dressing-gown. 'I woke and you weren't there.'

'I'm coming now, Clemmie. Was just peering into Gordon's eyes and thinking of his stoicism in the face of barbarism. Hitler is modern barbarism and he knows that he will have to break us in this island or lose the war.'

Clementine sighed. 'Yes, darling, but it's so late. It's vital you get at least a little sleep.'

As they gained the top of the stairs Winston halted. 'I've told Beaverbrook that in the months to come, Britain must build a bomber force with which to defeat Germany. If we don't, there's no way through. But in the meantime Hitler will turn the might of the Luftwaffe upon us to try and shatter our spirit, and our prime consideration must be to build fighter aircraft until we've broken his attack. Clemmie, we need fighter aircraft!'

'Darling, there's no doubt you're right, you don't have to convince me, but it's nearly four in the morning and we can't build them this minute.' She moved on to the bedroom. 'So please come along.'

As he followed her he mumbled something about leaving No. 10 and going to live in Whitehall above the War Rooms but Clementine was already back in bed.

On 18 June Winston Churchill gave the speech he had completed in the middle of the night to the Commons, and four hours later broadcast it to the peoples of the world. He spoke to inspire the nation and the Commonwealth to resolution and resistance.

Mussolini had thrown off his mask on 10 June, 1940 and joined Hitler announcing war on Britain and France. The Italians had already begun to attack the ports of Malta, Gibraltar and Alexandria in the Mediterranean, and on 14 June the Nazis had goose-stepped into Paris and Churchill could see that France would soon seek an armistice with the Germans. He was conscious that the successful evacuation of hundreds of thousands of troops from Dunkirk had briefly buoyed the British people but he knew too, that wars were not won by evacuations. He ended his speech with a rousing battle cry.

'. . . the Battle of France is over. I expect that the Battle of Britain is about to begin. Upon this battle depends the survival of Christian civilisation. Upon it depends our own British life, and the long continuity of our institutions and our Empire. The whole fury and might of the enemy must very soon be turned on us. Hitler knows that he will have to break us in this island or lose the war. If we can stand up to him, all Europe may be free and the life of the world may move forward into broad, sunlit uplands. But if we fail, then the whole world, including the United States, including all that we have known and cared for, will sink into the abyss of a new Dark Age made more sinister, and perhaps more protracted, by the lights of perverted science. Let us therefore brace ourselves to our duties and so bear ourselves that, if the British Empire and its Commonwealth last for a thousand years, men will still say, "This was their finest hour".'

Tears welled in Samantha's eyes as she sat alone and listened to Mr Churchill's speech in her flat in South Audley Street, Mayfair. At his final statement she experienced a great swell of emotion and she stood and crossed the room. 'Yes, Mr Churchill, yes,' she said and touched the walnut top of the wireless set.

Sam had cut a picture of the Prime Minister out of a magazine and she had it stuck up over her bed. Each night she said the same thing to it as she climbed into bed. 'You're no film star, Mr Churchill, but you'll do me.'

She had arrived in England on 2 June. Most people were travelling in the opposite direction, away from Great Britain. The American government had urged its nationals to return home and Sam had been lucky to set sail from New York on a liner which was being sent over to bring Americans back. There were very few passengers, and on the Atlantic voyage she had felt lonely and vulnerable after leaving Lenny. When she found she was seated with an officer at the dinner table, she had been flattered by his attentiveness. Randolph Knowles was thirty-one and very engaging in his uniform. She danced with him the first night of the crossing and by the fourth night he suggested she sleep with him. She had not. When they arrived in Portsmouth he kissed her goodbye. 'Write to me and I'll come and see you the next time we're here.' She had smiled and agreed, but had little intention of acting upon it.

The Sunday she arrived at Portsmouth Docks she was told of the Dunkirk Evacuation and thought of the wonderful photographs she could take. She asked where she could go to see the troops arriving back, but the official behind the counter at the Customs House shook his head. 'You won't be going anywhere, love, not till you have your pass and identity card – and they won't be forthcoming for at least twenty-four hours. We can't just let people wander about willy nilly; there's a war on. So don't leave Portsmouth and be at the Town Hall at three p.m. tomorrow.' He looked past Sam down the queue. 'Next!'

The following day she went to the Town Hall as requested and while she waited she read the *Daily Sketch* newspaper with its heading: DUNKIRK DEFENCE DEFIES 300,000 GERMANS: *Mr Anthony Eden Secretary of State for War broadcasting last night said more than four-fifths of the BEF have been saved . . . The epic of Dunkirk continues on its breathtaking way . . . already more men have been rescued from the trap than could have been thought possible.*

When it was Sam's turn the card was not ready and to her frustration, by the time her papers were in order the Dunkirk evacuation was over.

Portsmouth was full of soldiers and sandbags, and on the way up to London she began to see more signs of the country at war. Large anti-aircraft balloons floated over airfields and factories, and she realised they were to prevent dive bombers approaching their targets. At railway stations there were sandbags along the platforms and officials in tin hats. The Red Cross collected coins from passengers and there were signs and posters all about with rallying messages aimed at aiding the war effort.

In London she contacted a *Newsweek* correspondent who rented space at the *Daily Telegraph* office in Fleet Street. Victor Bradbury was a man of medium height with a shock of black hair. He took her for a drink at the Savoy and they talked over her assignment.

He helped her with accommodation. 'I know a place in South Audley Street. That's in Mayfair.'

Sam had given him a look of dismay. 'Mayfair? I don't know much about London but I know that's one place I can't afford to live.'

'But you can. It's run by friends of mine, Amelia and George Broome, funny old pair, but honest and straightforward. They're from Somerset originally and the whole building was left to them. Amazing really. The rent's moderate for all their swish address and I reckon if you say you've been sent by me then there'll be a little extra off.'

Sam smiled. 'Great!' Then she questioned him about getting around and taking photos and he told her that she would be stopped often and asked for her identification. 'You'll get used to it,' he said quaffing down his whisky. 'The police or the military will want to know who employs you. You see, there are a lot of restrictions on what can be shown in the local press, but when they realise you're working for an American publication they'll be more lenient on you.'

'Right,' she nodded.

'Do you want to go on somewhere to eat?' he asked, eyeing her appreciatively, but Sam shook her head. 'What I want to do is walk back to my flat, get my bearings, get to know London.'

'Well, drop in and see me anytime.'

Sam found it harder to walk across London than she had anticipated: all the street signs had been removed, and many of the thoroughfares were barricaded. All the monuments were encased for protection and many of the glass windows of shops were boarded up. The streets were lined with sandbags, and barbed wire stretched across the squares. Parliament Square was covered with both and Sam could not resist lying on the ground and taking a shot of Big Ben and the Houses of Parliament through the coils of a barbed wire entanglement. She was challenged there by a guard just as Victor had warned her, but when he had examined her papers and she explained she was from *Newsweek* magazine in New York he let her continue.

She wrote to John Baron immediately on taking the flat – Number 4 on the second floor. She had no idea where he was; since war broke out his address had been an RAF clearing house. She wrote to the Air Ministry and asked for information on her brother's whereabouts. She also wrote to Haverhill, and gave them her address and told them about her assignment and new job and new flat, and how it felt to be in London. She asked them to write to her often.

Please write a lot to me. I love to receive your letters. I am on my own here and I have finished with the life I was leading in New York. But I am confident of my ability to take pictures that will show the world what it's like to be in Britain at this dreadful time.

I love you all and miss you,
Sam
PS Please tell Veena I would adore a photograph of Storm. I know I gave her one of my old Box Brownies so surely she can take a photo for me. I wrote her a letter before I left New York but she'll need my London address now. Please give it to her.
PPS Have you heard anything of Cash? And I'm trying to find JB.

Victor's friend the landlady welcomed Samantha. She told her the rules and regulations of the establishment and gave her a quick lesson on the blackout curtains. 'Draw them each dusk and for pity's sake don't open them till daylight. We'll all be in trouble if you do. The Air Raid Wardens around here are a strict lot. The nearest government shelter if you ever need it is at the crossroads with Curzon Street but it's pretty cramped.' Then she gave a thin smile. 'It's a pleasure to have a real boarder. I've got two military types on the ground floor and most of my other flats have been taken over by the

453

Ministry of War; don't know what goes on in them but people come and go all the time.'

'Should you be telling me this?' Sam asked, having only that day noticed signs in a café reading *Be Wary Whom You Talk To, The Most Innocent Face Can Belong To A Spy.*

Mrs Broome had taken offence at that; her meagre mouth pursed. 'Well, I never! I don't need reproof from the likes of you. I'm a member of the Women's Volunteer Defence Force, I am.' She sniffed. 'And you – supposed to be a friend of Victor and all.'

'Excuse me, Mrs Broome, I just wanted to point out that you don't know me really. I could be anybody.'

The landlady endowed Sam with a withering look as she left the flat, discharging a final remark on the landing. 'Be sure you pay your rent on time.'

Sam felt she had made an enemy but she was surprised and impressed when the next morning Mrs Broome came to her. 'I got to thinking last night, having my cigarette and a small gin as I always do. You were right yesterday, Miss Slade. I admit it absolutely. I shouldn't be talking loosely to anybody, not to anybody at all and I take your point and wish to apologise.'

Sam smiled. 'Well, thanks, Mrs Broome. Truthfully I didn't want to upset you.'

Then the woman added, 'But you should still pay your rent on time.'

They both laughed and were more at ease. 'I know you're on your own, dearie, so any time you want a chat or just some company come down to the basement. This is a swanky part of town but we're just plain folk. George's father made his money in mines, and as well as a farm and a pub, left this building to him, but my George doesn't stand on ceremony and he'll be more than happy to lay eyes on a good-looker like you.'

In her bed at night under the picture of Churchill with lights out and the blackout curtains wafting in the breeze through her windows Sam listened to music on the wireless and imagined JB; remembering all the times they had danced together and how his arms felt around her. She saw his face and heard his voice and was conscious of the sadness living inside her.

Once, just before midnight, 'These Foolish Things (Remind Me Of You)' filled her tiny bedroom and she remembered the last time she had danced to that tune: it had been with Cash the night he took her to Prince's, the most glamorous eating place in Sydney. She could see him now, standing up and bending down to her as his wayward lock of hair stirred on his forehead and his hand took hers to lift her and lead her to the dance floor. 'Come, m'lady,' he had said and they had been the cynosure of attention; she in her backless silver gown and Cash in his dark grey pin-striped suit. They had danced, her head resting upon his shoulder and his face pressed in her hair.

She had lost both Cash and JB, and as the lyric and melody filled her mind, tears slid out from under her eyelids and drifted across her temple into her hair.

Sam began her assignment by looking for children in the West End and Central London and taking photographs of them, playing in the parks, climbing on the anti-aircraft guns and walking hand-in-hand with their parents or nannies, and being taught in the schoolroom. After three days she pressed further afield to St John's Wood and Hampstead and then later to South London and the East End and Docklands.

There were some glorious June days and the smell of summer was on the air. It was not like the dry blanket of heat that descended over the world in a Queensland summer, but she found it warm and comfortable with temperatures in the mid-seventies, and that, to Londoners, she soon found out constituted a perfect summer's day.

The air raids on England began in earnest in June but for a time London was virtually unaffected for they were confined to aerodromes and munitions factories and the docks and shipyards of eastern seaboard ports.

Sam read a lot of newspapers to familiarise herself with England. Obviously a majority of the news was about the war and every now and then about celebrities. Already the conflict was taking its toll even on the famous, for one of the first newspapers she read gave a lot of space to the actress Joyce Phillips and the death of her fiancé, a popular air ace called 'Cobber' Kain who had killed himself doing victory rolls after he had shot down his seventeenth enemy aircraft.

It was towards the end of June that Sam noticed Australian and New Zealand troops in the streets. She took dozens of snaps of them and photographed a smiling band of khaki-clad boys in front of the Strand Theatre which had been designated as the 'Australian Forces Official Social Centre', and was decorated by a huge sign hanging above the entrance with a kangaroo on the left-hand side and the words AUSSIES *Your London Home* beside it. After posing for her photographs, four of the Australians introduced themselves to her and she had gone inside and had a drink with them. All four had asked her out but she had declined, and as she took her leave and walked from the foyer she was approached by a Lieutenant.

'Excuse me, I'm Andrew O'Rourke from Roseville in Sydney and I'm just making a list of the ladies who are here so that we can invite you to the Regimental Dinner we're giving in a fortnight.' As he spoke to her she noticed a tiny chip on his front tooth, and when he smiled it helped to give him a sort of swashbuckling appearance. She was reminded of Cash and his gold filling on his eye-tooth.

'My name's Samantha.'

He grinned and replied with a mock bow. 'How do you do. By that accent you hail from Australia too.'

'Yes.'

'Samantha who?'

'Samantha Slade.'

'Look, there's a war on and nothing ventured nothing gained. Three of my mates are taking girls to a dance hall called the Locarno over in Streatham on Saturday night. I'm told it's great fun, and I . . . Well, I don't have a date. Would you do me the honour, Samantha Slade?'

Sam laughed. 'I've already said no to four soldiers inside.'

'Ah,' he grinned, showing the chipped tooth. 'Then don't break five Aussie hearts in a row. Now you must say yes.'

Sam succumbed. 'All right.'

'So where do you live?'

She gave him the address and he doubled up as if he had been shot; then he recoiled towards her. 'Oh my God! You're a rich heiress, you live in Mayfair. That means you can pay for the drinks.' He burst into laughter.

Sam smiled and shook her head. 'My goodness, are you always like this?'

'Always. I'll see you Saturday at nineteen hundred; that is, seven o'clock.' He grinned again.

The following Saturday, looking forward to the night ahead, Sam carried her shiny black and chrome Speed Graphic camera and went across the river to Bermondsey.

She photographed children playing cricket in the street with an old bat and a tennis ball and then arranged them outside a boarded-up butcher shop and by a fruit barrow in front of a barricade of sandbags. Afterwards she sat in the gutter and talked with two girls and two boys: Bernie, five and Gerard seven and the girls older, Kate, eight and Jennifer nine.

'Do you know what the war is?'

They all nodded.

'Well, what is it?'

Kate, a smart child, answered. 'It's bad. The Germans are fighting us with soldiers and we're fighting them.'

'With soldiers,' added Gerard.

'Do you know why the war began?'

This did not elicit an answer until after many seconds of silence Jennifer replied, 'I think the Germans hate us.'

'And we hate the Germans,' Gerard added solemnly again.

And now little Bernie touched her to draw her attention. His dark eyes appraised her as he spoke. 'I been with me mum away in the country and now we're back. I've got a sister, and she came too.'

Samantha knew that thousands of children and their mothers had been evacuated from London as early as the

457

previous September; she was also aware that a lot of the families had now returned.

'Do you think you'll be taken away again?'

Bernie smiled. 'Hope so. I like the country.'

Jennifer shook her head. 'No, I don't think so. Me mum has to work.'

'War's bad,' opined little Bernie, and Jennifer, twining her plaited hair around her finger, agreed. 'Yes. It's Hitler, he's bad.'

'We have to be brave,' Bernie added. 'Mummy said so.'

Samantha stood. 'Thank you.' She took a handful of sweets out of her pocket. 'Now before I give you these I want you to climb up on those sandbags across the street so I can take a nice photograph of you all sitting on them.'

The children ran to do her bidding and she took some wonderful shots of them lying and sitting and making faces.

Afterwards she walked across to give them the sweets and as they began to jump down to the ground Sam heard another child call out from across the street, 'Who are you and why are you taking photos?' Sam looked around into the face of a girl aged about thirteen with red hair and lively eyes.

'That's Joyce,' Bernie shouted, jumping down and putting his hand out for his share of the sweets.

'I'm taking photographs for a magazine in New York,' Samantha answered Joyce as she came over.

The girl looked at her in disbelief. 'Come here Bernie,' she demanded, putting a protective arm around her little brother. 'I'm his sister,' she eyed Sam, 'and I've come to take 'im home. Mum wants him. Are you really from New York?'

'Originally I'm from Australia. It's a long story but I work for a magazine in New York.'

Joyce was looking at her wide-eyed.

'What's New York?' Bernie asked.

'A city in America,' Sam answered. 'Here, I've got an idea. You stand with your sister and I'll take you together.'

Bernie liked the suggestion and moved in front of Joyce. She had her hands on his shoulders and the sandbags were piled behind them. The sun had disappeared and rain threatened, and as Sam adjusted a flash bulb a nun came walking along and the other children all turned to look at her. Sam snapped the picture just as Bernie poked his tongue out and the nun passed by the back of the stacked sandbags. It turned out to be a memorable shot, distinctively different: Bernie and Joyce in the foreground with the head and shoulders of the religious sister, her body hidden by the sandbags, and the other children caught in the motion of turning to gape at her; the sort of photo her old boss Lester Arnott at *Time* would have called 'magic'. Weeks later *Newsweek* carried it full page as the lead-in to Sam's story.

That night Sam put on her backless silver dress and tied her hair up on her head. She wore jewellery that Cash had given her: a gold chain round her neck, sapphire drop earrings and the sapphire brooch he had arrived home with in the middle of the night after their wedding. She had no illusions about them now. She knew they were all stolen.

When Andrew O'Rourke saw her he whistled and Amelia, who had come up from the basement to see her off, waved to them from the front door. She was pleased to see Samantha going somewhere special with a nice-looking fellow, and when she went back down to George and poured herself a gin she sat in front of the wireless. 'I'm glad Sam's getting out. She's been in every night since she arrived. That's not healthy for a girl her age.'

The Locarno was richly decorated with soft lights. Sam entered on Andrew's arm to Adelaide Hall's voice filling the dance hall and they searched for and found, Andrew's mates seated with their girls on the encircling balcony.

Andrew introduced Sam and they ordered drinks. One of the boys, Stephen Bladier, a Second Lieutenant from Newcastle, had the *Daily Sketch* newspaper tucked under his arm and he brought it out to show them. 'Look at this.' It was a photograph showing Australian ex-servicemen with Prime Minister Robert Menzies in their midst, all before the Cenotaph in Martin Place in Sydney. There were flowers over the monument and the men carried their hats in their left hands and were saluting with their right.

Stephen handed the paper to Andrew, who read aloud while Samantha looked over his shoulder:

"'Mr Menzies, the Australian Prime Minister, surrounded by ex-servicemen pledging allegiance to the war effort. Two days earlier Mr Menzies introduced a National Emergency Bill which placed Australia's entire resources at the Government's disposal to fight the war."

'Makes you proud, doesn't it?' Andrew said.

'Yes, it does,' Sam answered, 'and homesick.'

'Too right,' spoke up Barry Gresham, a Second Lieutenant from Rockhampton.

'Ah well now, that's what we're here for,' declared Della, Stephen's date, an almond-eyed girl with bright red lipstick. 'We're here to make you forget you're homesick.' She snuggled into his side. 'Come on, who's for a dance?'

Stephen lifted her hand and kissed it and the two of them glided away arm in arm to the melody of 'Begin the Beguine'.

Sam and Andrew talked of Australia and Sam's work. She told him about the photograph she had taken that day of the childen with the nun and the sandbags.

'Sounds like a wonderful snap to me. Anyway, you must be pretty damn good to work for *Newsweek*. I've never met a woman photographer before. You know, I bet when they say Sam Slade's coming to take pictures they think they're getting a man, and then you turn up! Some man!' He laughed and she did too, for that had occurred in the past. Later they danced to 'So Deep Is the Night' and 'This Can't Be Love', and all eight of them were on the floor when the band played 'Roll Out the Barrel' and they all sang in unison, along with the hundreds of men and women around them. It was a merry night and Andrew made her laugh a lot; the feeling of war was far away. The last song played before the National Anthem was 'There'll Always Be An England' which was hardly a dance tune but the hundreds there managed to sing and step along to it at the same time.

It was close to one in the morning when Sam and her soldier got off the bus in Park Lane. They had tried to get a taxi but there were none to be found and as they strolled along, Andrew took Sam's hand. His clasp was firm and strong and she felt comforted by it.

'Thanks for coming tonight, Samantha. I had a wonderful time. Hope I wasn't too much of a joker for you.'

'I like to laugh. And it was nice being with a few Aussie blokes.'

'It was nice being with you.'

They were approaching the Dorchester Hotel and across Park Lane they could see the silhouettes of the massive anti-aircraft guns in Hyde Park. The hotel wore its wartime disguise: there were no lights and the tall windows down the façade could not be made out. Screening the entrance were the ubiquitous piles of sandbags.

Andrew pointed to it. 'I've heard tell that's the swankiest place in London. They say it's made of reinforced concrete which probably makes it the safest too. How would you like to have a nightcap there? You look like a queen and I'd like to show you off just once more tonight.'

Sam was flattered. 'All right.'

They crossed to where the black shapes of cars stood along the front and as they came inside the shield of sandbags to the entrance steps the doorman was holding up a blackout curtain to let two people out.

The illumination in the foyer behind gave enough light for Sam to see the RAF uniform.

JB! Oh God, it was JB! Sam halted in shock.

Andrew, pausing at her side, asked, 'What's wrong?'

She stood stock-still as she watched JB hand the doorman a coin then turn to the girl beside him – a girl whose hair lifted in the breeze – a girl who could almost have passed as a double for herself. Sam's eyes were trained on them as her brother slipped his arm around his companion and drew her to him before they came on down the steps into the darkness. JB did not look towards Sam or Andrew who stood to the side.

'God, it's dark out here,' said the girl. 'Where's your car?'

As the doorman remained holding up the curtain Andrew led Sam into the lighted foyer and now he could see how very disturbed she was. 'Who were they?' he asked.

'Andrew, please, just excuse me for a minute. Please understand. I'll be right back.' And with that Sam hurried out into the night again.

She could make out the dark shapes of the couple just disappearing. 'JB?' she called loudly. 'Wait!'

She saw her brother pull up as if he had been hit by a bullet. He said something to the girl and she looked round into the night to see who called but Sam stood in deep shadow. Sam heard him say, 'Please, wait in the car,' and his companion moved reluctantly away and was immediately hidden behind the barricade of sandbags.

John Baron turned slowly and made his way back. 'God! Sam? What are you doing here?'

She took his hands and fought back the overwhelming desire to cry. 'JB, JB.'

'Sammy, please. What are you doing here?'

'Didn't you get my letters?'

'No.'

'I'm here working for *Newsweek*.'

'What happened to *Time*?'

'Oh God, JB, I'm just so happy to see you.' She still held his hands.

A few minutes before, John Baron had felt agreeably tipsy; now he was uncomfortably sober. 'Sammy, I'm with a girl.'

Sam's voice was cold. 'I noticed.'

'I'll come and see you. Where are you staying?'

'Just around the corner.' She gave him the address. 'It's run by a Mrs Broome.'

'I've got to report to Biggin Hill tomorrow at 1700 but I'll come to you first.'

'Promise?'

He hesitated. 'All right. Look, I've got to go.'

Sam met his eyes. 'Hug me. Just hug me, for Christ's sake.'

He stepped forward and took her in his arms. He held her for only a moment, just enough time for them both to remember. Then he dropped his arms and walked away.

'So who was he?' asked Andrew, who had come out to find Sam and now stood at her side in the darkness.

'My brother.'

'Oh yeah? Do you take me for that big a dope?'

'I'm telling you he was. Now do you want that drink or not?'

He looked hard at her in the night light. 'Only if you do.'

Sam took a long deep breath. 'I do. I do.' And Andrew slipped his hand along her arm and they re-entered the Dorchester.

In John Baron's car driving away along Park Lane a similar conversation was taking place. Alex's forthright nature had led her to question him immediately he rejoined her. 'Your sister? Then why didn't you bring her over to meet me?'

'I would have but she was with a friend; it was awkward.'

Alex looked sideways at JB. Of course she believed him. She had no reason whatever to doubt him. But she could sense his agitation, feel the rigidity of his body in the car beside her.

'Why have you never mentioned her before?'

He replied almost sharply. 'Do I have to tell you everything?'

Alex took her time before replying. She spoke calmly. 'No, JB, you don't have to tell me everything. But I've known you now for almost a year. We corresponded while you were in France and I've seen you two and three times a week for the past month. You and I are . . . well, I hope we are . . . more than friends. There's nothing about me you don't know. I suppose I'm just surprised that you meet your sister in the street in London and you don't even bring her over to the car to say hello.'

John Baron did not reply and after a minute or so Alex spoke again. 'We don't have to talk about it any more. I don't want to upset you.'

'You don't.'

When he pulled up outside the house in Kensington where Alex stayed with a friend of Jane she turned to him and touched his cheek. 'Are you coming in for a minute? After all, tomorrow's your last day of leave.' She sighed. 'I don't know exactly when we'll see each other again.'

John Baron met her eyes in the darkness. 'Alex, you're a mighty brave girl. I wouldn't be surprised if you get a medal for what you did at Dunkirk. You and Jane both. You said that you were motivated to go there by thinking about me. Believe me, I realise what that means.'

'Do you?'

'Yes.'

Abruptly, without any warning, he was kissing her passionately. Alex was in love with JB and to have him kissing her this way was one of the things her heart desired. She encompassed him in her arms and held him tightly to her.

When his mouth left hers his voice was thick with emotion. 'I'll come in for a few minutes.'

They walked up the steps hand in hand and when they were inside the door, John Baron took her coat and hung it on a hook in the hall, then he drew her out of the well-lit hallway into the darkness of the drawing room where he kissed her again. His hands ran down her back grasping her bottom and bringing the front of her body in hard against his own. She knew he wanted her and it was the only thing that filled her mind. 'I love you, I love you,' she repeated inside her head, as his hands slipped back up to her breasts.

'Where's your room?'

She took his hand and led him up the stairs to the front bedroom where she slept, a room decorated in country-garden style with chintzes and flower patterns in the curtains and the cushions. She moved across and sat on the pink satin bedspread looking at him with eyes of love.

He undid the buttons on the front of her evening dress and pushed it down to her waist, taking her brassière with it, and drawing his tongue down the side of her neck, he murmured, 'I need you, Alex. I want you.'

And Alex willingly gave herself up to him. She did not analyse why it was tonight that he needed her; her whole consciousness was overpowered by the fact that it was so. The reality was that he was loving her and desired her. A question she did not ask herself was – why now?

And as he ran his hands greedily across her nakedness

and covered her nipples with his mouth Alex abandoned herself to JB's wishes. She admitted that she had desired John Baron to love her almost from their first meeting. To have his hands upon her and his mouth caressing her was bliss, and when he slid between her legs she whispered what she had longed to say to him, 'I love you, JB.'

In South Audley Street a slightly drunken Sam was led up the stairs by Andrew who used the key to let her in and helped her up to the landing and into her flat.

At the Dorchester she had drunk three nightcaps hurriedly and Andrew had watched her with a thoughtful expression.

Before he closed the door he asked, 'Are the blackout curtains drawn?'

'Yes, but we never get any bombs dropped so I don't know why we bother.'

'Don't tempt fate, Samantha.' He switched on the light. 'Anyway, it's the rules. Good night.'

She gave a tiny giggle. 'You don't have to go,' and she stepped forward into his arms. His hands were on the naked skin of her back and Sam liked the warm feeling of them.

'Oh yes, I do.'

'Oh no, you don't.' She leant in towards his mouth.

He slipped his grasp to her wrists and held her at arms' length. 'Now listen to me, Sam. I don't know what the hell seeing *your brother* did to you tonight, but I don't like it. I'm not staying here, I'm going back to the barracks. Now I've got a bit of a journey ahead of me and I don't know how I'm getting there. So good night, Sam.'

'I'll cry if you go.'

'Then cry. I'm not taking advantage of this situation. You're not using me to get over whatever it is that ails you. Now I'm attracted to you, that's for sure. And I hope you come to the Regimental Dinner with me next week like I asked you, but now it's good night.' He put the key down firmly on the table and walked to the door. As he opened it he expressed more of his feelings. 'I prefer to be wanted for myself, Samantha.'

The door closed and she listened to his footsteps on the stairs. Finally she heard the front door open and close and she switched on the wireless and went to bed with the unshed tears floating in her eyes.

Chapter Thirty-one

John Baron woke as dawn inched under the blackout curtain. He could hear Alex's regular breathing beside him and he slipped out of bed and dressed in the semi-darkness.

He opened the door and moved into the hall, searched through his pockets, came across the Dorchester bill from the night before and wrote on the back of it: *Alex, You were wonderful. I'll be in touch as soon as I can. John Baron.*

He walked quietly to the side of the bed and left the note on the table under her evening bag, noticing for the first time the small blue and white porcelain deer he had given her for her twenty-first birthday under the lamp. He looked down at her momentarily before he left the room and carefully descended the stairs with his shoes in his hands. He put them on at the front door.

As he drove away into the empty Sunday-morning streets of London he was thinking about Sam – and the girl who looked like Sam.

He had taken a step with Alex last night that he had been avoiding. He was patently aware that Alex was in love with him. She had never hidden her adoration of him and when he ran into Sam last night he had been caught so unawares that his confusion of feelings had swelled up volcanically inside him and bubbled over. He had needed desperately to love either Sam or the Sam substitute, and the Sam substitute had been willing and available.

She was a lovely, warm, genuine, brave, honest girl and he felt overwhelming guilt for using her that way. And on top of it all he was supposed to see Sam today! No, he could not do that.

He accelerated towards Epsom where he and Twig had

taken a cottage for the month of their leave. This afternoon they were reporting to the squadron, or what was left of it, at Biggin Hill.

He was back in the war after a month of easy days. He admitted that he had enjoyed the hours he spent with Alex. She and Jane had come up to the cottage and cooked a couple of times. They had sat on the little terrace overlooking the racecourse with the sound of woodpeckers in the trees and it had been as if there were no war.

Once when Twig had gone down into the village alone John Baron and the two girls had talked about Dunkirk. Perhaps to dispel their memories, to release them from the weird delirium they recalled; and then perhaps they talked about it simply because they had all been there, experienced it, the three of them in the sea.

Twig had been the one to tell him that Alex and Jane had helped evacuate men from Dunkirk. Jane had revealed it to him over the telephone. At first John Baron had been disbelieving, but he had come to realise it was true. And when he found out that Alex had been motivated by the thought that he could possibly be one of the stranded, he came to understand how much she loved him.

He had finally analysed his feelings for her and accepted that he was attracted to her because she reminded him of Sam. But she was not Sam – and after this month of seeing her regularly he was becoming more aware of the real differences; and strangely enough they had not displeased him. But now he had taken the step of making love to her, of giving her a reason to believe he felt for her as she did him, and he knew that was not so.

It was a very confused John Baron Chard who arrived back at the cottage and packed for his departure to Biggin Hill.

Sam awoke with a heavy head and looked at her bedside clock. 10 a.m. She immediately recalled all that had occurred the night before and she dragged herself out of bed, drank two glasses of water, bathed, washed her hair and dressed and had tea and toast.

For the next two hours she sat in her lounge room waiting for JB, full of expectancy.

But at one o'clock she was still alone and she became apprehensive. Amelia Broome knocked on the door at half past the hour with a plate of fresh scones. 'Just popped up to give you these. How was it?'

'Oh, it was very nice. Andrew looked after me and we danced and we even went to the Dorchester for a nightcap. So swish. It was all . . . Well, it was all very nice.'

Amelia smiled. 'I'm so glad. Will you be seeing him again?'

'Perhaps.' Sam could see her landlady was on for a chat and she just could not face up to the questions. 'Look Mrs Broome, I'd love to come down for a talk this evening, but right now I'm waiting for somebody.'

'Andrew?'

'No. My brother.'

Mrs Broome looked surprised. 'Didn't know you had one.'

'Yes, he's in the RAF. So if you don't mind?'

'Of course love, I'll be off. Oh, give him a scone when he comes. Made with my mum's recipe; George loves 'em.'

Sam closed the door behind her and looked at her watch. JB had said something about being somewhere at seventeen hundred. Well, that was only a few hours away.

Why oh why wasn't he here?

By the time 4 p.m. came round Sam was lying on her bed in tears and the sharp rap on her door startled her. She bounded from the bed and came running in anticipation to call through the door. 'Who is it?'

'Me, love.' It was Mrs Broome. Sam's face dropped.

'Telephone call for you, it's your brother.'

Sam's face lit up again. She quickly dried her eyes. 'I'll be right down. Please tell him I'm coming.' She dashed into the bathroom and dabbed some powder around her eyes and as she hurried out and down the stairs she rubbed lipstick on her mouth. She smiled to Mrs Broome as she entered the basement flat.

'Over there.' The landlady pointed to an alcove where the phone was attached to the wall.

'JB?'

'Hello, Sammy.'

'Why didn't you come?'

'Listen, Sam, when I woke up this morning I just didn't think it was a good idea.'

'What?'

'Seeing you at your flat alone, together like that. Please, Sammy, understand.'

'Two minutes – are you extending?' came the inflexible voice of the operator.

'God, we've only just begun talking,' Sam reacted angrily.

'I said two minutes, are you extending?'

'Yes yes,' John Baron replied, dropping in more coins. 'Go ahead.'

'You there, Sam?'

'Yes.'

'I'm going back to the squadron in an hour. Fact is, I'm on my way. I just stopped at a phone box out here in Kent to call you.'

Sam did not answer.

'Sammy, are you there?'

'Yes.'

'Biggin Hill airfield, that's where I'll be. Listen, Sammy, the first chance I get I'll be in touch. I know where you are now. You know where I am. We'll spend some time together, I promise.'

There was a long silence and her voice was cold. 'You promised to see me today.'

He made a frustrated sound. 'Sammy, please, you know why I didn't!'

'No, I don't.'

'Don't be silly. I'll take you to the theatre. We'll have a night out together. Talk about a lot of things. I'm glad I know where you are. I hope you've left that Lenny bloke you were tied up with in New York.'

She paused. 'Yes, I have. Who was that girl who looked like me?'

'Sammy, not now, please. Just wait. I'll explain it all. I'll be in touch again soon.'

'When?'

'Soon. I'll come up to London.'

'JB . . .'

'Yes?'

'I really want to talk to you. There's so much to say.'

'Time's up!' came the obdurate voice again.

'But it can't be . . .'

'Bye, Sam.' He hung up.

Sam put the receiver back in its hook on the wall and took two deep breaths to control herself. 'Thanks, Mrs Broome.'

'That's all right, dearie, any time. Come back later and we'll have a natter.'

'Yes.' She walked slowly up the stairs.

She spent what was left of the afternoon cleaning her flat and she was surprised to hear Mrs Broome's knock on her door a few minutes after seven with news of another telephone call.

'Telephone, Samantha. Andrew this time.'

Andrew's energetic tones came down the line. 'How are you today, Samantha?'

'Good. Thanks for last night.'

'Which part of it?'

'All of it.' She paused. 'So you got home all right?'

'Sure did. Hitched a ride with a military ambulance . . . picked it up on the Edgware Road.'

'Good.'

'Listen, I'm ringing to be sure you're still coming with me to the Regimental Ball next Saturday?'

There was a brief silence during which Andrew waited.

'Yes, Andy, I'll be coming.'

'Great. We've got to get you out here to St Albans. I'm told there's a train leaving London at eighteen thirty and one back at twenty-three-thirty. I can't come up and get you because I'm on duty until eighteen hundred myself, but I can take you home.'

'Then how will you get back to camp?'

'Don't worry about me, I'll find another ambulance if I have to. Look, I'm using a military phone here in the barracks. Better go. See you next Saturday, Samantha. I'll be at St Albans' Station waiting for you.'

'Thanks. I'll be there.'

'Oh, and Samantha?'

'Yes.'

'You looked beautiful last night.'

Sam sighed. 'Thanks, Andy.'

She heard the click as he hung up the receiver.

As she left the telephone alcove, she wondered if she had been right to agree to go with him. She felt lonely in London with only her work to occupy her. She knew that she missed JB more than ever, and while she never believed she could have missed Cash she had to admit that sometimes she did. God, she was only twenty-three after all. Andrew was a diversion, and a pleasant one.

'Mrs Broome?' she called and the landlady answered from the kitchen. 'Yes, love?'

'Can I have that natter with you now?'

'Of course, come on through. George and I are just having our first gin.'

As Sam entered and sat down, Mrs Broome lifted an old felt hat up off the table. It had two thick U-shaped pieces cut out of the crown. 'I'm making a pair of slippers out of this, got the idea out of the *Daily Mail*. You make the uppers out of the crown and the backs out of the brim and use canvas for the soles; then a colourful old scrap for lining. Second pair I've made. So glad George didn't throw the hats out.' She looked across at her husband who sat drink in hand, beside the small window with a view up to the street. 'Nearly did, didn't you, love?'

George nodded and Mrs Broome swept on. 'I'm making patchwork cushion covers as well. All going to help the war effort. We have a pick-up here for this sort of thing every month.' She crooked her finger at George. 'Come and pour a drink for Samantha. What'll you have, love?'

'Actually I've got a bit of a heavy head. Think I overdid it last night.'

'Tea or coffee then?'

'Yes, coffee please.'

'There you go, George love. I think we've got a bottle of coffee and chicory in the cupboard. See to Samantha.'

George winked at Sam as he passed by. Amelia Broome noticed and gave a squeaky giggle. 'That's my George. Doesn't say much, but appreciates us girls.'

Sam smiled and settled back on the kitchen settee.

John Baron found a surprise awaiting him when he and Twig arrived that Sunday evening at Biggin Hill. Situated on a high point of the weald, or moorlands, of Kent, 'The Bump' as it became known to fighter pilots returning home from the other side of the Channel, guarded the front-line southern counties and approaches to London. It had been chosen by Air Chief Marshal Hugh Dowding to be Senior Sector Station of Number Eleven Group RAF which had group headquarters at Uxbridge.

Already operating from Biggin Hill were Squadrons 32 and 610, and as John Baron halted his second-hand Rover at the guard hut, a unit of the Local Defence force – about to be renamed by Churchill 'The Home Guard', were marching by.

John Baron handed the Corporal on duty their passes.

The young man checked their names on his clipboard before he took the pencil from behind his ear and ticked the paper.

'Password, please.'

John Baron looked round at Twig. 'Do you know it?'

'How could I? I've just arrived here with you.'

John Baron leant out of the window. 'Look, old man, we've just been posted here. Back after a month off. We fought in France and at Dunkirk. Now you've got our passes and you've just marked us off on your sheet there.' He pointed to the clipboard. 'So you know we're genuine. Let us through.'

The Corporal's chin shot forward stubbornly as he handed back the passes. 'Can't let anyone by who doesn't know the password, sir.'

'Shit,' spoke up Twig. 'How were we supposed to find it out if we haven't been here?'

The Corporal bent down to shoot a hostile look beyond John Baron to Twig before he turned back to the guard behind him and instructed the second airman to pick up the telephone.

'Park over there please and wait.' The Corporal pointed to the side of the road near the guardhouse.

'But this is ridiculous. You've just marked our names off on your list. We're obviously expected.'

'Sir?' The Corporal's voice rose and his chin inched further out. 'My orders are not to let *anyone* by who doesn't know the password. Wait over there please, sir.'

John Baron backed up and parked, and fifteen minutes passed during which he got out and sat on the bonnet in the sun and Twig began whistling 'Way Down South In Dixie' until finally he gave up and closed his eyes.

Eventually the Corporal marched over. 'You can enter the airfield now. You've been officially recognised.'

'I should bloody well think so,' Twig commented, waking up.

As John Baron turned to get in the Rover, he decided that the Corporal was probably right; rules were rules, and to be pleasant he asked, 'So how's everything?' not really expecting an answer, but to his surprise, the Corporal was positively voluble now.

'Gawd! How's everythin'? Well, sir, I can tell you, we've 'ad squadrons comin' and goin' out of our ears. Six hundred and ten, two hundred and thirteen, two forty-two, seventy-nine . . . all here for the Dunkirk evacuation.'

'Don't forget two twenty-nine and thirty-two,' the second guard reminded him. 'They came and went as well.'

'Yeah, but thirty-two are back now,' the Corporal replied in a quarrelsome tone, 'so they're not in the count.' He flicked his finger at the Rover. 'And now you lot have arrived. Must be the busiest airfield in the country, as well as being bombed by blasted Jerry almost every second day. Craters everywhere and most of the buildings are makeshift.' He waved John Baron on. 'Oh, by the way, sir, just now on the telephone we've been asked to inform you that Wing Commander Macarthur says that you are to report to his office at eighteen hundred.' He pointed with his clipboard. 'Living quarters are over there: don't know how Jerry's managed to miss them. There'll be a batman waiting. Wingco's office is beyond by the dispersal huts. You can park your car round to the right, sir.'

'What an enlightening little fire-cracker he turned out to be,' Twig asserted as John Baron drove through the gate.

When they stood before Robert Macarthur, he saluted them. 'Welcome back after your rest. Hope you feel refreshed. Dunkirk was tough, bloody hard on everyone and you all managed marvellously.'

'Thanks sir.'

'Did you have trouble getting past the checkpoint at the gate?'

They both nodded. 'Yes.'

He grinned. 'Seems all you boys were stopped – the whole blasted squadron. Something about not knowing the password. Good man, that Corporal Shelly. No spies getting by him!' He looked down at his papers and back up to them. 'I've a message here for you, Chard, to speak with Air Vice Marshal Park on the telephone in the morning. Bring yourself back here at ten hundred tomorrow, will you?'

Keith Park was the AOC – Air Officer Commanding, 11 Group. A New Zealander, he had been a Royal Flying Corps fighter pilot in World War I and had shot down twenty of the enemy. Unlike Air Chief Marshal Hugh Dowding, who headed all of Fighter Command and was known as 'Stuffy' because of his remote and austere manner, Park was a competent and approachable leader and popular with his young fighter pilots. Fighter Command in England, Wales and Scotland was divided into four groups: 11 Group covered south-east England and included Biggin Hill; 10 Group covered south-west England; 12 Group central and northern England and 13 Group Scotland.

Smartly at 1000 the following day John Baron reported, though it was forty-five minutes before he heard Keith

Park's steady voice over the line. 'Chard, the Air Ministry are impressed with your six kills and how you handled yourself getting home after being shot down – Dunkirk and all that. There's a DFC in it for you . . .' he paused '. . . and, as David Flinders is moving to Twelve Group, you've been promoted to Squadron Leader in his place. Congratulations!'

John Baron felt a swell of excitement: a Distinguished Flying Cross and a promotion! What a double.

'Why, thank you, sir. That's wonderful. That's great!'

'You'll remain at your current station, Chard. I know your squadron's been badly depleted. Too many good men lost. We're in the process of building you back up to strength.'

'Yes, sir. Thanks.'

'And Chard?'

'Yes, sir?'

'We're counting on you.'

John Baron was the toast of the mess that night.

Chapter Thirty-two

Late September, 1940

A chill westerly wind was delving into every corner of Haverhill. The dogs lay inside the kitchen near the woodstove for warmth and Ledgie knitted a cardigan as she sat at the kitchen table with a strong pot of tea in front of her listening to Constance who read aloud from the *Queensland Times*.

'"*With bombs dropping all over London even in daylight now, the city workers can watch from the streets the dogfights taking place in the sky overhead between the RAF and the Luftwaffe. The enemy have struck at the very heart of the capital, bombarding it constantly in an attempt to terrify. Destruction is everywhere and the mounting death toll of the innocent and helpless citizens continues into the thousands but the spirit of the Londoners is not dampened.*

'"*King George in a speech this week, instituted a new decoration to be known as the George Cross and paid tribute to the Air Raid Precautions Services, saying their devotion in the face of grave and constant danger has won new renown for them, that the walls of London may be battered, but the spirit of the Londoner stands resolute and undismayed*".'

Ledgie shivered. 'Makes me tremble it does to think about it, those poor Londoners. And our two babies there, one in the sky fighting those horrible Nazi hordes and the other, foolish enough to be takin' herself there, where she's got no business to be! It was bad enough when she went to that New York place, but why oh why didn't she come home instead of going to England?'

'Ah Ledgie darling, there's no answer to that. Whatever it is that drives Samantha is beyond me. I'm still heart-broken about the break-up with Cash. Somehow I always believed they were right for each other. Oh, he could be wayward and she's strongwilled, but to me they fitted together like bread and butter.'

Ledgie clicked her knitting needles together and moved her toes in the direction of the stove. 'Aye, me darlin' I agree, and a wonderful dreamy-lookin' pair they made. I'll always see them standing at the altar lookin' into each other's eyes, that I will and no mistake.' Her tone mellowed in recollection. 'That Cash always had a way about him – couldn't help but be fond of the lad.'

There was the sound of a car entering the yard and Charity and Tess sat up, ears pricked.

'Well, go and find out who it is,' Ledgie told them and as if they understood, they trotted out onto the verandah and began to bark.

Constance stood up. 'Must be strangers. I'll go and see.'

As she moved onto the verandah and commanded the dogs to be quiet, an order they did not heed, she saw her husband and Wakefield walking over to a grey Humber automobile.

The dogs had decided to investigate and were now charging down the steps as Ledgie called from inside, 'Who is it?'

'Don't know. Two men. Ben and Wakefield are talking to them.' And with that Constance returned to the kitchen, drawing her cardigan firmly around her middle. 'Oh, it's cold out there.'

'Supposed to be spring . . . doesn't feel like it.' Ledgie poured out tea from the pot. 'Here, darlin', have another cup.'

Fifteen minutes later they heard the vehicle leave and their two men and the dogs traipsed up the side verandah stairs and into the kitchen.

'Detectives again,' Ben enlightened them as he came through the door.

'Not Cash?'

'Afraid so,' answered Wakefield, easing himself into a chair.

Ben nodded. 'Same blokes again – Noble and Seymour, the ones who came last year. Said they're joining the army soon but they're still working on the murder of Dexter Wilde.'

'But Cash had nothing to do with that,' declared Ledgie, and Constance's cheeks drained of colour.

'Well, the case isn't closed. They've never found the murderer. And now some bloke's mentioned Cash's name in connection with Wilde. A man who recently died in prison, name of Creedy . . . ?' He turned his head to Wakefield who supplied the full name.

'Creedy Fulbrook, I think it was.'

'That's right. He died in Bogga Road gaol a week or so ago and on his deathbed he showered light on a few crimes, one being Dexter Wilde's murder.' He fell silent and Wakefield took up the story.

'Apparently this Creedy fellow "got religious" before he died and confessed a lot of things. Said Cash had come to him the night of the murder, seems he had some sort of *business* relationship with Cash – God knows what. The police said this Fulbrook fellow was a fence and small-time crook. Anyhow, he seems to have named Cash as involved in the murder in some way and they want to fingerprint him . . . that's if they can find him.'

'I don't believe it,' Ledgie affirmed. 'What a load of tripe!'

Constance appeared as if she were going to cry and Benjamin came round the table and hugged her. 'They want us to let them know if we hear from him, or become aware of where he is. Left us a phone number and their address at Police Headquarters in Brisbane.'

His wife looked up at him. 'Do you believe it?'

Ben let out a loud breath. 'Sweetheart, I don't know what to believe. Cash was a bit wild, yes – but murder? No, I don't think I believe that.'

'I wouldn't believe murder either,' agreed Wakefield. 'He was hard to rile, always cool-headed. But you know

479

they say that sometimes hides a violent temper. But in Cash's case we've no reason to believe it.'

Benjamin bit his lip in thought. 'We all know Sam told us Cash lied to her and she said that we didn't understand what he was really like. So perhaps there were other sides to his character that we didn't perceive.'

'But murder?' exclaimed Ledgie. 'Such a suggestion. Why? It's like saying *I'm* a murderer.'

Wakefield let out a peal of laughter. 'Your looks can kill, Ledgie old darling, that's for certain.'

Ledgie, whose legs were bad these days, did not move but she threw a ball of wool at him and it unravelled as it spun across the room. 'Now you can just roll that back up for me, you, you Frenchman!' she commanded and Wakefield, grinning widely, did as he was bidden.

It was not three hours since the police had left when Hardy Medcott arrived with the post from Boonah.

Benjamin and Wakefield had gone out to where the planting was taking place on the far side of the property and Crenna brought in the small sack of mail and dropped it on the table in front of Ledgie who was just putting a fruit pie in the oven. 'I'll sort them and take mine.' Which Crenna did while Ledgie washed the flour off her hands before she picked up the remaining letters and called out to Constance who was dusting the dining-room furniture.

The two women sat near the warm oven as Constance selected the order in which to open them. 'John Baron! We'll read his first and these others are just mainly bills. Oh my goodness!'

'What?'

'One from Cash, can you believe it? And those men only here looking for him this morning.'

'Well, read John Baron's first, me darlin', then Cash's.'

Constance tore the envelope open. It was only short, for as he explained:

We are day and night being scrambled to fight the Hun. I don't get a lot of rest but we sleep when we can. We've lost a lot of fellows, so the squadron is full of

480

new faces these days, and sooo young. Makes me feel like an old man. I feel responsible, being the Commander of the squadron and it's hell when I lose a bloke.

I miss you all and Haverhill. I can picture it with all of you having an evening drink on the verandah, with the jasmine weaving its blooms along the railing and Tess and Charity at your feet, with a tepid breeze wafting up from the brook. Gosh, I'm looking forward to the end of the war and just sitting there looking out to the hills for at least a year or so!!

Give my best to the Birnum family especially Veena and Storm.

Your ever-loving son, and nephew, John Baron

Constance wiped her eye with her apron. 'Always makes me sad when we get a letter.'

'There, there, me darlin'.' Ledgie comforted her by leaning forward and brushing Constance's hair back with her hand. 'Now to Cash. Look, it's postmarked Townsville.' She gave a fond smile. 'He does get around, that boy.'

It too was short. He told them he was well and in north Queensland at present.

I'm trying to do my bit for the war effort, but won't go into detail on that.

Enclosed is a little note for Sammy – would you be kind enough to post it on to her? I don't know her address these days, but you will.

I'll write again when I have time but it could be quite a while so don't count on it. I'm fit and well. Give a hug to Storm for me. Oh yes, and one for you too, Ledgie, you old charmer you!

Yours ever,

Your son-in-law, Cashman

Ledgie sniffed. 'Signing himself son-in-law and writing to Sam; still carrying a torch for her, I'll be bound.'

'Yes. I'll send his envelope to her in my next letter. *Doing his bit for the war effort* – wonder what that means?'

Then a serious expression crossed Constance's face. 'Oh dear! Ledgie, Ben and Wakefield will feel obliged to let those detectives know about this.'

Ledgie was silent for a time while she turned away to the stove and rubbed her hands together. Then without looking round she said, 'If we don't tell them, my angel, they won't feel obliged to do anything.'

Constance sat looking at the back of Ledgie's grey hair while she continued to warm her hands. Finally Constance spoke. 'I can't lie to Ben, Ledgie.'

'Not asking you to lie, darlin', just telling you not to say anything.'

Constance moved across to Ledgie and stood by her and the elderly woman lifted her bony hand and clasped the arm of her surrogate child. Then Constance knelt down before her as she had when she was a little girl many decades before and rested her head on Ledgie's bony lap. The old lady stroked Constance's hair with a tender loving touch. 'There, there me own darlin', precious as you are. Let's make a pact. No lies, just silence . . . that's the best idea in this matter. Nothing said and nobody hurt.'

Samantha edged a little closer to Amelia Broome. The last explosion had been very near and the flashes of light had shown even through the black-out curtains. Sirens were wailing. She had lost count of the nights like this: the bombing, the hellish noise, the sky bright with searchlights and ack-ack fire and the pit of her stomach somewhere near her mouth.

The Blitz on London had begun in earnest on 7 September with a twelve-hour day-and-night raid by four hundred German bombers; for each bomber a person had been killed and sixteen hundred others had been hospitalised: at dawn there were nine conflagrations, nineteen major fires, forty serious fires, and a thousand smaller fires. The London Fire Brigade could not contend with them and the next night they served as beacons for the returning German bombers. Every day and night since, the assaults had continued.

George Broome had disappeared at the first warning signal and gone down the street to the public shelter. Sam and Amelia had accompanied him the first night, but it became so over-crowded and claustrophobic that Samantha had decided if she were going to die at German hands in a bombing raid, that was that, and she would have to take her chances. Amelia felt the same way, so each night since, they had come down into the Broomes' basement flat, sometimes to the cellar, at other times they just sat in the kitchen like tonight.

Amelia sighed. 'It breaks my heart to think of Sandy.'

Sandy was the Broomes' cat. They had not seen him since 7 September. Amelia had searched all over the West End to no avail.

'The poor cats and dogs of London,' she grieved, sipping her gin. 'I'm furious with that bloody Hitler. My darling baby missing and God knows where he is, or whether he's dead or alive.'

'Yes, the animals have suffered dreadfully,' Sam agreed. 'So many of them obviously terrified by all the blasted noise. God, we're terrified, so why wouldn't they be?'

Amelia wiped her eye. 'Think I'll have another gin.'

'Good idea.'

The Luftwaffe's real targets were the docklands. On both sides of the Thames, they had taken the brunt of the devastation, Bermondsey and West Ham being continuously hit and the destruction spreading out to the surrounding districts. And, as well, on some nights, like tonight, bombs also arrived in the West End.

'Thank God we've got the anti-aircraft guns firing back,' Amelia said as she rose and poured two gins. Little did she realise that they were ineffectual against the aircraft in the night sky. She added tonic water and with a trembling hand passed one to Sam. 'You know since that huge crowd gathered outside Liverpool Street Station and demanded entrance to the Underground and Mr Churchill opened it all up, most people seem to head there. Perhaps we ought to go to the Underground tomorrow night. It's hard to stay dignified, good-humoured and brave when the bloody bombs get this close.'

Sam smiled. 'Yes, it is. It's just that I'm claustrophobic at any time, I now know. Didn't before. I was brought up in the wide open spaces, used to ride with the wind in my hair heading for the hills. I suppose that has a lot to do with it, since when I'm cheek to jowl with others in a confined space I get very panicky.'

'The Underground's much bigger than the other shelters. You might feel all right in there, love.'

'I might.'

Amelia had just taken a mouthful of her drink when there was an earth-shattering noise in the street. She let out a yell, and at that moment the single lamp went out and the floor beneath their feet shook as pieces of the window fell broken to the floor behind the blackout curtain.

'Oh good Lord! That was close,' the landlady moaned in the darkness, and giving a slightly hysterical giggle, added, 'but I didn't drop my drink.'

Sam switched on the torch and Amelia lit a candle.

'Yes,' Sam answered, pulling back the curtain to peer up to the street, 'that one can't have been far away.' She thought she could see flames up to the right. 'I can hear screaming . . . Amelia, I'm going up to see.'

Her friend's eyes were fearful in the candleglow. 'No, Samantha, leave it to the authorities. Stay here. It's too dangerous out there.'

'I'm going,' and with that Sam grabbed her Speed Graphic camera – it was always with her – and hurried up the stairs as Amelia continued to shout for her not to go out.

In the street there were flames dotted all over where incendiary bombs had fallen and Sam quickly saw that the main explosion had been at a clinic up on the corner with a chemist shop beneath. It was on fire and the front had been blasted away. There was a crater where a telephone box had stood and an ambulance with engine smoking was crumpled into a telegraph pole.

There was no one in the street but herself, and she ran towards the rubble and fire as dust rose in the air and the red flames seen through it coated the scene in an unearthly orange light. It was all surreal. God in heaven! What must it be like down in the East End if it's this bad here?

She could hear the anti-aircraft guns blasting away in Hyde Park and up near Marble Arch. However, Sam knew her arithmetic and was sadly very aware that hitting aircraft moving across London at over 200 m.p.h. was a game of chance; the odds most definitely with the bombers. They flew high and the searchlights rarely exposed them. 'You buggers are getting it all your own way!' she shouted as she hurried down the street.

Sam could hear someone crying as she came to a halt in front of the heaps of stone, wood and glass which had been the front of the chemist shop. She stood on a pile of dirt. 'Where are you?'

The driver staggered from the ambulance on the corner. He had cut his head but otherwise looked unhurt. He sat down on a large piece of plaster and put his chin in his hands. 'I'll be all right in a minute,' he said.

'There's someone trapped; help me if you can,' Sam called and he stood up and came unsteadily over. A moaning sound continued from under a pile of rubble and Sam began to pull the pieces of stone away as another explosion boomed from the direction of Oxford Street and the ground beneath her feet shook. She kept on with her task and revealed an arm covered in blood. Her stomach heaved but she controlled herself. 'Hang on, just hang on.'

She kept lifting pieces of stone and now the man began to help. They uncovered the woman's head as a burning beam crashed to the ground only a few yards away. The woman's face was covered in dirt, cuts and blood, and she continued to groan. Her dress was torn and her shoulder, cut and bleeding, was exposed.

Sam stood up and took a flashlight photograph of the ambulance driver and the woman, half her body still covered by rubble.

'Here, what're you doing?' the man asked angrily.

Sam knelt back down and continued to move debris as she answered, 'I work for an American magazine. This will help show them what you're going through.'

'Oh, right enough,' he replied much more accommodatingly.

Suddenly four men in helmets arrived. 'Out of the way, love, we'll take over now.' And they helped Sam to her feet.

'Go on,' said one with an ARP armband. 'Off you scarper. You've done well, but you shouldn't be out in the street.' And they got to work immediately, talking comfortingly to the woman and removing the wreckage at the same time.

Sam lingered. 'Can I just take a photograph of you please?' she asked, removing another flashlight from her pocket and fitting it in the chome reflector as she spoke.

'She works for an American magazine,' the ambulance driver explained. 'It'll show 'em what's goin' on here.'

'Well, be quick about it, and then get to a shelter.'

Sam took her shot: the five men lifting the woman covered in blood, with the debris of the bombed-out shop behind and the ambulance with its crumpled bonnet hard against the telegraph pole. While it was not in her Children series, she sent it back to New York anyway. It was used many times and became an iconic shot of the London Blitz.

She was on her second series of photographs now. The first, 'Children in War' had been carried over six pages of *Newsweek* and highly praised by the pictorial editor. Carter Brinkwood, his assistant, had immediately agreed to a second assignment and Sam was now on the payroll. She was continuing with her children theme: this time 'Children in Fear from Above'.

Tens of thousands of children and their mothers had been evacuated last September when the war began, and ironically only recently many returned; just in time for the carnage from the bombings to begin. Sam knew the authorities were removing them again and she was photographing that, but there were still many children about.

'As I said, off you scarper,' the air-raid warden commanded, pointing sharply down the street and Sam moved off to the wails of ambulance sirens drifting on the air. She walked along, her treasured camera under her arm, amid bursts of light and flames from the incendiaries up on rooftops and along the pavement, while the noise of distant explosions continued.

As she came to the block of flats and ascended the steps she thought of JB. He was probably up in the air tonight fighting the bloody Luftwaffe. She prayed for his safety.

He had kept his promise and taken Sam to a show. They had gone to the Palace Theatre and seen *Chu Chin Chow*, a spectacular based on *Ali Baba and the Forty Thieves*. Jerry Verno had played Ali Baba and at the beginning of the Third Act when explosions from the Luftwaffe bombs could be heard even above the music of the band, Jerry had held up his hands for silence and stepped forward to the front of the stage, where he addressed the audience. 'Sheikhs and Princesses, if you want to move out to a shelter, please do, but I can't leave my forty thieves so I'll continue singing and dancing for your amusement.'

Thunderous applause had met his announcement. And nobody had left the theatre.

There were numerous curtain calls and finally Tom Kinniburgh, whose character had been Abdullah, took off his turban and as the theatre trembled from a nearby violent explosion, he began to sing 'Maybe It's Because I'm a Londoner, That I Love London Town'. The chorus had taken it up, it was so wonderfully incongruous with them all in Arab costume, and within a minute everybody in the theatre had risen and was singing loudly.

They were keyed up with excitement when they exited the theatre. JB took Sam to the Café de Paris nightclub; here, in the splendour of its décor, they ate supper together. The bombs were continuing to drop intermittently and some of the patrons departed for the shelter, but they did not leave their seats.

'We didn't get hit in the theatre and we won't be hit here,' JB asserted.

He looked wonderful in his blue uniform with the diagonally striped ribbon of the DFC sewn on his tunic, and when he bought a bottle of champagne from the fast diminishing stocks, Sam had lifted her glass and clinked his with a toast. 'To the future, may we both be happy . . . and in love.'

He was uncertain what Sam meant by that, but he drank the toast anyway and afterwards told her how he had escaped from behind the enemy lines when he had been shot down.

She listened, her body rigid, the intensity of her emotion showing in her eyes. 'Oh JB, to think the buggers nearly shot you.' She took up his hand and there was the old electric feeling as their fingers met.

Later they reminisced about Haverhill and days gone by. Towards the end of the night he took her hand again.

'Sammy, the girl you saw me with that night at the Dorchester . . .'

'I was wondering when you'd get around to her,' Sam answered.

'Please hear me out. Her name's Alex. She lives with her family outside Sandwich, a little place in Kent.'

'Well, that's convenient to Biggin Hill, isn't it?'

He gave a small moan of frustration. 'Please, Sammy. She's in love with me.'

Sam met his eyes. 'Who isn't?'

'Sam, don't do this. I want you to understand. You *must* understand. Please. She's the first girl I've ever . . .'

His sister sat watching him. She withdrew her hand. 'Go on.'

'You're not making this easy. I've taken out a lot of girls over the years, some I liked more than others, but none that I cared deeply for. Alex is the first girl who has meant anything.' He looked earnestly into her eyes and exhaled loudly before he added, 'Other than you.'

'Are you going to marry her?'

'For heaven's sake, no, I'm *not* going to marry her! I'm simply informing you about her.'

Sam picked up her glass and drained it. 'Do you think you like her because she looks like me?'

'Hell, Sammy, how do I know? Yes, I suppose so. At first. But it's not that now. I never even think of that any more.'

Sam looked down at her hands beneath the table, eyeing

the gold wedding band she still wore. 'I'm sorry, JB, forgive me. I've been goading you.' She lifted her eyes. 'God, the happiest days of my life were in Queensland when we were growing up.'

'Snake Hips' Johnson, the band leader, slowed up the pace on 'This Can't Be Love' and as a couple glided by, holding each other close, Sam turned her head to them, but she wasn't watching the dancers for her sight was on the distant memories in her head and her expression softened.

'The way we used to ride hell for leather across the property with you on one side of me, Cash on the other. And how Ledgie would look askance at us when we all came home dirty and dusty.' She smiled to herself. 'I can see you and Cash diving into the water-holes and laughing your silly heads off about some dare or other. And how many times did I photograph you two on that motor bike of Belcher's? And rehearsing for the Christmas concert? Wonderful times. We were kids, eh?' Now her expression hardened. 'But kids grow up.'

'Yes, they do.'

The waiter came by and they ordered coffee.

'Darling?'

She sighed. 'Yes?'

'Do you ever hear from Cash?'

'No. Sometimes I wish I did. I wonder where he is, that's for certain.'

'What was it that really broke you up?'

She shook her head. 'Ah JB, manifold reasons, dear brother. None of which matter now. Cash is a decidedly unusual man. He marches to a different tune, as they say.'

'Yes, he does. Always did. But one thing I truly believe is that he loved you.'

A wistful look crossed her features. 'Yes,' she replied. 'He just didn't know what to do about it.'

It had been a night to remember and when JB took her home he hugged her on the front steps. 'I'm sorry you're here. London's so damn dangerous.'

'I know,' she replied, 'but somehow I was always going to be here. And that's that.'

'I'll stay in touch,' he promised. And he had. He telephoned her every Friday night.

And now, as Samantha thought of the possibility of his being up there in the bomber-filled sky she took a deep breath and entered the front hall to hear Amelia's worried voice call, 'Is that you, Samantha?'

'Yes, I'm here.'

The landlady appeared up the staircase as Samantha explained, 'There was a woman caught under the bomb blast, but they're getting her out. I took a photograph of it for the magazine.'

The following day Samantha was on her way out when Amelia came up with a letter in her hand. 'Arrived this morning. It's from Australia.'

Sam read it on the bus to Paddington where she was headed to photograph children who were being evacuated to Wales. As she unfolded her mother's letter, another smaller envelope fell out. She recognised Cash's handwriting and ripped it open.

M'lady Princess,

Thought I'd start off that way. Get your attention!

I'm in the Army and I've changed my name. No one knows this but you. I'm posting this in Townsville, last chance to write anything significant – once we're out of the country the censors will read every word.

We're being shipped out sometime soon. Rumour is Dutch New Guinea first, then Malaya or Singapore. They've made an officer out of me.

Just want you to know, wherever you are, that you are often on my mind. I was going to add 'and always in my heart' but I don't want to sound like I miss you that much!

Hope you got without that Lenny creep! Oh boy, Sammy, he wasn't for you.

The cops came to the flat in Sydney just like you warned they would, but I avoided them.

Gosh, Sam, if I ever clap eyes on you again I'll tell you a few things. I'll tell you all sorts of things.

I reckon you should return home to Haverhill, but when did you ever take any notice of me?

Look after yourself, m'lady. I messed things up, I know. That's me!

I sure hope this letter doesn't go down on a torpedoed ship, and that your beautiful blue eyes do in fact get to read it.

Take care of yourself, if not for me, then for the world. It needs you, kid.

Cash

She held the page and looked out of the window where spatters of rain hit the glass. Tears were welling in her eyes and she was furious with herself. She was crying too often lately . . . had to be the damned war! People on the bus were all looking at her.

She decided she must pull herself together. She wiped her eyes with the back of her hand and took a deep breath and stared across at the newspaper the woman opposite was reading. It was the *Daily Herald* and the headlines ran: BUCKINGHAM PALACE BOMBED AGAIN. Sam made herself think about that and how she could get round there this afternoon and take some photographs.

John Baron gazed around the dispersal hut. It was raining outside with low cloud and a strong east wind, so he had taken the opportunity to bring his pilots together for a briefing.

For over two months now the squadron had been in the forefront of the battle in the sky. Biggin Hill, Manston, Lympne, Hawkinge and West Malling were the front-line airfields for the protection of London. There had been days like those between 30 August and 3 September when hordes of Junkers had borne down on the airfield and pounded it every day, destroying the operations room and leaving craters and smashed and burning buildings all over the station. But they had set up a temporary operations room in the local village, found billets for those without quarters and rebuilt the buildings one by one.

Most of the pilots seated in front of him were new but there were old faithfuls like Twig, Henry Garner and Tom Hopkins dotted around the room. The face he was most pleased to see back with them was that of Harry Fairbanks, from South Africa, the squadron's baby. He had bailed out over the channel during the Dunkirk evacuation and had been picked up by a minesweeper and eventually brought back to Dover.

John Baron smiled at him now and briefly studied the other upturned faces. He had come to know some a little better than others. It was always the way – a few stood out: 'Tubby' Manders, a kid of twenty, was over-confident and acted as if he knew it all: Warren Dempster had already shown he was overbearing and belligerent in the two weeks he had been with them, and Gardiner Doyle at twenty-three was an enigma; he remained in his room rather than socialise with the others and he had been out sick a number of the days since he had arrived. Almost half of them were new, and many were hastily trained volunteers from Bomber Command, Army Cooperation Squadrons and Coastal Command. It was the same everywhere, all squadrons were undermanned. John Baron was not going to remind them but the wastage in fighter pilots was running at a hundred and twenty a week.

John Baron greeted his men. 'Good morning. It's a bad day for flying and a good day for a briefing. Some of you are brand new to the squadron and others have been into battle with us a few times. You all know your Flight Commanders, Twig Russell and Henry Garner. Now, these past few weeks we've had very little time to do much else other than fight, sleep and eat . . .'

'Well, I found some time, sir,' the joker of the squadron, twenty-four-year-old Arnie Townsend, called out and the others all laughed.

'No doubt, Townsend,' John Baron grinned. 'Some of you old hands don't need this briefing and much of what I'm about to say, you know, or have found out for yourselves, but let's go through these points once more for everybody, new or old.

'You are now all operational pilots in the truest sense of the word, but I cannot impress upon you often enough that it's the enemy fighter you never see that gets you. When I was hit over France during the Dunkirk evacuation, that was my experience. I didn't see the Heinkel until I was in a dive with a gaping hole in my wing. The point I want to make here is, be swivel-headed from the moment you begin taxiing out and don't stop looking round until you've taxied in.'

'Has anyone ever been hit as they taxied in or out?' queried a new recruit.

John Baron nodded, and glanced to Twig.

Twig stood up and looked around. 'Harvey Harrelson, Number One Squadron, and I, landed at St Pol on the first of May . . . Taxiing in I looked back, and there he was in flames. A Stuka had come out of nowhere and dived on him.'

'Shit,' uttered somebody in the back.

John Baron nodded. 'Quite. So use your mirrors, yes, but look around. And that's why we have a "weaver" the one who's often guarding our rear when we're in formation.

'We all know the value of height, and of trying to come out of the sun, and as a rule it's better to stick together if you can: you can help each other more when a dogfight starts. Now another little tip I've learnt: the distance of the enemy is invariably twice what you think, so don't open fire too soon. We've all done that and used up our ammunition too fast. A three-second burst is sufficient to make a kill, so don't waste your ammo. Oh, and obviously don't open fire until you're certain it's the enemy.'

'Yes,' affirmed Henry Garner, puffing on his pipe. 'I was fired on by a Frenchman outside Amiens one day. Thank goodness he missed and I rolled away so he saw my markings and realised what he'd done. Came up and waved apologetically later but I was in no mood for friendship.'

Ken Clarke, a twenty year old from Coastal Command

in Scotland made a comment. 'Sir, if Jerry's bullets have been getting too close we've been doing the barrel half-roll, then making sure we pull back on the stick when we're on our side . . .'

'Yes, that's it – straight out of the manual. And then rudder into a steep dive with aileron turns.'

The group murmured agreement.

'As I said, you should all have been aware of this before you joined the squadron: this is a reminder class. One thing I noticed yesterday and I'll mention no names . . . When we were in that dogfight with the 109s over the Thames estuary, somebody was shouting incoherently. Now I know it's hard to remain rational and calm, but you must maintain silence unless you have something important to say. Remember, when you spot the enemy: one, say who you are; two, speak slowly; three, report all hostile aircraft, not just those nearest; and four, always use the hours of the clock system, with you as the focal point and give height above or below you.'

Harry Fairbanks shook his fair curls and raising his hand for attention said, 'When I was hit and bailed out over the Channel I learnt something that might be of importance some time. I was in a spin and I was feeling faint so I turned the oxygen full on and that revived me enough to bail out.'

'Good point,' John Baron agreed.

'And I remembered what the Wingco had always pumped into us; to get out on the inside of the spin, so I did that but I'd dropped the ripcord and I did panic a little when I knew I was outside and falling. I was praying a lot at the time and when I looked down I couldn't see it, then I remembered what Alan Deere, the high-scoring New Zealand pilot with Fifty-four Squadron, told me. *"If you need to find your ripcord pass your right hand down the centre of your chest till you come to the quick-release knob then move it left along the wide strap. You'll find it."* And I did. So that's a tip for you fellows.'

'Well said, Harry baby!' And the squadron gave him a round of applause.

John Baron nodded. 'And one thing you might not quite realise, you fall at approximately one hundred and twenty feet a second, which is much slower than you fall inside the diving aircraft, so you've usually got plenty of time to pull the cord.' He rested on the table behind him. 'Any questions?'

One of the converts from Bomber Command, a twenty-two-year-old called Miles Sweetzer had one. 'What's your opinion of taking up larger formations, sir?'

'Well, I for one would like larger formations in the air. Too often these days we're meeting fifty, sixty, seventy of the enemy, especially on mega-bombing raids. But some people argue—'

At that moment the telephone rang. It was Operations. 'We're plotting a couple of suspicious aircraft coming in directly towards you, from the east about ten miles out at the moment. Can you get a section up?'

John Baron looked dubious. 'I can't send my boys up in weather like this. The cloud's pretty low over here. It's too risky.'

'Are you sure?'

He took a deep breath. 'I'll go.' He dropped the receiver and headed to the door. 'I'm going up. Looks like a few of the enemy are headed our way.'

The squadron moved as a body towards him. 'Not without us,' Tom Hopkins said.

John Baron put up his hand. 'I'm not sending any of you up in this weather, it's closing in. It's too bloody dangerous.'

'Then why are you going?'

'Because I'm in charge.' He grabbed the door handle, but not before he noticed that Gardiner Doyle had remained standing at the back of the room and had not moved forward with the others.

Twig came to the door. 'Be sensible. Take me and Henry; we're old hands at instrument flying, you know that. Come on, JB.'

'I'll go alone.'

Twig's voice became very sober. 'I wouldn't like to have to disobey you, Squadron Leader.'

John Baron relented. 'All right. But no one else move – that's an order.'

The three ran to their Spitfires in the rain.

The squadron had been equipped with the new aircraft in July. John Baron had loved the Hurricane but he was a Spitfire convert, had been ever since his first flight in one a year earlier after he had won the lottery in the mess.

It was virtually an instrument take-off and within seconds they were in cloud. He called over the radio to Twig and Henry but the static was terrible.

He experienced that feeling which always came to him in prolonged cloud, as if the world were not real and only the vapour world existed. At 4,000 feet they shook free of the clinging milky mist into the open free blue sky. 'That's better,' crackled Twig's comforting voice in his ear.

Then suddenly his radio went dead: water must have leaked into it. 'Koala to Panther, can you hear me?'

Twig did not reply.

'Koala to Kiwi. Do you read me?'

Henry did not reply.

They continued their climb up into the encompassing blue, looking around for the enemy aircraft. Levelling out at 24,000 feet they still saw nothing. He looked round at Twig and Henry and they both waved.

Then he saw the black dots straight ahead and below. Christ! There must be fifty or sixty! Ops had said two!

As they came closer he could distinguish that many of them had two engines and a wide wingspan: Messerschmitt 110s! Stacked to about 23,000 feet above bombers, Dornier 17s, at about 16,000 feet. A feeling of dismay overcame him. They were obviously headed for a daylight bombing raid on London. This was a completely different formation to the couple that Ops had tracked, and without the radio he could not tell them.

He waved again to his companions who signalled that they too had seen the enemy.

All the three Spitfires could do was climb into the sun again and come down to pick off an aircraft at the edge of the formation. John Baron did exactly that, swooping down upon them out of the sun at 360 m.p.h.

He latched onto a 110 and fired, veered behind it and fired again; a flash burst behind the escort fighter's starboard engine and flame and black smoke spewed out. Out of nowhere he was almost colliding with another one and he broke off and found himself in the centre of a bewilderment of Messerschmitts to right and left, blurs and flashes and broken formations. He instinctively ducked as one ripped across above him very close, cannons blazing. Immediately there was another one in his sights, close; 300 yards away. He hit the firing button and spun his head around. There was one behind him, and he rolled away in textbook style.

Then he saw Henry with two 110s on his tail and he called into the radio, 'Kiwi, get out! There are too many!' And suddenly his radio was crackling into life; Henry had heard him.

'Roger, Koala.'

'Twig, where are you?'

'I can see you. I'm below and behind. Just hit a bastard. He's on fire. Oh boy! Look! Two o'clock.'

Hurricanes! A squadron of them! Charging in like the cavalry in a bad Western movie.

'You beauty!'

Down to John Baron's right was the 110 Twig had hit, diving to the clouds dragging an orange sheet of flame. A man jumped out – too soon! The parachute was instantly ablaze, the body fell like a stone . . .

As they flew home, the cloud over Biggin Hill was dispersing and just before they landed Twig made a victory roll!

But that evening the weather really closed in thick and glutinous, and as John Baron told his boys to relax, for there would be no sorties tonight, he noticed Gardiner Doyle slip out of the door and run into the rain towards the living quarters.

At 1800 he asked for Doyle to come and see him and duly Doyle arrived. John Baron pointed to a seat and the pilot sat.

'You seem to be pretty much of a loner, Doyle.'

The young man looked uncomfortable. 'I like my own company, sir.'

'Yes, so I've noticed. You've had a few days out sick since you arrived at the Bump.'

Doyle moved in his chair and folded his arms. 'I get bad headaches.'

'And what do you attribute them to?'

'Don't know, sir.'

'Look, son.' John Baron was only six years older than the man in front of him but he felt ancient by comparison. 'This war's not easy for any of us. Combat's a strain, especially the type we have to face. Sometimes talking can be a release. Do you understand me?'

Doyle's face became almost sullen. 'I suppose so, sir.'

'I know there's a lot of chaffing and joking and messing around that goes on, and fellows like Tubby Manders and Warren Dempster can become a bit much, the way they swagger around. Arnie Townsend's jokes mightn't be to everybody's taste either, but if you spend more time with them, you'll find they're all going through the same gamut of emotions that you are. It might be better for you if you socialised just a little more.'

'I'm all right, sir.' The statement was bordering on belligerent.

'I didn't say you weren't Doyle. I'm the leader of this squadron and I have all my boys' interests at heart.'

The young man did not speak.

'Now your headaches might just be your way of showing a certain amount of strain. So go out sometimes. Join the boys at the White Hart. Get to know them. Let your hair down a bit.'

Doyle sat up straighter and dropped his arms to his sides. 'What's the point of getting to know them?'

'What does that mean?'

'Well, what's the point of making friends with fellows who might soon be dead?'

John Baron paused a moment. 'You were with Bomber Command, weren't you?'

'Yes.'

'And you volunteered for Fighter Command?'

'Yes.'

'Then listen, lad. You're here because you chose to be. Now drop that attitude of fellows soon being dead. We're trying to teach all of you ways of staying alive. Take my advice, and get to know your fellow pilots. It can help you feel the team spirit and that can make all the difference when you're up there.' He pointed skywards.

Doyle said nothing.

John Baron stood and smiled and the boy rose and saluted.

'Now I'd like to see you at the White Hart tonight, Doyle.'

The squadron spent the night at the White Hart Hotel in Brasted, often called Biggin Hill's second mess. The ground crew and other station personnel preferred the closer pubs like the Old Jail and the Black Horse, but the pilots made their way to where Kath Preston, the landlady, looked after them with a smile.

She moved along the bar in spotted red and white jacket and set up the beers for them, and most of the squadron, except for Miles Sweetzer who was a teetotaller, drank themselves into a glorious haze.

Gardiner Doyle was there, but he did not look pleased about it and John Baron noticed that while he talked to a few of the boys he spent a lot of the evening outside on his own.

As John Baron stood under the low wooden beams leaning on the bar with Tommy Hopkins they could hear the group behind them laughing wildly. This was the release of the tension and taut nerves living inside every fighter pilot: one hour down on the ground in a normal situation, the next hour up in the sky with death hovering just beyond his wingtips.

Arnie Townsend's voice came loudly over the top of the others: 'And like the day Sweetzer yells into the R/T, "Quick! Three o'clock below! Thousands of them! Oh Lord, bloody thousands," and the voice of Blue Leader comes back cool and controlled, "You donkey, they're barrage balloons!"'

This brought foot stamping and peals of laughter and Sweetzer put his face further into his lemonade.

Twig extricated himself from the babel and mirth and came over, put his arm around John Baron's shoulder and in his pleasing Southern drawl, confided, 'I've decided to do it.'

'Do what?'

'Marry her.'

'Jane?'

'Of course. We talked about it on the telephone this evening. And we reckon that none of us knows what the hell's going to happen, so we might as well be together now.'

John Baron who was tantamount to tipsy wobbled slightly as he thumped his friend on the back. 'Great stuff! When?'

'Soon as possible. Engagement party's this weekend.'

'Well, I don't know the girl in question,' Tom said, lifting his beer high in the air, 'but she must be crazy!'

Twig pretended affront and turned his back on Tom. 'Alex is the bridesmaid – and you will be the best man, old buddy, won't you?'

'Delighted.'

Twig edged in confidentially. 'There are a couple of guys from Ninety-two Squadron who've invited us back to Southwood – they've got a jazz band and everything over there. I reckon we should all wander round and celebrate. Those boys stay up till dawn. You can come on my motor bike.' He looked round to Tom. 'And *you* can walk.'

Southwood was a large house two miles from the airfield in Buckhurst Road, where most of the pilots of 92 Squadron were billeted.

John Baron shook his head. 'Sorry, old man, my bed's calling.'

The following morning Air Vice Marshal Keith Park was

at Biggin Hill. He had flown down in his Hurricane which was his way of getting around Eleven Group's airfields, and after a tour and a parade of the squadron he took John Baron aside. His kind eyes were serious. 'Whether you admit it or not, Chard, you're tired. You've been in the forefront of battle now close to twelve weeks . . . too long. This has been brought to my attention so I decided to speak to you today. Ideally we're attempting to move battle-weary squadrons to quiet sectors every six weeks. But because most of your boys are just new chums, they'll remain here. You, we're moving out for a bit of rest – and the others who fought with you in Dunkirk.'

'But, sir—'

'Don't protest – it's decided. You're off to a quiet zone in Ten Group for a while, Russell's getting his own squadron with Twelve Group and so are Garner and Hopkins.'

'They deserve it, they're fine officers. But I'd like to formally protest, sir. I don't feel tired.'

'No, perhaps not, but that doesn't mean you aren't.'

Park's face was sombre and John Baron had no option but to accept the Commanding Officer's decision.

'When's the move to take place?'

'Next Tuesday. Group Captain Grice will give you your orders. So say your goodbyes.'

'I'll miss Biggin, sir. Got fond of it in the last three months.'

Park's voice softened slightly. 'Who knows, you might be back.'

'Who's taking over my squadron?'

'Man called Tuck.'

'Do you mean Stanford?'

Bob Stanford Tuck was already making a name for himself. He and Al Deere had been the top scoring aces at Dunkirk.

'No, and not Friar either. Patrick, actually. Good chap who's been out for a bit with a back wound.' Park saluted, indicating the meeting was over.

'Right, sir.' John Baron lifted his hand in reply and walked away towards the dispersal hut.

Keith Park called out before he had gone six paces. 'Oh, by the way.'

John Baron halted and turned.

'We're making you a Wing Commander. For a while you can help train some chaps who are badly in need of flying experience and then come back to action.'

John Baron broke into a smile.

'It doesn't quite finish there either. You, Forrest and Garner have been awarded the DSO.'

John Baron's smile widened. Now he had the Distinguished Service Order to add to his Distinguished Flying Cross.

'So congratulations.' The Commanding Officer saluted again.

'Yes, sir. Right, sir. Thank you.'

'And one other thing.'

John Baron could hardly believe there was more.

'Sir Hugh wants to see you.'

'Sir Hugh' was Air Chief Marshal 'Stuffy' Caswell Dowding, the Commander-in-Chief of Fighter Command, whose headquarters were at Bentley Priory, Stanmore in Middlesex.

'He wants to talk to a few of you fellows who've been in the thick of it about leading up larger formations and what tactics work best in the air. Friday morning at 0900.'

'Absolutely, sir.'

'The meeting will be at the Air Ministry in London. So I'll see you then.'

'Right, sir.' John Baron grinned. 'Is that the lot, sir?'

Park laughed. 'For the present.'

Chapter Thirty-three

Sam moved past the National Emergency Washing Service van and the line of women waiting with their piles of soiled linen: this was one of the dozens of free emergency services now available throughout London for people who had been bombed. It still intrigued Sam the way the British people stood politely in line waiting their turn; there never seemed to be any queue jumpers.

She crossed the road and entered the railway station. This was the second day she had come to Paddington to photograph children leaving for Wales, the whole evacuation covering a six-day period.

There were hundreds of children collected in every corner of the station, all aged between five and fourteen and in family groups of two and three siblings; all with their brown baggage label tags hanging from lapels or tied around their necks or pinned on. The labels gave their names and home addresses, and a section number, known as a party number. Duplicate labels appeared on all luggage.

Sam collected eight children to sit on their suitcases and hold up their ration books with a train engine behind. She had taken a series of shots when the sharp voice of a London Council Marshal, one of dozens there to organise the departure, called, 'What d'you think you're doing?'

Sam turned to her. She had been questioned so many times that she carried her identity card and her press pass in the outer pocket of her jacket. She handed them to the woman. 'I'm an official photographer for *Newsweek* magazine, New York. I have permission to photograph the departing children.'

The woman studied the papers. 'How many pictures will you be taking?'

Sam sighed. It was an absurd question. 'I've no idea but I'll be as fast as possible.' She put her hand out to three of the children who had begun to wander away. 'Please, girls, come back here.'

The woman spoke irritably. 'Well, be quick about it, it's a big enough mess without you in it.'

Sam was challenged twice more by female Marshals before the children were all finally inside the carriages.

She continued to shoot pictures of them at the carriage windows, and as the train began to pull away she stood watching it pick up speed. She had just fitted a bulb into the flash on her Speed Graphic when her head came up to see a little boy leaning out of a carriage window shrieking, 'No, Joyce, no!' Automatically Sam took the shot of the child in terrible distress, the tears rolling down his cheeks. And then the carriage was gone and the train too, only the rear van in sight and fast disappearing.

Sam was positive she had seen the upset little boy before, and as she turned a girl of thirteen or fourteen stood bereft on the platform, all alone and sobbing. She hurried down to her. 'What's wrong, dear? Shouldn't you be on the train?'

The girl lifted her tear-marked face and suddenly Sam recognised her. 'Joyce, it's you, isn't it?' Sam recalled her from the day over three months before, when she had photographed the children and the nun and the pile of sand-bags in the Bermondsey street.

'Wasn't that your little brother leaning out of the train window?'

The girl replied through her sobs. 'Bernie . . . I had to trick him,' and she broke forth into a new flood of tears.

Sam put her arm around Joyce's shoulders and the girl lifted her face to her comforter. 'I said I was going with him, but I can't, see? Mum needs me, I've got to go to work. She needs the money. So I took him here and then when the train was moving, I jumped off.'

'Oh no, how awful for you. Both of you.' Sam hugged the girl to her.

'What's happening here?' It was the voice of the first Marshal who had challenged Sam earlier.

'Nothing,' Sam replied.

'Looks like something to me.'

'There's a little boy all alone on that train. His name's Bernie . . . ?' Sam looked down at Joyce to supply the surname.

'George.' She began to cry again.

'Bernard George. His sister's had to leave him on the train alone.'

'And why's that?' the Marshal asked antagonistically.

'Look, can't you see the girl's upset enough! I'm taking her with me. You do your job and make sure there's someone at the other end to take care of little Bernie George. He's all alone, for God's sake.'

The Marshal took a note of the name on her pad and Sam, with camera and bag over her left shoulder and her right arm round Joyce ushered the girl along. They went to a Lyon's café and after a cup of tea and a scone the teenager was more composed.

'Now don't you worry,' Sam spoke confidently. 'That woman back there was a bit cranky but I'd say she does her job pretty well and she'll make sure there's somebody proper to meet your little brother. There were a number of schoolteachers on the train too, so you can be certain Bernie will be all right.'

Joyce lifted grateful brown eyes to her new friend. 'You're a nice lady.'

'And you're a nice young woman to be staying here in London and helping your mother. That's a wonderful thing to do.' Sam delivered Joyce to the bus stop and the girl went off, in a calmer, happier state.

Back in South Audley Street, Sam passed by the bombed-out chemist shop with the sign:

WARNING!
No Looting
The penalty for Looting Can Be Death
Anyone found on these premises unofficially
Will be taken in charge

These signs were all over London now: strict measures for difficult times.

When she climbed the stairs there were two messages waiting. One was from Andrew confirming that he would see her on Saturday night, and the other was from Victor Bradbury, who had left his Fleet Street number for her to call.

She did.

'Hello, Samantha. I'm wondering if you'd be interested in meeting me and a few friends tonight? We're off to the French Canteen in the Astors' House in St James' Square. Thought you might like to come along. Lots of French soldiers. Don't know if that appeals to you or not.'

Sam smiled down the telephone line. 'Appeals to me? It does. I have an uncle who taught me French. His mother was from Champagne. Count me in.'

'Good. We'll meet you there at six thirty.'

That evening as she walked towards the house the music could be heard down on the street corner. Victor was waiting outside for her and they went in together. There were various servicemen present, mostly soldiers and airmen, and she had a pleasant time conversing in French and drinking beer which seemed to be in plentiful supply. When the usual bombing raid began at dusk, she was talking to a lady called Frances White; a woman with an English father and a French mother who had been handing out the beers.

'Perhaps we should go down to the shelter,' Frances said as people moved by, making for the stairs.

'I'll take my chances above ground,' Sam replied.

'*Vous êtes une femme courageuse.*'

'*C'est a voir,*' Sam replied, smiling. 'Truth is, I'm simply claustrophobic.'

Frances gave her a penetrating look and then disappeared. Sam assumed she had taken her own advice and gone to the shelter.

At eleven o'clock Victor found Sam dancing with a French Foreign Legionnaire. The sound of the bombs crept

506

closer and the room was becoming less crowded. People were drifting away to the shelters.

'We've decided to stay the night, Samantha. It's going to be impossible to get home. The explosions are all over London. There are beds downstairs.'

Sam nodded. 'All right. I'll stay too.'

Even though the bombs landed as close as 100 yards away, the Astors' house survived another night unscathed. Sam went to sleep on a makeshift bed in the hall at about one-thirty and at six o'clock the all-clear sirens sounded and breakfast was served.

Frances White brought Sam a cup of hot sweet tea. 'Everybody stayed last night.'

'So I see,' Sam replied, gazing round. They breakfasted on toast and jam and at eight o'clock she, Victor and the others took their leave.

'Come and see us anytime,' Frances said to Sam. 'You don't have to be accompanied; there are lots of nice men here.'

Sam laughed. 'Thanks, I will.'

An hour after Sam departed from the French Canteen, Twig and the boys of the squadron hurtled out of their deckchairs where they waited and scrambled to their Spitfires. They headed up into a clear sky to intercept Luftwaffe formations the radar had picked up apparently heading to Lympne, Eastchurch and Detling airfields. They met Junkers 87s and 88s.

While the squadron was away Biggin Hill itself received a surprise attack and some of the boys from 32 Squadron managed to get up in the air to meet the enemy. It was not a heavy raid and John Baron, who had spent the morning in his office, suspected it was a few renegades from the attacks on the other airfields who found themselves over Biggin and thought why not? As he ran across to an air-raid shelter with his notes for the coming Air Ministry meeting under his arm and machine-gun bullets of a Ju87B spitting through the grass nearby, he was grateful that his Spitfires were elsewhere and not on the ground to be damaged.

Close to an hour later his own men returned. A few craters dotted the aerodrome and part of the field had been blasted, but there was enough for the boys to land upon, and while they would have to manage for a time without a dispersal hut, the damage was not too devastating, not like some of the previous raids when the airfield had been closed for repair days at a time.

As the squadron landed, John Baron was inspecting the damage out near the landing strip. He saw Twig's aircraft, first to land, and he walked over to meet him. Others were taxiing in and a number of pilots were already on the ground as a line of erks crossed the field. Twig strode towards him and as he removed his helmet and drew closer John Baron could see the worried look on his face.

'Shit! We lost Tubby Manders and Ken Clarke. I can't believe it – saw them both go down. And Tommy Hopkins limped into Detling with a damaged wing.'

'Oh no.' Glancing over Twig's shoulder John Baron noticed two men rolling on the ground. 'What's going on over there?'

'Don't know.' The two friends hurried across the field to the pilots on the grass grappling with each other. As they neared, others of the squadron arrived.

'What the hell's going on here?'

'Don't know, sir,' Arnie Townsend answered, looking round.

'No idea,' Harry Fairbanks declared. 'As I jumped out of the cockpit I saw Dempster throw a punch at Doyle.'

Henry Garner arrived at the same moment, and as none of the younger pilots moved to stop the fight John Baron, Twig and Henry pulled the protagonists apart.

'You bloody coward!' Dempster shouted.

Doyle's lip was split and bleeding and blood ran from his nose.

'All right. Let's hear about it,' John Baron ordered.

Doyle looked sullenly down at his feet and Dempster nursed his right arm. 'Christ, sir,' Dempster declared, 'Clarke wouldn't have bought it if this bastard hadn't disappeared. We were diving at three Junkers – Clarke, me and him,' he pointed at Doyle, 'and suddenly this bugger's gone, wheeled away from the fight into cloud and we don't see hide nor hair of him until we're back here.'

'Did anyone else see any of this?'

Nobody answered directly but there was a discontented rumble and their expressions said a lot.

Twig lifted his thumb in the direction of dispersals. 'Off you all go. Move!' And John Baron addressed Doyle and Dempster. 'I'll see you two in my office at nineteen hundred.'

JB frowned at Twig and Henry, who remained. 'I've been concerned about Doyle. I had a talk to him on Monday evening.'

Henry gave a thoughtful grunt. 'I'm aware he keeps a lot to himself.' He glanced at Twig. 'You're his Flight Commander – does he get windy in a dogfight?'

Twig shrugged. 'Well, he's not the first one diving in there, that's for sure. But accusing the guy of cowardice? Dempster's a bit of a bully, you know. He could have made a mistake.'

'Yes, I know that,' John Baron agreed.

But when he interviewed both of the young men later, it was hard to judge what had really occurred. He saw them separately; then together. Both told their stories. Doyle was edgy and nervous and perspiring. Dempster was aggressive and insisted that Clarke 'bought it' because Doyle had not backed him up. 'We'd agreed to take one of the enemy each. And suddenly he's not there.'

John Baron grounded the two young men. 'You two don't fly until I've spoken to you again. I'm at the Air Ministry on Friday and I'll see you both on my return.'

The next afternoon John Baron's telephone rang. It was the Duty Sergeant. 'Someone's just taken off, sir. I didn't know of any patrols right now and there's been no call from Ops. Aircraft doesn't belong to Ninety-two or Seventy-two, so he must be one of yours.'

It was not long before John Baron found out that the missing Spitfire had been taken up by Gardiner Doyle. They never saw him again. It was believed he ditched in the English Channel.

In his room he had left a note. It read: *I'm not like the rest of you. I just can't do this. I'm scared.*

John Baron felt guilty. Was there more he could have done? Should he have read the signs earlier? Why did he not recognise that the boy needed help?

'Hell, JB,' Twig remonstrated with him, his Deep South accent suddenly very noticeable, 'we're all scared at times. There's a bloody war on. He had no monopoly on fear. We really don't have time to psychoanalyse every blasted kid we meet.'

'Thanks, mate. I know you're trying to make me feel better.'

'Feel better, hell! If there's any blame then we're all in it. I was his Flight Commander and Scott Day didn't notice anything either.'

Scott Day was the Squadron Adjutant, who was counsellor, confidant and friend to the young pilots.

'So, *sir*,' Twig asserted, 'you can ease up on the guilt business.'

John Baron slapped his friend's shoulder affectionately and walked away. But he requested that his new posting be delayed.

'I'd like to stay with my boys a little longer. This is not a good time for me to leave.'

His request was denied.

As the Station Commander Dick Grice put it to him. 'You're tired, and you're being sent to a well-earned rest. Just take it. Pilots are dying all the time.' He looked at a list in front of him and ran his fingernail down it as he spoke. 'This week alone we've lost John Bryson, Edward Males, Paul Davies-Cook, Dennis Holland, Trevor Oldfield, David Ayers, Howard Hill, Peter Eyles, John Paterson and your two boys yesterday. And now this Doyle fellow commits suicide. I don't want to sound unfeeling, JB, but you've got to get this into proportion. The others died heroes, we can't waste too much time and emotion on a poor kid who just lost his nerve.'

'But he had nerve enough to ditch into the Channel.'

'Yes,' the Station Commander nodded soberly. 'And took a very expensive aircraft with him.'

The following day John Baron presented himself at the Air Ministry building in King Charles Street near Downing Street at 0850 and found Douglas Bader there too.

Since June Douglas had been the Commander of the Canadian 242 Squadron and had brought them from an unhappy rabble, tired and demoralised after Dunkirk, to one of the premier squadrons in the Force. His men loved him, but there were those who resented him for his brusque, sometimes arrogant approach. Yet no one could deny his skills and competence, and he had already led (by British standards) some large wings into the air; no doubt that was why he was here.

Douglas flicked his forefinger at his friend's ribbons. 'Impressive!'

John Baron pointed. 'Where are yours?'

'Only just heard I've received this one.' He touched JB's DSO ribbon. 'Thelma will be sewing it on for me this weekend.'

'Lucky devil. Cresney attached mine – could fall off any minute.' Tim Cresney was John Baron's batman. 'Anyway, congratulations.'

Bader sat down. 'They had me here on my own a couple of weeks ago.'

'Heck, Douglas, they must have decided yours wasn't the only point of view in Fighter Command.'

Douglas rose to the bait. 'Now you listen here, JB. The way we handled big formations at Duxford should prove that putting up equal numbers against the enemy works, instead of just bloody twelve or so against a hundred.'

John Baron lifted his palm. 'You don't have to convince me.'

The door opened and Air Vice Marshal Keith Park entered with another fighter pilot in tow. They recognised Robert Roland Stanford Tuck, the Commander of 257 Squadron at Debden in Essex and the leading British fighter pilot during Dunkirk with ten certainties and a probable. He wore the ribbon of the DFC. An elegant young man of twenty-four, his uniform looked as if it had been pressed a minute before and his pencil moustache was trimmed in a neat line. Bader and Tuck had met before; Bader grunted at him and Tuck nodded.

Keith Park smiled. 'Come on boys, there's a lot of brass here, as you chaps say, and we've been talking tactics on and off since breakfast. It's time they had your thoughts.' The three fighter pilots followed him into a carpeted room with a long cedar conference table. John Baron had never seen so many Air Chief Marshals, Air Vice Marshals and Chiefs of Staff in one place – all the big brass of Fighter Command: Hugh Dowding, Sholto Douglas, John Slessor, Christopher Brand, Philip Joubert de la Ferte, Trafford Leigh-Mallory and Keith Park as well.

Dowding glanced to the empty chair at the head of the table. 'We're expecting Sir Charles back at any moment. Please all take a seat.' His pale eyes viewed the newcomers.

A lady in a black uniform was serving tea and then the door opened again to the Chief of the Air Staff, Sir Charles Portal.

'Good morning,' he said to all present and they sat down.

'We've been discussing fighter tactics so we thought we should talk to some Squadron Leaders. We heard from you a couple of weeks ago, Bader, so just reiterate briefly what you said then.'

Douglas stood.

'You can sit if you like.'

He shook his head. 'I'll stand.' Bader cleared his throat. 'As I said previously, we've been re-learning what you all found out in the last war – that height controls the fight, that coming out of the sun is paramount, that you knock the enemy out if you wait till you get close to fire, and that the economy of the battle is to put up large formations against large enemy formations.

'We know we'll have more of a chance with a hundred of our fellows against a hundred of theirs, it's just common sense. And in today's war it's the man in the air who knows

512

what's going on, not the controller on the ground. The fighter pilot knows where the sun is. I think I said last time that the sun should be plotted on the operations board; well, I still feel that way. The man in the air should be the one to decide how, when and where to meet the enemy. However my main thrust, gentlemen, is my belief in the large wing formations.'*

Portal nodded and waved his finger at John Baron and Stanford Tuck. 'Do you two agree? Let's hear from you, Chard. Forty-four Squadron, isn't it?'

'Until next Tuesday, yes sir.'

'So?'

John Baron stood. 'Well, there's no doubt at all about what Squadron Leader Bader says regarding height, the sun, and going in close to the enemy to fire. They're good standard rules that we teach all our recruits. And I tend to agree with him about larger formations. I personally believe that large wings should be taking off and gaining height when the enemy is building up over France, giving us time to advance in a mass attack as they come across our coast.

'Having said that, I am not referring to the forward stations in Eleven Group; we wouldn't have time to get up in the air to do this. We're in the front line and the enemy are over us almost as soon as the radar picks them up. I think we work better in smaller groups because we are fighting more of a defensive battle. For a start, if we sent up large numbers from any of the forward stations, we'd be seen for miles and would probably be attacked while we were still climbing. But Twelve and Ten Group can definitely take up large wings, and certain stations in Eleven Group that aren't frontline. Being further afield they have the time to be up in the air prepared and waiting.' He looked at Keith Park who smiled encouragingly at him. 'The enemy are bombing Bristol, Liverpool, Hull, Coventry – all over Britain now, so I'm all for larger formations when there's time for them to meet the coming attack. Squadron Leader Bader also makes a good point about decision-making in

* see Large wing formations: *Endnotes*, page 812.

the air. Obviously the radar picking the enemy up in the first place and giving us their position is a wonderful bonus for us, but to actually find the enemy we do often have to search around a bit and go higher or lower than Operations initially direct us.'

'And what about you, Squadron Leader Tuck?'

The debonair Tuck rose as John Baron sat.

'There's a lot to be said for what we've just heard. But tactics will always continue to be a matter of opinion and discussion will inevitably go on. What the previous Squadron Leaders have said is true. But as Squadron Leader Chard presented, often the size of the fighting group is conditioned by the amount of time you have to intercept the bombers, in which case smaller formations are much better. As for the fighter pilot deciding where and when he should attack, we know he often does. But the controller has the radar information. He must make many of the decisions based on facts of which the man in the air is totally unaware.'

'But that's defensive,' Bader spoke up. 'If you're up there, you're the best judge of what's what!'

'Did I interrupt you?' Tuck asked, looking round.

Bader coloured slightly but shot back. 'I advocate "offence" as the best "defence" for Britain; that's what I'm saying.'

'Thank you Squadron Leader Bader,' Dowding declared, 'Go on Tuck.'

'In my opinion, sir, Eleven Group can't have big wings. If you're further back, then probably. I'm told that down at Manston which is the furthest forward airfield, to get height one often has to fly inland first and then turn back to the enemy. That's very time-consuming and every minute counts.'

There was a lot more discussion and the brass seemed divided about the large wings. Later, when the three visitors were ushered out into the hall Douglas was still pursuing his point of view and when they found themselves on the street, his zeal had not abated.

John Baron remained composed. 'We know you're

enthusiastic, Douglas, but what matters is what those blokes back there think.'

'I know that, you clot, and I'm not advocating big wings from Kent or Surrey, but we'll have to continue to fight for what's right.'

'Right being in *your* opinion,' Stanford Tuck said quietly before he walked away.

Douglas exhaled loudly. 'Oh hell.'

John Baron grinned. 'Does you good to have some opposition.'

'But what I'm saying is just common bloody sense.'

As Douglas went on John Baron looked up and caught the warmth of the sun on his face. 'Now to alter the subject. Are you coming to the engagement party?'

As he took in what his companion had said, Bader's warlike blue eyes blinked in the sunlight. 'Engagement party? Oh yes, Jane and Twig. Jane telephoned Thelma. Not sure how in hell we'll get there, but wouldn't miss it.'

Chapter Thirty-four

Harriet strolled down the stairs at Castlemere. She caught sight of her image in the long mirror on the landing and gave a gratified smile. A string of pearls glistened upon her throat and she was certain that her velvet cobalt-blue gown would be the envy of all the other women in attendance. She had bought it in Paris before the war; it was fitted at the waist and dropped in a moulded flair to the floor. She knew that some might say the pearl and diamond ring on her left hand was ostentatious, but any such statement would be motivated by deep-seated envy and she lifted her hand to see its reflection in the mirror. Her skin was still smooth and unlined; she used creams on it every day of her life and she did facial exercises which an old gypsy woman in the New Forest had shown her twenty-eight years previously. As she eyed the mirror she thought she must be experiencing what the Old Masters must have felt when they looked at a work of ideal proportions. There was such satisfaction in perfection!

She glided into the drawing room to where her husband Edward sat nursing a gin.

He looked up admiringly. ''Evening, darling. My my, you do look a treat.'

Treat was not a word Harriet would have used to describe herself. 'Yes, thank you,' she replied as she swirled by Lillian Cardrew who appeared from the kitchen.

'Oh Harriet,' her sister-in-law said, halting to adjust her spectacles and look at her. 'You look wonderful. What a beautiful gown.'

Harriet fitted a cigarette into her slim black holder. 'Yes, it's Parisian.' And she meandered out onto the terrace.

The engagement party was taking place in Sandwich at

the home of the Levinsons, friends of the Cardrews. With petrol rationing and calls for people not to use private transport, it was easier to travel to Sandwich by rail, and it was a short walk by the Roman ruins to the Levinsons'.

The only ones needing private transport were those at Castlemere and Nicholas had saved enough petrol for the round trip to the village.

Harriet had heard her brother say that he had only one dozen bottles of Pol Roger champagne left but that he would use six tonight and save the others for the wedding.

She eased herself down into a chair, lit her cigarette and sat watching a rabbit edge out of the high grass onto the lawn. His nose twitched as his head gyrated from side to side. It was soothing watching the little creature and as she drew on her cigarette a scornful smile was inching its way across her mouth.

Tonight she was to meet the grown-up John Baron Chard! At last. To meet the devil who existed because of that French harlot and her whoring. All that her first husband had left had been spirited from her, his lawful wife – all seized by the Chards; by Benjamin and his meek mealy-mouthed little Constance.

How she hated them all and how deeply she hated this man who had grown from the half-French brat. She recalled the day over twenty years ago on the clifftop in Yorkshire. Pity the little demon hadn't fallen into the ocean. She leant back in her chair and drew on her cigarette.

Suddenly Mrs Blake appeared at her elbow. The woman had been at the Levinsons' all day helping to organise the food and drink for the party. She was flushed from the pace of the evening's preparations and as she spoke she wiped her hands on her apron. 'Mrs Barrington, Mrs Cardrew has asked if you would be kind enough to go down to the cellar for a bottle of brandy. Apparently the one she has is only half-full and she'd like to take another to the Levinsons' – that is, if there's one left.'

An expression of astonishment covered Harriet's face. 'In this gown? Has she lost her senses? Tell her not to be ridiculous.'

'Mrs Barrington, I'd go myself but I'm up to my ears in—'

Harriet stood and walked away.

Mrs Blake sighed and departed. She had expected the rebuttal. 'Don't know why I bothered to ask the so-and-so; I knew I'd end up going meself.'

As Harriet stormed down the stone steps to the croquet lawn her brother came out from the drawing room. 'I'm driving the first group into Sandwich now. Edward's going down to the car, are you coming?'

Harriet turned to him. 'Are you certain? I'm not going to come in to stand and wait for other people.'

'I'm absolutely sure,' her brother confirmed and she came back up the steps and took his arm.

The car driven by Nicholas, containing Harriet, Edward, Lillian Cardrew and her middle daughter Kate left the front of the house as Alex came into Jane's room, her face aglow with excitement. 'Oh Jane, it's so romantic! Engaged now, and married in a fortnight. I'm so happy for you.'

Her elder sister looked up from her seat at the dressing-table. 'Thanks, darling. Do up my top buttons, would you?'

Alex moved behind her sister and began buttoning her dress. 'Jane?'

'Yes, darling?'

'I've been meaning to ask you something now, for a while.'

'What is it?'

Alex took a deep breath. 'Have you? I mean, have you and Twig . . . Well, you know.'

Jane eyed her sister in the mirror. 'Are you asking if we've done it?'

'Well yes, I suppose I am.'

Jane frowned. 'For heaven's sake, that's personal.'

'Oh darling, I know, and don't answer me if I'm being too rude. It's just that I wanted to know.'

'Why?'

'Well, I mean you love him and everything. You're going to marry him. I just wondered if you'd done it yet, that's all.'

Jane put down her comb and turned to face her sister. 'No, we haven't. Twig's wanted to often, but I won't. If he loves me he can wait, that's what I told him.' A smile broached her mouth and her voice dropped confidingly. 'But do you know what?' She took up her sister's hands and stood up with her.

'No – what?'

'When he gets all hot and bothered, I let him feel my breasts. And a few times I've let him touch between my legs.' Then her voice became pontifical. 'But as for going all the way – no! A man doesn't respect a girl if she does that.'

Alex dropped her sister's hands. 'Yes, right, darling. Well, thanks for telling me. Now come along, you look beautiful. We should go down and wait for Daddy to come back.'

And as Alex left the bedroom ahead of her sister and walked along to the top of the stairs Jane touched her shoulder and she looked back.

There was a sly expression in Jane's round eyes. 'You haven't gone all the way with JB, have you?'

Alex was always honest; it was just the way she was. It was not a conscious thing, she just did not deal in duplicity. 'Yes.'

'Oh, you damn silly girl. Now you'll never get him.'

Alex sighed and looked down the stairs to where Mrs Blake waited, brandy bottle in hand, and as she descended she answered, 'What's done is done. And I love him no matter what.'

By half past eight everyone was at the Levinsons'. Twig, JB and the boys of the squadron had finally arrived a few minutes before, after a long wait at Canterbury Station for a connection.

The gramophone was playing and guests danced and drank. Patricia and Carolyn Blackburn were there and so was Meryl, red nails sweeping through the air to make her point as usual. In fact there were a lot of people John Baron recalled from Alex's twenty-first birthday party, though there was no sign of Trevor Braithwaite, her former boyfriend. The men of the squadron made themselves at home and Douglas puffed on his pipe in a corner of the room, propounding his big wing theory to Tommy Hopkins and Arnie Townsend, avid listeners.

At dusk they heard aircraft in the sky and the eyes of every pilot lifted to the ceiling

Lillian Cardrew looked around frowning. 'In this part of the coast, we hear them almost every night and day. We've had five aeroplanes come down in the fields not a mile away, two ours and three theirs.'

Kate Cardrew shivered. 'And when they bomb Manston Airfield it sounds like it's across the road.'

Alex was dancing with John Baron as the noise of the aircraft echoed along the river. She wore the bracelet he had given her for her twenty-second birthday and she admired it on her wrist now as she spoke. 'I suppose we're safer here than many places.'

'Yes. The large cities are the worst.'

'Does that matter to you? That I'm safer here?'

'Now, Alex, what on earth does that mean?'

A sheepish expression crossed her face. 'Oh, I don't know, I'm just a bit strange tonight. Forget I said it.'

John Baron stopped dancing but continued to hold her in his arms. He looked her squarely in the eyes. 'Alex, you know that your safety would always be important to me, so let's not play silly games with one another.'

'I'm sorry, JB. You're right.'

Suddenly somebody put 'Run Rabbit Run' on the gramophone for the fourth time and as usual the boys of the squadron began to sing, their voices lifting enthusiastically. Soon everybody was singing and laughing and as 'Run Adolf' resounded round the room John Baron left Alex to get a beer.

He was served by Nicholas Cardrew and as he walked across to talk to Douglas and Thelma, a gloved hand clasped his arm. He looked round into the dark fathomless eyes of Alex's aunt.

'Oh, Mrs Barrington. Enjoying the party?'

Harriet examined him and he realised it, though he had no idea why.

In fact, Harriet had been studying him the entire evening. Studying him and detesting him. He should never have been born. And if he were to be born then he should have been hers, not that French witch's; it was all her fault, taking the only man she had ever loved!

Harriet remained holding John Baron's arm and stared keenly at him. He bore John Baron's name, and God damn it, he was a replica of her first husband, that was the hardest part to bear!

Finally she replied, 'Oh yes, I'm enjoying it *now*. Are you?'

'I am.'

'You're little Alexandra's friend, aren't you?' She slipped her hand through his arm and drew herself into him. 'I'd like to talk to you.'

John Baron knew only what Alex had told him about her aunt: that she was her father's elder sister, had been married three times, was very wealthy and very selfish, and mostly difficult. The only other thing he knew he could tell by just looking at her: she was remarkably youthful-looking for her age. She could have been in her early forties, rather than fifty-nine.

'Let's go outside where it's cool.' She led him across to the door through the blackout curtain and onto the terrace. It was a mild night, the moon rode the clouds and John Baron could not help but look up to the sky.

'Now,' Harriet said, her eyes trained upon him in the gloom, 'tell me: how do you feel about adoption?'

John Baron drew his eyes down from the clouds. 'I beg your pardon?'

'I said how do you feel about adoption? You know, of children.'

'That's what I thought you meant.' John Baron was a little nonplussed by the question; it seemed a very odd way to begin a conversation. 'Well, I've never thought about it at all. I suppose it's good if people want to do it.'

'Do you know anybody who's adopted?'

John Baron gave a rumble of laughter. He could not help it, this was really odd.

'Why are you laughing?'

He looked at her by the light of the moon. She looked composed and in charge of her senses, very elegant and beautifully dressed. But she was obviously quite mad. Alex had said nothing about her mental state.

'Mrs Barrington, I'm laughing because this is a most peculiar conversation.'

'Oh, you think so? Well answer this. What do you think about people losing their rightful inheritance?'

John Baron shook his head in amused amazement. 'I'm sorry for them.'

Harriet took a cigarette from a silver filigreed container and began to fit it into her cigarette-holder. 'And do you have an attitude regarding loose foreign women stealing other people's husbands?'

Now John Baron really was dumbfounded, but very definitely amused. 'I'm afraid I don't. I thought you and I might spend a few minutes in small talk, I didn't expect you to launch forth questioning my attitudes to particular practices in society. But I must admit it's a change.'

And now Harriet laughed, a grating sound. 'Do you love your parents?'

'That's the best one yet,' John Baron chuckled. 'Did you love yours?'

Harriet sniffed and stepped quite close to him. He could smell the sweet aroma of her. 'Now, young man, listen to this. The fact is, I know your—' and at that moment both Alex and Edward came through the blackout curtain together.

Harriet spun around in annoyance. 'What do you want?'

'Harriet dear, you should be inside.'

'Daddy's about to make a speech. Come on, JB.'

A groan of exasperation came from the woman as she followed Edward inside, and John Baron noticed the way she tore the cigarette from the holder and threw it on the ground.

'What's wrong with your aunt?' he asked as Alex led him back into the noise and laughter.

'What do you mean? What did she say?'

'She was asking me the most absurd questions about my thoughts on adoption, inheritance law and adultery.'

Alex shook her head. 'Oh JB, Aunt Harriet's an enigma. There's no explaining her.'

'And she was pretty furious when you interrupted.'

'Oh, that's natural. She likes to be in charge. Though I must say she's been mad keen to meet you. which is really strange for she rarely shows interest in anything but herself. Daddy and Mummy put up with her because she's Daddy's sister, that's all.' She shrugged. 'Jane, Kate and I have known since babies what she's like.'

As Nicholas Cardrew made his speech, John Baron became very aware of Harriet's eyes upon him.

Nicholas hugged his engaged daughter to him as he spoke. 'My wife and I were amazed when Jane said she wanted to get married without delay. At first we were against it, especially to a Yank!' This drew laughter and a round of applause from the RAF boys. 'But when we talked to these two young people and realised that they want to create as much joy for each other as they can, now, when the war makes everything uncertain . . . when we saw how in love they are . . . then we accepted that they're right to grab happiness and we give them our blessing.'

He kissed Jane and Twig said, 'You're one of the few men I'll let do that now, sir.'

The six bottles of champagne were poured and the couple toasted, and Twig replied to his intended father-in-law's speech.

'As you all know, I was born in Florida . . .' catcalls and whistles greeted this.

'I actually left Tampa, my home town, because I thought I was in love with a girl who preferred someone else. I carried that disappointment for a long time until I met an English girl who altered my life. I suddenly knew that what I had felt back in the States was not the real thing at all. I felt entirely differently about this girl. She didn't make me feel blue or rejected, she made me feel wonderful and I knew I'd found somebody that I want to be with for as long as I live, and the miracle is that she feels the same. This is a really swell party and I'd like to thank Mr and Mrs Cardrew and Mr and Mrs Levinson, also Mrs Blake who's been sweating it out helping prepare everything. And Jane and I would like to invite all of you here tonight to our wedding in two weeks' time. It'll be in an RAF chapel; we're not sure which one yet, but you'll all know.' He bent forward and kissed Jane and the guests all applauded.

The night finished with laughter and good spirits and most of the guests a little tipsy except for Douglas and Miles Sweetzer who had imbibed only lemonade.

The RAF boys were sleeping overnight in the downstairs rooms at the Levinsons' and a number of the other guests were staying with the Cardrews.

As John Baron saw Alex to her father's car she asked, 'When will I see you again?'

'Soon. Perhaps you can come north and see me?'

She smiled so widely in the darkness he could see the gleam of her teeth.

Suddenly Harriet was at their side. 'Squadron Leader Chard?'

He turned to her with a droll smile. 'Yes, Mrs Barrington?'

'Could I have a moment with you, *alone*.' The last word was enunciated clearly.

'Oh Aunt Harriet, please, I'm trying to say good night to him.'

'And I want to speak to him!' She drew John Baron a few yards away and spoke in an undertone. 'I must see you again. It's of the utmost importance that I speak with you alone somewhere.'

John Baron scratched his chin. 'To continue our discussion on my opinions of life? Or are you a German spy, Mrs Barrington?'

There was enough light to see that Harriet did not find this amusing. 'Don't be stupid, I'm very serious. I can come up to London any time, or further if need be. I've travelled long distances to see you before.'

John Baron did not know what the hell that meant; this woman was astounding.

He felt the paper she pushed into his palm. 'This is my telephone number in Canterbury. My housekeeper will take a message day or night. It's imperative that I see you again. I have something to tell you which no one else in the world will.'

'JB?' It was Alex behind them. 'We're going now.'

'Infuriating child,' Harriet hissed, and clutching John Baron's arm whispered, 'You *must* see me.' Then she turned away, calling, 'Edward, are you there?'

'Over here, Harriet. I'm at the car.'

'What did Aunt Harriet want?'

'To see me again.'

'Good heavens. Why?'

'Why indeed?' John Baron said, steering her in the darkness to her father's car where Edward held a torch in one hand and the open door for Harriet in the other.

John Baron kissed Alex and she slipped in beside Jane in the front seat.

As the vehicle drove off into the night Twig ranged up beside John Baron whistling 'Way Down South in Dixie'. They stood for a few moments before Twig began wiping Jane's lipstick from his mouth. 'Gosh, I love that girl; she'll make the best wife – and what a great party!'

John Baron grinned. 'Yes, it was, and different from any other party I've ever been to in my entire life.'

The next day John Baron and Twig returned to Biggin Hill just in time to be scrambled.

In the previous week the weather had closed in and the bombers had not appeared as often, but Ops reported a pack of Messerchmitts darting in from the south, apparently heading towards London and the north.

When he led the wing through a misty layer of cloud at 20,000 feet and levelled off at 22,000, John Baron saw an empty sky. He took them back through the thin cloud and sat there with the vapour above their heads so that nothing could surprise them. They kept their eyes peeled for the enemy but saw nothing.

The controller had said they were at 20,000 feet, and

knowing where he would come in from if he were the enemy, he led the wing 40 degrees west and climbed again. He suspected they had probably wheeled west, gained height and were now coming in from there.

John Baron's pulse accelerated; he was getting like Douglas, disregarding the controller and going where he believed the Huns would be. It was catching! His gaze skimmed the horizon line all around, then he heard Tommy Hopkins in his ear, 'Red Leader calling Koala! Bandits at four o'clock below.'

John Baron could see only two black dots, hardly the formation the controller had spoken about. 'Koala to Red Leader, take Ironforce and investigate.'

Ironforce was Miles Sweetzer's call sign. JB observed the two Spitfires peel away and as they did, he suddenly saw a swarm of black dots, like tiny bees. A mass of them. Too many to be British. So the bastards *were* over in this direction. He rammed his throttle forward as his voice blasted stridently in his squadron's earphones. He did not identify himself this time, they knew his voice. 'Enemy aircraft eleven o'clock below!'

The Spitfires shot forward into battle to meet what evolved into two formations of Messerschmitt 109s with makeshift bomb racks fitted under their slim bodies. Must be fifty of the bastards! Anger rumbling inside him John Baron decided to go straight for the middle of the formation!

'Red and Yellow sections line astern, line astern! Follow me. Blue section remain as top cover.'

As he bulleted at them he saw 109s scattering; black crosses filled his vision, wings rolled right and left and the sun sparkled like lightning on passing Perspex! He hit the firing button and charged. Sweeping down beneath a 109, the massive flock divided and splintered. He glimpsed Henry and Arnie Townsend wheeling to the right after a couple of them and suddenly, directly in front of him, were three more. He squirted a stream of machine-gun bullets and almost instantly pieces lifted from the tail of a Messerschmitt and it dived like a seal for the cloud.

His blood was pumping and he perspired – back in the action! Below, another 109 was curling out of a turn and he swept down upon it, giving it a three-second burst of fire. Bits spun off its port engine and flames leapt out, followed by black smoke as it revolved in the air and dropped like lead beneath him. He was raging now and looked around for more. He steep turned and followed a 109 streaking away towards the east. Charging after it he pressed the button again, but it was too far away and scuttling like a demon for home. He looked around and wondered what he had wondered so often before. How could so many aircraft disappear so fast?

He was down at 8,000 feet and he twisted his head around searching for his boys. Through strands of misty cloud below he could see black smoke rising in four places. Funeral pyres to Messerschmitts. he hoped! Then the thought that they could be his own men dampened his spirits.

He saw one lone Spitfire and cruised up alongside it. It was Tommy Hopkins with his patently recognisable paint job, a Saxon axe dripping blood along his fuselage.

Tommy grinned under his oxygen mask and lifted one, no two, no *three*! fingers, indicating what he believed he had destroyed.

John Baron smiled. 'In your dreams.' But gave him the thumbs-up as the controller's voice broke into his ear. 'Weather closing in along the coast and up the Thames estuary. Return to base immediately.'

Back on the ground he watched his boys come in, along with rolling threatening clouds. It was always nerve-wracking waiting to see them arrive home. He counted them. They were all here, all exuberant and all cheering and yelling.

Later he was required to explain why he had disobeyed the radio telephone instructions.

The Station Commander, Dick Grice tapped his pipe on the window-sill of his office while John Baron defended himself.

'I just knew they weren't going where Ops were saying

they were heading. They always try to come out of the sun no matter what time of day it is. I just used my common sense and found them.'

John Baron thought of Bader putting the very point to the brass that morning and while Douglas was often pugnacious about it and probably disobeyed simply to prove his point, that had not been John Baron's reason. Today he had simply been aware of where the enemy would come from; he had really believed it and it had turned out to be so.

'Look, sir, getting up-sun before the enemy is the main thing. Squadron Leader Bader was propounding this very point at the Air Ministry.'

'And you've proved him right this afternoon?'

John Baron grinned. 'Looks like it.'

Between 1700 and 1900 it rained heavily, but after that the cloud dispersed and there was a moon at 2130 in a mostly cloud-free sky when the telephone rang in the officers' mess.

'How many of you can night-fly over there?'

'Four of us, but there are only three of us here in the mess.'

'Can you get up now? The Huns are going for Brighton.'

'Brighton? What the hell for?'

'We don't know.'

John Baron, Twig and Tommy climbed fast into a clear night sky and headed south. They flew across the whole south coast for an hour and saw nothing. No bombers, no fighters, no searchlights, nothing.

John Baron called over the R/T. 'We've found nothing.'

The controller's voice came back. 'Yes, they disappeared. You can head home.'

'Oh, bloody marvellous,' John Baron retorted. 'Always fun to leave the warm mess and fly around up here like clots. Thanks a lot.'

Ops did not answer.

They swung round and as they came towards the Bump, eyes narrowed peering through the night, they caught sight of the flare-path. 'Good, home's ahead.'

Abruptly Twig's voice burst into his ear. 'Panther to Koala, my engine's coughing, I think I'm running out of petrol. But I can't be! Hell, maybe I've got bullet-holes in my tank! What the devil's wrong?'

'Koala to Panther. Are you all right?'

'It's still coughing. Oh, that's just swell. It's cut out altogether. It's dead.'

John Baron felt a tingle of alarm. Force-landing a fighter in daylight was dangerous but at night was nearly impossible.

'Listen to me: bail out. Don't try landing it. I repeat, *bail out*.'

Twig's Southern drawl magnified. 'And lose the aircraft? Dicky Grice would never forgive me. No, Koala, I'll force-land it.'

'Don't try that,' crackled Tommy's voice. 'Do as Koala says.'

Twig joked in their ears. 'I'm going in on two good wings and a prayer. Don't worry.'

John Baron and Tom held off and watched the dark shape of Twig's Spitfire as his nose dropped and he began to glide down in a series of S turns over the flare-path, then suddenly they couldn't see him at all. They heard him say, 'Cross wind. Shit, I'm losing her . . .' and abruptly his voice cut out.

Down below them there was a single spurt of fire like a plume from a flame-thrower followed by a plethora of sparks bursting upwards as Twig crashed. With their hoods open for descent John Baron and Tommy heard the explosion.

'Jesus Christ.'

Without speed, caught in the sudden cross wind, Twig had flipped over and clipped the roof of the sheds at the edge of the strip. He had ended up over near the hangars.

By the time they landed, the Fire Brigade and an ambulance were at the scene.

When the inferno died down they pulled out Twig's body but it was not recognisable.

John Baron stood there beside what was left of the

smouldering Spitfire. Suddenly the war had become too personal. The tears streamed down his cheeks as Tommy and the Duty Sergeant tried to calm him. He kept repeating, 'For God's sake! For Christ's sake! This wasn't even his war and we didn't need to go up tonight at all!'

At 2300 John Baron forced himself to telephone Jane. She had been asleep wearing her new diamond ring with her left hand resting on the coverlet.

At her mother's call, she drew on her dressing-gown and hurried downstairs. At first she did not comprehend what John Baron was telling her, and when she asked him to repeat it and realisation flooded into her brain, her throat constricted as if it were paralysed.

Silence. She could not speak. All John Baron could hear were her broken-hearted sobs.

'Are you there, Jane? Did you hear me? I'm so very sorry.'

Chapter Thirty-five

January, 1942

Samantha put down the letter and wiped her eyes.

Andy . . . Gone just like that! Dead in the Western Desert. She did not even know where. Damn Rommel and his rabbble! And damn all the bloody Nazis. Another good Australian gone! She picked up the letter again and reread it for the fourth time. It was in a clear oval hand:

Dear Samantha,

I have never met you but I feel like I know you from the way Andy spoke about you. All the time. It was Sam this, and Sam that. I'm the bringer of really sad news and I'm sorry to say Andy was killed on 15th November. I don't know when you'll get this letter, or if you ever will, what with all the sinking of ships going on in the Med, but I'll write this in the hopes it reaches you.

Andy asked me to write to you if ever he copped it. I reckon he thought he was going to marry you. There's no doubt he loved you deeply.

His family in Sydney will be officially notified and if ever you want to write to them, this is their address:

Mr and Mrs Jack O'Rourke, 22 Chelmsford Avenue, Roseville, NSW, Sydney, Australia.

Sorry to have to write this. Andy was a real good bloke, one of the best, and I'll miss him.

With best wishes,
Peter Brownlow (Lieutenant)

PS He had just been commissioned a Captain so you can be really proud.

Sam wiped away another tear. She did not want to be alone tonight. She would go down to Amelia and George in the basement and spend the evening with them. They had turned into true friends and were so good to her, like a surrogate family. Amelia would give her a black-market gin and they would have a laugh. That was what she needed tonight: to laugh like Andrew had always made her do.

She moved across to the sofa where she sat and sank back as she had seen Andy do so many times. She thought of the final night she had ever been with him, last May. He had sat here in this very seat looking up at her.

They had been out earlier for it had been a wonderfully mild night with broken clouds drifting across a three-quarter moon. As usual they had carried torches, for with London in total darkness, the only way of getting about was with a flashlight. This of course was always held down to the feet so that no beam showed to the sky. White lines were painted on kerbsides and down the centres of the street and at the bases of lamp-posts to assist pedestrians and drivers.

In the comfortably mild temperature they had walked home from the Astoria ballroom after going to the theatre in Leicester Square where they had seen *Gone with the Wind*. At the cinema they sat in the expensive seats, one shilling and sixpence each, and Sam thoroughly enjoyed it; in fact, she thought it was perhaps the best film she had ever seen. She had been sad when Rhett walked away from Scarlett at the end, but at least there was the promise that sometime in the future Scarlett would win him back. It was a long movie, and afterwards with the nightly bombs falling on the docklands and the sky divided by the stark cords of light searching the sky, they had caught a bus to the Astoria and danced to Billy Cotton's orchestra.

Andrew had held Sam very close and she could feel his warm breath in her hair. He had seemed unusually quiet all evening long, and when a Sergeant in uniform tripped carrying a drink and Andy made no quip about it, Sam knew there was something really wrong.

She had asked, 'Andrew, what is it? You're so quiet.'

'Nothing, Sam. Just thinking about things, I suppose.'

The last melody before the National Anthem was 'The Very Thought of You' and she felt sad and pictured her brother and Cash, and remembered the past, as Andy guided her across the floor.

All night they had continued to hear explosions in the direction of the docklands but no bombs had fallen in the West End, and as they made their way up the steps to her building Sam had turned towards the violent red flashes in the sky. She remembered the girl Joyce and her mother and she hoped they were all right. 'The poor docklands, there must be nothing left.'

'There were ships in today, that's what the Huns will be after.'

'Coming in for a drink?'

'Yes, I will tonight.'

Inside Andrew had sat on her sofa, eased back and crossed his legs at the ankle. 'Good film.'

'Yes, wasn't it?'

She poured him a beer and sat beside him. He took a mouthful then slipped his arms around her and drew her to him and kissed her for a long time.

'Come on, Andy, what is it?'

He ran his finger down the neck of her blouse to the crease in her breasts, then he bent his head and kissed the spot. 'Now that the big brass believe Hitler won't mount his invasion of Britain for a long time, I'm off to North Africa. Most of the desert wrested from the Italians by General Wavell has been taken back by bloody Rommel. They want us out there.'

Then Sam had understood. 'Ah, so that's why you've been quiet.'

'Yes, I suppose so.' He lifted his sunbrowned hands to the sides of her face and drew her head to his, kissing her lips and lingering upon them. He was sure he was in love with her. When he raised his mouth from hers he gazed into her eyes. He could not read anything there to tell him how she felt. 'So it looks like I'll be spending Christmas in the Western Desert.'

Sam moved out of his arms, stood and poured herself a beer.

Andrew believed she was a single girl. She had never disillusioned him. She took a mouthful of her drink, standing looking down at him. 'When do you go?'

He ran his gaze over her from her abundant hair to her breasts and slender waist, down the blue crêpe-de-Chine pleated skirt to her ankles. She was a damn good-looking woman. 'Soon. I think this'll be the last time I see you . . . for a while.'

She walked over to the wireless and turned it on. Vera Lynn's voice filled the room, suggesting that they would meet again some sunny day.

'Well, that's pretty appropriate,' Andrew asserted, rising and coming to her. He took her in his arms and kissed the side of her neck. 'Sammy, you feel tense. Relax. I'll come back.'

He turned her mouth up to his and covered it with his again. Sam sank into his arms and her body melded along the lines of his. So Andrew was leaving. She would be on her own again.

He was looking down at her with his brown eyes and olive skin; there was something innately Australian about every nuance of Andrew; just being with him made her feel as if she were back in the sun and the heat of the land that had nurtured her. Perhaps that was why she had begun to sleep with him a few months back, or perhaps it was just the war. It did that to you; made you need people. Made you want the arms of a man around you. Made you want to wake up with someone beside you.

And hell, she had decided years ago that if you couldn't be with the one you loved then you might as well love the one you were with. And Andy was such a nice guy.

'Will you wait for me?' His voice was tender in her ear.

Just for a moment she dearly wanted to say that she would, but in the same instant she knew that she could not, and she would not. To saddle a good man like Andrew with the mélange of emotions that made up her feelings would be unconscionable.

But tonight was not the time to tell him; not when he was off to the Western Desert believing that he loved her.

'Andy,' she said, pressing into his chest, 'you're the best thing that's happened to me for ages. But there's a war on. It wouldn't be fair to either of us to promise anything. We've been happy together, but please just leave it that way for now. We can stay in touch, and who knows?' She stood on tiptoes and kissed the lobe of his ear. 'Why are we standing here? Let's go to bed.'

Her fingers laced through Andrew's and they had trailed off to the bedroom.

Sam sighed so deeply it shuddered out of her and she came back to the present and the sofa where Andy would sit no more. She looked down and rubbed the pile on the plush cushion seeing his smile that showed his chipped tooth and hearing his infectious laugh.

The noise of aircraft droned in the distance. Were they coming this way? She rose and turned off the light then crossed to the window and slid aside the blackout curtain to look at the sky. It was a clear cold January night. She gazed in the direction of the docklands and as she did she saw the searchlights flash across the sky and the explosions begin. She shivered. A year ago Hitler had taken to bombing all the other major cities in an effort to terrorise the British public in general.

She worried all the time about her brother. The death of his best friend, Twig, had impressed upon her the constant danger all servicemen lived under. And now with Andrew gone it sharpened her fear.

Presently she met her brother about once a fortnight. She was calmer in his company these days and she tried not to be sad. Oh, she still loved him, but it was subtler now and their hours together were wonderful times of harmony when mostly they talked of home and Haverhill, the family and Cash.

It still bothered Sam that JB saw Alex Cardrew, the girl

who looked so much like herself, but hell, she and JB both had their lives to live. Sam had never been introduced to Alex. JB had never suggested it, and that suited Sam. It was something she preferred to avoid anyway.

She closed the drapes and felt her way along to the light switch and turned it on as 'These Foolish Things (Remind Me of You)', lilted hauntingly from the wireless. She swallowed hard to stifle the memory that sprang to her mind. But the music had its way and Cash's forelock was dancing on his brow and he was taking her in his arms. 'Come, m'lady,' he said as they glided across the dance floor in time to the melody. She was running along Seven Bob Beach in her carefree yesterdays, indifferent to the world's woes, glowing in the hot wind and waving to her crazy husband who lay laughing and watching her on the yellow sand.

'Oh God, I'm such a mess!' she said aloud, walking firmly across and flicking the switch to turn the wireless off. 'Now pull yourself together, Sam, you damn fool.'

She moved deliberately to the table and folded the letter from Peter Brownlow. Beside it was another piece of paper with an address in Westminster upon it. She was to go there tomorrow to see Frances White. Since first meeting her at the French Canteen at the Astors' she had run into her many times at the Free French Forces Club and in a pub in Baker Street where French servicemen gathered. Frances had something important she wished to discuss and Sam had agreed to see her. Sam had mentioned to Frances how she felt she wanted to do more for the war effort, how these days she was frustrated by merely taking photographs of the effects of war, and that was when Frances had suggested they meet up tomorrow. And now the death of Andy had so angered and upset Sam that she was even more convinced of her sentiments.

She took the paper with the address and placed it beside her Speed Graphic camera which she touched lovingly. It had served her well. *Newsweek* had asked her to go to Belfast again. She had been there from August to October last year and Carter Brinkwood wanted her to return for another assignment.

She was pleased she had a date to meet her brother the day after tomorrow though he could not see her until the afternoon. He had said something about first meeting up with a woman called Harriet who had been pestering him on and off for ages. She was some relation of Alex Cardrew . . . an aunt or something.

She turned from her camera and picked up her heavy cardigan to wear downstairs to Amelia and George's.

Before she left the flat she glanced back at the empty sofa. Tonight was for remembering Andrew: a man who had loved her.

Three hours later and seventy miles away at Castlemere, Harriet stood with a glass of Scotch in her hand puffing on her cigarette. Earlier she had listened to the wireless. All sorts of current tunes had been played tonight, including some of her favourites: 'A Nightingale Sang in Berkeley Square', 'When the Swallows Come Back to Capistrano' and 'These Foolish Things'.

She took a mouthful of her drink and looked skywards. An aircraft was coming, and it was dangerously low overhead. She hurried to the blackout curtain and drew it aside in time to see a black shape shoot by only yards above the house. Everything shook and for a few horrible moments she thought it was going to strike the house. She gathered her fashionable warm stole around her and passed out through the French doors onto the terrace in time to hear the nauseating sound of its collision with the trees in the distance. She was surprised that it did not explode immediately and so she remained watching until two minutes later the expected blast came with flames reaching into the cold moonlit sky.

The war was such an annoyance, spoiling all sorts of social events. Wimbledon and Ascot no doubt would be cancelled again this year and they used to be such an essential part of her calendar. That confounded Hitler: she really would like to give him a piece of her mind.

The cold was seeping through her wrap so she drew again on her cigarette and returned inside. She moved to the fire. It was pleasant being alone here tonight. Alex had gone to bed early and Nicholas, Lillian and Kate were all away for a few days in Shropshire visiting Jane. After her fiancé's death the girl had gone to pieces and her mother had taken her to a cousin up there where she had remained ever since.

All unmarried women between nineteen and thirty had been conscripted into some form of war work and Jane had become a Land Girl or something; Harriet was not exactly certain.

While the family were in Shropshire Harriet had decided to come and stay with Alexandra who had been transferred to the Ramsgate area as a telephone censor of some sort, and so lived at Castlemere all week. Not that Alex appreciated her sacrifice. She would take merely one drink and then start knitting vests for the fighter pilots. It astounded Harriet, the girl must have completed hundreds.

But during her stay at Castlemere one good thing had occurred. Harriet had prevailed upon Alex to set up a meeting with John Baron Chard. So finally after being constantly thwarted she was to meet with the witch's child in London the day after tomorrow. Four times in the past she had set up meetings and each time the infuriating man had cancelled because of the war. But this date was definite. He was on rest from operations and so his time was more like his own.

Alex had explained that after months in forward squadrons fighting the enemy, all pilots were given periods of respite, known as 'rest from operations' after which they would return to their fighter squadrons again. In the Chard man's case he was presently assigned to an Operational Training Unit, an OTU, in Lincolnshire where as a Wing Commander he had been given the position of Chief Flying Instructor on Spitfires.

After Harriet's conversation with him at Jane's engagement party and what she had since learnt by quizzing Alexandra, she was positive that he did not know anything about the circumstances of his birth. This made her smile. Actually the extent of the waiting made the thought of

538

telling him even more piquant. How delicious it was going to be to reveal all that had lain secret, and in hurting him she would deal a body blow to those miserable wretches who had nurtured him: Benjamin and Constance. Her face tightened and her lip wrinkled in distaste as she visualised them. Oh yes, and that Ledgie vixen too; she would be a wizened old prune by now. That gave Harriet a certain satisfaction and her expression brightened.

She finished her Scotch and wandered over to the drinks cabinet and poured herself another. Nicholas's liquor was fast disappearing. Everything was so hard to get with this damn rationing, though she knew a fellow in Canterbury who had continued supplying her. It was on the black market, of course, and outrageously priced, but having to do without was just not to be borne.

Catching a glimpse of herself in the mirror on the wall she smoothed back her hair and admired her firm chinline before she lit another cigarette and sat down again, lifting her foot in the air in approval of her gold shoes. They were exquisite; another Parisian purchase before the war. It was such a frustration not to be able to pop across the Channel and spend a weekend at the Plaza Athénée. It was the one time she used to enjoy her husband Edward's company, for he spoke French and was so useful interpreting for her. She wondered momentarily what had happened to the vendeuse in Madame Guirad's, the chic salon in the Champs Elysées where she had shopped. Thinking about France reminded her again of the half French brat who was now a fighter pilot. That led her to take an extensive mouthful of her drink. She could hardly endure the forty-eight hours' wait now that the meeting was finally a certainty.

For a time she did the daily crossword in the newspaper and when she could not think of the last two words to complete it, she discarded it and sank back into the cushions of the armchair, just luxuriating in front of the fire.

A minute later she heard more aircraft droning in the distance and realised she had not drawn the blackout drape back over the French doors. As she rose to do it, she noticed Peaches, the cat, looking in. But suddenly Peaches streaked away across the terrace and the door in front of her eyes burst open.

Harriet reeled back in shock.

A man stood there.

'Good Lord! Who are you?'

He did not reply. He was holding a revolver and there was blood on the arm of his ripped jacket and the side of his face. He looked weary. Then she took in his clothes; he was in a pilot's uniform but not a British one!

It flashed through her brain. The aircraft in distress which had buzzed overhead and crashed to the north!

'You're German!'

'Are you alone?'

'So you speak English?'

'I said are you alone?'

Harriet shook her finger at the pistol he held. 'Stop pointing that thing at me, you German upstart.'

'Shut up!' He spat the words out. 'Or I will kill you. Killing an Englishwoman will not trouble me, I assure you.'

Harriet shivered. She received the impression that he meant what he said so she fell silent.

His accent was thick but his English was understandable. He looked around. 'Now you must answer me. Are you alone?'

'There will be people returning to this house very shortly.'

He stepped closer and waved the pistol in her face. 'Then you *are* alone?'

She did not speak.

He shoved her and Harriet fell back a step and lifted her hand in defence. 'Don't do that!'

Now he stepped forward menacingly and pushed the gun in her face. 'I'll do as I please. Answer me. *Are you alone?*'

She decided that she had better answer, and so she lied. 'Yes, I'm alone. But my brother will be here soon.'

'Take me to the kitchen. I need water.'

Harriet walked ahead. Her heart had speeded up and was pumping furiously but she was calculating what to do. Castlemere stood alone on all four sides, the nearest house

540

was Darcy Newell's a quarter of a mile away. Alex was asleep upstairs and there was no one else around.

In the kitchen she turned to the German pilot as he sat with a thud but continued holding the pistol straight at her. His left arm was injured and he was breathing heavily.

'Get water, get some food and put it in a bag. Hurry!'

'I'm not used to hurrying for Nazis.'

'Shut up and move. I saw a boat at the end of the garden, on the river. How do you start it?'

'Good heavens how would I know? You fly an aeroplane, you work it out.'

'Shut up.' Blood was dripping from his fingers onto the kitchen rug. She could see he was weakening but his gaze never left her and the gun continued to point threateningly.

'Give me the water.'

She poured it out and placed the glass on the table. He reached forward and took it up and drank it all. 'Now get the food.'

Harriet took some fruit and cheese and bread and put it on the table.

'Give me another glass of water.'

'You won't be able to sail the boat down the river, there's ice in many places. And you're wounded.'

'Shut up.'

'And you're over-fond of that phrase.' She poured more water and as he picked up the glass it slipped from his hand and shattered loudly on the floor.

He exclaimed and hit the table with his fist. He was young, perhaps twenty-two. He looked scared: scared men did foolish things. He stood and moved to the door and looked into the corridor while continuing to hold the gun upon her.

'Get me a flashlight and put the food in something.'

She took a torch from the shelf near the pantry and found a string bag for the food hanging on a hook behind the door.

'Now put water in something.' He waved the pistol at her again as he took a teatowel and wrapped it round his wounded arm. '*Schnell*.' He returned to the table and tied

541

a knot in the makeshift bandage with his teeth and gunhand before he sank back into the same chair and rested his wounded arm on the table-top.

Harriet found a Thermos flask and filled it with water. She was desperately hoping he would faint. He looked as if he might.

She turned to him with one of her faux smiles. 'Would you like to lie down? There's a comfortable sofa in the next room.' She pointed. 'It's so cold outside.'

This did not please him. 'Shut up you stupid woman!'

And this did not please Harriet. She was frightened but she was also insulted. 'Now look here, I'll not be called stupid! I've given you water and food and you've shown your gratitude by pushing me around, continuing to wave that thing in my face and telling me to shut up.'

He stood up from the table and, wobbling slightly, waved his pistol at the door. 'Do as you are told, bitch of a woman!' He pointed to the string bag. 'You carry the food and water. We go to the boat. Move!'

She gave him a defiant look. 'I'll need a coat, it's freezing out there.'

He was unsteady on his feet but he followed her through to the front hall where she took her overcoat, gloves and scarf from the closet. Then he gestured with the pistol and they departed through the drawing room and the French doors which banged shut behind them. He was certainly weakening and Harriet was now praying under her breath that he would drop dead.

He pushed her across the terrace. 'Don't do that!' she shouted. 'I might slip.'

'Move, woman, or I'll kill you.' There was fury as well as fear in his voice now. He pushed her again and she shrugged off his hand and proceeded.

Alex woke with a start and opened her eyes. There had been a noise somewhere – downstairs, she thought.

She knew her aunt would still be up.

The fire had gone out in her grate but the embers were still giving warmth. Through her window beyond her half-open curtains she could see the moon, a cold iridescent silver in the sky. This was the second time she had woken tonight. Earlier she had heard the terrible noise of an aeroplane buzzing low above them, crashing in the trees not far away and exploding a few minutes later.

But all seemed quiet now. She rolled over and closed her eyes and was just slipping back into sleep when a door slammed. She opened her eyes again. Then she heard raised voices on the terrace below.

What was going on? She rose and moved to the window box, opened the window and a wall of cold air hit her. She shivered and looked out.

There was a ray of light thrown from the open French doors and she recognised her aunt and another figure. She leant out of the window, trembling with the cold. 'Aunt Harriet? What's going on?'

The Messerschmitt pilot flinched in surprise and spun round to the window above. He brought the pistol up and in fear fired.

The bullet exploded into the wood at the side of Alex's head. She screamed and fell back into the room.

At the same second Harriet took her chance. She dropped the string bag and lashed out to knock the gun from the man's hand. He cried out but he did not release the weapon and now Harriet flung herself at him and grappled for possession of the gun.

They staggered across the stones of the terrace, the German grunting and perspiring from his loss of blood. Harriet's face was determined, his was mixed with fury and fear. Tottering wildly they half fell down the steps and suddenly the pistol discharged.

Harriet screamed, bent double and reeled sideways onto the croquet lawn.

The German pilot stumbled but he steadied himself and hesitated for a second to watch Harriet sinking to her knees, then he grabbed the bag of food and ran unsteadily down the path towards the river.

Harriet screamed, 'German bastard!' as she collapsed into the pool of blood pouring from her smashed shoulder.

Upstairs, Alex had picked herself up from the floor and raced in terror from her room down the stairs to the front hall where she ripped open the gun cupboard and tore her father's shotgun from the stand and grabbing two cartridges from the box on the shelf shoved them into the barrel. She took off the safety-catch pin and ran through the drawing room to the French windows. With her heart pulsating wildly she moved outside.

The terrace was empty and she called, 'Aunt Harriet?' The reply was a groan from the body she saw crumpled on the lawn beyond.

She looked around for the attacker and warily stole to her aunt and knelt down. In Harriet's shoulder was a great hole and a pool of blood oozed out from beneath her, blackening the stones of the terrace. Alex, with her mind in turmoil, thought she might faint, but she made herself walk across the lawn and look around through the trees. She could see nothing and knowing her aunt was still alive, she ran back to her.

'The little upstart shot me,' Harriet groaned as Alex half-carried, half-dragged the woman in through the curtains to the drawing room.

Then Alex heard the cough of the engine of the *Capability*! She tried to calm herself. *Think clearly, Alex. Think.*

She raced to the telephone in the front hall and rang the operator. She knew the girl who worked on the local exchange at this time of night.

'Oh come on, Ena! God, come on,' she said aloud. Finally Ena's voice came across the line. 'Number, please.'

'Ena, it's Alex. There's been a terrible shooting, I need a doctor urgently. Oh, and I need Constable Brackford. Hurry, for God's sake!'

'Alex? Alex Cardrew?'

'Yes. Ena, hurry!'

'Where are you?'

'I'm at home, at Castlemere. Oh Ena, hurry hurry.'

'You say there's been a shooting?'

'Oh God, Ena! Just get a doctor here quickly and put me through to the police.'

After a long time a sleepy voice announced, 'Constable Brackford speaking.'

Now Alex was beginning to cry. 'Constable Brackford, it's Alex. Please come quickly. My aunt's been shot . . . badly, and I think the man who did it is stealing our boat.'

At the other end of the line, James Brackford snapped into wakefulness. 'Alex?'

'Yes.'

'Now calm down, lass. You say your aunt's been shot?'

'Yes.'

'Are you alone?'

'Yes.'

'Stay where you are. Don't go out. I'm on my way.'

He replaced the receiver and looked up to see his wife standing at the top of the stairs. 'What's up love? It's one in the morning.'

'An emergency down at the Cardrews'.' He ran back up the stairs past his wife to the bedroom and began pulling on his trousers as he gave instructions. 'Alex says her aunt's been shot. Now phone Dr Kenny and ask him to come over to Castlemere straight away. Oh, and see if you can get hold of Les Brooke from the Home Guard. Tell him to get over there too.'

As he hurried from the bedroom and down the stairs he picked up his rifle and was out of the door and on his bicycle before his wife reached the phone.

Six hours later as dawn stole across the terrace at Castlemere, Alex slept. She had been in a state of shock when the Constable and the doctor had arrived at the house but she managed to bring herself under control, and after answering their questions she was finally put to bed by Mrs Blake who had come to the house along with the Constable's wife.

Dr Kenny dressed Harriet's wounded shoulder and gave her an injection for pain and Mrs Blake sat with her throughout the hours of the night. It was clear to all that Harriet was in a dire condition. 'There's no point calling for an ambulance. It's subjecting her to more trauma and she's dying. Can't last more than a few hours.'

The German Messerschmitt pilot had been captured by the Home Guard downriver at Richborough where he was attempting to make his escape in the *Capability* and had become lodged up against a section of ice.

The Cardrews, away in Shropshire, were at a remote farm without a telephone so it was left to the police to contact them at daylight.

Harriet drifted in and out of consciousness until the dawn's mellow light greeted Mrs Brackford as she entered with a smile of empathy and cup of tea for Mrs Blake.

'Come on, dearie, drink this, then you go down and have some toast and take a nap. I'll look after Mrs Barrington till Doctor comes back.'

Mrs Blake rose and pointed to the woman in the bed. 'Has her husband been told?'

'Yes. From what I understand he'll be here post haste.'

'What a terrible business.'

'Isn't it?' The Constable's wife eyed Harriet's pale hand on the coverlet where a ruby sparkled on her third finger. 'She was never a favourite of mine but I wouldn't have wished this upon her.'

'True,' agreed Mrs Blake charitably as she rose from the chair and stoked the fire.

A moment later Harriet stirred. Her eyes opened and through a haze she focused on the two women above her. When she spoke, her voice was weak but still replete with authority. 'Who's here?'

'Oh Mrs Barrington, it's Emma Blake and Mrs Brackford the Constable's wife.' Mrs Blake crossed to the bed.

Harriet's eyes rotated in her ashen face. She felt dizzy. 'My whole body hurts. What happened?'

The Constable's wife spoke quietly. 'You were shot.'

Harriet recalled the German pilot and what had happened. She grimaced. 'Am I badly injured?'

The two women looked at each other, not knowing what to say, and from the silence Harriet guessed the gravity of her state.

'I must see John Baron Chard . . . Alex's friend.'

Mrs Blake thought the dying woman was delirious.

'There, there. Don't worry about anything. Dr Kenny's coming back shortly. He'll look after you.'

Harriet closed her eyes and groaned. Then drawing on her meagre reserves of strength she spoke as forcefully as she could. 'Don't be a damn fool. *Get . . . Alex . . . now*. It's imperative.'

Mrs Blake's eyes lifted skywards and Mrs Brackford put down the cup of tea on the night-stand and explained, 'But your niece is asleep, dearie. She's had a terrible night, what with everything.'

'And I haven't?' Harriet snarled, as she tried to push herself up but slipped back groaning. 'Damn it, woman. Do as I say. Wake her.'

Mrs Blake sighed. 'All right. I can see there'll be no peace if I don't.'

Three minutes later she re-entered with Alex in pyjamas. Mrs Blake had already explained her aunt's odd request and Alex frowned as she leant forward over the bed.

'Aunt Harriet?'

Harriet took a rasping breath and her body trembled. 'I must speak to Chard . . . John Baron Chard.'

Alexandra knew her aunt had intended meeting with JB the following day but she was amazed that she would still wish to see him under the dreadfully altered circumstances.

Harriet forced herself to raise her right hand. With the fingers so refined and nails so elegantly painted it hovered in the air before Alex's eyes. 'Alexandra, am I dying?'

The girl did not reply.

'Am I?'

Alex nodded and her eyes filled with tears as hesitantly she answered, 'I think you might be.'

Now there was frustration in her aunt's tone. 'Then do as I damn well say. Get the blasted man immediately!' Harriet's hand dropped back to the coverlet and she groaned again.

Alex's confusion was apparent and Mrs Blake, feeling sorry for her, advised, 'Do as she asks, love. I think it'll be best if you do.'

Alex wiped her eyes and left the room, went immediately downstairs, grabbed the telephone, rapidly turned the handle on the column and lifted the receiver to her ear. When the operator answered, Alex recognised her voice. 'Penny, it's Alex Cardrew. I urgently need to speak to the airfield at Kirton-in-Lindsay.'

This was where John Baron was taking his six weeks away from his fighter squadron.

'Kirton-in-Lyndsay in Lincolnshire?'

'Yes.'

'The lines are all out. We're not making any connections north of Essex, Alex.'

'Oh Lord. Do you know when they'll be operating again?'

'No.'

'Penny, please help me if you can. I'm in a terrible state. My aunt's dying and she wants to speak to a friend of mine up there.' She thought she was going to cry and took a deep breath. 'He's Wing Commander Chard, at Kirton-in-Lyndsay, an instructor.'

Penny's voice dropped markedly, replete with sympathy. 'Oh Alex, I'm so sorry. I'll do what I can. As soon as the lines are back I'll call you straight away.'

The young woman hung up and remounted the stairs to her aunt's bedroom. Harriet had forced herself to remain conscious and as Alex approached the bed she waited expectantly.

'The lines are out to his air base, Aunt Harriet, but as soon as they're back we'll get a call; a friend of mine's on the switchboard.'

'Just make sure he comes here. That's all.' Harriet beckoned her niece to her side with a frail gesture. 'I want to tell you something, Alexandra.'

There was a mild expression on her aunt's face and the young woman approached the bedside with an expectation of at last hearing some affectionate words from the dying woman.

As Alex bent her head towards her, Harriet met her eyes. 'Promise me you will make sure the . . . damned undertaker puts pink lipstick on my mouth. I cannot bear the thought . . . of any other colour.'

Alex sighed and straightened, a look of resignation in her face.

'Did you hear me?'

Alex nodded. 'Yes, Aunt Harriet, I heard you.'

The woman closed her eyes, seeming to drift into sleep, and Alex wished her parents were home. Mrs Brackford wiped Harriet's forehead with a damp cloth and Mrs Blake put her arm around the young woman and guided her downstairs.

At 8 a.m. Dr Kenny came and brought a nurse – a capable-looking woman called Kerston – in a blue uniform with a white apron who took over, allowing the Constable's wife to leave.

After the doctor had examined his charge he found Alex and Mrs Blake in the kitchen where he stood by the warmth of the Aga oven and was given a cup of tea. He rubbed his high forehead in thought. 'I'm amazed Mrs Barrington's still with us. She can't live through the morning. It's nigh impossible.'

But he was proved wrong. Harriet had a reason to live.

At ten in the morning Alex's father telephoned. He and her mother were on their way to the railway station and hoped to be in Sandwich by nightfall.

Nicholas Cardrew's voice was agitated as he spoke to his youngest daughter. 'The police said Harriet's been shot by a Luftwaffe pilot who crashed not far from home?'

'Yes, Daddy. Dr Kenny says she's dying. I think she'll be gone by the time you get here.'

There was a brief silence on the other end of the line before her father said resignedly, 'I see. Well, it's a roundabout journey but we'll get there tonight sometime. You're not on your own?'

'No, Daddy. I've got Mrs Blake with me and a nurse too. It was all in the middle of the night. Aunt Harriet was fighting him down on the terrace and he shot at me at my window.'

'Oh darling, you've been very brave. Your mother wants a few words.'

She could hear her father tell her mother that the German had shot at her then Lillian's voice sounded down the line. 'Oh, sweetheart, how terrible for you. It's awful about Harriet but we're so proud of you.'

Alex took a deep breath. 'Thanks, Mum. They caught the pilot who shot Aunt Harriet.'

'Good, darling. Right, we'd better go or we'll miss the train. It leaves in a few minutes.'

'All right, Mummy. But I think Aunt Harriet will be gone when you get here.'

'Oh dear.'

'She keeps asking to see JB. I don't understand it. Anyway, you'd better go.'

'What? What was that about JB?'

'Two minutes.' The operator's voice crossed the line. 'Are you extending, please?'

'But I haven't any more coins.' Lillian Cardrew's anguished tones sounded in her daughter's ear.

'Then finish your conversation now please and hang up,' the operator replied.

'Oh no, please don't cut me off.'

'Put in more coins or hang up, please.'

'Don't worry, Mummy, I'm all right,' Alex shouted down the line.

'Alex, no! Don't let JB—'

The line went dead.

Alex put down the receiver and shook her head, confused by her mother's words.

At 2 p.m. the phone rang again. It was Penny at the telephone exchange. 'I've got Kirton-in-Lyndsay on the line.'

After being transferred twice Alex finally spoke to John Baron's Sergeant. JB was out in the field.

'I'll ask him to call you, miss, as soon as he returns.'

The Sergeant was true to his word and an hour later John Baron called back and Alex explained about her aunt's situation. 'Aunt Harriet says she must see you at all costs. Can you come?'

'Of course I'll come, but to see you first. You've been through a lot.'

Alex became emotional again and her eyes welled with tears. 'I'm all right. It's just that talking to you makes me want to cry.'

'Oh thanks.' He gave a small laugh.

'I don't mean it that way. I'm perfectly all right. It's Aunt Harriet who's in the terrible state. Doctor's amazed she's hanging on.'

'She's a strange one. It doesn't make sense that she desires to see *me* on her deathbed. But then she never has made sense to me. You know I was finally seeing her tomorrow after all the missed meetings.'

'Yes, perhaps that's why she wants you.'

'I'll fly down as soon as I can.'

'Oh, that's wonderful, JB. Thanks.'

'Have you contacted your mother?'

'Yes, Mum and Dad are on their way home. They'll be here this evening or sometime tonight.'

'Good.'

'JB, please hurry. I'm feeling lonely and Aunt Harriet seems so very desperate.'

'I'll be there as soon as I can.'

Edward Barrington arrived at 2.30 p.m., his face pale and grim, and he spent three hours beside his wife's bed but she did not open her eyes.

The doctor came and went every two hours and as the chill day ebbed Harriet came back to a feeble consciousness to see Edward looming over her lovingly. She looked past him to Alex who stood at the end of the bed. 'Where's Chard?' she sighed.

'What's that, darling?' her husband asked.

'Chard, get Chard,' she whispered, her eyes fixing upon Alex with all the determination left in her soul.

Edward turned questioningly to the girl as she replied to her aunt, 'I spoke to him, he's coming. He'll be here as soon as he can.'

Edward faced back to his wife and lifting her limp hand asked, 'Why do you want this man, sweetheart? What can I do for you, darling? Let me help you.'

For answer she shook her head.

Half an hour later Mrs Blake set the table for the evening meal though none in residence seemed interested in food, except for Nurse Kerston.

In the cold twilight the doctor was back again and Edward was crying softly. 'I know Harriet had a mind of her own, that she could be brittle and sometimes cruel, but she's my wife and I . . . well . . . Damn it, she suits me. I don't want to lose her. I love her.'

Dr Kenny nodded gently though he eyed the man with disbelief. He knew Harriet well and could not believe that she could inspire such depth of feeling in anyone. But he was not about to argue. 'I understand,' he said. 'But prepare yourself, she must give up soon. I'm astounded she's still alive.'

Harriet's breath came now in gasps, and her beautifully moulded mouth drooped sideways. Nurse Kerston wiped her smooth forehead with a cool towel and remarked, 'I can't believe she has no lines, no lines at all.'

And Edward with unrestrained pride in his voice claimed, 'She never has had.'

Her eyes were closed but they knew she was conscious for every now and then she whispered, 'Is Chard here?'

And when Edward and Alex informed her, 'He'll be here very soon,' she answered, 'Promise me you will leave him with me alone . . . when he comes here. Promise me.' And they did.

It was almost dark outside and Alex was downstairs waiting for him, when John Baron arrived. She ran to him and he enveloped her in his arms and kissed her lips tenderly.

'Aunt Harriet still asks for you though she can hardly speak at all now.'

'Are you all right?'

Alex nodded. 'I'd prefer you saw Aunt Harriet, then we can talk.'

John Baron held her round the waist as they mounted the stairs and entered the bedroom.

Edward turned expectantly and John Baron took his hand

in a solemn greeting. They moved to the bed as the nurse moistened Harriet's lips with a wet cloth. 'Your visitor's here, Mrs Barrington.'

Harriet did not move

Edward lifted his wife's fingers and kissed them. 'Darling, Wing Commander Chard's here at last.'

As if lightning had struck her, Harriet's eyelids lifted! She gazed at the newcomer and with obvious strain she managed to raise her fingers and wave dismissively at the others. Alexandra, the nurse and Edward trailed out of the door.

John Baron bent down and spoke quietly. 'Mrs Barrington, what is it you want of me?'

As Harriet's concentrated gaze latched onto his he felt something akin to physical impact, so forcible was the look she cast up to him.

Harriet took a deep rattling breath. He was here with her! Alone at last; after all the waiting, she had him here.

It was her first husband's face wavering before her – John Baron. He was so handsome, the only man she had ever loved. The only *person* she had ever loved. She felt as if she drifted downhill, but she gathered all her strength to focus upon him: the epicentre of her vision, of her concentration, of her entire being.

She blinked and he repeated, 'Mrs Barrington, what is it you want of me?'

Her hand lifted and her forefinger with its manicured nail aimed at his face. 'You and I have met . . . before.'

She saw the child in front of her on the clifftop; his fair hair gleaming in the sunlight and the sea birds whirling in the air and calling wildly all around. She looked into his innocent blue eyes and saw his trust and the smile of delight at the cakes she gave him.

John Baron frowned. 'What do you mean? When?'

She focused on the grown-up face. 'In Yorkshire. On the cliffs . . . when you fell.'

And back into John Baron's mind came the day with 'Auntie' and the exciting ride in the trap, the cakes and the abundant grassy slopes with the smell of ozone and birds banking in the air.

He studied the smooth pallid face before him. 'My heaven! Auntie? Were you Auntie?'

Harriet nodded and smiled to see the expression of confusion spread over her visitor's face.

'Yes. And I am dying. So believe everything I tell . . . you.' She paused for breath. She felt as if she were in a dark place and falling; her mind clouded for a minute but her strength of will brought her back to him, back to his blue eyes and face – the face he *should not* own!

Even through the finite haze of death enveloping her she recognised his concentrated look, his earnest desire to know what she would say. He was totally absorbed in her words.

John Baron could see she was dying. Her hand fell to the coverlet, her face was drained of colour, her eyes were glazed; she was drifting away.

He put his own hand over hers and the contact seemed to momentarily revive her.

Harriet found his eyes again and plunged down deeply into her being to find the power to push out her final words.

'Your mother and father . . . are *not* your real parents. Neither of them. You are not . . . their son . . .'

She saw his face alter: the shock, the disbelief, followed by doubt, misgiving, and finally pain.

'Your mother . . . was a French whore!'

John Baron flinched and stood upright, moving a step back from the bed.

A hiss of air escaped from Harriet's lungs as the final vision she had on earth was of John Baron, his face fraught and bewildered. She had completed her task! A smile of triumph lifted her mouth.

And in contrast to the venom of her last words, the planes of her face slipped into repose as if she were leaving the world having performed a veracious and saintly deed.

A mighty thrill eclipsed her soul and the expression she wore into the neverending blackness was pure and serene.

Chapter Thirty-six

John Baron stood rigidly looking down at Harriet's body. He was overwhelmed, his mind numb, submerged by the implication of her message. It could not be true. It could not be true! He was utterly vanquished by what the dead woman had told him.

He stepped away from the bed, shaking his head as if to relieve himself of the import of her words.

He urged his feet to move towards the window, which he threw open to a blast of cold air. He grasped the sill, opening his mouth wide to gulp in the air. Darkness had virtually descended but he could discern the croquet lawn, the garden, the hedges, and the elms and sycamores down near the river. He thought he saw a flock of grey birds flying in the gloom. They looked like doves; the bringers of peace! But there was no peace. Not in his own world or the world at large.

He heard the door open behind him and turned to see Nurse Kerston bustle in with a tray in her hands. Behind her followed Edward. As they crossed to the bed he spoke.

'She's dead.'

Edward let out a groan and hurried to the bedside where he knelt down.

The nurse put down her tray. 'Why didn't you call me, Wing Commander?' She fussed by him and closed the window.

'She died just now . . . Just now.'

Edward lifted his head, his eyes brimmed with tears. 'Did she have a message for me?' His face was full of entreaty; filled with hope.

Through the numbess that constricted his mind, John

Baron registered the man's words and with compassion lied. 'Yes. She said you were a wonderful husband.'

With a grateful sigh Edward's face sank into the sheet beside his wife's arm as the nurse crossed to the fireplace and put on another log.

With one backward glance at the bed John Baron left the window and walked to the door. He passed along the landing to the top of the stairs with a faraway look in his eyes and coming up towards him was Alex.

'Oh, JB, there you are. Is Aunt Harriet . . . ?'

He nodded.

'What did she want you for?'

He did not answer. He marched, robot-like, down the carpeted steps towards her and now she noticed his pallor and the expression on his face.

'JB, what on earth is it? What's wrong?'

He walked past her to the foot of the stairs and stood rigidly on the marble floor of the foyer beside the table that held the telephone. She followed him and took him by the arm, looking up into his face.

'JB, what did she say to you?'

He shook his head, then he enveloped her in his arms and hid his face in her hair.

She spoke gently. 'Oh darling JB, please tell me what's happened. Please.'

He did not reply, he just continued to hold her tightly to him. When finally he stepped back from her he gently stroked her face. 'Alex, I'm going now. Don't ask me to stay . . . I can't.'

'But JB, I don't understand.' Bewildered, Alex clung to him.

'Please, dear Alex, just accept what I say. I know you've been through a lot, but Mrs Blake is here and the nurse, and your parents will be home soon. I don't wish to be mysterious but I can't stay. I can't talk. I've got to be alone.' He kissed her forehead and then turned and walked out of the door into the night.

Alex began to cry and hurried to the doorway to watch his black figure disappear down the drive. In her upset state and complete frustration she looked skywards. 'Damn you, Aunt Harriet, what have you done? You couldn't even die without hurting people.'

Half an hour later Lillian and Nicholas arrived home in tandem with Dr Kenny on his bicycle. Alex's parents had walked in light rain from Sandwich Station carrying their cases.

They took off their coats in the welcoming warmth of the front hall and Lillian enveloped her youngest daughter in her arms.

The doctor took Alex's arm. 'Perhaps you should go up to bed. I'll explain things to your parents tonight and you can fill them in on the details in the morning. I've a little sedative for you.'

'Yes, darling,' her father said. 'You listen to Dr Kenny.'

But Alex moved out of the doctor's grasp. 'No, really I'm all right. I'll take the sedative if I need it later but I want to be with Mummy and Daddy now.'

The doctor relented and left the family with Mrs Blake who had refreshment for them. She made sure they had enough to eat and drink and then she departed for the night. Nicholas saw her to the front door and helped her into her raincoat. 'What a terrible day, and thank you for all your help, Mrs Blake. I know you've been a tower of strength.'

Upstairs the doctor found Edward remaining by his wife's body, and in the mood for handing out sedatives, he gave the poor man one and Edward promised to take it.

Down in the kitchen with her parents Alex explained all she knew, and as she came to the end of her tale she said, 'I don't know how long the pilot was here for I'd been in bed for hours. It was the French doors banging as they left which got me out of bed.'

Nicholas shook his head. 'My poor sister.'

'Daddy, I don't want to trouble you more, but . . .'

'What? Tell me.'

'Well it's just that she badly upset JB about something just before she died. I mean, she was on about his coming here all day long. Never let up, like a broken record.'

557

At that moment Edward and Dr Kenny came in and Alex fell silent.

Edward greeted Nicholas and Lillian.

'We're so sorry,' Lillian said, hugging him.

He mustered a smile. 'She looks beautiful even now.' He cast his gaze to the ceiling indicating where she was. 'Like a porcelain doll she is. And she gave instructions about the lipstick she wants put on.'

He turned to Alex who looked up with a sigh. 'Yes, Uncle Edward, I'll make sure it's the right pink.'

'Thank you, dear.' He patted her shoulder. 'Does anyone mind if I go to bed? The doctor's kindly given me something to take. I need it.'

Nicholas spoke for all of them. 'No, Edward, you go. Best thing to do. In the morning we'll discuss everything that needs to be done.'

Edward looked grateful and moved to the door where he halted and turned back. 'Alex's friend JB told me she thought I was a wonderful husband.'

'As you were, Edward,' Lillian declared and the man thanked her with a weak smile of gratitude, then turned to Alex. 'Did he say what the urgent matter was that Harriet wanted him for?'

The young woman shook her head.

'Ah well. That was my Harriet, always something important she had to attend to.'

He wandered out of the door and the doctor took his leave with the words, 'You know where I am if you need me. Nurse will remain until morning. Don't hesitate to call me.' He smiled at Alex. 'I heard you received the George Cross for going over to Dunkirk.'

It was true. Alex and Jane had received the medal from the King himself. The Mayor of Ramsgate and the Lifeboat Association had nominated the two Cardrew sisters for their bravery.

Alex looked embarrassed. 'Well, yes.'

'I reckon you deserve it again for how you handled things here last night until we came.' He smiled at Nicholas. 'You've got a good one in her.'

'Thanks. I know.'

When they were sure the doctor had gone, Nicholas eyed his daughter reluctantly. 'You were speaking about JB.'

'Yes. Aunt Harriet pressed me to get him here and I did. I swear she stayed alive just to tell him whatever it was. And it must have been devastating for he came out from her with his face all white. Lifeless. Then he left.'

'That's all?'

'That's all. He said he had to be alone and walked right out of the front door and never looked back. I was so infuriated with Aunt Harriet . . . even though she was dead.'

Lillian heaved a loud sigh and patted her daughter's arm. 'Ah darling, she was always one for distressing people. Hard to believe your father's her brother.'

Nicholas shook his head. 'I remember her as a young woman; she wasn't always like that.'

Lillian smiled tenderly. 'You lie very nicely, dear, but I think we know better. Still she's gone and we should be charitable.'

'Daddy, have you any idea what she told JB?'

Nicholas Cardrew met his wife's eyes before he answered his daughter. 'I'm not sure, Alex – perhaps. And I'd like you just to trust me. It's not something I can tell you. It's for JB to do that.'

Alex was absolutely baffled by it all. 'Oh Daddy, that's not fair.'

'Fair or not, sweetheart, that's how it has to be.'

The following day John Baron kept his engagement with his sister.

They met in Lyon's Corner House at Marble Arch.

Sam was sitting at a table covered in a checked cloth waiting for her brother, her overcoat draped across the back of the chair. She was gazing in the opposite direction as he came towards her and halted a few tables away. He stood watching her: the way she played with the small menu card, toying with it between her fingers; the attitude of her head, slightly on one side. His chest felt tight. Was he to believe what the dying Harriet had said? That this woman with her

559

abundant hair falling to her shoulders sitting waiting for him was not his sister?

He had spent much of the night awake analysing all he could recall from his first memories. They were all of Bridlington. He could not remember very much before his fall from the cliff, except for two things: the birth of his darling sisters with their cherub faces and the feeling he had experienced knowing they belonged to him and his parents. And he recalled his seventh birthday very clearly . . . Armistice Day. He could remember the unbounded joy in the very air of the land and how he had ridden on the dray into town and sat on the piano while fat Mags Fishburn played and everybody laughed. He remembered Wakefield finding him and giving him the wooden aeroplane on the footpath.

He thought he recollected a little cat that had been his pet, but he was not sure. He definitely recalled Grenville, his dog. That was everything from his early life. His parents had always been . . . his parents.

Sam half turned in his direction, still playing absent-mindedly with the menu. She looked thoughtful as the rain splashed on the pane of the window behind her head.

He moved in to the table and she realised he had arrived. 'Darling,' she said as he bent to kiss her cheek. 'You sneaked up on me.'

'Did I?'

Sam's mind had been elsewhere while she waited for her brother. She had been contemplating what had occurred at the meeting with Frances White the previous day. It had upset her equilibrium but had given her so very much to consider.

As agreed, Samantha had gone to the address in Great Smith Street near Westminster Abbey, to an unattractive grey stone building. She was met by a commissionaire with gold tassels on his shoulders and when she mentioned Miss Frances White he nodded and took her up a flight of stairs with boarded-up windows on a landing, to a first-floor room.

Frances met her at the door and took her coat and folded it, placing it on a chair. Beyond, a man sat at a table. He

560

had greying hair and looked trim and fit. Sam guessed he was in his fifties. The spacious room was remarkable in being almost totally devoid of furniture: there were four chairs, a table and one small cupboard. Upon the floor was obviously new carpet.

'Miss Samantha Slade, this is Major Eric Jaffer.' They shook hands and Jaffer swiftly ran his eyes over her from head to toe; not in a licentious way but as if he assessed her as a physical specimen.

'Sit down.'

Sam did, on the spare chair.

Frances asked, 'Would you like a cup of tea?'

'No, thanks.' She glanced questioningly at her friend and Frances spoke again.

'I know you're wondering what this is all about, Sam, and I'm grateful to you for coming along. But this is really Major Jaffer's interview.'

'Interview?' Sam queried.

Jaffer cleared his throat. 'Ah, let me get to the point, Miss Slade. We, that is the people Frances and I work for, belong to a special branch of the armed forces. We're interested in people who speak foreign languages – in this instance, French – and who are young and fit. Who could be trained in hand-to-hand combat, to jump out of aircraft, scale walls and who wouldn't mind doing things which come under the heading of *dangerous*.' He paused, because it was round about now that most of the people he interviewed (up until recently only men) caught on to what he was referring to.

Sam did not let him down. 'Are you talking about spying?'

He shook his head. 'This is different, though in certain conditions very much the same. Our people are highly trained, skilled in the use of all sorts of weapons and explosives. They have specific qualifications and they do their job, just as spies do, in enemy-occupied territory.'

'Sabotage?'

Jaffer smiled as he might upon a clever student. 'Exactly! You are ahead of me, Miss Slade.'

'Look, Major, I think perhaps it's time I mentioned that I'm married. I'm actually Mrs Slade.'

'Oh?' He glanced at Frances, who shrugged.

'Samantha didn't tell me that.'

'No, I don't as a rule. I think it's my business.'

The Major frowned. 'That might make a difference.'

Sam lifted her hand in negation. 'No, it won't. My husband and I are not together. Haven't been now for over two years. I just wanted to set the record straight.'

The Major's frown dissolved though he shot another sharp glance at Frances. 'I thought your people had delved into *Mrs* Slade's background?'

'They did, but nothing about a marriage came up.'

He gave her a look which suggested the investigation had not been good enough, but he went on with a smile to Sam, 'We're trying to subvert, disturb, confuse and upset the enemy as much as we can: we blow up their bridges and their factories and troop trains. We immobilise where possible.'

'And this is done in France?'

'In all enemy-occupied territory, but in the case we speak of, yes in France.'

'And that's why you're interested in me? Because I speak French?'

He looked again at Frances and this time the woman replied, 'Yes, Samantha, that's one of the main reasons, though usually we like people who've spent time in France, which you haven't. But you have other qualifications like being able to handle a camera.'

Sam was eyeing Frances and seeing her anew. She was no longer the nice friendly woman who met her for coffee and saw her in the evening at clubs. She was a scout, a person with a keen eye for those she thought might suit recruitment. For the first time Sam saw the efficiency in Frances White and couldn't help but wonder if that was, in fact, her real name.

Jaffer looked down at his notebook then back up at her. 'Mrs Slade, if you have no interest whatever in what I'm telling you we can finish now.'

A silence hung in the room. No one spoke and Sam took her time to answer. 'Please go on.'

Jaffer did not smile but a certain regard for his visitor appeared in his expression. 'Our organisation was formed eleven months ago. We're a Special Operations Executive and, as I mentioned previously, up until now we have only trained men, only sent males into enemy territory, but as from this coming spring we'll be enlisting females. You're one of the first we've spoken to.'

'Let me get this straight,' Sam cleared her throat. 'Frances has chosen me because she thinks I'm suitable and might be interested, and now you're asking me if I would like to train to become one of these special . . . saboteurs?'

He met her eyes. 'Yes, we are. But we'll give you plenty of time to think about it. We don't need an answer for months yet, and let me say one other thing which is of maximum importance. Something which I must ask you to think about. The enemy don't like what our Special Operatives do. If they're caught, the enemy react with violence – with brutality.'

Sam nodded. She knew, as every thinking person did, about the German SS, the Gestapo, about the Nazi death camps, about what they were doing to the Jews. 'I understand.'

'Do you have any children?'

'No.'

'Are you in contact with your husband?'

Sam thought of Cash, his cocksure manner and his self-opinionated grin, his lock of hair dangling cheekily on his brow; the way he called her 'm'lady'. Why was it she only remembered the things that had attracted her? She shook her head. 'No, we're completely separated.'

'I'm sorry to ask such personal questions but do you have a current boyfriend?'

'Not anyone special.'

That pleased Eric Jaffer; people with no emotional ties were preferable. 'And my understanding from Frances is that all your family are in Australia?'

'Yes, except my brother who's here in the RAF.' Frances nodded. She knew this.

563

For the first time Jaffer wrote something down in the notebook in front of him. 'I must ask you not to mention this interview to anyone. I mean anyone at all. As you can understand, whichever way you decide, today must remain top secret. No one must ever suspect what has gone on in this room. And if in time you agree to join us, no one must ever suspect what it is you really do.'

Sam took a deep breath; suddenly it had become very cold in the almost empty room. She shivered. 'So you give your people aliases?'

Jaffer stood up. 'Yes, and we give our people legitimate service positions of some kind to satisfy their families and friends. But Mrs Slade, if ever we talk again, we'll go further into that.'

Sam stood.

'Now you won't be seeing Frances again at the clubs or the pubs, but she'll be in touch with you. And if you feel you need to see me at any time, just telephone this number.' He handed her a card. 'But I would like to hear from you in a month or so anyway. To see how you think about things then. So I'll make contact.' He smiled a warm encouraging smile.

Frances took Sam's arm and as she moved to steer her away Major Jaffer asked abruptly, 'How do you feel about all this, right at this moment?'

Sam shook her head. 'I don't know.'

'Good,' he replied confidently. 'That's the best answer.'

In another minute Samantha was down the stairs and the commissionaire had let her out into the street. It was as if in a trance that she had made her way to Lyon's Corner House and waited for her brother.

'Well,' JB said, sitting down at the table with her. 'I'm sorry I'm late but it's taken me quite a time to get here in the rain.'

'Oh, that's all right.'

The waitress appeared at their side. 'What'll you be having?'

'Coffee for me,' Sam answered.

'Tea, please.'

'Anything to eat?' She pointed to the menu Sam still held. 'We haven't got the scones but the tea-cake's nice.'

John Baron nodded. 'The tea-cake sounds just right.'

As the girl turned from the table and the two siblings smiled at each other neither noticed the veil floating in the other's eyes.

'So how's everything?' John Baron asked. 'What are you up to?'

'Oh, the usual. But actually *Newsweek* want me to return to Belfast. Said they want more of the same. I was telling the story of the shipbuilding and the locals.'

'And how do you feel about that?'

Sam rested her chin in her hands. 'You know what? I'm not sure. At first I felt inclined to go, but now, well . . .' She gave a half-hearted smile. 'What do you think?'

He did not answer for an extended period; he seemed to be thinking as he leant back in his chair and said, 'Sammy, in the end it's up to you.'

Sam hardly noticed that her brother was vague. She was back in the spacious room with Jaffer. His smile so sincere, his concern for her abundant . . . but with recruitment in mind. And with Frances listening on the other chair a few feet away.

'But I'd like your point of view,' she replied, looking down at her hands.

John Baron tried to concentrate on Sam's coming decision but now that he was with her his consciousness was again overcome by Harriet's revelation. Could it be true that this woman was not his sister? That he could have loved her, married her? Taken her for his own? He studied her as she gazed down at the table.

The waitress arrived with the tea and coffee and momentarily brother and sister took notice.

'Thank you.'

'Tea-cakes are on their way.'

John Baron gave the imitation of a smile. 'Did you enjoy being out there last time?'

'In Belfast?'

'Of course.'

'I think so. Carter was really pleased with the set of shots from there last year.'

'Then it's up to you.'

Neither seemed to notice the circuitous conversation.

Sam sipped her tea and examined the poster on the wall opposite. It depicted a beautiful woman surrounded by three men in uniform. The caption read: *Keep Mum she's not so dumb! Careless talk costs lives!* The implication being the beautiful woman was a spy! Sam brought her eyes back to her brother as he glanced out the window. 'The rain's stopped.'

'Good, we might go to the shooting gallery then.'

It was something they usually did when they were near Marble Arch. They were both true shots and when Sam won she enjoyed handing the prizes to her brother in mock condescension. Though as he put it, 'I have managed to hit a few enemy aircraft, you know!'

The waitress reappeared with the tea-cake and as John Baron took a slice he nodded. 'Yes, we'll go to the gallery.'

They spent fifteen minutes there and they both won, but not large prizes. Their eyes were not as good today. They handed the packets of cigarettes to a passing stranger.

They walked down Oxford Street together and turned into Bond Street where a number of the fashionable shops had boarded-up windows. As the early January dusk descended they halted in front of a jeweller's window where Sam eyed the pieces, though with less enthusiasm than was usual. By the time they reached Piccadilly it was almost dark. Sam was heading to the Ritz where she was to meet Victor Bradbury, the *Newsweek* correspondent and the man who had first taken her to the Astors' where she had met Frances.

Sam took out her torch and John Baron accompanied her by the pile of sandbags outside the Royal Academy where they crossed the wide thoroughfare, virtually devoid of vehicles. A chill drizzle began and as they reached the awning outside the front door of the hotel John Baron took hold of his sister's shoulders and gazed at her in the enveloping gloom. He folded the collar of her coat in and drew the back of his hand tenderly down her smooth cheek.

Even though Sam was still overwhelmed by the quandary she faced, for the first time she noticed his preoccupation. 'What is it, JB?'

'Nothing. I just wanted to look at you.'

She gave a self-conscious laugh and hugged him. 'You can hardly see me in this light. When do you go back to the squadron?'

'Not for a month.'

'Do you know where?'

'We'll be back at the Bump again.'

'How long will you be there?'

'A couple of months.'

'Well, thank heaven Biggin's close. I'll still be able to see you.'

'Look Sammy, about Belfast. I suppose the best thing is—'

She shook her head. 'Oh, don't worry about Belfast. I'll probably go, but I'm beginning to think I might even join one of the women's services.'

This surprised her brother. 'I thought you were obsessed with photography?'

'I think I'm obsessed with winning the war.' She sighed and ran her hand across his ribbons. 'Andy was killed in North Africa.'

John Baron knew Andrew. In fact, he had been pleased that a good reliable man was in Sam's life. He had met him only a couple of times but he had liked the fellow.

'Oh Sammy, I'm so sorry.'

'Yes. He was a real nice bloke.'

'He was in love with you, Sammy.'

'I know.'

'But you weren't with him, right?'

'Right.' She gave him a hard look. 'You knew that.' Then a tear edged over her lid. 'But I liked him a hell of a lot. God, I really did.' She dropped her head into his greatcoat.

John Baron wrapped his arms around her and held her

and kissed her forehead. Just for a fleeting moment he wondered if he should tell her what he knew, but immediately quashed the thought. Why throw her into the same appalling confusion as himself? And in any case, he must find out if it were true.

He tilted her head up and thought how very much like Alex she was. He took out his handkerchief and wiped her eyes. 'Look, do you want me to stay? I'm only going down to Shepherd's to meet up with some of the fellows.'

Shepherd's was the pub where the RAF boys congregated in Shepherd's Market, a little enclave of lanes that ran off Curzon Street in Mayfair.

Sam shook her head. 'No. My friend Victor will be here any minute. He's always early. I'm all right, truly I am. I'm just bloody enraged about Hitler and the rotten Germans.' She gave a smile. 'Off you go and ring me next week.'

He kissed her again and walked off into the fine rain.

She watched him for a minute, his long stride taking him away in the drifting rain, and a wistful look passed across her face before she spun on her heel and walked past the elderly doorman who held back the blackout curtain for her. In the foyer of the Ritz a buzz of activity met her and she handed her damp overcoat to the attendant.

She had not told JB but she had been dating Victor for two months now. That was another reason why she was even more upset about Andy's death; she felt guilty. She had slept with Victor twice now.

As she walked through to the women's lounge she caught her reflection in one of the huge gilt mirrors and she halted. She pondered the face looking out at her. What use was this woman? While fine men like Andrew were dying she was taking pictures. Yes, they were helping the American public to see what was going on over here and now that the USA was in the war after the Japs had bombed Hawaii last December, she had a lot of new ideas for stories on American servicemen in Britain. But was that enough?

And she had begun a liaison with Victor Bradbury. Why?

The reflection could not answer that. It simply shook its head sadly and moved out of sight into the women's lounge.

When John Baron turned into White Horse Street off Piccadilly it had begun to rain more heavily and he ran the last 100 yards to Shepherd's pub, arriving as the evening session began with the place crowded as usual. Oscar, the publican, had just brought up the lift behind the long wooden bar. It was used to hoist the barrels of beer from the cellar to the bar, but today instead of a barrel, four pilots had emerged somewhat tipsy and very loud after having spent the hours of the afternoon drinking his ale down in the underground room!

The whole place had erupted in laughter even though Oscar and Mrs Oscar as they called his wife, appeared to take a dim view of the matter.

It was not long before JB was hailed in the crowded room and he turned to see the white-toothed smile of Johnny Johnson. Johnson had been flying with Douglas Bader just south of Le Touquet in France when Douglas had been shot down the previous August. It was Johnny who had telephoned JB to give him the bad news.

JB remembered the phone call in precise detail. It had been Saturday, 9 August, and an hour after he had returned from escorting a bomber raid on some German shipping in Cherbourg when he was told there was a telphone call for him from Westhampnett in Sussex.

Johnson was on the line. John Baron knew him but had never received a call from him and he sounded disheartened. 'I've bad news, I'm afraid. Dogsbody went down today over France. One O Nines. Last I saw of him, he was on the tail of one.'

John Baron took a gulping breath. 'Oh hell.'

'Yes. Woodhall called the Ops Room in Chichester and they've checked—'

'Excuse me, sir. It would be preferable if you did not use place names.'

It was the telephone censor cutting across the line. This was the job that Alex did: listening in on calls to and from airbases to ensure no one gave too much detail. The enemy could be listening.

'Oh yes, sorry,' Johnson answered. 'Just upset, I suppose.'

'That's all right, sir,' the girl replied politely.

JB was finding it hard to believe. Douglas had seemed invincible: domineering, dogmatic, brave and breezy. 'You're sure he went down?'

'Reckon so. We did a search of the Channel.'

'Does Thelma know?'

'Yes. Cocky's with her.' Cocky was a twenty-one-year-old pilot whom Douglas had been grooming. He was a sparse-framed gangling lad who had shown great prowess in the air. The youth revelled in telling one particular story about Bader. He was flying back over the Channel one day and ranged up beside Douglas and what Cocky Dundas saw almost had him fainting at the controls. For there was Bader flipping back the top of his cockpit. As the boy watched astounded, Bader proceeded to unclip his oxygen mask, shove his pipe into his mouth and strike a match and puff away. As Dundas put it when telling the tale, 'I would have loved a cigarette myself, but no normal man lights a naked flame in a Spitfire cockpit! And to cap it all Dogsbody gives me two fingers and flies on.'

Well, it appeared that the formidable Douglas Bader was mortal after all! He had gone down today. John Baron replaced the telephone receiver and looked at his watch and then out of the window. The August sky was darkening fast. The oaks on the other side of the lane were gloomy sentinels in the encroaching night and there was an awesome stillness in the air.

He moved to the window and took a deep breath gazing out at the summer twilight. All the Spitfires were down from the sky and the ground crews would be placing the chocks under their wheels, wrapping the cockpits in their covers and making sure each aircraft was ready for dawn. Soon the Beaufighters would be rising in the air on their night patrols. And Douglas? He was somewhere in France, or ditched in the Channel; or the unthinkable – dead.

John Baron had gone to the mess that night and drunk too much. Douglas Bader was a legendary figure throughout the RAF and many were already mourning his loss. Through the days that followed most of the RAF waited tensely until the news came that Wing Commander Bader was a prisoner-of-war.

The fact was that when Douglas's aircraft had been hit, his right tin leg had been caught fast in the cockpit and as he attempted to exit he had pulled and tugged on it fiercely until it had snapped off allowing him to bail out. Had his leg been real, it was believed that he would have gone down with his aircraft.

Johnny Johnson had been one of those in the escort that accompanied the bombing raid upon which was dropped a spare set of legs for Bader. They landed ten miles south of St Omer where he was a prisoner in hospital.

And now in Shepherd's as Johnny Johnson ordered beers and introduced his companion to John Baron, the newcomer said, 'I haven't seen you since Douglas was shot down.'

Johnny's face grew serious. 'That's right. We still miss him.'

'I heard you've painted your Spitfire with *Bader's Bus Company Still Running* on the side.'

Johnny grinned. 'Too right. Let's drink to him, shall we?'

They had just raised their glasses when a five-man bomber crew entered the side door affecting the same positions that they manned in their aircraft – three facing forward, two behind – and, mock firing with their hands and making ack-ack and machine-gun noises, they pushed their way, still holding formation, through to the front door and out into the street.

The entire bar erupted in cheers, whistles and cat calls as they disappeared.

Later, in heavy rain and a little worse for wear, John Baron wandered back to 128 Piccadilly where he was staying the night at the Royal Air Force Club. Elsey, the door porter, tipped his cap to him as he came in and John Baron decided he might as well be thoroughly drunk so he headed to the small, men only, bar. In the hustle and smoke he sipped a Johnnie Walker Black Label whisky – the only place in London he knew where you could find it. He was picturing a young straight-backed girl sitting astride Aristotle with her hair undulating on her shoulders in the breeze. He remembered the little indentation where her slender neck met her body and the smooth brown backs of her hands on the reins: just the way she was the day he had said goodbye to her and left for Melbourne.

Chapter Thirty-seven

Cash woke. He had been dreaming of Sammy again; dancing with her, his fingers resting on her waist and his face pressed into her hair, overwhelmed by the intoxicating smell of her.

For a moment he thought he was in the bedroom of the flat in Double Bay but he soon discarded that illusion as he opened his eyes to look sideways into the steamy night where his arm stretched out towards a rubber tree and the glimmer of light from the dying embers of a fire greeted his vision. Beyond in the ebony night the jungle loomed and the slithering, jumping creatures of the swamps yodelled interminably.

'Lieutenant Wade?' It was his Sergeant Curly Dunne who had been with him on the western plains of New South Wales before they had sent Cash away to make an officer out of him.

'Sorry to wake you, Lieutenant, but Taber, Carvolt and Johnny Q are back. And Johnny Q's brought three of his Malay mates.'

Cash sat up and yawned. 'Sure, Dunne. Where are they?'
He pointed across the clearing.
'What time is it?'
'0230.'

Cash moved off the groundsheet and followed his Sergeant who was taking swipes at the interminable mosquitoes.

Johnny Q was Cash's number one spy: a man about Cash's own age, he was a mixture of Chinese and Malay and had been with Cash six months now. He came from a wealthy Penang family and had been to university in

England, and his hatred of the Japanese, who had killed his brother in the Sino-Japanese war, made him a welcome member of Cash's band.

Cash greeted his men warmly. Corporals Taber and Carvolt were his best scouts; they saluted and picked up mugs of tea from Richards the cook.

Jack Taber was usually quick to grin but he looked serious in the night light. Cash had decided it was time Taber became a Sergeant; in fact, he was officer material and Cash had said so in a recent report.

The young man consciously affected the appearance of a brigand and over his jungle-green uniform he wore a bandolier full of bullets and a pistol thrust at a rakish angle through his belt next to his jungle knife. He cut a dashing figure, but one irreconcilable with the parade ground; not that it mattered here. When he spoke he showed a gold edge to his front tooth. Cash somehow liked the fact that his own eye-tooth carried a gold filling and that his protegé, Taber, had a front tooth the same.

Taber gestured over his shoulder with his thumb. 'There's a Jap bivouac about two miles up the road, sir. The little weasels have hopped off their bicycles for the night.'

'How many of the bastards are there?'

'We reckon about a hundred and fifty or so.'

'So two of them to one of us.' Cash smiled and looked at his watch. 'Right. Well, we'd better plan a nice dawn surprise for them.'

'Yes, but I reckon you should hear what one of Johnny's mates has to say first.'

Cash looked at the three Malays. The local population was divided. Some worked for the British, some for the Japanese. Malaya supported a complicated society and those who carried grudges against the British had fallen quickly into the Japanese service as they poured into Malaya, just as those who were loyal to the British remained working with them. And there were Chinese all over the peninsula. An oft-used local quote ran: 'Malaya is a country owned by the Malays, run by the British for the benefit of the Chinese.'

Cash shot a sceptical glance at Johnny Q. 'Are your mates trustworthy?'

Johnny Q nodded and pointed to one of the men he had brought in. 'I grew up with Butik. His word is his bond, as you say. He is a friend and he brings information from the north.' Johnny Q spoke in fluent, well-enunciated English and his bronze eyes studied Cash. 'I will have to interpret.'

'Then let's sit down.'

A groundsheet was thrown over the drenched grass.

Private Richards, the cook, handed Cash a cup of tea and he drank it: hot and sweet without milk. They had not had milk for months.

The Malay began to talk fast, gesturing with his hands, and Johnny translated.

'There was fighting at Muar and on the river, all along the Bakri Road and the ten-mile causeway to Parit Sulong and the bridge. Your Australian Colonel, I think his name is Anderson, was led into an ambush but he and others fought their way out. This man Anderson is very brave. There was constant artillery barrage and machine-gunning. Japanese aeroplanes dive-bombed from the air and tanks were brought in, but they were repelled. Many tanks were destroyed by the Australians. And Indian soldiers fought with them, but Japanese reinforcements arrived all the time. Finally the Australians made a last attempt to take back the bridge, singing that song "Waltzing Matilda", but they were cut to pieces. At one point on the Bakri Road there were less than a thousand Australians against a host of fifteen thousand Japanese.'

Here Johnny Q asked the Malay a question and the man shook his head.

'What did you ask?'

'If any of the Australian units were identified. He says he thinks some were men of the Nineteenth Battalion.'

Cash's expression altered. They were the boys he and Curly had begun army life with on the open plains outside Bathurst.

Johnny Q's educated sing-song voice rose again. 'The Australians and Indians retreated from Parit Sulong. They destroyed trucks and field equipment but could not take the badly wounded – they were left behind – about a hundred Australians and perhaps a few dozen Indians. They remained at Parit Sulong. The Japanese tied the prisoners' hands behind their backs with rope or wire. They were made to sit in a ring facing each other. Some were nude. The Japanese soldiers stood behind them and smashed at them with rifle butts.

'Around dusk the officers were tied together, and then so too were the other ranks. Many of the prisoners were lashed, mostly with wire, and they were kicked repeatedly. Then they were machine-gunned.

'Some time later the Japanese soldiers poured petrol over all the prisoners and set them alight. Some who had not died from the bullets were still conscious. There was much screaming. They were then battered with rifle butts again – and stabbed many times with bayonets.'

Cash closed his eyes momentarily as if to block out what he had just heard. 'Is this man sure of what he says?'

Johnny Q's expression remained impassive. 'He is sure. His cousin was an informer with the Japanese right there at Parit Sulong.* Three days ago he came over to us.'

Taber's head was in his hands.

Richards and Dunne were silent.

'Jesus H Christ.' Cash rose and moved away looking into the jungle. He stood, back to them for two minutes then he turned sharply and signalled for his chief informant and the two scouts and Dunne to follow him.

'It is interesting how you Australians always use the name of your God when you're angry.'

'Do we?' Cash shrugged. 'Now tell me about this bloody gang of Japs up the road. I'll feel better once we've wiped them off the face of the earth. Is it a bicycle unit only or have they got vehicles?'

Johnny Q shook his head. 'No vehicles.'

'They're probably waiting for the armoured units to catch up before they move on.'

Carvolt, a twenty-three-year-old dentist from Dubbo,

---

*Parit Sulong, massacres at: see *Endnotes*, p. 815.

agreed. 'I'd say so, sir. When we saw them coming through the trees at dusk last night the majority were laughing and joking as if they were riding to a football match.'

'We'll give the bastards a football match.' Cash eyed his men in the vague night light. Tired and weary they were, but with plenty of guts. *The boys of the 19th had gone in singing 'Waltzing Matilda'. The Japs had poured petrol over them and set them alight.* His stomach turned.

'Any other Japs in the vicinity?'

Carvolt looked round to Johnny Q who shook his head. 'We didn't see any. Not for five to ten miles, I'd guess.'

Taber was in accord. 'It seems there's just this lot. They've only put out two forward sentries to the south, and not very far from camp, perhaps a hundred to a hundred and fifty yards. Shows how damn sure they are they've got no opposition around here.'

Cash's mouth set in a grim line. 'Fine. The more cocksure they are, the better for us. They won't be expecting an ambush. What's the best way there?'

Taber answered. 'Straight up the road to a junction about a mile away with a deserted kampong to the east. They're bivouacked about another mile or more beyond that point but we need to leave the road and cross the jungle. Johnny Q knows a track through. We might be able to ride some of the way on our motor bikes and go on foot from there.'

Cash looked dubious. 'I don't think so. Can't chance their hearing us. We're best to leave the vehicles here and have them brought up to the junction for our getaway. I want all of us in place half an hour before dawn.' He glanced at Johnny Q. 'Now draw me a plan of their camp.'

Curly Dunne took out a dog-eared notebook and a pencil and handed them to the Malay while Carvolt leant in with his torch and Johnny Q began to draw.

Cash and Dunne knew something the others did not. They had been ordered to move south at first light: to retreat to Singapore. The war here in the Malayan Peninsula had gone badly awry and the British, Indians and Australians were falling back to the causeway and crossing into Singapore Island. He had received orders on the radio at

2100 and had been told not to delay. But after what the Malays had just told him, he could not in any conscience retreat when a hundred and fifty were just two miles away and asking for it. Too bloody tempting to resist! He was perfectly calm but he felt violent and his personal anger and revulsion had to be alleviated.

What had happened since 8 December had been staggering. The Japanese had launched their own form of Blitzkrieg and had come down through Siam like a shark after a seal: neutral one day and in full military flight the next. At the same time that Pearl Harbor in Hawaii had been attacked, devastating Japanese air raids had begun in Malaya and been quickly followed up by their troops on bicycles. Thanks to the money Great Britain had spent on the network of roads across Malaya the Japanese were riding down the peninsula following their air attacks and being reinforced from the sea. They carried their bicycles across rivers and streams and continued through the jungle on the perfectly paved roads. Each man carried a sub-machine gun strung across his chest and a rifle on the handle bars, and each company had its own bicycle repair unit.

Twelve months previously, when Cash arrived in Malaya, he had prevailed upon Colonel Anderson, his Commanding Officer, to allow him to train two platoons in Commando battle tactics and the hand-to-hand fighting he had learnt from Charles Hartford, one of his instructors back in Australia when he had been training to be an officer. Cash was certain that the sort of Commando warfare Hartford had taught him would be an ideal way to fight in the jungle.

Hartford had been in the Boer War and had been impressed by the mounted Boer units who made fast striking raids against the British troops. They had fought the natives in the same way. The Boers would rarely stand and fight, they would hit and run. He had spent time in the Middle East with British Special Forces and a Lieutenant-Colonel named Dudley Clarke who was expanding this 'hit and run' philosophy for mobile units.

Hartford, even at sixty-three, was still a physical fitness

expert and Cash's physical prowess, his strength and his abilities for climbing and stealth had made him the perfect pupil. Hartford had spent long hours showing Cash all he knew. 'Carry the war to the enemy' had been his catch-phrase.

Colonel Anderson had submitted Cash's idea to High Command; permission had been swiftly granted. The Colonel had said to him, 'It seems we're indulging your enthusiasm, Lieutenant. Apparently there are already one or two British Commando Units operating in Malaya but the powers that be appear keen to have yours.'

'Thank you, sir.'

'Though the belief is that when and if the Japanese strike, the war will be won or lost at sea.'

'Do you believe that, sir?'

'I'm not sure.'

The result had been that Cash was given two crack platoons to train and when the Japanese bludgeoned down from Siam he was ordered to hit the enemy wherever he could. He had done exactly that, but there was no stemming the deluge of the advance.

As December rolled into January the news became increasingly worse and when the Australians heard of the destruction of the British battleships the *Prince of Wales* and the *Repulse* seventy miles south of Kuantan on the Malayan east coast it was hard not to become disheartened.

Within a week, the battles that Butik had described had begun on the west coast at Maur on the Sungei Muar River, twenty miles inside Jahore and about ninety miles from Singapore Island. Amongst the defenders were three battalions of the Australian Eighth Division who had fought fiercely, holding out against the might of the whole of the Japanese Imperial Guards Division for seven days.

Cash had been told by his Malay spies that finally they were overcome by sheer numbers, but he knew his mates would have fought like lions! Hell, they were plainsmen, country boys shaped by the sun and the open spaces; they would have given a good account of themselves. From what he could gather, Colonel Anderson and some of his men had made a dash to the north then swung east to fight the Japanese again.

Cash was not a man for prayers but what he had heard tonight from Butik brought him close to praying for those boys of the Eighth Division and their Commanding Officers, Brigadier Maxwell and Colonel Anderson. He had always admired Anderson's astounding physical endurance and knew him for a brave soldier with a completely rational and fair attitude who inspired his men to great heights.

The news just got worse and worse. Yesterday, from what he gathered from Williams, the wireless operator, and from Johnny Q's contacts, two fresh divisions of Japanese had landed at Endau on the east coast and were engaging the Twenty-Second Australian Brigade at Mersing further south.

The rest of the Australians and other British forces were being drawn up to defend the road south from Mersing to the causeway leading to Singapore itself.

The British forces were also fighting at Keluang in the southern centre of the peninsula. This meant there was a line of defence running across the middle of Jahore but Cash was uncertain what was going on down the left flank since the stand at the Muar River.

One thing was now certain: they were fighting an enemy without conscience.

Cash and his men examined Johnny Q's drawing and decided on the angle of their attacks before Cash sent Taber and Carvolt off for a quick hour's rest while he lingered with Curly and Johnny Q.

The spy proffered explanation. 'In Japanese eyes it is a disgrace to be taken prisoner, that's why they treat them so badly.'

Cash halted and spun round. '*Badly?* That's a bloody tame word to use for what we just heard. Inhuman bastards! How about the old homo sapiens' emotion called compassion?'

Johnny Q's liquid gaze roamed acoss Cash's face. 'Perhaps they do not have it.'

Cash strode away and ran into Richards the cook. 'Here,

sir.' He handed Cash an open tin and a spoon. 'Have some bully beef. I've got one tin per man left and five tins of biscuits.'

Food? He could not eat! 'No, but make sure each man gets a ration before we set out. Wake them in half an hour.'

The Private saluted and moved away, hitting out at the ubiquitous mosquitoes.

Dunne eyed his superior. 'When will we be falling back to the causeway, Lieutenant?' Curly Dunne had been standing by Williams the radio operator when the message to withdraw to Singapore had come in. It had been particular. The brass wanted them back but they had asked specifically for Lieutenant Wade himself to return. He was to present himself at Fort Canning.

Cash cast a hard look at his second-in-command. 'As soon as the attack's over. If we can surprise this one last lot of sleeping monkeys, I'd retreat in a happier frame of mind.'

'Yeah, me too.' Dunne sniffed and wiped his nose on his wrist. 'It all makes ya feel sick.'

'Indeed it does.'

Dunne followed Cash to the jeep where they stashed the Thompson sub-machine guns – Tommy guns. 'They must have been planning this for years. The speed that this has happened has caught us with our bloody pants down.'

Cash agreed. 'You're right, Curly. The bastards might have been planning this while you and I were in knee-pants. You know all those Japanese barbers and photographers in every town in Malaya?'

Dunne did. It was true. 'Yeah.'

'All spies for sure! For years they'll have been sending back information to Tokyo. Remember those eager little photographers who kept offering to develop our film for next to nothing? And most of the bloody brothels in Singapore had Japanese girls in them. So what do you reckon?'

Dunne spat on the ground. 'I reckon you're right. I had my hair cut by a Jap barber a few months ago in Jahore Bahru. Asked me my Commanding Officer's name while he massaged the back of my neck. I told him I couldn't say, but I knew in my heart he'd get the info from somebody.'

'Patience – that's what they've got; more than any Westerner will ever realise. Oh yes, they've been preparing this invasion for bloody years, all right. Fifth Column little bastards everywhere.'

'Yep. One thing's certain, it's given the old boys of Kipling's *tin mines and rubber planters' clubs* a bloody shock.'

'You can say that again. Their comfortable little world with tiffin at two and gossip for dinner, will never be the same.'

Cash spent the next hour in preparation and ten minutes before they moved he gathered his seventy-one men together. Ambushes were their speciality. He did not need to tell them much, just who he expected to take out the sentries and what positions to go in from. He looked over their faces in the light from their two hurricane lamps which were guarded like gold. Stephen Daily from Blainey, their Quartermaster, somehow managed to hide the kerosene and dole it out as necessary.

'Now I've got something to tell you that'll stimulate you even more than usual. It'll make you want to annihilate these little bastards up the road. I can tell you I'm as motivated as hell and I want you that way too.' He revealed what Butik had told him to the increasingly incredulous and appalled soldiers.

'Johnny Q will verify what I've said.'

The man nodded. 'It's true.'

Silence. No man spoke. They looked around at each other.

'Right, let's move out!'

Four men who could hardly walk were left with the motor bikes and jeeps. They had tinea very badly, for in the damp, humid conditions soldiers became victims to extreme cases of this fungal skin condition. Once these men heard the start of the action they would ferry the vehicles up to the road junction for a quick getaway.

It was raining again when the platoons departed. Rain was the daily constant; nothing ever dried out thoroughly and all was soggy.

Cash led his men out.

The Australians made good time to the road crossing by the deserted kampong. The villagers had long gone.

From there they proceeded along Johnny Q's track in single file: walking in the eerie gloom through the eternal rain and the compact universal jungle, where swamps, streams and rubber trees filled the world and the pitch black was broken only occasionally by glow-worms in their thousands lighting up the endless rubber plants, the bamboo and the thick twined swollen *varicose vines* of the threatening jungle.

Each man held the bayonet scabbard of the man in front to keep together. They slid in the mud and staggered over hidden logs and vines until they emerged onto another road within 300 yards of the Japanese encampment where blessedly the rain abruptly ceased. They gathered around Cash in the darkness.

How I love the night even in this blasted steamy heat! Excitement prickled through him.

Johnny Q pointed to the enemy position and then moved off with Carter and Dale, the two youngest of Cash's soldiers and coincidentally the two swiftest at dispensing death. Cash and his men waited as the minutes passed.

'They're taking a while,' Bluey whispered.

'Yes.'

'It must be ten minutes. What's happened?'

Cash shrugged.

The men were getting restless. The time dragged. And it was twenty-seven minutes before they saw the dusky figure of Johnny Q, Carter and Dale emerge from the shadows.

'What the hell kept you?'

'The blasted sentries had moved. And there were three, not two.'

'Oh great. Well, I hope nothing else has altered, like some bloody reinforcements arriving.'

'No, Lieutenant. Still only the same number.'

'Good. Let's go.'

The troop moved forward with utmost stealth. The enemy were camped at the side of the road in a dip between a host of young rubber trees and low swampy ground. The plan was for half Cash's force to crawl on by the camp on the far side of the road and attack upon the enemy's flank. The Japanese would be caught unawares between the two platoons and the swampy ground.

The glow of dead fires could be seen but there was no movement.

Crawling along the roadside Cash led the first party, and Curly and the others began to edge into the jungle on the near side of the sleeping enemy. Due to the delay in taking out the sentries pale wisps of dawn light began to illuminate the sky before they were in position, and as Cash signalled for his men to hurry he saw one of the Japanese stand up and walk towards the jungle on the opposite side of the camp.

The man disappeared into the undergrowth and some seconds later an abrupt howling yell broke from him and the camp burst into life. Instantly Cash realised he must have found a dead sentry.

Bluey's troop reacted immediately. Mills Bombs hurtled through the air and the Australians on the south poured forward into the camp.

The Japanese staggered to their feet guns blazing and Cash leapt up and charged across the road pulling the pin from a Mills Bomb with Carvolt and Taber doing the same at his side. The noise was ear splitting as bits of shrapnel spat skywards and the sound of sub-machine guns rent through the dawning light.

The enemy were superior in numbers but the Australians had the value of surprise. They were upon the Japanese at the south of the camp before most of them were out of their sleeping bags. Two dozen thudded back to the ground before they had lifted their bodies upright.

But the enemy facing Cash were up, guns in hand, as Cash and his men came bounding across the road at them hurling their grenades then blazing away with their Tommy guns. Four of the enemy pitched forward and about twenty ran up the incline towards Cash and his two companions who dropped on their knees and kept firing. Bullets whizzed over their heads as the front row of the enemy fell but the others came on and met Cash's men in hand-to-hand combat.

One Japanese actually ran right into Cash, collided with him as he rose, and they spun a few feet away from each other. The man swung round firing his sub-machine gun but Cash was upon him and the bullets flew skywards as Cash thrust forward with his bayonet full force into his stomach, exactly as Harford had taught him.

Beautiful! Textbook! Centre of the solar plexus.
Rip upwards!
Dead in a second!
Perfect!

Blood spat out of the man's stomach over the steel blade as Cash retrieved his weapon, spinning on his back foot to intercept another arrival. This soldier was undersized and slashed with his bayonet at Cash's knees but, in ballet-like fashion, he jumped and swung his bayonet in an arc straight into the enemy's head. It sliced off his ear and the Japanese went down as Cash shot him at point-blank range.

Cash whirled round taking in the scene. Every soldier was now fighting hand-to-hand. The fury of the Australians was unleashed, and they fought ferociously.

'It's beautiful, like a football match, eh? Well, guess who the football is, you bastards!'

Cash's cries spurred his boys on. 'Kill them! Kill them!'

It was all over in another three minutes.

They counted the Japanese dead: one hundred and fifty-one, for the loss of seven Australians and fifteen wounded.

Cash stood and looked down at the dead Japanese. *Good, a hundred and fifty-one of the little sadists gone west.*

'Hey, look at their shoes, sir.'

Cash did.

'Why the cloven soles, sir?'

'Easier for them to climb trees to spy ahead.'

'Gawd!'

'Shoot each one through the head,' Cash shouted, eyes wild. 'Make sure we leave no survivors!'

Taber, Japanese blood on his forehead and down his trousers, lifted his pistol in the air. 'Yes, sir.'

'We were flamin' motivated all right,' Dunne said, wiping his mouth with the back of his hand as he spat on the ground.

Johnny Q, who had remained fifty yards down the road while the battle raged eased himself into the ranks of the victors, gazing inscrutably at Cash. 'Best we leave fast,' he advised.

'Right, boys. Pile the bloody bikes in a heap and hoist a few Mills Bombs in. They won't ride these again.'

He felt good. He felt heady. What a dawn! He was expert, and it was easy. Shame about his dead boys. He hated to lose his boys. Hell. Real shame. He turned to Dunne. 'Can the wounded walk?'

'Five can.'

'Then carry the ten who can't and move out as soon as we've blown up the bikes. Where are the boys who caught it?'

Dunne took him to the dead men. He knew them all, like brothers. One more thing he had against the Japs. He touched each man on the face, gently at the side of his eyes. Dunne watched him with pride, Johnny Q with a look that was unfathomable.

Immediately afterwards he crossed to the wounded men. They were remembering Butik's account of Parit Sulong; there was fear in their eyes. 'Don't worry, boys, we'll get you out. No one stays behind.' He gave them a quick grin and turned away, catching Johnny Q's eye. 'Is the fastest way out the way we came in?'

'Of course.'

'Then let's move.'

The jungle groped at them on the way back as it had previously on the way in; the human convoy moving more slowly now with the wounded. And as they came out at the crossing there were the vehicles all lined up and ready to go.

'You beauty!'

'How'd it go?'

'Bloody wonderful.'

The soldiers began climbing aboard as Williams called out from the back of the wireless truck, 'Lieutenant Wade, message coming in.'

Cash turned to Curly. 'Get all the men aboard.' He strode over.

A voice crackled out of the receiver. 'Is that Commando Twelve?'

Even though there were only three Commando Units operating in Malaya they had given them high numbers in an attempt to fool the Japanese into believing there were more.

'Yes, come in. Who's calling? Over.'

'What is your position? Over.'

'Who are you? Identify yourself.'

'Give me your position, please.'

Cash looked at Williams, and repeated, 'Identify yourself.'

'AIF Headquarters here. Is that Lieutenant Wade?'

Cash was getting a bad feeling. 'Are you boys from Sydney?'

'Sure. Sydney yes.'

'Ever been to Luna Park?'

A moment's silence. 'Sure, funfair on the harbour, near the bridge.'

'Right. What's your favourite ride?'

'Repeat please?'

'Do you like the underwater ride?'

Another silence. 'Yes, sure, the underwater ride, we like it a lot.'

Cash smashed his hand down on the top of the radio. 'Cut the connection now!'

Williams did. He was a boy from Wellington and had never been to Sydney. He looked up to his leader for an explanation.

'There is no underwater ride! They were Japs.'

'Jees, sir.'

'Wanted to know where we were so they could strafe us,

587

no doubt. Move out!' Cash raised his hand high in the air and jumped into the forward jeep beside Taber at the wheel.

An hour later as they were heading down to a junction where they would join with the main road to Jahore Baharu, they heard explosions in the distance and the drone of aircraft.

'The Japs are having their first fun of the morning somewhere.'

The enemy utilised fast, well-equipped aircraft, the Navy Os, and the old Brewster Buffalo fighter aircraft that the Australians and British put up against them were almost useless. The Allied pilots fought with the will and spirit of their brothers in Britain but they were overwhelmed by superior numbers and modern equipment. Every town and airfield had been bombed and strafed. All the raids were in daytime when the pilots could clearly see their targets. Why bother with night flying when there was little opposition except from the ground fire?

Cash and his boys were hit by enemy aircraft fire three times on the main road and each time they scattered into the trees and lost vehicles and were held down for half an hour or more until the Japanese either gave up or ran out of fuel and departed. They arrived at the bottleneck at Jahore Bahru as another sultry dusk slid quickly across the tropics.

Trucks, motor bikes, armoured cars, all manner of vehicles and soldiers and civilians on foot fought to enter the causeway, while overloaded sampans and small craft sailed unsteadily for the island. It took Cash's command all night to move four miles and cross to Singapore Island. But finally the boys of the Twelfth Commandos were singing as they rolled into Kranji:

> I touched her on the knee – how ashamed I was!
> I touched her on the knee – how ashamed I was!
> I touched her on the knee; she said, 'You're
> rather free!'
> Oh Gord Blimey how ashamed I was!

And on and on as the verses became progressively more indecent.

They ate breakfast with a unit from the Forty-fourth Indian Brigade and that was when Johnny Q came to him. 'I'll be leaving Lieutenant Wade. You do not need a spy now you're on the island fortress.'

'Where will you go?'

'I don't know. I have a sister out at Tengah in the north east. I will go there to begin with.'

Cash took off his watch. It was solid gold and he was very fond of it. He had 'acquired' it in Sydney before the war. He handed it to Johnny Q.

'I don't need payment. I hate the Japanese.'

'It's not payment. I want to give it to you. You've been a friend.'

The man's smooth face melted into a smile. 'I suppose I have.' He took the gift. 'Thank you. You are a curious man, Lieutenant, but you engender great loyalty.'

Cash took his hand and winked. 'Thank you. Goodbye, Johnny; be careful.'

That afternoon Cash and his soldiers rumbled into the camp at Pasir Panjang and the following morning Cash presented himself, hastily compiled reports under his arm, at Fort Canning where to his surprise even the sentries on duty appeared to be expecting him.

Within ten minutes he stood before Major Stacey, an Intelligence Officer on General Bennet's staff, in a small office over-stuffed with filing cabinets.

He saluted and handed across his reports.

'No doubt it's all here, but I've been told to congratulate you and your men.' Stacey pointed to a chair. 'We're aware of the way you harried the enemy. Well done.'

'Yet the enemy seem to be at our gates, sir.'

'Indeed.' The furrow between his eyes deepened. 'I cannot see how we can hold out too long. We need reinforcements in a hurry. You know, I've always believed that one British soldier was worth ten Japs.'

His visitor made a wry sound, replying with supercilious expression. 'Perhaps this time there are eleven Japs, sir.'

'That's not funny, Wade.'

'Sorry, sir.'

Stacey looked depressed. 'Even the reservoirs of water can't last with the way the troops and civilians are pouring into the island. And heavy air raids began here yesterday.'

'Yes, we were strafed as we came out from Jahore. I've got sixty-three men out at Pasir Panjang and I don't know what to do with them.'

Stacey gave him a strange look and opened a folder on his desk before he answered. 'Fact is, you won't be doing any more with them.'

'What's that, sir?'

He tapped the folder in front of him. 'In here is a request that might surprise you. It seems the police in Brisbane are interested in tracing any man in the AIF with your exact description.'

Cash did not speak or move but his eyes widened momentarily.

'Something about a killing. Do you know anything about a killing in Brisbane, Wade?' He looked down. 'In August 1936?'

'No, sir.'

'Well, as much as we would like to help the police back home, the powers that be here have other things on their mind, like saving this island.'

'I reckon, sir. Me too.'

He inclined his head. 'The other item is an order that sends you on your way out of here.'

Hell, they're sending me back to Brisbane! His hand clenched at his side. 'What does that mean, sir?'

'It means that someone has decided that they don't care if you are involved in a killing in Brisbane, you're valuable. And when the Army thinks you're valuable they're a law unto themselves. You're to leave here by flying boat to Java this afternoon. Your battle tactics are wanted somewhere in Europe is my understanding, and it seems you'll be headed to the Mediterranean, Malta's the place mentioned here.' He tapped the folder. 'I've been instructed to give you your orders. You're to leave your reports here with me but to take copies with you.' He pointed out through a glass-topped door. 'There's a good secretary at your disposal. She'll type up your report.'

Cash felt the relief trickle through him. But then he thought of his men.

'You're to be at the seaplane anchorage at Tanjong Rhu at eighteen hundred.'

'Excuse me, sir, but I don't want to leave my men. If I'm to be transferred or whatever the hell it is that's happening to me, I'm no good without them.'

'That's not how we see it. You're the one with the knowledge. You trained the platoons. Two other Lieutenants will be going out with you, they also ran their own shows like you did. You're the valuable ones.'

'And I have no say?'

Stacey looked irritable. 'Christ man, you're in the Army. You take orders. Now get out. In my opinion you're bloody lucky to be leaving here. I'd like to be coming with you.'

Cash saluted and headed to the door. As he took the handle Stacey asked, 'Are you from Queensland, Wade?'

Oh, bloody cute!

'No, sir. I grew up in New Zealand. Was born in New South Wales.'

'Right.'

Cash closed the door behind him. These Intelligence Officers were not stupid.

Back at Pasir Panjang he found it hard to farewell his men. It was an emotional hour and he visited the wounded in hospital and the others all hung round him until he mounted the jeep and drove away. Taber and Carvolt, Dunne, Carter, Dale and Richards climbed on the vehicle and rode to the front gate with him where they fell off into the long grass shouting their goodbyes.

He had led these men for eleven months but it might as well have been eleven years; their bonds born of the same experiences – ones you could not share with outsiders. The historians wrote about the convict mateship ethos already in the Australian character; well, if that were true, all they had undergone together here had just bloody magnified it. These blokes were his brothers.

591

He looked into Jack Taber's eyes for the final time and quickly turned away. Tears had not stung Cash's eyes since Sammy had left him, but his head was rotated from the driver much of the way back into Singapore town.

The last view he had of Singapore Island was one he carried with him for ever. As he climbed aboard the small craft which was to take him out to the flying boat, a Chinese priest in black frockcoat was sitting with a small boy fishing on the wharf. The heavy tropical dusk was oozing over the seashore as the child began to cry out with glee. The priest helped him reel in a fish and as Cash skimmed across the gloomy waters and the clouds lowered over the harbour both physically and metaphorically, the child, unaware of the hatred and angst looming down upon his island, lifted, with peals of laughter, the fish from the sea.

That very day Winston Churchill departed from the Commons with a sprightly step, his forward stoop momentarily disappearing as he turned to his private secretary. 'I must speak to Roosevelt as soon as possible.'

He had just faced a no-confidence vote in Parliament and had defeated it 464 to a single vote against.

Churchill had recently returned from the United States and Canada, his visit prompted by the Japanese attack on Pearl Harbor on 7 December and the declaration of war by the United States.

He and his new overt ally, the President, had planned for ultimate victory and he had come home sanguine about the future but to a catalogue of present trouble: three weeks before, two British battleships, the *Prince of Wales* and the *Repulse,* sent with four destroyers to protect Singapore, had been sunk near Kuantan on Malaya's east coast, and the Commander-in-Chief Admiral Sir Tom Phillips had been drowned. Battles had been fought and the British, Australian, Indian and Chinese troops had fallen back in front of the Japanese who were overrunning the Malay Peninsula and now threatening Singapore itself. In tandem with this, Rommel and his forces in North Africa were taking command of the desert and pushing the Allies back towards Egypt.

Churchill's Parliament had been impatient with him, for the war was not going their way, but he had defended himself so masterfully that it was said by a colleague that 'one could actually feel the wind of opposition dropping sentence by sentence.'

'There is much to do,' he mumbled as he rode in a jeep back to the Annex, a fortified stone flat overlooking St James's Park and above his underground War Rooms which had been prepared in 1938 in anticipation of massive air attacks on London. The War Rooms accommodated the War Cabinet and Joint Planning Committee.

Once there, not allowing himself the luxury of enjoying his victory, he lit a cigar, went down to the bunker and called on one of the two Atlantic telephone links to President Roosevelt, his counterpart across the Atlantic.

'I am troubled by events in Malaya. And the Australian and New Zealand Prime Ministers need aid. We need reinforcements to go to Singapore immediately.'

But immediately was impossible.

On 15 February, Cash was in India on his way to Europe when he heard Singapore had fallen the previous day. There was a place in his heart that opened wide with pain. He knew his sixty-three boys would never have surrendered. He knew as a given truth that they would never have allowed themselves to become prisoners of the Japanese, not with their knowledge.

How can it be that you're all gone? But gone you must be.

He saw them making their last attack. Charging madly into the oncoming Japanese: Taber, eyes wild, grinning at death, Tommy gun in hand striding out in front of Carvolt and Carter, Dale and Dunne, the rest of the two platoons racing on behind them. Shouting and singing 'Waltzing Matilda' as they ran, relentless-eyed, into the enemy.

The eager bronze sons of the red earth and the wide open plains, of freedom and clear golden sunsets and crisp

morning skies. The boys of the Australian Imperial forces!
His boys! Lions all!

Tears were beginning to be familiar.

*Hell, those sixty-three would have taken hundreds of Japs
out with them! No white flags for them! They wouldn't have
rolled over and surrendered. They would have given those
little bastards a whopping great big blasted surprise!*

Three months later Danny Defoe received a letter from
India.

17 February, 1942
Hello Danny,

*I've asked a girl I've met to post this for me to
avoid the British forces' censors. I think I can trust
her. She tells me the normal Indian post office doesn't
read the letters out of here. I'm going to believe her.
But God knows what the Indian post is actually like
. . . You might never get this, but if you do I want you
to know I'm all right.*

*It's as hot as hell here. Everywhere I've been is
the same.*

*I'm on my way to the island of Malta in the
Mediterranean Sea, but I've been in Malaya and
Singapore where the bloody Japs seem to be overrunning the place. They're a rotten enemy, sadists I
reckon like the Nazis. Birds of a feather flock together
– I lost a lot of great blokes in Singapore. All dead,
I know that for certain in my heart. I left sixty-three
of them there, all boys I'd trained. You would have
loved them, Dan. Just like us, they were. They liked
a drink too, like you and me. They would have given
a mighty good account of themselves that last day on
earth, I can tell you. They would have shocked those
little yellow buggers.*

*I get to wondering what this whole blasted war is
all about. The world's mad, of course. And one
supposes that at some time in the future there'll be
peace and in fifty years or so the new generations*

won't even care about what's happening now and we'll probably be on good terms with the enemy. That's pretty bloody depressing so I'll try to dispel that speculation with alacrity.

Stay healthy, lad, and not too many cigarettes, eh? Remember you promised to stop by the time I get home.

I miss Sydney and the beaches and the late nights with you. Ha ha – if you know what I mean.

Look after yourself and for heaven's sake stay out of gaol. You don't need to do any jobs, you've plenty of moolah till I get home.

Your pal, C.

PS Enclosed are two messages that I'd like you to post on to that address in Queensland I gave you.

Danny received the letter and he took the notes and posted them at the GPO in Pitt Street the same day.

Chapter Thirty-eight

John Baron entered the long reading room where the shadows had begun to gather between the leather chairs, and looked around. He saw Nicholas Cardrew's uplifted arm and strode past the trails of rising smoke from the cigarettes and pipes of the men with newspapers.

The two shook hands and John Baron sat in a wing-backed green chair.

'Thanks for seeing me, sir.'

'No trouble. I had to come up to London anyway and as the club hasn't been taken out by enemy bombing it's a good place to meet. What'll you have?'

'Oh, a beer will be sufficient, thanks.'

Nicholas who had a beer in front of him ordered another one from the elderly waiter and smiled at his visitor. 'They've run out of most spirits here but the beer seems to be holding out. Now, how can I help you, my boy?'

'I think you know the reason I asked to meet you.'

The older man nodded. 'Perhaps, but it's best I hear it from you.'

John Baron grasped and ungrasped his hands, before placing them palm down on each knee. 'Before your sister died she told me that she knew I was not the son of the people I believe to be my parents. She said I was the child of a Frenchwoman. She spoke badly of her . . . called her a whore. I know very little of your sister. She seemed entirely different from the rest of you . . . of your family. Alex has always told me she was only motivated by her own needs and desires and that she couldn't be relied upon. But the fact is, the woman was dying when she told me these things. And she reminded me of a day when I had

596

seen her before, once as a boy in Yorkshire. Do you know anything about that, sir?'

Nicholas shook his head. 'No, I don't.'

'Then it doesn't matter. She had made arrangements to see me many times. I now realise why, and through circumstances,' he gave a weak smile, 'like having to fight a war, I always cancelled our meetings.' He glanced momentarily down at the floor and his voice dropped. 'She must have been prompted by a very powerful hatred.'

Nicholas was looking at him with an uneasy expression. 'Yes, my sister was one to hold grudges.'

'So, sir, I'm here because I imagine you are the single person in this land who will be able to tell me the truth.'

'Are you sure it's what you want?'

'To know the truth?'

'Yes.'

'I'm sure. Can you tell me?'

Nicholas had tried to prepare for this, analysing what he knew and what Harriet had speculated. It was difficult for him. Unlike his sibling he did not wish to cause pain and he could see the anguish in the man before him.

He sighed. 'I can only tell you what I know, which in truth is very little, mainly just Harriet's speculations about you.'

'And what were they, sir?' John Baron could see the older man was very ill at ease and this made him believe even more that what had been said to him might be true.

The beer arrived and was placed on the low table beside John Baron as Nicholas began resignedly. 'What she said to me is virtually what you have repeated from her today. All I know as fact is that Harriet's first husband was a man called John Baron Chard, which of course, is your name. I was younger than her and the marriage did not last many years, about five, before he left her and went to France. You see, my boy, that's really all I do know as absolute fact. He returned to this country before the Great War began and died here. I would say that was in early 1914 from memory. My sister was obsessed with him. And I have only her word on anything else.'

'And what would *anything else* be, sir?'

Nicholas sighed. This was not easy for him. His daughter was in love with this man. 'JB, my sister was a trouble-maker. I don't really give great credence to her theories.'

'Yet I'd like to know what they were, if you don't mind.'

The older man did mind but he could see no way out except to lie and that was not in his nature.

'All right, JB, but remember what I'm saying is second-hand I do not have proof of it. Harriet *said* you looked like her first husband; you reminded her of him completely. She said there had been a child born of a union of his in France and that her first husband's cousin had taken the child as his own and gone to Australia.'

John Baron sat back in his chair. 'Do *you* think I resemble her first husband?'

'As I said, I didn't see him often. But perhaps there are similarities.'

'I look a lot like my own father – that is, the man whom I have always believed is my father . . . the man I *want* to be my father.'

Nicholas sat forward and tapped John Baron's knee. 'That's it – there you have it. You want him to be your father. Take my advice, JB. He *is* your father. He brought you up, moulded you, has given you all you have and loved you. Leave it there, lad. He's your father all right.'

The younger man studied Nicholas for a few moments in the silence that fell between them.

'Sir, there's so much you don't know.' He paused and thought a little before he went on. 'This might sound shocking, but there was a time when I was in love with the girl I call my sister. I love her even now, though time has forced me to hold her in a different part of my heart. And I hope you understand when I say I began to see your daughter because of the striking similarity she has to Sammy. Though it's . . . not the case now.' He looked down at his hands. 'I'm confused and angry.'

Nicholas had not expected anything like this and he did not speak as he reflected upon what he had just heard while the day waned and the shadows in the smoke-filled room met and mingled with each other.

John Baron broke the silence. 'I don't know what I feel any more.'

'What you've just told me is a lot to take in and accept, young man.'

JB nodded. 'I realise that sir, but I had to tell you now for one thing is certain: I must know the truth about myself. Where did they live, sir?'

'Who?'

'Harriet and her first husband.'

'They lived at Brokenhurst in the New Forest.'

'And did Harriet's husband actually have a cousin who went to Australia?'

Nicholas hesitated. 'I cannot answer about Australia reliably. I have only Harriet's word on it. But I know he had a cousin for they ran a shipyard together.'

'A shipyard?'

'Yes.'

John Baron nodded to himself before he spoke. 'We ran one in Yorkshire when I was a child. The coincidences seem very great.'

Nicholas admitted to himself that they did.

'And what was this cousin's name?'

Inside Nicholas gave a sigh of relief for he had never known. 'I don't know, son.'

'But as you said, my name is John Baron Chard sir, the same as Harriet's husband.'

'Yes, it is.'

'My parents have always led me to believe that I was born in Lymington in the New Forest.'

It was patently obvious that Nicholas was at best uncomfortable. 'JB, I've told you all I know. But I have a question for you. Do you intend to continue to see my daughter?'

'Sir, I can't answer that. The reality is I can't think of anything else just now other than my need to find out the truth.' John Baron took up the beer and drank before he placed it back on the low table beside his chair and stood. 'Thank you, sir. I appreciate your coming here to see me.'

* * *

The following afternoon under dark skies John Baron rang the bell outside the Lymington Register Office.

It took seven minutes for the information to be given to him. There was no baby's birth registered in the name of Chard in 1911. He asked the woman to check the years before and after. There were no Chard births at all.

The woman chewed her pencil. 'Are you the person in question?'

He hesitated. 'Yes.'

'You sure you were born here?'

'That's what I've always believed.'

'Did your family move away?'

'Well, yes, but I think it was some time later.'

The woman nodded. 'Most people were very proud to register their children but occasionally busy people, or the opposite if you know what I mean, forgot for a time. There was a fine and all for late registers, but rarely was it applied. Where did they move to?'

'Yorkshire.'

'When?'

'I'm not sure but around 1914 I think.'

'Goodness, that's years after.' She chewed her lead pencil again. 'You wouldn't think they'd forget for that long.' She smiled. 'Your mum still alive?'

'Yes.'

'Well love, just ask her.'

'Thank you.'

He wandered along Mill Lane to the dock and there on the seat were two elderly men smoking pipes. Seagulls strutted along the low stone wall behind them.

He greeted them and in friendly fashion they answered.

'Have you lived here long?' he asked.

One laughed, showing missing teeth. 'All our lives, laddie, all our lives.'

'Then would you recall Mr and Mrs Benjamin Chard who ran the boatyard here before the Great War?'

There was immediate recognition.

'Remember them? Of course we do. Bert here worked at the yard for years, didn't you, Bert?'

'Best years of me life. A good man was Mr Chard and his cousin, too. Ran it together they did till Mr John Baron went off to France.'

John Baron shivered as he felt the first drops of rain on his face. He drew his greatcoat around him as he asked his next question. 'Did Mr Benjamin have any children?'

Bert shook his head. 'Not a one. Well, none before they left here, anyway. And that was fast, like. Off they were the end of the first year the war started, I reckon it was, now I think of it. Never heard of them again. Though I think about those days a lot, you know. Old Jacob Scammon took over the yard and things were never the same. Went to pot after the war, it did. Shame about that.'

'True,' his companion remarked, puffing on his pipe and eyeing the drifting rain.

John Baron swallowed hard, contrived to say, 'Thanks,' and walked away across the stones of the dock.

The following day he was in the old town of Bridlington. He recalled a little of the main thoroughfare though he had not come often into Bridlington proper as a child.

He found the Register Office and the sign outside read: *Open weekdays 10 a.m. to 2 p.m.* A woman in a grey overcoat was just locking the door as he confronted her. 'Oh excuse me, I'm sorry to be so late.'

She spun round ready to reprimand, a glowering expression behind her black-rimmed glasses but the subject of her rancour was so good-looking in his RAF uniform that she merely cleared her throat and turned back and opened the door.

'Would you mind checking a birth date for me? The eleventh of November, 1911.'

'Goodness!' she exclaimed. 'Eleven eleven eleven. That's very auspicious. That's a lucky date, that is – Armistice Day thrown in and all. My old mum used to say eleven's the luckiest number there is.'

John Baron looked unconvinced.

'What was the child's name, please?'

'John Baron Chard.'

'I'll just get the files for that year.' She crossed to a stack of cabinets, opened a drawer and leafed through. 'Only sixteen births that year, but none of the name you say.'

'Could you look later?'

She bit the corner of her lip. 'Yes, they sometimes registered late that's true. I'll look in early 1912.' She did. 'No, nothing there.'

He gave her a grateful smile. 'I know this might sound odd, but I think that the birth might have been registered very late – I mean years late . . . Would you be kind enough to look in 1914 and '15?'

A perplexed expression crossed her face. 'But that would be very strange. People were proud to have their children. Waiting that length of time would be absolutely extraordinary.'

'Nevertheless would you mind please?'

She believed it useless, but who could refuse a man who looked like this and with ribbons for bravery on his tunic. She removed the files from the cabinet and placed them on a table. 'Nothing in 1914.' She pursed her mouth as she searched further. 'Good Lord! Here it is! I can't believe it. Registered in 1915, Friday the eleventh of January. I'm amazed. And look – there's a notation here.'

He came round the corner of the table to stand beside her.

She pointed as she announced: '"NB. Irregular: late notification of birth of male child, John Baron Chard. Seven and six paid in for offence committed".' She moved the document nearer the light. And John Baron saw the signatures:

Benjamin Chard, Father and *Egbert Lacy, Assistant Registrar.*

The woman was dumbfounded. 'I've never seen anything like this before. And only signed by an assistant to the Registrar! My mum's often told me the Registrar in those days was a lovely fellow, killed in Belgium, as so many were; name of Orlando Taff. The way she still speaks of him I'm sure she was soft on him. Bad days they were and they've come upon us again.' She heaved a sigh. 'It's strange the Superintendent didn't sign this, but there you are and close to thirty years ago, so there's naught to be done about it now, but I'd call it most unusual practice.'

John Baron picked up the form and held it.

'Do you want a copy?' the woman asked. 'Though I won't be able to have one done till tomorrow when I have help for a half day. It'll cost five shillings.'

'I would like one, yes. And thank you so much for all this.' He placed the form back on the table and moved to the door.

'By the way who was the child?'

He turned back. 'A relation of mine. I'll be back tomorrow for the copy.'

She gave him a searching look. 'Right you are then. Just see me.'

As he closed the door behind him she was speaking to herself. 'I'll have to ask my mum about the Chards, she'll remember them sure as sure. Knew everybody, did Mum.'

John Baron walked off down the street and hesitated outside the ancient church of St Mary and St Nicholas where something prompted him to enter by the tall wooden door and pause inside. He would have been very surprised to know that Benjamin had found himself in here twenty-seven years previously after registering the false birth notice.

But what filled John Baron's mind as he eyed the ancient walls was the recollection of seven years before in the other St Mary's, thirteen thousand miles away across the world and the great sadness that had carried him inside to meet the Catholic priest. The guilt, the sickness he had felt: how he had believed himself contemptible for his indecent feelings towards his sister! His sister?

No! *Not* his sister. Nothing he had felt had been wrong. Nothing had been wrong. Nothing had been wrong . . .

He leant forward and grasped the back of the wooden pew in front of him and his vision blurred. He remained head bent as he pictured his family on the verandah at Haverhill so far away. The two who had brought him up and loved and nurtured him.

Mum and Dad, whatever your motives were, I know they

were good and wonderful, for that's what you both are. Whatever the reason, I know you did it all for me. How could you possibly have guessed that Sammy and I would care the way we did?

He suddenly realised that Ledgie and Wakefield must be partners to the secret. He stood up as he wiped the back of his hand across his eyes and focused on the altar in the distance where a cross gleamed in the low light.

He thought of the turmoil the world was in; his feelings simply mirrored the whole damn thing. He shook his head and turned and walked out into the street.

The winter dusk was falling when he kept the promise he had made to his mother on his final departure from Haverhill on his way to England. He found the gentle green rise behind the town where little Vivian had been buried twenty-three years previously. Her moss-covered grave rested beside a copse of leafless beeches, and clumps of ice from the previous day's snowfall still clung to the grass near the headstone.

Vivian Chard
Our Darling Baby
Left us at 2 years and 4 months on 4 April 1919.
Suffer the little children to come unto me.

Beloved daughter of Constance and Benjamin
Sister of John Baron and Samantha
Godchild of Millicent and Wakefield.
Thy will be done.

John Baron sat for a long time on the overgrown grave and stared at the boles of the naked trees until the wind bit through his greatcoat, and in the darkness he rose and walked slowly back into town.

Four days later he telephoned Sammy and was pleased just to hear her voice.

'Sam?'

'Gosh, JB, this is a nice surprise.'

'Look, I'm sorry I wasn't much help about Belfast when we met last.'

'Don't be silly. That's all right. I'll probably go.'

'Really?'

'Yes. Victor Bradbury's going; so we'll be working together.'

'The new boyfriend?'

Sam sounded irritated. 'I suppose so.'

'I thought you said you might join one of the women's services?'

'JB, going to Belfast for *Newsweek* doesn't preclude me from doing that when I come back.'

'If you go when will it be?'

'Oh, in about two weeks or so.'

'I'm back on active service soon.'

'Oh dear, when will I see you?' There was a long pause. 'JB? You there?'

'Yes.'

'Can we see each other before you go back to fighting?'

'Sammy, let me ask you something.'

'What?'

'Are you happy?'

'Oh my heaven. You ask me that on a telephone. That's a question for a long grey afternoon of rain.' She gave a giggle. 'I'm not sure I've ever been happy since the days when you and I and Cash charged like mad things along Teviot Brook upon our horses.' She laughed again. 'Those were the days.'

He sounded forlorn. 'Yes, weren't they?'

'JB, are you all right?'

He gave a grim smile down the line. 'I'll call you next week and I'll try to see you before you go to Belfast.'

'Good. Perhaps we could go back to the Marble Arch shooting gallery so I can slaughter you.'

'You and whose army?'

She laughed again. It was so good to hear that sound.

After hanging up he walked back to his office and sat looking out of his window at the bleak Lincolnshire afternoon until Sergeant Norris, his Canadian aide tapped on the door. 'Your meeting with Group Captain Chadwick's in five minutes, sir.'

When the meeting was over he telephoned Alex.

She was excited to hear from him but couldn't help saying, 'I've been so worried about you.'

'No need to be.'

The forthright Alex was quick to reply, 'Oh, you think so? You walk out of here like a haunted man and I don't hear anything from you for seven days and I'm not supposed to be worried?'

'Alex, please. Just leave it, will you. I'm telephoning now to say I'm all right.'

Her voice softened. 'Look, I'm pleased to hear from you, really I am. But JB, I hate being in the dark. I know that whatever Aunt Harriet said devastated you, and I'm aware that Daddy knows something about it. Whatever it is, can't you confide in me?'

There was a hesitation. 'I will one day but till then you've got to trust me.'

She heaved a quiet sigh. 'I miss you. When am I going to see you?'

'I'll be in touch.'

The disappointment in her voice dripped down the line. 'Oh.'

'Alex, I've asked to return to active duty. I'll be posted to a squadron in about ten days.'

She tried to brighten. 'I could come up to you.'

'I'm pretty busy here at present. Listen, Alex. The truth is, I think we should have a moratorium for a while.'

'What on earth does that mean?'

'In this instance, to temporarily cease seeing each other. Look, this isn't easy to say. I—'

'Oh, I see – a *temporary* break from each other.' She took a deep breath. 'All right, JB, if that's what you want.' She tried to sound matter-of-fact but a nuance of defeat crept into her voice. 'I don't know what's going on.'

'I'm sorry, Alex.'

She swallowed hard. 'Are you? Look, there's something you should know.'

'What?'

'I've volunteered to drive ambulances in London. I'm going to be staying with Jane's friend Kerry Kelly. You'll remember her flat – it's in Kensington.'

John Baron certainly remembered it. He felt bad. 'Right. What do your parents think?'

'They understand my feelings.' She paused.

'London's dangerous, Alex.'

'That's the whole point, JB. I want to help win the war.'

He was silent so she continued. 'The lady downstairs there has a telephone.'

'Two minutes – are you extending?'

'Oh hell,' Alex replied and rattled off the number. 'Did you get that?'

'Yes.'

The line went dead.

Chapter Thirty-nine

New Year's Eve, 1942

As midnight approached at Haverhill there was the benefit of a slight breeze which brought the temperature down marginally even though it still read 84 degrees Fahrenheit on the thermometer attached to the wall by the kitchen door. The ladies in attendance on the verandah all fanned themselves.

Marjorie and Randall Slade and Henrietta and Hank Thomas had joined the ranks of those at Haverhill to enjoy a mild celebration for the New Year.

Electricity had arrived the year the war began and so there was a hanging light now, around which the moths clustered in profusion while beneath it Constance smiled at Benjamin and as Wakefield counted down the last ten seconds to the New Year she leant across to kiss his lips. 'I hope this year is a better one, darling.'

'Yes, my lovely girl, I hope so too.'

Wakefield cried, 'It's midnight,' and lifted his glass. 'To the end of the war!'

The gathering repeated the toast and drank.

Randall Slade looked meaningfully over at the host and Ben took the hint and rose to his feet amid polite applause. He glanced around the faces and his eyes rested softly on seven-year-old Storm who was asleep on Crenna's capacious lap. As the years had passed Veena and her child increasingly spent more time at Haverhill until now they lived here, as accepted members of the extended family. Under Ledgie's tutelage Veena had turned into a marvellous cook and now that the elderly woman found the worst of the heat too debilitating, Veena had taken over the kitchen. She and Crenna had become great friends and they accepted Ledgie's chiding with remarkable fortitude.

As Ben began to speak he smiled at Ledgie who lifted her yearly glass of sherry in his direction.

'It's the New Year and 1943 has arrived. None of us knows what it'll bring. But our greatest wish is for the war to end. Over the last twelve months we saw the Japs advance in our direction. As we know, Singapore fell into their hands and so too did the Philippines, Java, Burma and much of the South Seas. Then their air raids followed on Australia itself in Darwin, Wyndham and Broome and while they attacked no further we in Australia were made to feel vulnerable.

'But we've had Allied successes as well. We stood our ground in the Battle of the Coral Sea between New Guinea and Queensland when the Americans came to our aid and our Air Force fought from the aircraft carriers alongside them, and now the Australian Army, Navy and Air Force are fighting back with the Yanks all over the South Pacific. We've got boys fighting the Japs in New Guinea at places like Milne Bay and what the newspapers tell us is becoming known as the Kokoda Trail. And we know about the American victory at the Battle of Midway last June so we're starting to give the blasted Nips a run for their money.'

The group broke out clapping and Randall Slade shouted, 'And don't forget the Australians are fighting along with the Brits against the Germans and Italians in North Africa and the Middle East.'

Benjamin nodded. 'Too right, so the war continues and all we can do is support the war effort and hope that the right side wins.'

'Hear, hear!' Wakefield raised his glass while Ben paused and looked at his wife who was at that very moment knitting a vest to go in a Red Cross parcel to troops in cold climates.

'And we who are gathered here know the constant fear of having our children far away fighting for freedom. JB's in the Royal Air Force and his mother and all of us worry

609

for him every day. And Samantha's in London where they're still constantly being bombed.'

'Don't know why the silly gel doesn't come home,' Ledgie interjected, her cheeks pink from the alcohol.

'They're doing what they believe in,' Wakefield proclaimed and Ledgie gave a grunt of irritation.

Ben raised his hand for quiet. 'While we're talking of our children we must mention Wesley.' He glanced at Henrietta and Hank Thomas. 'He's just joined the Navy and gone off to Sydney.'

Wakefield put down his glass and applauded loudly.

'And even though we haven't heard from Cash in a long time I think we should speak of him tonight.'

Constance shot a glance at Ledgie, for two notes from Cash had arrived in an envelope posted at the GPO in Sydney about four months before. One had been to Sam, and Constance had posted it on to London. The other had been to them all, but the women had not shown it to the men in fear of the Brisbane Police calling again and a slip being made by Wakefield or Ben.

Marjorie Slade looked round at her husband; they had not heard from Cash. Randall Slade shook his head disconsolately as Ben went on: 'We all believe Cash is doing his bit somewhere. In fact, in our hearts we're sure he is, for there was one thing about Cash and that was he wasn't afraid of anything. So let's all stand and drink to our kids who are fighting for the freedom of mankind against the greatest evils humanity has ever known.'

They all rose and declared, 'To our kids!'

'May they come home safely,' Ledgie added spiritedly. 'Hear, hear!'

Wakefield turned to Ledgie. 'Now, *ma chérie*, how about playing us "Auld Lang Syne"?'

Ledgie protested but she moved to the piano and they all held hands and sang. And afterwards, continuing in the spirit of the evening, their voices lifted in 'My Old Dutch'. Everybody was staying the night so the little party went on until around one-thirty and then as Wakefield carried Storm into her mother's room and the others trailed off to bed, Constance took Marjorie Slade's hand and drew her aside.

'I've got a secret to tell you.'

The woman's eyes opened wide.

'I know Cash is estranged from you but you'll remember once before we received a letter from him and he said to tell you and you only, that he was all right.'

Marjorie remembered. 'Yes.'

'Well, we've had another, not four months ago. I haven't said a word to the menfolk for those policemen still call out here from time to time asking about him.'

'They visit us too.'

'And the men might say the wrong thing.'

Marjorie smiled in agreement. 'Too right.' She bent her head and Constance noticed a stray curl fall forward on her brow, just the same way that Cash's did, and before she realised what she was doing, she tucked it back into Marjorie's hair and the woman, pleasantly surprised at the intimacy, gave her a friendly smile. 'Thanks.'

Constance cleared her throat. 'Well, dear, don't say a word but this will set your heart a little more at rest.' She took a folded paper out of her pocket and handed it to Cash's mother who moved down to the light to read it.

Dear Mum and Dad Chard, Ledgie and Wakefield,

A pal of mine in Sydney will send this on to you.

I'm on my way to the European war zone. The big brass seem to want me over there. Anyway, this is to tell you I'm well and to ask you to post the letter herewith on to Sammy as I have no idea where she is.

Please be kind enough to tell my mother I'm all right because I know she's a worrier.

I miss Queensland but where I've been I've had enough of tropic heat for a while, I can tell you.

Stay beautiful, Ledgie, and I'll see you all one day.

It was signed with a C.

Marjorie lifted her eyes to Constance. 'He *is* in the Army, or the Navy, or something, I always knew he was.' Tears

611

formed in her eyes as she returned the note. 'Thank you so much. I feel better now.'

'Hey, you two.' Benjamin stood at the kitchen door. 'I'm turning off the lights. You can chatter away all day tomorrow.'

Marjorie gave Constance a thankful smile and the two women said good night.

As Cash wandered along in the light rain with his companions he wondered what his old mate JB might be doing tonight; he was probably in the officers' mess being waited on. There were times he really missed JB. And Sammy? Hell, he missed her all the time. Then he thought of Danny back in Sydney. He could picture him in his little retreat behind the stadium, probably alone and sipping on a beer and having a cigarette.

He turned to his three companions as Matt Fleming, a Second Lieutenant who idolised Cash, remarked, 'Here comes the heavy rain again.'

'Yeah, well that's this town. Rains a lot.'

On Cash's other side Lieutenant Phillip Boyd gestured with his thumb at a side thoroughfare. 'I can't see a thing. Point that torch along here. I think I know where we are.' And as the beam of light explored ahead he announced, 'I thought so. That's a real toffy pub. We'll get a drink for certain. Come on.' And he charged ahead in the rain followed closely by his comrades.

'Congratulations!'

'Have another glass, *sir*.' Henry Garner laughed from where he stood on a chair holding up a bottle of wine. He lifted it dramatically and began to pour it over the castle of glasses stacked one on top of the other on the bar.

Henry was now a Wing Commander, had been for seven months and was stationed at Debden. He had come over to the sector station at Martlesham Heath to celebrate New Year's Eve and John Baron's recent promotion to Group Captain. Tommy Hopkins was there as well; his squadron was not far away at Duxford. The three had enjoyed a marvellous few hours of reminiscing about the early days in France and discussing where each of the old squadron's pilots were now.

The mess at Martlesham was getting louder as midnight approached. A gramophone played and smoke drifted across the ceiling in the hullabaloo.

Martlesham was where Douglas Bader had commanded 242 Squadron from December 1940 to March 1941 and where Douglas had begun to lead many of his 'big wings' out over enemy-occupied territory. JB's squadrons flew the new MARK IX Spitfires, had just been re-equipped with them, and his boys were gently ragging him about the consequence of his recent promotion. 'You'll be *flying a desk* as a Station Commander in no time.'

Lou Edmont, a young ace with three kills to his credit reached up and gingerly eased a glass off the top tier and handed it to John Baron who took it and smiled at the sea of faces. 'Let's hope this blasted rain stops because we come to "stand-by" first thing tomorrow. The Huns won't be taking New Year's Day off.'

A general groan sounded because 'stand-by' – sitting in the cockpit, waiting for immediate take-off when enemy aircraft were sighted – was very unpopular.

John Baron went on, 'And tomorrow afternooon we've got a rendezvous with a squadron of Blenheims. We're going to be their close escort and top cover to a nice little target across the Channel.'

His boys cheered and someone shouted, 'It's coming up to midnight!' And there was Vera Lynn's voice again echoing through the mess telling them, 'We'll meet again.'

Twenty minutes later the Commanding Officer excused himself and shook Henry and Tommy's hands and with a backward glance towards his men, shouted over the clamour, 'Get some sleep, you lot! You'll be on deck at sun-up!'

Someone shouted back, 'Thank God it's midwinter, sir!'

John Baron smiled as he strode out of the mess; that was true, it would be close to 0800 before dawn. He pulled his greatcoat around him and hurried across in the jet-black night to the Operations Building. Inside, a single bulb lit the corridor as he passed along it and opened his office door and switched on his light.

Glancing automatically to see that the blackout drape was drawn he crossed to his desk where he picked up a sheaf of papers. He was working on the escort of a large bombing raid planned to hit targets in the Moselle Valley a week hence. He looked at the top sheet of paper, hesitated and put it back down thinking about his loved ones.

A few days before Christmas he had received a fat envelope from his parents – they would always be that no matter what. Inside the envelope were letters from all his family. Two pages from his mother and two from his father, three from Wakefield, one from Ledgie in her failing hand – that had depressed him. One page from Crenna and even one from Veena who lived and worked at Haverhill now. On the bottom of her page had been twelve kisses with rings for hugs from little Storm. They had brought him up to date with everything in their lives and his father had ended his message with: *Remember where your home is, son. When this war ends I hope you'll come back to us. My great wish is that you continue to run this property as your own one day.*

He sat on the edge of his desk as he pictured his family 13,000 miles away across the seas and he twisted the gold ring on his little finger that his parents had given him for his twenty-first birthday.

Since he had learnt about his origins John Baron had spent a lot of time searching his soul.

Finally he had decided to tell his parents what he knew and to ask them all the circumstances surrounding his birth. But that was not a thing to accomplish by letter: it was something to do after the war, face-to-face – although he had written a letter to be delivered in the event of his death, telling them what he knew. It was lodged with a firm of solicitors who kept their records in a small village in Wales away from the possibility of loss through bombing. In it he revealed Harriet's last words and his own conclusion that he was the son of a Frenchwoman and John Baron Chard,

Benjamin's cousin, but more than that he did not know. He told them he loved them as if they were his true parents; that he needed no others, and that Ledgie, Wakefield and Sam had made his life full and wonderful. He mentioned nothing about his feelings for his sister for he would never wish to hurt them in any way.

He had seen Sam only three times during the year though they telephoned each other about once a month and he had made a point of taking her to the theatre for her birthday just three weeks ago. He had spent the year trying to accept what he now regarded as the truth.

His emotions towards Sammy remained complex. He knew that he loved to be with her and to hear her laugh, but he also knew that he had acknowledged her as his sister for three decades. The terrible heartache of Christmas 1934 was long behind them. He was not really sure how Sammy felt. It was something he never asked.

Thinking of Sam brought him to thinking of Alex.

He had only spoken to her once since Harriet's death and that had been shortly afterwards. But he was thinking of her tonight as a New Year edged its way into the world. Last New Year's Eve they had spent together and had made love in the small hours of the morning. He wondered where she might be now. At the flat in Kensington, or home at Castlemere? Or somewhere else with some other bloke? That thought bothered him as he sank forward onto his desk, his head in his hands.

The grandfather clock in the corridor outside struck twelve and Ed Monroe took Samantha in his arms and kissed her deeply. She wriggled out of his embrace as he said, 'I hope the New Year turns out to be a good one, darling.'

The room was filled with war correspondents and men and women in uniform; all the major publications in London and the USA were represented as well. They had taken a room at the Savoy Hotel to throw a low-key party, and with rationing at its height and only beer and wine to drink, it was a pleasant surprise when bottles of port and brandy appeared as the New Year came in.

'Come on, you two,' laughed Brian Jacobs, correspondent for Columbia Broadcasting, lifting one of the port bottles high. 'Let's drink to good news this year.'

'Like the war's ended?' Sam asked as he planted a quick kiss on her mouth and smacked his lips.

'Ah, my dear Samantha, I wish it could be – but I very much doubt it.'

Ed Monroe held out his glass with one hand as his other found Sam's waist. 'Well, whatever's coming let's enjoy tonight.' He was a New Zealander, a Captain with an Infantry Division based near Weybridge. They had met in October at a New Zealand Forces Club where all ranks were included, both Officers and Non-Commissioned Officers, and their 'Tui' female volunteers had all come over from New Zealand to staff them. Apparently a Tui was a bird, a honeyeater with attractive green-blue plumage.

Staffing the New Zealand clubs and canteens with girls from home was the idea of their own General Freyberg and it had given them a refreshing homely feel different from many others.

The result of meeting Ed had been the end of her relationship with Victor Bradbury, and even now as Ed threw down his drink, Sam saw Victor pushing his way through the mêlée towards her and she slipped out of the soldier's grasp. 'I'm going to the ladies' room.'

'Hurry back, it's not the same without you.'

As she headed to the door Victor caught up with her. 'A New Year kiss, for old times' sake?'

She met his eyes. 'All right.'

He pulled her to him and covered her mouth with his though she quickly ended the caress and stepped back. 'Have a good year, Victor.'

'I miss you,' he said with conviction.

She touched his arm, shook her head and moved away.

Out in the corridor Sam hurried along to the ladies' room and when she left it instead of going back to the party she walked up the short flight of stairs and stood beside a window which fronted onto the Embankment. This part of the hotel had been damaged more than once when enemy aircraft flew along the Thames in attempts to bomb the Houses of Parliament nearby.

Sam deliberated a moment and then slipped inside the velvet blackout curtain and pressed her face to the glass. It was freezing and she could see nothing. London was black and wet. She took off her long gloves and touched the pane with her fingers, trembling with the cold. She was thinking of the year gone by. She had just done the same old things. After the meeting with Major Jaffer she had felt ready to do what he asked, but then as the days passed her conviction waned and she had phoned him and told him she wished to delay her decision. He had been charming and polite. 'I understand perfectly. I must say you're the sort of person we need, Mrs Slade; people of your quality don't come along too often. If ever you alter your mind you know how to contact me. The number you've called today will always be in service.'

She had gone to Belfast with Victor, and *Newsweek* were more than satisfied with her submissions. Recently they had given her the option of accepting an assignment with the American Pacific Fleet and she knew that was really an honour. She was considering it. Then when she had met Edmund Monroe something had clicked between them. They had a lot in common. Perhaps it was that he was from the Antipodes like her, for they seemed to think alike. He had come from a sheep property near a place called Tauranga, and he loved horses and animals and the open countryside. He contrasted sharply with Victor who was an urbane journalist; she just felt happier with Ed.

Footsteps and voices sounded on the stairs outside the drapes where she remained unmoving, feeling the velvet at her back until the sounds died away. Then, pulling on her gloves, she whispered into the blackness around her, 'I'm thinking of you all, my darlings. All of you: Mummy and Daddy and Ledgie and Wakefield. What I wouldn't give to hold little Storm in my arms and wander along the brook taking snaps with Veena. And I'm thinking of you, my dearest brother and yes, Cash, you too. Even you. I wonder where you are?' She rested her forehead on the icy glass for a moment then stepped back. 'Hell,' she said aloud as she pushed her way out through the heavy drapes to the interior again. 'Come on Samantha, buck up,' and she began to hurry down the steps so fast that she collided with a serviceman coming up.

'I'm so sorry – Oh my Lord God!'

They both halted in amazement, eyes locked.

'Sammy! What are you doing in London?'

Cash, in officer's uniform, was standing there on the step below regarding her and looking wonderful, his ebony curl suspended on his forehead.

'I live here. What are *you* doing here?'

He grinned. 'Long story.' He took hold of her hands. 'Ah, m'lady, just let me look at you. I've dreamt about this.'

She suddenly felt bashful, like a schoolgirl. It was ridiculous but she could not help it. His fingers were squeezing hers through her gloves.

She was the last person he had expected to meet. He had believed her to be in the States with Lenny the Loser but no, here she was before him and looking a dream as always with her hair tumbling to her shoulders and her eyes the colour of a beaut clear Queensland sky. God, what a girl!

'You look great, Sammy.'

'So do you. But how on earth did you get here?'

He slipped his hand up to her arm. 'Let's find a seat and talk. I've got three mates somewhere but they'll be all right.'

As she allowed him to lead her up the stairs he continued, 'I've been trying to find out where JB is without any success. I've only been here three days and I'm off to Wales in the morning.'

She felt a little surge of disappointment to hear that.

'Why? What's in Wales?'

'They're going to teach me advanced parachute jumping, whatever that means, and a few other little tricks.'

He paused at the top of the stairs and she halted beside him. She could not believe Cash was here in the Savoy in London with her.

'Sammy, I've dreamt about you in Australia, Singapore,

Java, India, Syria, Malta and a little hell-hole in Egypt called El Alamein which I got out of only a couple of weeks ago.'

Sam knew of the third great battle that had been fought and won at El Alamein in October and November. So Cash had been there! She supposed nothing about Cash could ever really surprise her. She noticed the Major's crown on his shoulder but the badge he wore on the cap under his arm she had never seen before. It looked like a pair of angels' wings with a dagger striking down through the middle, and a banner underneath had *Who Dares Wins* embroidered upon it.

Cash was studying her. 'Hell, Sammy, all we need now is for JB to walk in and we'd have one of the world's great reunions going!'

She laughed, a happy carefree sound.

'Do you see much of him? He's here, isn't he?'

'Oh yes, as much as I can. He's in Essex – just been promoted to Group Captain. I can tell you how to get in touch with him.'

He paused then and looked searchingly at her. She was smiling at the mention of JB, her eyes bright and merry, and just for a second he wondered if he should tell her that JB was not her brother, but he dismissed the embryonic thought.

Surely part of her smile was for himself?

She looked up at Cash, truly delighting in being with him, unmindful of anything else. 'I received your messages. They took a long time to get here via Mum but I was glad you sent them.' She recalled the day on the bus when she was reading one and how upset she had been.

He grinned. 'I'm only pleased they made it to you.'

'I didn't know where to reply.'

'No.'

She sighed and played with the fingers of her gloves. 'Gosh, we made a mess of things, didn't we?'

'Uh huh! We definitely did.' He took her arm and steered her through into a lounge. 'Now, m'lady, where should we—'

'Samantha! What's going on?' They turned to see Ed

619

Monroe. 'I've been looking everywhere for you.' He took her free arm and there she stood beween them.

The two men glowered at each other for a moment then Cash released her. 'Are you with this bloke?'

Sam's mouth opened but Ed answered, 'Yes, she is. Look, Major, this lady and I are a double. She's my girl.'

Cash took a step away and Sam half raised her hand towards him before it fell back to her side.

Cash's voice was leaden. 'Are you his girl, Sammy?'

'I . . . oh Cash . . .' She turned to Ed with a pleading expression. 'Ed, listen to me. I must speak with the Major. This is important. Please just wait here. Please don't cause a fuss.'

'I don't like this, Sammy. It's bad enough being in the room downstairs with that Bradbury bloke who wants to be all over you.'

Cash's mouth formed a tight line as Sam drew him further away into the lounge. Ed did not move, he remained where he was, staring at them, while Sam spoke.

'Cash, I'm so pleased to see you. Listen, this is a little awkward.'

'I'd say it's bloody awkward.' She saw the disappointment in his face and it hurt her. 'This galah's all indignant and waiting for you, and there's some other fella on the make downstairs.' A brittle sarcastic note edged into his voice and the eager light in his eyes withered. 'Just as a matter of interest, exactly how many have there been since me?'

She blinked. His words were like a physical blow. She had felt so thrilled to see him and now this had happened. 'Oh Cash, listen to me, please. It's not like it looks.'

He shook his head and now his tone was flippant. 'Oh really? Isn't it? Don't explain, Sammy. Hell, there's a war on and a girl's got to have company. Helps her through the night.'

'That's cruel, Cash.'

'Yes, it is. Who are you working for these days, Sam? Or perhaps you don't work any more, perhaps you just . . . ?'

'Cash *don't*, please. I work for *Newsweek*, an American

magazine. Look here, take my card, this has my home address and telephone number – well, my landlady's telephone, that is.' She fumbled in her purse and found a card and handed it to him.

He took it without looking at it and put it in his pocket. 'Do you write home, Sammy?'

'Oh God, yes, Cash. Of course I do.'

He stepped back from her and she came a pace closer to him but he raised his hand to halt her and deliberately moved away again. 'Then remember them and remember they love you and might not be happy to know how you're conducting your life.'

'Oh Cash, don't judge me. I was so happy to see you. Don't you want to see me again?'

She found it impossible to read the emotions that washed over his features. 'I'd rather not be just another one of your retinue, Sam.'

She felt ill.

'Ah, m'lady, why do I let you do these things to me?' He accomplished a brief smile. 'It was really good to see you, Sammy. Look after yourself and be careful who you get hooked up with.' He spun on the heel of his boot and walked away.

She wanted to run after him, justify Ed and Victor, everything. But then how could she?

'Well, thank goodness *he's* gone.' Ed's relieved tones sounded in her ear and his hand went round her waist. 'Come on, Samantha darling, let's get back to the party. Noël Coward's down there playing and singing. You'll like that.' He gently steered her to the corridor. 'Anyway come on, who was he?'

Who was he? Who was he? Just my husband, that's who he was. Just my husband . . . Just my husband.

She did not answer, she simply wiped her eye with her gloved hand.

'Listen, Samantha. It doesn't matter who he is. Just tell me sometime when you're ready. All right?'

She looked back to the empty doorway where Cash had disappeared before she cast her eyes to Ed. 'It's the war,'

621

she said, sniffing and clearing her throat. 'You get so damned sentimental during wartime.'

Cash's companions saw him as he entered the room on the ground floor where they had been drinking with three Wrens.

'Here, Major!' Phillip Boyd called out, waving from the centre of the room.

Cash pushed through to them.

'Thought we'd lost you,' Matt Fleming grinned, throwing down the remnants of a pint of beer.

The Wren who had been talking to Phillip took one look at Cash and sidled over to him. 'Where've *you* been hiding?' She had striking eyes; they affected a green colour in the electric light.

'Oh, nowhere. Just with my wife.'

'Wife? Are you kidding?'

'He hasn't got a wife!' Phillip laughed, putting his arm round the Wren and drawing her back towards him. 'Have you sir?'

Cash gave a quick wry smile and strived to lighten his voice. 'No, I haven't, Lieutenant.' He pulled the Wren purposefully back in his direction. She did not resist. 'I haven't now and I never did have.'

Driving rain and sleet hit the windows of Castlemere as Lillian Cardrew adjusted her spectacles, lifted her champagne and announced, 'It's nice to be with good friends and it's a rarity to have all our daughters at home together, so let's drink to the coming year, may it be better than the previous ones – and here's to the end of the war.'

'To the end of the war,' declared Nicholas and at his side Norman Levinson proclaimed, 'Hear, hear!' as he sipped on the champagne.

Suddenly Jane bent her head, obviously distressed, and her mother moved protectively to her side. 'Now, sweetheart, what's wrong?'

Jane was still not over the death of Twig even though it was more than two years before. She worked hard in the

Women's Land Army, on farms and properties, but her emotions were always close to the surface and she was quick to cry. She moved into her mother's embrace. 'Oh Mummy, this is the champagne Daddy was saving for our wedding.'

Her mother comforted her. 'Oh darling. Now don't start to cry. There, there.'

Lyn Levinson turned to Kate and Alex. 'There's so much sadness. To think that just because of one awful man so many people are hurt.'

'It's not quite that simple, darling,' her husband remonstrated. 'Hitler needed support. He didn't plunge the world into war on his own. No doubt he wants to rule most of it and divide what's left with his Jap cohorts, but the Germans as a whole allowed it to happen. If he died tomorrow I think the Nazis and the German war machine would keep on rolling.' He glanced at Nicholas. 'What do you think, old man?'

'I think you're probably right. They'd make a blasted symbol out of the bastard then. I'm sorry, excuse me for swearing, ladies.'

Alex moved across to her father's side. 'We have heard swear words before, Daddy.'

'Yes, but usually not from me.'

Alex took a sip of her drink. 'Anyway, Hitler's the one who stirred them up in the first place! You know that swastika's just so grotesque, and their salute is menacingly ugly. They're just so suitable for him, I reckon.'

'That's my sister!' Kate proclaimed. 'No opinions.'

'To alter the subject slightly,' Lillian said, pointing to the French windows where the rain could be heard spattering against them, 'the only good thing about this weather is that it keeps the Huns at home.'

'Yes,' agreed Nicholas, 'and it allows our fellows in Bomber and Fighter Command a night off, eh? Not to mention fellows like us in the ARP and the Home Guard.'

Norman lifted his glass. 'Let's drink to all our soldiers, sailors and airmen and everybody fighting for freedom all over the world.'

And Jane added, 'And to those who died for it.'

'Yes, let's do that.'

They all drank the toast and Kate switched on the wireless and the music of Glenn Miller's band playing 'In the Mood' filled the room. He was followed by the ubiquitous Vera Lynn, singing of blue birds and white cliffs and peace.

They joined in and Alex rose and retreated into the front hall. She had not seen JB since he had walked out on the night her Aunt Harriet had died. She had spoken to him once on the telephone about a week after and he had not called again. She had written him a letter every week for seven weeks and then she decided she was demeaning herself and stopped.

Her father would not speak of it. He had maintained what he had said on the night of Harriet's death: that it was not his place to tell her anything and that it was for JB to enlighten her; though when he added, 'It might be for the best if you don't see him again anyway. He's a very confused young man,' it had just upset her more.

Nicholas was calm and thoughtful, and unlike his sister did not wish to harm. He had deliberated on what JB had told him almost a year ago in his club in London and had decided to do nothing more. He knew his daughter loved the fellow, and he was prepared just to wait and allow matters to take their course.

Alex had tried to understand, but the whole affair had left her in miserable confusion. She remembered last New Year's Eve; how JB had held her in his arms and loved her. Well, she was another year older now, though no wiser, she was sure of that. She wiped her eyes with the back of her hand and took a gulp of champagne.

Kerry, her flatmate, kept introducing her to fellows, but how could any of them compare with her lost fighter pilot?

She listened to the rain on the hall windows. It was already New Year's Day. What would this year bring? She looked wistfully over at the telephone and finished off her glass of champagne, turned round and took two steps back towards the drawing room when the ringing halted her.

She hurried across and lifted the receiver. Who would call at this hour?

'Can I speak to Alexandra, please?'

She had to steady herself. 'JB?'

'Yes.'

'Where are you?'

'At an airfield in Essex. Look, I just wanted to say that I hope this year's a better one for all of us.'

'Oh, so do I. It's so good to hear your voice.'

'Good to hear yours, too.'

'Really?'

'Really.' He heard her sigh. 'How are your parents and Jane? And Kate?'

Alex did not want to talk of them. 'They're all well. How are you?'

'Me? I'm the usual. Making it as hard as possible for the Huns.'

She gave a small laugh and a brief silence fell.

JB broke it. 'I might have some time off, the weekend after this.' She held her breath. 'Could I come down to see you?'

Should she try to sound casual, as if it didn't matter? When it did so very desperately. 'I see. The weekend after the coming one?'

'That's right.'

She knew she should act as if she were considering it. After all, eleven months had gone by and now out of the blue he called. He obviously believed he could just pick up the telephone any old time and she would jump at the chance of seeing him. She should make an excuse. Give him some of his own back.

'Well, the fact of the matter is, JB . . . it's that I don't think I . . .'

'Yes?'

She hesitated, then out it tumbled. 'Oh darn it, what's the use of pretending? When do you think you'll be here?'

Winston Churchill could hear the rain on the windows of the Annex. He stubbed out his cigar and stood in the lamplight looking down at his desk as he took out his fob-watch: 0200, 1 January, 1943.

A Cabinet meeting in the War Rooms at 1900 had been followed with a shared drink. He had made an exception to his rule of no alcohol in the bunker. By midnight he and Clemmie were alone, except for Smokey the cat who even now mooched around his feet.

There was much work to do. He must leave for Casablanca within two weeks to meet President Roosevelt, and Stalin too if he could make it, though the fighting in Stalingrad might keep him in Russia. His mouth turned down at the thought of Joe Stalin.

It was mooted that the French Generals Guiraud and De Gaulle would be called to the Casablanca meeting. A great deal needed to be covered and he looked forward to strengthening his growing relationship with Roosevelt. Winston had agreed to fly out there to save time. He liked to have Charles Wilson, his physician, along with him on his journeys away from Great Britain. Charles had no penchant for flying but he would have to come.

Suddenly Smokey jumped up on the chair and unconsciously he stroked the cat as it purred beneath his fingers. He looked at his hand, well-formed and smallish, the only feature he bore that he believed was reminiscent of his father Randolph. For some reason his father had been on Churchill's mind tonight. Not that he had ever been close to him or even conversed in any depth with him, though he would have given his right arm for a true sign of intimacy from his parent. No, in the twenty years he had known him, Randolph Churchill had remained remote.

The lines of Winston's rotund face settled into deep thought. He had adored his mother Jennie who had been his shining star but she too had shared little with him as he grew; it had been left to his nannies to love him. He shook his head as he ruffled Smokey's fur.

The night his father died in the house in Grosvenor Square he remembered being woken. He had been staying on the far side of the square and had run across the snow-covered ground with the icy winter wind stinging his face. Was it one or two in the morning?

The burial took place in Bladon churchyard on 2 January, three days after. Soon to be forty-eight years ago! He could still picture the dainty diamond brooch in the shape of an arrow his mother had worn on her black dress. For a moment he wondered what had become of it. His father had left a litany of debts and disarray.

Churchill knew he was the sum total of all his life experiences. What homo sapien was not? And there had been bad and difficult times, but made less so with Clemmie at his side.

He thought of his monetary losses in the stock market crash and his years in the wilderness of the previous decade. They had been hard to bear, but in retrospect his lowest point had been after the car accident in New York almost ten years ago.

He had been in his mother's homeland for a lecture tour and seen traffic lights for the first time. One night crossing Fifth Avenue from Central Park he had looked the wrong way and been knocked down by a car. The result had been deep head and scalp wounds, some down to the bone, bruises all over and two broken ribs. The poor driver had shown such concern and worry. Hadn't he been a mechanic or something?

They took him to Lennox Hospital, on the West Side and kept him there a few days.

Winston dropped his head forward in thought and his shoulders drooped. He and Clemmie went to the Bahamas after that. And there he had felt most keenly despondent. Aftermath of the accident, he supposed.

He tapped the wood of his desk with his middle fingernail. It seemed to always break low, perhaps due to an injury when he was a child.

Now why was he recalling these miserable points of his life tonight? With a new year dawning this very day?

Perhaps because he believed the war was far from over, yet he did not feel tired and knew he was up to the task. He experienced no dejection about the state of the war. He believed in his armies and the armies of freedom. They would overcome in the end – though Stalin and his Communism would be the threat after that, he was certain. Still, one evil at a time!

Hitler, Mussolini and Tojo – what a twisted triumvirate! Great Britain and much of the Commonwealth had been fighting them for three and a quarter years in every theatre of the war. It was fortunate he could leave much of the Pacific War to the Americans now. The President was a sterling man with good ideas, and the many millions of men he could rally to his armed forces would make the vital difference in the end.

Winston grunted and sat down, brightening visibly as he picked up his port and drank. His jaw came forward as he mulled over the past year.

Even though it had started appallingly with the Fall of Singapore and too many of the South Sea Islands, the two decisive sea battles – Coral and Midway – had been won, and in August US marines had landed on the Solomons.

And while for years they had played tug-of-war with the Germans in North Africa and they had lost Tobruk and Mersa Matruh in June, the tide had turned and the recent great victories of the British Eighth Army offensive in Egypt had taken place at Alamein. Montgomery had been brilliant, and given the Allies the first clear-cut success of the war. Erwin Rommel, the lauded German strategist, had come up against Montgomery the brilliant, and Monty had executed his victory with precision!

And now Allied shipping was returning to the Mediterranean. Malta had held out against all attack and the whole island had been awarded the George Cross; and with the recent victories in North Africa he felt confident this coming year would see the Allies advance against Mussolini in Sicily and Italy itself.

He drew a map of Europe towards him and peered at it. The German drive in Russia was being met with an unparalleled defence in Stalingrad, that bastion of the Volga. The savage hand-to-hand fighting in the city's battle-scarred streets and buildings was a life or death struggle unknown

628

in the history of man. The Russians were making Hitler and his chums in the Reichstag pay a high price for any conquest they might have there.

He ran his finger towards France and Germany.

1942 had seen low points like the failed Dieppe raid in August, but the Strategic Air Bombing of German industrial centres like the Ruhr Valley were beginning to have an effect. The Avro Lancaster Bomber and improved navigational devices based on radar were making a difference, and the Americans had brought in their B17s.

Smokey, who had settled comfortably into his chair, looked up indignantly as Winston nudged him aside and sat down.

Churchill was aware that the war was costing Britain dearly, not only in physical destruction and sale of foreign investments, but Britain had lost a quarter of its national wealth whereas America, which did not experience bombing or blackout, was seeing the Gross National Product actually rising by 50 per cent.

He put his elbows on the desk and held his head in his hands for a few moments. Armageddon brought with it a massive price!

Indeed, there was much to discuss with the President in Casablanca.

He lifted his head and touched a tall pile of folders at his right hand. He must see Anthony Eden tomorrow – no, today! Perhaps he should go through those notes now?

The sound of a soft footfall outside the door gave him his answer. He grunted, finished his port, rose and spoke. 'All right, Clemmie, I'm coming.'

Chapter Forty

Dawn on New Year's Day arrived into a sky of broken cloud as John Baron and his squadron, wrapped in thick layers against the seeping cold, climbed into their cockpits to sit at 'stand-by'. They wore their masks and gloves ready for immediate take-off.

The sign that enemy aircraft had been sighted and they were to take off, would be the firing of a Verey light flare from the Operations caravan situated to the right of the runway. Instructions would come over the radio once they were airborne.

John Baron's mind wandered over many things including his phone call to Alex the night before. Now that he had made contact he was looking forward to seeing her, although he would not have blamed her if she had told him to go to hell.

They sat at 'stand-by' for well over an hour, squirming in the cold and restricted limits of the cockpit. John Baron thought of Cash as he sometimes did in his quiet moments and wondered where his old friend might be. He could not help but miss Cash and his singularities. There was no one like him, no one at all. He felt sure he would be doing his bit somewhere. Cash might have liked the easy life but he would not have wanted the world run by the Germans and the Japs.

No red Verey light spat into the sky and finally, when heavy mist rolled in over the field, the squadron 'stood down' and went into breakfast.

John Baron spent the rest of the morning in his office and by noon when he arrived in the mess for lunch the mist had gone, the rain had ceased and the sky was again stacked with broken cloud, the sun appearing in intermittent bursts.

At 1300 he briefed his men about the operation.

'Our target is a group of three German oil refineries in Southern Belgium near the French border on the Schelde River. We've been chosen to escort the Blenheim bombers because it's a short-range mission well within the Spitfires' capabilities.' He looked across at Michael Self who had run out of petrol and ditched into the North Sea and been rescued swiftly only a month ago. 'We've all run out of juice once or twice because of our limited range and we know what that's like; but there's no need to worry on this one.'

Michael Self crossed himself. He was a religious boy from St Ives in Cornwall.

'New orders have come through and we won't be the close escort squadron. We are now the cover only, so if we do see any bandits we'll take them. Let's go.'

Fifteen minutes later, the squadron was in the air. They rendezvoused with the Blenheims and their escort southeast of Clacton-on-Sea and the bombers flew 500 feet below.

As they crossed the Channel John Baron looked down. The water appeared bleak and lumpy; in fact, the sea would be so cold that a pilot who ditched would be dead in less than an hour, and so choppy that the fragile dinghy that fighter pilots carried would be awash in no time. Not an afternoon to bail out over the Channel! He shivered even though he wore a thick woollen scarf tucked into the top of his flying suit and with his Mae West and parachute, he filled the cramped cabin.

They reached the target without incident, flying the last twenty miles in through heavy flak from ground fire.

The bombers were deadly accurate, and the refineries, one minute fixed solidly there below in the crepuscular light, were transformed the next into towers of red, orange and blue flame.

As one Blenheim went in it was hit in the wing and slid into a wobble like a cork at sea, but got rid of its bombs and gained height again.

The sun was nearing the horizon as they viewed the lumbering bombers being hugged by their escort as, in a pack, they turned for England.

Two minutes later John Baron saw black specks over his right shoulder.

'Tally ho! Four o'clock high!'

'Shit!' It was Red Leader's voice – Lou Edmont. 'Yes, bandits – flaming dozens of them.'

John Baron banked into a steep turn, announcing decisively: 'Red and Blue sections follow me, attack in pairs and stay together if you can.' He knew the close escort would remain with the bombers.

The enemy were spread in 'line abreast' and were charging straight at them.

John Baron sized them up. 'Plenty for everybody. Koala going in.'

The 109s were diving down towards the Spitfires in the darkening sky, all combatants speeding at each other with startling pace. One came straight at John Baron and he fired rapidly in the few seconds before he hauled on the stick and put on full rudder, diving aside as the 109 shot by overhead.

He pulled up and turned back to see a 109 dropping in flames to the deck. His! He knew it. A thrill surged through him as he headed back to the other fighter aircraft. He glanced around and saw another black shape spiralling downwards to the earth. One of theirs, he hoped. Heavy cloud was forming and rolling in from the south. Another few minutes and it would be too dark for combat.

He was looking around when something slammed into him! The impact slewed him sideways. What the hell was that? His Spitfire lunged forward as the black shape of a Messerschmitt ripped by. The black shape must have hit him!

He wrenched back on the control column but it collapsed towards him. Oh no! The altimeter was spinning like a catherine wheel. He looked round and realised part of his tail was gone. Then to his shock he saw the fuselage was missing too!

God, half the aircraft had disappeared! The 109 must have actually collided with him. Sliced right through the Spitfire!

Suddenly he could smell high-octane fuel. *Get out fast!*

He released the hood, disconnected the oxygen and radio, pulled the Sutton harness release on his chest and stood. The icy wind tore at his face as he pushed his head out of the cockpit, the noise horrendous in his ears. He looked down and felt dizzy, as if he were already tumbling over the side; his mind was filled with falling and cliffs and seagulls screeching, as if he should just stay where he was and fall like this for ever . . .

No! He must get out or he would go down with the Spitfire. He forced himself back to reality, feeling the atmosphere suck at him like a giant mouth as he hurtled himself out. The next second, he was free of the cockpit and alone with the cold universal night.

Floating!

Gliding in tranquillity . . .

No! Snap out of that illusion!

He pulled the ring on his parachute, felt a tug upwards as it opened and an aircraft shot by him, nearly taking his chute. He shut his eyes. That was close!

He was sorry to lose his Spitfire. He thought of the koala holding the Aussie flag painted on the fuselage. Disintegrated!

It was freezing as he fell through the sky and he prepared himself for the collision of arrival back on earth. It came with a heavy thud! He rolled over and lay still in snow a foot or so deep.

Absurdly into his mind came the thought of the rugger match he had agreed to play in on Sunday. His squadron were taking on Henry's boys over at Debden. Damn! He had been looking forward to it. He was on form.

He wondered whether he was in Belgium or France. Not that it mattered – the Germans occupied both. Sitting up, he moved his arms and legs and lifted his shoulders up and down. Nothing was broken, though his thigh felt a bit tender. He was in a field in empty countryside.

He gathered up his parachute and remained where he was for a time. The sky was stocking with cloud again and the light was failing. He hoped that no rain would fall. He stood up and began to look for somewhere to spend the night.

He shivered but it was not as cold as it had been at 15,000 feet. He delved inside his flying jacket and found his compass. He carried a ten-pound note, a box of matches, a map of Belgium and France and three chocolate bars. They were the sum total of his belongings.

What should he do? Head for the coast, he guessed. This was his second stint behind enemy lines and he did not like the feeling. Though this time was going to be a bloody sight more difficult than the last, for attempting to pass himself off for a Frenchman now would be well-nigh impossible without the papers and identification which the invaders made everybody carry.

He crouched down and put the compass on the ground to rapidly ascertain his bearings. Then he began to walk in a north-westerly direction. It was hard going though the snow was not deep and he tripped over logs and pushed his way through bracken. Night descended and after about an hour he crossed a small hill where he saw the black shape of a hut ahead near trees and he approached it cautiously. His night vision showed him a roadway which led to a bridge. Warily, he walked up and tried the door of the hut. It opened and he bent over and entered then closed it behind him and, lighting a match, looked around – shovels, seed bags and a scythe. It was not the Ritz but it was better than sleeping out. He ate a chocolate bar and arranged the seed bags into a sort of mattress to lie upon. And with the disconcerting picture of his warm bed and the cocoa that his batman brought him each night looming in his mind, he lay back and tried to go to sleep. Hours, hours of thinking passed, before sleep came.

He spent a cold uncomfortable night and he dreamt of being on the Harley Davidson with Cash driving like a wild man through a chilly, windy night out to Haverhill. He awoke with the dawn. Eating another chocolate bar he opened the door and edged out into the daylight. Through the straggling formation of oaks was the roadway and the bridge. He stretched and looked all around, noting only low hills and fields. His gaze returned to the road as suddenly around a bend beyond the bridge, two motor bikes and a lorry appeared, heading straight towards him!

He threw himself back behind the hut and hit the snow. They were Germans and he had the sickly feeling that they had seen him.

He was right.

He heard them pull up. The trees were widely spaced and would give no real cover, but were his only hope. Bent double, he ran.

'*Halt!*'

The first sweep of bullets went over his head.

'*Halt!*'

He knew the next volley would go in his back. He stopped.

'*Hände hoch! Und undrehen!*'

His German was scant but he was sure of what they were shouting, he put up his hands and turned around.

Two approached him. One continued to shout at him in German, holding a sub-machine gun upon him while the other walked right up and ran his eyes over John Baron as he smiled. His English was good. 'Ah, a British pilot. Well, now I can tell you, you've reached the end of your war!'

Samantha had woken on New Year's Day to the sound of knocking on the door of her flat.

She looked at the clock – 9 a.m. God, she had not arrived home until three! She slipped out of bed and shivered with the cold as she drew on her warm dressing-gown. 'I'm coming!' She hurried through and opened her front door.

Cash!

She was dumbfounded. 'I thought you were going to Wales?'

'I am. But there's something I really need to tell you.' He took off his cap.

She stood aside. 'Come in.'

He entered and looked around. Nice flat. Good taste. 'You were asleep?'

'Yes, but that's all right. I'm so pleased to see you. Do you want coffee? Tea? I have a little, though with the rationing I run out fast.'

He shook his head.

She found it hard to believe that he had come to her after last night. But she was delighted that he had, and now after the initial surprise, her face broke into a smile. 'Won't you sit down?' She pointed.

His eyes lit on the sofa and he imagined the big New Zealander of last night sitting upon it. That only steeled the conviction in his mind.

'No thanks, Sammy, I won't be here long.'

'Oh?' It was a disappointed sound.

'I'm here to set you free at last, m'lady.'

'What does that mean?' Then she understood. He was going to ask her for a divorce. She sat down heavily in a chair opposite him, her face clouding.

He paused and waved his fingers in a circular motion in the air as if looking for a place to begin. 'Sammy, I've seen and done things since the war started that have altered me. Oh,' he gave a semblance of his cheeky grin, 'I'm still trouble, that hasn't changed. But what I want to say is this: I know why you ran off with Lenny the Loser. Oh yeah, sure, you wanted to be a big-time photographer but the main reason was something else. It's the same one that drives you on now, getting involved with one fella after another.'

'Cash, please . . .'

'No, m'lady, let me say this. It's taken me bloody long enough to get the conscience to do it.'

She fell silent.

'I used to make a point of making you feel bad in Sydney by implying things about you and JB. Things that made you unhappy but things that I know to be true.'

'Cash, why are you bringing this up now? That's all gone by.'

'Sammy, this is hard to say so please be quiet. The fact

636

is this: I knew then, and I know now, that you've always been in love with JB.'

She shook her head and lifted her hand. 'That's not true. Don't, please.'

'But darling, it's all right. You can be! You could have married him and not me. Hell, you should have! He's not your brother.'

Her head shot up and her eyes enlarged.

'Yes, m'lady it's true. You can love him as much as you want. I've lost you. The fact is, I guess I never had you, and it's time I did the right thing and released you to love him.'

A flush was creeping up her neck to her face and a minute nerve in her cheek twitched. 'Why are you saying this? *Why?*'

'Because it's true. Look, Sammy I've never told you before because I just always hoped like hell you'd eventually love me the way you love him. But after last night, realism has finally found its way into my brain. I don't want you skidding from one bloke to the next, you're better than that. Hell, you're m'lady, for God's sake! The truth is, and I know you'll hate me for it, but so what? I deserve it. I've known you weren't brother and sister since JB turned twenty-one.'

Sam flung her hands round in the air. She shook her head and crossed to him and grabbed his arms. 'What the hell are you talking about? This isn't true.' Her eyes were wild.

'Darling, it is. I overheard a conversation on the verandah at Haverhill between your parents and Ledgie and Wakefield the day before JB's twenty-first birthday. It's true without a doubt that you and JB are not brother and sister.' He sighed. 'Hell, the truth is, I eavesdropped.'

Her nails were digging into his forearms. She was weaving her head from side to side in disbelief.

'Remember the night you went to JB's bedroom?'

'Oh God!' Her hands left him and shot to her mouth.

'Yes. I saw everything. Heard everything. I was on the verandah outside in the dark. Look, I'm a bastard. I never

637

deserved you in the first place. I kept it a secret knowing how you both felt. I've no excuse, Sammy, except for the fact I wanted you for myself, because I've never loved anyone the way I love you and I never will. But hell, girl,' he attempted to smile, 'I've gone and got religion or something, because last night I came to terms with the whole rotten mess I've permitted to happen. Me, I'm to blame. It's time I released you two. Allowed you to have each other.

'It's easy to see that Lenny and the New Zealander last night and the bloke at the party downstairs and God knows who else, are in your life because they're all substitutes for JB. Heck, that includes me too. And it's about bloody time you were able to have him.'

Sam's eyes were brimming with tears. 'No, no, no,' she repeated.

'Start divorce proceedings any time you like, sweetheart. I'm the guilty party. You know I've been a burglar and a liar, a cheat and a trickster. I've lied so much I hardly know what's real, but the one single thing in my whole life that's been truth, a bloody *beacon* of truth, is my love for you. *You* are the real truth in my life, m'lady . . . You . . . Just you. Always were. Always will be. So hear me. JB *is not* your brother.' He tried to smile again but could not, his lips merely twisted. 'Now in a couple of hours I'm off to Wales and then Scotland and God knows where after that, so it's good riddance to me. The war suits me, Sammy. I'm one of those it suits.'

She could not speak; she simply stood there looking at him.

He stepped forward and took her shoulders and gazed down into her eyes, right down into her. Then he moved back, and the look he gave her was infinitely sad.

'I've never said sorry for anything to anybody in my life, but I'm saying it to you today. Goodbye, m'lady.'

He took a deep breath and mustered a ghost of a smile.

She watched him leave, heard his footsteps on the stairs, and the sound of the front door slamming.

She did not move.

She could not move.

For a time she could feel nothing; it was as if all her senses had been violated. There was a moment when she was quite sure her heart stopped beating.

At last she stirred and with leaden footfalls moved through to the bedroom where she cast herself upon the bed and drew her body into the foetus shape, hugging herself and moaning softly at the unutterable pain that kept running in waves through her.

Chapter Forty-one

Samantha had finally drifted into sleep. It was after 2 p.m. when she woke and rose, made coffee and sat and listened to the wireless, though if she had been asked to name what she heard she could not have done so.

Her heart and mind were elsewhere, 13,000 miles across the sea. She was in JB's arms dancing to 'Tea for Two' at the Christmas concert, skimming across the stage with a carefree tread; she was on Aristotle's back and racing JB to the turn along the trail by Teviot Brook, her hair flying in the wind and a peal of laughter echoing from her; she was photographing him with his hand in the air to show off the ring he had been given for his twenty-first birthday. She was walking into the stable and seeing him for the first time after he had come home from Melbourne for her wedding, the late-afternoon sun animating the blue of his eyes. He held out his fingers towards her and said, 'Hello, Sammy. You're gleaming.'

She pictured herself in her wedding dress of lace and silk with clusters of orange blossom over each of her ears. JB was holding her close within his arms and they were upon the dance floor. A tear was running down her cheek. What had he said to her then?

'Don't cry, sweetheart. Cash is all sorts of strange things, but he does love you, I'm positive of that.'

Cash, her husband. A picture of him on his knees asking her to marry him floated in her mind. The inscrutable way he contemplated her as he waited for her answer.

Cash the conscience*less*, at last motivated by conscience, coming to her this morning: 'The one single thing in my whole life that's been truth . . . is my love for you. *You* are the real truth in my life, m'lady. You . . . Just you. Always were. Always will be. So hear me. JB *is not* your brother.'

Sam had never smoked a cigarette in her life but if there had been one to hand she would have. As it was, she had a nip of whisky left in the bottom of a bottle. She drank it straight down and went in and took a bath and washed her hair.

At 4 p.m. she walked across to Hyde Park and around the Serpentine. It was very cold but not raining and the sun kept intermittently appearing in vain attempts to warm the first afternoon of 1943. There were slivers of ice all over the Serpentine and four hardy ducks sat determinedly on one by the Lido. She felt bleak like the world was these days, and she turned her steps to Rotten Row where she stood beside the grey, uncompromising shapes of the anti-aircraft guns pointing to the sky. Then as the early winter dusk enveloped her she headed for home.

As she came in the front door, she met Amelia.

'There you are, love. Would you like to come down for a drink later? George got three bottles of beer from an ARP fella, and I've used some of my flour ration and made a few scones.'

Sam tried to smile. 'Thanks, Amelia. Around eight?'

The landlady saw her distress. 'What's wrong, love?'

Sam did not reply.

'Bad news?'

Sam shook her head. 'I can't talk about it, Amelia, but I'd like to come down and have that drink later.'

For a landlady Amelia fell into the unusual category of not being a busybody. She did not press the matter. 'That's it, love. You come on down around eight.'

At the appointed time Sam descended the stairs and Amelia and George welcomed her, not that the ruminative George was suddenly vocal; he simply waved as she came in and poured her a beer. Then he went back to cleaning the blocked sink in the little kitchen.

Sam helped Amelia to collect the clean white ash from the embers of the fire before they put on more wood and built it up again for warmth. They spooned the ash into jars for Amelia to take to the Women's Auxiliary. It was used as scouring powder and also helped to remove stains from china and tin and other metals. Sam too collected ash from her own fireplace upstairs. Then the two women sat and listened to the gramophone while Amelia darned two of George's socks.

Sam found it therapeutic to be in the cosy downstairs flat and sipped her beer and ate a scone and was comforted by the landlady's constant chatter.

At 10 p.m. Amelia was generously spreading her last knob of butter ration on a scone for her visitor while Sam protested, when the telephone rang.

Amelia looked at George. 'Who's that going to be at this hour?'

George, by now ensconced in the big chair by the fire, roused himself enough to shrug and Amelia rose and answered it.

'Yes . . . Yes, I can. She's here with me, actually. . . I see. Just a few moments, please.'

Sam realised the call was for her and she stood and crossed to the telephone in the alcove as Amelia handed her the receiver with the words, 'RAF Martlesham calling.'

Suddenly Samantha had a very bad feeling.

'Samantha Slade.'

'My name's Edmont, Lou Edmont. I met you once with your brother.'

She remembered. 'Yes.'

'Can I come and see you tonight? I know it's late.'

'Why?'

'You know there's a censor listening.'

Samantha did know. All military establishments and many of the civil ones had telephone censors listening for breaches of security. In fact, it was the job JB's friend, Alex, did.

'Yes.'

'All I can tell you and I'm very sorry to have to do so, is that your brother's missing over Belgium.'

Sam tried to answer but she couldn't.

'Look, I'll be at your place in an hour, and I'll explain

all I know. I'm getting a ride in with one of our Air Force vehicles. Did you hear me?'

Her voice shook as she forced a reply. 'Yes.' Then she put back the receiver and turned to Amelia. The colour had seeped from her face and she stood there helplessly.

'Oh my dear, what is it?'

Even George was sitting up watching from his position by the fire.

'My brother. He's missing.' Sam's torso dropped forward as if she were a stringless marionette and Amelia rushed to her and took her in her arms.

'Oh God no!' The anguish in Sam's voice was pitiful to hear. 'I can't bear it. This is too much. All too much to bear.'

George was on his feet and he helped his wife to steer the near-collapsing Sam to the sofa.

'Oh no no no no,' Sam kept repeating as her friends gently eased her down and George hastened to put two cushions behind her head.

Amelia kissed her and stroked her hair. 'Now, dear, it'll be all right.' She glanced at George. 'Get a blanket, love.' And he hurried off.

While he was gone Amelia tried to comfort her. She had opened the door to a Major at 9 a.m. this morning and she was well aware that what he had told Sam had upset her badly just from the way the girl had looked this afternoon; and now this right on top. 'Listen, love, I reckon this is the second lot of bad news you've had today, and that's just too terrible. I'm so sorry. But let's calm down. Your brother's *missing*. That can mean he'll turn up any old minute. You'll see, I'm sure it won't be as bad as you think.'

Sam brought her gaze to her friend and simply shook her head. She looked so pathetic and lost that the woman took her again in her arms and hugged her tightly, talking to her as she would a child. 'There, there, darling, now don't you take on so. It'll be all right. You'll see.'

But it was not all right.

Lou Edmont was in South Audley Street by 11 p.m. and

Sam saw him in her flat with Amelia at her side. He explained that no one had seen JB hit but when he had not turned up at a home airfield by 2200 – three and a half hours after all the other Spitfires had landed – they had to assume he had been shot down.

Her face was distorted with grief. 'So you don't know whether he's dead or not?'

Lou shook his head. He was greatly affected by the loss himself, as so many of them were. John Baron Chard had become a legend in the RAF like others before him. Three and a half years in action and still going strong until today. Some of the younger pilots, including himself, had thought him invincible and they had been buoyed up and confident when flying with him.

Tears filled the young man's eyes. 'The boys at Martlesham will be lost without him. I've spoken to a few of them already. The mess is like a morgue tonight, and will be for a long time to come. I know that Mike Self, one of our lads, has gone off to the chapel for the night.'

Sam simply sat there eyes red and puffy.

She said goodbye to him at her front door, and even in her own shocked state, she noticed his desolate look and took his arm. 'All we can pray is that he's a prisoner.'

'That's right. I'll let you know the minute we hear anything.'

Amelia stepped forward and put her arm around Sam. 'Thanks love, we'd appreciate that,' she called as he marched away.

Amelia stayed the night with her and the next afternoon reporters were on her doorstep. John Baron's fame had brought them. There were pieces in the *Daily Mail*, the *Daily Sketch*, the *Telegraph* and the *Evening Despatch*: mostly with the small headline. HERO DISAPPEARS OVER BELGIUM.

Sam had been due to go down to Cornwall on assignment but she remained in London waiting, with her head spinning and her thoughts whirling. She too had come to believe that JB was invincible. She had always hated Hitler and the Nazis; always thought them vile and cruel, but now she began to be overwhelmed by her loathing of them.

She stood in front of the mirror and scrutinised herself. She counted the men she had been with and shook her head. Cash had got that part right; she had simply skidded from one to another.

The following day was Sunday and it rained heavily so she remained indoors and wrote letters to her loved ones in Australia while Amelia kept popping in and out in an effort to cheer her.

On Monday morning the streets were still awash and she went out in her raincoat to the Post Office. She did not want to make the telephone call from Amelia's flat.

She stood in a cramped booth with a tiny spider in a web in the corner. She supposed cleaning telephone boxes was not high priority for the war effort. The operator put her through and a man answered. 'Peter Larkin, can I help you?'

'Is Major Eric Jaffer there, please?'

'Could you give me your name?'

'Samantha Slade.'

Fifteen seconds later she heard Jaffer's voice. 'Mrs Slade? It's been a year or so, hasn't it?'

'Yes. Can I come and see you?'

'Of course.'

'I've altered my mind.'

That same afternoon Samantha wrote her letter of resignation to Carter Brinkwood at *Newsweek*.

The next morning a hand-delivered letter came for her. It was from Major Jaffer requesting her to be at Number 4 Hyde Park Square that same day at 4 p.m.

She was amazed at how calmly she prepared for it after the turmoil of the previous days. But she admitted that, since she had stopped crying and weeping and made the commitment to her life-changing decision, she felt a sense of purpose she had not known in years. In fact, she eyed herself again in the mirror to see if there were any obvious transformation, for she had never experienced such a sense of resolve and intent as she carried now.

It was after 3 p.m. when she left the flat and came down to the ground floor, leaning over the stairwell to call down to the basement to Amelia, informing her she would be away for a few hours.

The sun was out and the leadlight colours in the front door sparkled as she opened it and halted.

A young woman stood there, hand poised to knock. She looked at Samantha in amazement.

Alex could not believe her eyes! She froze where she stood on the doorstep, fist in the air. The woman she was looking at was so much like herself! The same olive skin and Titian tint to the hair that tumbled to her shoulders: high cheekbones and slight fullness to the mouth.

'My heaven!'

Sam of course knew exactly who Alex was. She recalled the night outside the Dorchester years ago when she had seen this girl with JB.

'Good afternoon, Alexandra,' Sam said.

Alex quickly grasped the situation. 'You're Samantha?'

'Yes.'

Sam closed the door behind her and stepped down to the landing beside her visitor and now Alex could see Sam was taller than she was and that there were other contrasts between them.

'I came to see you about JB. Do you know?'

'That he was shot down? Yes, I do.'

Alex took a deep breath. 'I just thought, perhaps . . . Well, the fact is that we both care about him and I suppose I just wanted to commiserate.'

Sam would never have made the move to meet Alex but now that the girl was here she decided not be rude. 'I understand, but I'm off to an appointment and if I don't keep going I'll be late.'

'Oh.' Alex looked disappointed.

'Where do you live?'

Alex pointed back towards Park Lane. 'Over in Kensington. I'm in the Ambulance Service there.'

'I thought you were a telephone censor?'

Alex nodded. 'I am but I help out with the Ambulance Service too. I'm off duty this afternoon and I thought I'd come over. I've known where you live for ages and I know how special you are to JB. And now he's been shot down I wanted to meet you. I thought you'd be upset too.'

Sam couldn't help but warm to the girl. She seemed so sincere. 'I am. I just couldn't believe it.'

'Me neither. I hadn't seen him for a long time. The truth is, for nearly twelve months. I missed him so much, you see, and then out of the blue on New Year's Eve he telephoned me. He was travelling down to be with me this coming weekend.' Alex's eyes welled with tears.

Automatically Sam reached out and took her arm. 'Oh yes, I know. I've been a mess since Friday night too.' She came to a decision. 'Look, I'll be tied up for a few hours but I could meet you later. Do you know the Rambler? It's a pub over your way in Rutland Mews. They do nice sandwiches even with the rationing.'

Alex smiled. 'I'll find it.'

'I'll meet you there at seven.'

Alex watched Sam stride down the steps and along the street. She was still in surprise over the similarity between them and she had the uneasy feeling that JB might have been attracted to her because of it.

She stood there thinking. She knew that Kerry, her flatmate, would be home this afternoon. She made a decision to go and see her and walked firmly down the steps to the street.

Sam walked to Hyde Park Square where her knock on the door brought a bearded porter who recognised her name and took her to a downstairs flat.

Major Jaffer himself opened the door with a smile. 'Come in.'

They shook hands and he led her through to a perfectly normal sitting room with chintz-covered chairs. Only the two of them were present though she could hear voices in a room beyond.

He opened the dialogue. 'You say you've altered your mind. Why?'

'Many reasons. I've always been inclined to work for you ever since my first interview, but in recent times I've definitely decided that I'm not doing enough by just photographing sides of the war for *Newsweek*. Actually I suppose I've always felt that way. I want to do so much more. I'm young and fit and my brother's just been shot down over Belgium.'

He nodded. 'Yes, we know.'

'Do you?'

'You mentioned your brother at our last meeting. Fact is, I know a great deal about both of you now. I've obtained a clearance on you from MI5. I did it just in case I ever heard from you again.'

'So you *expected* to hear from me again?'

'Let's just say I'm trained to assess people.' He offered her a cup of tea which she refused, then he asked, 'So all of what you tell me has made you want to risk your life; to be trained and to go into enemy territory on secret and dangerous missions?'

'Yes.'

'And you won't change your mind?'

'No.'

He picked up a sheet of paper on the sofa beside him and tapped on the wall. A woman and a man entered. He introduced them as Vera Atkins and Captain Martin Denning.

'They're going to accompany you over to Portman Square where a lot of matters will be discussed. The last time we met I mentioned that our people have legitimate service positions to satisfy family and friends. You'll be given a commission in the First Aid Nursing Yeomanry, the FANYs. Have you heard of them?'

'Yes. I think they do all sorts of auxiliary work.'

'That's right. They do everything from driving Officers around Britain from camp to camp to helping the Red Cross and serving in canteens. They also carry out duties overseas in other theatres of war, so any time you leave the country you have cover. The other important aspect is that they're the only women's service under the Army Act permitted to carry weapons.' He gestured to Vera and David. 'So these two will get you enlisted and give you the aims of our organisation and the purpose of the training which you'll do.'

He looked at Vera. 'When will the training begin?'

'Once we get Mrs Slade enlisted, which I'd like to do in the next couple of days.'

Sam lifted her hand towards the woman. 'Look, if I'm going to be working closely with you, shouldn't we be using Christian names?'

A glance passed between Vera and David. They liked this. It showed the new recruit had ideas of her own. 'Of course we should, Samantha. Though I must warn you, we won't be using Samantha after today. We'll allot you a new name at each stage of your training.'

'Oh?'

Martin Denning explained. 'You'll use a series of different names so that everybody you come in contact with, even the other agents, will have difficulty in keeping track of you.' He pointed to the door. 'So we'll get over to Portman Square and start, if that's all right with you?'

'Perfectly.'

'Good.' He winked at her, and she was reminded of Cash, and a wave of sadness flooded her as she shook hands with Major Jaffer and followed her new companions out.

Alex was waiting for Sam when she walked into the Rambler.

Sam hesitated in surprise as she saw her sitting in a booth near the bar. 'You've cut your hair?'

Alex shrugged. 'Yes, my flatmate did it this afternoon. I think it makes me look less like you.'

'Oh, so that was the intention?'

'Yes. Perhaps I'm silly, but when I saw how much I resembled you I suppose I just wanted to make a statement that I'm *not* you, even though JB'll know nothing about it.'

Sam shook her head. 'You don't believe that was the attraction, do you?'

649

'I'm sure it must have had something to do with it.'

Sam decided to be generous. 'I'd say he liked you for yourself. I'm only . . . his sister, after all.'

'Yes, but a sister he treasures.'

'Thanks, that was a nice thing to say. Let's hope he's still alive to treasure me.'

They ordered a cheese sandwich – the choice was only cheese or egg – and they drank a beer.

Sam told Alex she had joined the FANYs that afternoon. 'That's where I was going when we met, to the recruitment office.'

'Gosh, that's wonderful. To give up a highly paid job like yours.' Alex was looking at her companion with admiration. 'I mean, we're conscripted, we have to join something, but you don't.'

'It's just that I'm sick of Hitler and the Nazis and I felt I wanted to do more.'

Alex nodded and took a mouthful of her beer. 'You know, that's why I joined the Ambulance Service too. I didn't have to because telephone censoring is regarded as an essential occupation, but if we all do our bit we'll win this and life will get back to normal.'

'Normal – what's that?'

They both grinned and Sam said, 'JB told me about your George Cross. Congratulations.'

'Thanks.'

'Did you go to the Palace?'

'Uh huh. It was all very posh. The King's a lovely man.'

And so the evening went along, and a couple of American sailors bought them a drink around nine o'clock and offered to walk them to the bus stop. They refused politely and it was all taken good-naturedly so they strolled down to Brompton Road alone.

'I could almost walk home from here,' Alex remarked as they reached the corner of the main road and she shone her torch ahead, 'but in the dark I'd better not.'

'Yes, well, goodbye.'

Now Alex surprised Sam. 'If you don't mind, I'd like to keep in touch with you.'

Sam had liked Alex much more than she could have believed, but it was the wrong time for her to begin a friendship. She did not like lying but she had to. 'Look, I'm going off to learn how to drive lorries next week. Somewhere over near Wales, I think, so I'll be hard to contact.'

'Oh.' There was real disappointment in Alex's voice. To her Sam was the nearest thing in this world to JB and it had become important to her to keep a connection. Alex's straightforwardness prevailed. 'I'm going home to Sandwich on Sunday. Two of JB's closest friends are meant to be coming: Henry Garner and Tommy Hopkins. They were the ones who let me know about JB actually. Do you know them?'

Sam had met Tommy. 'I know Tom.'

'Then why don't you come with me? I mean, meet Mummy and Daddy. The trains are a bit unreliable but I always manage to get there.'

Two people arrived beside them at the bus stop and with the gleam thrown up by the four torches Sam could just make out Alex's face. She did not know what to say.

'I'm not sure.'

At that moment Sam's bus arrived.

'Please come,' Alex said.

Sam relented and handed her new friend a card. 'This is my *Newsweek* address – my landlady's telephone number is on the back. I'll still keep my things at the flat, I guess.' She mounted the bus.

'I'll call you on Friday night,' Alex shouted out as the vehicle pulled away.

Chapter Forty-two

September, 1943

Cash glanced across at Second Lieutenant Matt Fleming as he continued his final briefing. The young man grinned. He was fast becoming to Cash what Jack Taber had been in Malaya. That bothered Cash. He did not want to get close to anyone. You got close – they bloody died on you.

He pointed to the map in their midst. 'So we slip off the sub here between Guernsey and Jethou and paddle in the dinghies to the Guernsey shore. The sub waits for us and we land here . . .' he tapped a black cross on the map '. . . meet our contact, then cut across country to the railway line. If we come in this way from the north-east we've got it on good advice that we won't meet much opposition. There's a slave labour camp here: poor bloody Polish Jews.' He pointed. 'It's mighty close to the single-gauge railway and we have to pass it to lay the charges but our information is there's a copse of trees between it and the track which affords cover to any movement along the railway line itself.'

'And so we detonate as much of the track as we can?' Lieutenant Roger Crystal asked, his forehead lined in concentration.

'Yes, we're carrying enough fuse wire and explosives to blast over a mile of track and with any luck we can use Mills Bombs on a few hundred yards more on our way out.'

Cash edged his finger along the map. 'We need to cross this land where there are probably dirt roads and glorified paths. There's only one main road across the island and that runs from St Peter Port and we don't go near that.

Blowing up the railway means that the Organization Todt, their infamous bloody construction mob who abuse the slaves, will be out of work for a while, and the building of the blasted casemate bunkers they're proposing to raise all along the west coast will be halted. The railway delivers the cement, steel and heavy equipment across the island.'

Captain Damien Kirkland bent his fair head across the map. 'So while we're blowing up the railway you'll go in and get Dietrich, sir?'

Cash nodded. 'That's right.' He gazed round their blackened faces. There were twenty-six of them: twelve would go in with Cash and twelve with Kirkland. 'We land on the beach, meet our local spy "Ragtime", climb up the cliff and he'll take us in.'

Matt Fleming glanced at Kirkland. 'And *you* don't detonate until 0230, by which time *we* should have despatched "Dibber" Dietrich and his pal Sühren into the next world.'

'Yeah,' declared Private Ludlow. 'The only good Huns are bloody dead Huns.'

'Well, that's original,' replied Matt, thumping him on the back.

General Max Dietrich, known as 'Dibber' had been born into a military family in Bavaria in 1894. He was an early recruit to the Nazi Party and soon after they rose to power he became a member of the Prussian Assembly and the Reichstag. He had commanded Hitler's bodyguard for a year – the 'Führerbegleitbatallion', and had been instrumental in raising two SS Divisions. British Intelligence had found out that he was in Guernsey on a visit of short duration during which time he was approving the plans for the complete fortification of the island. He was staying at Farley Manor, a house three-quarters of a mile to the north-west of St Peter Port.

When war began the residents of the Channel Islands had been given the option to evacuate to Great Britain or remain. The majority of the islanders had evacuated but 21,000 had remained on Guernsey. Immediately the Germans invaded, anyone born in England or with military connections had been deported to the continent and the inhabitants came under curfew and strict rules. But there were a few who resisted and on the shore where Cash and his raiders were to arrive they hoped to meet one: code-named 'Ragtime'.

Thousands of slave labourers had been brought in and died from the appalling conditions, cruelty and overwork, especially on the island of Alderney, where almost all the original 1,400 inhabitants had been evacuated to England in 1940 and the handful remaining had been removed to Guernsey by the invaders. Alderney was now merely a fortification and the Nazi Organization Todt were intending to make Guernsey the same.

At times on Guernsey numbers of the male inhabitants were rounded up to assist the slave labour, but in the main the local population was left to supply food: to fish and produce salt and vinegar, and grow tobacco. But any boats that went to sea carried German guards.

Cash moved his finger to the position of the manor house. 'It would appear that because the German Occupation force on Guernsey is so large it's made them less cautious in guarding the General. He has a mistress with him and the manor house, our objective, has a three-foot-high stone wall around it. Soldiers are in residence – one platoon, we're informed – so there'll probably be sentries. We're told Dietrich's aide, former Gestapo Colonel, Joseph Sühren, is in the objective with him. He too has a mistress along.

'Not that any of you should have difficulty in recognising them if they're in uniform, but if they're not, be sure you know their faces. Take another good look at the photographs.' He gestured to them where they were taped to a cluster of steel pipes running along the deckhead. 'Dietrich has a round face and a mole on his left cheek; Sühren's thin and clean-shaven. We're told his eyes are pale and his hair's fair.' The picture they had of Sühren showed him clutching the hand of a boy of about nine, a member of the Hitler Youth, and as Cash ended with, 'Right, that's it. Go and have a hot cup of something and stand-to for dusk,' Matt took up a crayon, leant over, and quite skilfully drew a dagger through the necks of Dietrich and Sühren.

Two hours later as they leapt from their four rubber

dinghies and pulled them towards the black figure that appeared on the shoreline in the moonlight, Cash looked across to Matt, the pale gleam of the young man's eyes the only thing visible in the murky night. He, like all of them, wore a balaclava and was covered in black from head to toe.

'Hide the dinghies in the brush.'

Cash grinned in the night. *I love this. I love the darkness. Oh yeah, I'm alive!*

His excitement was building as he called quietly to Kirkland and Lieutenants Boyd and Crystal, 'Come with me,' and moved swiftly to the figure on the shore.

'Ragtime?'

'Aye.'

From what they could see of their contact he was a stocky man in his middle years.

'There are twenty-six of us; we'll separate into two parties at the point on the railway line. I understand we need to cross it to get to the manor house?'

'Aye. It seems quiet up there tonight. The last two nights it's been music and dancing and noise.'

'You're sure the targets are there?'

'Quite sure. I saw them arrive in a jeep just before curfew; they had women with them. Follow me.'

They distributed the charges between them. It took four men to carry the fuse wire and Matt Fleming hoisted the detonator onto his shoulders. They all carried Mark 11 Sten guns with silencers.

The full September moon gave ample light and they followed Ragtime along a track up the cliff, then crossed open land for a time. From what they could see in the moonlight it looked a scenic place; one of the boys had mentioned sailing around Guernsey before the war.

Cash, trained to remember landmarks, noted clusters of rocks and copses of trees.

They came to semi-wooded land and crossed a couple of dirt roads, after which Ragtime halted and pointed. 'The railway track's ahead and Farley Manor's this way.'

'Right.' Cash's men gathered around him as he spoke in a hushed tone. 'When we reach the railway line you begin immediately placing the explosives. And be careful as you pass the labour camp.' He looked at Ragtime in the weak illumination. 'How long in time from the railway track to the manor house?'

'Seventeen minutes.'

'Right.' He tapped Damien Kirkland's shoulder. 'We'll give you and your boys until 0200 before we go in. By then you'll have the charges laid along the railway line. We'll take out the sentries then Dietrich and Sühren. Our aim's to remove the targets silently. Give us half an hour to complete our part of the mission. Detonate at 0230.'

He turned to Ragtime. 'I'm told there's another way back from Farley Manor to the cove. Once the track blows, this area will be crawling with Nazis.'

'Yes. I'll show you where it starts before I leave you. It leads straight to the clifftop and along to the cove. You can't miss it.'

'Don't say that, Ragtime. Whenever people say that, it's the kiss of death.'

'Oh, sorry.'

Cash pointed behind him. 'Kirkland, Crystal, you and your boys go back the way we just came in.'

'Right, sir.'

'But should any sort of battle ensue, you detonate the railway line immediately, get back to your dinghies and return to the sub. Don't wait for us.' He glanced round their eyes in the wan night light. 'Good luck, boys.'

The objective, Farley Manor, sat solidly on a slight rise in the moonlight, the low stone wall surrounding it. An armoured car was parked at the front steps and three jeeps and a lorry in the yard. Two sheds and a copse of trees stood behind the house on the west. Phillip Boyd turned to Matt Fleming and whispered, 'The bastards seem to be pretty blasé, lights everywhere.'

It was true, there were no blackouts or even brownouts at Farley Manor for electric lights glared from many rooms within.

Cash and his men lay in the grass 150 yards away and

he sent Privates Ludlow and Skinner in to reconnoitre. They came back smiling, their teeth gleaming in their blackened faces.

'We got right up to the house. One of the sheds is the sleeping quarters for the troops. Look to be about twenty of them. There's a fire at the back of the building with three soldiers around it. They appear to be on duty but they're certainly not circuiting the place. Not a bloody sentry in sight. Easy access into the objective, broken window into the corridor outside the room where the targets are. They're drinking in what appears to be a main hall. There are four officers in all, and four women.'

Cash looked around to Ragtime. 'Our information is that the bedrooms are off a corridor behind the main hall.'

'Yes, that's right.'

Skinner traced a line on his palm in the moonlight. 'I'd say the bedrooms are on an extension of the corridor we'll enter through the broken window.'

Ragtime nodded. 'Probably.' He lifted his hand in a north-easterly direction. 'See that building on the rise?'

'Yes.'

It looked like a disused farmhouse about 300 yards away.

'Victor Hugo spent some time in that when he exiled himself here and wrote *Les Misérables*.'

Cash cleared his throat. 'Yes, well, that's interesting, Ragtime, but history's not on the agenda tonight.'

'However, the track out of here starts behind it.'

'Ah well now, that's different.'

'It runs down a long hill to a cluster of cottages, about six in all, and after that it's only a couple of hundred yards straight to the coast. There you turn left and in another three-quarters of a mile you're back at the cove. It's shorter than the way we came, but it's rougher. I'll be off now. I've got a way to go to get home.'

Cash shook his head. 'Oh no, Ragtime. One of my men will accompany you over to the farmhouse first. Show him *exactly* where the track begins. Then you can go home.'

In the pallid light Cash nodded to Matt and he began to move out with the man.

'Thanks, Ragtime.'

'Just win the bloody war,' Ragtime whispered in reply.

At 0200 they fitted their silencers to their pistols, took up their Sten guns and went in.

It was now the still of the night and they moved cautiously.

Cash's heart was pumping. *Love this. Love it. Love it.*

He left three of his men, Deese, Curtis and Kemp, by the vehicles in the front yard. The rest crossed in the shadows to the side of the house where the entry window lay.

Cash signalled for six of his men to remain in the bushes near the house, and with Matt and Privates Ludlow and Skinner he crept to the eastern corner of the building where a garden seat stood beside a hedge and three yards beyond, the trio of German guards still sat round the fire. Ludlow pointed to one of the sheds fifty yards away, denoting the one in which the troops slept.

The Commandos knew their routine. Cash with his usual stealth moved away to a position by one of the ash trees and the other three tensed in place by the hedge. Cash then made a scraping noise on the trunk with his knife.

The guards looked up.

'*Was war dass?*'

'*Wahrscheinlich nur 'ne herrenlose Katze.*'

Cash continued the noise.

'*Ich sollte besser nachschauen.*'

One of the Germans stood and walked over to investigate. He was so secure he left his rifle at the fireside while the other two kept smoking, hardly raising their heads.

The soldier proceeding towards Cash flicked his torch around as he approached the trees. The moment he was within reach, Cash stepped out, flung his left arm round the man's face and using his jungle knife in his right, sliced open his throat. Blood spurted over Cash's wrist while, at the same second, Matt, Ludlow and Skinner sprang upon the soldiers at the fire. One managed a strangled shout but they were dealt with in three seconds. The Commandos eased the dead men to the ground and pulled their bodies back behind the hedge.

Cash and Matt left Ludlow and Skinner to watch the troop shed, and returning to the others, they eased themselves along the wall of the building. Cash peered into the room where the General had been drinking earlier. He saw the thin-faced Sühren, two other officers and three women. No General! He must have gone to bed.

The Commandos returned to the broken window leading into the corridor, climbed through it and crept along noiselessly, Cash trying each door leading off the corridor in search of the General. He came to one that was locked and decided this was probably the one. He indicated for two men to remain there on watch and moved with the rest of his men along to the door they assumed led into the main hall and Sühren.

Cash signalled for them to use their pistols and if possible to avoid killing the women.

Silently he turned the handle, flung open the door and burst in. One woman was so drunk she merely sat there grinning, the other two screamed. And as the German officers rallied in defence, Cash, Matt and Lieutenant Phillip Boyd, who had each immediately marked their man, brought their pistols up and fired. There was a woman on Sühren's knee and he pushed the unlucky girl into the gunfire as he stood and drew his own revolver, but Cash had thrown his knife and one of the others had fired again. Sühren sank to the floor, surprise frozen on his face.

Gunfire sounded in the distance!

'Shit, something's gone wrong at the railway track.'

Cash looked at his watch. 'Only fifteen minutes before it was to be detonated. Hell!' He bent down and retrieved his blade from Sühren's chest. His tone was tense. 'Find the General.'

The drunken woman had revived and the two females clutched each other in terror as the Commandos bustled back into the hall.

Now the rattle of gunfire began at the back of the house.

'The bloody platoon's awake!'

Matt put his pistol in his belt and raised his Sten gun. 'With this racket the whole island'll be awake. Entire bloody place is only nine by five.'

Cash was stimulated; his eyes gleamed as he ran along to the door where he had left the two Privates. He kicked it in and hurtled into the room. The beam from Matt's torch hit the bed and the figure of a woman with horrified eyes clutched the sheet to her naked body. There was no Dietrich!

Matt shouted, 'Where's Dietrich?' And the woman shook her hand at a door on the far side of the room.

They ran to it and kicked it open. It led to a bathroom. Empty! A door on the far side was swinging on its hinge.

Grenades exploded in the yard and Cash shouted to Matt, 'Get back outside and help finish off the platoon, I'll find the bastard.'

Matt turned and ran and Cash charged through the door. He was in another well-lit corridor which led to a sitting room. He dashed across the room, knocking over a chair, through another open door and out onto a patio. His men were fighting to his left, but glancing right he saw a hefty figure running for the corner of the building. Dietrich!

He vaulted off the patio and suddenly a bullet ripped across the side of his neck. He spun round and a German soldier came running out of the shadows with bayonet levelled. Cash brought his Sten gun round and fired. Nothing. It was jammed! The soldier was upon him, all he had time to do was use the Sten gun as a club. As the bayonet came at him he leapt back and swung the sub-machine gun, knocking the blade aside. The man grunted and went down on his knee, but still holding his bayonet thrust back towards Cash's midriff. The front of Cash's black jacket ripped open but wielding the Sten gun, he smashed it with all his force into the side of the soldier's head. There was a crunch and the German slipped to the ground.

Without hesitation Cash flung himself around and ran after Dietrich, realising that all his men were fighting at the back of the house where the German troops had been sleeping.

He heard the engine of a jeep turning over. Dietrich was escaping!

Gunfire and grenades continued exploding in the north-west where he knew Kirkland and his other boys to be. A blasted battle was ensuing over there! What the hell had happened to blowing up the track?

As he reached the corner of the house the ground shook from a series of blasts, as all the colours of the rainbow expanded in flames to the sky.

You beauty! Kirkland and Crystal had detonated the railway line!

But the jeep was moving and Cash, always a powerful runner, raced like he did that night back in Sydney when the cops were after him – catapulted over a hedge and charged at an angle to meet the General. He tried again to use his Sten gun but it was useless and at the same time Dietrich fired his Luger PO8 and the bullets spat across Cash's right shoulder. Cash was bounding headlong at the vehicle as it gathered speed towards a gap in the wall. He took a mighty spring and as the vehicle passed him, he landed in it and cannoned into the Nazi, who lost control of the wheel. The jeep slewed sideways, hit the low wall and hurled the two men to the ground where they tumbled together into a bush.

Dietrich, who still clutched the semi-automatic pistol, fired again. His bullets went into the night sky.

Cash felt his head hit something but his hand was on his quarry's wrist as they rolled across the grass into the dirt of the driveway. They fought for the pistol, grunting gutturally in each other's ears, sweating and growling, but Cash was fit and strong and twenty years younger than the Bavarian and he brought his knee up with all his force as he tore at the pistol barrel. The General groaned in pain and his finger squeezed again just as Cash yanked the gun upwards. The bullets smashed into Dietrich's eye and he moaned, quivered, went limp and lay still.

Cash rose from him and stood a moment above him. The man was wearing only his trousers; the upper part of his face was gone, nothing but a bloody mass. *The only good Nazi General is a bloody dead Nazi General!*

He bent down and released the Lüger from the dead man's hands. For five seconds he turned it over, studying it. Nice weapon. Snakeskin on the handle, barrel polished to a high shine, gleaming in the moonlight. Spoils of war after all! He held it in his palm, it balanced, felt just right.

Abruptly he took a sharp breath. 'Nah! Those days are over.' And he tossed it hard into the bushes and stood up to see his men come running through the shadows of the building towards him.

Matt's shoulder was covered in blood. 'Copped one,' he announced as he tried to smile. The wound looked bad.

Boyd glanced at Dietrich on the ground. 'Mission accomplished, sir.'

'Mmm.'

'We're all here but Deese. He bought it, though we got most of them before they were really awake.'

'Damn it, Deese was a good bloke.' Cash paused, and picked up his Sten gun. He pulled the trigger and bullets ripped into the ground. 'Now it bloody works!' Suddenly he could hear vehicles not far away. 'Sounds like we've got visitors. Move out, everybody. On the double.'

As they ran out past the body of Dietrich and up the rise towards the deserted farmhouse, Cash's eyes were on Matt assessing the seriousness of his wound.

He looked over his shoulder and saw four sets of headlights coming along the dirt road towards the manor house. And by the time they had reached the old farmhouse and Matt had pointed to the track behind it, German troops were piling down from the lorries and spreading out.

The commandos started sprinting down the slope to the collection of houses snuggled in the vale. 'Won't take them long to be looking for us. Shit! What's that?' Over to their right another set of headlights appeared to be heading towards the cottages they had to pass.

'Stay on the track. If it gets there before us circuit the village.'

Matt was breathing too heavily, keeping pace at Cash's side. 'Ragtime said not to leave the track . . . it's all broken

662

ground around the village . . . and some places you can't get through.'

'Give me your Sten gun and just run as fast as you can.'

Matt protested but Cash took it and pushed the boy ahead of him.

Down they raced, heads twisting right to watch the approaching vehicle. Their breathing and grunts echoed on the night air for there was now silence in the distance. Whatever battle had started near the labour camp was over!

Running in the night! Ah, how he loved running in the night! But the edge of thrill was gone for he was concerned for the wounded boy who ran at his side.

They were nearing the village and it looked like they would be through before the Germans arrived but Matt was slowing down, he was losing speed and, with his whole left arm dripping blood, he began to falter.

Cash carried his own gun hoisted over his shoulder and Matt's in his right hand. 'Come on mate you can do it. We're nearly there.' He took Matt's arm.

Boyd and the others were already in the village lane and passing the second of the six cottages while the lorry closed in from the right.

Cash was calculating the possibilities. They had to get through the lane without being seen otherwise the Germans would follow them to the cove!

The first of the cottages was just ahead when Boyd came running back to them. 'Give me Fleming's gun sir. You'll be able to help him more without it.'

Cash handed him the weapon. 'Come on, Matt, we'll make it.'

Matt was obviously tiring but he was still on his feet and as they passed the second cottage Cash thought he saw faces at the window.

It was a hundred yards down the lane through the six cottages and Matt was weakening all the time. He had slowed to a walk when they caught up to the other Commandos standing waiting in a pack.

'There's only one lorry coming, sir,' Skinner said. He

was nineteen, physically perfect and brave as a cockerel. 'We can easily take 'em out.'

'I agree we can, son, but if we stand and fight they know exactly where we are and others will be here in no time. We can't risk leading them to the cove. Keep moving – that's an order. Get back to the dinghies and have them ready in the sea when we get there.'

Skinner looked dubious in the moonlight and Boyd began to speak. 'I'll stay—'

'Get going. Give me Fleming's Sten and if we don't turn up, you lot get back to the sub.'

'Are you sure?'

'That's an order. *Go!*'

Reluctantly the Commandos trailed off as the lorry turned into the end of the lane and the beam from the headlights hit the dirt, illuminating the fronts of the cottages.

Matt had lost so much blood that he began to sway. He turned to Cash where they stood on the track leading off through the tall grass, his eyes white in the night. 'I'm going to slow you down too much, sir. Please leave me here and get going.'

Cash gave a rueful smile and a dismissive grunt. 'Shut up, soldier. We're going together. If the Germans see us, we hit the ground and hold them off as long as we can. And with the way I feel about these bastards, that'll be until we run out of bullets.'

He took Matt's arm to lead him away, expecting the lorry to disgorge its soldiers onto the village lane and take the consequences, when to his amazement, the vehicle backed up, turned around and drove off the way it had come.

A wheeze of relief escaped from Matt. 'What's going on sir?'

'Don't know, but let's not analyse it. Let's go.'

Gunfire sounded again in the distance as he supported Matt, half-dragging him to the cliff path. Ten minutes later the young man had lost so much blood he collapsed and Cash hoisted him on his shoulders and carried him. All the rest of the way he heard intermittent fire and noticed torch-light sweeping inland.

With the burden of Matt Cash slowed to a walk and finally staggered along the cliff path to the cove where he saw a shape running towards him. He let the boy slip from his shoulders and brought his Sten gun up, but to his relief it was Roger Crystal, who had been at the railway track.

The Commando hurried up to Cash in the moonlight as he caught his breath. 'Are you all back?'

'All except Captain Kirkland, Moss and Hargreaves.'

'What happened?'

As they carried Matt between them Crystal explained. 'Everything went like clockwork until four guards at the slave camp came out through the gate with a pack of dogs. The bloody Alsatians must have sensed something or smelt something because they ran right up to Captain Kirkland, Moss and Hargreaves who were coming back from setting some of the charges. That's when hell broke loose. We finished off the dogs and the guards all right, but the whole camp was awake by then. I bet the poor bastards in there hoped we'd come to save them. Anyway the Captain ordered us to move out, and so as not to lead them here, he made sure they followed him in another direction.'

Cash gave a grim smile. 'Good man.'

When they reached the cliff path the others were waiting. 'Get down to the boats and someone stop Fleming from bleeding to death on us.'

Each craft had a motor fitted to the back. They had not used them on the way in to keep silence but now on the way out, time was of the essence.

Cash pointed out to sea. 'Take three craft and get going. Skinner and Kemp stay with me.'

Crystal paused. 'We'd rather all remain, sir.'

Cash rounded on him. 'What's going on tonight? Don't you lot understand orders? Get into those dinghies and get back to the sub, right now!'

That was pretty clear! The nineteen men so commanded clambered into the craft and left.

Cash sent Skinner up the cliff to wait at the top. 'If they're not back in ten minutes we'll have to leave. There's a German destroyer in the harbour and we don't want to be around when dawn breaks.'

They could hear the occasional volley of gunshots echoing on the night air. Once they heard the explosion of a Mills Bomb and a return of fire.

'Shit, where are they?' Kemp asked, holding the rope of the rubber craft and kicking small stones with the toe of his boot as the moon slipped behind a cloud.

Cash counted the minutes. *Come on, Kirkland, old man. Come on.*

Suddenly there was a volley of gunshots up beyond the clifftop and Skinner's voice called 'Oh Lord, here they come with the whole bloody German army after them!'

'Push the boat out, Kemp, and start the motor.' There was a small chop to the sea and Cash and Kemp thrust the craft to where they were knee-high in the water as Skinner came scuttling down the cliff followed by Kirkland, Moss and Hargreaves.

They leapt and bounded over rocks to the shore as beams of light appeared on the clifftop.

The motor jumped into life, the Commandos jumped into the craft, and Kemp headed the dinghy through the black choppy water out into the Strait of Little Russel as bullets spat across the night, and Cash, the only one with any rounds left, returned fire.

Back aboard the submarine heading for Plymouth Hoe Cash sat in the galley with his boys all around. He lifted the beer in front of him and the boys cheered.

Across from Cash, Betty Grable in a pink swimsuit smiled coquettishly at him from a large poster. It reminded him of Sammy in her swimsuit on Seven Bob Beach. Reckon she gave Betty a run for her money any day! Would she ever realise how much he loved her? Nah, not a chance now. Ah well, that was life. And he would miss her all the days of his, that was for sure. He wondered if she had told JB the truth yet? He wished them luck. He hoped one day when this bloody war was over that he would see JB again. He still thought of him as the best damn friend in the world, other than little Danny in Sydney. Yes, and dear old Ledgie. He smiled to himself, thinking of her sharp tongue.

Hell JB would probably smack him in the mouth, and he'd let him do it. After what he'd done to him. He shook his head. Shit! He had better not develop a conscience. That would never do!

'Major?'

Cash looked up to Crystal who stood beside him. 'Fleming's wound's been dressed, sir, and the doc says you can go in.'

Cash found Matt Fleming, shoulder bandaged and lying in a bunk.

As Cash bent through the watertight door, the Second Lieutenant's eyes lit with pleasure.

'Thanks, Major. I owe you one. I would have been a gonner without you.'

Cash winked. 'Just don't get in the way of a bloody bullet again; that's an order.'

'I won't buck that one, sir.' The young man grinned. 'It was all a big success.'

Cash was thinking of the one he had lost. 'Yes, it was. Except for Deese. I don't like to lose good men.' Into his head flooded Taber and Carvolt, Dunne, Carter, Dale and Richards and all his boys in Malaya. Unconsciously his shoulders sank, his head dropped and he stared at the floor.

The astute young man with him spoke quietly. 'Did you lose some other good men?'

For some seconds Cash said nothing while Matt watched him. Then he gave a brittle laugh and slapped Matt's unharmed shoulder as he moved to the entryway. 'The best there are, son; the very best. Men it made me proud to walk beside. And they wouldn't want me moping about it either, that's how they were.'

He was at the door when Matt called, 'Won't be surprised if you get the Victoria Cross for this one, sir.'

Cash hurled his words over his shoulder as he bent and stepped out. 'Don't be bloody silly.'

But it was not, for in the event, that is exactly what occurred.

Chapter Forty-three

Samantha hit the ground and rolled over, jumped up and looked round.

'Perfect!' she heard Martin Denning shout through a loudhailer as his jeep rumbled down the hill towards her.

A thrill of satisfaction ran through her.

'Now fold it and hide it!'

She pulled the parachute in towards her, folded it as fast as possible and looked round. A thick gorse bush grew beside a rock and she ran over and stuffed it between them.

'Now get on that bicycle and we'll see you back at the house,' Denning's voice boomed again as he drove off and began shouting to 'Bart', another trainee who had just landed a hundred yards away.

Sam ran to the bicycle and climbed on. This part of the training was almost enjoyable with the autumn breeze in her hair and some sunshine sneaking out from behind the clouds as she headed for the Scottish West Coast twenty miles away where they lived in a house overlooking the Sound of Arisaig.

There were fourteen men and three girls in the second-last stage of their training. They had been here six weeks and would leave the day after tomorrow. The schedule was hard and tough, often drastic.

She had long since realised the significance of the badge Cash had been wearing on his cap on New Year's Eve. It was that of the Special Air Service, a branch of Commandos, the 'army within the army' who used the latest weapons and had been given Churchill's blessing to carry the war to the enemy. They were an elite task force and were often airborne. Many of her teachers over the past nine months had been such men. She was not surprised at all that Cash would end up in such a Service. He was perfect for it.

She and the others had been educated by experts of all kinds, civil and military, who instructed them how to use revolvers, rifles, Sten guns, Tommy guns, hand grenades and bombs; they learnt about explosives: how much was needed to blow up a bridge, a building, a factory. They were taught to paddle canoes and to avoid booby traps and how to kill with a knife.

They were instructed on how to read maps, use a wireless and tap phone lines; to scale cliffs, firstly during daylight and then at night, always burdened with packs and weapons, then coils of fuse wire and explosives. They rope-walked between trees, holding one line with their hands, their feet on the other. They waded across streams in the early hours of the morning and climbed into buildings and over roofs, jumped from heights of ten and twelve feet and learnt how to roll to avoid injury. They tackled difficult assault courses both in daylight and darkness; trekked in the mountains sometimes for twenty-five and thirty miles, often in bitter weather: once Pamela and Sam – now known as Delilah – became lost and to Sam's great embarrassment had to be rescued. She made sure it never happened again. Finally they were shown how to live off the land, catching rabbits, pigeons and other birds, and to tell which were edible berries.

Originally they had trained in parachute jumping outside Manchester at an establishment named Ringway, and were now in Scotland to put the finishing touches on advanced parachuting and raiding using live ammunition.

Often, to her surprise, Sam had revelled in it. At each stage of the training the unsuitable men and women had been weeded out and now they were almost veteran. The only thing she did not care for was being bitten by midges during the long night hikes.

Sam sang a French song as she rode along. Her French was practised daily and by the time she reached the large country house on the cliffs it was almost dark. Seven of the group had arrived and she was the first woman in, just

669

beating Pam by six minutes. Martin Denning congratulated her.

'What would you like? A beer?'

She shook her head and called out as she bounded up the stairs, 'No, thanks. All I want is to have a nice bath, wash my hair and put on some make-up.'

Martin turned to Vera Atkins who stood beside him. 'She's still a woman!'

'Of course,' Vera replied. 'That's her charm: gritty and manly one minute, seductive the next.'

Two hours later the seventeen sat at dinner with Martin at one end of the long refectory table and Vera at the other.

At ten o'clock Martin lifted his glass and stood up. 'Tomorrow's our last day. You've all come through brilliantly and we're proud of every one of you. Two lorries will be here at dawn the day after to bus you back to the rail station near Mallaig, so if you want to celebrate, do it tonight. You'll be required in the morning at 1000 for a final target practice and then at 1400 for your last parachute drop wearing full kit and carrying Tommy guns.'

This was met with a round of groans.

Martin smiled. 'Listen, it's in daylight so don't complain. You'll attack a small armoured division on your way in. And then it's goodbye to Arisaig. Thank you for your dedication, and good luck at finishing school!'

This was a reference to the last and in many ways, most important stage of the course, the psychological conditioning. They were all going to different places. Sam was bound for the home of Lord Montague of Beaulieu in the New Forest. The Lord was in fact only sixteen and away at Eton, and his trustees had given the house over to government use. There, Sam would take her fifth name and this time her new identity. At Beaulieu she would complete her secret agent's skills. Learn how to merge into the life of Occupied France; memorise all the uniforms of the Nazi Army; become au fait with the German military and espionage systems and remember their codes and cyphers; rehearse her assumed identity until she could be woken in the middle of the night and fall immediately into it. All conversation would be in French. There she would be born anew. There she would be made ready to 'go into the field', as they at SOE termed active service.

That night Sam got a little tipsy and when she and Pam, Vicki, Terry, Bart and Irwin arrived at the top of the stairs together at two in the morning and Bart playfully suggested the girls did not go back to their own rooms but came into the male dormitory accommodation with them, Sam wagged her finger in the air. 'Get out, you cheeky mug.'

'Ah, come on Delilah, be a sport.'

'Buzz off,' she said, looking down her nose and Vicki giggled. 'Or we'll give you a rabbit killer.'

They all laughed and tottered off to bed.

There was gloom in the air when they departed from each other in London. They were aware that it was unlikely they would meet again, unless they were ever to do a job together. They were also aware of the seriousness of what they had all trained to become.

They shook hands on King's Cross Station and hugged each other. Pamela, Sam and Vicki, who had become so close, clinging a little longer than the men.

When Sam arrived in South Audley Street wearing the khaki uniform of the FANYs with the insignia of cross in circle on beret and lapels, Amelia welcomed her warmly. The landlady had been more than generous, keeping all Sam's belongings in a small flat on the ground floor.

'You can have the flat for nothing, love, whenever you're back in London. It's a lot smaller than what you had before, one bedroom, a bathroom, little kitchen and weeny sitting room, but I never let it out as me old gran lived in it till she died in the spring of thirty-seven. Sentimental, that's me.'

'But are you sure?'

'I'm positive. I'd like you to use it. It'll be nice to have you here when you're in London.'

Sam had lost contact with most of her social set, though Victor Bradbury still telephoned and left messages with Amelia. Victor and Amelia had always been friends and Sam believed that her landlady would really like to see

671

them back together again. Ed Monroe had gone off to Italy and though Sam still went to the Forces clubs she avoided getting entangled with anybody. She had no inclination to, and in any case, she knew very well that Vera and Martin Denning did not want her involved with anyone special. They had said more than once: 'Better if you don't have a boyfriend. They tend to ask awkward questions.'

The first night back in the metropolis Samantha surprised herself by telephoning Alex and asking to see her.

Alex was delighted to hear from her. 'You're back for how long?'

'Oh, just a week or two.'

Alex laughed. 'Have you ever been to the Studio Club in Knightsbridge?'

'No, but I'd like to go.'

'I've got Friday night off.'

Sam was pleased. 'Good. We could meet at the Rambler first, have a drink and walk over.'

'Yes. Seven o'clock all right?'

'Perfect.'

When they met the two women smiled and they sat in the same booth as many months previously. Alex could not help but say, 'Samantha, you've been out of touch for so long I was beginning to think you might never call again.'

Sam felt a little awkward. 'I know it's been a while, Alex. It's the job, you see. I'm off a lot of the time driving old Generals around but I really enjoyed that Sunday last winter out at your home and meeting your parents. They did get my letter of thanks, I hope?'

'Oh yes. Mummy keeps asking about you, actually. At last I'll have something to tell her.' Then a thought crossed her mind. 'You know, perhaps you could send me a card sometimes from wherever you take your top brass.'

Sam knew that would not be happening. She hated lying but it was now to be such a part of her life she might as well get used to it. 'Alex, being in the FANYs isn't simple. Sometimes we're rushed off to other theatres of war at a moment's notice and I can't let you know that. I'm all over the place. But look, I'll promise you something. Whenever

672

I'm in London I'll make sure we see each other. How's that?'

Alex met Sam's eyes. She liked Sam, she really did. 'That suits me, Samantha.' Then she sighed. 'I miss your brother an awful lot, you know. Let's talk about him for a while.'

They knew John Baron was a prisoner-of-war; had known since six weeks after he had been shot down. Both women had waited, fearing that he had been killed, but finally the message had come via the International Red Cross who were the distributors of such news.

Sam paused. Being asked to talk about JB to Alex was pretty difficult. She did not know whether to laugh or cry, but after a brief hesitation she began with her first memories of him. She mentioned that she had been one of twins and had grown up with her brother a focal point of her life, how she admired him and how he had always been wonderful to her. And when she found she did not want to burst into tears, that speaking of him was easier than she thought, she related much about their lives in Australia and even told Alex about Ledgie and Wakefield, her parents and Haverhill.

Finally Sam even spoke of Cash. She did not say what had broken them up, she simply spoke of the happy times – clowning around in the water-holes of Teviot Brook, riding with him and JB across the miles of open country, photographing them on the Harley Davidson; then after their marriage, their mornings on Seven Bob Beach and starting her photographic studio in King's Cross. She even divulged how his hair fell over his forehead.

Alex watched her new friend. She felt that Samantha was paying her a great compliment, which indeed was true.

Finally when Sam realised how long she had been talking she faltered. 'Oh Alex, I do beg your pardon. I've just been going on and on and we were supposed to go to the Studio Club.'

Alex smiled. 'Heck, we can go there anytime.' She pointed to the drape over the window beside them. 'Anyway it's pouring down, you can hear it.'

Sam felt comforted. Each time she was with Alex Cardrew she liked her more. And as Alex turned round to the elderly waiter and ordered a cheese sandwich for them Sam said, 'Don't you think it's my turn to listen to you?'

Two months later Alex heard from Sam again. It was just before Christmas and as Alex knew she was not on duty on Christmas Day she spoke to her parents and they all agreed to invite Samantha to Castlemere.

Kate, who was in the WAAFs, could not get leave but Jane had managed to return home and they all arrived at Sandwich Station late on Christmas Eve.

The weather contrived to be traditional, snowing early on Christmas morning so that the grounds of Castlemere were dusted white. Small gifts were given and Mrs Blake baked a chicken. No one asked how it had appeared; they simply enjoyed it and said what a genius she was. In the afternoon they all took a walk north towards the Roman ruins at Richborough. They did not attain them, for with the coming early winter night they only strolled a mile or so and turned back but it was a cheerful event and they were laughing as they crossed the stone bridge to trail along the Stour back to Castlemere. Jane and her parents were ahead and Alex and Sam walked side by side.

Sam was talking. 'It's been so kind of your parents to have me here. Just for today I'd forgotten all about the war.'

Alex smiled. 'I'm glad you came.'

'I wonder how long the war will last?'

'We all wonder. Sometimes it's hard to remember what life was like before the war. No rationing, people able to make plans, children living natural lives, and all your friends alive. You know, in the last fortnight I've heard of five boys in my social set who've been killed. One was my flat-mate's boyfriend.'

Sam drew her coat more firmly around her as the wind lifted along the Stour. 'Yes, I've lost friends too. Everybody has. The cream of the country's being wasted.' Sam thought of what she was about to do. She was soon to be dropped inside France to photograph German secret documents in a munitions factory. She was going to pose as a secretary and had learnt to type and to take satisfactory shorthand in French. She had already had a dummy run at a factory in the Thames estuary where everything had gone well, but the first week in January it would be the real thing in France, with the ever-present Gestapo. Her 'nom de guerre' was Angélique Levet . . . Angélique Levet . . . Angélique Levet . . . Suddenly she realised Alex was speaking.

'Sorry, Alex, what was that?'

'Do you worry about your parents in Australia?'

'I used to, but now that the Yanks are down there in fairly large numbers I worry less.'

'Don't you miss them?'

'Oh God, yes. They went into shock when they were informed that JB was a POW. I think they were like the rest of us, believing he was invincible. In every letter they ask me to go home, but I can't do that.'

Alex paused at the water's edge by a holly bush. She extended her gloved hand and picked a sprig. 'I can't help but think of JB in a prison camp. It must be hell not knowing how long you're in there for. I mean, here we are – we're free and the war's dampening our whole existences, but just imagine being locked up and not knowing whether it's for another year or two or three or four.'

'Yes, or for ever, which could be the case if we lose, God forbid! They'd probably kill the prisoners-of-war and then it wouldn't just be the Jews and political prisoners in the slave and death camps; the Nazis would begin exterminating on a much broader scale.' Sam shivered as she spoke. 'What a world that would be.'

Alex had been holding the sprig of holly up, intending to push it through the buttonhole on her coat collar and then pick another for Sam, but her friend's words were so depressing she simply dropped the leaf in the snow.

'Oh God, Sam, we must win. We simply *must*.'

Sam thought again of what she was about to do. 'Yes, Alex, we must. I'm going to try to be positive about that. The alternative is unthinkable.'

They walked on in silence, each with her own thoughts, until they saw Castlemere in the distance and the group ahead turned round to wait for them, then Alex spoke. 'You know, I miss your brother very much. He really made me feel complete and all I want is his happiness. I've written him a letter every week since I found out he's a POW. I don't know if he ever gets them, probably doesn't, but I feel better writing them. I'll wait for him however long he's in the damn camp and when he gets out, if fate dictates he still wants me, then I'll be the happiest girl in the world. But do you know what?'

Sam shook her head. 'What?'

'If he decides he wants someone else, I'll be broken-hearted, but if she makes him happy – then I'll be content.'

Sam was studying her, thinking about her brother who was not her brother. If only the woman beside her knew . . . She looked hard at Alex. 'What an unselfish thing to say. You mean it, don't you?'

Alex nodded. 'Yes.'

'You must love him very deeply.'

'I do.'

Sam returned to the flat on 27 December and as she let herself into the building she saw Amelia and George's suitcase sitting in the front hall and Amelia's voice echoed up the stairwell, 'Is that you, Samantha?'

'Yes.'

The landlady spoke as she mounted the stairs. 'Victor came after you'd gone on Christmas Eve.'

'Oh?'

'He left a card. I put it on your mantel. He was so sorry he missed you and I told him to telephone you this week. I think he'll ask you somewhere for New Year's Eve and you should go, it'll do you good.'

Sam made a longsuffering sound in her throat. 'Yes, Amelia.' And as she turned to open the door of her flat George arrived. He had heard the last part of Amelia's statement.

'What about the other one?' he said, as he picked up the suitcase and walked back to the stairs.

'Yes, yes,' Amelia replied in an irritated tone, 'I was coming to that.'

Sam paused with her key in the lock. 'What?'

'Well, we were just leaving for Windsor when a soldier turned up.'

'Did he leave his name?'

'No, but I reckon I know who he was.'

'Well, come on Amelia, this is like drawing teeth.'

'It was the Major who came to see you last New Year's Day.'

Cash. Oh God. 'Did he leave a message?'

'Yes. He said to tell you he was passing through London on his way overseas. That he didn't know if he'd ever be back here but he wished you a good Christmas.'

'Did . . . he seem disappointed that I was away?'

'I couldn't guess at that, love.'

'Did he leave a note or anything?'

'No.' Amelia sniffed and eyed Sam. 'Now I'm not prying love, but what's he to you?'

Sam shook her head. 'Nothing.'

The landlady closed one eye. 'Nothing? For somebody who's nothing he has the ability to get you right agitated.'

Sam shook her head. 'I'll tell you about it one day.' And she let herself in and closed the door.

An hour later as the cold winter night descended on London and the shadows swelled inside Sam's little flat, she sat peering at four photos she had spread out over her kitchen table.

JB was laughing out of a 10 x 8 and she and Cash on their wedding day smiled out of another. In the third she was riding pillion behind JB on the motor bike (Cash must have taken that!) and in the last one Cash, curl easing down his brow, nursed little Storm on the front steps at Haverhill.

Sam had forbidden herself to cry but she heaved great sighs as she pored over them. When it was too dark to see, she stacked them up, pulled the blackout drape, switched on the light and put on the kettle.

Sam met David Maitland Flinders two hours before she

flew out to France. 'Angélique Levet, this is Laurent Vauban!'

'How do you do?'

David/Laurent was a Captain. He had been with the Special Operations Executive since its inception and he had been five times 'in the field', which was somewhat of a record. His mother had been French, his father English and he used to live and work in Belgium and Southern France before the war. Married to a Belgian girl who had been killed in the Blitzkrieg, he made his way to England when France fell. He was instrumental in organising early Resistance movements with such well-known SOE heroes as Charles Staunton (real name Philippe Liewer) and was on the Nazis MOST WANTED list.

Returning to France was dangerous for Laurent but he had opted to go and had grown a moustache for this mission. He was organising part of the widespread deception plans which were being leaked to the Germans about the Allied invasion of Europe. Laurent was an integral part of a cozenage, code-named 'Ultra' which enabled the Allies to monitor German response to the misleading information and thus alter their own strategies accordingly. While Normandy was the chosen spot for the Allied Invasion, Ultra indicated to the Axis powers that it was Calais. The South of France had also been mentioned.

Sam had been brought by Vera Atkins in an armoured car to a large country house in southern Kent, well concealed by oak trees from the road. They were met at the massive cedar front door by Martin Denning.

She and Vera appeared to be the only women in the building and as they passed through the hall she looked into the various dining rooms and bars where she saw RAF pilots and Special Forces Officers.

'They're going out on other missions,' Vera told her and Sam thought of Cash and scanned every face.

She and Laurent ate a meal together and he explained that he would be parachuting in with her.

'I'll be leaving you with trusted Resistance fighters in Évreux while I travel to Rennes to an underground group

I established. I'll be in constant touch and once you have the documents you will pass them to me. We'll then get you back out of France. I'm told you're a whiz with a camera.'

'Well, photography's been my life. I believe I'm getting the smallest camera in the world tonight – specially made for this sort of work.'

After the meal Vera took Sam to an upstairs room where she received a French suit and a blouse. The jackets being worn in wartime France were longer than those in Britain and everything must be authentic. 'The Resistance will supplement you with further clothing. We supply one outfit in case you have to change immediately, but there's just so much you can fit into a knapsack.' Everything she took with her was made in France, even down to her toothbrush. She was given 100,000 francs which was equivalent to £600 and when she asked, 'What about make-up?' Vera smiled. 'I knew you'd get to that.'

She handed her a small green plastic case containing lipsticks, powder, rouge and a French cleansing cream.

'Now,' Vera said as Sam brushed her hair in a long gilt mirror, 'are you sure you have nothing English on you?'

'I'm sure.'

'You'd best put on your travelling kit.'

Sam took off her English clothing and left it on the bed and changed into French underwear and a specially zippered flying suit for the journey over.

Finally Vera gave Sam a wallet. 'Your identity card and papers, ration cards and clothes coupons. Also writing paper and a pen.'

Sam placed them in her knapsack and faced back to the mirror. Vera came behind her and looked across her shoulder to meet Sam's eyes. 'Are you ready to go, Angélique?'

Sam nodded. *'Oui.'*

'You clearly understand your mission?'

'Yes, I'm to stand in for a secretary in the manager's office at the Concorde Munitions factory in Évreux. It's all been arranged by the Resistance. The girl, Fleur La Basse, will be ill for a week, and longer if I need it. I'm her temporary replacement. All my papers are in order. I'm to photograph secret documents. Once I have completed the mission the camera and exposed film will be given to Laurent and we'll return to London. How, I'll be informed at the time.'

Vera nodded. 'Angélique, you were chosen for this particular mission because it can only be carried out by an expert photographer who has been trained in all the skills you have. You'll need to work with extreme speed and under stressful circumstances. But we all believe you can do it.

'The Allies are mounting a great invasion of France and the documents you'll be photographing are of plans for the prototype of a fast amphibious tank.' She smiled. 'And we want them. Once you're inside the factory you'll have to find out where they're kept. Our contacts in the Resistance will have more to tell you.'

She walked to the door and rapped on it and Martin Denning entered. 'Evening, Angélique.' He was dressed in civilian clothes and he opened a portmanteau and handed her a key. 'We're told this key will open almost any door and we think you might need it.' Then he took out the smallest camera Samantha had ever seen.

He handled it lovingly and presented it to Sam. 'This is a Minox. It was actually invented by the enemy but now we have them.' He pointed to a chair and Sam sat down while he described the features in detail.

It was as she had been told, small enough to fit in her hand. She was in wonder. 'How will I carry it? I mean, conceal it?'

'You'll be given a special handbag with a false bottom. You should carry both camera and key in there.' He turned to Vera. 'Has that arrived yet?'

'I believe it's downstairs.'

'Right, let's go. Laurent will be waiting. It's a perfect night for flying.'

They descended the wide cedar staircase and Sam noticed the pattern on the carpet and the shape of the bannister rails; they were striking, all knights in armour. She registered such things now.

In a room on the ground floor with blackout drapes over long green velvet curtains covering a wall of windows Laurent greeted her with a smile. 'Ready to go to France?'

'Yes.'

A black leather handbag stood on a table and a small white phial lay beside it. Martin picked up both. 'This is the handbag, Angélique. Laurent will show you the secret compartment on your way across the Channel in the Lysander. Now this is the L pill which you should carry with you at all times. Inside the straps of your brassière there are tiny pockets where it goes. You can refuse to take it with you. It's up to you, of course.'

Sam knew what the L pill was. L stood for Lethal. It was provided for the act of killing oneself if torture was unbearable or a situation seemed hopeless.

Sam paused and looked at the small white phial. *How brave are you really, Sam? If the Gestapo catch you and they do to you some of the inhuman things you've been told, will you be able to stand it?*

She could feel the back of her body cosily warmed by the fire in the grate behind her, but the front of her was chilled. She stared down at the container for some seconds before she lifted her head and looked into Laurent's eyes, into Vera's eyes and finally into Martin's eyes. 'I'll take it with me,' she said as she held out her hand.

Chapter Forty-four

The weather was surprisingly good for a January night: cold and clear with cirrus clouds trailing their ice crystals at 25,000 feet. The Lysander flew low over the Channel and as they crossed the French coast a Messerschmitt came out of nowhere and fired a burst at them, they dived and made a few extreme turns and the fighter for some reason lost interest but it was Sam's first taste of being a target, and ever a realist, the truth of her position struck home.

Outside the town of Évreux in the fertile valley of the Iton and sixty-seven miles west-north-west of Paris, the Lysander was guided in on shortwave signal from the Resistance fighters below. The aircraft made a long swoop and Sam and Laurent stood on the threshold looking down into the blackness. Laurent saw a flickering light below, and said, 'Now!' and Sam stepped out into the air. She was falling through the night sky, pulling her ripcord and floating down, down.

She landed easily in about a foot of snow, rolled over and scrambled to her feet. Her knapsack was strapped to her front for she carried the parachute on her back.

Her eyes roved the night and she saw Laurent – a black shape upon the white field – come down about 200 yards away. She folded up her chute and then she heard low voices call in French, 'Laurent? Angélique? We're over here.'

She replied in French. 'Yes I'm Angélique.'

Two figures ran up to her, one holding a torch low to her feet.

'Welcome to France. I am André, this is Étienne.'

'Thank you.' She shook hands and one took the parachute from her. 'Follow us, we have bicycles in the lane.'

Laurent was already running towards them with two other figures.

Soon the knapsacks were strapped to the back of their bikes and they rode fifteen miles towards Évreux. Twice they left the road and hid behind trees when the headlights of lorries appeared from the opposite direction, and three times they had to alight and carry their bikes through thick snow for a hundred yards or so but the rest of the journey was quiet. As André explained, 'It's after curfew so there are only German vehicles on the roads.'

Sleet drifted down upon them and Sam was so cold she could not feel her feet when they finally rode into the yard of a solitary cottage. It was outside the town and was the home of a married couple in the underground movement.

They were Babette and Christophe and welcomed everyone with smiles. Sam halted in amazement to see a repast waiting on the kitchen table for them. Upon a clean blue and white checked cloth lay wonderfully aromatic chicken with potatoes and leeks. Babette was also preparing thick steaks on the stove, and slices of buttered bread lay in a white porcelain dish. A wood stove warmed the room and Sam felt the chill at last easing from her.

'How is it you have such a lot of food?' She was thinking of the strict rationing in England and the tiny slivers of meat they saw about once a fortnight.

'The Huns want everything grown for their forces, so there's plenty of food in France, especially in these country areas. Go ahead and enjoy yourself.'

André, Étienne and the other men who had met them on landing did not stay, but after Sam had removed her papers and make-up and items for the following day, they took her knapsack with them. She could not ride into Évreux the following morning with a knapsack; it might arouse suspicion. Her ultimate destination was a house in the town where she was to stay with her 'cousins', but as it was past curfew they could not take her there now. The knapsack they would deliver in a milk van in the morning and her

683

wardrobe of French clothing would await her. Tomorrow she and André would ride into the town on their bicycles as if they had just been out for a genuine morning's spin in the country.

Once André, Étienne and the others had departed Sam and Laurent and their host and hostess ate, and Laurent asked Christophe many questions before they ended the meal with a brandy and went to bed.

Babette provided her nightdress and Sam lay there thinking how wonderfully normal it all seemed in this house, and yet she knew that was an illusion.

It did not take Sam long to fall asleep but before she did so, she recounted her identity as Angélique. She had been born in the town of Roubaix and had travelled around Northern France as a child, eventually going back to Roubaix and studying typing and shorthand. When the war started she worked in munitions factories near Amiens and then Rouen.

Originally Sam had been told she would be from Amiens, but that had altered in the first week of her final course at Beaulieu in the New Forest.

Sam had received a shock when Vera had come to her and announced, 'We're worried about your French accent.'

'You mean I don't sound French?'

Vera gave a weak smile. 'Mmm, that's what we mean. So we're giving you a different background. First we thought we'd have you come from Alsace Lorraine, but the Germans would expect you to speak German if that were authentic, so we've come up with another idea. We've decided you were born in the far north, right on the border with Belgium in a place called Roubaix. The accent of the Northeners is more like yours. So you'll need to memorise the streets, cinemas, shops, parks, gardens and public buildings of Roubaix as well as those in Lille and Rouen. The good thing is you won't need to know anything about Evreux where you're going to relieve at the Concorde Factory because you've just arrived.'

Sam had groaned. 'It's a fine time to tell me my accent's awful.'

'No, not awful, but not quite pure.'

Sam thought about Wakefield and how he had always praised JB's accent. Now she looked back, he had rarely praised hers!

The next day Samantha was woken at ten in the morning. 'My goodness, I've slept late.'

'That's what we wanted you to do.' Babette's dark hair was caught up in a pink ribbon, and she looked fresh and clean as she smiled. She handed Sam a white towel and Sam noticed how soft it felt. 'There's a washroom at the back of the house. Please use it. I've put three jugs of hot water in there and the room's warm because it's next to the kitchen. There's a dressing-gown on the door hook.'

'Thank you.'

'Breakfast will be ready when you come through to the kitchen. Laurent said to say goodbye and that he will see you next weekend. André's already here to brief you.'

Sam and André rode their bicycles into Évreux to the house she was to stay in with her 'cousins', Émile, Anna and André. They were halted at one checkpoint but the guards merely gave their identity cards a quick glance.

Twice on the way Sam noticed WANTED posters on the walls and she shivered to see Laurent's face upon them. Underneath were the words, *Known as Alain or Guillaume*.

The following Monday morning Sam arrived at the Concorde Munitions factory. Everybody was searched on the way in and the way out. Each time she had to present her identity card and papers, and place her handbag down on the large oak desk which the guards used as a table, and each time she was body-searched and a guard went through her bag and handed it back to her.

She worked in a small office with Danielle the manager's senior secretary. Danielle, a lugubrious girl who rarely smiled, was Norwegian and spoke fluent German and French. The manager was a Frenchman called Balzac, a local and a collaborator. One small coal fire sat in the corner of the room next to Danielle's desk, so a lot of the day Sam shivered. Two other secretaries worked in an outer office and wore their overcoats the entire working day.

André had given Sam her instructions: they were simple. Find the top-secret document which they knew would be called file *Q105*, and photograph it.

Sam kept watching but the first day went by without any Q files being requested. On the second afternoon Balzac asked for one and Danielle left the office, returning with it a few minutes later. She carried the keys to the central filing room on her belt and when she left the office had told Sam to 'remain here'. Sam noticed she returned the file at the end of the day and she quite casually asked, 'Are all files meant to be returned before we leave?'

'All files must be back in the central filing room before *I* leave, yes.' She spoke dismissively. 'It doesn't apply to you as you won't be handling any. You're temporary.'

The third morning, a French-speaking guard was on duty as Sam arrived at the factory. He wore the uniform of a Sergeant of the *Werkschar*, a type of factory Gestapo. His eyes were an intense blue, his chin square and his hair was fair: an archetypically pure Aryan. He asked, 'You're new here, aren't you?'

'Yes, just relieving.'

'When were you last at home?'

'At home?'

'Yes, in Roubaix.' He tapped her identity card.

'Ah, about a year ago.'

The French-speaking Nazi looked closely at her. 'I was there in 1940.'

Sam's stomach tightened.

He mused a moment. 'I liked it. What's the name of that popular café where the clown dances? Or at least he used to then.'

Sam did not know anything about a clown dancing but she had memorised the names of two of the most popular cafés. She tried hard to give a nonchalant smile. 'Do you mean the one in the Rue Jules Verne?'

'I think I do.'

'La Chalice.'

He returned her smile. 'That's it – I used to go there all the time.'

Pulse quickening, Sam picked up her handbag and moved on. The next day to her relief he was not on duty.

This was now her fourth day at the factory and as yet she had not learnt where the secret files were kept.

Her luck altered at lunchtime.

Two of the manager's four secretaries took lunch from noon to 1 p.m. and she and Danielle went from 1 to 2 p.m. At 12.15 p.m. Danielle was away from her desk when Balzac, face flushed, rushed out of his office. 'Where's Danielle?'

'Out in Light Armaments I think, sir.'

He was obviously upset. 'The stupid girl, she has all the keys. She's never here when I need her! I want a file, *Q79*, now – immediately.'

'I'll go and find her, sir.'

'Yes, yes. Hurry. I must have it.'

Samantha hastened along the concrete corridors to the staircase that took her down to the Light Arms department. There she found Danielle. 'Mr Balzac's very upset, he needs *Q79* straight away.'

'*Mon Dieu!*' She was already carrying two thick cardboard folders in her hands.

'I'll take those for you,' Sam offered.

It was obvious from the expression on Danielle's face that the papers she carried were not for ordinary eyes. She hesitated.

Sam pushed her point. 'Mr Balzac's not in a very good frame of mind. He seems upset.'

Danielle's natural frown deepened; she hesitated before coming to a conclusion. 'You carry these and come with me.' She appeared to prefer to keep an eye on Sam rather than let her wander off with sensitive information.

The Norwegian girl hastened back up the staircase followed by Sam.

Once on the managerial floor the women hurried down two connecting hallways and through a dark green door which Danielle unlocked with a key from her belt. They passed though a small anteroom to a second door which

687

the Norwegian unlocked the same way. She switched on the light to reveal a room of cabinets in rows. All had large drawers with padlocks.

'Stand here,' Danielle instructed her and she walked down an aisle to the left. She glanced back at Sam by the door as she bent and unlocked one of the padlocks and opened the drawer. Sam noted exactly where she was.

She bustled back past Sam with the document. 'Come on. He gets so mad when he has to wait.'

She locked both doors behind them and they ran to their office where Balzac stood fuming. He snatched the file from Danielle's hands and slammed the door behind him, and the Norwegian girl, in turn, snatched the folders from Sam.

The rest of the day, uniformed men came and went visiting Balzac. Danielle was called into his office more than once, and in the late afternoon two Generals and a Colonel arrived. When it came to the day's end, the two secretaries in the outer office departed as usual and Balzac asked Danielle to stay late and to join him in his office with his visitors. The woman was halfway through the typing of a letter and she told Sam to complete it and take it to the postal department.

When Danielle disappeared into Balzac's office, Sam hastily finished the letter and left. Coming towards her in the corridor was an SS Corporal in the *Werkschar*. They often just patrolled the halls. Sam found even the black uniform itself disturbing so she did not look at him, and as she took the corridor to her left he called, 'Where are you going? That's not the way out.'

Sam held up the letter. 'I must deliver this to the postal desk for Monsieur Balzac before I leave.'

He nodded and passed on.

Sam hurried down the corridors to the green door. Looking right and left she used the skeleton key and to her immense relief it worked. It also opened the second door. She did not switch the light on but took out a small torch she carried and closed the door behind her and locked it. Then she crossed to the aisle she had seen Danielle enter for the *Q* section. Her key opened the top drawer.

With slightly trembling fingers she went through the Q files. 105 was missing!

She stood there, mind blank for a second. What now? Her heart accelerated.

The only conclusion was that Balzac must have the plans of the prototype tank right now in the meeting with the Generals. Every moment was becoming more dangerous. She would have to try again tomorrow.

She let herself out of both doors, locking them behind her, and hastened along to the staircase and down into the hall which led to the postal desk.

The postal officer, a bespectacled man with a Hitler moustache, was closing the door as Sam ran up to him. 'Here's a letter from Monsieur Balzac.'

'Why are you so late?'

'We're awfully busy up there.'

'Why isn't Danielle delivering this?'

'She's in a meeting with Monsieur Balzac.'

He took the envelope and went back into his room. Sam hurried on and departed the factory with fast-beating heart.

The following day was Friday and as Sam came in the gate and showed her pass it was snowing. She felt nervous when she saw the French-speaking SS guard was on duty again inside the factory entrance, and he gave her a smile as she came up to him. She managed to respond in kind.

He took a cup of coffee from the shelf behind him and sipped it as she placed her handbag down.

'Nice handbag,' he remarked.

'Yes, thank you.'

He looked in it as usual while the female guard ran her hands over Sam.

'You carry a torch?'

'Oh yes, always. These days it's dark so early.'

'When are you going back to Roubaix?'

'I'm not sure.'

'You're only relieving here, aren't you?'

'Yes.'

The woman guard completed her frisking.

Sam's chest was beginning to tighten.

'Where are you staying?'

'With my cousins. Look, I told Mr Balzac I'd be in early this morning. I'd best be going.'

'Come down here at lunchtime. We can talk about Roubaix.'

'Yes, yes, I will if I can.' She gave him another quick smile – she hoped it looked natural and not self-conscious – picked up her handbag and moved away. His eyes followed her.

Danielle appeared more morose than normal when Sam arrived in the office. 'I was here until half past nine last night. I'm tired.'

'Perhaps Monsieur Balzac will give you the afternoon off.'

Danielle made a disgruntled sound. 'That'll be the day.'

Sam was beginning to think she was going to need the following week to complete her task. But the Nazi guard had her worried. He was asking too many questions. If only she could conclude everything today.

At lunchtime she was anxious, hoping the guard would not come looking for her. She went to the canteen briefly and attempted to leave on her own but Danielle accompanied her. Sam knew she needed between ten and fifteen minutes to accomplish her task and she was calculating ways to do this when shortly after lunch Balzac came into their office. He spoke to Danielle. 'I'm going out for an hour. I need you to accompany me.' He gave a cursory glance at Sam. 'If my telephone rings, you can answer it at Danielle's desk. It's the same line. Explain I'll be back by half past three.'

'Yes, sir. Of course.'

Danielle gathered up her handbag and coat as Balzac locked his office door.

Sam waited twenty minutes before she took the tiny Minox camera and skeleton key out of the false bottom of the handbag, slipped them into her pocket and walked into the outer office. She paused in surprise, for the *Werkschar* Corporal she sometimes saw in the corridors was sitting on an empty desk talking to Annette, one of the two secretaries. All three looked at her.

Sam held up the two envelopes she carried. 'I must take these to the postal desk for Monsieur Balzac.'

The Corporal said something in German and unfolded his crossed legs as the light caught the gleam on his black boots.

Annette translated. 'He said he'll deliver the letters for you.'

'That's kind,' Sam replied lightheartedly, 'but I have to leave the office anyway. I need to go . . . well, you know where. So I might as well do both.'

Annette translated again and he shrugged as she brushed by his brooding figure and he returned to talking to the secretary.

Sam, looking right and left, hurried through the corridors to the green door. The managerial floor was mostly quiet, thank heaven. Moving as fast as she could she opened, closed and locked the two sets of doors. Again she took out her torch and opened the Q drawer.

Stay calm, Samantha.

Her hands fumbled for *Q105*. This time it was here!

She rested the torch on the top of the cupboard and opened the file. Eleven pages! She crossed back, and turned on the light. If she heard someone coming she would have time to switch it off but what she would do after that she had no idea. She put the secret documents down on the floor. They were indeed of a tank and it was indeed amphibious. The words were all in German.

She took deep breaths to steady herself placing each paper on the floor and skilfully lining up her shot and taking it. She knew she was perspiring even in the freezing concrete room.

Calm, Samantha, calm. It's only Balzac or Danielle who come in here and they're both out.

She photographed the final page, thought she heard something and froze. But all was quiet.

She replaced the file, padlocked the drawer, put the minute Minox camera back in her pocket, crossed to the door, unlocked it, switched off the light and moved out. In the outer room she repeated her actions and was about to ease out into the corridor when she heard footsteps outside. She leant on the door, heart thumping, but the sound of the steps faded.

Once outside she locked the green door and walked as swiftly as she could to the staircase. Bounding down the steps, she turned the corner to see a group of people coming towards her. Many wore the white coats of the Heads of Department. They eyed her as she hurried by into the post desk. No one was there so she dropped the letters in the basket on the desk and scurried back to the managerial floor.

As she turned the corner to her office she saw the SS Corporal and another man ahead of her and when she opened the outer office door the Corporal glanced back.

Annette gazed up as she came in. 'You were a long time. I was just going to come looking for you. What happened?'

Samantha patted her stomach. 'Must have been something I ate at lunch.' Regaining her office Sam glanced at the wall clock. It had taken her sixteen minutes.

She replaced the Minox and the key back in the secret compartment of her bag. All she had to do now was to get out of the factory and no one would ever be aware that the photographs had been taken. File *Q105* was in its drawer; the two doors were locked, the camera and key were in her handbag! She only had to wait until 5 p.m. to leave. It was now four minutes to three.

She began to have wild thoughts that she had not switched off the light in the top-secret filing room. When Danielle and Balzac arrived back, it was twenty to four and within fifteen minutes Balzac requested File *Q105*!

Danielle returned with it and went into him and Sam calmed herself.

She was on tenterhooks until 5 p.m. and tried not to look eager to leave. Danielle accompanied Sam to the ground floor and out to the entry where they were searched. Sam was again relieved to see the French-speaking SS Sergeant was not on duty.

It was dark as she pushed her bicycle through the main gate and allowed herself a small sound of relief. But the relief vanished into apprehension as she saw him waiting under the street-light.

'Angélique!' he called and Sam could do nothing but head towards him.

His fair hair was covered in a dark hat. 'How are you?'

'I'm well, thanks.'

'I finished early today.' He was in civilian clothes and wore a heavy greatcoat with a fur collar. 'You did not come to visit me at lunchtime.'

'No. We were busy.'

He gave a strange smile and she noticed a dimple near his mouth. 'Why don't I come round to your house tonight? Perhaps we could go to a café and have a drink. Chat about Roubaix. You know, seeing we didn't at lunch.'

Sam prayed her anxiety did not show. The last thing she wished to do was give him her address; it could jeopardise the whole Resistance movement in Évreux. The wind was whipping along the street now and Sam shivered. 'It's not really a nice night for going out.'

'Then we could remain in.'

Oh God!

'You *are* staying with your cousins, aren't you?'

'Yes, so you see it's not really my place to invite people home. But look, on second thoughts I could meet you at a café. Do you have a favourite here like you did in Roubaix?'

He grinned. 'As a matter of fact I do. It's three streets from here near the bombed-out baths. It's called La Lune Bleue. Do you know it?'

Sam did not, but she smiled and declared, 'Yes, I think so. Would seven-thirty be all right?'

Curfew was at eleven.

'Of course. Where do you live, by the way?' The acute blue of his eyes was picked up in the glow from the single street-lamp above.

Sam's chest tightened. She attempted a carefree tone, hoping desperately that she succeeded. 'Around the corner from the Rue Petit.' She swung her foot onto the pedal of the bicycle. 'So I'll meet you at La Lune Bleue at seven-thirty.' She made herself wave to him as she pedalled away. She did not live anywhere near the Rue Petit.

André's house was low to the street. She unlocked the front door and pulled the bicycle into the stone hall with the icy wind at her back.

'André?'

He appeared at the other end of the hall smoking a cigarette. 'Angélique?'

'I got the photographs.'

He ran down to her and hugged her; he looked boyish in his delight. 'Wonderful! And Laurent will be here tonight. The timing's perfect. We'll try to ship you out on Monday, weather permitting. It's so damn cold I think we'll be getting more snow; that might hold us up.'

He looked so happy Sam hated to tell him about the SS Sergeant but she knew she must. 'André?'

'Yes.'

She gave him an account of what had happened.

His mood darkened. 'Do you think he suspects anything?'

She shook her head. 'There's nothing to suspect. But if I spend a night with him and he talks in detail about Roubaix, well then . . .'

She followed André through to the kitchen where she put the kettle on the stove and sat opposite him.

He picked up a pencil and began to make notes on a pad, speaking as he wrote. 'We must get you out tonight. Once seven-thirty passes and you do not turn up at La Lune Bleue, the SS Sergeant will start to wonder why, and when you never arrive, he'll begin to make enquiries about you. You gave him the wrong address which is good, so there's little to connect you with us unless we're already being watched. Laurent's arriving after dark at Christophe and Babette's. We'll go there now. There's only one checkpoint we must pass but I'm afraid you must leave your clothes and knapsack here. To take anything will arouse suspicion. Anna and Émile will not be home until late and I'll leave them a coded message. Wear two lots of everything under your overcoat and more if you can, and bring only your handbag with whatever will fit in it.'

They reached Babette and Christophe's in the dark of the bitter evening and when André was preparing to return to Évreux, Laurent arrived. He brought bad news of the Underground group in Rennes. It had been infiltrated and when he arrived there, many had been arrested. He had moved on immediately to Le Mans and Caen where the news was better and they were beginning to plan for the expected liberation of France. Laurent's local spies were diligently passing out the false information that the landings would be in Calais.

After André had departed they went into a back room of the house behind locked doors and listened to the BBC's 9.15 p.m. broadcast. There were messages in the simplest of phrases: one was 'Jack and Jill went up the hill' and Laurent gave a grateful smile for it meant that tomorrow night a drop of ammunition which they had been waiting on for months would be made in a field east of Le Mans.

Sam slept in the same little room she had used a week ago.

She was up early, and dressed and helping Babette fry ham and eggs as snow drifted onto the kitchen windowsill outside, when she saw André ride into the yard.

'I didn't know André was coming back this morning.'

Laurent jumped up from where he had been sitting at the scrubbed oak table. 'He wasn't. Something must be wrong.'

Babette stood stock still then she dropped the egg she held and ran through to the washroom, calling to Christophe as André leapt off his bicycle and came hurrying in.

His eyes were bloodshot and though he appeared to have shaved he still wore the same clothes as last night. 'Émile and Anna have been arrested.'

Babette's hand stole into Christophe's.

'I arrived back at the end of our street just before curfew and the Gestapo were already there. I saw them taken from the house into the van and driven away. I dared not go back. I went to one of our members on the outskirts of town and remained there. But it seems that some others have been arrested also.'

Laurent walked to the window and looked out as André said, 'I'm almost certain I was not followed here.'

Sam felt sick. 'Do you think I had anything to do with it? Because I didn't meet the SS Sergeant?'

André shook his head. 'No, I think that's coincidence.'

Christophe tried to sound positive. 'Perhaps they've only been taken in for questioning. Sometimes the Gestapo round people up and question them and let them go.'

'Or they end up in Fresnes. And are never seen again,' Babette said in a monotone.

Fresnes! Samantha knew of the Gestapo prison outside Paris. It was now filled to overflowing. From there inmates were moved on to the hellish prisons inside Germany itself.

The Nazis had built the infamous Dachau, Buchenwald, Flossenburg, Mauthausen, Theresienstadt and Ravensbruk even before the war began and had been systematically exterminating prisoners there ever since.

Sam shivered, for she knew of Belzec, Sobibor, Majdanek and Treblinka where there was a combined killing capacity of 60,000 human beings per day, and Auschwitz, Chelmno, Belsen and Natzweiler were names that meant death by chemicals or horrific neglect.

Fresnes was the first step in their direction.

The little group in the kitchen looked silently at one another, and it was Christophe who spoke first.

'Now darling,' he said, bringing Babette's hand to his lips and kissing it. 'Let's not be alarmed. Let's concentrate on what to do.'

It was decided that André would not go back into Évreux, but that he would travel south through a network they hoped still existed, to join the Maquis at Châteauroux. The Maquis was a paramilitary Resistance group that worked mostly south from there in what had been Vichy France, the unoccupied zone which had collaborated with the Germans until Hitler, in usual fashion, broke his word and took it over in early 1942.

Sam and Laurent would make their way to the coast via

Caen, as planned, and pick up the small craft that was being sent by SOE to carry them and the precious film back to England.

They waited until nightfall to say their goodbyes. Sam hugged Babette close. 'You are so brave to stay,' she said in the woman's ear and the woman smiled and kissed her. Then she pushed Sam back to arm's length, and studied her. 'And none but the brave would leave the safety of Great Britain to come here.'

As Sam pedalled the country roads through the drifting snow of the long night her mind was replete with thoughts of André and Babette and Christophe. She prayed that they would remain safe and kept picturing Babette with her dark hair caught up in the pink ribbon.

The weather was so bad that it was another ten days before Sam and Laurent were safely aboard a motor boat. They finally arrived in England after twenty hours of bouncing around fighting the seas of the English Channel and were met south of Portsmouth by Vera Atkins and Martin Denning.

Sam and Laurent were driven to Daleton, a country house used by SOE in West Sussex, where each was taken through the mission step by step.

That first night back in freedom after the hours of questions Sam was sitting sipping a brandy in a plush maroon velvet chair when Laurent came in to say goodbye. His dark eyes regarded her with respect. 'You were wonderful. I hope we work together again. Goodbye.'

She hugged him and he left with Martin.

Sam turned to Vera. 'Will he be going back?'

'Yes. He wants to reorganise the Resistance in Rennes if he can, to have them ready to aid the Allies when they liberate France.'

Sam shook her head. 'He's so brave. They all are. And they live in constant horrible fear.'

Vera nodded. 'I wonder in years to come if people will ever understand any of this?'

* * *

Later, when Sam lay between white sheets under a pile of blankets in a cosy bedroom upstairs at Daleton she thought for the first time in weeks about her family – about Cash and JB. She was exhausted and drifting swiftly into sleep when she wondered what Cash and JB would think about her if they knew?

As Sam slept, John Baron too slept but not as comfortably. He was in a freezing dormitory hut in a prisoner-of-war camp in Germany where ice caked on the glass both inside and out and the men slept in layers of clothes. A single coal heater for each hut made an ineffectual attempt to warm the area and for much of the day and night men huddled around it.

After being captured, the first POW camp John Baron had been sent to was south of Minden, and when he had been brought before the Camp Commandant, a man with red hair cropped almost back to his scalp, he had informed his new prisoner of many rules. At the end he added, 'I don't allow Red Cross parcels here.'

John Baron had replied, 'According to the Geneva Convention for the protection of prisoners of war, Red Cross parcels must be distributed on arrival.'

The German edged slightly forward on his metal desk and answered him in passable English, 'The Geneva Convention was drawn up by a bunch of old women.'

John Baron's immediate thought had been escape and he and three others had mounted one in March 1943 from a work party taken outside the camp to tend the roads. They were caught and punished in solitary confinement: cells an arm's width wide with one bunk.

After his punishment John Baron had been transferred to Stalag Luft 111 at Sagan where many of the inmates recalled 'Tinlegs' Bader who had arrived there in April 1942.

They told John Baron that he had been wanting to escape from almost the minute he arrived. Some remembered him with deep and abiding admiration, telling how he had 'Goon baited' ceaselessly. The Germans were known by the prisoners as Goons and annoying them was the constant joy of the inmates. Bader was the master of the craft. When the Germans marched by singing their songs he would organise the prisoners to whistle opposing melodies to make them lose step. When the 'ferrets' – the name given to the Germans in blue uniform who snooped around searching the camp – found an escape tunnel, he would crowd the prisoners around and sing, 'Hi ho, Hi ho, It's off to work we go' . . . Whenever there was a chance to deride them he would, and there were often times he would openly defy them.

A section of the camp adored him, others disliked him, wanting only peace and quiet and thinking he went too far and that reprisals would follow. There was a third group who approved of a certain amount of Goon baiting but believed it judicious not to overdo it.

A story was recounted to John Baron which had become legend in Stalag Luft 111.

Because of Douglas, life at the camp finally became a series of 'dogfights' on the ground. The inevitable reprisals had begun and privileges – like remaining outdoors after sunset – had been removed. Those loyal to Douglas had doggedly held with his point of view, that maximum non-cooperation was their only form of defiance and defence.

But ultimately Douglas had been singled out as the one to be removed. He was informed that he was being transferred, and to be ready to leave the next morning. Douglas had asked defiantly, 'Where am I going?'

'Where you will be more comfortable, as it is not comfortable here, for anyone.'

'I'm not going. Take me to see the Commandant.'

'The Commandant will see you on the way out tomorrow.'

'No, he damn well won't. I'm not going.'

The German snapped an order and a rifle was levelled at Douglas's head.

Bader stood there, jaw pushed forward, daring the guard to shoot as the moments dripped by. The tension was electric. Then abruptly the soldier was ordered to lower his rifle.

The following morning and afternoon passed with Bader still resistant and towards dusk a company of guards in battle order marched out of the German administrative compound next to the camp: fifty-seven of them in webbing and helmets with rifles and bayonets fixed. The prisoners all rushed to the wire while Bader remained inside his hut.

The Senior British Officer, Group Captain Massey, reasoned with both the Commandant and Bader. He was now concerned that Bader's legion of supporters might do something wild, that the company of guards might begin shooting, and men would be killed.

Douglas saw the point.

He stomped out of his hut and down to the gate, then he turned back and smiled at his supporters who all cheered, before he walked over to the fifty-seven man guard. To everyone's amazement he strolled down their ranks inspecting them. Suddenly there was something absolutely farcical about an entire company of soldiers arranged in battle order to suppress one legless man.

The prisoners burst into laughter and it was as if the Germans saw the absurdity too, for the tension dissolved and Bader walked away whistling.

John Baron could not help but smile at the account. That was Douglas! The *enfant terrible*. You either loved him, or hated him. The Germans had met their match with Bader!

John Baron would not have been surprised at all to know that Douglas had frustrated and upset his captors so often that he had finally been removed to Colditz Castle, the so-called impregnable fortress where the 'incorrigibles' were ultimately sent.

At that same camp, Stalag Luft 111, a very large camp, John Baron again tried to escape. He was the second most senior officer, and when the tunnel they were digging was discovered, he was caught, given solitary confinement again and sent to his current camp: again in a vast compound for RAF officers only and this time in the Rhineland. It was much like the others but was for 'repeat offenders' as the would-be escapists were called. He was well aware that the next step was internment in Colditz Castle.

This current camp consisted of the same drab grey wooden barrack huts circled by trodden dirt paths etched into the ground inches deep: the caged humans like caged animals, paced round and round. They were fenced in by a tripwire and two walls of thick barbed wire inside a twenty-feet high fence which was buttressed by tall sentry boxes on stilts. Sentries sat with machine guns, and search-lights roved the camp at night.

The daily ration of food per man consisted of three slices of black bread, two or three potatoes, some soup and ersatz coffee, the variety in the diet being occasionally a portion of blood sausage. Red Cross parcels got through here and joyously augmented their allowance from time to time.

As morning dawned and a distant bugle sounded from the *Kommandantur* – the German guards quarters – the early risers left their bunks to sip the ersatz coffee and wait for *Appel* – the roll call – after which the stale, black bread breakfast arrived.

The man in the next bunk to John Baron was Anton Plzac, a Czechoslovakian Wing Commander who had escaped his country when the Germans invaded on 15 March, 1939. He had been in his aircraft on an early-morning reconnaisance flight and had just kept on flying and landed in Switzerland. From there he had made his way to England, joined the RAF and fought back. He had been shot down the previous February.

John Baron and Anton Plzac had struck up a friendship, and after *Appel* they walked on to the exercise field where prisoners who wanted to discuss anything privately usually strolled. They called it 'the circuit'.

At 1000 they arrived at the hut used for recreation where the escape committee gathered, a group of seven who were elected by the prisoners to evaluate escape schemes. At the door sat a man on watch to alert them if any guards approached.

In the past many prisoners had proposed half thought-out ideas, so finally in most camps, escape committees, sometimes known as the X Committee, for anonymity, were elected to decide which plans made sense. John Baron was

701

one of the two senior officers in the compound. The other, Group Captain 'Tiger' Milford, was in fact the SBO (Senior British Officer), having attained the rank earlier than John Baron. For the previous six months John Baron had chaired the escape committee and only relinquished the position when he decided he had a proposal which he wished to present.

It was strange for him to be putting forward an idea and not sitting in judgement. Sam Collier, a Wing Commander and now president, stroked his beard and nodded for John Baron and Anton to begin.

John Baron leant forward on his stool. 'Even though this is a camp for officers only and the Geneva Convention states we should do no manual labour, we all know that a work party of fifteen to eighteen of our men is marched out through the front gate every day between 0930 and 1100 to chop wood. The time it leaves varies: some days it's very early, well before 1000, and some days it's late. The Goons on the main gate change at 1030 and we have ascertained that the new guards are in fact unaware whether the work squad has departed or not. If they don't see it pass them through the gate, they simply assume it was taken out before they came on duty.

'Our idea is as simple as it gets. We just march out of the front gate.'

Collier glanced at the other members and Junior Christensen, an American Squadron Leader said, 'Go on.'

Now Anton spoke. 'This camp's so large that there are often new Goons on guard so it's quite feasible that the ones on duty don't actually know the faces of the Goons taking out the work party.'

Collier nodded, for that was quite true.

'Our intention is to be ready with a second work party hidden in here. We'll be rehearsing a play or something, and as soon as the guard changes, we'll exit, form up outside and march via Hut 44 where the party is usually rounded up, and go on to the main gate. They'll assume we're the genuine squad starting late and open the gate. I speak pretty good German so we'll choose five others who are all, or mostly all, fluent in German. They'll pass for the guards. And there'll be eighteen prisoners. As soon as we're out of sight of the camp we'll disperse.'

Anton paused and John Baron went on excitedly, 'So you see we need six Goon uniforms and the others will escape in their own clothes. Hall's incredible with props. He can make the false wooden rifles. Actually I think there are two already in props from the last concert. The pass that the guards carry is often cursorily looked at because it is such a normal everyday happening, but we must have it of course.'

Squadron Leader Charlie Hall had worked in the London theatre before the war and was a brilliant designer who could make anything. In fact, the talent inside the wire was often remarkable.

'Now there'll be some who want identity papers and it'll take time for our forgers to make them and for the handicraft boys to come up with the uniforms . . .'

Now Anton jumped in. 'There's a civil airfield outside Merzig which isn't far from the Luxembourg border and in a straight line to Lympne not more than three hundred miles. The Group Captain and I intend to hightail it to the civil aerodrome, steal an aircraft and fly home! We'll wait until early summer, probably May or even June when the weather's better. We want to give the plan every chance and it'll be warmer for those escaped prisoners who'll be sleeping out.'

There was silence from the committee and John Baron, who in his time as president had heard some ridiculously half-baked, hare-brained schemes, could not believe they were unenthusiastic.

'So,' he asked, 'come on you lot, what do you think?'

Collier looked round at the others. 'Best proposal I've heard in bloody ages!'

'You bet,' agreed Christensen. A rumble of affirmative sounds now greeted them.

Anton jumped up and punched the air.

Chapter Forty-five

April, 1944

Winston Churchill and Anthony Eden stood in front of the Mercator's projection of Europe in the Map Room of the War Rooms bunker underneath King Charles Street. Military duty officers moved in the background. They had been discussing the 'boot' of Italy where the Allied invasion continued.

The Germans were falling back but it had been a slow, hard winter and British General Harold Alexander was still bogged down south of Rome and the American Fifth Army under General Mark Clark had sustained heavy casualties. The Third Battle of Cassino was raging, where the New Zealanders and Indians were fighting it out with the first German Parachute Division, the Polish and French Corps were battling on the Gustav Line, and there was bitter fighting on the Anzio beachhead.

Last September Mussolini had been deposed by the Fascist Grand Council and placed under house arrest in the Apennine Mountains where German airborne troops had raided and removed him to Germany. Mussolini was now set up by Hitler as the head of a fascist administration nominally in control of German-occupied Northern Italy. Mussolini had rounded up all those he could find who had voted against him the previous September and had them executed as traitors. This included his own son-in-law, Ciano, even though his daughter had pleaded for his life.

Eden pointed to Salo where the dictator now spent his days. 'So the vainglorious *Il Duce* continues as nothing more than a pathetic puppet of the Reich.'

'Indeed. It's a phantom republic he runs from Lake Garda.'

'I wonder how one feels after executing a son-in-law?'

'I wonder.' Winston gave a characteristic rumble in his throat. 'It includes all the elements of Renaissance tragedy.' His gaze came back to France. 'Have Montgomery and the Cabinet arrived for the meeting on Overlord?'

'I believe the Cabinet are here.'

Overlord was the code-name for the planned Allied Invasion to liberate Europe. The need for short-range fighter support dictated that the Normandy beaches in France had to be the place for the landing, but widespread deception plans were afoot to fool the Germans into thinking it was Calais. It was proposed for the force to land at dawn on 5 June, in the event, due to bad weather, it was a day late.

As the two men moved into the corridor they met Leslie Rowan, WSC's private secretary.

He looked at his notebook and then at the PM. 'Mary called by earlier to see you, sir. She said to tell you she would come back again tonight.'

Mary was WSC's daughter who was with the battery in Hyde Park; his other daughter Sarah was an officer in the WAAF. Both girls had accompanied him overseas the previous year: Mary to Canada and the USA, and Sarah to Cairo and Teheran.

Churchill nodded.

'And the King's been in touch. He'd like to speak to you at 1700, if convenient. I've just received a letter from him for you.'

The King followed the course of the war with close attention and was anxious over many aspects of it.

Winston cleared his throat. 'Right, arrange it please. What else?'

'After the Cabinet meeting you have a telephone call across the Atlantic to speak with the President. Topic: the Eastern Fleet and the ocean war against Japan.'

Since July 1943 technology had provided a new scrambler so that the Prime Minister and the President of the United States could hold TransAtlantic conversations confidentially. Before *Sigsaly* – the code-name for the technical equipment – there was an ever-present fear of the enemy tapping the line.

'Thank you, and I want to speak to Brooke.' Churchill growled. He was referring to the recently promoted Field Marshal Alan Brooke, his principal strategic adviser.

'Right, I'll organise that. General Montgomery will arrive in half an hour, sir.'

The PM coughed. 'Soon as he does, bring him in.'

He coughed again and his secretary asked, 'Are you feeling all right sir?'

Churchill had been very ill in January with pneumonia, and had been forced to take a few days off in bed; his staff were still very aware that he had returned to the affairs of the war too soon.

The Prime Mininster gave him a withering look. 'Of course I'm all right,' he snapped, and followed by Anthony Eden, he headed along to the Cabinet War Rooms.

Through the carefully guarded bunker he moved down the main reinforced concrete corridor past the sign which read *cool and wet*, denoting the weather above. A Royal Marine orderly opened the door and all the members of the War Cabinet stood at the Prime Minister's entry. He placed his red box of State papers down on the desk and sat in front of the map of the world on the wall behind him.

He looked around their faces: the Chancellor, John Anderson; the Secretary of State, Anthony Eden; Home Department Secretary of State, Herbert Morrison and the others of his inner circle: Ernest Bevin, Clement Attlee, Oliver Lyttelton, Edward Grigg and Lord Woolton.

'Gentlemen, Overlord dominates today's agenda.'

'It's code-named Overlord and it will begin on June the fifth.' Martin Denning was speaking to Sam, who sat opposite.

'That's why we want our operatives in France. To organise as many of the Resistance groups as we can into para-military forces, so when the Allies advance in from the Normandy beaches, the Resistance movements will cause as much general mayhem for the Nazis as possible and thus help our advancing armies.'

Sam nodded in thought as Martin continued. 'We need our agents there to do the distribution of the weapons that we'll send in with you, and to help organise the sabotage. Some of you will work with our Special Forces Officers who will come in closer to the date of the liberation or during the landings themselves.' He ran his finger across the map of Normandy. 'You know some of this area from your last mission?'

'Yes.'

'Because in the main the Germans expect operatives to be men, not women, someone with your expertise can accomplish a lot.'

'Yes, I understand that. It's always said that women are less likely to be spotted than men.'

'We've just been informed by two of our operatives, one a woman, that nearly a hundred of the Resistance group in Rouen have been arrested and imprisoned, which means, in effect, that it's wiped out. The man in charge of our group in Le Havre, a schoolmaster called Roger Mayer, has been sent to Dachau.'

'Oh God.'

The woman he spoke of was Violette Szabo, a beautiful young widow whose husband had been in the French Foreign Legion and died earlier in the war. She was an amazingly brave operative who would be murdered in Ravensbrück and leave an orphan, an infant girl.

They were conversing in a country house in Somerset where Sam had done a refresher course and taken on the new identity of Camille Cabot. As Martin spoke the rain spattered on the casement window behind him and the day died beyond the weeping willows at the edge of the lake in the middle distance.

'Yes.' Martin sighed and observed her with his dispassionate gaze. 'Now there's one thing I wish to stress. I know you've volunteered for this mission, but you've been in the field once. There's plenty of work you can do here. You don't have to go again.'

Sam pictured Babette with her oval freckled face and her dark hair pulled back with a pink ribbon. She often thought of Babette, her strength and dignity in the face of terrifying fear; she thought of her brother in a POW camp; she thought of André and wondered if he had reached the Maquis without being caught; she thought of Laurent, who she knew had been back to France again recently; and she thought of Cash, a Commando in the Special Air Service.

'I want to go.'

He nodded. He had expected Samantha to say that. It was intriguing to him but most of the men and women who had been in the field once opted to go again. No doubt all his secret agents were driven by something. He was uncertain what it was with Samantha but whatever it was worked for the cause.

'We have agents going in to join up with the Maquis and some who're already working with them. But you'll be closer to the initial advance. 'There's a semi-paramilitary group,' he smiled, 'that's if you can have such a thing, in the hills near Caumont. They don't have many weapons but they're long on guts. They operate often at the edge of the prohibited coastal zone.'

'There'll be two drops. Number one: you, and three nights later number two: guns and ammunition. We want you in there first so that you can make sure the weapons are distributed and used properly.'

Sam seemed to be concentrating on the rain outside as she asked, 'Isn't this something a man should do? I mean, aren't most of the fighters in the group I'm to join, men?'

'Yes.'

'And you expect me to go in and control them?'

'We believe it's possible. Sam, the fact is that most of our operatives are in the field. We've people now in every country under the Nazi yoke. Yes, we could probably find a man to send but we think you can do it.' He picked up a jug of water that lay on the table between them. 'Your radio operator will be a man, but it's your mission.'

'Right.'

'You'll be getting support after you're in there anyway. Laurent will be bringing men to join yours.'

'That's an agreeable surprise. He's just the best there is.'

'Funny, but he says that about you.'

'Who's the wireless operator?'

'He's one of the boys you trained with in Arisaig. You knew him as Bart, now he's Guy.'

Sam grinned. 'I remember *him*. He suggested we girls sleep in the male dorm the last night of the course.'

Martin laughed. 'Good for him. Did you?'

Sam pretended shock. 'Of course not.'

'At the same time that we drop you we'll drop in Bourgogne, Champagne, Brittany and L'Auvergne which is so hilly and mountainous that it's ideal for guerrilla fighting.'

'That's the Maquis country.'

Martin poured water into a glass and drank as Sam smiled. 'I'll be very happy to see Laurent again.' Then she pointed to the water. 'Martin, the yard arm's in positive shadow, don't you have anything stronger?'

He called a waiter and ordered two brandies.

'Sam, there's something I must say to you.'

She lifted her gaze.

'I don't like this part of the job.'

She shrugged. 'Whatever it is, Martin, spit it out.'

He sighed. 'Obviously the Nazis know we're planning an invasion of Europe. The preparation and the amount of weaponry and manpower we've got sitting near our Channel ports hasn't gone unnoticed. You know we've been deceiving them into thinking our destination is Calais and not Normandy, and some of our double agents have been brilliant in this regard. So, I must ask you: if in the event you were taken prisoner and it was prior to, or during the Overlord operation, and they questioned you about it, we'd be very grateful if . . . under pressure . . . you confirmed our deception. Because you see Sam, even once we've landed we want them to believe that the real landing is simply a diversion: that we are mounting a second and major attack on Calais. This way they keep their northern forces in position and don't rush them down to Normandy.'

Sam picked up the drink that had just arrived. 'This pressure you're talking about I assume is torture?'

'Yes, Sam, I'm afraid it is.'

Sam looked past him to where little rivulets of water flowed down the window pane. She actually liked the rain; perhaps it was being brought up with so much sunshine. The rain cleaned things and made the earth smell good. She took a long breath and brought her gaze back to her companion. 'Right, Martin. I understand. If I need to . . . I'll do that.'

Martin sat forward and tapped the table with his fingers. 'Why don't we go to the Astor the night before you fly out?'

She eyed him for a moment. The Astor nightclub in Piccadilly was a famous night spot. 'You want to take me on a date, Martin?'

'I want to make sure you enjoy the night before you go out into the field again, Samantha.'

She paused and took a sip of her drink. 'Sure. Why not?'

That same night the deluge covered all of southern England, and as the door in the Kensington ambulance station opened and wind and rain entered along with Mrs Periwinkle, the Station Officer, Alex looked up from where she sat writing.

'Rotten night, Alexandra.'

'Yes, it is.'

'Is that a letter or a report?'

It was quite obviously a letter that Alex was writing but she replied politely. 'I've completed the report, Mrs Periwinkle. I'm off duty in twenty minutes. This is a letter.'

'Boyfriend?'

Alex took a deep breath. 'I'd like to think so.'

The Station Officer sat down opposite. It was said that she was jealous of Alex's George Cross and as a rule she certainly did not converse with the young woman but it appeared that tonight was different. 'Ah my dear, don't waste your time if it's not going anywhere. I did that in the First War and he lived through it, came back, and married someone else.'

Alex really did not want to hear that: she had other hopes. 'But then you found Mr Periwinkle.'

'Well yes, I did.' For a second or two Alex thought her senior officer was about to launch forth into a confidence. The woman lifted her hands as if she were about to pray and then she returned them to her sides and with a sigh stood up and crossed to the door. 'And a decent man Mr Periwinkle is too,' she announced. 'According to his own lights. Now it's time I had a cuppa.' She opened the door and called back over her shoulder. 'Oh, and Alexandra, don't get too used to these quiet nights without bombs where you can be lolling around and writing letters. I imagine Hitler's got more up his sleeve yet.'

'Yes, Mrs Periwinkle.' And Alex went back to JB.

A week later Sam was at the Astor. She and Martin danced to 'As Time Goes By' and 'In the Mood' and as a couple on the dance floor began to jitterbug, they paused and watched. Later they sat with a drink and listened to 'Coming in on a Wing and a Prayer'.

It was close to midnight when Sam suddenly pointed to a girl dancing by. She was glamorous with large eyes and beautifully defined brows.

'I know her – she's Australian. I'm sure she was in a parachute class I did at Ringway.'

Sam crossed the floor to her. The young woman was with four or five others, all laughing and obviously enjoying themselves. 'Excuse me, weren't you at Ringway with me?'

The girl beamed, jumped up and hugged her. 'For heaven's sake, yes, I remember you!' she declared. 'Weren't you Delilah?'

They were both a touch tipsy and Sam hugged her in return.

'Yes. I often wondered where Samson was.'

They both laughed and the girl with the big eyes asked, 'Are you, you know, going into the field?'

Sam nodded.

'Bloody hell,' the other girl giggled. 'Me too.'

So they hugged each other again and when the band broke into 'We'll Meet Again', Sam quipped, 'Don't forget your poem.'

And the big-eyed girl grinned. 'Implanted on my brain, dear.'

This was a reference to the few lines that all agents took as their own code, so that in communication with London they could be identified.

Sam had chosen four lines she herself had written years before:

> All the places I have been,
> And all the loneliness I have seen
> Were beauty a million multiplied
> If only you were by my side.

Sam did not know it, but the other girl's was a mite less poetic and a lot more bawdy, which suited her sense of humour precisely for she tried not to regard the deadly enemy too seriously and kept a devil-may-care attitude:

> She stood right there, in the moonlight fair,
> And the moon shone through her nightie.
> It lit right on the nipple of her tit,
> Oh Jesus Christ Almighty!

Sam went back to Martin and as she sat he eyed her.

'You know her, I suppose,' Sam remarked.

He nodded. He knew exactly who the other young woman was. Her real name was Nancy Grace Augusta Wake and he was aware that she was off to Maquis country tomorrow night.

They stayed until after 2 a.m. and Nancy Wake and her friends waved to Sam as she departed.

As they walked in the cool night to Audley Street Sam asked, 'Do you often take your operatives to nightclubs?'

His voice had a serious edge. 'Never. Until tonight.'

Martin made no attempt to kiss her good night, for which

Sam was grateful. He was charming and easy to be with, but she was not attracted to him and in any case, for the last hour at the Astor, she had been thinking of Cash, for the band had played 'These Foolish Things (Remind Me Of You)'. She could not help it, but every time she heard the song she saw Cash's face with his hair stirring on his forehead and it always managed to disturb her.

'Good night, Martin. I had a lovely time.'

'Good night, Samantha. I'll see you tomorrow.'

The following day when Sam was about to leave the flat Amelia knocked on the door and Sam let her in. The landlady's right hand was in the pocket of her checked apron. 'I came to say goodbye.'

'Thanks.'

Amelia regarded Sam's FANYs uniform. 'So where are you off to this time?'

'Not sure. Scotland, I think.'

Amelia closed one eye. 'What? Driving old Generals around again?'

Sam laughed. 'No. I think I'll be working in some coastal defence canteens.'

'You sure?'

'Now what does that mean?'

'I don't know Sam. I really don't know. I just get this strange feeling about you.'

Sam laughed again. 'For heaven's sake, Amelia.'

'No, love, I do.' She stepped closer. 'I've known you for years now, Samantha. I've seen you happy and I've seen you sad. And I've seen you alter. There's a determination in you these days. And it's since you joined the FANYs, but it's not just that. You're different from the girl who always had a fella on her arm. Very different.'

Sam shook her head. 'What a lot of rot.'

'No, darlin' it's not – no matter how you protest. George has seen it too. You come and go and I wonder about you.' She was peering at Sam and shaking her head.

'Amelia, I don't know what's got into you.'

'Well, don't mind about me, it's just that I want you to take this.' She brought her hand out of her pocket and opened it to reveal a tiny black cat made of ebony, with a minute gold chain around its neck.

'Oh, it's lovely,' Sam said.

'And it's lucky. It was my gran's. She lived right in here in this very flat and it was here she gave it to me the day before she died. Superstitious old biddy she was, and she passed it on to me, no doubt about it. She said, "Amelia, this'll keep you safe." And you know what, I like to believe it has.' She gave the flash of a smile. 'We didn't get hit by any of those Hun bombs did we?'

Sam shrugged. 'Not yet.'

Amelia took Sam's hand and turned up her open palm and placed the tiny cat in it. 'Now you take it. I'm darned if I know what it is you're really up to, and I'm not asking, but one thing I know for certain: it's not going to any canteens or drivin' any old Generals around. You can't fool me any more with that.'

The landlady stepped quickly forward and took the young woman in her arms and kissed her. Sam felt as if she were going to cry but she took a deep breath and controlled herself.

Amelia's eyes were wet as she stepped back. 'Now you be careful and off you go to wherever it is you're goin' and remember we're waiting for you here. So you darn well make sure you come back to George and me.'

Sam swallowed hard. 'Oh Amelia, thank you, my dear, good friend.'

At the SOE flat in Orchard Court Vera and Martin awaited Samantha. This was where agents usually had their final briefing a day or two before they left on a mission and it was where Sam was to meet the car which would transport her out of London to the airfield.

As she came in the front door a man walked out of one of the rooms. He was slender, six feet tall with ample lips and a cool gaze. Martin turned to him. 'Colonel Buckmaster, this is Camille. She's off to France tonight.'

Everyone in the Special Operations Executive knew who Colonel Maurice Buckmaster was. He was the head of

General De Gaulle's secret service: the French section of SOE.

He smiled, running his cool eyes over her and he did not use her code name. 'How do you do, Samantha?' He held out his hand.

'How do you do, sir?' She tossed her hair back over her shoulder with her right hand and then grasped his extended palm.

'I'm aware you've been in the field before, and brought back something that the Prime Minister himself was most interested in. I've been asked to thank you for it. That was fine brave work you did. Wonderful.' His eyes gleamed with sincerity.

'Thank you, sir.'

He was still holding her hand. 'So you're off tonight?'

'Yes.'

'Come home to us.'

'I'll try to do that.'

He released her hand and Sam saluted and Buckmaster returned it.

Chapter Forty-six

Early June, 1944

There was a crisp summer breeze blowing from the pine forest down the slope to the compound of the POW Camp as the prisoner watching the main gate bent down and tied his shoelace.

This was the signal being waited upon by the twenty-four would-be escapees in the fake work squad back in the recreation hut. As the prisoner stood up, the sign was repeated by a man standing in the compound near Hut 12.

And so the message was passed along to Hut 51, the recreation hut. Junior Christensen, on watch inside at the window, turned and proclaimed, 'Old guard's gone! New Goons in position. Go!'

'Good luck, buddies,' he said as he opened the door and John Baron, Anton and the other twenty-two men, six of them in German guard uniform with replicated rifles over their shoulders, slipped out and lined up outside the hut.

John Baron lifted his rifle to his shoulder. 'March.' And the three columns moved off between the huts. In the usual pattern of a work party, the eighteen prisoners tramped along out of step and the six guards marched.

They headed towards Hut 44 where the track leading to the main gate began.

They made steady progress through the compound past the rows of huts and on by the circuit where a desultory soccer match was in progress. Once past the players they came by three extensive rows of huts and on to Hut 12 where they took a sharp right turn and issued into clear sight of the barbed wire fences and the main gate.

A dozen or so men watched them from windows where the blackout shutters were latched back during the daylight hours.

The normal procedure as a work party approached was for the main gate to begin to swing open and once an accompanying guard had handed over the pass, the body of prisoners continued on through.

John Baron's eyes were fixed on the gate. They were fifty yards away, forty-five, forty, thirty-five . . . *Hell, open the bloody gate! Come on, what's going on? Thirty yards from the gate. Shit! Twenty-five . . . Ah good . . .*

The gate began to groan and swing back. The boys all marked time and Anton crossed to the nearest guard and handed him the folded pass – made with meticulous care by one of prisoner Charlie Hall's forgers. The German glanced down at the paper and handed it back to Anton. Then he did a quick count of the number of prisoners going out and said, '*Sie haben achtzehn männer?*'

Anton nodded. '*Ja, achtzehn.*'

The guard smiled. '*Alles klar. Gehen sie weiter.*'

The gate was now completely open and the so-called prisoners began to move forward but Anton threw up his hand and halted them. Then he neatly folded the paper and put it back in his pocket before he lifted his hand again as a signal for the work party to proceed.

Smart move, Anton. Now we don't look too eager. Eyes straight ahead . . . Walk by in natural fashion . . .

The German guards watched the prisoners pass and the gate shuddered closed behind them.

On they went . . . thirty yards, forty yards, fifty, fifty-five. No shots had been fired, no sirens wailed. Seventy yards . . . a hundred, a hundred and twenty-five. *Slow down, don't pick up the pace! We'll soon be into the woods. Don't hurry. Maintain the lackadaisical step.*

At 200 yards the track veered into the forest of pine trees and in another forty yards they were hidden from the sight of the camp. It was as if the prisoners released a universal sigh as they broke ranks and with speedy farewells – 'Goodbye, good luck' – they all evaporated into the trees, and the track which had held twenty-four men ten seconds before, now stood empty.

John Baron and Anton ran through the woods leaping logs and bracken. They had a map which showed the POW camp and surrounding area for twelve miles of the Rhineland towards Merzig.

Their vision was to secure over six hours' start if all went well. The genuine squad usually returned between 1600 and 1700, so the alarm should not be raised until evening *Appel* at 1730.

From the prison camp to the civil airfield was approximately ten miles. Once through the wood they had to take the road. It ran for about five miles, passing through two small villages. It appeared from the map that at that point they could again cut across country for three miles, passing through another pine forest, and come out along the Saar River which would bring them very close to the airfield.

They gained the road and began marching along. This part of the country was fairly sparsely populated and they still carried their phony rifles intending to pass for two German soldiers off duty and out for a walk.

In the first village there was no one in the open and once through it they began to ascend a long hill. On the crest they looked down a valley and saw a lorry coming towards them so they left the road and walked into the field a short way. The lorry passed and they took the road again.

As they approached the second village they were overtaken by two men on bicycles who greeted them and Anton replied.

There was only one street through the cottages, a cluster of fifteen or twenty dwellings with a small hotel in the centre. They saw the men on bicycles dismount and go into the hotel and as they passed it one elderly man sitting outside with a beer smiled and spoke. '*Guten Tag. Schönnes Wetter Heute.*'

Anton replied, '*Ja, ist es.*' And they kept on walking.

They drew glances as they marched by the front of a bakery where a man and woman sat, though no one spoke.

As they came to the last stone cottage a small child of

around six ran after them and walked beside Anton, stepping out and talking. Anton patted him on the head and they kept up the pace but the child continued along with them.

'*Wo gehen Sie hin?*' he asked.

Anton told him they were out for a walk. The little boy asked if he could come. Anton and John Baron did not halt and the Czech replied in the negative, telling the boy to return to his mother. But the child asked them where they were from and Anton replied that they could not continue to talk as they were on a special military hike.

The boy was keeping up with them and ran round to John Baron's side and asked to see his rifle but not knowing what he had said, John Baron ignored him. Anton again repeated for the child to return to his mother.

They were wondering what to do if the boy persisted in accompanying them when a female voice called loudly from the village street and the child reluctantly halted and turned back. With an ever-quickening pace they continued until once out of sight of the village they entered the woods.

'Little nuisance.'

'Yes. Nosy little bugger. Asked to see your rifle.'

'He's a candidate for the Hitler Youth Movement.'

They made slow going through the pine forest this time, for Anton began to complain about his foot. 'This bloody right boot's scraping the back of my heel.' He sat down on a log and removed his boot. A huge blister sat on his skin. He began to wrap it in a piece of cloth he took from his pocket as John Baron eased himself down beside him and, taking out some cheese he had saved from the last Red Cross parcel, handed a piece to his companion. The prisoners hoarded food items for 'escape rations' and the Escape Committee doled them out to those leaving, but John Baron and Anton had not taken very much because they expected to be on their way quickly.

Once through the pines they came to a grassy plain and eventually to the Saar River: it was 1930 hours and back at camp, *Appel* would be starting.

They continued on open land for a time until they came

to a large building not shown on the map and with the appearance of a factory. A wire fence enclosed it, stretching from the river up the incline in the distance.

'We'll have to skirt it.'

They kept to the trees which dotted the slope and detoured about a mile until finally they could see the airfield. It was about 800 yards away across a road.

John Baron took out another piece of cheese. 'The airfield's civil and we're inside German Rhineland so it's unlikely to be guarded. Soldiers with guns might draw attention.'

'We can leave them at the side of the airfield when we get there, in the grass or something.'

They descended the slope. Crossing the road was the only hazard but they waited in the bracken until all seemed clear and then ran.

They took cover in a clump of ash trees and noticed a gate in the perimeter fence about forty yards away. No one was moving about inside the airfield but because Anton spoke German he ventured closer and inspected the gate. He came back to John Baron, grinning. 'No lock of any kind on it.'

'That's good, we can simply walk onto the field.'

'Yes.'

By now it was after 2000 and there were no aircraft in sight but the early summer evening stretched ahead of them so they remained confident. But half an hour later two men closed and locked the doors of the four hangars.

'Blast, that's it for today. We'll just have to wait for morning.'

Anton turned a bleak gaze to his friend. 'So much for being in England tonight.'

They thought it would be safer to spend the hours of darkness back up the slope in the long grass so they clambered up the hill between the trees. They slept the night there, eating the last of the cheese and a small tin of ham and saving the six bars of chocolate they had brought between them for the following day.

They passed an uncomfortable night on the ground

fighting the swarms of insects that found them agreeable prey, and they were awake with the light.

Then it began to drizzle.

They ate two chocolate bars each and walked down towards the airfield. As they did so, three lorries of soldiers passed by on the road and they ran back into the trees. Of course they were well aware that by now all train stations, bus terminals, post offices and police stations would have been alerted of the twenty-four-man escape from the POW camp.

They were thoroughly soaked when at 0800 the door to one of the hangars was opened and two men went in. Shortly afterwards an aircraft taxied out and rolled around behind the buildings out of sight.

'Probably fuelling up,' John Baron remarked.

It was proven so, for the machine revealed itself about half an hour later and took off.

Nothing happened all morning until finally the rain ceased and the small road became increasingly busy so they found themselves hiding in the trees most of the time.

They were both drenched, and when the sun inched out from behind the cloud they took off their tunics and laid them out to dry on a rock in the sun amongst the verdant bushes.

From time to time a man in a uniform came out from one of the buildings and crossed to a hangar and disappeared.

Two freighters landed at 1400 and 1430 but on both occasions only one crew member climbed out and went into the huts while the other remained in the aircraft. Around 1500 a single-seater biplane was pushed out of a hangar with a pilot already aboard and it took off to the east.

By 1600 they had eaten the remainder of their chocolate and were becoming anxious. More lorries full of soldiers rumbled by on the road and each time they hid in the bracken. Another hour passed and John Baron turned to his companion. 'We'll have to risk walking into the open hangar and taking one of the aircraft.'

'But what about fuel?'

'That's a chance we'll have to take. The biplane that left earlier didn't fuel up before take-off.'

'True. You're right, we've hung around here all day – come on, let's do it.'

Their tunics were semi-dry and they put them on and left their rifles behind a rock, walked smartly up to the fence and through onto the airfield. They made straight for the hangar that had held the biplane. The door was open and they entered.

Ahead stood an old Junkers F13 passenger aircraft.

'That wouldn't get us home even fully fuelled.'

Anton slapped his friend's shoulder. 'Hey, look at that.'

It was a Dornier.

John Baron smiled. 'It's a twin-engine reconnaissance aircraft. Perfect. Come on.'

They hurried over to inspect it and as John Baron put his hands up to climb on the wing a voice growled, '*Was machen Sie?*'

They swung round to see a *Feldwebel*, a non-commissioned officer, glowering at them. Anton saluted and John Baron followed suit as the Czech replied that they were inspecting the aircraft.

'*Warum?*'

Anton gestured to the fuselage and said they had been told to clean it.

A sceptical expression crossed the *Feldwebel*'s thin face. He walked right up to them. Each had grown a day's beard and looked as if they had slept in their uniforms. They could see he thought they were deserters. The soldier gestured with his thumb to the hangar door. '*Raus! Sie dürfen nicht hierein.*'

Anton grabbed John Baron's arm and pulled him away. They hurried out and round the side of the hangar where another *Feldwebel* and a Private approached.

They both saluted the NCO and swiftly slipped past a petrol truck to a narrow alley between the huts where they could see out to the airfield.

John Baron could feel his bid for freedom fading. 'Where did these bloody soldiers come from all of a sudden?'

'That NCO back there thought we were deserters.'

As they stood there in indecision a monoplane came rolling towards them, quickly followed by another. They taxied up in front of the hangars.

John Baron found his enthusiasm returning. 'Junkers 33s.'

'Yes.'

These were sturdy monoplanes with a single Junkers L5 engine and fixed landing gear. The Luftwaffe used them for instrument and navigational training. Anton slapped his hands together. 'They've got a range of around 500 miles. Oh Lord, Lympne here we come!'

'Yes, if they're fuelled up.'

'Even half full they should make it.'

'That's if the bloody crews leave them unattended.'

They hid behind some oil drums and watched. To their delight the two crews, each of three men, alighted, left both aircraft standing, and strode over and entered a hut at the edge of the airfield.

'Come on.'

The escapees walked straight over to the first aircraft and climbed inside.

Anton flicked the switches for the ignition and the fuel tank. 'Oh blast, we'll have to wind it up. There's no electrical starting. You'll have to get out and do it.'

'Me?' John Baron replied in amazement. 'I don't speak German, you clot. Out you go.'

'Shit,' Anton proclaimed as he scrambled back out through the roof and jumped down to the ground. He grabbed the propeller with both hands, forcing it round, and at that moment the door of the hut at the airfield's edge opened and one of the crew came out. For a second or two he stood there watching Anton then suddenly he waved his arms and shouted. Anton gave a furious heave to the propeller and as the engine coughed into life the German shouted again and sprinted towards the aircraft waving his arms excitedly.

Anton waved back to him and vaulted up onto the wing as two others ran out behind the first man dashing towards them.

As the Junkers began to turn and roll away, the closest German yelled something to the other two and one whirled round and raced back to the hut. Anton was now climbing through the roof into the cockpit and John Baron was heading the aircraft back down to the runway.

Now five men appeared from the huts all shouting and screaming. Two lifted pistols and began shooting at the monoplane as it gathered speed and the first of the Germans, who was now running beside the Junkers, hurtled up onto the wing.

'Bloody hell!'

The German stood up and cast himself at the roof of the cockpit, grabbing the side of the window and hanging on.

John Baron was accelerating and Anton rose to meet the invader. He balanced half out of the cockpit roof and began fighting the German to force him from the fuselage.

The two were struggling, the aircraft was gaining speed and suddenly a bullet spat through the Perspex of the cockpit and both men lurched back in shock. The outsider lost his grip and tumbled from the wing as John Baron reached high speed and the monoplane began to lift with a hail of pistol bullets ricocheting off the undercarriage.

'Oh sweet Jesus!' Anton shouted, easing himself down to a sitting position. 'We did it!'

John Baron began to whistle 'Waltzing Matilda' and the Czech, who had never heard the tune, soon picked it up, and as they lifted up across Luxembourg and wended their way in and out of bunched rain cloud, they continued to whistle.

Suddenly Anton stopped. 'They might send up a Messerschmitt after us.'

'Let's hope not.'

John Baron had been eying the instruments and now he pointed to the fuel guage. 'There isn't enough juice to reach England. I don't think there's even enough to cross Belgium and land near the coast.'

Anton attempted humour. 'Look, if we climb high enough we should be able to glide there.'

'Mmm.'

They were at 12,000 feet when they saw four small dots at one o'clock high and watched them keenly as they became aircraft. But they did not deviate from their path and passed by overhead.

About three-quarters of an hour later the fuel gauge was pointing to zero and a few minutes on, as dusk descended, the Junkers hicupped and the engine died.

'Oh boy, here we go.'

'I think we're actually somewhere on the border of Belgium and France.'

'I was around here during Dunkirk,' John Baron announced as they watched the darkening earth rising up towards them.

'Gawd, that's a town over there, JB. Stay away from that!'

They shot over a river and a village and still the Junkers 33 stayed airborne. Anton's tone was sober. 'So down to earth. I just hope we don't get captured again straight away.'

Careering on they saw below a long straight road with vehicles upon it, another stream, some farm buildings, then a forest where they continued to hold just above the tree-tops, coming into earth fast. John Baron could see open land ahead and held the aircraft as steadily as he could but there was a crunch as the undercarriage clipped the top of a tree and they wobbled from side to side and descended to earth.

John Baron was still pulling her nose up as they braced and hit the ground with a thud. The Junkers bounced in the air to dance another fifty yards, hit a tree, swerved sharply left and clunked into a solid trunk.

JB shook his head and blinked.

Anton suddenly began to laugh. 'Oh, lovely landing, JB!'

It was darkening quickly now and they did not like the smell of fuel in the cockpit so they vaulted out onto the port wing and down to the ground. The other wing had broken completely from the fuselage and lay forty yards away.

Anton winced as he stood up on the ground. 'Ouch, my heel didn't like that.'

'We'd better get away in case it goes up in flames.'

They ran from the wrecked aircraft and into a lane, Anton limping. At the end of the thoroughfare they crossed a small wooden bridge but still the Junkers did not catch fire, and remarkably, it never did.

'Right – the first thing we must do is discard these German tunics. We'll look better in shirtsleeves.' They took them off and threw them into a clump of bushes and bracken.

Noticing a sign in the fading evening light, they read: *Béthune 12 kilometres* and John Baron declared ruefully, 'So, La Belle France instead of Mother England!'

'They say there are two collaborators in every ten French, and seven who're openly on our side.'

'What's the other one doing?'

'Heaven knows. Anyway, with a bit of luck we'll run into one of the seven.'

It was very quiet as they continued along the lane in the pleasant evening temperature. The sky blackened and the evening star made an appearance and the aroma of honeysuckle floated on the air while crickets clamoured behind the hedgerows.

John Baron was feeling unreal. From sixteen months of the bleak restrictions of the POW camps to the night of sleeping in the long grass, to the airfield and the stimulation of stealing the Junkers, to this gentle innocence of a quiet country lane. He was heady with the eccentricity of it all.

At his side Anton halted for a moment. 'My foot's burning. I think I'll take off my boot.'

He sat down in the lane and John Baron patted his shoulder. 'We're going to have to take a chance and knock on a door.'

They walked on, Anton now carrying one boot – until they came to a road. A cottage lay on the far side and fifty yards on, what looked in the darkness like a country pub.

'Let's try the cottage.'

'The pub might be better. We could go round the back of it.'

John Baron felt dubious. 'I just feel better about the cottage.'

'All right,' his companion agreed. 'Anyway, this is where you take over. I've played the German-speaking part, now you take the stage.'

They crossed the road and stood outside the stone cottage. There was no garden and the front wall of the dwelling met the footpath. In the night light they could see flower boxes at the windows and a knocker in the centre of the door.

They rapped on the wood.

Nothing happened though they could hear children inside.

They knocked again and after a short time the door inched open and a man inquired who they were and what they wanted.

John Baron replied that they were escaped British prisoners of war and needed help.

The man looked out at them. A light shone in the interior and vaguely lit the faces of the two men in the street. He paused before pointing to the right. '*Allez vite de l'autre côté de la maison et attendez moi.*'

Anton turned to John Baron. 'What did he say?'

'He said to come round to the side of the cottage. I told him we were escaped British POWs and that we needed help.'

They did as asked and found the man standing near a shed at the back.

He spoke again and John Baron translated for Anton. 'He says this area has become dangerous, but that there might be someone who will help. He says to call him Gaston and we're to follow him.'

The Frenchman headed off through a gate in his back fence and led them for about a quarter of a mile along a forest track until they saw a row of cottages in the mild illumination of the night.

At the first of the dwellings the Frenchman knocked on a side door and called softly, '*Je vous apporte un paquet.*'

The door creaked open and a bearded man looked out.

Their guide explained their presence and the bearded man shook his head, saying he would like to help but that friends he knew in the town had been taken in for questioning yesterday and he dared not. He then pointed in the darkness and suggested a person who still had 'connections'.

Gaston asked who it was and the man spoke to him in a low tone that neither John Baron nor Anton could hear.

Gaston then signalled for them to follow him again. 'It's about a mile away, all cross country.'

John Baron translated for Anton as their guide set off at a swift pace and Anton protested, 'Not so fast. I've only got one shoe on and I keep standing on grit and stones.'

They arrived at a stream and Anton bathed his heel for a few seconds as they crossed on stepping stones. On the far side they took a path through a stand of beeches and up an incline to a road. Once across it they entered another copse of trees where they could see so little they had to hold the shoulder of the man in front, and a hundred yards on they climbed a fence, covered fifty yards of open ground and passed by a shed where they halted. There was not much light from the mostly overcast sky but there was enough to see a lonely cottage on a gentle slope.

The Frenchman rapped on the back door. A curtain was moved aside on a window next to the door, before it was pushed open by a woman who leant out, one arm on the windowsill. She appeared only as a dark shape before them backlit by a pale light.

Gaston said he had been sent to her by William; she asked who his companions were and he replied escaped prisoners of war.

She shook her head. '*Non.*' And said that now it was too dangerous to be helping anyone to escape.

At this point John Baron spoke. He told her they would be grateful for anything, even a bed for the night, and that they would leave first thing in the morning.

She asked where they had escaped from and he told her. Then she asked their rank and serial numbers and he told her. She eyed them from her position in the window and shook her head again, declaring that it would be foolish of her to help. That the Gestapo were everywhere and had rounded up people in the district.

John Baron then asked if there were anyone else she could advise them to approach in this vicinity.

At this point, Gaston decided he did not want to take the risk of guiding them anywhere else and he abruptly departed. The woman watched him hurry away but remained leaning on the sill. She spoke again, telling John Baron that she had taken too many chances in the last four years and was not going to take any more. One of her dearest friends in Bapaume had just been arrested by the Gestapo. However, she would pass them out some food and give them clean clothes. Then she added that JB's accent was so good he could pass for a Frenchman.

She closed the window and disappeared while they waited in the dark and John Baron explained what was happening.

After about four or five minutes the window opened again. She passed out two shirts, two pairs of trousers and jackets and a cloth cap, and told them if they did not fit there was little she could do about it as they were all she had. She then said she would find food for them to take.

Anton held up a pair of trousers in the weak light and declared, 'Heck, John Baron, we could both fit into these, old boy.'

The woman was in the act of turning away. She flinched, halted, and looked back. Neither man noticed her action for they were concentrating on the clothes. She frowned as she studied the two escaped prisoners.

Now she spoke in English. 'What are your names?'

John Baron turned to her in surprise. 'You speak English?'

'Yes, I always have. I was educated for some years in England.'

Anton smiled. 'I'm Anton Plzac from Czechoslovakia.'

'And I'm John Baron Chard from Australia.' He smiled.

She did not speak for some seconds and when she did it was very slowly. 'Come forward, please.' She pulled back the curtain and opened an interior door so that a beam of pale light fell upon her visitors.

She leant there in the window eyeing them for a time before moving silently away. They heard her push back a bolt on the door and it swung open. 'Come in.' Her voice shook slightly. 'I have altered my mind. I shall do what I can to help you.'

The two men entered carrying the clothes she had just given them. Bolting the door behind them she led them through to a small kitchen lit by one light and gestured for them to sit upon two ladder-backed chairs.

They did and looked around. It was neat and scrubbed. Red and white checked cushions on the tiny window seat matched the curtains. It was snug and a delicate feeling of cheer prevailed which the two men felt forcefully after the long months away from anything graceful, cosy or womanly.

She moved past them to the pantry and as she did so, John Baron noticed her right hand. It was made of wood!

'I shall bring you some food,' she said as she disappeared, 'and then you must wash. I'll heat water for you.'

When she was out of sight Anton shook his head. 'What brought on the change of heart?'

'Don't know, old man, must have been our charm.' Then John Baron whispered, 'Did you see her hand?'

Anton shook his head.

'Her right hand's missing. It's made of wood.'

In the small stone pantry Antoinette Desaix sank against the wall. She felt faint. Her head was dizzy, her heart beat quickly. *John Baron Chard.* The man in her kitchen was called *John Baron Chard.* And his face was the same!

Using her mouth she removed the ring she wore on her left hand and dropped it into her pocket.

Sam was thinking of John Baron. She rested against a substantial rock under cover of a wooden shelter. It was raining. She did not have many quiet moments, but when she did she thought of JB or Cash and wondered how they were. Being a prisoner of war must alter you. How could it not? All the things you loved and held dear somewhere in the remote distance, never knowing if you would see them again.

She stood up and gazed down the hill through the scattered trees. This hill was unusual in that there were rock formations along one side which afforded a certain amount of cover. Two small buildings where her Resistance group lived, were secreted up here, elevated and well back from the road, and unless you knew where they were, sheltered by the shape of the hill, the rocks and the trees, you would drive by on the road below without ever suspecting.

She had been in France for over a month following SOE's orders and organising her group of Resistance fighters. Every day more joined and in less than forty-eight hours, the landing on the Normandy beaches would begin – the start of the liberation of Europe!

It had not been easy for her, arriving out of the night sky with just Guy, but she had proved herself and stood up to this motley collection of freedom fighters, and by the time Laurent had joined her the men already trusted her, and with his final stamp of approval, they had completely accepted her.

She and Laurent, along with Jacques, had planned a series of attacks to coincide with the Allied forces landing and heading in towards them. Jacques was their able 'lieutenant', an ex-musician who continually hummed as he went about the camp. He was thirty-five and all muscle, and he spent hours every day doing callisthenics in a clearing between their huts.

Fifty more men had bolstered their little army in the past week. Bren light machine guns, Sten guns, explosives and ammunition had been dropped by London within three days of Sam's arrival, and with the distribution of that the group felt more secure. Before, their arsenal had consisted of a meagre three pistols and knives between two dozen men. Now even with the expanding numbers they had enough for all, though Sam did not hand out Bren or Sten guns randomly. Each man had to be recommended by Jacques and prove his credentials in the Underground before he was approved to carry one of those.

Tonight they were to blow up a small arms distribution warehouse outside St Lô on the banks of the River Vire. Guy and four of their men were presently away stealing bicycles. With the growing numbers they needed the transport.

Hearing a movement behind her, Samantha spun round to see Clément, one of the group. He carried a tin cup and stood looking at her for a few seconds before he moved in and handed it to her. 'I've brought you some coffee.'

Coffee was a treat and hard to get.

'Thank you.' As she took it from him he covered her hand with his own. He was in his early thirties, a solid man with long eyelashes framing attractive sleepy eyes.

She retracted her hand. 'Don't do that, Clément.' He had done this sort of thing before. Found her when she was alone and touched her arm or her hand. Once he had stroked her hair and as she had moved out of his reach, he laughed.

She stepped away now and sipped the coffee. He came close to her again and she moved around him.

'Are the men set for tonight?'

He nodded.

'We'll leave as soon as it's dusk. I hope Guy's back. We need him to radio London first.'

Clément smiled. 'He will be. Stealing a few bicycles shouldn't take long. I can do it in ten minutes.'

She met his gaze. 'Then you should have gone along.'

'I'd rather be here with you.'

Sam placed the coffee down beside her Sten gun, on the smooth surface of a rock. 'I've told you before. I'm here to do a job for British and French Intelligence and that's what I intend to do.'

'What's wrong with me?' he asked, an injured expression on his face.

'Clément, there's nothing wrong with you. My priority's fighting the Nazis. I'm interested in *nothing else*.'

He gave her an odd look and she turned from him. 'Tell me as soon as Guy and the others are back.'

She felt his hand on her shoulder and she did not move. He spoke in her ear. 'Camille, you're a beautiful woman.

I'll be good for you. You need a man – I can see it in your eyes.' The next second his warm palm slid down the inside of her blouse onto the bare skin of her breast. His fingers found her nipple and in the same moment he turned her body against his and brought his mouth down over hers.

In one movement she leapt away and put out her hands but he kept coming. He was determined now.

'Clément, don't do this!'

But his eyes were hungry and he caught her arm. 'Come on, Camille. A little loving will be good for us both.' He began to drag her back towards him.

He was leaving her no option but to fight him the way she had been taught.

She laughed and feigned weakness and he grinned. 'That's better, little Aussie girl.'

She allowed him to pull her closer and as he did so she spun sideways in one movement and brought her elbow with all her force into his ribcage; then, steadying herself on her left foot and throwing all her weight into her next action, she struck him in the testicles with her right knee as she thumped the heel of her hand into his chin. She deliberately avoided his nose for she knew how to kill a man that way.

His head shot back and he cried out and went down like a pricked balloon. His body skidded into the bracken and he lay there looking up at her.

She retrieved her Sten gun as he rolled over and began to rise.

'I'll repeat it. I'm here to fight the Nazis. I don't want to fight you. I picked up a saying years ago when I lived in New York. It fits this occasion. *Wise up, Clément. Wise up.*'

She stepped round him and walked back to the huts.

Four hours later they were lying in the trees outside the small arms warehouse on the riverbank.

One of the local Resistance members worked at the distribution house; and he was on night duty and had ensured a side gate was open in the barbed-wire fence. Guards

733

patrolled all night but at 2300 most went into the canteen for a half-hour break and left depleted ranks of only four men patrolling, instead of twelve.

Laurent turned on his stomach and signalled for them to move out. He, Sam, Jacques, Clément and two others, Giles and Henri, crawled through the brush and at exactly 2301 cautiously entered the well lit gate. Behind them waited twenty others in the woods. The explosives had been smuggled in twenty-four hours earlier and they found them as planned in a drum sitting beside the entrance to a metal walkway which took them straight to the side of the building. Doubled over they ran down the walkway which was lit by bulbs every ten yards.

In a shadowed area Jacques and Clément crawled under the warehouse floor. Sam and Laurent handed them the charges from the drum, while Laurent kept glancing continually towards Henri, a nineteen year old who stood on watch twenty-five yards back near the entrance to the walkway. Giles waited further afield on vigil near the gate.

They had rehearsed this over and over and had the timing down to twenty-six minutes. During the half hour that the majority of the guards were in the canteen only one patrol passed this point.

Fine rain had begun to fall and Sam tasted it on her lips as she handed Clément an explosive.

He looked up at her. 'Aussie girl?'

'Yes?'

He sighed. 'I wish to apologise for this afternoon.'

Sam smiled at him 'I accept it.'

He grinned and his teeth gleamed. 'Good. I'm very sorry I did it, and I'm glad we are friends again.'

Clément had no sooner said this than the whole area snapped into brilliant light and sirens began to wail.

'Jesus Christ!'

'We've been had!'

They heard gunfire outside the fence as Henri shouted, 'Oh my God!' And the next second they saw him fall in a hail of bullets.

Sam spun round as Clément and Jacques threw themselves

out from under the building and stood up beside her. Laurent shouted, 'I think we'll have to fight our way out!'

Sam pointed down to where bags of concrete were stacked under an awning against the tall wire fence and yelled above the tumult, 'If we get behind them we might have a chance to shoot a hole in the wire.'

They charged towards the concrete bags as bullets spat in the air around them and a dozen German soldiers appeared where Henri had fallen.

Sam and the three men blazed away at the oncoming Germans and made a dash across the yard, but before they reached the cover of the concrete, they were hit by machine-gun fire. Laurent stumbled from a bullet in the shoulder and Jacques, hit in the knee, collapsed to the ground. Clément fell dead. Sam was not hit at all but her Sten gun was knocked out of her hand as bullets slammed into it; she kept running and threw herself down behind the awning. She rolled over and was in the act of rising and pulling her pistol from her trouser belt when she saw the black boots appear in front of her eyes.

The rain spattered upon the shining leather.

Sam knelt with the raindrops hitting her cheeks and as she lifted her gaze across the uniform she met the cold eyes of an SS officer who stood holding a Lüger at her head.

Chapter Forty-seven

Code-named Overlord, the landings in France to begin the liberation of Europe were twenty-four hours late. The invasion had been set for the early hours of Monday, 5 June but the weather was so bad and the seas in the English Channel so rough that the liberation of Europe began on Tuesday, 6 June.

Overlord was the greatest amphibious operation in the history of the world.

At 2200 hours on 5 June, 130,000 British, American and Canadian troops in five assault groups departed ports in southern England in convoys of 6,939 vessels which sailed via mine-swept corridors across the English Channel to the Normandy beaches for a dawn landing at 0630.

Airborne Assault Groups went into the fields of Normandy via parachute and glider. The 6th British Airborne Division and 86th and 101st American Airborne Divisions of Commandos, paratroopers and SAS were landed. In all 23,490 men were dropped from 2,395 aircraft and landed from 867 gliders.

In the minutes after midnight on 5 June – in an operation recognised as the finest piece of navigation in the history of flying – four Horsa gliders, their pilots using only a compass and a stopwatch, landed within yards of the two bridges over the Orne River and its canal, and within eleven minutes the 6th British Airborne had taken both bridges from German hands.

D-Day had begun!

Sam woke. She was lying on straw and for a second

wondered where she was. But the pain in her face and her body and the gnawing agony that shot up from her fingers through her right arm jogged her memory.

She was in a Nazi gaol which had been constructed only the previous year in the wood east of the village of Cormolaine. The irony was that, had her captors only known it, the hide-out Sam and her arm of the Resistance used was only about six miles away.

She thought she had been here five or six days and she recounted them in her head.

The first morning she had been given some cold broth and then taken out of her cell to an 'interview' room, a concrete square with one desk and one chair and a single window high in the wall. The man who had interrogated her had been in the German service uniform of a Captain and he presented himself as desirous to help her. She had maintained silence.

Sam knew that usually the Gestapo were out to get information as quickly as possible, knowing that once a few days went by the prisoner's contacts had time to disperse and alert others in the Underground.

So she was surprised when the second and third days went by with virtually affable questioning conducted by another man in plain clothes, though obviously Gestapo. He had begun in the same soothing manner, telling her the people she worked for in London did not care about her and that they would willingly let her suffer and die: that she had been used by them and that she owed them no allegiance. He had promised her he would help her if she told him where the hide-out was. 'For we know all about you, you see . . . Camille.'

Sam had told him, 'Go to hell!'

The fourth day it had been a different man again. This time he was young and clean-cut, possibly three or four years younger than herself and was dressed in normal street clothes; he was also unmistakably Gestapo. He spoke good English in a self-assured manner and he began in the same way, telling her she would be taken care of if she told him where the hide-out was. He informed her that the two men caught with her had disclosed a great deal already and that she should be like them. That if she would name people in the movement and help her captors, she would be taken immediately to an hotel and given warm food, a hot bath and new clothes.

Sam had looked derision upon him, knowing full well that Laurent and Jacques would never talk. 'Of course you Nazis are always understanding, fair and kind.'

He had actually smiled and replied, 'Yes.' And offered her a cigarette. She allowed him to place it in her mouth and then she spat it at him and hit him in the face!

He recoiled in shock.

'Pig!' she had said and turned away.

He screamed out and two guards came running in and dragged her away to her cell. About half an hour later two women arrived and beat her with sticks until she passed out.

The fifth day became very serious.

It was the same individual, only this time he did not present himself solicitously; he told her that if she did not talk today he would 'have to help her to remember'.

'You are not as pretty as you were yesterday,' he said, pointing to her bruised face.

'Neither are you,' she replied.

He clicked his fingers and two well-dressed men entered. One in a blue suit opened a leather bag and took out what were obviously instruments of torture. The Gestapo interrogator then asked her again to name her comrades and to tell him where her hide-out was.

She peered at him. 'In a very short time it will be you sitting here having to answer the questions.'

He hit her bruised face with the back of his hand. Then he shocked her. 'We know who you really are, Samantha.'

Her eyes must have shown amazement.

'Ah yes, we have our own network, you know.' Then he smiled again. She found it grotesque. 'And your two companions have been most helpful.'

Now Sam knew he was lying again for neither Laurent nor Jacques were aware of her true identity and she knew in her soul that neither of them would ever reveal it even if they had known.

'Go to hell,' she said.

They strapped her to a chair and lifted her right hand and placed it in a vice so she could not jerk away.

'You have lovely nails. It will be a shame to lose them.'

Sam tried to look steadily at him, though she was unsure if she succeeded.

He now spoke in an off-hand manner. 'There has been a small attempt to invade us.'

Ah! Thank God Overlord had begun!

'A small attempt' you say to try and fool me. You'll soon find out how small the British and American armies are, you bastard! Whatever happens to me, you pigs will eventually be stopped.

'Do you know anything about this landing?'

'You and your kind disgust me,' she replied, looking away.

The man in the blue suit applied pincers to her thumbnail. They dug into her flesh and she bit her lip so as not to cry out as he ripped the nail off.

As they gouged into her forefinger she steeled herself to concentrate on the happy days of her past with Cash and JB, charging on Aristotle's back down the slope to the brook path, racing the boys with the Queensland summer wind in her hair, but the hellish pain overtook her mind and she slumped forward.

They tore out each of the fingernails on her right hand, one after the other. She was uncertain whether she screamed or not when they ripped out the last nail. She knew her body slipped sideways in the chair and she drifted in and out of consciousness while the Gestapo continued to ask her about the landings and where the Resistance hide-out was.

Over the years the Nazis' methods of torture had become known and the people in the Resistance had told Sam about the electric shock treatment and icewater baths, where prisoners were virtually drowned and revived only to have the action repeated over and over again. She knew that people were beaten until their organs were pulped, that prisoners were hoisted on pulleys up and down until their shoulders dislocated, then they were suspended upside down and their ankles broken. All this coursed in her head along with the brain-numbing torment as his voice, always in a monotone, asked the same questions over and over.

At one point he reiterated that her two friends had talked, and through the haze of agony she heard herself say, 'Then, smartarse, what are you doing here with me?'

He reacted violently, kicking over her chair, and her face slammed into the floor. She thought her nose had broken for blood spurted out all over the place.

She blacked out but they threw cold water over her to revive her.

And again came the refrain. 'What do you know about the beach landings?'

She thought she would vomit; she felt violently ill and the agony in her arm and face was making her confused, but into her violated mind came the words Martin had said to her back in England: *You see, Sam, even once we've landed we want them to believe that the real landing is simply a diversion. That we are mounting a second major attack on Calais. This way they won't rush their northern forces down to Normandy.* And she knew this was the time; they would believe her now, for they would think she had taken all she could stand.

She made herself say, 'Please just don't hurt me any more. All I've ever known is that the landings are to be around Calais.' She looked up at her torturer's face and saw the satisfied expression upon it as it wavered before her eyes.

Inwardly she smiled and then she fainted.

And now she was awake and lying on the straw. With her left hand she fingered the strap in her brassière where the L pill was secreted. Sam had always wondered how brave she would be and she knew she could not stand much more. She thought to take the pill immediately for she believed that soon they must move her. The Allies were heading in towards them. She would be sent on to either

Fresnes or just straight to Germany. There was no route for a secret agent except to end up in a death camp. And in between now and then there would probably be more torment.

She imagined her darlings on the wide verandah at Haverhill with the sun going down behind the gums and the whisper of a breeze rustling the jasmine vine. She saw her father and mother arm in arm, laughing at something Uncle Wake had said and Ledgie regarding them from the kitchen door. She smelt the glorious aroma of bread baking in the oven and pictured little Storm run by Ledgie to the verandah steps where Veena waited to envelop her in her arms. She heard Crenna shout that dinner was ready and she saw Cash and JB race each other up the side steps to be first at the table. Then she tasted her tears as they slipped from her eyes and ran across her cheek to the straw.

She sat up and pain shot through her. Her face ached and her body ached but when she touched her nose she realised it was not broken. She manifested a wan smile.

Even though you're contemplating death, Sammy, you're vain enough to be pleased your nose isn't broken!

While she had been unconscious someone had bandaged her right hand and a tin of water lay nearby. She sipped a little, continuing to mull over whether to take the pill or not.

Abruptly the door to her cell opened.

One of the women who had beaten her came in with a bowl and a wooden spoon and put them down beside her. The food looked inedible, some type of grey porridge, but Sam decided to try a little. She managed to eat half: it did not actually taste as vile as it looked – or perhaps it was just that she was starving.

She had no sooner put down the spoon and sagged back against the concrete wall than the same woman came back; perhaps she had been watching through a spy-hole.

'Get up. You're being transferred.' She reached down to help the prisoner to her feet but Sam gathered all her strength and shouted, 'Don't touch me!' The woman stepped away and Sam forced herself to rise and stand upright. She sank against the wall momentarily before walking unsteadily out of the cell.

The woman led her along the same corridor as always but this time they bypassed the 'interview' room and continued on to turn a corner where two interior windows sat in the wall. Sam peered in the glass as she passed and saw that while she was still recognisable, one side of her face was badly swollen and her eyes were black.

Twice she stumbled but straightened up and walked on, and at the end of the second corridor they exited into a sterile concrete yard with grey walls about twelve feet high. It was dusk and the shadows in the yard fell on two guards who marched up to Samantha and escorted her to an iron gate in the wall which the woman unlocked. Sam found it hard to walk without stabbing pain but she willed herself to hold her head high.

Outside the gate two more guards stood by a small black lorry. The sides were closed in with black canvas. A swastika was painted above the tailboard. How she despised that symbol.

They pushed her towards the vehicle and she shrugged off their touch. 'Don't!' she said as forcefully as she could.

'Get in!'

She eyed the guards. 'Leave me alone.' And she bit her lip to keep herself from crying out as she lifted her bruised body up and scrambled into the vehicle. Inside on a torn blanket lay Laurent and Jacques. Jacques was unconscious but Laurent tried to smile. His leg was bandaged and his arm was in a sling. He turned bloodshot eyes to her. There were bruises all over him and he slurred his speech when he spoke. 'Camille, it's good to see you.'

Sam eased herself down onto the blanket beside him. 'Oh, it's so good to see you too.'

'No talking!' one of the guards shouted as he climbed in and sat on a wooden form built into the side of the lorry. Another followed and a third stood on the backboard, rifle in hand as the truck pulled away.

Sam closed her eyes, trying not to concentrate on the searing pain that filled her mind. She thought about being a child again when the world had been a joyous place and life had held no horrors or ugliness.

Jacques remained unconscious. He had a great gash on the side of his neck and his breathing was laboured. Laurent lay beside him regarding her and she touched him gently just to comfort him. His eyes smiled. She was still thinking about the L pill and finally she decided that she would take it before they tortured her again.

They had travelled perhaps a mile and a half when suddenly she saw a black Citroën racing by recklessly on the narrow road and a few seconds later there was a screech of tyres, a machine-gun volley and the lorry lurched sideways, slamming into a tree. Sam tumbled into the nearest German guard and they both fell to the floor as Laurent and Jacques slid into them. The guard sitting near the back of the vehicle braced himself but skidded sideways and the one on the tail fell into the bracken at the side of the road.

Three men carrying Sten guns bolted out from behind an oak tree at the side of the road. They fired and the German in the bracken fell dead in the act of rising.

The soldier at the back of the lorry lurched forward to grab his rifle which had slipped across the floor, but a knife hit him in the throat and he toppled sideways with a scream. The other guard scrambled to his feet and managed to get one shot off but dropped in a hail of bullets.

Sam heard a brief scream from the front of the vehicle and then two men jumped up into the rear of the truck beside her.

One bent towards her. 'Camille?'

'Yes.' She brought her eyes up to her deliverer and his face swam before her . . . The untidy curl of black hair dangled on his brow! But it could not be! She must be delirious. Cash! Oh God in heaven, Cash . . .

Cash was dumbfounded! He could hardly speak as he took her arms. 'Oh, Sammy. I had no idea it would be you!' He lifted her to her feet. 'M'lady, my darling girl . . . what have they done to you?'

She fell forward into his arms as he kissed her bruised face and the tears flooded from her eyes.

He carried her down to the ground. 'Let's get out of here!'

And now she saw the other men were helping Laurent to his feet and supporting Jacques.

Cash carried Sam to the front of the lorry where she saw men in Commando uniforms with Tommy guns and motor bikes. They had been waiting at this point for the ambush.

'Move out as fast as we can,' Cash shouted. 'Huns could be along here any minute!'

One of the Commandos opened the door of the car and Cash tenderly put his precious burden into the back seat. Sam regarded him; it was as if she were seeing him for the first time and she marvelled at the miracle that had brought him to her. She whispered his name and the word lingered on her lips. 'Cash.'

Within another minute she was leaning on him in the back of the Citroën with Jaques unconscious beside her and Laurent in the front passenger seat, while they sped along the country road with two Commandos on a motor bike in front and six Commandos behind in three motor bikes and side cars.

As they headed east on a back road Cash looked down at Sammy in the fast-falling night. She was asleep, her darling face bruised and swollen, her neck and arms cut and her hand wrapped in a blood-soaked, dirty bandage. A great rage swelled through him and his hatred for the Nazis, already powerful, overwhelmed him.

He had been sent to hijack a German lorry that was transferring two captured agents and a leading Underground figure. He had been told one was a woman, but never could he have believed it would be Sammy. The last time he had seen her she had been in London living the high life of a foreign correspondent, or so he had thought. Obviously a lot had happened between then and now.

He had been informed of this mission back in England on the damp grey afternoon of 5 June. Overlord had been set to begin the night before but had been delayed because of bad weather and would now start at midnight.

Cash and his men were part of the British Sixth Airborne Division assaults and he had just come out of a final briefing with Major John Howard, the officer in charge of the Horsa glider Commando assault on the two Orne River bridges at the extreme left of the British attack.

A Sergeant hurried down the corridor and saluted. 'Which one of you is Major Wade?'

Cash nodded. 'I am.'

'I have a request for you to report to Headquarters. General Stampson wishes to see you.'

Cash turned to Howard. 'I'll see you tonight.'

Cash knew the General well. He found him seated at a table with two men whom Cash already knew and a third he did not. Empty tea and coffee cups made an awkward pattern on the tabletop in front of them.

Cash saluted.

'Wade, I think you know Colonel Buckmaster of SOE and Colonel Thomas of MI5.'

'I do.'

'And this is Colonel Seaward of American Intelligence.'

'How do you do, sir.'

'We've something we'd like your opinion on, m'boy.'

Cash grinned. Stampson always called him m'boy.

'We've got a situation in Normandy where two of our agents, a woman code-named Camille and a man code-named Laurent are being held by the Gestapo. They were captured along with a leading Resistance fighter, Jacques La Tour.' He looked across at Buckmaster. 'I think you should take it from here.'

The Colonel nodded. 'We know our people are held in a gaol east of a village called Cormolaine. It's a purpose-built prison to hold any on our side they take in the Manche and Calvados Departments of Normandy. There was an informer who's already been dealt with by the Underground themselves. We've learnt this from the radio operator who went into the field with Camille.

'We have it on reliable information that if our three people don't talk they'll be transferred on Saturday or Sunday to Fresnes.' He stood. 'Here let me show you.'

They all moved across to a table where a map of France was unfolded. He pointed. 'Both hide-out and gaol are inside the sector into which our American allies will advance from the beach-heads. That's why Colonel Seaward's here.'

The American Colonel now spoke. 'If we can lend any assistance we will, but my understanding is that it's a British operation. Nevertheless we'll be advancing towards you and we'll make contact as soon as we can.'

Buckmaster tapped the map where the gaol was located and glanced at Cash. 'We're informed that you and your men have become the most successful raiding party in the Special Forces. And as these three people are very valuable to SOE it's been suggested that you take a dozen men, go in, and ambush the transfer vehicle.'

General Stampson touched Cash's shoulder. 'So do you think you can do it, m'boy?'

Cash took this with equanimity. 'Yes. How do we get in? That part of the country does have Panzer Divisions around.'

Buckmaster smiled. 'Your normal descent method. Parachute. The Resistance will meet you.' He drew a cross on the map with a red pencil. 'All airborne units will be dropped in the early hours of tomorrow. Our radio operator, code-named Guy, will be at the drop point waiting with the others for your arrival. It needs to be a precise descent but I think we can leave that to our RAF fellows.'

'When I've accomplished the mission, what do I do with the agents and the Resistance fighter?'

'Their hide-out's in the hills north of Caumont; apparently it's pretty well concealed. Anyway, the informer did not know where it was so it's still operative. We expect the American advance to be there within a few days of your ambush. All you need to do is remain until the Americans push into your sector.'

Cash gave a strange smile. 'No way home? That's unusual.'

The American Colonel was studying the map. *'We're*

going to be your way home, Major, and if we're held up I guess you've been in tight spots before.'

'Mmm, just one or two.'

Colonel Buckmaster was thinking about Sam, code-named Camille, as he had seen her on the single occasion he had met her: the same night she had flown into the field about six weeks before. She had tossed her shock of hair back over her shoulder and greeted him. A young woman with a strong face and smooth olive skin: a beautiful girl. She and Laurent were two of their finest. And from what he was told, this Commando in front of him was one of the ablest they had.

He held out his hand to Cash. 'Bring them home if you can, Major.'

Cash grinned and nodded his head, and his black curl danced above his eyes. 'I'll do my best, sir.'

And now Cash continued to observe the sleeping woman beside him in the back seat of the stolen Citroën. It had belonged to a collaborator in St Lô. The Resistance fighters had killed him and taken it as he left his stud farm outside the town this morning.

Sammy! God, he had dreamt about her so often. What had brought her to this? A bloody secret agent? And here he was, a Commando. And JB a crazy fighter pilot. Heck, was there something in that blasted water back home in Teviot Brook?

He shook his head. For himself there could have been no other way, not now when he looked back on it. Let's face it, he had joined the Army to evade the police, but in Malaya and Singapore, it had become personal, a war he wanted to fight. The Nazis and Nips had to be stopped.

History showed that man had an evil side: rampages and excesses were rampant from Attila the Hun to the Spanish Inquisition. No continent had escaped crazed and violent warlords. But nothing in all history had the scope and magnitude of the combined depravity of the Nazis and the Japanese. And if you were unlucky enough to be on the planet when these abominations arose, well – you got caught up in it! Hell! He was no angel! But it was your duty as a human being to resist.

747

'We're here, Major,' the Commando at the wheel informed his leader as he turned off the road into the darkened yard of a horse-breeding farm.

'Right! Pull round behind the barn and we'll dump the stolen Citroën, then we'll wait till midnight and make our way up to the hide-out.'

Chapter Forty-eight

10 June, 1944

The destroyer *Kelvin* sped through the rolling grey waters of the English Channel at the start of her return journey to Portsmouth. On deck stood Winston Churchill, and at his side the South African Field Marshal Jan Smuts and English Field Marshal Alan Brooke.

In Field Marshal Brooke's words, they had enjoyed 'a wonderfully interesting day' and he was 'dog tired and very sleepy'.

Four days after D-Day Winston had finally received his wish to go to Normandy to view the beginning of the liberation of Europe. He and his two Field Marshals had been accompanied by the American Chiefs of Staff, General Marshall and Admiral King. They had taken the PM's train down from London and sailed over from Portsmouth to France.

On the way across they had continually passed convoys of landing craft and minesweepers while overhead, wings of aircraft escorted them.

Mr Churchill had smiled when he saw his 'brain child' being constructed in the Channel off Arromanches in the centre of the Normandy assault area. It had been code-named 'Mulberry' but was currently known as 'Winston Harbour' after himself. It was a roadstead of 1,235 acres, six miles of flexible steel – a floating harbour with floating piers attached to the sea bed which allowed more than 7,000 tons of goods, vehicles and heavy equipment to be landed daily to supply the troops engaged in the Battle of Normandy.

Churchill had thought of it years before, after the failed Dieppe raid. He knew the Allies would need the facilities of a port for the assault on Europe but the German concentration of defences was so heavy in the ports that they would be unlikely to take and hold one, as Dieppe had proved, so Churchill had come up with the idea of a floating harbour. There were in fact two of them, one for American use off St Laurent (which sadly would be badly damaged by a storm and rendered useless) and this one for British and Canadian use. They had been constructed in pieces in Great Britain and Canada and had been towed across and were currently being fitted together.

Within a few days of Churchill's viewing of his concept off Arromanches it would be fully operational and remain so for the duration of the liberation.

As the Prime Minister's party sailed closer to the Normandy beaches they were surrounded by craft of all descriptions and on the sand they were met by General Bernard Montgomery, known affectionately to the free world as 'Monty'.

Monty had conducted them through his headquarters and they had generally surveyed that small portion of France now in Allied hands. The only action they had witnessed had been some anti-aircraft fire during a German air raid on Courseulles Harbour.

And now, as evening fell and Churchill eyed the water billowing from the bow as the destroyer cut through the sea, Brooke, holding the rail beside him said, 'So, Prime Minister, you got your wish to go to France.'

Churchill grunted. In his mind he had been thwarted for he had missed the landing itself! He, in fact, had deeply desired to be on the deck of a cruiser on the night of 5 June and the morning of 6 June to watch the momentous historic event which had been so much in his mind and which the Allies had planned for years.

As he had said to Brooke before the landing, 'I have formed a view over many years which is: that any man who has to play an effective part in taking the grave and terrible decisions of war, should – when sending so many others to their deaths – share in their risks, even if it's in a small way. As a result of what I saw in the First World War I'm convinced that Generals and High Command should observe the conditions and aspect of the battle scene. I've seen grievous errors made through the silly theory that valuable lives should not be endangered.'

To that end he had discussed his presence at the landings with Admiral Ramsey who had assumed control of all operations in the English Channel. They had decided that Churchill would embark on HMS *Belfast* in the late afternoon on the day before D-Day. The *Belfast*, a sleek cruiser, was one of the bombarding craft attached to the centre British Force and it had been agreed that Churchill would spend the night on her and view the dawn attack. The PM had then desired a tour of the beaches.

Ramsey, for better or worse, had felt it his duty to explain to General Eisenhower what had been mooted and the American Commander had protested at Churchill's taking such risks. Nevertheless Churchill had prevailed and the affair gave the appearance of being settled. Then matters became complex. Winston had lunched with King George a week before D-Day. The two princesses, Elizabeth and Margaret, who had remained in London and not been evacuated to Canada as had been suggested by Parliament, had joined the men briefly as they sat down. And on their departure, the King had asked where Winston intended to be when the Normandy landings took place.

The PM informed him, 'At the landings themselves.' And suddenly King George became enthusiastic to go along as well. But the following day the King had a change of heart, obviously having thought deeply overnight upon the matter. Perhaps the Queen had influenced him, but he had arrived at the belief that it was too dangerous, which of course it was, to have the two leaders together within the battle front.

He had written a letter to Winston stating that for the sake of the country and Empire they should not risk being killed. He had ended the letter with the words:

The anxiety of these coming days would be very greatly

increased for me if I thought that, in addition to everything else, there was a risk, however remote, of my losing your help and guidance.

Churchill still had been very inclined to go. But another meeting with Admiral Ramsey had been followed by a second letter from the Monarch arriving a few days later. It ended with:

I ask you most earnestly to consider the whole question again, and not let your personal wishes, which I very well understand, lead you to depart from your own high standard of duty to the State.

The King had won. Winston remained in England and had now taken what he believed was a tame inspection of the aftermath, so Brooke's platitude had drawn merely a grunt.

The Prime Minister's eyes remained on the churning sea a few seconds more before he left the Field Marshal at the rail. Walking amidships he ran into Admiral Vian who proposed that before returning to Portsmouth, they could sail along and watch the bombardment of the German positions by the Allied battleships and cruisers protecting the British left flank.

This was more like it! Churchill's eyes flashed. 'Good. Let's.'

Up to the bridge they went where Vian gave the order and the destroyer shot between two battleships that were firing at 20,000 yards, and Winston began to smile. His smile widened as they continued on through a cruiser squadron that was firing at 14,000 yards and finally they were within 7,000 yards of the shore; and Winston's smile was set in place.

He turned to Admiral Vian. 'Since we're so near, why shouldn't we have a plug at them ourselves before we go home?'

The Admiral answered, 'Certainly.'

And in another two minutes all the destroyer's guns fired at the coast.

'Well done!' Winston beamed and Smuts at his side proclaimed, 'Wonderful.'

752

They were now well within the enemy's range and after another brief burst of fire the Admiral thought it best if he removed his precious charge from the line of fire, and gave orders for the ship to turn and move out with full speed.

But he had made Winston happy. The Prime Minister had experienced first-hand his own little taste of the liberation of Europe, and it was a very agreeable Winston who stomped into the officers' wardroom and smoked a cigar, drank a brandy and then slept the four hours back to Portsmouth.

As the Prime Minister sailed back to Portsmouth John Baron sat and watched Antoinette Desaix wash the dishes under the oak beams of her kitchen while Midi her black cat sat on the windowsill near her. Beyond the window, branches of trees swayed in the strong summer breeze. The woman worked fast with her single left hand and utilised her other wooden hand amazingly well.

Fifty times during the ten days John Baron had been hidden in her home Antoinette had wanted to take him in her arms and tell him the truth, but she had not. During their conversations she had learnt how much he loved and admired the two people who had raised him and each time she had held her tongue.

'They brought me up marvellously. Our home was always full of laughter. My mother is kind and my father is an exceptional man.'

Antoinette knew this. She remembered the twenty-four hours in Benjamin Chard's company, and how strong and reliable he had been.

'Uncle Wakefield has lived with us since the end of the Great War; he taught me French, and my mother's nanny lives with us too. Now she's a dour old soul but she idolises my mother and I suppose loves us all. She used to dote on my friend Cash even though she pretended she didn't. We call her Ledgie. I actually had twin little sisters but one died. The other is just the most special woman. Her name's Samantha.'

'That's a lovely name.'

'I call her Sam.'

One evening Antoinette opened a bottle of Dom Perignon champagne which she had been saving since the war began and she rested her elbows on her kitchen table and contemplated the two airmen. 'Tell me more about yourselves and your parents. Did they shower you with gifts?'

Anton had exclaimed, 'What? In Czechoslovakia? During the Depression we were lucky to eat, let alone be given gifts, Antoinette.'

'And what about you, John Baron?'

'The same applies really – though they always tried to give me things I wanted, I suppose. I can remember Uncle Wake making dozens of model aircraft for me and painting them himself. My room was full of them.'

Antoinette smiled. 'What did they give you when you became a man?'

'Do you mean for my twenty-first birthday?'

'Perhaps. I suppose so.'

'Actually, I must say I was surprised by that present.' He turned to Anton. 'And it was during the Depression, too. Goodness knows where they found the money.'

'What was it?' Anton asked.

'A gold ring. It fitted my little finger as if they had measured it. Unusual, with gold ridges running round it and a small triangle of gold extending from it. They had my name engraved on the inside.'

Anton had laughed. 'Lucky you, to receive such a gift.'

Antoinette sat there in silence. She was overwhelmed by the memory of asking Benjamin to give it to her son, 'when he is a man'. And Benjamin had kept his promise, just as she had hoped he would. She saw his father, his real father, in her mind's eye placing the ring on her finger, one half with *Antoinette, my love always* engraved upon it, the other with *John Baron*. She opened her mouth to ask John Baron where it was when he enlightened them. 'Bloody Huns took it from me in the first camp. That was the end of it.'

And tonight, in less than an hour, JB and Anton were to depart. John Baron stood from the table and picked up the tea towel to help Antoinette dry the washed plates as she protested.

He smiled. 'Let me, I want to help you.'

Anton had gone into the room they shared to rest before the journey. Antoinette and Franchot Benoit, a friend, and the leader of the depleted Resistance movement in this part of France had worked ceaselessly to obtain the papers and the passes to smuggle them out of the country.

Everyone knew of the landings in Normandy approximately 200 miles to the south-west, but the German concentration of troops and armament in the northern areas around Dunkirk, Calais and Bologne had not yet been depleted. This of course was owing to the deception, fostered by agents like Sam, that had tricked Hitler and the German High Command into believing that the landing in Normandy was to mislead them. It had given the Allies those vital days to make bridgeheads into the countryside.

John Baron felt comfortable with the woman beside him. She had been kind and caring to them both and hidden them until the plans were now arranged and very soon they would leave her. He was somehow sorry about that.

For a time she had been tentative with them, almost tense, and he had put that down to the fact that she had just decided on the spur of the moment to help them. In fact, the morning after she had taken them in they had told her again they would move on, but she had reacted quite vehemently, saying that they must not leave: that she desired greatly to help them and that was that.

Since then she had seemed happier as each day passed. After the rigours of the prison camp they had not minded the confines of this neat and tidy cottage, for her smile had rarely faded. At first they had called her 'Madame' but she had soon dispensed with that and asked them to call her 'Antoinette'. She appeared to enjoy cooking for them and had even made alterations to the clothes she had given them to ensure they fitted, using her one hand with amazing dexterity. She had gone out on her bicycle to see Franchot Benoit and arrange forged papers and organise their departure. They were aware of the constant danger; they owed her so much and in the last few days John Baron had thought that after this hellish war was over he would come back here just to see her.

She seemed a little on edge tonight. No doubt it was because they waited for the Resistance to arrive with the bicycles for the ride towards the coast. Because John Baron spoke good French, Franchot and Antoinette had decided to take the chance of sending them into the restricted coastal zone where they knew they had men who could organise their departure by boat.

John Baron studied Antoinette as he stood at her side. He guessed she must be in her sixties for her hair was mostly grey and her face had begun to show the ravages of time, but her bone structure was attractive and there was a gentility about her that must have made her most alluring in her youth.

She had been fearful to let them out of the house even though the dwelling was remote. But one afternoon it had been so warm and oppressive inside that she had consented to their sitting in the breeze in the shade between her back door and the shed. Elm trees made a third wall and the one open side had a view down the track which led to the road below so that they could see anyone coming.

The two men, used to the long, dull hours in the prison camp, had played cards for a time and then Anton had fallen asleep on a blanket in the shade of the elms.

Antoinette had kept her gaze on the road below and had talked to John Baron about many things. She told him that she had never married and that she had lost contact with her own family decades before. She informed him she had been an interpreter in the American Embassy in Paris for eighteen years after the Great War. 'I only came back to this part of the country two years before this war began. I used to live here many years ago.'

The sun had found John Baron and as he lifted his fair head it was bathed in light. Antoinette felt a swell of love and swivelled quickly back to the road below.

John Baron watched her. He could smell the faint aroma of honeysuckle which always clung to her and there was something clean and comforting in it.

'Do you have a special friend?' she asked suddenly. 'I mean a girlfriend? Was there someone before you were shot down?'

John Baron hesitated momentarily. 'Yes, I suppose so. Her name's Alexandra Cardrew – she's English.'

'Tell me about her.'

And he did. And when he had completed his description – which took many minutes because he told Antoinette about Alex's George Cross and her voyage to and from Dunkirk as well as all the other details that made up the young woman in his mind, he paused and added, 'I carried a letter from her out of the prison camp with me, hidden in my shoe. It was one of two that reached me though in it she said she wrote two every week. So there must be over a hundred floating around on censors' desks in Britain and Germany. Guess I was lucky to get two really.' He took the letter from his pocket and on an impulse said, 'Would you like to read it?'

Antoinette was surprised. 'Are you sure?'

'Yes, I'd like you to. I'd like to know what you think.'

It had been written five months before and told of the cold winter days with the snow on the ground and how Alex had skated on the frozen pond in the garden at Castlemere. She told him of the pup her mother had brought home, a stray she had found roaming the streets of Ramsgate. They had called her Cleopatra. She mentioned seeing Sam and how they had become friends. Originally when he read that, JB had felt odd. Alex signed off with love and her postscript had been in typically candid Alex style: *So JB wherever you are remember we think of you all the time . . . Especially me.*

Antoinette completed reading it and quickly glanced down to the road before she smiled across at him. 'I think she sounds wonderful. Just right for you, and the way you spoke of her just now . . . Well if you could have seen yourself talking, I think you would have realised that you're in love with her.'

John Baron did not reply. He took the letter and tucked it in his shirt pocket and within another minute Antoinette had suggested they return inside so they woke Anton and moved in through the back door.

John Baron was thinking about that afternoon now as he stood beside Antoinette at the sink and lifted another plate and dried it.

She glanced round at him as she let the water out of the bowl and wiped her hand on a towel and her black cat Midi jumped from the windowsill to the floor. 'Thank God the British have landed in Normandy though it could be six months before they get here, or longer.'

'Yes, it could. But I have the feeling it'll be quicker and I think it's the beginning of the end for Hitler.'

'*Les Bosches!*' She proclaimed it like a curse. 'They turned this part of France into a morgue in the Great War . . . and now they spawn that monster Hitler.'

'You're right, he's hardly human.' The wind rattled the window again as he asked, 'Antoinette I don't mean to pry, but what's your surname? When I think of you in the future I don't want to just think of you as Antoinette.' He laughed. 'And I'll need to know if I try to find you again.'

She moved away. 'Would you?'

'Yes. I'd love to come back here after this rotten war's over and see you again in happy times when La Belle France is free.'

John Baron did not notice the flush begin to creep to her neck as she busied herself putting the plates and dishes away. 'That would be very nice.'

In the days he had been here Antoinette had found out quite a lot. He was so confident and natural and unaffected that it was obvious Benjamin Chard had brought him up wonderfully well.

'They'll be here for you soon,' she said abruptly. She hated to lose him but she would be so relieved to see them gone. She had ridden into Béthune today and visited a forger called Jean Levant. He was the only one within 100 miles who had the stamps which the escapees' forged papers must carry, to allow them into the restricted coastal area. The papers, she and Franchot had acquired from another source.

Tonight they would make a thirty-five to forty-mile bicycle ride and tomorrow they would enter the restricted area. Tomorrow night they would leave for England in a small boat which would wait for them some miles north of Dunkirk.

But Antoinette remained concerned about confiding in Jean Levant. She had never met him or dealt with him before but had been informed by Paul, another friend, that only three weeks ago someone who had gone to him for a stamp had been arrested a few days later. They were not sure whether to connect the arrest with Levant or not.

Antoinette had talked the matter over with Franchot and he had suggested she take the precautionary measure of telling Levant the wrong date for the flyers' departure from her cottage. So today when she met the forger in a small back room behind his garage she had told him that the departure was set for the day after tomorrow when in fact it was tonight. She had to be careful to make him believe it, for normally once the papers were in order the smuggling of the escapees would begin immediately. She lied and said that one of the men had hurt his ankle and they wanted to give him another forty-eight hours' recovery before they made a long ride; she also lied and told him they were heading south towards Amiens. Her hope was that if Levant *did* work for the Nazis, they would not feel the need to rush to her cottage tonight.

Her whole being was concentrated on seeing her son away to freedom. Providence had brought him back to her after thirty years, the single person she loved more than anyone except his long-dead father.

She looked at her son and pride swelled through her.

John Baron noticed the tender expression and it surprised him. 'Antoinette, you still have not told me your last name.'

'Ah have I not? It's Desaix. Come, let us sit more comfortably in the sitting room while we wait.' The room faced the track which led down to the road.

As they left the kitchen he decided to say, 'Is it too rude of me to ask what happened to your hand?'

She did not look round as she led him through the narrow

759

hall, the heels of her shoes clicking on the stone floor. 'I was run over by a train. It was an accident a long time ago.'

'I'm so sorry.' And he was.

'I was taken to a convent, the Great War had started and *les Bosches* were coming. I thought I was dying, and the nuns did too. At one point a young novice even believed I had stopped breathing; that I was in fact dead. But I was not,' she smiled, 'as you can see – though I was gravely ill for many months. When they evacuated the convent they took me with them.' She entered the sitting room and sat on the arm of her green and white patterned sofa where she could see through the window. 'Are you completely ready to leave?'

He patted his pocket where his forged passes lay. 'Yes. I cannot thank you enough for hiding us and for what you've done.'

'I am content to have been able to help.'

He studied her. 'Thank you is not enough, nowhere near.' And as he regarded the softness of the planes of her face he felt an overwhelming urge to tell her what he knew he could tell no one else. 'Antoinette?'

'Yes.'

'You know I have wonderful parents . . .'

She swallowed. 'Yes. You have told me about them and your home at the place called Haverhill so far away in Queensland.'

The breeze was rising to a wind and they could see the branches of the trees swaying through the window. It would soon be dark and the Resistance would arrive.

John Baron leant forward. 'I met a woman in England who asked to see me when she was dying. She told me that my mother and father are not my real parents. That I am the son of a Frenchwoman.'

Antoinette shifted on the arm of the sofa, lifted a cushion and put it back down. She was amazed but tried not to show it. Her heart quickened.

I can tell him everything. He knows he was adopted. So I can simply tell him I'm his mother.

He was looking at her, waiting for her reaction.

But if I tell him who I am, ah the confusion for him . . . the shock, the complexity. What if he does not want to leave me? But he must. He must be saved. No matter what, my son must get away tonight.

She heard her voice far away and thin. 'I see. Do you believe her?'

'Yes, I do. She was a mixed-up person, beautiful but completely selfish and motivated by her needs only. But there's no doubt what she said is true.'

Antoinette guessed exactly who she was. Harriet. Her beloved John Baron's legal wife. The seconds passed as she sat there playing with the tassel on the cushion, her eyes riveted upon the man speaking.

'For a long time I was in shock. And I've told no one, no one at all . . . until tonight. Somehow I wanted to tell you. To ask your advice. You've never had children or a husband but I feel you are full of love, and you have such gentle strength. I'd like to know what you think.'

Ah, to hear her son say such things . . . . She could hardly bear it. She sat there gazing at him willing herself to be strong and not break down.

'Antoinette, being in a prison camp gives you a lot of time to think. Days on end without change. Sometimes I feel I should tell my parents. Find out the truth – learn what really went on and where I come from.'

She wanted with all of her heart and mind to go to him. To hold him in her arms and tell him, but it was the wrong time, the wrong time. She could not risk it. He *must* get away tonight.

She swallowed. 'If they have never told you, John Baron, it's because they don't want you to know.'

'Well, yes, that's obvious. And I don't want to hurt them.'

She hesitated and spun her body to the window. 'But you would if you tell them what you know, wouldn't you?'

He thought of his mother then, with her loving heart, how she had hated him to leave home, how easily hurt she was. He thought of his father Benjamin, the man who had given him all the honest values of his life. 'Yes, you are right, I would hurt them. Especially my mother.'

Antoinette felt dizzy. 'Then perhaps it's best to leave it the way it is. Not to say what you know. You were happy before you found out, weren't you?'

He admitted that most of his life had been perfect. That was, until suddenly he had desired Sammy and everything had altered.

But if he analysed it all rationally and considered what had happened since that time: the RAF, the camaraderie, the action – there was no doubt he had been fulfilled and happy. And during it all he had thrown off the guilt he carried because of his emotions and Sam.

He answered her as she rounded to face him again. 'Yes, my life was happy before I knew, and I've had time to come to terms with it since, so except for being in the flaming prison camp I was happy. And I'll be happy again once I return to England and help finish this rotten war!' He peered at the woman opposite him who seemed so interested in his answer. He liked her so much. She was a wonderfully brave and amazing person. He wanted to know a lot more about her, but there was no time. He was due to leave.

Antoinette was so grateful to Benjamin. He had made an outstanding man of her son. All those years ago when she believed she had been dying she had given her darling baby to a good man. Tears started to form but she rose quickly and walked to the window to peer outside.

She had even gone to England after the war and tried to find the Chards. Now she realised they had gone to Australia. So she had lived without her darling child all these years: bereft and angry at first and later in dismal acceptance.

She wiped her eyes with a swift movement and composed herself as much as she could. 'Then, John Baron, if you really want my advice, I say you should not destroy the ones who love you so, by telling them what you have learnt.'

As she spoke she saw four men ride through the quickening dusk up the track to her house. They climbed off their bikes and left them against the broken fence as she watched. Two ran off the way they had come and the others walked to her door.

She spoke over her shoulder. 'Our friends are here. Go and wake Anton.'

She opened her door and greeted Franchot Benoit. The second was her friend Paul.

'We have a long ride – are they ready?'

She knew she could not be brave much longer and she drew Franchot away along the short corridor to her kitchen. 'Just a few minutes first.' She quickly took paper and a pencil and wrote a page in great haste as Franchot stood watching, then she removed the ring from the pocket of her dress and slipped it in an envelope along with what she had written.

She handed it to her friend. 'Franchot, this is a most vital request and more important to me than life itself. Please make sure the one called John Baron receives this – but not before he's on the boat to England. It's imperative he must be on the boat.'

Franchot took the envelope and put it in his waistcoat pocket. He liked Antoinette and would do as she asked. 'I understand.'

They returned to the sitting room to see the others waiting at the door. Antoinette crossed to them and Anton hugged her. 'You've been wonderful.'

John Baron contemplated her from under his cloth cap. He looked so like his father she had to hold her breath. Then he smiled at her and her heart missed a beat. 'Goodbye. Any thanks are inadequate. You're wise, Antoinette Desaix, and I've listened to you.' He paused. 'I shall do as you say though there are things I'd dearly like to know.' He stepped forward and enveloped her in his arms.

She knew the tears were waiting in her eyes ready to fall as her lips touched the skin of his face and an infinite joy swelled through her. She tried to lighten her voice as she said, 'You will know one day, without causing any pain to anyone – I'm sure of it. I will miss you. Goodbye.'

He hugged her close. 'Not goodbye. I'll see you after the war.'

And then he was gone.

She watched them mount the four bicycles in the gloom and ride away. And her heart left her and sailed along in the night beside her son.

An hour later Antoinette had not moved. She sat on the sofa as night enveloped the cottage. Franchot had told her that in the hills to the west near Desvres there were three hundred people of the Resistance: that the numbers grew each day and that many such small armies were banding together all over France emboldened by the Allied landings in Normandy. He had advised her to pack and to go there.

But she had not. She was loath to abandon her cottage and her cat Midi who even now sat at her side. The bloody *Bosches* were always turning people out of their homes, making refugees of them – or slaves. Or worse.

The most important thing of all was that her son was on his way to freedom. She remembered the night so long ago at the start of the Great War when Benjamin Chard had come to her to take her and her son to safety in England. She imagined the tiny John Baron with his father's blue eyes, felt the softness of his body against hers. She rocked herself in remembrance with her arms taut across her body.

Suddenly she heard a noise outside and Midi sprang to the floor.

She was not surprised to see movement in the dark of the yard or to hear the battering begin on the door, even though she had thought perhaps they would not come tonight.

Now her listlessness left her and she ran through to the pantry where she kept her pistol. It was always loaded. She raced back and stood feet planted firmly on the bottom step of her narrow stairway as the door burst open.

Remaining there, hands behind her back, she watched a soldier enter. As he saw her, he stood aside to allow the two Gestapo police to enter. She waited until they walked through her sitting room across her pale flowered rug and halted in front of her.

'Antoinette Desaix?' The German's smug manner suggested she was already his prisoner and he was in complete charge.

She smiled and nodded. 'Yes.'

'You are hiding two escaped prisoners of war?'

She nodded again. 'Yes.' And brought her gun from behind her back and shot him though his self-satisfied face. The second Gestapo screamed in amazement but before he could move she shot him too. They both fell dead at her feet. The soldier who had stood back to let them in flung his rifle up to fire but she pulled the trigger a third time and he crumpled to the rug, blood surging from the hole in his forehead.

By now the enemy soldiers outside came charging in and Antoinette, smile still firmly fixed on her mouth, took a fourth German out of the world with her before they blasted her with a sub-machine gun from the doorway.

She staggered back, her smile turning to a laugh as she thought of her son on his way to freedom, and as her body writhed full of bullets, rotating on the staircase, she saw her soulmate in the distance. He sat at the other end of the boat, the oars resting at his side as they floated along under the overhanging branches. His boater hat had fallen forwards at a jaunty angle and his voice floated gently in her dying mind.

'Ah, my sweet darling, you have visited upon me such love as I did not know existed.'

She gave a tiny smile. Now was the time to tell him. The perfect time. 'John Baron?'

'Yes?'

'I am going to have our child.'

The ride towards the coast was arduous. Knowing the area intimately, Franchot took them by as many backroads as he could but that extended the time and it was nearly seven hours later when they reached their destination, a lonely house through an avenue of trees, on a hill outside the restricted zone.

A man and a woman who introduced themselves as

Claude and Maria, awaited them with sandwiches and wine and John Baron, Anton, Franchot and Paul ate and drank gratefully. They fell asleep immediately afterwards and spent the following day mooching around the farmhouse anxious to leave but knowing they were to wait until four in the afternoon when Jean Baptiste, the man who would accompany them into the restricted area, would arrive.

At one point during the long hours of the day John Baron took out Alex's letter and re-read it. He recalled his first meeting with her and how he had been attracted to her because of her resemblance to Sam, but later, attracted to her for herself, her wonderful, sincere, straightforward self. And he remembered what his new friend Antoinette had said to him about her.

A porcelain clock with Roman numerals stood on a dresser by the front door and as the gold minute hand came up to five to four in the afternoon a man on a bicycle pedalled at speed up through the avenue of elms.

'It's Jean Baptiste,' Maria announced from the window.

In another minute he was inside the tall room and greeting them as John Baron and Anton stepped forward ready to depart.

'I have something to tell you,' he said, his face serious with the news he brought. 'Antoinette is dead.'

Franchot crossed himself, Maria murmured, 'Oh no!' and the others mumbled in shock, but John Baron flinched noticeably and walked quickly away to the far side of the room. He was engulfed in a wave of sorrow, he could not speak, he was about to cry and knew that tears flooded his eyes. No, he did not want Antoinette to be dead. He wanted to come back after the war and see her again in happy times when France was free.

Anton asked, 'How do you know? What happened?'

'We received a coded telephone call this morning. It happened last night, apparently not long after you left. The Gestapo came to arrest her, two of them and four soldiers. Our contacts believe that they thought you were still there. But this is the part which is wonderful. She had an old pistol. She shot both Gestapo agents and two German soldiers before they killed her.' Jean Baptiste spoke softly, his eyes staring into the distance. 'Well done, Antoinette my dear, dear friend.'

John Baron spun round to them and raised his hand for silence. 'We killed her. If it were not for us she'd be alive.'

Franchot moved across the room and took his shoulders firmly. 'Don't say that, friend. Antoinette was no fool. She knew her options. She desired to help you and she did. I think she decided what she wished to do, and simply did it. Remember her for the magnificent woman she was. That's what she would want.'

John Baron hung his head.

Franchot led Jean Baptiste down the corridor a few paces and quietly gave him Antoinette's envelope explaining her wishes. 'It was her last request so we must be sure to do as she asked.'

Jean Baptiste took the letter. 'I will do it.' Then he returned to his charges. 'We must be leaving now.'

John Baron and Anton departed from Franchot and Paul, Maria and Claude with handshakes and grateful smiles and warnings to be careful, and rode down the hill along another back road.

They passed three checkpoints and each time presented their papers. The guards glanced down, read them briefly and waved them by. But at the fourth checkpoint on the outskirts of Dunkirk the German soldier spoke French and took his job more seriously. The sun was descending in the sky and his shadow fell ominously towards them as he walked up to Jean Baptiste on the first bicycle. 'Where do you work?'

Jean Baptiste answered, 'Usually down at the Canal de Bourbourg. Today we were further along.' He waved his hand in the general direction from whence they had ridden.

'So your name's Jean Baptiste Dupont?'

'Yes.'

'Are these bicycles yours?'

'Yes.'

'How long have you had them?'

'For years. Mine was my father's.'

'And who are you?' He pointed to John Baron, who

handed over his papers and replied in perfect French, 'My name's Alexandre Caron, these are my papers. And I too have had my bicycle a long time.'

The German eyed the papers and held the pages up to the evening light as John Baron tried to look as nonchalant as possible. He was worrying about Anton who could speak no French.

The guard strode over to Anton who realised what was happening and quickly decided to speak in German. He handed across his papers and began in the man's native tongue. 'My name is Michel La Boure. I was born in Alsace Lorraine so I've spoken German all my life and I like to practise it. I hope you don't mind.'

Their false birth-places appeared on their papers and Anton's did read Alsace Lorraine.

They all held their breath praying this would please the guard and that he would not return to French to continue the questioning.

To their relief he replied in German. 'What are you doing here? Were you a transferred worker?'

Anton shrugged. 'No. A woman – she's now my wife. She's from these parts.'

The guard, who had been frowning till now, nodded as if he understood all about women and as they waited, pulses quickening, he grunted and waved them by.

They rode on.

They avoided another vital control point by detouring through a wide sewer, and by nightfall had skirted a number of sea batteries and were in a shed on the seafront north of the town. There was constant activity about half a mile away and armoured vehicles came and went. At ten o'clock Jean Baptiste tapped his watch. 'We must go. Leave your bicycles here and come with me.'

Out along the beach they walked, the sea breeze carrying the smell of ozone into their lungs, their shoes sinking into the sand. After ten minutes by the light of the starry sky they saw an outcrop of rocks.

Jean Baptiste called softly, 'Alleraman? Alleraman?' And a voice replied, 'Jean Baptiste?'

The escapees scrambled into the narrow boat with tall bulwarks, hurrying their goodbyes. 'Thank you, thank you for everything. See you after the war.'

Alleraman, the sailor, spoke in English. 'We must row until we are far enough away from shore to use the motor.'

As they sat at the oars Jean Baptiste handed the envelope to John Baron. 'This is from Antoinette. She said to give it to you when you were in the boat for England. Goodbye and good luck.' He and the sailor pushed hard on the craft and it lifted into the sea as Alleraman jumped aboard, and headed them into the black rolling waters of the Channel.

As John Baron had no light to read by, it was hours before he opened Antoinette's letter.

They were picked up by a British minesweeper midway across the Channel. Alleraman's boat was hoisted aboard and when the two escapees proved who they were they were toasted in the mess.

In the excitement of the rescue John Baron had forgotten the envelope until he had been given a berth in the crew quarters and was undressing. He turned it over in his hands as he sat down on the bunk. Being rescued was like a dream, and would have been a marvellous dream but for Antoinette's death.

He opened the envelope and the ring fell out on the bunk. He picked it up in wonder and it lay in the palm of his hand near his lifeline. A shiver ran through him as he clutched it and read:

My Darling Son,
  For that is who you are.
  I could not tell you, for all I desire in this world is for you to leave & return to England where you will be safe. Providence brought you to me & I have exulted in having you near.
  Your real father was John Baron Chard, Benjamin's cousin, & I was the wife of his heart & mind. He completed my life. The dying woman you

*visited was his legal wife – still bitter, it seems, after
so long a time.*

*Your father lived with me here in France & you were
born. He went back to England to obtain a divorce but
he died & the Great War began. Benjamin & he were
very dear to each other & Benjamin came to France to
rescue us – you & me. You were a baby of two.*

*The train accident happened as we crossed
Northern France & the wonderful irony is, the three
of us were to leave for England from Dunkirk! Near
where you will leave for safety.*

*I thought I was dying, so in the convent I gave you
to Benjamin to bring up as his own. He has done the
most splendid job & my heart bursts with pride.*

*I have seen you, lived a short time with you & held
you briefly in my arms – my lips have touched your
face. Joys of such magnitude, they have glorified my
soul.*

*So you see, my wonderful son, you do not need to
hurt the 'parents' who have nurtured you & made you
the fine man you are. You know it all now. They are
the best of people.*

*Whatever happens to me, don't be sad. My greatest
desire is to join your father & I feel the need to be
with him very soon.*

*Weep not for me, but live with the knowledge that
I love you for ever.*

Antoinette, your mother.

His fingers shook as he read it again, and then once more.
Antoinette Desaix was his mother! The ring was a duplicate of his own except for the little triangle of gold and he
realised now that if put together they would have fitted
neatly into each other and made a perfect whole. He looked
inside. *Antoinette, my love always.* And his ring had read:
John Baron.

He had felt so much for her. No wonder he had felt good
with her, comfortable and comforted and enjoyed a bond
he could not explain.

She was dead. She was his mother and she was dead.

He lay for a long, long time looking into the night as the minesweeper cut through the sea, visualising his mother and father so far away and remembering how they had loved him and brought him up. He pictured them with Antoinette. Finally he went to sleep with tears in his eyes and Antoinette's gold ring on his little finger.

Chapter Forty-nine

Sam sat looking down through the trees to the road in the distance. In a couple of hours the sun would slide behind the horizon. She had seen German armoured vehicles pass half an hour previously and the thunder of cannons and mortars in battle could be heard clearly now. Back behind her towards the encampment, members of the Resistance moved about cleaning weapons, tinkering with their bicycles, smoking and talking.

In the days since Cash had rescued her she had regained her strength. She had been in superb physical condition before the torture and the beatings, and while her hand would be a long time healing, the rest of her, apart from scratches and bruises, was mending swiftly.

She had trouble remembering the rescue except for the fantastic moment of recognising Cash. She knew she had drifted into sleep at his side in the Citroën and she recalled how solid arms had carried her through woods and across a stream and on up here to the hide-out.

She recollected feeling strange and awkwardly bashful when Cash had stripped her and bathed her sore and tender body with a gentle touch. He had dried her and called her 'm'lady' and lifted her and put her to bed. The next day when she awoke she realised she had slept the clock around.

Sam was aware Cash had avoided her since. There were nine other women here, strong robust girls of about twenty-one who carried their guns like men and smoked cheroots and told bawdy jokes. They had nursed her after the first night and he had not come near her except for once briefly each day to see how she progressed.

She had found herself watching for Cash and remembering

all sorts of times they had shared together, like the day after their wedding when in the noonday sun they climbed to the top of the rise in Queen's Park in Ipswich and Cash had kissed her and she had quixotically named the spot Mount Farest. 'Because it's far away from worldly care and it's where we rested.'

She heard footsteps rustle in the grass behind her and wheeled round expectantly, hoping it would be Cash.

It was Laurent and she tried not to appear disappointed.

'Ah, there you are Sam.' He knew her real name now as she did his. It was Captain David Flinders, though she would always think of him as Laurent.

'How are you?' she asked, consciously brightening.

He grinned. 'Great. Funny how being out of those bastards' clutches makes you feel well, wounds or not.'

She nodded. 'Yes.'

Jacques had died in the night. He had been so badly beaten that many of the bones in his body had been broken and they believed one had pierced his lung.

They had buried him this morning in a spot overlooking the road, a green glade in a haven between the rocks. Sam was thinking about him as she said, 'The Gestapo are fiends out of hell all right. I wonder if they'll be brought to justice?'

David shook his head. 'We'll get some of them but not all. They'll go to ground.'

Sam frowned. 'But surely we'll win?'

'We must. And you know what? Then I predict there'll not be one member of the bloody Nazi Party to be found anywhere. Suddenly they'll all disappear.'

'But we'll get Hitler and the leaders and the death-camp Commandants! Tell me they won't be able to hide?'

David sighed as the breeze lifted the tails of the blue kerchief he had tied around his neck. 'I hope that's right, Sam, I truly hope so, for the sake of brave, dead men like Jacques.' He gestured back over his shoulder to the camp. 'I came out to tell you there's a sudden meeting being called. Apparently the Major has information that makes him believe we should be abandoning the hide-out.'

Sam felt hurt that Cash had not come for her himself,

but she stood up and followed David back to the clearing between the huts where dozens of men milled about.

Lieutenant Matt Fleming, Cash's second-in-command, was sitting in their midst flanked by the ten other Commandos. Guy, the radio operator, sat cross-legged on a huge rock, his arm round Noële, one of the young women.

Sam's gaze roamed and caught sight of Cash talking to Fleur, a nubile girl of Amazonian proportions who wore her men's trousers too tight and her shirt opened to expose the tops of her breasts. Sam recognised the emotion that assailed her; she was jealous. As he left Fleur and strode into the centre of the gathering Sam pushed her way through the men to be close to him.

He smiled at her as she came near and she felt womanly and to her annoyance, partly shy.

Wakefield would have been proud to hear Cash speak fluently in French to the freedom fighters and then translate for his own men. He pointed to Ludlow and Skinner who had been with him in Guernsey. 'Our scouts have been out and they inform us that the battle you can hear is between a Division of SS Panzers and the Americans. There are German reinforcements heading this way and our feeling is that we need to abandon this hide-out tonight, because by tomorrow it'll be the middle of the battlefield.'

Matt handed him a long stick and as the motley group of fighters clambered on rocks and boxes to look down at the ground at his feet, Cash drew in the dirt.

'This is where we are, and these are two points where we think we can meet the vanguard of the American advance.' He looked across at David. 'Captain Flinders and I will lead our command out before sundown. We think it's best to find the Yanks in daylight. Don't want to be mistaken for Nazis and get swatted by friendly fire. Good luck to you all.'

As the British special forces mingled with their companions of the Resistance to say goodbye, Samantha took Cash's arm. He turned aside to her, a questioning expression on his face. 'You all right, Sammy?'

'Well, yes, I am . . .'

'Then get moving. Not that you've much to take but I assume you can still carry a Sten gun in your left hand.'

She bristled. 'Hell, of course I can, and I can use it with my left hand too.'

'Good for you,' he grinned and marched away. She felt cheated, and when she saw Fleur making straight for him she remained to watch.

'I shall see you after the war,' the young woman said and stood on her toes and kissed Cash on the mouth.

Cash smiled and patted her cheek. 'You never know.' Then he strode away from her shouting, 'Let's move!'

Sam felt such a sense of jealous injury that she turned sharply in case anyone saw her face and she hurried off to pick up her weapon.

Half an hour later Cash's small group rode down the hill on bicycles, motor bikes and sidecars. Sam had hoped Cash would ask her to ride with him but he had gestured for her to climb into a sidecar and for Matt to ride the attached bike.

Skinner positioned himself behind Cash and they bumped down the undulating hill, weaving in and out of tree trunks which were already immersed in the yellow-gold light of the last hour of the day.

Once on the narrow road Cash and Skinner moved ahead 100 yards in front of the main body of Commandos, the sound of intermittent gunfire rumbling to them across the landscape. They rode slowly and cautiously for a few miles before Skinner turned them down a side track. 'The Aure River's about a mile over there,' he said, pointing across open country.

A couple of hundred yards on the cavalcade gained a main road bordered by hedgerows. A cluster of abandoned houses sat at a crossroads and apple orchards reposed in neat avenues down to the river.

The sun had disappeared and a fiery rose afterglow was swelling up from the horizon into the dying summer sky. Sam looked up into the mellow beauty and thought how it contrasted with the ferment and disorder of the war.

Cash spoke over his shoulder to Skinner. 'I don't like being on this main road. Is this the only way?'

'We'll only be on it for about half a mile, Major. Once we're over the rise we can shoot off across country, I'm pretty sure. If everything's the same as it was earlier, the Germans should be over there and the Americans straight ahead beyond the hill somewhere.'

Cash raised his hand and waited for his men. 'I'm going to the top of the rise.' He took his field-glasses out and held his Tommy gun across his lap as he and Skinner sped up the slope.

Halfway up, Cash brought the bike to a screeching standstill.

There, looming over the rise not 300 yards away was the bulk of a lorry full of soldiers, quickly followed by another – and they were not American!

Skinner flinched. 'Oh shit! They've seen us!'

'Well of course! We're in the middle of the bloody road!'

Cash spun the motor bike around, tyres complaining and tore back down the hill shouting, 'Oh great, Skinner! Good scouting! So much for your Americans over the hill!'

Then Skinner let out another wail.

Ahead on the bitumen road past their motor bikes and bicycles, four more German lorries with armoured vehicles and tanks behind them, trundled inexorably towards the abandoned houses at the crossroads.

'Now we're hemmed in, front and back! It looks like a whole division of bloody Panzers.'

Skinner was shouting in Cash's ear. 'Hell, Major, I know the Yanks are just back there somewhere. Their front should be within half a mile of here, I'm certain. What the hell happened?'

'Good question, Skinner.'

His men were already charging into an apple orchard as Cash raced up to them. 'Panzers!' He jumped off his bike as soldiers began emerging in large numbers from the lorries and swarming out like bees towards the fleeing motor bikes. Cash shouted, 'Our only chance is the river!' And he and Skinner returned a burst of Tommy-gun fire while the others roared through the orchard wheeling in and out of the apple trees.

Sam swung round in the sidecar and using her good hand fired a volley at the first group of Germans.

Cash raced over to Sam and Matthew. 'Come on, move!' And those of his special forces who had been on bicycles now straddled the sidecars and kept firing at the Germans who were running down the road to the orchard.

Bullets hit tree trunks and burst upon branches as the Commandos continued their hectic ride through the apple trees; those in the sidecars were firing back at the Panzers and Cash was giving thanks that there had been no rain for days so that the ground was hard enough to allow the bikes free passage.

But the Panzers were emptying from the lorries in their scores as the motor cycles careered on down the gentle incline towards the water. From one orchard they crossed a track into another, and when they came to the river's edge they halted and the Commandos went into battle order behind their motor bikes.

The sky was darkening quickly now and the moon was already up as Cash turned to Sam, his eyes gleaming, his black lock perched on his brow. They stood close together on the riverbank. 'Into the water, Sammy! The current's flowing fast here. You're a top swimmer, even with one bad hand; it'll take you down to the American lines.'

Sam shook her head. 'No.'

'That's an order, Sammy. Go!'

'You can't order me, I'm not one of your men.' She grabbed his arm. 'I don't want to leave you, Cash.' Her throat hurt and tears stung her eyes. 'For God's sake, I—'

He gave a quick glance back to where the Germans, hundreds of them in a dark host, pressed through the apple trees. Then he rounded on her. 'I wish . . . Ah hell, m'lady, take good care of yourself.' And he pushed her straight into the river. Then swiftly lifted his thumb to Matt. 'And you, Lieutenant – after her. I expect you to see her to safety.'

Matt hesitated, peering at the other Commandos who

waited, battle fashion, ready to fire at the enemy who were now almost within range.

'But sir?'

'Get going!'

'Yes, sir,' he replied and directed a burst of fire at the enemy before he dived into the water.

'Now!' Cash yelled to his men. 'Give it to the bastards and you, Ludlow, jump into the river. I want each man to enter the river at thirty-second intervals. The rest of us will continue holding them off. It's getting darker by the minute and the way the current's running it should be sufficient to have you all downsteam out of range before the bastards get here.'

Ludlow grinned. 'Yes, sir!'

And Cash eased himself down beside Skinner as bullets spat off the front of the motor bikes and the forbidding mass of Germans swelled towards them.

'Love the dark,' Cash whispered to himself as he began to fire.

Sam pulled herself into the shallows and felt her feet sink into mud. She saw the dark shape of Matt a few yards behind her. There was the glow of a fire about a hundred yards away and the moon revealed trees ahead. Suddenly a voice shouted in English, 'Halt! Who goes there?'

'Friends!' Sam shouted in reply. 'British, let us come in, please.' She had left her Tommy gun behind on the river-bank but Matthew had managed to come downstream with his.

'Drop your weapons!' It was an American accent. 'Hands over your heads, move forward slowly.'

As Sam staggered in the mud towards the soldier she saw two more emerge behind him. 'God bless America,' she said as she reached him and sank down on the grass, her hands still over her head.

Within fifteen minutes after the first arrivals all the unit including Guy and Laurent had issued from the river. The only one missing was Cash.

Sam and Matt had done the explaining and dry clothes

had been found but Sam would not change; she stood down by the shallows watching the black water for her husband.

At first they thought they could hear gunfire coming from upriver, but that had faded and Matt now waded over to stand in the water beside her.

'Samantha, you should change your wet clothes.'

Sam shook her head. 'Not until he comes. Why is he so long?' She looked at the young man and he could see the whites of her eyes. 'What if he were captured. Oh God!'

Matt shook his head. 'I can't see the Major surrendering. He just wouldn't. It's not in his nature.'

That only made Sam shiver. The alternative was unthinkable. 'He made sure we all got away.'

Matt's voice lowered. 'Yes, that's how he is. He saved my life last September in Guernsey. I'd be dead or a prisoner now if it weren't for the Major. Look, it's pretty obvious you're in love with him.'

Sam took a deep breath and it trembled out of her. 'Is it? Well, I wish it were to him.'

She turned her gaze back to the water, scanning the river, praying, hoping. Another minute passed while Matt waited at her side. And then she saw it . . . a dark shape broke out of the moon's silver shimmer on the inky surface. It moved towards them.

'Oh God. Thank You.'

Cash was emerging and she began to struggle through the muddy water, her damaged hand lifting out, stretching in love towards him, her heart singing . . .

'Cash, my darling.'

He pushed his way out of the river and she pushed her way in. They met thigh-high in water and she reached him and hugged him, the river swirling around them as if encouraging her embrace. She kissed his soaked face.

'Now, now, m'lady, what's all this?'

'Oh Cash, it's you I love, I love you more than anyone.'

Cash blinked, water dripping from his chin in the moonlight. 'Ah hell, m'lady, you've never loved me. This isn't genuine.' His arms had remained at his sides and he began to move on by.

'Oh Cash, stop. Please listen to me.'

'No, m'lady, you listen to *me*. We're in a war and all this is playing on your feelings. It'd confuse anyone. You've been bloody tortured and I saved you. Sure, you're grateful. Come on, honey, let's not hurt each other any more. I'm different now. I'm not playing that game.' He waded on a few staggering steps past her and saw his men on the bank as Matt entered the river and moved towards him.

Now Sam's voice was caught in her throat and she still clung to him with her good hand as he trudged on, bringing her with him. 'Please, Cash, listen. It's not gratitude, it's real. It's you I think of when I hear sad songs. It's you I dream about and want to be with. Hell, I don't care what you've done, whether you've been a burglar or even a blasted highwayman! I love you so much it hurts.'

He looked round in the moonlight. His voice was weary. 'Sammy come on, we both know you love JB.'

'No, I don't. He's my brother! That's who he is and who I want him to be. No more, no less. Will you listen to me? It's you I want.'

Matt had reached them and Cash took hold of the young man's shoulder. 'Matt, old boy, I think I need to lean on you. I . . .' He blacked out and slid down into Matt's strong grasp.

Suddenly Sam saw the dark gluey substance on his back as he sank towards his lieutenant and she realised. 'Oh no! He's been shot!'

The other Commandos were surging around him and carrying him ashore and Sam stood knee-deep in the river suddenly all alone with a summer breeze at her back.

'Hell, Cash,' she said, tears glistening in her eyes. 'Why don't you ever listen to me?'

The following morning Cash woke on a stretcher bed in the American forward camp. He looked around and saw Sam, hair drawn back in a knot at the nape of her neck, her bandaged hand resting on her lap and a book in the other. She was backlit by the sun that streaked through the tent flap as she bent over him and he saw the tenderness in her expression.

'A surgeon took the bullet out of your back,' she smiled. 'You'll live.'

'Good. I was hoping for that diagnosis.'

'Matt'll be in shortly. He's making arrangements for our transfer across to the British sector.'

'Good. Back to work.'

Sam shook her head. 'I doubt you'll be fighting for a while. The war should be over by the time you're fit.'

He grinned. 'Just goes to show you still don't know me, m'lady.'

She touched his hair. 'Oh yes I do.'

'You know what, Sammy? I had a mighty strange dream last night.'

She was peering intently at him.

'I dreamt you said you loved me, and not JB.'

She shook her head and her eyes welled with tears. 'That was no dream. That's real. Now hear me for once. It's not gratitude or thanks, it's a fact. I think I knew it a long time ago, but the New Year's Day you came to my flat to tell me the truth and to say goodbye, hell, I was shocked and in disbelief, but when I got over it I knew, and I've been certain ever since.'

He was slow to smile. 'And JB?'

'He's wonderful. A wonderful brother and I love him. But I don't want him to be anything else.' She took a deep breath. 'Oh Cash, don't keep me in suspense like this. Please. I was jealous of Fleur. Please say you still love me. Cash, say it – please?'

He attempted to sit up and winced.

'Let me help you.' She took up two pillows with her good hand and made an effort to stack them behind him but with her bandaged fist it was not a great success. He was tilting sideways and she could not hold him. She tried to put her body between him and the floor but with his greater weight he was sliding and she was fumbling, and in amongst the movements his lips met hers. It was a long time before he lifted his mouth and when he did, he was grinning through his pain, the sun glinting on the edge of gold on his eye tooth. 'You know, m'lady, some things don't alter. I've always loved you, and I guess I always will.'

She was covering his face with kisses and he was tilting off the bunk. He groaned with pain but she was still kissing him as they collapsed in a heap.

'Ouch!'

He was on top of her, his black curl dangling, when Matt bent through the tent flap.

'Oh heck! Sorry!'

He began to retreat as both looked up from the ground and Cash called out. 'No, don't leave, Matt. I need you to help me up. My wife's pretty helpless with her bandaged hand.'

Matt shook his head. 'Wife? You mean you're married?'

'I do. But it took us a hell of a while to know it ourselves. Now help me up. I like being kissed but I can't stand the pain.'

'Yes, sir.'

Sam was lying on the grass laughing through her tears as Matt came in and lifted his Major back to bed. Cash caught Sam's eye over his Lieutenant's shoulder. 'Sammy, I once said, "Nothing good happens in daylight", but this morning might have altered my mind.'

175 miles away across the English Channel in London, Alex lifted the dead girl's head. She was about seven and her hair was fair and curly. Alex kissed her forehead and the child's blood smeared on her mouth. 'Goodbye, little one,' she whispered as two air-raid wardens came across the rubble with a stretcher.

'I'll carry this one,' Alex decided with a sigh.

The V1 had hit an infants' school and seventeen children between the ages of five and seven were dead.

The V1s, in German the *Vergeltungswaffe 1,* the 'Retaliation Weapon', had begun to hit London on 12 June, 1944. They were in fact a pilotless monoplane and Hitler's secret weapon to attempt to cower Britons once again. Londoners had quickly come to call them 'buzz bombs' and the rule of thumb was that if an engine of the V1 was still going when it travelled overhead, those below were safe. It was when it cut out and began to drop to earth that it was time to take shelter.

Alex sighed as she saw the air-raid warden pulling another arm from the heap of stones and mortar in front of her.

Things had been quiet in London for a long time and with the Allied landing in Normandy the whole country had been optimistic. And now this.

She walked back to the ambulance with the child in her arms and handed her over to Sue the driver who had delivered Alex to the bomb scene.

Sue shook her head. 'Makes you cry.'

'Yes, it does. There are only three alive. Shirley's already driven them off to hospital.' Alex could do no more. 'I'll head back to base.'

'Right. I think we need a stiff drink tonight.'

'Mmm.' Alex climbed in beside her and the ambulance drew away.

She and Sue did have the drink that evening in the Hare and Hounds on the next corner to the ambulance station, but at 7 p.m. Alex said good night and she walked home in the evening light. She came along Kensington Church Street and halted for a moment looking in the window of an antiques shop and eyeing a splendid piece of Minton Celadon with cherubs and winged figures encircling a wide shallow vase. She wondered if anyone bought antiques these days. Spending money on artworks seemed trivial when innocent children were dying because the Nazis wanted to rule the world.

She strolled on, trying to lift her spirits, and was soon into the High Street, and not long after, walking down her own road towards the white Victorian house she shared with Kerry. She thought of JB – he was never far from her mind – and decided she would write to him tonight. She wondered if any of her letters ever found their way into his hands in the prison camp.

As she neared her building she saw someone sitting on the stone steps that led up to her door.

She did not think much of that at first but as she drew closer she saw the dark blue of the clothes he wore. Was it an RAF uniform? Suddenly she was walking faster and then she was running. The man stood up as he saw her coming and she realised who it was.

Emotion flooded to her throat, her eyes filled with tears. Her heart was bursting with love.

And as if all the gates of heaven opened along with the opening of his arms she shouted, 'JB! JB!' and ran along the pavement, tears springing to her eyes. He was here! It was a miracle and he was here!

She ran straight into his arms with the heady summer breeze at her back as he lifted her and covered her face with kisses.

And then she heard the words she had prayed every night for years to hear, 'Alex, my darling, how I've missed you. How I love you.'

Chapter Fifty

Four months later Cash sat on the verandah of the military convalescent hospital on the outskirts of Portsmouth. He was to be discharged in twenty-four hours and would rejoin his unit in ten days' time. His boys were fighting in Holland and he was keen to be with them. Even though Paris had been liberated and Allied troops had pushed on through Belgium and towards Germany, the war was not over yet. He had been reading about paratroops in Arnhem, where it seemed the fighting was pretty tough. He let the *Daily Mail* slip from his fingers and peered up at the sky. The sun flirted with making an appearance through dark clouds. He was expecting Sammy and they would probably take a walk if it did not rain.

Dreamily he eyed the bunched clouds, and glancing down to the perimeter hedge he noticed a man in RAF uniform striding across the grass towards him.

With surprise and pleasure he rose to his feet as John Baron reached the stone steps, mounted them and walked along the verandah. Smiling widely, Cash put out his hand to his visitor and John Baron halted in front of him, took a step forward and punched him solidly in the mouth!

Cash reeled backwards and fell into his chair.

'Hell, JB?' He made no attempt to rise as he nursed his chin and a tiny blood spot appeared on his lip. 'You could've broken my jaw and I'm a wounded man.'

John Baron shook his head. 'You're not wounded. You're leaving tomorrow.'

Cash blinked as he dabbed his mouth with his finger. 'I suppose I know what that was for.'

'I'm bloody sure you do.'

'So Sammy's told you everything?'

'She has.'

Cash opened his mouth and wriggled his jaw. 'Funny, you know, I've always thought you might sock me.'

'I should bloody well flog you. All those years you held out on me. What sort of a friend were you?'

'Not a very good one.'

'Damn right! Lie after lie . . . burglary. It would have done you good to have gone to gaol.'

Cash stood up and pushed his chin forward. 'So do you want to hit me again?'

John Baron shook his head. 'You're not worth it.'

Cash extended his hand. 'JB, I'm really happy to see you. Hell, it's been too long.'

John Baron stood regarding him as Cash kept his hand out. 'Look, I've only said this once before in my life, JB, and that was to Sammy. Now I'm saying it to you. I'm sorry. Believe me, I mean it. I let you and Sam suffer for years and I wouldn't do it if I had my time again. War does that to you. Changes you. Makes you able to distinguish the valuable. My single excuse is that I loved Sammy and wanted her for myself.'

His palm was still extended.

His visitor said nothing, he simply contemplated it.

'JB, you're the best friend I ever had, other than a little bloke in Sydney I've got to look after. Listen, I've given up all that stuff I used to do. I've matured.' He met John Baron's eyes and winked.

John Baron took a long deep breath and could not help but smile. Cash was incorrigible.

Slowly, very slowly, he raised his arm and stretched out his hand. They touched palms. 'Matured – really? Well, time will tell about that.'

They stood there eying each other. Suddenly Cash stepped forward and hugged his friend hard. 'Heck mate, I've missed you.' Then he moved to arm's length and felt his jaw. 'You pack a hell of a punch.'

John Baron nodded. 'I'd remember that if I were you.'

Chapter Fifty-one

Tuesday, 8 May, 1945: VE Day – Victory in Europe

The Prime Minister, Winston Churchill, stood waving his right hand high in the air, his left resting on the drape covering the front of the balcony on Buckingham Palace. A roar lifted from the tumultuous crowd in the forecourt and along Pall Mall as Union Jacks flapped in the breeze and Winston made the Victory sign with his fingers.

To his right stood Queen Elizabeth and to his left King George V. They had paid him the great compliment of flanking him on either side and allowing him to be the centre of attention. Princess Elizabeth in uniform stood next to her mother and Margaret Rose next to her father. Winston turned to the King and smiled. The monarch and his wife had worked ceaselessly for the war effort and the people of Britain and the Empire recognised it.

Another roar rose from the crowds below and 'Land of Hope and Glory' lifted spontaneously and resounded along Pall Mall. The unconditional surrender of the Nazis saw the manifestation of an outburst of delight across the globe. Jubilation echoed through the streets of London, across Great Britain, around the liberated countries of Europe and over the world to USA, Africa, India, Australia, New Zealand and beyond. Democracy had prevailed.

The people were weary of war, worn with nearly six years of strict rationing and austerity, of seeing their loved ones and friends die. They had staked their entire existences on fighting for freedom: how truly they deserved their triumph! Winston's eyes gleamed with unshed tears as he allowed himself this moment of pure joy.

He had broadcast a Victory in Europe message to the world earlier in the day and a ceasefire was in operation on all fronts in Europe. Japan was yet to be subdued and the Pacific War continued with the Australians, Americans, British and other Dominion troops still engaged, so even though his heart was triumphant, it was with mixed emotions that he viewed this joyous day.

Winston had seen the telegrams and messages which had begun to arrive in their thousands even before he had left 10 Downing Street this morning: marvellous touching messages from countries everywhere. One from Anthony Eden he recalled: *Without you this day could not have been*.

Yes, he had believed in himself, as if his whole life had been a preparation to defeat Hitler, and he had believed in the British people and in the Empire and the Commonwealth: but his War Cabinet and his Chiefs of Staff had been tireless too: Air Chief Marshal Charles Portal, Admiral Dudley Pound and after his death Admiral Andrew Cunningham and the man who had become his great friend – Field Marshal Alan Brooke even though there were many times they had disagreed. For they all knew, every decision made had not proved correct, but human beings were not infallible and man had no crystal ball. The Allies had finally cowed the Nazis and the Reichstag was in ruins as it deserved to be. Germany and the European Axis powers were in disarray.

Hitler, unable to face up to defeat, had blamed the German people, saying they had betrayed him and that they had proved unequal to his leadership: all typical of such a malformed mind. His death had been craven: he and his mistress had committed suicide on 29 April.

As the throng below in the Mall cheered again, Winston thought of his friend, Franklin Roosevelt, who had collapsed during a sitting for his portrait and died swiftly only twenty-six days before. His death had been at the supreme climax of the European War and had come as a massive shock to Winston. He had felt Roosevelt's passing as an irreparable loss; theirs was a lasting friendship forged in the fire of war and Winston had conceived an admiration for him as a statesman and been confident in him as a true friend.

Roosevelt's brilliant idea of Lend-Lease – though initially opposed by isolationist opinion in the USA – had allowed the President to sell, transfer, exchange, lease or lend equipment and armaments to Great Britain when she and the Empire had stood alone after the collapse of Europe. For an entire year and a half they had fought against Germany and the Axis powers, until the American entry into the war in December 1941.

'. . . In Franklin Roosevelt there died the greatest American friend we have ever known and the greatest champion of freedom who has ever brought help and comfort from the New World to the Old.'

Suddenly at Winston's side the Queen spoke. 'What a wonderful day, and we've all waited for it for so long.' She looked around at the Prime Minister and her voice softened. 'Thank you.'

Winston smiled and raised his hand in the air again as the cheering continued to lift from the Mall. 'I think I shall go out amongst the people this afternoon in Whitehall.'

The King was enthusiastic. 'Yes, do. There are tens of thousands who will want to touch you, Prime Minister.'

They remained on the balcony as the crowds below continued to grow and when at last the Prime Minister and the Royal Family left and moved inside there were photographs taken in the palace with the War Cabinet and Chiefs of Staff.

Later Winston did walk through the rejoicing people in Whitehall and hands touched him and voices praised him and individuals were overjoyed to be near him. In the afternoon he stood on the balcony of the Ministry of Health with the Union Jack draped in front of him and the members of the War Cabinet around him and as the day passed, the capital echoed with continuing celebrations of victory.

And late that night after all the excitement around him had quietened and his colleagues had disappeared, Winston found himself alone as the unique day faded.

He sat smoking a cigar thinking of Clementine. She was in Russia at the invitation of the Soviet Government and the Soviet Red Cross, on a five-week goodwill tour in recognition of her Red Cross Aid to Russia Fund which had given so much relief to the Russian people. It was strange timing for her not to be at his side.

Winston lifted the whisky and soda in front of him and spoke aloud to himself. 'To you, my love, Clemmie, I miss you most of all, today of all days.'

He rose and walked to the window placing his glass on the sill. He studied the back of his hand where the veins linked in blue-green pattern across it. It was an aging hand. But he had needed age – age and experience of life – to wage the long struggle he had finally won.

These war years would always be with him: each battle and stratagem would stay with him for ever. All the judgements made and defeats taken and the successes built upon; the endless studying of maps, the conferences with leaders and Chiefs of Staff and the flights under assumed names to the various fronts; even the personal concerns like his son Randolph's narrow escape from death when his aircraft crashed in Yugoslavia.

Six years of perpetual vigilance.

He gazed at the street where the triumphant crowds continued their revelry throughout the city even though a gentle misty rain was falling. The tiny drops on the pane in front of him covered the glass like the haunting suspicion that had been forming in his mind for years. Even on this day of overt glee he was oppressed by forebodings about Joe Stalin. His darling Clemmie was in Russia and would come home soon, but he knew that in the weeks and months to come Stalin would greedily annex 'as payment for his part in the victory' as much of Europe as he could. Winston was aware that in accepting Russia as his ally he had 'joined hands with the devil' to defeat Hitler; but it had been the only way. Europe was still in crisis and needed to be rebuilt; the millions of displaced persons had to be helped, there was much to do, and he was deeply concerned for the future of countries like Czechoslovakia, Hungary, Poland and the Baltics. He knew Stalin wanted them. They would simply slip from one ogre to another.

He took a rumbling deep breath. But for this moment he

must indulge in the glorious satisfaction that Hitler's depraved 'Mein Kampf' was over.

Winston finished his Scotch, put out his cigar and moved across to his desk where he picked up his book of Victorian portraits and opened it at his favourite painting of Gordon of Khartoum. He read again what he had written in lead pencil beside it many years before: *The whole fury and might of the enemy must soon be turned upon him.*

'Well,' he said aloud with the glimmer of a smile, 'it was and we defeated it!'

Then he closed the book and went with victorious and solid steps to bed.

Across London in Audley Street Alex and Sam followed Amelia and George up the front steps of the block of flats, and as George paused in the darkness and fumbled in his pockets for the keys, the singing of 'Run Rabbit Run' floated to them from the South Street corner where a party was still in progress. George began to hum along with the singers and even though a fine rain was falling the mood of glee could not be dampened.

They had spent the afternoon and night in canteens: American, Canadian, New Zealand, Indian, Australian and South African, and at each one they had been welcomed along with soldiers, sailors, airmen and ordinary Londoners. In the Canadian canteen they had become caught up with two Bermudan soldiers who had been wounded in Holland and were convalescing, and they had all danced and sung and listened to entertainers but they had lost them at the Indian canteen and now as George found the keys and unlocked the door, Amelia's voice sounded a little husky from a night of singing and shouting. 'Half past three and I don't feel a bit tired. What a day it's been.'

George bent down and picked up a *Daily Mirror* newspaper which had been lying on the table in the hall. The headlines shouted VE-DAY! PUBLIC HOLIDAY TODAY AND TOMORROW.

Sam yawned. 'I think we'll be off to bed. I'm going round to SOE headquarters in the morning to see Vera and

Martin. They'll be working with the Red Cross to try and find our missing agents. I want to help.'

'Yes, I'm for bed too,' Alex agreed. 'I have to catch the train home to Castlemere at some stage of the day.'

George grunted a cheerful good night and headed for the stairs to the basement flat.

Amelia shrugged. 'In that case, as you're all deserting me, I've no option.' She called after her husband, 'I'll be down in a minute, love,' then she turned back to Sam. 'I suppose you'll be leaving us soon, now that you're back with your husband and this lot's finally come to an end.'

Sam smiled. 'Yes, but it'll take months before Cash is demobbed and I want to help find as many of our missing operatives as I can, so we'll be around for a while.'

Amelia shook her head. 'To think you were a spy, love.'

'A secret agent really, Amelia.'

The landlady shook her head. 'That's a spy to me. Dangerous and all it was and I picked up on it. I just knew you were doin' something terribly brave – you ask George. I used to say to him, "Whatever she's doin' it's secret and dangerous."' She sighed. 'I'll miss you terribly.'

Sam kissed her. 'And I'll miss you, but we can write, and who knows? You might come out to Australia and visit us.' She delved into her handbag and brought out the little ebony cat with the minute gold chain around its neck. She smiled at Amelia. 'It's been almost everywhere with me.'

'Oh love, I hope it'll continue to keep you safe for me.' Amelia looked as if she might cry and Alex stepped forward and slapped them both affectionately on the shoulders. 'Now now, let's not get maudlin. Nothing's going to happen for a while yet.'

Half an hour later Sam and Alex were in pyjamas, teeth cleaned, faces scrubbed and hair brushed. They slipped into bed and Sam put out the lamp as Alex spoke. 'I'm so happy we're going to be sisters-in-law.'

'Me too.'

'I wonder exactly where JB and Cash are right now?'

'They're probably still out celebrating with their mates. You know what men are like.'

They knew Cash was with his unit in Germany and JB was a Station Commander in Hampshire.

'Yes, I think at last I do. I can't wait to see JB.'

'I can't wait to see both of them.' Sam turned on her side in the darkness and lifted her right hand from under the cover to rest it on the sheet. Her four fingernails had grown back but she would never have a thumbnail. When the Gestapo had ripped it out, the bed of the nail had been permanently damaged. She had already had two operations on it and it ached from time to time, but hell she was alive. She rubbed it gently as she thought of how she had altered. She would be thirty this year and she loved her husband with a deep abiding feeling. She knew she would go to the grave wanting and needing Cash. JB would always be a hero to her and she would always love him too, but her desire for him had died long ago, when she had turned from a girl into a woman; and she felt solace in the knowledge that Alex was the right wife for him.

Sam smiled as she felt Alex snuggle down into the bed beside her and whisper, 'I know I'm going to love Australia and Haverhill. I can picture riding the trail along Teviot Brook and I can see the cattle grazing. I can even imagine the sudden summer storms and the way the kookaburras laugh in the gum trees.'

Sam gave a tired giggle. 'Stop. You're making me homesick and you haven't even been there yet.'

'Do you know, Mum's already talking about bringing Dad out to Haverhill in a year or two? It's all so exciting. But I think we'll get married here before we leave. We don't want to wait.'

Sam answered in a slow, sleepy voice. 'Good idea.' She yawned. 'You'll love it at Haverhill. It's a bit too hot sometimes, but heck, that's all right. And they'll all love you . . . I can see Mum now fussing to make sure everything's just so before we get there. And Ledgie'll be telling everyone what . . . to . . . do . . . ' Her words faded.

Alex listened to her friend's measured breathing and said, 'Good night, Sammy,' but the woman beside her did not reply even though she was not quite yet asleep. She was dreamily visualising Babette, her dark hair caught up in a pink ribbon, the way she had seen her the last time in her kitchen outside Évreux. How she prayed that she and Christophe and André were safe. She would do what she could to find out.

Two months later in July 1945 the public of Great Britain went to the polls for the first time in ten years.

The result* was known on 26 July, and that morning just before dawn, Winston woke with a stabbing pain, as if in ominous foreboding. By noon it was clear that his Conservative Government had been defeated by Attlee's Socialists. Clemmie, who had returned from Russia some weeks before, and who, as usual, was attempting optimism for her beloved husband, took his hand at lunch and said, 'It may well be a blessing in disguise.'

Winston looked her in the eye. 'At the moment it seems quite effectively disguised.'

On 14 August, 1945 Japan surrendered after the Americans dropped two atomic bombs: the first, a uranium-based bomb, on Hiroshima and the second, a plutonium-based bomb, on Nagasaki.

The Second World War was completely over.

The entire free world and many of the vanquished, released after years of suffering, rejoiced.

One month later on 15 September, Douglas Bader stomped across the airfield at North Weald and slapped John Baron on the back. 'So, you old bugger, we survived,' Douglas said as he wrapped a blue polka-dotted scarf round his neck.

John Baron grinned. 'Yes, Dogsbody, and I beat you home as well. You had to wait until you were freed.'

'You were just lucky,' Douglas rejoined. 'The blasted Goons must have been asleep the day you walked out.'

They were soon joined by Air Chief Marshal 'Stuffy' Dowding and members of the elite Few like John Ellis,

---

* Result of July 1945 election: see *Endnotes*, p. 815.

Dennis Crowley-Milling, 'Hawk-Eye' Wells, and Bob Stanford Tuck. They milled around and chatted and then Bader called, 'Let's go!' and they moved to their aircraft. John Baron could not help but think how sedate it all was in comparison to the days when they had raced and climbed into the cockpit, hearts accelerating.

The Victory flypast over London was to celebrate peace, 15 September being the fifth anniversary of what was known as the climax of the Battle of Britain. Bader led the procession of 300 aircraft and they took off into a cloud-covered sky and sailed across the rooftops of London while hundreds of thousands cheered from below.

John Baron remembered the boys who had not lived to see this day, and Twig loomed in his mind. He imagined his friend bouncing out of his Hurricane, a broad grin on his face after they had come back from their practice run over the North Sea when they had emptied their machine guns into the waves; the first time John Baron had ever flown a Spitfire.

He could not recollect the exact conversation but he could easily recall Twig's cool Southern drawl and it had gone something like:

'Hey JB, how did the Spitfire handle?'

'Bloody beautiful.'

'Looks an absolute dream.'

'It is.'

'Must say I loved killing the North Sea! You bet!'

Twig, full of life, the Florida boy who fought with the Royal Air Force. John Baron took a deep breath as he peered across the grey sky to where Douglas's Spitfire led them through the haze and he said softly, 'Twig, wherever you are, old man, I hope you're still whistling "Dixie".'

Later they had drinks and John Baron left Douglas to spend time with Tommy Hopkins, Henry Garner and Lou Edmont who, to his delight, were all there, but it was too soon to talk of the war and the dogfights; emotions ran high and memories were too recent. That was for the years to come when the doldrums of peace gave them the desire to relive the Battle of Britain.

On this day they soon trailed off, but not before Douglas had booked John Baron for a game of golf at Wentworth Golf Club the following week.

'I'm determined to get my handicap down below five,' Douglas stated, arms akimbo, as they parted.

John Baron smiled. 'Douglas, legs or no legs, if you're determined . . . You will!'

He did.

Chapter Fifty-two

Sydney, early December, 1946

Cash rolled away from Sammy's naked body and her hand caressed the scar on his back as he sat up and slipped off the bed.

He turned back and brushed her lips with his. 'I won't be long, m'lady.'

Her fingers toyed with his forelock. 'I'll be waiting, and tell Danny I'm all for it.'

'I will.' He took her hand and kissed her thumb and its missing nail. 'I love you, Sam.'

Sam's eyes filled with tears and she sat up and hugged him. 'How lucky we are to have survived.'

An hour later Cash entered Danny's dilapidated dwelling behind Sydney Stadium where he had been so many times prior to the war.

Danny was so thrilled to see Cash that for the first minute he could not speak and when at last he could, he blurted out, 'I gave up the fags, Cash!'

'Good on you, mate. I knew you could do it.'

Danny poured a beer and kept admiring Cash's uniform, and running his fingertip across the Victoria Cross ribbon. 'Jees, Cash, ya make a bloke so proud! Ya're a flamin' hero! Fair dinkum ya are. Guess I always knew ya would be but.'

'Dan, Sammy and I are back together – permanently, I reckon.'

The little man grinned. 'I knew that girl'd come to her senses one fine day.'

'She's been a brave woman, Dan. I'll tell you all about

it in time but she did a hell of a lot more than most people could even comprehend. She received four medals, one from France. She's done more than her bit.'

Dan shook his head in wonder. 'Sounds like medals aren't enough.'

Cash met his friend's eyes. 'You're no fool, Danny. There's no way they are. No way in this world.' He paused in thought for a moment then his voice lightened. 'You remember when I left you to join up I said we'd take a cruise on a ship after the war?'

'Sure do.'

'Well, we will. But first I want you to leave here and come and live with us in Queensland.'

The little man's mouth formed a silent O.

'Sammy and I are going home to her parents' place. It's a big property with lots of horses.'

Danny grinned, showing a broken tooth. 'I like horses, Cash.'

'You can ride all day and fish and help me put up a house. We're thinking of building on the rise up from the brook not far from the main homestead, with a nice little place for you right on the water's edge.'

Danny frowned. 'True?'

'True.'

'Ya mean ya really want me to live with ya, real proper like . . . Like a . . . relative?'

'Yes.'

He pondered a moment. 'So we're droppin' all the dodgy stuff then?'

'Yes, we are.'

'All of it?'

'Yes.'

'For ever?'

'Yes.'

'Shit.'

'I know, but it's time, Dan. And you remember how I said the Queensland cops were after me?'

'Yeah. It's why ya joined up. To give the buggers the slip.'

'Yes. Well, mate, I have to face up to it. I'm going to see the police in Brisbane after I'm finally demobbed here. But first I want you and Sammy to pack up all your belongings and go ahead of me to Queensland.'

Danny frowned and studied his hands and Cash took hold of his arm. 'Don't you want to come with me, mate?'

'Jees, Cash, it ain't that. But are ya sure Sammy wants me?'

'Bloody certain. I can tell you it's a menagerie up there; all sorts of people live at Haverhill, that's what it's called. You'll fit in like a charm. As well as the main household there's the Birnum family who reside in a cottage by a place called Cockatoo Hill and the sons do the horsebreaking and milking. You'll like those blokes and be able to help them. Sam's parents are steadfast and my oldest friend JB's the greatest bloke alive. We three can go down to Brisbane now and then for the fights. Nobody's stuck-up and even an old girl called Ledgie who comes on a bit cranky has a heart of gold.'

'Jees, mate.'

'Now come on, what do you say?'

Danny wiped the corner of his eye and sniffed. 'Sounds real beaut. Gawd, Cash, I'd go to the moon wiv ya and that's a fact.'

Cash stood. 'Then that's settled.'

Three weeks later, Brisbane, Christmas Eve, 9 a.m.

Cash entered the Central Police Station.

He strode in and stood with his palms resting on the counter as the senior Constable on duty eyed his uniform and insignia. 'Yes, Colonel? What can I do for you?'

'I'm here in reference to the death of a man in 1936.'

'Oh, now who might that be?'

'Dexter Wilde.'

'Just a minute.' He left the desk and passed a young Constable at a typewriter who watched him go and then brought his gaze back to Cash.

Minutes lapsed before the Sergeant reappeared with a

solid middle-aged man in plain clothes. He shook Cash's extended hand. 'I'm Detective Sergeant Jones.'

'Cashman Slade, how do you do?'

'Would you come this way please, Colonel.' They walked together down a corridor and entered an empty office where a window onto the street revealed a view of people passing by. Cash remained standing and Jones crossed to a cabinet in the sunlight near the window.

'The man you mentioned to the Sergeant was named Wilde, you say?'

'Yes, Dexter Wilde.'

'And the year was 1936?'

'Yes.'

The detective leafed through a drawer of files, lifted one out and opened it on top of the cabinet. He made a cursory inspection of the case and gazed back at Cash, regarding the deep magenta ribbon along with the others on his uniform. 'Is that the Victoria Cross you're wearing, sir?'

Cash nodded. 'Mmm.'

Jones glanced down at the papers on the cabinet top. 'So in regard to the Dexter Wilde case, what is it, Colonel?'

Cash stared at the detective. 'I believe I'm wanted for questioning about his death.'

Detective Sergeant Jones observed his visitor silently for a second or two. 'If you'll excuse me, Colonel, I'd like to familiarise myself a little with this before we continue.'

Cash nodded. 'Of course.'

The Sergeant took the file and left the room while Cash walked to the window and watched the street. A woman aged about forty with dark wavy hair to her shoulders passed by carrying a chubby girl infant in a floral dress and floppy hat. The mother had a comely face with strong dark eyebrows and the child appeared well fed and cared for. He regarded them, thinking how lucky they were to live here in Australia which had been virtually unaffected by the ravages of the war. He thought of the malnourished barefooted children and adults he had seen in the streets of Europe.

He remained there observing the vehicles and the

passers-by and gazing at the shoe shop opposite with Christmas decorations in the window. He thought of Sammy. She knew he was here this morning. Cash had finally told her about the death of Wilde a few weeks ago in Sydney when she was with him before his demobilisation.

She had been fearful for him and Cash had kissed her and said, 'Sammy, it was accidental. Wilde pulled the knife on me. I must go to the police and face up to whatever happens.'

The door opened behind him and Cash turned to see Jones enter. The Detective Sergeant had read enough of the case to know that Wilde was a seamy sort of character. He had been a known womaniser and there were two females named in the case who, when interviewed after his death, alleged he had raped them. Another thing was that the knife which killed him was in fact his own. It had DW etched in the handle and the woman who was at his house the night he died, recognised it as his. There had been apparent signs of a fight and it appeared Wilde and another person had rolled on the ground. All of which made Detective Sergeant Jones conclude that Wilde had pulled his knife on his adversary during the struggle. Hell, his guess would be that the man whom Wilde fought that night was probably a boyfriend of some woman Wilde had come on to.

The event had occurred over ten years ago and the two policemen who had been working on the case had joined the army and both been killed in New Guinea in 1942. He had known them – they had been right good blokes, Tommy Noble and Ron Seymour. Hell, there were so many gone! It was a completely different world from the one it was before the war.

He faced the Colonel opposite and contemplated his insignia and ribbons. The emblem on his uniform was that of the Special Air Service. He knew about it because he had studied medals and insignia and was teaching his son to identify them. The Colonel wore the Victoria Cross and the Distinguished Service Order and bar, as well as the

French Légion d'Honneur. Shit! He was a bloody hero and no mistake! It was a great honour to have him in the station.

He threw down the file on a desk, and his voice was matter-of-fact. 'This case is closed, Colonel.'

He extended his hand and Cash crossed the room and took it, meeting the Sergeant's eyes with a frank expression. 'When did it close?'

Jones hesitated a few moments, looking directly back at Cash. 'It closed when the two blokes working on it were killed by the Japs on the Kokoda Trail.'

Cash nodded. 'I see. And there's no plan to re-open it?'

'None. It's marked *Reasonable Assumption Death Accidental During a Struggle*. So if that was good enough for the two blokes working on it, then that's good enough for me.'

Cash continued to hold the Sergeant's hand for the space of another three or four seconds and as he did so Jones asked, 'Are you staying in the Special Air Service?'

Cash shook his head and released the policeman's hand. 'Demobbed in London two months ago and finally out of the army here, forty-eight hours ago. Though strange to say they're already asking me to rejoin.'

Jones could understand that; he suspected that men like this might be hard to find. 'Well, Colonel, it's not every day I get to meet a real hero. It's been a pleasure to have you in the station.'

'Thanks, Sergeant.'

Detective Sergeant Jones crossed to the door and opened it. 'You know the way out, Colonel. Good luck and a very Merry Christmas.'

Cash nodded. 'And to you. Goodbye.'

As Cash rode off the main bitumen road onto the dirt surface that led towards Haverhill it was close to three in the afternoon and the summer heat was dissipated by a strong breeze that swept down from Mount French across Boonah and along Teviot Brook.

Breathing the warm air under a dazzling sky he bumped along on the motor bike he had bought from Taylor & Son in Fortitude Valley after his visit to the police. He remembered the other Harley Davidson he and JB had owned together and how he had repaid JB for his half after his father had gone broke. And he thought of all the nights Cashman Slade had appropriated other people's goods. Well, the war had cured him of all that!

How differently he saw everything: what had been important before was no longer important, and what happened on earth could only be described as bizarre; none of it made sense. He had seen the finest die, and many of the less fine, live. None of it was equitable, nothing was predictable. He thought of Matt Fleming and their farewell on the Southampton docks as he and Sammy set sail for Australia. Thank heaven Matt made it through. But what of the others – his boys in Malaya? He saw Jack Taber, saw him sipping Billy tea in the jungle in his brigand's outfit; saw Dunne and Carvolt, Carter and Dale. Gone, dead – and for what? For the Allies to rebuild Germany and Japan and for it all to be forgotten in fifty or a hundred years.

But that was how it went on this third planet from the sun; the children never understood the previous generation's suffering. He laughed into the air rushing across his face. 'Hell, you can't take any of it seriously!' he shouted to the open road. 'I reckon there's some nutcase out there in a universal asylum who dictates what happens down here.'

He laughed loudly again and the sound was lost on the open country road as he bounced along.

At the same time John Baron sat facing Benjamin in the study at Haverhill. John Baron had just told his father he knew the truth about his birth. He had related how he had learnt it from Harriet in the first instance and then from Antoinette. He revealed meeting his real mother in France and had given his father Antoinette's letter to read as he took out her gold ring and placed it before them on the desk.

Though at first surprised and shocked, Benjamin had

803

listened calmly to John Baron's extended tale. He had remained silent until after he read Antoinette's letter, then he had folded it and placed it down on his desk and looked his son in the eye. 'It's hard for me to believe she didn't die. I would never have left her if I'd known.'

John Baron leant forward confidentially. 'I know that and she knew it too.'

'In her letter she suggested you should not tell me – but you have.'

'Dad, I thought about it and analysed it and I've told you now because you deserve to know. It wouldn't be right to hide it from you.'

Ben sighed. 'She gave you to me to bring up as my own.'

'I know.'

'It's a lot to digest, son.'

'I understand that, Dad, and I know why you and Mum and Wakefield and Ledgie kept the truth from me. You were doing it for me. I'm completely aware it was done out of love.'

Ben did not speak, he simply nodded and rose from his chair and walked to the window. John Baron followed him and they stood there side by side in the glaring sun as a magpie swooped down and landed on the verandah beyond. They watched it hop along the rail, its black and white plumage shining, its head darting up and down.

John Baron spoke softly. 'She was a beautiful person and in the end she died for me, Dad.'

'Yes, son, she did, and it makes me wonder what this human life's all about. Why she had to live all those years without you and only have you in her life so fleetingly at the end. Whole damn thing's a mystery. You know, I can visualise her now as I last saw her, her lovely face pallid, and ill unto death, as I thought.' Ben studied his son as the brazen Queensland light rested in his fair hair and brought it to gleaming. He shook his head. 'And you say that Sam and Cash and Alex all know everything?'

'Yes, Dad, they do.'

'I see. Well, perhaps all this was meant to be though I'm still staggered by it.'

'Of course, Dad, I understand.'

'I'll tell Wakefield for he'll accept it just like the great friend he's always been.' He cleared his throat and added, 'Though I won't inform your mother or Ledgie. I think it would be best to allow them to go on believing that you and Sam know nothing, if you understand what I mean.'

John Baron did; completely. 'Yes, Dad, I agree. They wouldn't take it quite the same way as you and Uncle Wake.'

At that statement, Ben gave the suggestion of a smile. 'True. I don't like to keep things from your mother as you know, but I think this is the exception.' He seemed to study the magpie out on the verandah rail as he lifted his hand to John Baron's shoulder and rested it there. 'Your real father was my dearest friend. I went to France at his behest. I brought you up as mine believing I did right by him. Your real father was the best sort of man there is.'

John Baron's eyes filled with tears. 'No, Dad, you're my real father. I've had a long, long time to think, day after day in the prison camp and almost every day since. I've waited until we were here face-to-face and I want to tell you one thing. I love you and Mum just as much as I ever did, even more if it's possible. You're the most wonderful parents a man could ever have.'

A tear broke over Ben's eyelid and slipped down his cheek.

'And Dad, I remember ten years ago you said to me that whenever we were alone in this study I was always telling you I was off somewhere. Well, this time I'm telling you I'm home to stay.'

Ben could not stop the tears from continuing down his cheeks and he took his son in his arms and drew him in close to his heart. 'Ah my boy, those are the words I've longed to hear.'

They held each other for an extended time while the magpie continued his dance along the railing and then abruptly propelled himself skywards at the sound of Sammy's voice rising staccato-like from the front verandah.

'Cash is here! Everybody! Cash is here!'

* * *

805

Cash had turned in the front gate past the green and white painted Haverhill sign and smiled to himself. It would be a good life here running the property with JB. It was what they both needed: days in the sun with the smell of the eucalyptus in their nostrils and the wide sky above: no bastard shooting at you and no risk of dying before sundown! And the nights out here were glorious! He looked forward to long walks after dinner in the purple shadows, embraced by the bush smells and the night breeze. Hell, he looked forward to just running through the bush at night. Just to run without danger for a change – now that would be great.

No doubt as time went by Sammy would want to work again, perhaps with one of the magazines, but she swore all she wanted to do for a year or two was be his wife. She reckoned she had experienced enough excitement for the rest of her life.

And Sam liked Alex. Their friendship was solid, had been moulded in dark unhappy times when they had consoled one another and brought cheer to one another. Cash had met Alex first in England during his convalescence after being shot. He liked the fact that she looked a little like Sam, made them seem more like sisters. The other thing Cash appreciated about Alex was her uncompromising manner. She did not prevaricate – and to Cash, who for years had embraced mendacity and fabrication, she was a semaphore of truth and it truly fascinated him!

He was riding through the avenue of poinciana trees when he saw Sam. She had been sitting on the verandah waiting and she sprang up and shouted before she jumped down the steps and came running towards him, her floral skirt fluttering around her long brown legs. A dog he did not know barked and ran with her and then he recognised dear old Tess, the kelpie, making her way slowly down the steps wagging her tail; she must be at least seventeen.

He brought the motor bike to a halt and reached out for Sammy.

Her eyes were concerned. 'How did it go?'

'The case is closed,' he said, kissing her lips.

Relief poured over her features. 'Thank God.'

He climbed off the Harley Davidson and stood on the carpet of fallen vermilion blossoms under one of the poincianas, when into his vision, issuing out onto the verandah, came a wonderful eclectic assembly of his in-laws and his friends. Constance held the hand of eleven-year-old Storm who was dressed in pale pink. Wakefield welcomed him. *'Tu es enfin de retour! Je te souhaite la bienvenue.'* Veena and Crenna supported Ledgie between them to help her down the front steps while along the side verandah emerged JB and Benjamin waving.

As they all hurried to meet him, a golf ball landed and rolled to his feet, and Alex, five iron brandished high, appeared around the side of the house with Danny. The little man was carrying a bag of clubs and when he saw Cash he dropped them and ran forward shouting, 'Jees, mate, we bin waitin' for ya all day!'

Cash hugged him with his right arm as he took hold of Storm in his left and kissed her. And as Ledgie reached the newcomer she wagged her forefinger. 'What about me?'

'You're as beautiful as ever.' He lifted her from the ground in an embrace and kissed her too.

'Put me down. You're as brazen as ever.'

Everyone laughed and the dogs barked, and Storm, excited by the wonderful homecoming, shouted, 'Merry Christmas, everyone!'

Two hours later the entire household, except for Crenna, Veena and Danny who were in the kitchen, sat on the verandah talking and laughing while Storm and Alex cuddled Tess and Hogarth, the two-year-old pointer, upon the top steps.

Veena and her daughter had decorated the Christmas tree and Danny had amazed them all by taking some remnants of dress material and Storm's paint box and fashioning the tiny golden angel which perched at the apex of the branches.

'Me old gran used to make dolls,' he had explained with a grin.

The moths were circling the light bulb and a breeze

stirred the jasmine vine which hung from the rafters in white spirals.

Sam bent down and kissed her husband's forehead as she refilled his beer and he gazed up at her. 'You know what, Sam?'

'No? Tell me.'

'I might even plod on over to Fernvale in a few days and see Mum and the old man.'

Sam was thrilled. 'Oh Cash, I'm so pleased you've said that. They'll love to see you. I'll come if you like.'

Suddenly Danny's voice crackled across the verandah from the kitchen door. 'I've been told to tell yuz that Christmas Eve dinner's served and the girls reckon if you don't come straight away the flies'll get it instead!'

From inside they heard Crenna's infectious laugh. 'First time I've been called a girl in twenty years!'

Wakefield and Cash helped the ninety-year-old Ledgie to her feet even as she scolded them. 'I'm perfectly capable on my own.' And Storm took Alex's hand and drew her along the verandah as the other members of the family stood and made their way inside.

Sam watched her mother kiss her father's cheek and slip her arm in his as they passed along the verandah. Her mother was wearing the gold pendant that carried the photo of little Viv inside. What a perfect marriage they had had: such trust and such love. She felt a confidence that she and Cash would be that way thirty years from now, and as her parents disappeared Sam hesitated for a few moments near the verandah railing toying with a blossom of jasmine on the vine that wound down the pillar from the rafters.

Haverhill . . . She had missed it so. The sound of a frog drifted up from the stream and she thought she saw the dark shape of a wallaby heading to the water. After all the angst and danger, the excitement and eccentricities of her life, it was just simply marvellous to be home, like a satisfying dream. Unconsciously she massaged her missing thumbnail as the breeze stirred the dark hair on her shoulders.

A moment later she turned round to follow her family,

and there standing behind her was John Baron, a soft expression in his blue eyes.

She smiled at him and he lifted his hand and touched her cheek.

'We went through hell, Sammy.'

'Yes, we did.'

'But we adapted, we survived.'

She nodded.

'This is going to be the best Christmas ever.'

'You bet.'

He grinned. 'Still using those expressions you picked up in New York.'

'You're not kidding!'

He laughed and she thought what a wonderfully happy sound it was; it spoke to her of her childhood and comfort and good times.

And now she too laughed with him as he put his arm around her shoulders and they sauntered along the verandah together towards the dining room.

'Don't eat it all!' John Baron shouted loudly to the family as they reached the door. 'Leave some for my sister and me.'

THE END

Endnotes

Chapter Twenty-seven (page 404)

Dunkirk:
Operation Dynamo, the evacuation from Dunkirk, ended on 4 June, 1940.

338,226 Allied troops had been shipped to England, 113,000 of them French. The 'Miracle of Dunkirk' had been achieved and a sense of deliverance spread throughout Britain and throughout the Empire.

861 ships, from warships to rowing boats, took part in the engagement; 243 of them were sunk by the Germans.

Some of the ships went back and forth more than once.

In the official list of ships which embarked troops it showed that of the 861 ships in the engagement, 372 were 'Other Small Craft'. The *Capability* was one of these.

The other, darker side to this miracle was:

The British Expeditionary Force had been compelled to abandon or, in many cases, destroy:

7,000 tons of ammunition
90,000 rifles
2,300 guns
120,000 vehicles
8,000 Bren guns
400 anti-tank rifles

By 22 June the French Marshal Pétain supported by General Weygand requested an armistice with Hitler. Under the terms agreed, Northern France and the territory north and west of Vichy were occupied by Germany. The French government moved to Vichy and became a government of collaboration with the Nazis while General De Gaulle and others escaped to England to continue the fight of the Free French. Nearly 2,000,000 Frenchmen were German prisoners and the casualties sustained by the British, French, Belgians and Dutch amounted to 390,000. German deaths were estimated at 40,000.

Great Britain now stood alone with the deadly enemy poised a mere twenty-three miles across the English Channel.

The stubbornness of Churchill and Great Britain supported by the Commonwealth were all that stood between Hitler and the collapse of freedom.

Chapter Thirty-three (page 513)

Large wing formations:
Douglas Bader's tactics were embraced.

An edict was issued by the Air Council that wherever there were two squadrons on one airfield they were to practise battle flying as a wing as often as they could, and that competence was desired as soon as possible. Large wing formations became accepted.

To invade Great Britain the Germans had to cripple Fighter Command. Göring told Hitler he would devastate the RAF by mid-September 1940, and based on that assumption, Hitler's plan was to send twenty-five divisions to land in England between Folkestone and Worthing on 21 September.

His plan was thwarted by the RAF.

On 12 October Hitler shelved his invasion, Operation Sea Lion, until further notice.

Prime Minister Winston Churchill in his address to the House of Commons on 20 August paid tribute to the fighter pilots of the RAF:

'The gratitude of every home in our Island, in our Empire, and indeed throughout the world, except in the abodes of the guilty, goes out to the British airmen*, who, undaunted by odds, unwearied in their constant challenge and mortal danger, are turning the tide of the world war by their prowess and by their devotion.

'Never in the field of human conflict was so much owed by so many to so few.'

*'British airmen': in 1940 'British' referred to all people of the Commonwealth and Empire. They were classified as British subjects and therefore called themselves British. This covered:

Australia
Canada
England
India
New Zealand
Scotland
South Africa
Ulster
Wales
And all Territories under the British flag, which were:
Aden
Antigua
Ascension
Bahamas
Bermuda
British Guiana
British Honduras
British Solomon Islands
Brunei
Burma
Cayman Islands
Ceylon
Cyprus
Dominica
Falkland Islands
Federated Malay States
Fiji Islands

Gambia
Gibraltar
Gilbert and Ellice Islands
Gold Coast
Grenada
Hong Kong
Jamaica
Kenya
Malta
Mauritius
Monserrat
New Hebrides
Nigeria
North Borneo
Northern Rhodesia
Nyasaland
Palestine
St Helena
St Kitts and Nevis
St Lucia
St Vincent
Sarawak
Seychelles
Sierra Leone
Somaliland
Southern Rhodesia
Straits Settlement
Tanganyika
Tonga
Transjordan
Trinidad and Tobago
Turks and Caicos
Uganda
Virgin Islands
Zanzibar

Parit Sulong:
The Massacre at Parit Sulong would have remained a
heinous secret for all eternity if not for the miracle of one
lone survivor, Lieutenant Ben Charles Hackney of the
2/29th Battalion AIF, a grazier in civilian life from Bathurst,
New South Wales.

Eight and a half years after the crimes of Parit Sulong,
in June 1950 in Los Negros, Manus Island, a War Crimes
Court heard his evidence.

Accused was Lieutenant-General Takuma Nishimura
charged with the murder of 110 Australian and 35 Indian
prisoners-of-war.

Hackney told how he survived beatings, machine-
gunning, rifle-fire, bayoneting and mass cremation on that
day at Parit Sulong. He told how he was kicked countless
times as he feigned death, particularly on the wounds on
his back and how he was battered over the head with rifle
butts and stabbed more than twenty times with bayonets to
see if he lived.

But live he did!

He spent thirty-six days crawling through the Malayan
jungle with his many wounds, with shell splinters and
bullets in his back, right calf and knee. He was recaptured
by Malayan policemen and taken to the infamous Changi
Gaol. There he wrote the tale of Parit Sulong and buried it
in a shell case which was retrieved after the war and used
as evidence at the trial.

Nishimura was found guilty. He was hanged at Los
Negros on 11 June, 1951.

Result of July 1945 Election:
Much has been written and many an analysis done on why
the Conservatives lost that election. In historical retrospect

the knowledgeable agree that it was not a rejection of
Winston Churchill the man, that the country recognised he
was the single human being who had done more than any
other to defeat the Nazis. The result of the election was
more an extempore desire to begin anew with all that
Clement Attlee and his promises of the welfare state
pledged.

Indeed six years later the country returned Winston
Churchill to power and he led it as Prime Minister until
1955.

Bibliography

Binns, Stewart and Wood, Adrian; *The Second World War in Colour*; Pavillion Books Ltd, London, 1999

Brickhill, Paul; *Reach for the Sky: The Story of Douglas Bader D.S.O., D.F.C.*; Collins Press, London, 1954

Bungay, Stephen; *The Most Dangerous Enemy*; Aurum Press Ltd, London, 2000

Burns, Michael G.; *Bader: The Man and his Men*; Cassell & Co. Ltd, London, 2000

Churchill, Winston S.; *The Second World War* Vols 1-6; Cassell & Co. Ltd, London, 1949

Colville, J.R.; *Man of Valour: Field Marshall Lord Gort V.C.*; Collins Press, London, 1972

Coombs, L.F.E.; *The Lion has Wings: The Race to Prepare the RAF for WW II 1935–1945*; Airlife Publishing Ltd, England, 1997

Darman, Peter; *Uniforms of World War II*; Blitz Editions, 1998

Deighton, Len and Hastings, Max; *Battle of Britain*; Wordsworth Editions Ltd, England, 1999

Ezell, Edward Clinton; *Small Arms of the World*; Stackpole Books, Pa, USA, 1983

Frayn-Turner, John; *The Battle of Britain*; Airlife Publishing Ltd, England, 1998

Harrison, Tom; *Living Through the Blitz*; Penguin Books Ltd, London, 1978

Jenkins, Alan; *The Twenties*; Book Club Associates, London, 1974

Johnson, Air Vice Marshal J.E.; *Full Circle: The Thrill-packed Story of Air Warfare 1914–1964*; Bantam Books Inc., New York, 1980

Johnson, Air Vice Marshal J.E.; *Wing Leader*; Chatto and Windus, London, 1956

Keegan, John; *World War II*; Parkgate Books Ltd, London, 2000

Kemp, Anthony; *Allied Commanders of World War II*; Orbis Publishing Ltd, London, 1982

Knowles, David J.; *Escape from Catastrophe: 1940 Dunkirk*; Knowles Publishing, England, 2000

Manchester, William; *The Last Lion – Winston Spencer Churchill: Vol I 'Visions of Glory' 1874–1932*; Abacus, London, 1993

Manchester, William; *The Last Lion – Winston Spencer Churchill: Vol II 'Alone' 1932–1940*; A Delta Book, New York, 1988

Mant, Gilbert; *The Singapore Surrender: The Greatest Disaster in British Military History*; S. Abdul Majeed & Co., Malaysia, 1992

Minney, R.J.; *Carve Her Name with Pride*; Chivers Press, England, 1987

Oddone, Patrick; *Dunkirk 1940: French Ashes, British Deliverance: The Story of Operation Dynamo*; Tempus Publishing Ltd, England, 2000

Ogley, Bob; *Biggin on the Bump*; Froglets Publications Ltd, England, 1990

Ogley, Bob; *Ghosts of Biggin Hill*; Froglets Publications Ltd, England, 2001

Oliver, David; *Fighter Command 1939–45; From the Battle of Britain to the Fall of Berlin*; HarperCollins Publishers, London, 2000

Parker, Matthew; *The Battle of Britain: An Oral History of Britain's 'Finest Hour': July to October 1940*; Headline Book Publishing, London, 2000

Price, Alfred; *Blitz on Britain 1939–45*; Sutton Publishing Ltd, England, 2000

Reid, Major Pat MBE, MC and Michael, Maurice; *Prisoner of War: The Inside Story of the POW from the Ancient World to Colditz and After*; Hamlyn Publishing Group Ltd, London, 1984

Taylor, Eric; *Heroines of World War II*; Robert Hale Ltd, London, 1995

Williams, Eric; *The Wooden Horse*; Collins Press, London, 1965

Wilson, Patrick; *The War Behind the Wire*; Pen & Sword Books Ltd, England, 2000

Wood, Derek with Dempster, Derek; *The Narrow Margin: Battle of Britain 1940*; Smithsonian Institution Press, Washington DC, USA, 1990

Ziegler, Philip; *London at War 1939–1945*; Arrow Books Ltd, London, 1998

Other Sources

Braithwaite, Brian, Walsh, Noele and Davies, Glyn; *Ragtime to Wartime: The Best of Good Housekeeping 1922–1939*; Ebury Press, 1986

Danchev, Alex and Todman, Daniel (editors); *War Diaries 1939–1945: Field Marshal Lord Alanbrooke*; Weidenfeld & Nicolson, London, 2001

Documents Relating to the British Home Front 1939–1945; Imperial War Museum, London, 1995

Hammerton, Sir John (editor); *The Second World War* Vols 1–10: August 1941 to June 1942; Trident Press International, 2000

Images of London; Evening Standard; Breedon Books Publishing Co., England, 1995

McDonnell, Leslie; *Insignia of World War II*; Silverdale Books, England, 1999

Patterson, Juliette; *Secret War: A Record of the Special Operations Executive*; Caxton Editions; London, 2001

Raby, Angela; *The Forgotten Service: Auxiliary Ambulance Station 39*; Battle of Britain International Ltd, London, 1999

RAF Manston Album; Sutton Publishing Ltd, England, 2001

Ramsey, Winston G. (editor); *The Battle of Britain Then and Now*; Battle of Britain International Ltd, London, 1989

Schweitzer, Pam (editor); *Living Through The Blitz: Londoners Remember*; An Age Exchange Publication, London, 1991

Shortt, James G.; *The Special Air Service*; Osprey Military, London, 1981

Soames, Mary (editor); *Speaking for Themselves: The Personal Letters of Winston and Clementine Churchill*; Doubleday, London, 1998

Swift, Michael and Sharpe, Michael; *Historical Maps of WW II: Europe*; PRC Publishing Ltd, London, 2000

The War in Pictures Vols 1–6; Odhams Press Ltd, London

Wheal, Elizabeth-Anne, Pope, Stephen and Taylor, James; *A Dictionary of the Second World War*; Grafton Books, London, 1989

World War II Vols 1–8; Orbis Publishing Ltd, London, 1973

WW II Air War: The Men – The Machines – The Missions; Chain Sales Marketing Inc., USA, 1998

Wynn, Kenneth G; *Men of The Battle of Britain: A Biographical Directory of 'The Few'*; CCB Associates, England, 1999

Yesterday's Britain: The illustrated story of how we lived, worked and played in this century; Reader's Digest Association Ltd, London, 1998

Vale Valhalla

Joy Chambers

In the 21st century the men who fought in the Great War have all but faded away, and only the memory of their sacrifice will be preserved. Between 1914 and 1918 soldiers from all over the world converged on the trenches of Belgium and Northern France: from Australia and New Zealand, Canada, England, India, Ireland, Scotland, South Africa, Wales and the far reaches of the British Empire they came to fight alongside the Belgians and the French.

VALE VALHALLA

traces the lives of a group of Australians through the years prior to, and during, the First World War, and reveals how they were forever altered by their sufferings in that singular and relentless conflict. The result of many years of research, VALE VALHALLA cleverly melds fact and fiction and is a compelling epic novel from the bestselling author of MAYFIELD and MY ZULU, MYSELF.

'An epic saga . . . meticulously researched . . . history skilfully combined with fictional characters'
Daily Telegraph, Sydney

0 7472 6088 5

headline

My Zulu Myself

Joy Chambers

Darlengi called out, 'John Lockley! Is it you?'

'Oh dear sweet Jesus!' John Lockley shouted. 'Yes, yes, Darlengi, I'm here!'

There was a moment of pure elation as they rushed forward to each other. Then they were in each other's powerful arms; hugging, laughing, shouting for joy, clasping each other like the treasure they thought lost for ever . . . Even the moon shone more brightly.

From the moment John Lockley saves the Zulu boy, Darlengi, from drowning they almost believe they are true brothers; born on the same day, never knowing their mothers, they spend their formative years together sharing a deep and abiding love for their country of South Africa. But when love intervenes in the young men's lives, tragedy appears, and all they hold dear is threatened as they fight to maintain a relationship across cultures and a deeply divided nation.

0 7472 4859 1

headline

Now you can buy any of these other bestselling Headline books from your bookshop or *direct from the publisher*.

FREE P&P AND UK DELIVERY
(Overseas and Ireland £3.50 per book)

Vale Valhalla	Joy Chambers	£5.99
The Journal of Mrs Pepys	Sara George	£6.99
The Last Great Dance on Earth	Sandra Gulland	£6.99
Killigrew and the Incorrigibles	Jonathan Lunn	£5.99
Virgin	Robin Maxwell	£6.99
The One Thing More	Anne Perry	£5.99
A History of Insects	Yvonne Roberts	£6.99
The Eagle's Conquest	Simon Scarrow	£5.99
The Kindly Ones	Caroline Stickland	£5.99
The Seventh Son	Reay Tannahill	£6.99
Bone House	Betsy Tobin	£6.99
The Loveday Trials	Kate Tremayne	£6.99
The Passion of Artemisia	Susan Vreeland	£6.99

TO ORDER SIMPLY CALL THIS NUMBER

01235 400 414

or visit our website: <u>www.madaboutbooks.com</u>